Don Anderson was born in Sydney in 1939 and has taught American Literature at the University of Sydney for the last thirty years. He has reviewed Australian, American and European literature for the *Age*, the *Age Monthly Review*, the *National Times*, and currently writes a column for the *Sydney Morning Herald*.

His articles have also appeared in the *Independent Monthly, Meanjin, Quadrant, Southerly, Island*, and *Westerly*. Many of his articles have been collected in the anthologies *Hot Copy* (1986), *Real Opinions* (1992), and *Text & Sex* (1995), and he has also edited *Enchanted Apartments: Sad Motels* (1989) and *Transgressions* (1986).

To Kate:
    Because no matter
what country it comes
from, you always
    appreciate beauty in
    words —
                Love You,
                    Molly

65 95

contemporary classics

The best Australian short fiction 1965–1995. Edited by Don Anderson

V

VINTAGE

This project has been assisted by
the Commonwealth Government
through the Australia Council, its
arts funding and advisory body.

A Vintage Book
published by
Random House Australia Pty Ltd
20 Alfred Street, Milsons Point, NSW 2061

Sydney   New York   Toronto
London   Auckland   Johannesburg
and agencies throughout the world

First published in 1996

National Library of Australia
Cataloguing-in-Publication Data

Contemporary classics: the best short fiction of the last 30 years.

ISBN 0 09 183075 3

1. Short stories Australian. I. Anderson, Don, 1939–

A823.010803

Design by Yolande Gray
Front cover photograph by Tracey Moffatt
Typeset by Midland Typesetters, Victoria
Printed by Griffin Paperbacks, Adelaide

10 9 8 7 6 5 4 3 2 1

Contents

	Introduction	**vii**
glenda adams	Reconstruction of an Event	**1**
jessica anderson	The Milk	**8**
thea astley	Hunting the Wild Pineapple	**39**
murray bail	A,B,C,D,E,F,G,	**56**
candida baker	The Powerful Owl	**67**
jean bedford	Country Girl Again	**80**
carmel bird	The Woodpecker Toy Factory	**89**
david brooks	Dr B. and the Students	**98**
peter carey	American Dreams	**112**
moya costello	Frank	**129**
anna couani	Xmas in the Bush	**139**
peter cowan	Party	**142**
rosemary creswell	New York, New York	**159**
gary disher	Syndrome	**171**
robert drewe	Radiant Heat	**185**
beverley farmer	Place of Birth	**203**
flacco	A Word in the Hand	**234**
helen garner	A Vigil	**236**
zeny giles	Miracle of the Waters	**262**
kerryn goldsworthy	A Patron of the Arts	**274**

Contents

peter goldsworthy	The Booster Shot	**287**
kate grenville	Look on My Works	**299**
marion halligan	Cherubs	**311**
barry hill	Getting to the Pig	**315**
janette turner hospital	Bondi	**348**
elizabeth jolley	Five Acre Virgin	**364**
joan london	Burning Off	**374**
angelo loukakis	Velodrome	**391**
richard lunn	The Duel Catalogue	**403**
morris lurie	Camille Pissarro 1830–1903	**419**
david malouf	Southern Skies	**428**
olga masters	A Good Marriage	**455**
james mcqueen	Nails of Love, Nails of Death	**469**
gillian mears	Afterthoughts	**488**
frank moorhouse	The Annual Conference of 1930 and South Coast Dada	**507**
gerald murnane	Boy Blue	**519**
hal porter	Boy Meets Girl	**533**
john tranter	Gloria	**561**
carolyn van langenberg	Hitler's Driver	**587**
ania walwicz	stories my mother told me	**595**
	dad	**598**
archie weller	Going Home	**601**
nadia wheatley	Women's Business	**618**
michael wilding	Singing Birds	**638**
gerard windsor	Botany Cemetery	**644**
tim winton	Thomas Awkner Floats	**650**
amy witting	The Weight of a Man	**661**
	List of Contributors	**679**
	Acknowledgements	**696**

Introduction

Here's how it began. March, 1994, a Thursday, 10.07am. My first-year English tutorial, twelve literate students, most straight out of high-school, a couple somewhat older, perhaps women of the world. As they settled down, one indicated that she wanted to sit next to her 'friend'. Thinking of deflecting them momentarily from the task at hand, Milton or Marvell or whichever dead white male, I said, invoking a living, Australian, female, ' "Two Friends": has any of you read Helen Garner?' This was not merely desultory, for I like to recommend Garner as a model of lucid prose, much to be admired and emulated. None had. 'Has any of you *heard of* Helen Garner?' I continued, recklessly. Not one. This was, you will note, before *The First Stone* thrust Garner into an inescapable limelight. I decided to ask the same question of my 11am tutorial. Same answer. So of twenty four first-year students who had chosen to enter the most venerable Literature school—not Communications, not Cultural Studies, note—in the country, *not one* had heard of one of its most esteemed short story writers. The H.S.C. system, whatever its virtues, must surely stand accused of a narrowness of focus, of breeding tunnel-vision. At home that evening, I told my wife, Angela, how shocked I was. She, ever practical, ever optimistic, said simply: 'Do an anthology.' Here it is.

Why the short story? Why its enduring popularity and importance in Australia, as the success and longevity of Bruce Pascoe's periodical *Australian Short Stories*, as its continuing presence in the quarterlies surely bear witness? Christina Stead, who wrote many, though her strengths resided in the sprawling canvases of her novels, observed in her essay 'Ocean of Story' (1968), that 'what is unique about the short story is that we all can tell one, live one, even write one down.' As one who judged the Bicentennial Short Story competition, I'm not sure I want to encourage that to be taken too literally, and would stress that the 'writing one down' demands skill of the highest order, perhaps a higher order than sprawling novels. Yet, as an Australian, I feel a sympathy with the democratic implications of Christina Stead's assertion. She continued: 'The short story is what everyone has and so is ever new and irrepressible.' This anthology bears witness both to the ever-newness of the Australian short story, as well as to its enduring connection to the traditions represented by the heroic figure of Henry Lawson.

Why 1965–1995? Apart from wanting to avoid the too-obvious 1968, thirty years seemed a neat period, and *that* thirty years a significant one. For something *did* happen to the Australian short story in the 'sixties or, if it did not in fact, enough people believed that it had for it to have achieved the status of the real. This happening has been considerably documented, notably by Michael Wilding, a contributor to this book, in his introduction to *The Tabloid Story Pocket Book* (1978), where he points to important cultural shifts in the 'sixties such as the breaking-down of repressive censorship legislation, to a burgeoning internationalism, eclecticism, and richness of literary culture. He observed that these had existed in the *eighteen-* seventies with Marcus Clarke, but had been reduced in the intervening century to an aesthetic which was 'narrow, utilitarian, insular, aggressively anti-experimental', and caused not so much by the nationalistic writers of the 1890s, but by the 'new nationalist theorists, critics and publishers and editors from the 1930s through the 1950s.' So, the *evenements* of the 'sixties and 'seventies in Australia were not merely a revolution but a renaissance.

Another contributor to this anthology, Kerryn Goldsworthy, in her essay on 'Short Fiction' in *The Penguin New Literary History of Australia* (1988) quoted two texts to document a significant shift in the fortunes of the Australian short story, sometime in the 'sixties. An advertisement in *Australian Letters* in 1958 read: 'Rigby Limited, one of the large Australian publishers, welcome any type of manuscript. Careful consideration given to all kinds of literary work *excepting short stories and poetry* . . .' (emphasis added). Against this she placed a 1977 observation by Frank Moorhouse, also a contributor to this anthology: '[In the early '60s] the new editor of the *Bulletin* told marketing guides: "The editor has recently tried to revitalise interest in the Australian short story and is anxious to secure short stories of Australian interest that break new ground."' The cultural shifts indicated in these two paragraphs, to which we should add the development of new arts funding (encourage-ment!) principles by the Federal government—I refer to the seeding activities of the recently much and unfairly maligned Literature Board of the Australia Council, our principal national arts funding body—and later by State governments, suggested that the time was ripe.

That it was, this anthology, I trust, bears resonant witness. For, despite its arresting cover, this is not intended as a 'cutting edge' collection. I produced one such in *Transgressions: Australian Writing Now*, a decade ago, and leave it to other, possibly younger, editors to do that today. Rather, *Contemporary Classics* is intended as a document of achievement, a substantial body of national work, and I thank my publisher for being prepared to countenance a collection of some six hundred pages though we were, for reasons of space and cost, obliged to omit some older writers such as Marjorie Barnard, John Morrison, Christina Stead, and Patrick White, who had lived into the period of this collection, but the bulk of whose short fiction was originally pub-lished earlier. My self-imposed guidelines were simple. The period to be observed, though it might be taken to refer to the author's living into those three decades, rather than the story's having been first published—let alone written—then. No extracts from novels. Each author to be an established short story writer by virtue of a combination of reputation and having published at least one volume of short fiction. The 'Australian' was straightforward, though not all were born here, nor have all resided here continuously, and Australian setting was irrelevant. As any editor is permitted to be a trifle flighty, I have broken all these rules, but not often, and not by accident.

I spoke above of the suppression and reemergence of traditions. Murray Bail, himself a contributor to this volume, has lamented: 'The realist tradition is the great curse of the Australian literature. It's part of that Anglo-Saxon pragmatic, prosaic, empirical heritage.' 'Empirical' as in 'empiricism' *and* 'empire', perhaps. It is true that the new generation writers of the 'seventies were reacting against the tradition of Lawson as it had ossified by the mid-twentieth century, but what impressed me, as I read for this anthology, was the persistence of a realist sub-stratum in Australian writing which, like the return of the repressed, manifested itself even in those writers at the vanguard of the new, 'experimental', wave. Though the influence of European writers and, perhaps especially, American ones is, as I have documented in my *Hot Copy* (1986) and *Real Opinions* (1992), significant in the 'seventies, Australian 'experimental writing' retains a strong affiliation with the tradition of Lawson: David Brooks, Peter Carey, Richard Lunn, Ania Walwicz, and, dare I suggest, Murray Bail bear this out.

I firmly believe two things about the short story. Firstly, it by its nature concentrates upon the importance of what filmmaker Eric Rohmer saw in his own work, the 'small moral decisions'. Secondly, though perhaps not as effectively as poetry, it can achieve a brevity and concomitant density not available to the novel. To demonstrate by going to an extreme: Italo Calvino hoped to edit an anthology of tales consisting of one sentence only, but could not find any to match that by the Guatamalan Augusto Monterroso '*Cuando despertó, el dinosauro todavía estaba allí.*' ('When he awoke, the dinosaur was still there.') Calvino dreamt of 'immense cosmologies, sagas, and epics all reduced to the dimensions of an epigram.' That *is* an extreme view, but short stories succeed insofar as they aspire to that economy. The stories here included will, I hope, convince those who need convincing, that economic rationalism or, much worse, intellectual and emotional rationalism, are not all that there is to life. Realism and reality are but part of a fuller life. There is the life of the imagination, the life of the spirit, to be found, among other places, in literature. Writing is a site of desire, as a great secular poet observed:

> Unreal, give back to us what once you gave:
> The imagination that we spurned and crave.

Don Anderson
The University of Sydney
September 1995.

It is a Tuesday morning. The doorbell wakes her up. She may have heard the footsteps on the concrete path leading to the front door just a second or two before the bell rang. The sun is high enough to light up the lime-green umbrellas and lollipop-pink houses printed on her curtains. The jacaranda tree outside her bedroom window casts a shadow on the wall. She has overslept.

Does it matter that it is the shadow of a jacaranda? Rather than dwell on the shadows and the type of tree casting them, just state what time it is. No scene setting, no exposition.

It is a Tuesday morning. The doorbell wakes her up. She has overslept. It is nine oclock. There is no sound in the house. No footsteps. She guesses that everyone has gone to work and forgotten her. The doorbell rings. She intends to get up and answer it, but instead decides to spend the day, and possibly all days thereafter, in bed sleeping. She closes her eyes and begins the drift back to sleep. The doorbell rings. She sits up with difficulty. Good manners prevail. It is rude not to answer and one spends years learning not to be rude.

It is not plausible, never to have been rude. Also, she

has to get up sooner or later, so why not answer the door? Why this repeating of the doorbell rings, the doorbell rings? Also, her thoughts and wishes are irrelevant and throw no light on the matter. It is necessary to state only what happens. No opinions.

The doorbell rings. It is nine oclock. Tuesday morning. She came in the night before, expecting them to be waiting up for her. All was quiet, and she was grateful. The father normally lies awake whenever she goes out at night. He longs to sleep. Then, after she comes home, he tosses and turns and grunts and growls in bed and finally gets up to walk around the house and let it be known that he has had no sleep and that nothing has gone unnoticed. The next day he gives a speech to the effect that the daughter is giving him grey hairs and driving him to an untimely grave. He often composes his epitaph, beginning 'They will rue the day' and ending 'and they will all be sorry when I'm gone.' The whole thing has become a laughing matter, a family joke.

No background. None of the above is necessary or necessarily true. Just what happens.

She goes out, comes home late, and goes to bed. The doorbell rings. It is nine oclock the next morning. Tuesday. She stands up then she falls right over. She lies on the floor. It feels pleasant enough. She can stay right where she is on the floor and continue sleeping. The doorbell rings again. She crawls to the door, hauling her dressing gown around her. She uses the door jamb to hoist herself up. In the hallway are her mother and her younger brother. They are steadying themselves against the walls. The smell of gas is everywhere. 'Is it an earth-quake?' she enquires. The brother starts laughing, stag-gering away from the wall, then back again to continue leaning against it. She has never heard him laugh so much. 'In case of earthquake, stay in the doorway. Safest place,' the brother says, laughing and laughing.

Not credible. They all think that there is an earthquake just because they are a bit dizzy and have to lean against walls? Simply not possible in this part of the world where there are no earthquakes. But if they believe there is an earthquake, why does the brother laugh? An earthquake is a serious business. Don't they smell the smell? Don't they immediately know that something is wrong? Do they really stagger and sway like that?

The doorbell rings. The mother, the brother and the daughter get up to answer it. They arrive in the hallway at the same time. The mother feels her way along the walls to the front door and opens it. She has an arm through one sleeve of her dressing gown. The other sleeve hangs loose over her shoulder and she clutches it to her heart.

There is no need for her to feel the way along the wall. There is no earthquake. Why does she move so slowly? Is that supposed to be a symbol of something? Why the fancy language, clutching things to hearts? Just the facts. What happens.

The mother rushes to the door and opens it. No doubt she has her dressing gown on properly. No one has said anything at all. It is the piano tuner at the door. He has come to tune the pianola. He has arrived early.

'It's an earthquake. Stay where you are,' the brother calls. He is laughing.

There is no earthquake. There are no earthquakes in this part of the world.

The piano tuner sniffs. 'What's the smell?' he asks. 'Not me, I didn't do it. I didn't make no smell,' says the brother. The daughter laughs. She thinks she will die of laughter. The mother turns her head slowly, more or less in the direction of her children.

There is no earthquake. No one is dizzy. Also inconsistent. The mother has already rushed to the door. There is no need for slow head turning, if any head turning at all.

The mother says, 'Don't speak that way in this house.' The brother says, 'I didn't do it, that's all I said.' The tears roll down his cheeks. The mother groans and leans against the wall. She shakes her head as if she has a drop of water in her ear. 'Where's your father?' she whispers. The brother says, 'When roses are red they're ready to pluck, when a girl's sixteen she's ready to drive a truck.' The mother says, 'You ought to be ashamed of yourself.'

No earthquake, no dizziness, no laughter, no elaboration, no metaphors. What happens.

The mother opens the door. It is the piano tuner. He has come to tune the pianola. He has arrived early. He says, 'What's the smell?' He walks past them into the kitchen. 'Everything's turned off in here.' He is checking the gas jets on the stove. 'What else have you got that's gas that could be leaking?' The mother replies, 'Everything in this house is gas. It's cheaper. We get the

4

appliances at a discount. Everything's gas.'

The brother says, 'Appliances and people, both.' The piano tuner says, 'What about in the laundry?'

Enough with the reconstructed dialogue. The facts. What happens.

The piano tuner says he can smell gas. The mother runs into the kitchen. She checks the gas jets. She throws open the windows and the back door. The piano tuner stays standing politely at the front door. The mother takes the daughter by the arm and leads her into the back garden. She leans her against the jacaranda tree and goes back to get the brother. The daughter holds on to the grey trunk and looks at the house. She sees the kitchen door painted blue, the window with her curtains, and the laundry door downstairs, also blue.

No trees, no doors, no curtains, no excursions into anyone's head. No fabrications. Only what happens. It does not matter, the tree or the colour blue. Forget the build-up and the climax. Just what happens.

The piano tuner stays at the front door. The mother rushes down the back steps to the laundry. The brother and daughter are following more slowly. The mother rushes back to the stairs and calls to the piano tuner to come and help. The daughter is at the top of the stairs and starts to come down. The mother orders her to stay where she is. The daughter walks on down and goes to the laundry door. There are rags and newspapers stuffed into the keyhole and the vents in the door and into the space between the door and the floor. The smell of gas is everywhere. The door is not locked. She pushes it open, coughing and retching at the gas. She holds her nose and goes in and turns off the laundry gas outlet which has been left on by mistake. Then they all go upstairs and wake the father up and they all have breakfast. The piano tuner tunes the pianola.

Not so. That pianola never got tuned.

The daughter stays at the top of the stairs, as she is told. The smell of gas is everywhere. It is the mother who rushes down the stairs and opens the laundry door. All the rags and newspapers fall to the floor. The father lies there on the floor on a spare mattress that is stored in the laundry. His face is next to the outlet. He lies next to the dirty clothes. He looks as if he wants to be found in time. They drag him out into the air, near the jacaranda, and he revives.

No tree, no embellishments, no opinions, no lies.

It is a Tuesday morning. It is nine oclock. The doorbell wakes them up. The smell of gas is everywhere. They have overslept, drugged by the gas. The mother opens the door. The piano tuner has come, early. The mother rushes to the kitchen. She checks the gas jets. She opens the back door and rushes down to the laundry. The brother and daughter follow her. There are rags and newspapers stuffed into the keyhole and the vents in the door and into the space between the door and the floor. The door is not locked. The mother opens the door. The father lies there. He is dead, having gassed himself. Less than half a minute has passed since the doorbell rang. If the piano tuner had not come early, they would all be dead now.

Later they remember that the daughter was out late

and was the last to go to bed. They ask why she did not notice the absence of the family joke and why she did not notice the smell of gas and why she did not avert the tragedy.

No, nobody actually asks anything like that. No need for denouement. This is an ordinary family, one of many such families in houses on streets. Nothing distinguishes it from the others except, today, this event.

When Marjorie's son Emlyn returned to Sydney from
Europe, he demanded to see the little flat she had rented
but had not yet moved into. She divined his opinion
from the way his feet came together in such an abrupt
stop on the threshold. 'See the nice broad window sill,'
she said, going briefly to sit on it. 'And I shan't be here
for ever, you know.'

He was in the tiny kitchen. 'It's not secure,' he
shouted.

'What?' She stood beside him. 'What isn't?'

'That.'

'A servery. Oh, good. I didn't notice that.' She
opened it with one finger. It was certainly dirty. 'It's for
the milk,' she said.

'They put kids through those.'

'Not in these parts, surely. There can't be much to
steal.'

'Everyone has a television.'

'I haven't.' She shut the servery. 'It's only for a while,'
she coaxed. 'Only till the divorce.'

Although it was one of Marjorie's rules never to do anything drastic in the January heat, it was in January that she had managed at last to convince her husband that she was serious about leaving him.

'No contentious matters at dinner' was another of her principles, but no principle could stand against the momentum gathered, and it was at the dinner table that she achieved that communication.

Bruce rose abruptly. The look on his face was murderous, as was the one brief and thickened sentence he spoke. Even in the immobility of her astonishment, she did not believe he would actually murder her, but did realise that such venom not only made impossible the amicable kind of divorce she had just proposed, but made it impossible for her even to stay in the same house. She packed two suitcases and went to a private hotel suggested in a hurry by her friend Carla. She went by taxi because, while she was packing, Bruce took her car keys.

The hotel, on the northern shores of the harbour, was a place of somnolent residents and soggy beds. 'Well,' said Carla, in Marjorie's room there, 'you did say somewhere cheap.'

Marjorie noticed that Carla avoided looking at her face. 'Poor old Brucie,' said Carla.

This was in 1976. The divorce laws had been reformed the year before, sweeping away grounds such as adultery, cruelty, and desertion, and putting in their place only breakdown of marriage. Carla said, 'He can't believe you can leave him, and not be legally punished.'

'Nonsense. He reads the newspapers.'

'But he can't take it in. It doesn't seem natural.'

'Oh,' said Marjorie, 'I dream about him.'

'He says it must be your change of life.'

'It probably is.'

'Well, Marj, in that case,' said Carla.

'Why shouldn't it be?' said Marjorie. 'Why shouldn't change of life be like adolescence? The two great changes. So? The two great chances.'

'Chances of what?'

'Exaltation. Remember?'

'Not really.'

'And suddenly seeing the truth. And knowing just how to do things.'

'Oh my,' said Carla. 'Perhaps now you'll be able to draw feet.'

Carla and Marjorie had been at art school together. Carla had become a commercial designer and had continued in it in spite of marriage and children. Marjorie, an illustrator specialising in botany, had dropped that, and all of her training, until the sixties, when, under the influence of a group of local women, she had begun to sculpt in the garage. But, abstract and incisive though her pieces were in conception, all turned out to have a trivial and fiddled-with look. Nor did persistence bring improvement. 'It's the surfaces,' she said. 'Like badly iced cakes.'

But when she returned to small-scale drawing, she found a new enjoyment in her materials, and an excitement in each day's first contact of pen or chalk with paper. She also discovered in herself a reluctance to say anything to anyone about these pleasures. Her stylish and accurate pen drawings soon began to earn her money, but even though the unsparing truth of her instinct told her she would leave Bruce, she did not face that truth to the point of providing for it, and remained lax in commission and shy about naming her price. All her drawings were of plants or objects, although she could usually manage a figure hovering behind the cooking ingredients, or a distant child in the garden. 'With its little feet behind the herbaceous border,' Carla would say. It was often Carla who commissioned these drawings. Now, in the hotel, Carla said, 'It makes it harder to find work for you.'

'I've a book of West Australian wild flowers to do. All from photographs. Easy.'

'Then for God's sake, get it in on time, and see that you get decent money. Have you got a lawyer?'

'Of course not. I always thought Bruce and I would talk, you see, discuss—'

'Oh, Marj, get one, get one.'

'Legally, I am sure I am—'

'Within your rights. Yes, but the law's a new one. Not many precedents. Martin, of course, won't—well, he can't can he?'

Carla's husband, Martin, was a lawyer. 'Of course he can't,' said Marjorie. 'Do you think I expected it?'

'Not really.'

'Does he recommend anyone?'

'No.'

'I see.'

'Sorry.'

'So I'm to be put in solitary.'

'Marj, give people time to get used to it.'

'I can't work here. I'll have to get a flat. Look, there isn't even room for a table. Carla, am I imagining it, or are you really trying not to look at my face?'

Carla laughed, abashed, and picked up her bag. 'It's just that I'm sorry for Brucie.'

But she still did not look at Marjorie's face, kissing her goodbye instead.

All the flats Marjorie saw in the territory familiar to her, the north and east, were too dear. It was Bruce's edict that they should communicate only through lawyers. Marjorie went to see her lawyer, who was named Gwen.

'Look, since I'm not claiming maintenance, or even my full legal share of our property, don't you think Bruce should allow me something to go on with? I've got a thousand or so in my own account, but the rest of it is all muddled up with his. I'm earning, but I must rent a flat, you see, working space. And here is a list of the things I need from the house. Basic, as you see. Bed, table, etcetera. But will you ask about the money?'

Gwen, like Carla, did not look at Marjorie's face, though for a different reason. A big peachy Rubens beauty, she set herself up to be looked at rather than herself do any surveying. She swung aside her waist-length hair and directed at her bookshelves the sweet pensive smile often seen on television, where she spoke on women's affairs. Her voice was very soft.

'I'm afraid he still insists that because you're the one who left, you're not entitled to a cent. Of course under the new act he's wrong, but I'm afraid it does mean that unless you're prepared to put out a good bit of money, you're going to have to wait till the case comes to court.'

'Which will be?'

As she watched Gwen shrug, Marjorie in her imagination cut her hair to shoulder length and removed some of her eye-shadow. She never made these fast and absent-minded rearrangements in the appearance of her friends; they simply seemed to take place of their own accord in suspenseful or awkward moments with people hardly known. 'Will it be,' she asked, 'say, three months?'

'More like six,' said Gwen.

'Then he's just being *mean*,' cried Marjorie, like a child.

'We so often express our injuries through property,' murmured philosophical Gwen.

'What about that list, then? Can Trevor persuade him to let me have those things?'

Trevor was Bruce's lawyer. 'Oh, I expect he can, yes. I'll ring him now.' Gwen put a hand on the phone and gave her delicious smile. 'Leave a hundred with Isolde on the way out, will you?'

Marjorie went south to Newtown, where she found a small flat—one room, kitchenette and bath—with good light, in a big old block set among patched-up terrace houses, small shops, and light industry. Her son Emlyn and his wife

Fiona returned from Europe two days before she was to move in. They had heard nothing of the separation. Fiona was agog but amused. 'It gave him a bit of a shock, I bet.' But sweat had broken out under Emlyn's eyes. 'Shut up, Fee. Mum, tell us what we can do to help.'

By now Marjorie was used to people who avoided looking at her face. She understood that Emlyn's modernity was in conflict with his grief and disapproval. All the same, she was pleased to see his censure deflected to Fiona, who only hugged him and said, 'Shut up yourself. Yes, Marj, what can we do?'

'I want to look at this flat you've taken,' said Emlyn, pushing Fiona away. 'Wouldn't you know this would happen when we're overdrawn on our Bankcard?'

'Don't worry. I've two books to do. You can look at the flat tomorrow.' Marjorie smiled at Fiona. 'And on Thursday, if you like, and of course if you can get time off, you two could help me to move. I've got this sore shoulder. Here, at the back.'

'Get it looked at,' said Emlyn with ferocity.

'It was the suitcases. It will go. If you like, you two could go with the carrier to pick up the things Bruce—your father—oh, what shall I call him?—anyway, the things he is letting me have for the flat.'

'You won't fit much in one room,' said Emlyn.

'I adore Newtown,' said Fiona.

'Fee got that dress from Valentino,' said Emlyn.

Marjorie laughed when she saw how Bruce had interpreted

her list. A weathered outdoor table with its two slatted
chairs, a folding bed, a pale-blue chest of drawers from
Emlyn's childhood, a bagful of worn linen and blankets, a
box of pots and pans without lids, and her worktable, stool,
and the old tea trolley on which she kept her materials. She
laughed out of the strained amusement she was finding it
more and more easy to summon, and because his meanness
relieved her guilt, and because she did not want to further
inflame Emlyn, but to co-operate with Fiona in keeping it
light and funny.

'Love that window sill,' said Fiona. 'Wow.' She sat on
it. 'I want it.'

'Well, mum, if that's really all?'

'Thank you, dears.'

'Come on, Fee. I'm late as hell.'

'See you soon then, Marjie.'

In the doorway Emlyn stopped, as he had done the day
before, and morosely surveyed the room. Fiona could be
heard running down the stairs. Unzipping the bag she had
marked FIRST THINGS, Marjorie hardened herself against
her son. She was tired. Her shoulder hurt. There would be
cockroaches. Emlyn had himself divorced his first wife
(under the old laws) in order to marry Fiona.

'I wish you would let me nail up that bloody servery.'

'I don't know how long they let you park down there,
Emlyn.'

As soon as he had gone, Marjorie abandoned the bag
and went to the window. As she had hoped, the sill was
wide enough, and broad enough, to contain her sitting
figure. She sat resting in the embrasure, her legs along the

seat, her back against the wall, her face turned to the window.

No tree broke her view of the street, which on this late afternoon was fairly busy with traffic and pedestrians. After a while she noticed that most of the people were burdened. Shabby young mothers bore heavy, sleeping babies. Women were weighted down on both sides with plastic sacks of provisions. Men carried bulging airline bags and packs of beer. Those waiting on the bus seat had bags and cartons on their laps or at their feet. Only the boys and those children not tethered by an adult hand were free. A group of boys, Aboriginal and white, came running. Knocking into each other, yelling, guffawing, inventing dangers, they brought a neat Chinese for a moment to the door of his grocery shop.

When travelling in Europe, Marjorie had looked down from hotel windows on traffic and human activity, but in Sydney she had lived all of her life from infancy in quiet neutral streets, where the neat squat houses were separated by splendid trees, and where almost the only pedestrians were school children. She had nursed a longing for the sea, and after the friendly divorce she had planned from Bruce, she had intended to find a small cottage near the beach where she had spent holidays as a child. She looked down on the street with an alertness that asked for no explanations, as if she were living only with her eyes. The cafe next to the grocery came alight through its netted shopfront. Lights came on in the terrace houses and revealed people cooking in corners of bedrooms. In the flats a television roared and was cut down. A phone rang; water throttled in a pipe. When heavy steps ascended the stairs outside her door, she was amused to be able to match them with the visible gait of a man she had just seen crossing the street. She got up and went to the peephole in the door.

She had never looked through a peephole before. The man had disappeared, but the distorted perspectives were mesmeric, and kept her there. The corridor looked so long, almost noble, but threatening too, the towering doors curving inward at their height. She told herself that one of those doors must open and admit a figure to her view, and under the alertness of this expectation, the scene grew more and more eerie. It was only a game, but when she withdrew her eye, having seen no figure, she was touched with solemnity.

She turned on the small battery radio Emlyn had left her, seized the bag marked FIRST THINGS, and took from it cleaning gear, a spray can of insecticide, and two rolls of Marimekko paper. She quickly washed the kitchen shelves, the drawers, and the servery, then lined them all with the paper. She refused to care that the chastity of the paper, its gloss and small vivid geometric daisies, made so sad the scarred and discoloured paint. In the room she took from among her work things a piece of card and a felt pen.

MILKMAN—When you see the servery door open, it
means I want milk.
Bottles only please. I don't take milk in cartons.
M.T.

She folded the card and set it like a neat tent on the paper. Beside it she put the clean milk bottle she had remembered to bring, and beside that, the exact money. She pushed open the outer door of the servery, and shut the inner one.

She held her breath as she rapidly sprayed insecticide behind the stove and refrigerator and along the skirting boards. On an explosion of breath she staggered out of the kitchen, kicking the door shut behind her so that the poison could lose its first stench while she ate and slept.

Carla had brought to the hotel that morning a little wicker hamper. As Marjorie examined its contents she compared herself to Carla. She would have remembered the wineglass, but forgotten the bottle opener.

She ate and drank in the window embrasure. The wine eased the pain in her shoulder, but relaxed her strained alertness and returned her burden to her. As bad, precisely as bad, as going back to Bruce, was the burden of her guilt. She longed above everything (everything but that) to be forgiven. She jumped up and stood boldly, with one knee on the sill, and finished the wine. She became drunk enough to be quite pleased with the improvisation of the folding bed, and to be comforted by the semblance of a cubby house given by the dim shapes around her of her unpacked, mismatched things.

In her dream, Bruce is hurrying to meet her, as he had done that time at the airport. He almost runs, shouldering his way through the crowd, his face congested with the familiar sizzle before his laughter would break. But in her dream, she was not appalled by his joy, as she was at the airport, having brought herself on the long journey to her irrevocable decision. In her dream, indeed, she is not at the airport, but is in the folding bed in the Newtown flat, and Bruce is advancing, one hand extended, across the floor. She sees behind his laughing face the floral curtains she has drawn against the street lights. She sees her worktable and trolley. She is amazed to be forgiven; the bliss of his forgiveness makes her gasp. She reaches for his hand and sees not the laughing face, but the malevolent face that had looked down on hers as he rose from the dining table. His extended hand would kill her. It presses on the bone between her breasts. She rolls off the bed to escape, and as she scrambles, sobbing, to her feet, she hears a loud crash, and a door slamming. She fumbles along the wall and finds the light switch. The room is exactly as it was when she went to sleep. The crashing is no longer loud; she recognises it as the joggling of milk bottles in a carrying crate. Her search for the light switch has brought her to the door. She rolls against it and puts her eye to the peephole. Far down the long and stately corridor she sees a dark little gnarled figure running weighted on one side with his milk and disappearing round a corner.

The suffocation in her chest becomes a searing pain. She considers a heart attack, but cannot believe in it. When the pain grips her entrails and forces her to a bowed position, she remembers the wine so quickly drunk. 'Fool!' she sobs. 'Fool!' But she is able to be amused by her ignominious cramped run into the kitchen. Milk will help. Even to envision the calm white bottle on the clean paper is a solace. She opens the servery. Her card stands there, and there, on the Marimekko paper, is her money, and there stands her empty bottle. The milkman has been, and has rejected her request. She drinks water, glass after glass. The pain leaves her belly, but spreads across her chest again, and goes on and on, attended by the old steady pain in the back of her left shoulder.

It seemed to help Doctor Furmann's powers of diagnosis if, as he tapped, as he listened, as he pressed fingers beneath her rib cage, he looked into the distance. But when she was dressed again, and sitting opposite him at his desk, he did look fully and very attentively at her face. He was a ferret-faced young man with notably intelligent eyes.

'I think you have a stomach ulcer.'

'Is that all?' said Marjorie.

'All? Ulcers are no joke.'

'No, but the worst pain last night was across my chest, and the pain I've had for weeks is behind my shoulder, so naturally, you know,' said Marjorie, with her shrugging, 'I thought, heart.'

'Would you prefer that?'

'I don't care one way or the other.'

'You're divorcing, did you say?'

'Yes, I did say that.'

Marjorie guessed by the sympathy in his eyes that he thought her the abandoned one. She would have liked the luxury of allowing him to think so, without the discomfort of deception. She said coldly, 'I left my husband.'

The sympathy remained. His splendid dark eyes reminded her of Emlyn's. His hairline was so uneven that in this pause she began to straighten it by electrolysis. 'It seems to me,' he said at last, 'that at your age, it doesn't matter who leaves who, not so far as my work is concerned. I want you to have an X-ray.'

'What will it cost?'

'Don't you belong to a fund?'

'My husband did all that.'

'You're still legally his wife.'

'Please give me a referral.' Marjorie knew she would pay for it herself. 'I'll go to a hospital.'

'You'll wait longer.'

'Never mind. I can take something, I suppose, in the meantime.'

He gave slow instructions as he wrote the referral and two prescriptions. 'No alcohol. And you don't smoke, so that's okay. No coffee. No aspirin. Not much tea. Eat little and often. If not solids, milk.' He handed her the flimsy sheets. 'If you find milk helps.'

'Milk!' Marjorie laughed, then lifted the top prescription and said sternly, 'Tranquillisers?'

'Don't indulge your opinions at the expense of your health.'

'But I told you, I must work.'

'Then take one when you stop work, and another at night. That pain in your shoulder, by the way, it's my guess that's referred pain.'

Coming home one day with her plastic sacks of provisions, Marjorie encountered the woman who lived in the next-door flat. Marjorie would have been diffident about knocking on this neighbour's door, but when she saw her in the mundane and undistorted corridor, she was bold enough to accost her.

'I wonder if you could tell me what I must do to get milk delivered.'

'Easy,' said the woman. 'Leave your money out. No money, no milk.'

'But that's what I do.'

'And I always leave the servery door open.'

'I do that, too.'

'Well, I get milk, no trouble. Except when I forget to leave the money out. Then I get a carton across at Wong's. It's no trouble to slip across to Wong's.'

'That's what I've been doing. But I like bottled milk. Besides, I just don't understand it.'

'Well, it's no good telling you to ask him. He comes at three-thirty. Why don't you ring the company?'

Marjorie rang the company in the smelly public phone booth on the corner. Her name and address were taken, and delivery promised, but the next morning, and the next, when she went to the kitchen and opened the little door, she saw only her note, her money, and her empty bottle. She knew her disappointment was ridiculous, but it was unconquerable; it gave a lagging start to her days. She went again to the booth on the corner, but vandals had been there, and the receiver lay smashed on the floor. She hoped it had not been done by the group of boys she had come to like and watch for. She walked to the post office and found an undamaged phone. The company passed her from person to person, and while waiting for someone named Miss Vinson, she was cut off. After that, she would open the servery door merely to exercise her cynicism, and would smile as she banged it shut.

Emlyn was furious with her for having no phone of her own.

'Mum, even professionally—'

'Emlyn, if you would listen—'

'Even professionally, it's crazy. Fee and I are financial again. We'll shout you a phone.'

'Emlyn, I've been trying to tell you, I've paid for my phone. I asked Harrap for an advance on the cookbook. They didn't mind a bit. It was amazing. Now I'm waiting for Telecom to connect me.'

'God! What a service! How long are you supposed to wait?'

She hoped that Emlyn was expressing his affection through this indignation, since at present he was inhibited in expressing it in any other way. She did notice also that he had begun to look at her face, though as often as not his glance would slip quickly to her collar.

'And what about this milk Fee tells me is so important

to you? Cartons are okay. We get cartons.'

'It's just that I wanted to get up in the morning, and open the servery door, and see it there.' She made the shape of it with her hands. 'And reach out, like that, and take it in. But you're right. Cartons are okay.'

Emlyn went to the servery and opened it. He picked up her note. 'What's he like?'

'I've seen him only once. He comes before dawn. I don't wake out of my drugged sleep. In the distance he was little and dark, not young. Don't worry about it.'

'I guess he doesn't read English.'

'That's not it. He wouldn't need to.'

'No. The bottle, the money. That says it.'

'Right. So.' She took the note, tore it up, then padded in her bare feet to throw the scraps into the carton of waste paper beside her worktable. She hoisted herself on to her stool and spread her hands. 'Look at all the work I've been given.'

'Mum, I had a go at talking to dad. Useless.'

'I don't want to know about it.'

'Yes, but look here, mum, this—' Emlyn slanted his head to indicate the room '—this just isn't a fair go. You need better legal advice than you're getting from that Mae West character. If ethics mean you're stuck with her, which is bloody nonsense in my opinion, instruct her to engage a barrister. Carla's husband would recommend someone. Or I'll find someone.'

'My dear—'

'Don't talk to me about money. Don't insult me.'

'My dear, I am here in this room, and I wish to stay

here, working every day, until the case is heard. I have set myself on a course. Don't divert me. Don't upset my balance. I mustn't fall off my rope.'

He was looking her full in the face, but as if it were the face of a stranger. After a while he said absent-mindedly, 'Right.' Then he said, 'When do you get those X-rays done?'

'They'll let me know.'

'You look well,' he said in the same tone. 'Fee was saying you're looking really good.'

'I feel fine.' Now that Emlyn had dropped his ferocity, she seemed to have picked it up. 'I don't believe there's anything wrong with me at all. And I don't need help. And I don't need to know anything about your father.'

'I get it,' he said. 'And anyway, look here, dad's okay.'

His sympathy had brought her to the point of telling him how intensely she was enjoying her work, but she drew back out of the superstitious fear that to reveal it was to risk losing it. She did not overvalue her work. She knew its first importance was that it earned her money, but she was surprised and grateful that in her present circumstances it could so deeply engross her, could give her such a sense of urgency. Every day in the humid heat of January, February, and early March, she rose and folded up her bed, ate her breakfast and bathed, then put on one of her loose dark batik dresses and went to her worktable. She pinned her hair high on her head to free the nape of her neck; she wore no pants nor bra, no jessica anderson

shoes. The dress itself was a concession to her visibility
from the street. Curtains or blinds reduced the light, and
she had besides become accustomed to making quick
little sketches of the people in the street, and dropping
them, done or half-done, beside her worktable, where
they lay gathering grit and dust. When she had to go
out for food, she put on pants and the rubber thongs
she had bought at Woolworths. She wore these same
clothes to the hospital, where she was given a barium
meal and X-rayed. She had to wait four hours, which
slackened her sense of urgency and made her feel restless
and tense. The urgency was exciting and exhilarating
except during enforced waits or when she had to go to
the city to collect or deliver work. She hated these occasions because she felt obliged to wear full underclothes,
a dress of a more formal sort, panty hose and shoes, even
make-up. To dress like this she felt as a serious and even
dangerous intrusion, and she would arrive back at her
flat in a state of anxiety or even of slight hysteria, and
would violently pull the hated clothes off her sweating
body. She wished she could afford couriers. If it were
Carla who had given her one of these jobs, Marjorie
would beg her to bring it herself. Carla riffled among
the drawings on the floor, casting some aside and picking
out a few at which she cocked her head and lifted one
corner of her mouth. 'It's no miracle that you can draw
feet,' she said one day. 'It's just this.' She tapped the
drawing she held. 'Practice, practice, practice.'

'I can draw feet because I need the money.'

Carla appreciated the humorous hardness of this.

Marjorie wondered if Carla believed it to be entirely true. Carla wisely nodded, in any case, as she returned the drawings to the dusty pile.

The glass of milk Marjorie kept on the window sill she covered with an envelope. Dust and grit gathered also in the servery, on the coins, the bottle, and the Marimekko paper. Although Emlyn had been assured by the milk company that there was no possible obstacle to Marjorie getting her milk, the servery continued to present, on each morning's sardonic inspection, the same picture as before. She pretended to Emlyn that his complaint had been effective; she did not want him to go on a crusade about a bottle of milk a day. He had already been on a crusade about her telephone, and whether or not as a result, it was now connected.

Once, in the early afternoon, hearing faintly the clink of coins, she slipped quickly from her stool and ran into the kitchen. The money had gone. Feet in thongs were slapping down the stairs. She heard the laughter of the boys, and yelled down the staircase after them that they were devils, as she had heard Mr Wong and the people in the street do. She did not replace the money, but in bed that night found the omission gave her a superstitious uneasiness, and impatiently she got up and put the three coins in the servery. The rolled newspaper she carried in the other hand was for killing cockroaches; she never went into the kitchen at night without it; another superstition she had developed was that insecticide would kill her as well.

The radiologist reported that Marjorie had a large ulcer crater on the posterior wall of the upper third of her stomach. As Marjorie read this, she heard Doctor Furmann remark, in a pleased and enthusiastic voice, that he had been quite right about that shoulder pain.

'Referred pain. Come here, and I'll show you the crater on your X-rays.'

'I can't stop work to have an operation,' Marjorie warned him swiftly.

'I don't suggest it. Now, that silvery area is your stomach. Now, see that dark intrusion? I'm tracing it, see? That's it.'

'And that is my monumental backbone. And those wavy things, which I must say are quite pretty, are my intestines.'

'If I may have your attention.'

'Perhaps I could wear myself inside out. Well, all right. It's awful. It's huge. It looks like the Gulf of Carpentaria.'

'Yes, it does. It's deep, all right. That one hasn't grown overnight. Well, it's our job to close it up. On each X-ray you will see it get smaller.'

She asked with horror, 'How often must I have these X-rays?'

'Every month.'

'And how many months will it take to cure?'

'That's partly up to you.'

'Give me some idea.'

'No less than three.'

'Which I suppose,' she said bitterly, 'means six.'

'Sit down,' he said, 'sit down. There's a drug recently developed. Cimetidine. Perhaps it's for the lucky future. I don't prescribe it yet. It's still at the trial and error stage.'

'Like the divorce laws.'

'I know it's no use telling you not to worry.'

'I thought not worrying was exactly what I had been doing.'

'I know it's hard.'

'I've been feeling so well,' she said angrily.

'Fine. You've responded to treatment. So now we're sure of our ground, we'll give you something stronger.' Again his voice went on as he wrote. 'These may have the side-effect of raising your blood pressure, but we'll keep a weekly check on that.'

'Weekly!'

'Yes, and give you something for it if the need arises. It's a matter of maintaining a balance.'

'Oh, I see. A balance.'

All the next day Marjorie lay on the bed in her nightgown, stubbornly reading out-of-date magazines. She read about Patty Hearst and Princess Caroline of Monaco and how to stretch your budget. Carla rang. Emlyn rang. 'Mind your own business,' she wanted to say. But their solicitude was her own fault, for having told them anything at all. So she said it was only a small ulcer, nothing really, easily fixed. She ignored a knock on the door, but when she got up in the evening, and saw the agent's card under the door, she remembered it was rent day. There was hardly any food in the kitchen. She got dressed and went over to Wong's.

'And your milk?'

'Yes, please, Mr Wong.'

Just before dawn on the following day, she dreamed again of Bruce. He stood at the dinner table, looking down at her. 'From now on,' he said, 'every mouthful you eat will poison you.' It was near enough to what he had actually said to make her rise and spend the remaining hour till daylight hunched in a shawl on her worktable stool, looking out of the window at the street cleaners, the garbage collectors, and the derelict men and bag women freshly routed from their cubbies. But just as she did not remember what she had read about Patty Hearst or Princess Caroline, so she did not now absorb what she looked at.

She was too tired to work that day. In the evening Emlyn and Fiona came and presented her with water biscuits, creamy cheeses, and a book on herbal medicine. They were still there when Carla came with her husband Martin. Carla bore the food of childhood, a milky rice pudding in a homely earthenware dish. Marjorie had to open the folding bed so that they could all sit down. She noticed that now everyone could look easily at her face, except Martin, and even he was able to address her in a natural tone of voice. The next day, via Carla, he suggested the name of a barrister Marjorie might instruct Gwen to engage. Marjorie refused. Though she had returned doggedly to her work, she could not afford to add this factor to all the others to which she must now adapt her balance. At the end of the week, when Doctor Furmann prescribed tablets for her raised blood pressure, she accepted the instruction passively and in silence, and as passively took the tablets at the ordered times.

She had lost her sense of urgency. She did her work faithfully, but without her former delight. One day, warmly complimented on it, she was startled, and took the piece back and looked at it again, and saw that, yes, it was better than she had done in her exalted state. She sighed with incomprehension.

Perhaps because the cool days had come, she no longer found it hateful to dress to go to the city. She did not dream of Bruce again, but although she increased her dose of tranquillisers, her sleep was often broken. When she heard the milkman's bottles jangling away down the corridor, she assumed that what had brought her awake was his banging her servery door. In the morning it was always shut, and she would viciously slam the inner door she continued to open for her inspection. Then one night, as she was about to go into the kitchen for water, she heard him stop outside her servery. It was not a full second before he banged the door and jangled away. She threw down her rolled news-paper, seized the money and the bottle, and ran in her bare feet down the corridor after him.

She caught up with him while he was scooping money from a servery. She stood with arms extended, proffering the money in one hand, the bottle in the other.

'What about me? Flat forty-one?'

He put two bottles into the nearby servery and shut the door. 'Good,' he said. He took the money and the bottle, gave her a full bottle, and picked up his crate.

'Wait! Why don't you deliver it?'

He was certainly Italian: small, lumpy though thin, with black mordant eyes and a look of disgust on his simian mouth. She had seen his counterpart among his comely people, and concluding him to be a relict, almost bred out by prosperity, she had been surprised that he had so often crossed her path. He had cheated her in five Italian cities, and in those same cities had directed her lost footsteps with kindness and even gallantry if she were quick to understand, and with testiness and contempt if she were not. In Sydney he had spared some of his time and authority to help her to buy unfamiliar food, and last year, when she had bent to the driver's seat of his taxi and offered a fifty dollar note he could not change, he had all but screamed his anger and abuse. She was in awe of his inheritance, the implant of poverty and unnatural labour. She said (for his English had been no better than her Italian), 'Everyone else,' and pointed to the row of doors, 'but not me,' and pointed to the door at the far end. 'Why not?'

He scowled as he put down his crate and took money from his bag. 'You do this.' He extended his hand, the money on his palm. 'I give milk.'

'That's what I *do*!'

But he had picked up his crate and was moving away, and when she called again for him to wait, he responded with what sounded like a curse, and gave a backward flip of his free hand. In none of his manifestations had he been patient. Herself cursing under her breath, she ran after him, but he had turned the corner, and when she reached it his only visible part was the small head bobbing down a narrow service stairway she had never seen before.

Without gratification she put the bottle of milk in the refrigerator. She knew he did not expect her to run after him in her nightgown every time she wanted milk. He meant her simply to pay him. Her end of the corridor was dimly lit. She put another three coins on the paper, then went out into the corridor and opened the servery door. The money was clearly visible in the light from her kitchen. But usually, the kitchen was dark, the inner servery door shut. She went back, shut the inner servery door, and turned off the light. And this time, she saw that it was difficult (though not impossible) to distinguish the coins from the small geometric daisies on the Marimekko paper.

In the morning she went out and bought sandpaper and a tin of white enamel. She sanded down the old cream paint and put fresh white paint on all planes of the servery except the base. For the base, she folded a sheet of layout paper to the right size. In the evening, after her work was done, she polished three coins and washed and dried a milk bottle. A soft laugh broke from her as she did this, and again as she slowly and ceremoniously set down the three coins. She did not know if he had failed to leave her milk because, in days filled with the same desperate impetus as hers had been, he had not bothered to give the second glance that would have distinguished the coins, or whether it angered him that he found them hard to see, and he was forcing her to show them as clearly as he had done when he had displayed them on his extended palm. She thought the latter more likely, but did not care, such was her certainty that the milk would be there in the morning.

Yet she could not have been so certain, because, in the morning, when she opened the door and saw it standing there in its simplicity, amazement preceded her delight, and amazement was in her smile as she reached out with both hands and brought it in. During the day she had only to think of the sight of it, standing there, for the sensation of smiling to spread through her whole body.

She did not continue to polish the coins, but took care to set aside for that use the cleanest ones in her purse. During her next restless night, when her wakeful period included half-past three, and she heard the milkman's fast padded steps, and the jangling of his crate, she listened intently enough to hear him take the coins and set down the milk. He did not slam the servery door. He closed it gently. She told nobody of the incident. Each night, she changed the white paper, and took pleasure in setting down the three coins in their invariable pattern.

She was disappointed when she studied her second X-rays with Doctor Furmann.

'What?' he said. 'Did you expect a miracle?'

'Yes,' she said.

'I thought you would be pleased. It's so much reduced.'

'Oh, it is,' she said, to appease him. 'Now it's like Spencer's Gulf.'

'You mean Spencer Gulf.'

'Your geography is as good as your treatment.'

'Next time it will be like Port Phillip Bay. Roll up that sleeve, please.'

In the winter, the sunless flat was cold all day. She bought a small radiator, but its heat made her lethargic, so after her morning shower she walked into fur-lined boots and swaddled herself in layers of clothes before she started work. She picked up her sketches from the floor, dusted them, and put them into different coloured folders in order of preference. Each time she added new ones, she found that her order of preference had changed. Though her divorce was not yet listed, she began to think of a garden, the smell of basil and geraniums, and the feel of a warm stone path under her feet. But when she studied advertisements for cottages at that northern beach, she felt less certain about wanting to live there.

Carla, when she came to the flat, would often, as she was about to leave, fall into the kind of silence that made Marjorie suspect her of hanging about to find a chance to say something about Bruce. 'I hope you don't think I'm going to put myself into reverse at this stage,' said Marjorie on one of these occasions. 'I mean, about the divorce.'

'No, I don't expect you can,' said Carla.

'It's no help to talk about it.'

'It was you who mentioned it.'

'It was you who so clearly wanted to. Tell me something. I can't get my money from Manzell and Rogers. I've sent my account twice. Do you know anything about them?'

Her divorce was listed the day after she had her third X-rays. These showed the ulcer crater reduced to the proportionate size, if not the shape, of Port Phillip Bay. 'Don't be over-confident,' warned Doctor Furmann. 'Don't relax your care. When is your divorce?'

'In three weeks.'

'Just what part stress plays is not known for certain.'

The day after this, Marjorie put some documents in an envelope, put money in her purse for Isolde, and went to the city to see Gwen. Early for her appointment, she decided to go to Nock and Kirby's to buy paint for the outdoor table and slatted chairs. It was a quarter to two; the counter was crowded, and while she was waiting her turn she saw Bruce standing on the downward escalator. He wore an unfamiliar tie, held his attaché case in one hand, a walking stick in the other, and was carefully regarding his own feet. When he reached the floor, he stepped on to it with a slightly fumbled and panicky step, then with one hip swinging wide, limped quickly away towards the George Street entrance.

Marjorie abandoned the paint and hurried distractedly out of the York Street entrance. She took four antacid tablets on her way to see Gwen, who was magnificent that day in magenta and purple. When Marjorie got home she rang Emlyn.

'Emlyn, I saw your father in Nock and Kirby's.'

'Did you?'

'Has he had an accident?'

'No, mum, he hasn't.'

'Then why is he lame?'

'Mum, we all saw your point when you said you didn't want to hear anything about him.'

'Yes, but now I've seen him, it's better if I do hear something.'

'Well, you remember his arthritis?'

'But that was nothing. He called them twinges.'

'It's something now.'

'Twinges. But I do recall,' she said, since Emlyn was silent, 'that most of the twinges were in one hip.'

'Right, that's where he copped it.'

'Will he always be lame?'

'I don't know. There are things they can do. He's going to a specialist. A top man. And anyway, mum, even if he is always lame, he's not the kind of guy who can't handle it.'

'No,' said Marjorie, 'he's not.'

But as she put down the phone she thought of how characteristic it was of them each that she should take the wound in the soft tissue, while he should take it in the bone. She sat with her hands folded, wondering if it was only bad luck that she had not found, at the right time, the right, miraculous seeming, gesture of conciliation; but after a while she jumped up and turned her mind to other things, knowing she could not afford to enter that labyrinth. She had collected her mail on the way upstairs, and was pleased to see that Manzell and Rogers had paid her at last.

After all, the house was nothing but an enormous barn, one gigantic living-room sixty by forty which was entered through the garage. Everything about the place groaned with bad taste.

Mr Pasmore ushered his guests—somehow his presence made us third person—from car to garage with the flair and pride of a talented lush, past rows of spigots labelled 'strawberries 7', 'pineapples 12', 'bananas 4'.

'It's simple,' he says twirling a pink gin, and he and his gin lean sideways with film-star lop-sided charm. 'But I'm so bloody lazy. Muscle-blood-bone-marrow-lazy.' His torpid eyes manage a practised twinkle. 'It's all mechanised now. Turn a knob and off race the nutrients. Saves a hell of a lot of trouble and the casuals do all the rough stuff. Weeding. Pine-grubs and so on. And I don't have to pause between drinks.'

He eases us into the living-room, which is split across one end by a twenty-foot curved tank of tropical fish, and twitches at a shoji screen. 'Bedrooms back there. Expand or contract a little according to taste. Makes the john a bit public, but then you can't have everything.'

Who has? But if I can horn in a bit on another's mummery . . .

I always seem to be explaining how I got where.

In a town like Mango social movements are amoebic—you'd better believe it, as they say in the US of A. I have dying memories of a middle-aged red-head on a bus to Florida: I want a meaningful relationship, she said. I mean I want to relate, she said. How do I get to express my total self? she asked. Baby, I say mentally, don't ask me, and dumped her in Jacksonville. Here there are these mercurial, spontaneous and apparently directionless surges to north and east; a lively fusion, a parting. The fusing can take eater and eaten by surprise: 'My *goo*'ness!' the little blonde had said in a bar somewhere off Madison, 'I didn't expect *this*!' It's not all carnal, I swear. Mere temporary interpretations, if you like, of what appears to be a strange new language which, despite the sameness of the semantic signals, is strange and new because the signals are given by a stranger. ('I've just changed guards!' Doc. Tripp commented bleakly after his third corrupt marriage.)

That's the fallibility of us. The new inflexion! Ah, *Mamma mia*! A new meaning. This body, this face, these fingers, talk *diff*runt! But they don't, of course; and reason asserts itself and the same dull old drone of the expected vision intrudes in those boardroom, barroom, bedroom cliche's I've heard, oh, I've heard, before.

I had moved, one translucent April, into a brief congruence that had originated as business and became shortly but intensely an ardent pattern of mutual succour. Mrs Crystal Bellamy, a calmly widowed South Georgian, impossibly researching the human geography of the north for a nonsense thesis, established a two months' base within the sticky filaments of my bed-and-breakfast web.

We passed swiftly from the manager-client nod to pleasant weather syllables to interrogatory clauses that contained all the primary fervour of two Vasco da Gamas colliding as they rounded the Horn. I'm interested in the violence of quick friendships. Snap up a pal! She was an articulate, golden-bunned lady with a certain piquancy of profile that was, at first encounter, blandly misleading. Be misled, I tell myself (and others, viciously), if only for the colour of expectancy. I am bearded now (arty or distinguished according to company), wooden-legged (the limp is captivating), and with a fringe of hang-ups, monstrous puritan-liberal growths like gall-wasp. No nodes on the skin, mark you: merely a flicker of epidermic sun-spotting—I call it bagassing—where the north has bitten me.

She wrestled me from Crusader Rabbit. My car became her car.

In a kind of tour-captain fever I distributed the country for her in hunks. We pursued lakes, craters, dams, limestone caves, ghost towns, abandoned mining camps, mission settlements, crocodile farms, hippie communes, sugar mills, prawn fleets, rich American marlin fishers, tin fossickers. We ranged north, south, west and, as far as weather would allow us, east. Her bun became sweetly loosened, my sun-spots increased, her note-book thickened. That's the how of it; and the specifics? Well, track them back to a well-intentioned buddy who wanted to prove we're not all grubbing away at the soil up here, that we're smooth, polished, and have swung quite nicely, ta ever so, into the sophisticated seventies.

So smooth that outside the house we are left gawking at a whopping heart-shaped swimming-pool filled with blue tears that blinked as a woman (his wife?) plunged from sight.

Mr Pasmore smiles at us.

'When Tubs emerges, if she does of course, she'll toss up some food. It's a pity in a way you didn't get here while there was more light. I could have shown you a bit more action. Muh-heen-while, I'll stiffen you a couple of stingers. You like that?'

We like that.

The sun took three drinks to go down. Mrs Bellamy gave an elegant paraphrase of academic purpose, and Tubs returned dripping from the pool and vanished behind a screen. Mr Pasmore did not seem to notice her.

'My, my!' he says, to Mrs Bellamy, 'we don't often get visitors of your calibre here.' Snapping the ice tongs. 'Another?'

We have another. Tubs emerges from the screen in a half-buttoned house-gown and heads straight for the bar where Mr Pasmore intercepts her with in-front-of-the-guests *bonhomie* and tells her she must meet these delightful people.

'Call me Crystal,' instructs Mrs Bellamy.

'Crystal,' Mrs Pasmore says obligingly and swigs a triple Scotch.

There are ice noises and Mr Pasmore puts heartbreak music on the tape-deck. Outside the world has gone black.

'What's for dinner, darling?' Mr Pasmore asks.

Tubs is a massive woman hewn from the one stone block. She stares vaguely at her handsome lug of a husband and momentarily her eyes cross with effort.

'There's a lobster somewhere.'

'Somewhere?'

'God knows.' She helps herself to another Scotch.

'Well, well,' Mr Pasmore says, smiling on us brightly, 'we'll just have to see if we can find it, won't we?'

The rummaging sounds from the screened-off kitchen section are terrible to hear. Tubs finishes off her drink and pours another.

'Crystal,' she says.

'Yes?' My bunned blonde registers polite guest stuff.

'Just musing,' Mrs Pasmore says.

We fight the conversation along for a bit, but it is only working two ways as our hostess sits with the lonely hootings of endless distances about her. From behind the screen it sounds as if a whole deep-freeze has been emptied onto the floor.

'My God!' Mr Pasmore cries flinging the screen to one side—and it's true: he's islanded on twenty square feet of frozen goodies. 'Got the damn thing! Afraid you'll have to wait a bit though. I need a drink after that.'

He comes back to us and bends spousily over his wife.

'I could kill you, my dear,' he says with frightful sweetness.

'Not now,' his wife says, regarding him for the first time. 'Not till after the guests go.'

'Certainly not till after the guests go,' Mr Pasmore says.

Beside me Mrs Bellamy quivers with hunter's instinct.

Mr Pasmore is savaging the gin bottle. 'Fuel stop! Just the briefest of fuel stops and we'll do it together. Well, we three will. I think Tubs has opted out, haven't you, Tubs?'

'In,' Tubs says. 'I've opted in.'

There's nothing like doing things together my dad, my mum, my teachers all, all unblinkingly, blindly told me. Oh, my God, there's not! Eventually we got our-selves sorted out with lobster pieces and salad balanced on our laps. ('Tubs gets the small one! She didn't help one bit, did dear old Tubs!') The tape-deck changed its mood and Mr Pasmore sat as closely as possible to Mrs Bellamy and became highly technical as he thanked the good God for all growing things: which appeared to include her.

'Moonrise at nine. If you want,' he suggests, 'if you like, we'll go in search of the wild pineapple.'

'My!' Mrs Pasmore made her first conversational gambit in half an hour. Crystal smiled at me, him, even Tubs, uncertainly.

'Yes, oh yes! We'll do it by car'—he chucked ice into vodkas—'and take a flash. Bring those. We'll need sus-tenance for the perils of the journey. Tubs won't come, will you, Tubs? She's rather had hunting the wild pineapple.'

But the moon was behind cloud as he backed his cumbersome elderly Ford from the garage and took it on full beam down the tracks to the paddocks. Our drinks slopped, but Mr Pasmore settled the car into low gear, steered with one arm curved affectionately round the wheel, and sipped elegantly. He was full of whimsy.

'No noise now,' he cautioned, disc-jockey style, as we bumped into the third plantation a mile from the house. 'Some of these big buggers might hear you. We'll go on foot from now on.'

Sitting in the well of the noisy dark we finished our vodkas. Mr Pasmore's manly and chipper handsomeness should have reassured, but he was just sufficiently not quite like a well-known actor to appear not valid. The car was parked below a crest in the road with sea visible now on our right, its blanched acres distantly alive.

'You right, old man?' he inquires, doing the wrong thing as I stumble getting from the car. 'It's not much of a walk.' I hobble my answer. 'Just keep those flashes down, eh? I always like the element of surprise.' He lopes ahead with ball-toe bounce.

If I say that at this precise moment Mrs Bellamy unloosed her bun and the moon came out, you will charge me with the wretchedness of symbol. She did and it did and under the sudden blaze of both I barely noticed the whisper of her fingers on my arm. 'Don't worry,' she hummed with musical southern accent in my ear. 'He's what we call slightly off-centre.'

And why should I care? It's these half-way, middle-term, middling, mean hucksters who demean my spirit. I've always had a taste for the circumferential.

'He'll want you to douse that hair!' And the half-smile from under it.

We caught up with him at the bottom of the slope where he stood, finger-lipping a warning as we came up. He was doing cautionary peerings at the stickle-backed fields, a hunter's ear cocked to the grainy night. Suddenly he lunged sideways, football-tackle mode, and in the prancing beam of his flash his distorted shadow heaved and buckled at the base of the paddock-line. 'Lights!' he roared. 'Lights!' The paddock-line was racketing with movement. His body reeled and dived in the quaking air: a shambles of convulsed half-tone.

'Got you!' The voice was cracking at check-mate. 'Goh-hot you!'

'Oh, my God!' Mrs Bellamy whispers beside me, beginning to laugh, to laugh and run forward. His lank shape banked against moonlight. From his hand dangled a huge humped fruit.

Mrs Bellamy was catching on, astute Mrs Bellamy. 'Did it put up much fight?'

Mr Pasmore grinned and I am aware of teeth, the wet curve of lip.

'A flick of the wrist. A mere flick of the wrist,' he says, 'and it was all over. I am,' he says, 'in pretty fair condition. Here. It's for you.' On the word, he tattooed her arms with spikes; the head spears stabbed her chin. He lit, post-coitally I think nastily, a cigarette.

'Why, thank you!' Mrs Bellamy cries. 'You've given me the ears and the tail. But, my God, it's like a barb-wire melon!'

'Now, I like that,' Mr Pasmore murmurs. He turns down his flash and drops a pally arm on each of us. 'I like that very much. In fact, I like that like I like the two.'

'The two?' she asks. I don't. We are limping to the car. Yes. All of us. I'll transfer any disaffection, muddled as I am by hair and pineapples and the clear indifference of hot moonlight.

He's suave again, opening car doors with busy elegant flourishes.

'Two—um—two casuals. Two pickers. We do seem to get a funny crowd round here. Not, mark you, that I carp. No, no. I do not cuh-harp.' He lets in the clutch. 'In fact, it makes a break in a dull life. We have, you might have noticed, a very dull life. It's not often we get visitors like you. Style. Articulateness. The world, as it were, come to pines.'

Despite the hair-flow Mrs Bellamy says rather tartly, 'You're making fun of us.'

'Mrs Bellamy—Crystal,' he says. 'As if. As very *if.* In a moment,' he adds catching my eyes, 'I'll have to make love to this delightful lady simply to prove her wrong. Wrong wrong wrong. No seriously—' Oh, you're a no-but-seriously man, I think sourly. But he isn't. There's no 'but'. 'Nothing happens. That's our problem. Nothing happens.'

He went gloomy on us for half a mile.

'You wouldn't care, would you,' he asks as the house lights shoot between the trees, 'to take a little excursion? It will give Tubs time to achieve her coma. We can visit the—er—two.'

'More human geography,' I whisper. Mrs Bellamy's tanned fingers were rolling her hair into a sausage, but the profile was still bemusing.

He didn't wait for an answer but reversed the car suddenly with millimetric genius, swinging on rutty tracks to grind back between 'strawberries 1' and 'bananas 3' to an eastern fork. Another half-mile—I am counting the death blows to my stump!—and a second house squatting on its moonlit hunkers, a half verandah'd timber box watching through narrowed eyes like Jason's (there's culture for you!) the grey metal spikes of millions of pineapples.

Mr Pasmore drummed a neat riff on the wall beside the open front door, the over-familiar, paternalistic-presumptuous tat-a-tat, tat-tat, and emitted hearty cries of boss-lure down a passage blazing with unshaded electricity. Space goggled back at us. He rapped again and after another blazing empty minute a lardy perspiring Greek, a cliché of a Greek, hands clasped somewhere where his heart should be, waddled his smiles towards us. I thought he was smiling, I say now.

'Georgy,' Mr Pasmore asks, 'may we come in?' He was already in. 'I've brought you two delightful visitors. They have been exploring the possibility of the pineapple. Do you like that? The possibility of? I mean we all know the positivity of, don't we? What we want, oh, what we all so want want want is the possibility of? Georgy, do you believe in the possibility of the pineapple?'

Georgy giggled and the giggle made ripples on his flesh. So what else could the poor bastard do? He giggled and his eyes stayed dark as our names were offered and instantly forgotten. The introductions fluttered away like blank paper and came to rest in the mauve cube of a sitting room which, too, was blazing like a bonfire of snappy magazine cut-outs tacked straight to the walls: glaciers, bad-lands, Alpine staccatos, palm-fringed nirvanas (they lie!—the motel complex has been chopped off by the fraudulent eye of the lens!)— all the clap-trap of plausible fable, while outside, outside, the grey lines of the armed fruit formed a desert of succulence.

There is a rhythm-bodied male of brunette intensity (even I can pick it!) shuffling cards by the window.

Mr Pasmore is saying with relish, 'And this is Tom. In fact, these are the tuh-who!'

Mr Pasmore can smile and smile and be, I am beginning to think, somewhat of a shit; but the young man's smile matches up to his, and his height matches and his accent is what I call all haggis and kilt.

'It's a bonnie sound,' Mr Pasmore says with whimsy. 'I come here to practise m'Scots.' He practised it a bit. 'Y' no theenk ah bung eet on a beet?'

'Two what?' Tom asks, shuffling cards and smiling tensely. He is superbly good-looking and muscular and Georgy watches him with a moist and jealous eye.

'Two? Why, most interesting, most remarkable, most most ... ' Voice-trail for hand-bafflement gestures. 'They are without a doubt'—turning to us—'the best couple of workers I've had in years. Yes, years. So many, so many bums hit the coast this time of year and all they want to pick is the pay. But with Tom and Georgy, now, it's different. They've been with me—how long is it, Tam?'

'Three years.'

'Three. Well, thruh-hee is a long time. A long time in these parts. Most of them move on after one season and you never see them again. But Georgy and Tom, now, are part of the place. When the pines are finished they stay on for the replants. Georgy and Tom. They solace my evenings. They will even, if asked nicely, make us coffee. And, if asked really nicely, make music.'

'Are you asking nicely?' Tom enquires.

'Very. Oh, very.'

Indifferently, Tom fishes a mouth-organ from his pocket, teases us with an insolent jig during coffee noises. The coffee waddles back, Tom does bravura stuff to Mrs Bellamy's entranced delight, and Mr Pasmore, clasping hands round his mug and surveying the room, appears to be consuming us, not it. I always know when I'm being eaten, even the most delicate of nibbles. But do the others? Somehow being punched in the privacy, not the privates, gives such stunning pain I'm reduced even below whimper-level to shiver.

Tom shakes the saliva out of his mouth-organ, takes a gulp of coffee, and inspects Mrs Bellamy's quince and cream with rapid glances that our host easily nets.

She fills the void. Fatuously. 'Have you always done this?'

'Done what?'

'Well, casual work? Farming?'

'I don't know about thens. Only nows.'

Mr Pasmore is delighted.

'How about a song, Tom? He's a great ballad man, you know.'

And instantly, with an abruptness that was offensive, Tom launched into virile tenor that rang and roared across the room, out the open window and over the acres of pines. ' "Och, Jock, where are y' trewsis?" ' he sang, aggressively comic for six verses of *double entendre* hammered home with professional poise and eye-twinkles at each of us in turn: while Georgy poured more coffee and smiled possessively and watched enviously as Mrs Bellamy finally hooked the singer's eye for an entire verse.

The fat happiness of his possession is shaken.

'A good boy, eh? Good voice, eh?' Nodding and observing. Mr Pasmore is beating time with a playful spoon; but Tom drowns the taps with flourishes, to wind up with a smasher of a bow to the lady whose corruptibility he is testing with mock hand on bogus heart.

'Oh yes oh yes! Only the most talented of puh-hickers!' Mr Pasmore cries. 'Only. I told you this is a show farm, my friends, my dear friends, and you are seeing the *spécialité de la muh-haison*!'

'You're surely quite an artist,' Mrs Bellamy says, reluctant to release that hand on the heart. At least she's got his eyes! 'I suppose you've done a bit of singing professionally, have you?'

'A wee bit. Here and there.'

'Oh, it was so good! Very, very good. Could we beg another?'

She's fusing. Relating. She's on the Florida bus. She's giving him the Martini eye in a singles bar. Her orbs glut on his hip-moves as he swings into a chair and rides it back to front.

'I . . . ' Georgy appeared to be gulping. 'I . . . I . . . ' His sausage fingers are plucking at her arm. 'I, too.'

I've seen it. You've seen it. We've seen it. Want me to conjugate all the forms of envy? It's rather nice, this, turning into a cipher recorder in the middle years, slapping my wooden-leg for comfort while I note—note, mark you—the gobbledy-gook of sad little human rivalries setting flesh aquake. Oh, I'm sad for them all right. Sad sad sad.

Crystal (the moment calls for intimacy) releases her eyes unwillingly to turn and stare, not resentfully—interestedly, at the fingers on her arm.

'I, too,' Georgy repeats.

'You sing?'

'No, no. An artist. I am an artist.' His eyes are on Tom with love and loathing. 'I paint. I am an artist.'

'An artist?'

Georgy nods and beams.

'Aye, he is that,' Tom agrees. I am the only one to catch the wink. 'Gie us a wee glance at some, Georgy.'

Mr Pasmore, raree-show proprietor, becomes golden

with pride. 'Come on, Georgy. Bruh-hing out those etchings, those fabled canvases. If you won't come and see mine,' he adds in a whisper to Mrs Bellamy. 'Eh?'

Georgy's eagerness, all gulps and agreement and smirks of tumid promise, is frightful. Bloated and puffy with his moment, he waddles off to the bedroom and we nurse our discomfort—I nurse mine; Mr Pasmore is asimmer with something—until he limps back with a shabby grocery carton that he heaves onto the table.

'There!' he says. And beams.

We wait.

He smiles before his backdrop of deadly cut-outs, centre-stage at last, clutching his moment.

'Go on, Georgy,' Mr Pasmore says lightly. 'Open up!'

Georgy folded back the cardboard flaps, did an all-thumbs fumble at a protective layer of brown paper, and scooped out half a dozen sketches that he spread on the table before us as if he were fanning a royal flush.

Spanking girls they were, big-thighed, vilely luscious cartoons of comic-strip emptiness, copies of an archetype sex goddess that came with the first fifty lessons. Kid-stuff. Clumsy. Crude.

What to say?

'Why, Georgy?' Mrs Bellamy says, not daring to look at his eager and waiting face, 'they're really good. Really.' She doesn't look at anyone but keeps shifting her fingers' desperate interest from one sketch to the next, a shade too enthusiastic. 'I'd really love to have one. May I?'

Does Georgy's delighted vanity then do to the others what it's doing to me? Does it?

He puts the sketches aside and purses his mouth critically.

'But that is before,' he says, 'before I am enrolled. These I have sent them. They are trials, you understand.' He is engrossed with explanation. 'To see if I can be an artist perhaps. And they take me, you know. They take me.' He can hardly contain his joy. 'Oh, very expensive. A lot of money. But you send away, you see, and they send you . . . there are fifty lessons. They say I have . . . ' He can't find the word and sausage hands wave helplessly.

'Promise, Georgy,' Tom says, helping him. 'They say you have promise. Lots o' promise.'

'That's it. That is what I have. Promise.'

He sucks the word with his head on one side. 'I am enrolled since two years now.'

He dives into the carton again, his pudgy arms milling around, and drags out another box. The two unused brushes lie beautifully beside unsqueezed tubes, three rows of them. The palette is unstained. Georgy runs his fingers lovingly over it.

'Fifty lessons.'

Below the paint-box is a great stack of gleaming knot paper. Reverently Georgy lifts the paper block out and places it carefully, gently, and perfectly square beside his other things. His fingertips keep stroking the paper.

'And all this,' he says. 'I am an artist.'

We all looked at the untouched, well-loved objects.

'How's about more coffee, Thomas?' Mr Pasmore asks. 'Or prithee a Scotch?'

But Georgy it is who hauls himself up. 'I,' he says, 'I make you more coffee. I make you beautiful coffee this time.' He is radiant with possession.

'And when are you sending in that first lesson, Georgy?' Mr Pasmore asks spitefully. 'When are you sending in the fuh-hirst, eh?'

I see Tom flash at him and catch the hate before the laugh.

But Georgy turns back to us from the kitchen door and he is still doped with the dream, wagging, smiling benignly, benignly, at the lunatic acres beyond the open window.

'Soon,' he says. 'Soon now.'

murray bail   A, B, C, D, E, F, G, H, I, J, K, L, M, N, O, P, Q, R, S, T, U, V, W, X, Y, Z.

I select from these letters, pressing my fingers down. The letter (or an image of it) appears on the sheet of paper. It signifies little or nothing, I have to add more. Other letters are placed alongside until a 'word' is formed. And it is not always the word WORD.

The word matches either my memory of its appearance, or a picture of the object the word denotes. TREE: I see the shape of a tree at mid-distance, and green.

I am writing a story.

Here, the trouble begins.

The word 'dog', as William James pointed out, does not bite; and my story begins with a weeping woman. She sat at the kitchen table one afternoon and wept uncontrollably. How can words, particularly 'wept uncontrollably', convey her sadness (her self-pity)? Philosophers other than myself have discussed the inadequacy of words. 'Woman' covers women of every shape and size, whereas the one I have in mind is red-haired, has soft arms, plain face, high-heeled shoes with shining straps.

And she was weeping.

Her name, let us say, is Kathy Pridham.

For the past two years she has worked as a librarian

for the British Council in Karachi. She, of all the British community there, was one of the few who took the trouble to learn Urdu, the local language. She could speak it, not read it: those calligraphic loops and dots meant nothing to her, except that 'it was a language'. Speaking it was enough. The local staff at the Council, shopkeepers, and even the cream of Karachi society (who cultivated European manners), felt that she knew them as they themselves did.

At this point, consider the word 'Karachi'. Not having been there myself I see clusters of white-cube buildings with the edge of a port to the left, a general slowness, a shaded verandah-ed suburb for the Burra-sahibs. Perhaps, eventually, boredom—or disgust with noises and smells not understood. Kathy, who was at first lonely and disturbed, quickly settled in. She became fully occupied and happy; insofar as that word has any meaning. There was a surplus of men in Karachi: young English bachelors sent out from head office, and pale appraising types who work at the embassies; but the ones who fell over themselves to be near her were Pakistanis. They were young and lazy. With her they were ardent and gay.

Already the words Kathy and Karachi are becoming inextricably linked.

It was not long before she too was rolling her head in slow motion during conversations, and clicking her tongue, as they did, to signify 'no'. Her bungalow in the European quarter with its lawn, verandah, two archaic servants, became a sort of *salon*, especially at the Sunday lunches where Kathy reigned, supervising, flitting from one group to the next. Those afternoons never seemed to end. No one wanted to leave. Sometimes she had musicians perform. And there was always plenty of liquor (imported), with wide dishes of hot food. Kathy spoke instantly and volubly on the country's problems, its complicated politics, yet in London if she had an opinion she had rarely expressed it.

When Kathy thought of London she often saw 'London'—the six letters arranged in recognisable order. Then parts of an endless construction appeared, much of it badly blurred. There was the thick stone. Concentrating, she could recall a familiar bus stop, the interior of a building where she had last worked. Her street invariably appeared, strangely dead. Some men in overcoats. It was all so far away she sometimes thought it existed only when she was there. Her best friends had been two women, one a schoolteacher, the other married to a taciturn engineer. With them she went to Scotland for holidays, to the concerts at Albert Hall. Karachi was different. The word stands for something else.

The woman weeping at the kitchen table is Kathy Pridham. It is somewhere in London (there are virtually no kitchen tables in Karachi).

After a year or so Kathy noticed at a party a man standing apart from the others, watching her. His face was bony and fierce, and he had a thin moustache. Kathy, of course, turned away, yet at the same time tilted her chin and began acting over-earnest in conversation. For she pictured her appearance: seeing it (she thought) from his eyes.

She noticed him at other parties, and at one where she knew the host well enough, casually asked, 'Tell me. Who is that over there?'

They both looked at the man watching her.

'If you mean him, that's Syed Masood. Not your cup of tea, Kathy. What you would call a wild man.' The host was a successful journalist and drew in on his cigarette. 'Perhaps he is our best painter. I don't know; I have my doubts.'

Kathy lowered her eyes, confused.

When she looked up, the man called Syed Masood had gone.

Over the next few days, she went to the galleries around town and asked to see the paintings of Syed Masood. She was interested in local arts and crafts, and had decided that if she saw something of his she liked she would buy it. These gallery owners threw up their hands. 'He has released nothing for two years now. What has got into him I don't know.'

Somehow this made Kathy smile.

Ten or eleven days pass—in words that take only seconds to put down, even less to absorb (the discrepancy between Time and Language). It is one of her Sunday lunches. Kathy is only half-listening to conversations and when she breaks into laughter it is a fraction too loud. She has invited this man Masood and has one eye on the door. He arrives late. Perhaps he too is nervous.

Their opening conversation (aural) went something like this (visual).

'Do come in. I don't think we've met. My name is Kathy Pridham.'

'Why do you mix with these shits?' he replied, looking around the room.

Just then an alarm wristlet watch on one of the young men began ringing. Everyone laughed, slapping each other, except Masood.

'I'll get you something,' said Kathy quietly. 'You're probably hungry.'

She felt hot and awkward, although now that they were together he seemed to take no notice of her. Several of the European men came over, but Masood didn't say much and they drifted back. She watched him eat and drink: the bones of his face working.

He finally turned to her. 'You come from—where?'

'London.'

'Then why have you come here?'

She told him.

'And these?' he asked, meaning the crowd reclining on cushions.

'My friends. They're people I've met here.'

Suddenly she felt like crying.

But he took her by the shoulders. 'What is this? You speak Urdu? And not at all bad? Say something more, please.'

Before she could think of anything he said in a voice that disturbed her, 'You are something extraordinary.' He was so close she could feel his breath. 'Do you know that? Of course. But do you know how extraordinary? Let me tell you something, although another man might put it differently. It begins here'—for a second one of his many hands touched her breasts; Kathy jumped—'and it *emanates*. Your volume fills the room. Certainly! So you are quite vast, but beautiful.'

Then he added, watching her, 'If you see what I mean.'

He was standing close to her, but when he spoke again she saw him grinning. 'Now repeat what I have just said in Urdu.'

He made her laugh.

Here—now—an interruption. While considering the change in Kathy's personality I remember an incident from last Thursday, the 12th. This is an intrusion but from 'real life'. The words in the following paragraph reconstruct the event as remembered. As accurately as possible, of course.

A beggar came up to me in a Soho bar and asked (a hoarse whisper) if I wished to see photographs of funerals. I immediately pictured a rectangular hole, sky, men and women in coats. Without waiting for my reply he fished out from an inside pocket the wad of photographs, postcard size, each one of a burial. They were dog-eared and he had dirty fingernails. 'Did you know these dead people?' He shook his head. 'Not even their names?' He shook his head. 'That one,' he said, not taking his eyes off the photographs, 'was dug yesterday. That one, in 1969.' There was little difference. Both showed men and women standing around a dark rectangle, perplexed. I felt a sharp tap on my wrist. The beggar had his hand out. Yes, I gave him a shilling. The barman spoke: 'Odd way to earn a living. He's been doing that for years.

Kathy soon saw Masood again. He arrived one night with his shirt hanging out while she was entertaining the senior British Council representative, Mr. L., and his wife. They were a cautious experienced pair, years in the service, yet Mrs. L. began talking loudly and hastily, a sign of indignation, when Masood sat away from the table, silently watching them. Mr. L. cleared his throat several times—another sign. It was a hot night with both ceiling fans hardly altering the sedentary air. Masood suddenly spoke to Kathy in his own language. She nodded and poured him another coffee. Mrs. L. caught her husband's eye, and when they left shortly afterwards, Kathy and Masood leaned back and laughed.

'You can spell my name four different ways,' Masood declared in the morning, 'but I am still the one person! Ah,' he said laughing, 'I am in a good mood. This is an auspicious day.'

'I have to go to work,' said Kathy.

'Look up "auspicious" when you get to the library. See what it says in one of your English dictionaries.'

She bent over to fit her brassiere. Her body was marmoreal, the opposite to his: bony and nervy.

'Instead of thinking of me during the day,' he went on, 'think of an exclamation mark! It amounts to the same thing. I would see you, I think, as a colour. Yes, I think more than likely pink, or something soft like yellow.'

'You can talk,' said Kathy laughing.

But she liked hearing him talk. Perhaps there'll be further examples of why she enjoyed hearing him talk.

That night Masood took her to his studio. It was in the inner part of the city where Europeans rarely ventured, and as Masood strode ahead Kathy avoided, but not always successfully, the stares of women in doorways, the fingers of beggars, and rows of sleeping bodies. She noticed how some men deliberately dawdled or bumped into her; striding ahead, Masood seemed to enjoy having her there. In an alleyway he unbolted a powder-blue door as a curious crowd gathered. He suddenly clapped his hands to move them. Then Kathy was inside: a fluorescent room, dirty white-washed walls. In the corner was a wooden bed called a 'charpoy', some clothes over a chair. There were brushes in jars, and tins of paints.

'Syed, are these your pictures?'

'Leave them,' he said sharply. 'Come here. I would like to see you.'

Through the door she could feel the crowd in the alleyway. She was perspiring still and now he was undoing her blouse.

'Syed, let's go?'

He stepped back.

'What is the matter? The natives are too dirty tonight. Is that it? Yes, the walls; the disgusting size of the place. All this stench. It must be affecting your nostrils? Rub your nose in it. Lie in my shit and muck. If you wait around you might see a rat. You could dirty your Mem-sahib's hands for a change.' Then he kicked his foot through one of the canvases by the door. 'The pretty paintings you came to see.'

As she began crying she wondered why. (He was only a person who used certain words.)

I will continue with further words.

Kathy made room for Masood in her house, in her bed as well as the spare room which she made his studio. Her friends noticed a change. At work, they heard the pronoun 'we' constantly. She told them of parties they went to, the trips they planned to take, how she supervised his meals; she even confessed (laughing) he snored and possessed a violent temper. At parties, she took to sitting on the floor. She began wearing 'kurtas' instead of 'blouses', 'lungis' rather than 'dresses', even though with her large body she looked clumsy. To the Europeans she somehow became, or seemed, untidy. They no longer understood her, and so they felt sorry for her. It was about then that Kathy's luncheon parties stopped, and she and Masood, who were always together, went out less frequently. Most people saw Masood behind this—he had never disguised his contempt for her friends—but others connected it with an incident at the office. Kathy arrived one morning wearing a sari and was told by the Chief Librarian it was inappropriate; she couldn't serve at the counter wearing that. Then Mr. L. himself, rapidly consulting his wife, spoke to her. He spelt out the *British* Council's function in Karachi, underlining the word British. 'Kathy, are you happy?' he suddenly asked. Like others, he was concerned. He wanted to say, 'Do you know what you are doing?' 'Oh, yes,' Kathy replied. 'With this chap, I mean,' he said, waving his hand. And Kathy left the room.

People's distrust of Masood seemed to centre around his unconventional appearance and (perhaps more than anything) his rude silences. Nobody could say they knew him, although just about everybody said he drank too much. Stories began circulating. 'A surly bugger,' he was called behind his back. That was common now. There were times when he cursed Kathy in public. Strange, though, the wives and other women were more ready to accept the affair. There was something about Masood, his face and manner. And they recognised the tenacity with which Kathy kep living with him. They understood her quick defence of him, often silent but always there, even when she came late to work, puff-eyed from crying and once, her cheek bruised.

Here, the life of Kathy draws rapidly to a close.

It was now obvious to everyone that Masood was drinking too much. At the few parties they attended he usually made a scene of some sort; and Kathy would take him home. Think of swear words. She was arriving late for work and missed whole days. Then she disappeared for a week. They had argued one night and Kathy screamed at him to leave. He replied by hitting her across the mouth. She moved into a cheap hotel, but within the week he found her. 'Syed spent all day, every day, looking for me,' was how she later put it. 'He needs someone.' When she was reprimanded for her disappearance and general conduct, she burst into tears.

In London, the woman with elbows on the table is

Kathy Pridham. She has unwrapped a parcel from Karachi. Imagine: coarse screwed-up paper and string lie on the table. Masood has sent a self-portrait, oil on canvas, quite a striking resemblance. His vanity, pride and troubles are enormous. His face, leaning against the teapot, stares across at Kathy weeping.

She cannot help thinking of him; of his appearance.

Words. These marks on paper, and so on.

Louise was born on a Monday; she was married on a Monday, and her cat was eaten by an owl on a Monday.

At first, Louise and Paul thought it might be an eagle.

'It can't be,' said Paul. 'It's the middle of the night.'

They were up at their beach-house sitting on a sofa watching television when they simultaneously, so they discovered later, experienced the spooky sensation of being watched. In fact, they had both already glanced through the glass doors, just in case, but there was nothing there. Neither of them thought to look up at the long, thin triangular wedge of glass which lay between the ceiling and the doors. It wasn't until Paul got up to make a cup of coffee that he happened to see the brooding shape perched on the pergola.

'Christ!'

'What?' Louise turned, followed his gaze, and could not believe her eyes. For there, staring into the room and gazing directly at them, was a huge bird.

'Is it an eagle?' said Louise, squinting up at the towering shape.

'It can't be,' said Paul. 'It's the middle of the night.'

When they had arrived for this particular weekend at their beach-house, which was perched on top of a hill backing onto a national park, they were laden down with their usual mountain of stuff—the cat and the dog, the computer, the backpacks and the groceries. Before the dog came into their lives it was not quite so crowded, it was just Paul, Louise and the cat.

Apart, that is, from the several months, which they do not even mention any more, when it was just Louise and the cat, or just Paul, because of the sudden and very surprising news that Paul had been having an affair for some months with a mousey acquaintance of theirs who was a regular partner in their Sunday morning tennis game on the weekends they were in town. This news had led swiftly to what their counsellor had called a 'trial' separation, although while Louise was undertaking the trial it felt as if her world had come to an abrupt and permanent end.

Paul had been put out when Louise had insisted on remaining in the Sunday tennis game.

'But that means I can't play,' he said at the time, sounding almost whiney, she thought.

'You and your friend can play somewhere else,' Louise said, with what she thought was considerable restraint.

'I haven't got any friends since I left you.'

Louise felt a surge of triumph. 'Well,' she said magnanimously, 'I suppose you can play this weekend. I'm going to the coast anyway.'

'Oh.' He looked crestfallen. 'You didn't mention to me you were going.'

What was it he thought he was up to, Louise had wondered to herself as she pottered around the shack with her pathetic single-person grocery bags. Even the raucous parrots living in the spotted gum outside their living room window managed a monogamous relationship. The magpies, Mr Hole-in-the-Head and Mrs Hole, had raised one noisy and ravenous offspring a few years back and were so evidently worn to a frazzle that they seemed to be practising some form of contraception because no other jangly baby Hole had made its presence felt. Mr and Mrs Hole seemed relieved, and rather plumper since they had given up raising babies. They were obviously happy together. Some days, Louise and Paul had noted in the past, Mr Hole-in-the-Head, having unearthed a plump grub, would offer his wife some of it. On other occasions, on one of their off-days, perhaps, he would keep it to himself while she scolded him noisily. Still, they were a couple, there was no doubt about that. They chased other magpies off their territory *immediately*.

'I can't believe I didn't chase *her* off,' said Louise, on one of her lonely visits, scooping up the cat and cuddling her close for yet another crying bout. Everywhere in the shack were reminders of her years with Paul, from the romance of a faded holiday snap to the more prosaic evidence of sandy bathers and shaving cream. But of all the things she hated most to see it was the recent painting of a Powerful Owl, which Paul had dashed off the day after the visitation. She had rarely seen him so fired up, and she'd got caught up too, searching through bird books for information; helping him mix his paints. At the end of the day she'd almost felt as if she had painted the picture; she had thought to herself, 'This is one of those experiences that we'll talk about when we're old. We'll say, Do you remember the Powerful Owl?'

At the time this nocturnal visit from a bird with such an extraordinary name seemed fortuitous. Almost, Paul and Louise said over breakfast the next morning, as if their house had been blessed in a pantheistic ritual. They had looked it up in the bird book the night before, and there was no doubt it was a Powerful Owl, *Ninox strenua*.

'It inhabits mountainous forests and scrubs,' Louise read out loud while Paul scribbled notes—the painting already talked about, already hanging in the air, only needing to be coaxed into existence. 'My God! You wouldn't believe what it eats—its main diet is possums and gliders—we're talking some owl here.'

Paul pointed to Molly, curled up in her favourite armchair. 'She'd better watch out then, she's smaller than a possum.'

Louise was shocked. 'Don't even mention it,' she said. 'What a horrible thought.'

It was Molly who kept her company through the endless nights of their separation. Molly who sat on her chest, purring away, delighted that the house rules had suddenly been broken and she was allowed in the bedroom. It was Molly who would decide when Louise needed entertaining, launching herself into an acrobatic routine at the drop of a whisker, her tail fluffed up and her paws beating an irate piaffe on the slate floor. It was Molly, too, who, distressed at being locked out of their bedroom when the separation was over—when Louise had won (thank God she had won)—developed an extraordinary habit.

The first time Louise felt Molly land on her chest, she sat straight up in bed. 'How the bloody hell did she get in?' she muttered to Paul—except that Paul was sleeping soundly beside her, and there was no cat in the room, let alone on the bed. Louise didn't bother to mention it to Paul, it was so obvious it was just her imagination, but as the months passed and Molly's daily activities became abruptly curtailed by the puppy, she took to regular flying visits. It became so commonplace that Louise would occasionally get out of bed and open the door, and there would be Molly, primly sitting with her paws together, a baleful stare in her amber eyes. 'You stop that, do you hear,' Louise would whisper. 'I know exactly what you're doing, and you can't come in.' Nevertheless she felt guilty that Molly was reduced to spiritual naughtiness in order to get her quota of attention. It seemed unfair.

In the beginning Louise never asked about the other woman. She did not want to jinx her and Paul's passionate reconciliation. But the questions ran around her head, all day, all night. Why had Paul found the mousey woman attractive? What was she like in bed? Was she funny? Paul always said he loved Louise's sense of humour. Did the mousey one have a sense of humour? If so, she hid it well. What did they do with their time together? Where did they go? Worst of all, the unaskable question—was he happy with her? And if he was happy with her did that mean he wasn't happy with Louise, and if he wasn't happy with Louise, why had he come back to her? Had he really come back, or would he leave again? If he left again would it be for the same mousey woman or a different one? Sometimes, not often, she would voice her fears and he always reassured her: 'It's over, it's all right, we're together and that's what counts.' What she wanted to know was how could he be so sure when she felt so unsure. It seemed the most grotesque irony that he should be the one to leave and come home so cheerfully optimistic, while she—who had been labouring under the delusion they were happy together—was left with this rattling insecurity which was quite unknown to her.

But the thing that bothered Louise most was the reason Paul had given for leaving during one of their vitriolic sessions with the counsellor.

'She writes about me,' he had said, not even looking her in the eye. 'It's like living with Woody Allen. I feel like everything I say or do is being noted for some future book.'

'But that's not true!' Louise could hardly believe her ears. 'I've always been a writer. He knew that when we met, and anyway, it's fiction.'

Paul laughed. 'Fiction, schmiction.'

The counsellor held up a warning finger. 'Here we go again,' she said, 'not listening to each other.'

Louise took no notice. 'And what about him?' she said. 'What about his paintings? Don't think I haven't noticed who he's been using as a model.'

The night that Molly went, the night she was eaten, Louise and Paul had decided to sleep separately. He wanted to finish a painting, and on such nights it might be two in the morning before he would leave his studio and come up to the house. Louise opted to sleep on her own, but before she turned in for the night, she plucked up enough courage to ask Paul her question.

'Are you happy with me?' she asked.

'Of course I am,' he said. 'We got married, didn't we? I love you, you know that.' He came and put his hands on her shoulders. 'Let it go, love,' he said. 'It really is time to let it go.' After he had gone to the studio, Louise sat outside for a while and Molly came too. The dog was shut up safe and sound in the laundry, hidden from the marauders who had been hanging around their house of late.

'We'll have to get that dog desexed immediately,' Louise told Molly. 'I think she's on heat.' Even as she spoke she could see the glowing eyes and scruffy coat of the labrador-cross from next door. 'Shoo,' she said crossly. 'Piss off.'

Powerful Owls, said the bird book, *are shy birds; they live in pairs and are strongly territorial. They roost in various tall trees—and not always together, in order to protect their territory. They eat birds and small mammals, gliders, sugar gliders, bush possums, rats, rabbits, kookaburras and magpies. They tear their prey apart and eat it piece by piece. Sometimes they take the rear end back to their roost, place it carefully on a branch and hold it all day in their talons before eating it when they leave the roost the next night. They nest at least fifteen metres above ground, using a hollow tree; the female lays two dull white eggs, and while she is nesting the male makes no attempt to guard the nest. They eat everything and regurgitate pellets.*

As Louise was cleaning her teeth she heard a familiar noise, the sound of miaowing from the roof. She stomped outside in her nightdress, put the chair on the verandah and reached up for the cat. 'Come here then, stupid,' she said, and hauled her down by the scruff of the neck. Molly followed her inside, and sat on the kitchen table looking out into the darkness.

Louise can never, no matter how hard she tries, rewind the film of that night. She can never hear again those pitiful miaows in the night and, this time, make the decision to get up—as she had done a hundred times before—and get the cat off the roof. Instead, when Molly's cries woke her, she shut out the noise, buried her head under the pillow and pretended she couldn't hear. Finally the miaowing and pacing stopped. But then, not long after, and still in the dead of night, there was a huge thump, as if a large branch had fallen on the roof. At the same time a shaft of pure white terror screeched through Louise's body—Louise felt the pain of the talons in her flesh and at that moment she and Molly became one. Louise lay in the dark and knew without a shadow of doubt that her cat had been taken off the roof by an owl, by *Ninox strenua*.

Looking back on it, Louise wondered how she ever got to sleep, how she managed to delude herself into believing that the cat was all right. But in a way it was easy, it was simply a matter of pretending to herself that nothing was wrong—that it had, in fact, been a branch landing on the roof. In the end she had slept until the dawn broke, when she started up with the strange sensation of some forgotten disaster. She immediately went out to look for the cat, but she was nowhere to be seen. She knocked on Paul's door, tears streaming down her face.

'Molly's gone,' she said. 'She's been taken by an owl.'

He was sleepy, surprised and sceptical all at once. 'She's probably just hiding in a cupboard,' he said. 'You know how she is.' He helped her look inside the house, and then he sat on the verandah watching as she walked through the bush, calling and calling. 'Do you want to stay here?' he said. 'She'll probably come back.'

'No, she won't,' Louise said. 'There's no point in staying, she's never coming back.'

They drove back to the city quickly, with Louise

snuffling into a hankie. When they stopped at the local garage, Paul got out to do the petrol.

'How are you today?' asked the attendant.

'Not so good,' Paul said. 'My wife thinks our cat's been taken by an owl.' He injected the words with a kind of male camaraderie, a sort of 'you-know-how-they-are' kind of sound.

'Bastards, those owls,' said the attendant. 'Our cat had a run-in with one, but he got away.'

Paul got back into the car looking white.

Why does she mourn so long and hard for Molly? She was, after all, only a cat. It is partly the manner of her going—as if she and Paul had prompted it all those months ago when they had seen the Powerful Owl on the pergola and Paul had remarked: 'She'd better watch out, she's smaller than a possum.' It is partly because Molly is a symbol of the relationship she and Paul shared before the mousey woman came on the scene. They had bought her in the early days when they first moved in together, and as it had become increasingly obvious there might not be children from their marriage, there was no doubt that Molly had somehow taken the place of family.

But there is something else which niggles away at Louise, something she does not understand at all, and that is that she has been finding it hard to write since Molly was taken. It is almost as if her familiar has left her; she has even been finding it hard to wreak a fictional vengeance on the mousey woman. It is as if her life is only pretending to be normal. It is as if there is something going on, something Louise should know about and does not know. Sometimes she wonders if it is because there was no corpse, no visible sign of death. Occasionally she likes to recite 'The Owl and the Pussycat' to herself; she likes to pretend that perhaps the owl took sympathy on the cat, and they are living out their lives somewhere with their little green boat on the edge of the sand.

Louise has a friend who is psychic. She talks easily about spirits and angels and devils as if these are everyday realities and not part of the unknown. The friend, who has had her name changed by deed poll to Venus, has often offered Louise a reading but Louise has always refused. Then, one day, over lunch, Louise finds herself talking about Molly, about her habit of astrally projecting herself onto the bed, and that night Venus rings her up.

'I've got my medicine cards here,' she says. 'Did you know that owl medicine is associated with clairvoyance, astral projection and black and white magic?'

Louise feels a shiver running through her body. 'Really?' she says. She thinks of Molly's neat black and white body sitting primly outside the bedroom door.

'Remember your Greek myths,' says Venus, who certainly does. 'Do you remember Athene?'

Louise thinks. 'She's the one who jumped out of Zeus's head, isn't she?'

Venus laughs. 'She is, but also her emblem is the owl. She has an owl on her shoulder, and the owl is the revealer of unseen truths—it lights up her blind side, and enables her to speak the whole truth. Right way up this card is about Owl befriending you and bringing you messages through dreams and meditation, wrong way up and it means that deception has been practised, by or against you. Owl tells you to keep an eye on your property and loved ones. Remember that Owl is always asking, "Who?"' She pauses. 'Louise? Does that make sense?'

Louise would like to say no but she would be lying. 'Yes,' she says. 'It makes sense.'

Louise puts the phone down, sits on the sofa and buries her head in her hands. For now she knows what she has suspected for some time—that Paul is still seeing the mousey woman, indeed, is not going to stop seeing the mousey woman, and that Louise's marriage is well and truly over.

'How did you know?' asks Paul ingenuously.

'I knew. That's all.' She has only one question left to ask her husband. 'Why?'

He puts his hands behind his back, as if distancing himself from her. 'Because I want children.'

'I see.' Louise feels strangely cold and divorced from her own body. She is cat, owl and mouse all at once. 'So you persuaded me not to have children because you didn't want any and now that you do, you're leaving me for someone who is young enough to have them. I see.'

Paul looks up at her. 'I still can't understand why you're throwing me out. Why can't we talk about this in the morning?'

That night Molly visits Louise for the first time since her death. When Louise feels the familiar sudden weight on the bedclothes, she is unalarmed and content. She strokes the imaginary outline, seeing the black head under her hand, the white chest and socks, the small silver rings on the tail. 'I don't know why you had to leave me, Molly,' she whispers. 'But I promise you one thing—this is something I'll never write about.'

But even as Louise speaks the words she knows she is lying. Even as it had happened to the cat, even as she had felt the talons in her back, she knew she would write about it. Just as one day she will write about Paul again, and the mousey woman, and anything else that ever happens to her, because she is Owl and she must eat everything, regurgitating the pellets of her memories, endlessly.

At last it was spring. The paddocks in front of the house were still sodden from the months of rain and until midday, when the sun was directly above the farm, the grass was covered in fine overnight cobwebs, sparkling with drops of heavy dew. Pale clear sunshine lay like moss on the flat fields which stretched from the house to the road.

When she went walking with the baby down the potholed track Anne could see the white nubs of new mushrooms all through the long grass. They would sit on the little wooden bridge over the creek while the baby threw in rocks and bits of bark, chuckling when they splashed. Then they would walk on to where the cows grazed next to the path and the little girl would try to pat them, stumbling and sinking in the clods of cow-trodden turf.

Anne watched her in a detached way. Her mind was still numb from the cold winter and what she saw as the gradual failure of her marriage. They had been saying, for the second year now, that it would all be better in spring. When they didn't have to get up at six and chop the kindling in the frost and shiver in the smoky kitchen until the fire caught . . . 'It'll be good then. We'll go on picnics and get baskets of apples from the old trees near the creek.' Terry was always the optimist. 'People will come and stay, you'll see. As soon as the weather is better.'

But she sensed that he was being held back by her reluctance and lethargy. His council job was routine, nine-to-five, with occasional stints in the hills. He would have liked to pack up his gear and set off for months at a time—really get into trees as he put it. They joked about it—she said 'Why couldn't you have stayed a maths teacher? Why wouldn't you settle for lunches at the pub and evenings at the theatre? What more has life to offer really?' and he'd grin his Peter Pan grin and say 'Yes, you've saddled yourself with Melbourne's answer to Gauguin—but at least I let you come too,'

Now she was pregnant again. She hadn't told Terry, she still hadn't decided not to get rid of it. Looking at the baby now, sitting happily in the reeds and muck she thought of a pun to tell Terry. Katherine of all the rushes. She grinned, she always laughed at her own jokes. She felt a bit better.

'Kathy. Come on. Time for yum.' She hugged the plump child to her. Fierce, fierce, she thought, is my love for you. I'd live my life in grief at the thought of killing off another Kathy. But in her head she was circling, crying—How? How? Can I be tied down by another one? I'd never be able to break free then. She'd have to make the decision herself. If she told Terry he wouldn't leave her any option. He often claimed he wanted six or seven children. He wouldn't make her have another child, but he'd never forgive her for getting rid of one.

Putting the little girl to bed after lunch she was suddenly overcome by the sheer physical effort of looking after babies. Kathy was still in nappies, she'd hardly be out of them when this one was due. I couldn't bear it, she thought angrily. Bound hand and foot by nappies and cot sheets and wet woollies. The ridiculous metaphor pleased her. God, I'm getting like my mother—making a joke of everything so she didn't have to scream.

She put the wet clothes into the trough and hung out the morning's washing, tripping over the rope of the sheep they had tethered there to crop the grass. She found herself drifting into fantasies of what she'd do if they owned this house. The farmer kept hinting that he wanted to sell. She sat on the garden wall muttering to herself. 'I'd have a kitchen garden here. With borders of marjoram and oregano and a hedge of rosemary.' A part of her these days wanted strongly to settle down. At times like this, with the baby asleep, the lamb bleating softly against her hand, the warm green grass rippling all around, it seemed a fine idea to buy a farmhouse and put down roots. 'We could make a lawn and the children could play here . . . ' She stopped herself. No, no, no. She wasn't going to be drawn in like that. She went inside to make tea.

She sat in the cold kitchen and thought of her old plans to live by herself with the baby. Nothing had come of them—she didn't like living here and her relationship with Terry was obviously deteriorating, but she was too apathetic to change, too overwhelmed by tiredness and routine.

That night friends came round. A painter who lived up the valley and his wife. They had no children and although they were a good ten years older than Anne and Terry, she always thought they seemed younger and more dashing. They grew their own dope and sometimes appeared with large plastic bags of it, recently cut down. Tonight they brought wine. Alec had just sold a painting and they were celebrating.

Sometimes Anne had fantasies of fucking Alec, although she didn't know him very well—he was a romantic figure to hang her dreams of freedom on. She never did anything about it. Since her affair with Nick she had been completely faithful to Terry. One drunken night she had told him about it and been appalled at the depth of his hurt and bewilderment. She had always assumed he knew what was going on. Now they had an understanding that they would talk it out before anything like that happened again. In fact now she had become the jealous one, afraid of the possibility of losing Terry while still wishing to escape herself.

That night they drank two flagons of red wine and argued loudly and hilariously about anarchy and revolution. Alec was blatantly anti-intellectual, furious and aggressive in his contempt for wishy-washy liberals, of whom he said Terry was a prime example. Terry withdrew into his charming complaisance, letting the others argue it out. If it was like this more often, Anne thought, I could contemplate it. But she knew this surge of energy and engagement was fleeting, dependent on new and stimulating people.

She went in to make coffee and Alec followed her. Terry was talking to Carol about horses, her obsession.

'I'd like to learn to ride,' he said. 'Is it very difficult?'

Anne made a sour face. The country was really getting into him, or was it Carol?

In the kitchen Alec was amorous. She stood stiffly when he put his arms around her.

'What's the matter?'

'Nothing's the matter. Are you usually so irresistible?'

'I thought I had perceived the odd signal that you might not be exactly averse . . . ' He spoke in a parody of a drunk's careful enunciation.

'Oh, well, of course I'm not averse.' She grinned. 'It isn't possible, that's all.'

'Well all right. OK. That's fine. Enough said. Sorry I asked!' He put the cups out on a tray. She was tempted to say more, explain it in detail, but it wasn't relevant. There was a tension between them now which was rather pleasant.

While Alec went to piss she took the tray in and stood quietly for a moment outside the door listening. She was fluttering with suspicion and the wish to be proved right. But when she opened the door Carol was asleep on the couch and Terry was changing the record. She put the tray down. Of course it was silly to suspect Terry, he'd come out with it if there was anything going on.

After they had left, the still sulky Alec half dragging Carol to the car, she said, 'I've never seen her get animated about anything except her bloody horses.'

'Yeah. It's interesting though. She's going to take me

riding tomorrow. That's OK isn't it?' he said, picking up her reaction. 'I'll look after the bub in the morning and you can get a rest. She's not calling for me until two.'

'Yes, of course it's all right. I hope you don't break your neck that's all.'

She brooded over it until she went to sleep and all the next morning while Terry took the baby shopping in the town. When she came down to it she didn't really care if he wanted to fuck Carol or not, she resented his freedom to even spend time with her. But I want to *own* him, she thought with a shock. This has really got to stop.

When he came back with Carol in the late afternoon, bruised and shaken from a fall, it was obvious that neither of them had any ulterior motives. Carol was rather irritable with him, she obviously thought he was hopeless. Still, even that sort of crossness can turn into sexual energy, Anne thought. She couldn't shake herself out of it. Every gesture, every word they uttered was sifted through the fine net of her jealousy until she finally had to relax and accept that there was nothing there. When Carol left, leading Terry's horse, muttering that she hoped it wasn't lamed by his carelessness, he gave an exaggerated sigh of relief.

'Jesus. Never again. I'm going to take lessons from the riding academy where they won't be so bad-tempered.'

So her last doubt was settled. She couldn't believe he was anything but genuine. Now the reaction set in. All afternoon, mulling over her jealousy, she'd been thinking of her pregnancy as her secret weapon. If she thought she was losing Terry she would tell him. Another baby would bind him to her with iron chains. Now she felt flat, cold, even let down. Her thoughts of the last twenty-four hours had been painful and frightening, but titillating in their way. I'll have to think it through again, she told herself.

During the next week she started to feel sick in the morning. Feeding Kathy her breakfast sludge made her retch. She'd have to make a decision soon or Terry would notice. One afternoon while the baby slept she went for a walk along the creek to where it joined the river. She sat down on a lichen-covered trunk and watched the swirling water. Frog spawn rimmed the pool and little purple grass-flowers were starting to poke out here and there. Everything seemed to be budding, flowering, gravid. Anne could feel the hormonal effects of pregnancy on her own mind. It would be so easy to give in to this longing to be part of the natural cycle, to be sucked in to the seasonal fertility. Oh God, she thought. There'll be baby lambs soon and then I won't have a chance.

One night Terry said, 'You're looking very down. What's the matter?'

'Nothing,' she said. 'Springtime depression. New life all around—and in here,' she pointed to her head, 'nothing new at all.'

'Why don't you go to town for a weekend? I'll mind the girl. Have a couple of nights out, get drunk, catch up on all the gossip. Go on.'

'Yes. I might,' she said, thinking, He's a kind man, I'd like to tell him and watch his pleasure. But she couldn't. She thought she'd put it off until she'd been away. She might talk to her friend Liz about it.

In the pub on Friday night it could have been a different universe. Anne felt tense among all the shouting laughing crowding people, some of them her friends. She saw Liz and pushed her way over to her. They kissed and talked and drank. By the time they left for a party she was fairly drunk. She hadn't said anything to Liz about being pregnant.

Much later, finding herself in bed with a man she'd known and lusted after years ago she started crying. He was alarmed and tender but she wouldn't talk about it. As much as anything it was the clumsiness of being with someone else after Terry. Different contours, different textures, new body habits to be learnt. It was very sad, but very fine, she thought drunkenly as she fell asleep.

In the morning he said, 'Can you come up to town very often?'

'As often as I like, I guess. I'll have to tell Terry why though.'

'What will he do?'

'I don't know,' she said. 'I really don't know. Does it matter?'

She went round to see Liz and collect her gear and make her arrangements. Then she rang Terry.

'How's it going?'

'All right. Listen Tez, I want to stay over till Monday night. Is that possible?'

'Sure. I'll take the day off. Having a good time? Drink? Drugs? Sex-crazed Carlton heavies?'

'All that.'

'How're you feeling physically? You looked very tired when you left.'

'I feel OK. I'm pretty sure I'll be better by Monday,' she said. 'I think it's one of those three-day wogs.'

She said hello to Kathy and sent him her love over the wires and then she went to meet her new lover for lunch. He was pleased to hear they'd have an extra night. He suggested that he could also take Monday off. 'We could have a picnic in the Gardens.'

'No,' she said. 'I've got an appointment on Monday morning. And after that I don't think I'll feel like doing anything much.'

My mother was a magger.*

A paling fence divided our garden from the garden next-door, and over the back fence lived Mrs Back-Fence. My mother and Mrs Back-Fence might have been posing for a cartoonist as they stood on either side of the fence, magging. Behind each woman was a rotary clothes line. We had striped tea-towels, white sheets, woollen singlets, pink pants, and knitted socks all hanging from dolly pegs. Some things were patched and darned, the mending being more obvious when the clothes were wet. It was unsafe to hang anything damaged but unmended on the line, for this would be noted by other maggers as a sign of degeneration in the family. And once, when a torn, unmended nightdress had got through the washing and as far as the line, our rabbit attacked it and shredded it so that it had to be thrown out. My mother and Mrs Back-Fence had floral aprons, and often their hair was set with metal butterfly wavers, covered by a chiffon scarf knotted at the front. They did not wear fluffy slippers. Instead they nearly

* The magpie is the scandalmonger of the woods. The verb 'to mag' meaning 'to gossip' derives from magpie.

always wore rather thick stockings and brown lace-up shoes, like nurses.

Over the back fence, these maggers passed hot scones wrapped in tea-towels, cups of sugar, bowls of stewed plums, and a continuous ribbon of talk. They sifted through the details of everything they heard and saw and thought, and arranged them into art. Children under the age of ten, considered to lack the ability to understand the narrative, were allowed to listen, provided they were still and quiet. (Today, magging usually takes place on the telephone, I think, and so a child listener becomes restless because there is only one side to the conversation.) The Crusaders took from the Arabian desert the seeds of the wild flowers which later became the glory of English gardens. The maggers scoured the lives of their relations and neighbours, and sometimes the lives of famous people, to shake out the seeds from which would grow undulating plains of exotic grasses and flowers giving colour and perfume.

One of the most hypnotic habits of the maggers was the constant use of possessive pronouns and parentheses. They constructed sentences which could go on all day in dizzy convolutions as one relative clause after another was added.

'Edna and Joe (his brother was Colin who married Betty Trethewey who later divorced him which was when he had his breakdown over the Kelly girl so that it was no wonder the business went down-hill) were having their twenty-fifth anniversary which was just before Easter which was early that year, and Pam (she's the daughter, you realise) was there with her fiancé who was Bruce French (his father had the hardware next to the Royal Park) when it turned out that Joe was electrocuted in the cellar which was where he kept the wine (they drank a terrible lot of wine in those days) and it wasn't long after that that Edna turned round married Bruce, and Pam went and lived next-door to them (this was fifteen years ago now) and she hasn't spoken to them since which is very hard on the daughter, Susan, who doesn't even know that Bruce is her father, not that Bruce can be certain himself really, but of course Edna knows and she has never forgiven Pam for not telling her she was going to have Susan when she was engaged to Bruce.'

As a child I never saw any Marx Brothers films. When I *did* see them, I was surprised to hear Grouch Marx using my mother's phrases. Trapped in her language, like fish in a net, were snatches and snippets from the Marx Brothers' scripts. Inserted into the magging of two women in a Tasmanian coastal town of the 1940s, the expressions of Groucho Marx had a curious lifelessness, and their meaning was elusive. But I, as a child, accepted the words at face-value, in faith, expecting to have their meaning revealed in good time. It took many years for things to fall into place. Perhaps the child who called his bear Gladly after Gladly the cross-eyed bear is an apocryphal child, but the story has a nice ring of truth. Harold be thy name. I applied the same unblinking acceptance to the name of the local toyshop. The end of the sign had fallen off, and so it was called 'The Woodpecker Toy Fact'. I even accepted the name of the toymaker as an ordinary name, and now I don't know whether it was his real name or not. He was called Jack Frost. At Christmas, he used to make wooden peepshows of the crib. You closed one eye and looked through the hole in the box. Inside, in an unearthly light were first the shepherds, then the animals, and further back, the baby like a sugar mouse in his mother's arms. The angels were in the far distance, wings sharp like the wings of swallows. And Jack Frost carved our rocking-horse. Even the name of the horse, Dapple Grey, I failed to see as descriptive, and thought of as Christian name and surname. I must have existed in a blurry blue mist where I waited for the words to acquire meaning. Something which I always connected with the verb 'to mag' was some stuff called 'Milk of Mag'. This was a thick, white, slightly aniseed, shudderingly horrible laxative medicine, the 'Mag' being short for magnesia.

I tried to join in some magging once. I made the mistake of thinking that if I introduced some fabulous fact, I would be included in the discussion. So I said that Jack Frost had told me he had made the original statue of the Infant Jesus of Prague. Nobody took any notice of me at all. Or so I thought. But after a while I realised that terribly silly lies were being referred to as wood-pecker toy facts.

'And then she tried to tell me the baby was premature. A woodpecker toy fact if ever I heard one. It is no mystery to me that he weighed nine and a half pounds. Nine and a half pounds! I ask you.'

There was a special quality to a toy fact. There was a

desperation—either to attract or to deflect attention. And a toy fact only became a toy fact after it had passed through the special sifting process of the maggers, and had received from them a blessing.

So I had generated a term which had drifted into the net of the maggers. Little did I know (as a magger would say) that the spirit of my words was being given the same weight as that accorded the words of Groucho Marx.

Over the years, the concept of the woodpecker toy fact has become very important and dear to me. I have lived here in Woodpecker Point on the northwest coast of Tasmania all my life. My parents have died and my sisters have all married and left the island. I live alone in the house with the rotary clothes line and the paling fence. Mrs Back-Fence is in a nursing home in Burnie, and I have never seen the wife of the Turkish man who now lives in the house. They have a baby daughter who sings Baa-baa-black-sheep sadly and endlessly in the garden. It is a very boring and irritating song, after a while. Jack Frost has disappeared. One of my nephews took Dapple Grey to the beach and left him there and he was washed out to sea. As these and many other things have changed, so the idea of the toy fact has changed and developed. The quest for the toy fact has gradually come to dominate my life.

Once when I was at the beach, years before the toy fact was named, I captured a star fish in my tin bucket. The tide was out, and there was a cold breeze coming in across the shiny wet sand. I was sitting on the pebbles which were shaped like eggs, and smooth, and all different kinds of white. I had the bucket between my legs so that I could stare down into it at the star fish, and I was given the ability to understand the shape of everything. The moment passed, and yet it has never left me. Five minutes later, the sky went darker, and a red-haired girl in a green dress came up behind me and grabbed the bucket. She ran off across the pebbles with the star fish. My second oldest sister chased the girl, and the girl defended herself with the spike of a beach umbrella. She drove the spike into my sister's lip, ran off with the bucket, and disappeared.

I think my quest began with the star fish. Perhaps if that girl had not stolen it when she did, had not injured my sister as she did, I might never have undertaken the quest. Then, when the toy fact was named and its nature defined in a rudimentary way, I sensed that there was a system of knowing things which could, if handled in the right way, lead to an understanding, the idea of which dazzled me. The simplicity and complexity of the star fish, punctuated in time by my sister's blood, and coupled with the glorious lie (which might not have been a lie) about Jack Frost and the Infant of Prague, suggested to me that if I assembled facts in a special way every minute of every day for years and years and years, I would eventually see something more beautiful and more wonderful than anything I could have imagined. It was as though I had a golden thread which I wove to make a net in which I caught the toy facts, trapping them, bright birds in flight, planets in amber. I have collected and assembled the toy facts in my brain, and I am still uncertain as to whether I will ultimately discover *The Toy Fact*, and so complete the pattern, or whether, by placing the final *Fact* I will produce *The Toy Fact*. The quest itself is, however, absorbing, and has, as I said, come to dominate my life.

It is not only a matter of discovering things, but of manufacturing from those things the toy facts in all their fullness and beauty. I sometimes think my golden net of facts is like a fabulous story I am writing in my head. Once when I was studying poetry at school, I used to think that everything was a metaphor, and said 'metaphor' in answer to every question.

'If we took a slice off the top of her head,' said the teacher, and I thought she was going to pay me a compliment, 'we would find that the only thing in there was a metaphor.' She meant to be insulting, but had stumbled on the beautiful truth. It was that remark of hers that set me on my final course. From then on, I did not have to pass any exams or do anything much at all. I have spent my time since that day listening to people, reading encyclopaedias, browsing in the library, sitting on the beach, and generally pursuing one toy fact after another. I cared for my parents when they were ill, and I have worked in the Morning Glory cake shop for the past ten years.

One day, I am going to know everything about everything. I will know what makes a Cox's Orange Pippin different from a Granny Smith. I will know what it is that stops hydrangeas from having any scent. I will see the pyramids being built and survive the Hundred Years' War. I will understand the nature of fire, and know the depth to which the longest tree-root goes down in the earth. I will know what sorrow is made from, what constitutes joy. I will have conversations with the sage of Zurich, afternoon tea with Chagall in his garden, speak to Polycrates the King before his crucifixion in Magnesia. There are bound to be times when I can think in Chinese.

Meanwhile, I live here in Woodpecker Point, not far from the ruins of the park where the deer and the peacocks used to roam. I prune the roses and the fruit trees and I talk to my finches.

I have a large collection of feathers, and am making a study of their colours. I am particularly interested at present in the iridescent colours which ripple and change on the necks of pigeons. They are formed when the light is refracted from the surfaces of the tiny scales which make up the feathers. I suppose some colours of reptiles and butterflies work on the same principle. I have spent a lot of time with butterflies, and can here, quite naturally, in the course as it were, of the conversation, mention a very high-class toy fact. This is the fact that the Cabbage White Butterfly arrived in Tasmania on the feast of St Teresa 1940, which was the day that I was born. We both arrived in Devonport, and have been constant observers of each other from the beginning. It is possible that the Cabbage White knows more about me than I know about it. I have a photograph of myself with a cloud of Cabbage Whites. I am three and I am standing among the cabbages in my maternal grandmother's garden, wearing a blue dress with the white edges that my grandmother knitted for me for Christmas. As these were the days before colour photography, the blue of my dress and the blue-green of the cabbages are tinted with inks. My hair is the colour of butter, and my shoes are magical red. The butterflies are untouched by the tinter's brush so that they possess a quality of ethereal purity which is lacking in the coloured areas of the picture. I have always been pleased that I had a grandmother who had Cabbage Butterflies in her cabbages. And I have the photograph to prove it. It was taken the day before Christmas, and on Christmas day, my grandmother died.

The night before they buried her, she came to me as I lay sleeping. She had taken by then the form of the smallest British butterfly, the Small Blue, so often found near warm and sunny grass slopes and in hollows. She was like a forget-me-not. She alighted on my quilt and smiled at me, sweetly, as she always smiled. And all she said was one word. This almost shocked me at the time, because she was a magger, like my mother. She had no doubt trained my mother. Well she smiled at me and she said:

'Listen.'

One morning, after a night of particularly disturbing dreams, Dr B. awoke to find he had become a text. Perhaps not entirely that, but the black points on his chest and neck, the thicker dots of beard as he shaved did make a pattern, and the raw red patches on his legs were now symmetrical, a Rorschach blot. What surprised him most, however, was not the text itself— it was, after all, quite undecipherable—but the calmness of his reaction, as if it had somehow resolved a matter long outstanding.

Something strange had been happening in room 401, or could have been seen to be, things thus designated being so often less matters of the truly bizarre than of altered perspectives, types of perception hitherto untried. Nor would it be so true to say that they were happening *in* 401 as to say that they were seen to happen *through* it, as if something in its air or light had assumed an uncharacteristic density, diffracting the normal activities of that place into unsuspected components.

Dr B. had noted something of its kind before, though that had been of so benign a nature that the possibility of a bizarre, disturbing source had not occurred to him. It had been a large group, all women. The one other male had fled before the third week of the course. Even Dr B. had had to experience a number of precarious moments before, relaxing, he allowed himself to be cajoled, ignored, even ungently disabused. When four of the nine became pregnant—one of them most mysteriously—he had himself conceived the notion that they had done it somehow to themselves, so openly did they seem to vilify their lovers, so evidently were they gravid with something he never quite dared mention.

To a party once (it was the kind of group you held a party for), he had invited two famous authors then visiting the city. Smoking, drinking, touching the writers as they talked, the women had devoured them. For half an hour Dr B. had hung about nervously, anticipating anger or offence, but then retired to an armchair by the stereo, to watch and marvel. One of the visitors, a poet, had been so taken by Ursula, her full, lactating breasts staining her dress unnoticed in the heat of her argument, that he had later written of them feeding the entire company as she talked, her bounty overflowing, crossing the floor, spilling out onto the balcony where it gathered into a wide white pool, the size and shape of the great mid-winter moon.

Eventually Dr B. had allowed them to set their own examination, given long extensions, seen the course open and turn and transubstantiate amongst its births and separations, infatuations and divorce. It seemed to him as if the path of the students through its texts had become itself an incalculable gestation, and he liked now, five years later, to think that his teaching had never been the same again. Perhaps he was right, but this new university was different, and that extraordinary atmosphere had never been repeated. If what was happening in room 401 had reawakened that earlier excitement in his mind it was only to expose its darker implications. It was hard to say where it had started. Once noticed, it had come to seem a broadcast that had gone on perhaps for centuries, but into which one tuned only with the greatest difficulty. Even now the things it had begun to tell him could not be spoken of without risk, or the ridicule that might ruin everything.

One day, in a third-year course, they had been speaking of the seventeenth century, and a student had marvelled at the intensity of John Donne's preoccupation with sexuality and death. Perhaps Dr B. had remembered Ursula, Pauline, Jenna as he tried to explain. Certainly, pausing overlong to collect his thoughts, he had remembered something else: the twilit room and the roses and Michelle, exhausted, sleeping at last mid-labour, the strong contractions continuing under the epidural, trying to expel the child that would not come and would not come.

Perhaps, he had said, *for the woman, death and sex are never far removed.* Certainly in Donne's time, given the difficulty of contraception, the high infant mortality, the perils of labour, any act of sex might mean a birth, any birth might mean a death. Perhaps the poet had tried so hard to know the one that he came to know the other, and had realised that as a maker of love he might also be a maker of death. *But you must know far more of such things than I could ever tell you.* And then he, Dr B., had felt a shadow in the room, a sudden tightening, and knew that it was just the truth. He felt weak, humiliated, whether before the students or the sudden ghosts he could not tell. Although it lodged itself in his mind as something he had been looking for, so stupidly simple it had taken years to find it, and although there had ensued a discussion in which he glimpsed, at moments, a familiar excitement, nothing more had seemed to come of it.

It had been a beginning nonetheless, for them as much as for himself. Some two weeks later he had arrived late, to find the group already seated. He caught the tail-end of a conversation. One of the students—a girl who attended irregularly, but who had been there on the earlier occasion—was speaking about medical tests. Thin, nervous, chain-smoking as she talked, she claimed that for almost two weeks now she had been unable to keep anything down. She would vomit after every meal, and was surviving on fruit juice alone. If that had been true, he thought, she would not be attending classes, but throughout the seminar his eyes kept returning to her. Drawn, pale, writing nothing down, saying little more after her opening disclosures, it seemed as if she had lost her stomach for words also. Why, then, had she come? Two weeks. He wanted to ask her when, precisely, her problem had started, whether it had ever happened before, but he did not have the chance. A week later, just before the seminar, he received a letter from Sydney, to tell him that for medical reasons she had had to withdraw from the course.

She was not the first to go—in fact there had been three already—and she would not be the last. He consulted the department's records. Yes, the others had withdrawn from other courses also, and there were medical certificates, one citing abdominal pains, another glandular fever. Dr B. had not much considered such things before. One's attention as a teacher was always of necessity on those present, those actually in the room. But now it was increasingly the gaps, the absences which preoccupied him, and not just of those who left a course entirely, but also of those whose attendance was erratic, who sought extensions, or whose work was never submitted. The patterns astounded him. Certain names and syndromes kept reappearing—unidentified disorders of the gut, the abdomen, behavioural and eating disturbances of undetermined origin. The suspicion of some as yet undiscovered link with his own discipline, perhaps even with the texts on his own course grew stronger, but how could he test it? One could not inject phrases, administer ideas like barium.

Although they scoffed at his suggestions, the medical friends he consulted served only further to convince him. The conditions he named occurred in nothing like such proportions in the population at large and, although the figures were closer there, not even elsewhere in the university. He had learnt from Freud how a word, a chance phrase overheard could trigger dyspnoea, aphasia, *tussis nervosa*. Why should it not be that the written or printed word had a similar power, that in the intimacy of reader and text some thought or idea could not take hold which could so disquiet, so distress, that it produced physical symptoms? Bulimia, anorexia, obsessive compulsive syndrome, myalgic encephalomyopathy: the categories were there, awaiting the signs, but they did little or nothing to explain their origins. Now, when a student came to him with a request for an extension, he would ask them more carefully why. Now, when someone did not appear for a seminar or tutorial for two or three weeks running, he would take the trouble to contact them. And whenever one of the familiar diagnoses occurred, as they continued to, he would ascertain as best he could where the particular problems had started, what it might have been that the student had been studying at the time.

It was not easy. A number of other factors intruded. But there were also incidents, connections too obvious to doubt. One disturbed ex-student came to him claiming quite specifically that it was his course, his seminars, the texts that he had taught, that had created a rift in his marriage, that, altering his mind, his attitudes, his expectations, had alienated his friends and left him wounded, isolated, in a position he could neither escape nor endure. Another, calling him for a reference some months after her graduation, revealed that she had been troubled for a considerable period by neurotic symptoms which began at a specific point in her final examination. Looking back through her paper, trying to find the precise point where she had faltered, where things had begun to crumble, at last he found something, a partly erased quotation, a fragment of an Empson villanelle, that might have been a clue.

Once his mind began to move along such lines, there seemed no shortage of evidence. In another course, on contemporary fiction, two older, married women had made friends, arriving and departing together, discussing tutorials over coffee, sharing resources. At first sceptical, they had become increasingly immersed, almost obsessive about the books they read, salvaging from them their hidden stories, finding in one novel in particular— a tortuous account of a marriage, the manipulation of children, an eventual matricide—an indictment of proportions Dr B. himself had never seen before, the bitter web of its ironies reaching into every corner of reality.

At some point—it must have been while working on this text—something had happened. It was late autumn, and a 'flu epidemic was sweeping the country. For over a month his classes had been severely affected, four or five students appearing where in the weeks before there had been a dozen or more. This, while amongst the more extreme he had experienced, was not particularly unusual and, although one or two of their children had been ill, the two friends had attended regularly. Pauline had a cough, it was true, and Marjorie had seemed tired and distracted, as if fighting something off, but while, as the winter continued, all but two of the other sufferers had returned, these particular problems had continued. At one point, halfway through a sentence, Pauline had had a fit of coughing so severe that Marjorie had had to fetch water for her, and thereafter, for several weeks, her cough had interrupted her almost every time she tried to speak. Meeting her once in the corridor he had asked about this, and she had joked that he seemed jinxed, that it attacked her only in his classes. She had said this with no sign of trouble and yet, when next she tried to speak in the seminar, the cough returned.

Marjorie, meanwhile, had continued to look drawn and distressed. She had been absent two weeks without explanation and had submitted an essay well below her usual standard. In class she seemed restless, inattentive, and once, near the end of the course, just after a point someone had made about Christianity, had rushed from the room and had not returned for her books until several hours later, her voice strangely husky, her manner artificially unconcerned. Afraid that he had offended her, he asked, at the time, if there might have been some misunderstanding, if there were something he might clarify. No, she said, she had simply remembered that her parking meter had expired. He had hardly seen her again. Soon after the course had ended, and finding that she had missed the examination, he asked another student about her, and was told that, at some stage during this period, Marjorie had left her husband, and that one of her children had attempted suicide. He felt disturbed that she had said nothing to him, but was told that she had said very little to anyone—that, indeed, she could not; that she had been in hospital for some weeks already, having lost almost half of her body-weight, and having lost her voice almost entirely.

Small wonder, then, that something had begun to happen to Dr B. himself—an insomnia, or partial insomnia, that left him only a few hours' sleep per night. This was not the first time this had happened, but it had never been so severe. At first he would lie awake trying to calm himself, to sleep again, but eventually would rise instead, and read, so as not to disturb Michelle. At three, four, five in the morning, he would find himself going over the books he had been teaching, looking for clues, finding them nowhere, everywhere, moved more than ever by a pain, a frenzy, a despair they seemed to hold at bay. The questions abounded. Why was it so often the women who suffered? Was it a pain, a frenzy *in* the text that they reacted to, or was it something beyond it? Could it be that the texts, the particular places of rupture were less important than the way they were now reading them—the habit of doubt, the multiplication of meanings, the reluctance to quiet alternatives? Or could it be that the writing itself, whatever else it was, was also something darker, a matter of expulsion, of expiation, of authors ridding themselves of things too painful to contain?

Towards dawn, his eyes heavy and his mind exhausted, he would catch himself nodding in his chair, and would return to bed. Almost always he would now dream vividly, often of teaching the very text he had just been reading. Instead of sitting as they normally did, calmly, rationally discussing the meaning, the author's technique, the students would seem unnaturally intense or agitated. Eventually one of them would begin to sob, or break into sudden violence, tearing papers, overturning furniture, throwing books from the shelves. Sometimes, between words, between lines of a poem, gaps would open so wide and so deep that they would all be sucked from their chairs and, like some manic parody of skydivers, fall into an endless blackness, reaching for hands or parachutes that were not there. Repeatedly, in one of the most disturbing dreams of all, Marjorie would begin to vomit, and it would continue, flooding the carpet, seeping out into the corridor, trickling down toward the second floor, a warm, sickly liquid, now milk-like, now dark as ink, in which there floated not only small fragments of food, but pieces of pencil, eraser, soggy fragments of manuscript, small clots of blood, short sections of a strange, black string. He would dream that he had fallen into it, was covered in it, was being swept away, and would wake suddenly, choking a scream, his sheets twisted and damp with perspiration, Michelle leaning over him frightened and bewildered.

It was after one such night that he first found the changes. Not instantly, but slowly as he showered, shaved, he realised that the indelible dark points on his chest not only made a pattern but were somehow extended in the fine lines in his eyes, that the patch of red, irritated skin on his right calf was matched exactly by that on his left, that the boil on his abdomen two weeks before was somehow connected to a small eruption beneath his chin, an outbreak upon his upper thigh. He went to several doctors, specialists and general practitioners alike, and in each case the reaction was depressingly the same: they would treat the symptoms only, break the problem into parts, look nervous or amused when he suggested something more.

The term ended. After a brief, troubled holiday during which he was much preoccupied with the events of the year and the unravelling hieroglyph of his own flesh, he returned to the university determined to scour yet again the things he had been teaching for their points of danger, their infectious places of blankness or upheaval. Slowly, carefully he went over them, page by page, line by line, exploring for their softnesses, their ambiguities, finding subtexts, countertexts he had not yet dreamed of, rents in the fabric, meanings redoubling or undoing themselves, characters and incidents flowing into each other, or turning about dark, elusive centres like the waters of whirlpools.

It was then, after eight or ten days of such intensive scrutiny, that it began to happen. At first a matter only of the most complex sentences—a difficulty, when he came to their conclusion, in remembering what it was that they had started with; a need to re-read, sometimes more than once, before he could put end with beginning, part with part—but the sentences grew shorter, less complex. Eventually, even the simplest resisted him. With less and less confidence he would embark upon the eight or ten words before him only to find, more and more often, that by the fifth or sixth he would be lost, floundering, needing to start again.

At first he thought it a matter of tiredness, of long-term exhaustion. He would begin each day well enough, and it would be only after several hours that the problem set in. But the attention-span shortened, the trouble occurred earlier and earlier. And then, one morning, within minutes of sitting down, he found himself not reading, not even trying to read, but merely counting the words, wondering idly what it could be that they were doing together, who had gathered them, what on earth it might signify.

It was not the alarming experience he might once have feared. After a few seconds of a purely physical distress, he found himself uncannily relieved, light-headed. When, after a few days rest, he sat down again at his books and found that the problem had persisted, the way seemed clear.

He sought and was granted an extended leave. Taking up a long-standing offer, he took Michelle and the child to a cabin in the mountains. For several weeks they hiked, picnicked, went sight-seeing, saw friends in the area. Then, when he felt he might be ready, and beginning with the simplest of texts, he began to teach himself to read.

It did not work. After a fortnight of promise, the trouble began again. At first Michelle attributed his subsequent silences, his distraction, his increasingly disrupted speech to a deep depression. But what began as the odd unfinished sentence, the occasional comment that had no context, became rapidly worse. By the time his colleagues at the university began to teach again, Dr B., still in the mountains, was reduced to almost total silence, the very gestures with which he now communicated becoming erratic, uncoordinated, harder and harder to follow. Michelle pressed him to return to the city and to consult a specialist, but at the mere mention of doctors Dr B. became angry and impatient. It was not clear, in any case, what kind of specialist might help. One day Michelle returned from a walk with the child to find him carefully pacing the floor, examining it closely as if checking for loose boards or some hidden trapdoor. He did this increasingly over the following days, examining again and again the same places, confining himself to a smaller and smaller area of the cabin. When he was not doing this or staring vacantly at the television, he would stand before the mirror in the tiny bathroom, examining his face, his chest, his ams obsessively, as if trying to read something there that Michelle could never see. It was before the mirror that she found him crouched one morning, apparently unable or unwilling to move independently, showing no signs of recognising her or of understanding anything she said. He put up no resistance as she led him to the car.

She was surprised when, a week later, she could not find him in the psychiatric unit into which he had been initially admitted, and where she had been visiting him daily since. He had been transferred, they said, to the University Research Clinic, for special observation.

She found him in the neurology ward. For two days— so extensive were the tests—she was able to see him for only a few minutes at a time, and unable to speak to anyone who could adequately explain the nature of the examination or what it was that they were looking for. On the third day, however, a message was waiting for her, and she was directed to the office of the chief neurologist.

A nurse at the hospital, he told her, had been concerned at what she had thought were Dr B.'s deeply
bloodshot eyes. On closer examination she had found
that, amongst the many tiny red veins discolouring them
were several strange black filaments. Exhaustive tests at
the clinic had determined that these were part of a
growth that had spread through much of Dr B.'s body:
not cancer—at least, not any form with which medicine
was yet familiar—but networked like the nervous or the
circulatory system, a web of slender black channels con-
ducting no detectable substance, serving no purpose they
could identify. Michelle could not help but notice, as the
doctor, on a fresh sheet of paper, tried to sketch a section
of this system for her, its remarkable resemblance to
writing. A kind of Arabic, or Aramaic, strange arcs and
curliques and jagged waves pulsing in the living flesh or
rising, as she suddenly imagined, like some ancient
shrapnel to the surface. To fall, as shrapnel might, in tiny
fragments, hard and dry and shining, into the palm of
the hand.

No one can, to this day, remember what it was we did to offend him. Dyer the butcher remembers a day when he gave him the wrong meat and another day when he served someone else first by mistake. Often when Dyer gets drunk he recalls this day and curses himself for his foolishness. But no one seriously believes that it was Dyer who offended him.

But one of us did something. We slighted him terribly in some way, this small meek man with the rimless glasses and neat suit who used to smile so nicely at us all. We thought, I suppose, he was a bit of a fool and sometimes he was so quiet and grey that we ignored him, forgetting he was there at all.

When I was a boy I often stole apples from the trees at his house up in Mason's Lane. He often saw me. No, that's not correct. Let me say I often sensed that he saw me. I sensed him peering out from behind the lace curtains of his house. And I was not the only one. Many of us came to take his apples, alone and in groups, and it is possible that he chose to exact payment for all these apples in his own peculiar way.

Yet I am sure it wasn't the apples.

What has happened is that we all, all eight hundred of

us, have come to remember small transgressions against Mr. Gleason who once lived amongst us.

My father, who has never borne malice against a single living creature, still believes that Gleason meant to do us well, that he loved the town more than any of us. My father says we have treated the town badly in our minds. We have used it, this little valley, as nothing more than a stopping place. Somewhere on the way to somewhere else. Even those of us who have been here many years have never taken the town seriously. Oh yes, the place is pretty. The hills are green and the woods thick. The stream is full of fish. But it is not where we would rather be.

For years we have watched the films at the Roxy and dreamed, if not of America, then at least of our capital city. For our own town, my father says, we have nothing but contempt. We have treated it badly, like a whore. We have cut down the giant shady trees in the main street to make doors for the school house and seats for the football pavilion. We have left big holes all over the countryside from which we have taken brown coal and given back nothing.

The commercial travellers who buy fish and chips at George the Greek's care for us more than we do, because we all have dreams of the big city, of wealth, of modern houses, of big motor cars: American dreams, my father has called them.

Although my father ran a petrol station he was also an inventor. He sat in his office all day drawing strange pieces of equipment on the back of delivery dockets.

Every spare piece of paper in the house was covered with these little drawings and my mother would always be very careful about throwing away any piece of paper no matter how small. She would look on both sides of any piece of paper very carefully and always preserved any that had so much as a pencil mark.

I think it was because of this that my father felt that he understood Gleason. He never said as much, but he inferred that he understood Gleason because he, too, was concerned with similar problems. My father was working on plans for a giant gravel crusher, but occasionally he would become distracted and become interested in something else.

There was, for instance, the time when Dyer the butcher bought a new bicycle with gears, and for a while my father talked of nothing else but the gears. Often I would see him across the road squatting down beside Dyer's bicycle as if he were talking to it.

We all rode bicycles because we didn't have the money for anything better. My father did have an old Chev truck, but he rarely used it and it occurs to me now that it might have had some mechanical problem that was impossible to solve, or perhaps it was just that he was saving it, not wishing to wear it out all at once. Normally, he went everywhere on his bicycle and, when I was younger, he carried me on the cross bar, both of us dismounting to trudge up the hills that led into and out of the main street. It was a common sight in our town to see people pushing bicycles. They were as much a burden as a means of transport.

Gleason also had his bicycle and every lunchtime he pushed and pedalled it home from the shire offices to his little weatherboard house out at Mason's Lane. It was a three-mile ride and people said that he went home for lunch because he was fussy and wouldn't eat either his wife's sandwiches or the hot meal available at Mrs. Lessing's cafe.

But while Gleason pedalled and pushed his bicycle to and from the shire offices everything in our town proceeded as normal. It was only when he retired that things began to go wrong.

Because it was then that Mr. Gleason started supervising the building of the wall around the two-acre plot up on Bald Hill. He paid too much for this land. He bought it from Johnny Weeks, who now, I am sure, believes the whole episode was his fault, firstly for cheating Gleason, secondly for selling him the land at all. But Gleason hired some Chinese and set to work to build his wall. It was then that we knew that we'd offended him. My father rode all the way out to Bald Hill and tried to talk Mr. Gleason out of his wall. He said there was no need for us to build walls. That no one wished to spy on Mr. Gleason or whatever he wished to do on Bald Hill. He said no one was in the least bit interested in Mr. Gleason. Mr. Gleason, neat in a new sportscoat, polished his glasses and smiled vaguely at his feet. Bicycling back, my father thought that he had gone too far. Of course we had an interest in Mr. Gleason. He pedalled back and asked him to attend a dance that was to be held on the next Friday, but Mr. Gleason said he didn't dance.

Oh well,' my father said, 'any time, just drop over.'

Mr. Gleason went back to supervising his family of Chinese labourers on his wall.

Bald Hill towered high above the town and from my father's small filling station you could sit and watch the wall going up. It was an interesting sight. I watched it for two years, while I waited for customers who rarely came. After school and on Saturdays I had all the time in the world to watch the agonising progress of Mr. Gleason's wall. It was as painful as a clock. Sometimes I could see the Chinese labourers running at a jogtrot carrying bricks on long wooden planks. The hill was bare, and on this bareness Mr. Gleason was, for some reason, building a wall.

In the beginning people thought it peculiar that someone would build such a big wall on Bald Hill. The only thing to recommend Bald Hill was the view of the town, and Mr. Gleason was building a wall that denied that view. The top soil was thin and bare clay showed through in places. Nothing would ever grow there. Everyone assumed that Gleason had simply gone mad and after the initial interest they accepted his madness as they accepted his wall and as they accepted Bald Hill itself.

Occasionally someone would pull in for petrol at my father's filling station and ask about the wall and my father would shrug and I would see, once more, the strangeness of it.

'A house?' the stranger would ask. 'Up on that hill?'

'No,' my father would say, 'chap named Gleason is building a wall.'

And the strangers would want to know why, and my father would shrug and look up at Bald Hill once more. 'Damned if I know,' he'd say.

Gleason still lived in his old house at Mason's Lane. It was a plain weatherboard house with a rose garden at the front, a vegetable garden down the side, and an orchard at the back.

At night we kids would sometimes ride out to Bald Hill on our bicycles. It was an agonising, muscle-twitching ride, the worst part of which was a steep, unmade road up which we finally pushed our bikes, our lungs rasping in the night air. When we arrived we found nothing but walls. Once we broke down some of the brickwork and another time we threw stones at the tents where the Chinese labourers slept. Thus we expressed our frustration at this inexplicable thing.

The wall must have been finished on the day before my twelfth birthday. I remember going on a picnic birthday party up to Eleven Mile Creek and we lit a fire and cooked chops at a bend in the river from where it was possible to see the walls on Bald Hill. I remember standing with a hot chop in my hand and someone saying, 'Look, they're leaving!'

We stood on the creek bed and watched the Chinese labourers walking their bicycles slowly down the hill. Someone said they were going to build a chimney up at the mine at A.1 and certainly there is a large brick chimney there now, so I suppose they built it.

When the word spread that the walls were finished most of the town went up to look. They walked around the four walls which were as interesting as any other brick walls. They stood in front of the big wooden gates and tried to peer through, but all they could see was a small blind wall that had obviously been constructed for this special purpose. The walls themselves were ten feet high and topped with broken glass and barbed wire. When it became obvious that we were not going to discover the contents of the enclosure, we all gave up and went home.

Mr. Gleason had long since stopped coming into town. His wife came instead, wheeling a pram down from Mason's Lane to Main Street and filling it with groceries and meat (they never bought vegetables, they grew their own) and wheeling it back to Mason's Lane. Sometimes you would see her standing with the pram halfway up the Gell Street hill. Just standing there, catching her breath. No one asked her about the wall. They knew she wasn't responsible for the wall and they felt sorry for her, having to bear the burden of the pram and her husband's madness. Even when she began to visit Dixon's hardware and buy plaster of paris and tins of paint and waterproofing compound, no one asked her what these things were for. She had a way of averting her eyes that indicated her terror of questions. Old Dixon carried the plaster of paris and the tins of paint out to her pram for her and watched her push them away. 'Poor woman,' he said, 'poor bloody woman.'

From the filling station where I sat dreaming in the sun, or from the enclosed office where I gazed mournfully at the rain, I would see, occasionally, Gleason entering or leaving his walled compound, a tiny figure way up on Bald Hill. And I'd think 'Gleason', but not much more.

Occasionally strangers drove up there to see what was going on, often egged on by locals who told them it was a Chinese temple or some other silly thing. Once a group of Italians had a picnic outside the walls and took photographs of each other standing in front of the closed door. God knows what they thought it was.

But for five years between my twelfth and seventeenth birthdays there was nothing to interest me in Gleason's walls. Those years seem lost to me now and I can remember very little of them. I developed a crush on Susy Markin and followed her back from the swimming pool on my bicycle. Then her parents moved to another town and I sat in the sun and waited for them to come back.

We became very keen on modernisation. When coloured paints became available the whole town went berserk and brightly coloured houses blossomed overnight. But the paints were not of good quality and quickly faded and peeled, so that the town looked like a garden of dead flowers. Thinking of those years, the only real thing I recall is the soft hiss of bicycle tyres on the main street. When I think of it now it seems very peaceful, but I remember then that the sound induced in me a feeling of melancholy, a feeling somehow mixed with the early afternoons when the sun went down behind Bald Hill and the town felt as sad as an empty dance hall on a Sunday afternoon.

And then, during my seventeenth year, Mr. Gleason died. We found out when we saw Mrs. Gleason's pram parked out in front of Phonsey Joy's Funeral Parlour. It looked very sad, that pram, standing by itself in the windswept street. We came and looked at the pram and felt sad for Mrs. Gleason. She hadn't had much of a life.

Phonsey Joy carried old Mr. Gleason out to the cemetery by the Parwan Railway Station and Mrs. Gleason rode behind in a taxi. People watched the old hearse go by and thought, 'Gleason,' but not much else.

And then, less than a month after Gleason had been buried out at the lonely cemetery by the Parwan Railway Station, the Chinese labourers came back. We saw them push their bicycles up the hill. I stood with my father and Phonsey Joy and wondered what was going on.

And then I saw Mrs. Gleason trudging up the hill. I nearly didn't recognise her, because she didn't have her pram. She carried a black umbrella and walked slowly up Bald Hill and it wasn't until she stopped for breath and leant forward that I recognised her.

'It's Mrs. Gleason,' I said, 'with the Chinese.'

But it wasn't until the next morning that it became obvious what was happening. People lined the main street in the way they do for a big funeral but, instead of gazing towards the Grant Street corner, they all looked up at Bald Hill.

All that day and all the next people gathered to watch the destruction of the walls. They saw the Chinese labourers darting to and fro, but it wasn't until they knocked down a large section of the wall facing the town that we realised there really was something inside. It was impossible to see what it was, but there was something there. People stood and wondered and pointed out Mrs. Gleason to each other as she went to and fro supervising the work.

And finally, in ones and twos, on bicycles and on foot, the whole town moved up to Bald Hill. Mr. Dyer closed up his butcher shop and my father got out the old Chev truck and we finally arrived up at Bald Hill with twenty people on board. They crowded into the back tray and hung onto the running boards and my father grimly steered his way through the crowds of bicycles and parked just where the dirt track gets really steep. We trudged up this last steep track, never for a moment suspecting what we would find at the top.

It was very quiet up there. The Chinese labourers worked diligently, removing the third and fourth walls and cleaning the bricks which they stacked neatly in big piles. Mrs. Gleason said nothing either. She stood in the only remaining corner of the walls and looked defiantly at the townspeople who stood open mouthed where another corner had been.

And between us and Mrs. Gleason was the most incredibly beautiful thing I had ever seen in my life. For one moment I didn't recognise it. I stood open mouthed, and breathed the surprising beauty of it. And then I realised it was our town. The buildings were two feet high and they were a little rough but very correct. I saw Mr. Dyer nudge my father and whisper that Gleason had got the faded 'U' in the BUTCHER sign of his shop.

I think at that moment everyone was overcome with a feeling of simple joy. I can't remember ever having felt so uplifted and happy. It was perhaps a childish emotion but I looked up at my father and saw a smile of such warmth spread across his face that I knew he felt just as I did. Later he told me that he thought Gleason had built the model of our town just for this moment, to let us see the beauty of our own town, to make us proud of ourselves and to stop the American Dreams we were so prone to. For the rest, my father said, was not Gleason's plan and he could not have foreseen the things that happened afterwards.

I have come to think that this view of my father's is a little sentimental and also, perhaps, insulting to Gleason. I personally believe that he knew everything that would happen. One day the proof of my theory may be discovered. Certainly there are in existence some personal papers, and I firmly believe that these papers will show that Gleason knew exactly what would happen.

We had been so overcome by the model of the town that we hadn't noticed what was the most remarkable thing of all. Not only had Gleason built the houses and the shops of our town, he had also peopled it. As we tiptoed into the town we suddenly found ourselves. 'Look,' I said to Mr. Dyer, 'there you are.'

And there he was, standing in front of his shop in his apron. As I bent down to examine the tiny figure I was staggered by the look on its face. The modelling was crude, the paint work was sloppy, and the face a little too white, but the expression was absolutely perfect:

those pursed, quizzical lips and the eyebrows lifted high. It was Mr. Dyer and no one else on earth.

And there beside Mr. Dyer was my father, squatting on the footpath and gazing lovingly at Mr. Dyer's bicycle gears, his face marked with grease and hope.

And there was I, back at the filling station, leaning against a petrol pump in an American pose and talking to Brian Sparrow who was amusing me with his clownish antics.

Phonsey Joy standing beside his hearse. Mr. Dixon sitting inside his hardware store. Everyone I knew was there in that tiny town. If they were not in the streets or in their backyards they were inside their houses, and it didn't take very long to discover that you could lift off the roofs and peer inside.

We tiptoed around the streets peeping into each other's windows, lifting off each other's roofs, admiring each other's gardens, and, while we did it, Mrs. Gleason slipped silently away down the hill towards Mason's Lane. She spoke to nobody and nobody spoke to her.

I confess that I was the one who took the roof from Cavanagh's house. So I was the one who found Mrs. Cavanagh in bed with young Craigie Evans.

I stood there for a long time, hardly knowing what I was seeing. I stared at the pair of them for a long, long time. And when I finally knew what I was seeing I felt such an incredible mixture of jealousy and guilt and wonder that I didn't know what to do with the roof.

Eventually it was Phonsey Joy who took the roof from my hands and placed it carefully back on the house, much, I imagine, as he would have placed the lid on a coffin. By then other people had seen what I had seen and the word passed around very quickly.

And then we all stood around in little groups and regarded the model town with what could only have been fear. If Gleason knew about Mrs. Cavanagh and Craigie Evans (and no one else had), what other things might he know? Those who hadn't seen themselves yet in the town began to look a little nervous and were unsure of whether to look for themselves or not. We gazed silently at the roofs and felt mistrustful and guilty.

We all walked down the hill then, very quietly, the way people walk away from a funeral, listening only to the crunch of the gravel under our feet while the women had trouble with their high-heeled shoes.

The next day a special meeting of the shire council passed a motion calling on Mrs. Gleason to destroy the model town on the grounds that it contravened building regulations.

It is unfortunate that this order wasn't carried out before the city newspapers found out. Before another day had gone by the government had stepped in.

The model town and its model occupants were to be preserved. The minister for tourism came in a large black car and made a speech to us in the football pavilion. We sat on the high, tiered seats eating potato chips while he stood against the fence and talked to us. We couldn't hear him very well, but we heard enough. He called the model town a work of art and we stared at him grimly. He said it would be an invaluable tourist attraction. He said tourists would come from everywhere to see the model town. We would be famous. Our businesses would flourish. There would be work for guides and interpreters and caretakers and taxi drivers and people selling soft drinks and ice creams.

The Americans would come, he said. They would visit our town in buses and in cars and on the train. They would take photographs and bring wallets bulging with dollars. American dollars.

We looked at the minister mistrustfully, wondering if he knew about Mrs. Cavanagh, and he must have seen the look because he said that certain controversial items would be removed, had already been removed. We shifted in our seats, like you do when a particularly tense part of a film has come to its climax, and then we relaxed and listened to what the minister had to say. And we all began, once more, to dream our American dreams.

We saw our big smooth cars cruising through cities with bright lights. We entered expensive night clubs and danced till dawn. We made love to women like Kim Novak and men like Rock Hudson. We drank cocktails. We gazed lazily into refrigerators filled with food and prepared ourselves lavish midnight snacks which we ate while we watched huge television sets on which we would be able to see American movies free of charge and for ever.

The minister, like someone from our American dreams, re-entered his large black car and cruised slowly from our humble sportsground, and the newspaper men arrived and swarmed over the pavilion with their cameras and note-books. They took photographs of us and photographs of the models up on Bald Hill. And the next day we were all over the newspapers. The photographs of the model people side by side with photographs of the real people. And our names and ages and what we did were all printed there in black and white.

They interviewed Mrs. Gleason but she said nothing of interest. She said the model town had been her husband's hobby.

We all felt good now. It was very pleasant to have your photograph in the paper. And, once more, we changed our opinion of Gleason. The shire council held another meeting and named the dirt track up Bald Hill, 'Gleason Avenue'. Then we all went home and waited for the Americans we had been promised.

It didn't take long for them to come, although at the time it seemed an eternity, and we spent six long months doing nothing more with our lives than waiting for the Americans.

Well, they did come. And let me tell you how it has all worked out for us.

The Americans arrive every day in buses and cars and sometimes the younger ones come on the train. There is now a small airstrip out near the Parwan cemetery and they also arrive there, in small aeroplanes. Phonsey Joy drives them to the cemetery where they look at Gleason's grave and then up to Bald Hill and then down to the town. He is doing very well from it all. It is good to see someone doing well from it. Phonsey is becoming a big man in town and is on the shire council.

On Bald Hill there are half a dozen telescopes through which the Americans can spy on the town and reassure themselves that it is the same down there as it is on Bald Hill. Herb Gravney sells them ice creams and soft drinks and extra film for their cameras. He is another one who is doing well. He bought the whole model from Mrs. Gleason and charges five American dollars admission. Herb is on the council now too. He's doing very well for himself. He sells them the film so they can take photographs of the houses and the model people and so they can come down to the town with their special maps and hunt out the real people.

To tell the truth most of us are pretty sick of the game. They come looking for my father and ask him to stare at the gears of Dyer's bicycle. I watch my father cross the street slowly, his head hung low. He doesn't greet the Americans any more. He doesn't ask them questions about colour television or Washington D.C. He kneels on the footpath in front of Dyer's bike. They stand around him. Often they remember the model incorrectly and try to get my father to pose in the wrong way. Originally he argued with them, but now he argues no more. He does what they ask. They push him this way and that and worry about the expression on his face which is no longer what it was.

Then I know they will come to find me. I am next on the map. I am very popular for some reason. They come in search of me and my petrol pump as they have done for four years now. I do not await them eagerly because I know, before they reach me, that they will be disappointed.

'But this is not the boy.'

'Yes,' says Phonsey, 'this is him all right.' And he gets me to show them my certificate.

They examine the certificate suspiciously, feeling the paper as if it might be a clever forgery. 'No,' they declare. (Americans are so confident.) 'No,' they shake their heads, 'this is not the real boy. The real boy is younger.'

'He's older now. He used to be younger.' Phonsey looks weary when he tells them. He can afford to look weary.

The Americans peer at my face closely. 'It's a different boy.'

But finally they get their cameras out. I stand sullenly and try to look amused as I did once. Gleason saw me looking amused but I can no longer remember how it felt. I was looking at Brian Sparrow. But Brian is also tired. He finds it difficult to do his clownish antics and to the Americans his little act isn't funny. They prefer the model. I watch him sadly, sorry that he must perform for such an unsympathetic audience.

The Americans pay one dollar for the right to take our photographs. Having paid the money they are worried about being cheated. They spend their time being disappointed and I spend my time feeling guilty, that I have somehow let them down by growing older and sadder.

This is a short history of my father's life. A short history of parts of my father's life. The history begins where I've decided to begin it: with a retelling of what Frank told me. I'm calling my father Frank, because that's his name.

Frank becomes a footballer.

At school Frank was trained by the Christian Brothers to be a footballer. Under their tutelage, he played against all the western suburbs schools.

This was a first-rate toughening process, further evidenced by Frank's brother Jack. Jack was normally a quiet man, but his eyes glazed over when he played football.

Frank played in the ⅝ position for Canterbury Rugby League, first grade, before he was sixteen. He had to put in three months training to a big bloke's one month. He was really too light (hence the ⅝ position).

He left the game early too—it was physically dangerous for him to keep playing.

Frank's working life takes an unusual turn, affecting the nature of episodes in his life as a footballer.

As a young man during World War II, Frank was drafted into the army. In a commando course, a sergeant said to Frank, 'Attack me. Go on, come at me and try and kill me.'

Frank attacked the sergeant.

At the hearing, the captain said to Frank, 'You almost killed the sergeant.' (The sergeant was still in hospital.) And Frank replied, 'That's what you trained me for.'

Under the Manpower Act, operative during the war, the railways requested labour for essential services. Frank joined the railways. The alternative was a protracted prison sentence. So Frank laboured on the railways, and the railways posted him to Junee in the west of New South Wales.

In Junee Frank played football. After he walked down the main street of this country town, there was nothing left to do. Besides, this being a country town, he got time off the railways for football training.

The following episode in Frank's life as a footballer is based on a text written by a friend and drinking companion, Richard McDermott, plumber. McDermott wrote the text so Frank wouldn't repeat it endlessly as oral history. Half-joking, half-serious, McDermott circulated the text amongst other friends and drinking mates as preventative medicine for his own sanity.

It was the '44 season, and when Junee played Cowra, Frank expected to win.

Cowra was playing on its home ground, but the home

ground was a hastily mown strip, bare in parts except for the odd pat of cow dung. The goal posts were forged from saplings.

The oddball locals toed the sidelines. 'Weak as piss,' said one of them of his own team. His felt hat was turned down, and he had a bumper between his thumb and forefinger. He grunted at Frank, 'They're weak as piss.'

Except for the Aborigine in its line-up, Cowra looked as promising as its home ground. And though the Aborigine had a large head and spindly legs, he also had odd socks and moth-eaten boots. 'Heart like a caraway seed,' growled felt hat. 'Not worth a knob of goat's shit.'

Frank won the first scrum, gathered on the burst, and deftly passed to his support. But there followed a black flash, a flurry of arms and legs, and the inside centre screamed in pain from a broken collarbone. Five minutes later the Aborigine tackled the full-back, who was carried off the field unconscious.

From then on, to avoid being tackled, Frank kicked the ball anywhere—even in his own twenty-five—to get rid of it. The game finished: Cowra 32, Junee 0.

Frank breasted the bar of the pub after the game. He wore his bravest face, yarned and joked with all. The locals were passing beers through the window to the Aborigines outside. Prominent among them was the footballer. Frank was half-frightened to go to the toilet, having to pass him along the way.

From his place at the corner of the bar, felt hat grinned, 'The trouble is we can't take him away on games—he wrecks the opposition's town.'

moya costello

The role of social and cultural politics in the premature ending of Frank's life as a footballer.

At Junee Frank had won the Maher Cup, the trophy for country players. Called the Old Tin Mug, Old Pot, or Win, Tie and Wrangle Cup, it was the icon of country supporters, the Davis Cup of western area rugby league.

So when Frank was transferred to Mudgee by the railways in '45, a local journalist made a story of it: 'Maher Cup for Mudgee.'

Frank couldn't think what he'd done wrong when a group of men in suits met him as he stepped off the train. They were officials of the Mudgee Rugby League Club.

For as long as anyone could remember, Mudgee had never won a season. But when Frank became coach and captain, the history of the town's team changed dramatically.

He used two six-footers he'd seen playing handball with strength and dexterity on the back wall of Mudgee Catholic Church. As coach and captain, and a Catholic himself, he could redetermine the composition of the largely Protestant team.

At one match there were over two thousand spectators—mothers, fathers, brothers, sisters, aunts, uncles, cousins and second cousins—to see Mudgee play and win a match on their home ground.

Frank drank at two pubs in town. He had a single drink out of politeness in the one that was full of analysis of the game by people who'd never played. But he stayed drinking at the other pub where the hardheads said of the opposition team, 'Make them eat dirt!' And Frank replied, 'I just want to win.'

On the selection panel for Mudgee Rugby League there was a wealthy squatter who wanted his son on the team. Frank could see the boy had no heart, and you needed heart to play league.

When Mudgee played against Lithgow Workers and lost, the squatter pointed the finger at Frank. Even though Lithgow Workers, of the ammunition factory— a team of desperadoes: thugs, criminals, army cheats— had never lost a game.

Payment for players and coaches was introduced after the war. Frank recommended professionalism to the six-footers, but they were from the landed gentry: what they could make at football was playlunch money.

Frank prepares to be a husband and father.

League could be a brutal game, and now Frank was moulding himself into a husband and father, he decided to quit.

He was engaged to a woman whose father had captained Balmain and had played for Australia against England.

He returned to Sydney to be married. He joined the public service as a clerk and, as one of his colleagues puts it, invented flexitime.

A personal memoir of my father.

Frank took us away to the beach every September school holidays. He packed only what was needed: 'a sandshoe and a galosha', while our mother packed away linen, underwear, T-shirts, and several sets of our home-made shorts-suits.

There was no one Frank's equal for booking the absolutely best holiday bungalows. They were ungla-morous, old-fashioned and right on the beach, at sleepy spots on the verge of discovery, along the central and northern coast of New South Wales: Ettalong, Tuncurry, Forster, Port Macquarie. He had an instinct for keeping just ahead of developers. We can never return to those places now saturated with development.

At Christmas time he printed T-shirts for himself with messages like 'Be Frank' on the front and 'I'm Frank' on the back. He displayed the T-shirts to guests who arrived during the day, and he pointed out his greeting cards, received and given. Guests laughed uneasily, wanting to appear to understand and not understanding these in-jokes.

At these celebrations he sang 'My Canary Has Circles under His Eyes' looking like one, birds being the regular household pets, though there were two dogs over a ten-year period. Escapee canaries and budgies, captured in the backyard, counted as his mates.

His presents were perfunctory: something from Coles; or else, perhaps, a transistor, from the back of a truck. My presents were perfunctory too: what could I get a man who didn't want anything? Not because he had everything, he just didn't want anything. Greeting cards and T-shirts with messages gave him pleasure. I bought special shaving soap, books and tapes: the 'My Word' series in print, *A Fortunate Life*, Frank S. singing 'I Did It My Way', Don Burrows's jazz, Don Bradman reminiscing; and once, tools: a stanley knife and a rectractable tape measure.

But Frank didn't have hobbies. Mother would say, 'I replace the tap washers; I fix the fuses; I hammer and nail.' It was all she could do to get him to paint, or mow the lawn. Instead, he took bets for an SP bookmaker, and privately dealt in football results.

The history continues as told to me by Frank. Football and, to a large extent, parenting are now behind him. He becomes a bookie's mate.

'There are a lot of mugs in racing,' Frank said, shaking his head and looking into the distance.

At the pub where he took bets, there were men he preferred not to deal with. But some might insist, if they thought they were on to a sure thing.

A bloke insisted he wanted a bet on My Philanderer. To prevent him screaming to the police, Frank said okay. The bloke started to move away without putting down any money. 'No steak, no gravy,' said Frank. If the horse had lost, Frank would be left trying to chase the money.

Frank sat drinking with his mates, listening to the race, telling them why he took the bet. My Philanderer won, but the bloke came up looking low, saying he was sure

The Philosopher was a hot tip. The Philosopher came in fourth. All Frank's mates said they were sure it was Frank's shout.

Frank hated the pedantry of the radio race commentators. 'My prognostication for the fifth at Randwick . . . ', one started saying. So Frank thought he'd try it on at his club with one of the blokes. 'Er, Bill,' he said, 'what's your prognostication?' Bill, with his ear to a transistor and a pencil and form guide in hand, panicked, scanned his form guide and asked anxiously, 'What? Prognostication? What race is he in?'

Once at the races with Frank, Mother said seriously, 'Oh, Blue Hydrangea!', spotting a name on the form guide. 'Mine's flowering now; I'll have a dollar on Blue Hydrangea.' The horse is 20-1, it's never won a race since birth, thought Frank, why doesn't she stab the form guide with a sharpened pencil in the dark? But the horse won.

Frank usually settled up with his bookmaker at one of Sydney's clubs. He hardly ever stayed, though the bookmaker might insist he have a drink while money was exchanged and pocketed in the corner within a group of big men built like Darlinghurst detectives.

During raids, staged like theatrical events in local pubs, the bookmaker had a pensioner clearly taking money: someone without a criminal record, who welcomed a bit of extra cash. The police would come in and lay their hands on him. The bookie would pay his fine and give him something for his trouble.

All day on the day that Fine Cotton was racing in Brisbane, Frank was taking bets. The rush was suspicious, so he rang the bookie: 'Do you want to take the bets on?' Frank asked. The bookmaker said yes, take the money, but recommended that Frank not bet himself: the horse wasn't running to form.

Though the substitution of a good galloper was supposed to be a secret, a trail of rumours snaked its way down the coast. The instigators backed it themselves and had others back it for them. Everyone knew about it from Brisbane to Thangool, Fiji to New Guinea.

The instigators were found out, and the bookie won because he didn't have to pay up. And though the bettors complained to Frank, they weren't going to the police.

Frank gave betting up when he landed at the club one day and there were more big guys looking like they smashed glass and ate it for breakfast. But this time they were the bookmaker's protectors.

History is written by the victors.

There was a clampdown, sometime in the late reign of the Wran Labor Government in New South Wales. However, in Queensland, the head of the TAB still took thousands of dollars in bets on credit, completely against the rules. And in the pages of the newspaper, Frank saw a big photo of a man dancing in a dinner suit—the same man who, when in prison, had been found printing form guides to his horse stud on prison equipment; now there he was photographed in the social pages, dancing at a charity ball.

When Frank recognised inequity, he pointed it out to his children. But like men of his particular generation, who were Irish-Catholic, working-class, Labor voting and left-wing, in his own life he remained immune to ambition and to the value and power of money.

Running along far away from the road. Along the shallow creek bed, the wide flat rocks just below the water, creamy brown. The creek is wide here and open for hundreds of yards until it makes a turn. And straight ahead above the blackberry bushes and foliage along the water's edge is the typical country house with a row of yellow pines up one side, white walls and a red roof. The mother, the father and the children are here. With friends. The adults stand on the beach made of river stones or on the big rock in the middle of the creek or on the bank, talking, talking. All day. They make sandwiches while they talk. They smoke cigarettes. They point at things. The sight of a parent's eyes following the pointed finger across to the bank on the other side of the creek or into the branches of a nearby tree. They gesticulate sometimes. The men put their hands in their pockets and take them out again. The women fold their arms or put their hands on their hips. They go for a walk very slowly while they talk. Along the road, across the ford, up the hill, round the corner. They stay away for hours, talking. The shadow of the hill falls over the creek. It grows cooler. They come back and organise dinner while they talk. The women talk to each other. The men talk to each other. The men talk to the women. They all talk at once. They set out the card table under the trees, light the kerosene lamp and play 500 while they talk. They miss tricks while they talk. The children go to sleep in the tents and wake up in the night and hear them talking. Then later they wake up and everything's quiet.

In the morning the father throws the dog in the water. The dog paddles madly to the shore. The father talks about snags in the river. They all discuss the difference between snags as in water hazards and snags as in sausages. Sausage dogs. Smoke. Children who've drowned. Bushfires. Snakes. Carpet snakes. The long grass. The blackberry patch. The tar baby. Was there such a thing as Brere Bear. The pyjama girl. Bulrushes. Flash floods. Flying foxes. The hazards of flying foxes. High tensile wires and electricity lines. Broken electricity lines hanging down into creeks. Fords with cars on them washed away in flash floods. River snakes. March flies. Bot flies. The difference between bot flies and sand flies. Maggots in sausages. Maggot stories. Meat safe stories. Ice chest stories. Milk delivery when milk was in pails. The bread cart. The sound of the bread cart. Draught horses. Old draught horses. Horses being sent off to the blood and bone factory. Horses in the city. Sewerage. The sewerage works. Polluted creeks. The correct drinking sections of creeks. The aeration process. Stagnant water. Boiling the billy. Billy tea. The Billy Tea brand name. The inferior quality of Billy Tea. Swaggies.

Gypsies. The cleverness of gypsies. Poverty. Bread and dripping. Sausages. Home-grown vegetables. Out-door toilets. Improvised toilet paper. The long summer nights. Mosquitoes. Marshes and bogs. Moonee Moonee and Brooklyn. The possibility of a mosquito breeding in the dew on a leaf. Bites. Bee stings. Allergies to bites. Death from bee stings. How to make a whistle from a leaf. Playing the comb. The mouth harp. The bush bass. Bottle tops. The corrosive qualities of Coca-Cola. Big Business. Monopolies. Bigger and bigger monopolies. Free enterprise. Russia. The idea of women working in men's jobs. Suez. American election campaigns. The Ku Klux Klan. The colour bar. The Iron Curtain. The Cold War. The ideals of communism as distinct from the practice. China. Industrialisation. Cuba. Atheism and agnosticism. The idea of the supreme being. The church in Russia. The Jews. Israel. The world wars. The next one. The fatalistic approach. The end of civilisation. The end of the human race. The inexorable continuation of the universe in spite of the human race. Humans as microscopic and trivial beings. The frailty of humans. The stupidity of humans. The innate badness of humans. Animal life and animals' code of behaviour. The rationality of animals. The fowls of the air and other biblical quotes. And now I see as through a glass darkly.

At the end of the last hand of 500, they remember other discussions they've had and that they always concluded with politics. The father turns down the tilly lamp.

He had been talking to the girl beside him on the lounge though she was unseen and his words perhaps unheard, for himself as if he had not phrased them. She might have materialised piecemeal in his mind, her black hair drawn smooth and tight to be held at her neck, the whiteness of the scalp where the strong hair was pulled back from her forehead, her full arms and the slope of her almost bare shoulders, her skin as if not much exposed to the sun and with its own flush of colour— these things came to him like unrelated aspects of different people. Her voice was quiet and without emphasis, it had perhaps met and parried his own, he did not remember. Looking about the room, he thought there seemed fewer people. Opposite, a man was unashamedly asleep in an armchair. The radio was still going and more couples than before were dancing.

He said, 'Shall we dance?'

'If you wish,' she said.

The square of carpet and the gleam of polished boards stretched endlessly in enigma. He contemplated it tiredly.

'I—perhaps I don't.'

'Neither do I,' she said.

He looked at her sharply, but her dark eyes seemed without expression. He could only accept her beside him as he must accept the people, the rooms, the noise.

'I'll have to go,' she said. 'I live quite a long way out, and the bus service is very curious at this time of the night. If it exists at all.'

'Where do you live?' He looked at his watch and realised then what seemed to have been part of the puzzle.

'North Beach,' she said.

'Have I—I mean, we've been talking quite a time?'

She smiled. 'You were drinking with the men for some time, I think. We've been chatting here for a while.'

'Yes,' he said. 'The bus—there might not be one now. Could I give you a lift?'

'Oh—it's much too far. And right out of your way.'

'No. No, there's nothing I'd like better than a drive now. I mean—I like driving—'

She smiled gently so that her irony was rather like a private joke between then. 'I know. And you could drive?'

'Yes. I'm not stupid about it. If you think I'm not capable—'

She put her hand quickly on his arm. 'Only teasing you. I'd like to.'

They stood up, and he saw that she was not tall, her plain dress was gathered at the waist by a vivid red belt. She said, 'I'll get my things.'

He saw no one he knew and by the time he had found his way into the hall again he could not be bothered seeking out his hostess to say goodbye. They would have forgotten him, anyway, as he would himself forget all of them. The tall fair girl had gone. If she had ever been there. His passenger was suddenly at his side and they went out to the cars parked along the kerbing and over the street lawns.

'This one,' he said. 'I'm afraid it's an open job—an M.G.—might be cold—'

'That's wonderful,' she said. 'Blow some of the stuffiness away.'

'You didn't enjoy it?'

'Well, not really.'

As she settled herself beside him she said, 'Nor you?'

'At first,' he said.

'It didn't work out?'

'No.'

He drove carefully, the cold air cleared his head, and on the long stretches when the suburbs and then the market gardens had given place to banksia and scrub he worked the car up, feeling it steady, vital, on the dark road. They spoke very little; when they came to the outlying cottages she directed him, until he stopped before a small house, one of a street where houses had been built spasmodically, additions erected as convenience and cheapness suggested. The road was too narrow to park at night so he drove off onto firm ground near the fence.

She said, 'That was a lot better than the bus. I could give you a cup of coffee—it's been a long trip for you—'

'If it's not a lot of trouble—'

'No. I think we might both find it do us good.'

He followed her through a picket gate and along a rough path. She went across a verandah that was latticed in, and when she turned on the light inside he saw on the verandah two bare folding iron beds, and an old wooden chair. He went into a kitchen that held a wood stove and a small electric stove, and in the centre of the room a wide table. Another room opened from the kitchen, though it was in the darkness he saw it was obviously a bedroom. She slipped her coat off and turned on the bedroom light. He could see the unmade bed, and there were clothes on a chair. At the foot of the bed two large suitcases were pushed together.

'Oh heavens,' she said. 'I came away in a hurry this evening. Don't look.'

She put her coat on the bed and turned the light out. As she began to heat the coffee she said, 'Shall we have some toast? The drive made me hungry. That was a wonderful car.'

'Nothing better if you like them,' he said. 'Though people that don't say a few harsh words.'

'I've never been in one before.'

She turned the toast in the toaster, looking at the browning square of bread. Her back was towards him, he saw the plain brown dress and red belt, her dark hair caught smoothly on her neck. She set the cups on the table, removing a cup and plate that had been used earlier from the end of the table. By them a book had been closed on the handle of a tea spoon as a marker. She buttered the toast and sliced it, and poured the coffee.

As she sat down opposite him she said, 'What do you do? I'm inquisitive, I know, but I like to place people. I can't with you.'

He smiled, seeing the vapour rise from the brown surface of the liquid in his cup. 'I'm a farmer.'

She looked at him for a moment, and he thought she might have been called attractive, she did not have beauty, a restraint, perhaps strength, imposed upon her small regular features denied beauty.

He lifted a finger of toast and she said, 'I'm beginning to see. You were once. All right, I won't intrude.'

'No. It isn't that. I was joking. My parents have a farm. I've been doing accountancy. I've not long been started on my own. A precarious living at the moment.'

'I see. It does fit.'

'I'm glad of that,' he said.

She laughed suddenly, and he realised it was the first time she had seemed relaxed. Without any reason he began to laugh with her, and then choked on the toast crumbs.

'Well,' he said, 'I don't know what's funny.'

'I said the cup of coffee would do us good.' She got up and brought the pot from the stove.

'Is this your place?' he asked.

'No. A girl I know is living here. She works in town, and this at least is not expensive. I'm only staying.'

'You don't work in town?'

'No. Albany.'

'That's quite a way.' He said it only because suddenly they seemed to have come upon that which was no longer clear and known and he could not see how to proceed.

'I'm going back tomorrow night.'

'Tonight?'

'Oh. Tonight.'

She fingered the book that lay with the spoon protruding from the pages. She said, 'Do you read much?'

'Figures,' he said. 'Millions of them.'

'Money.'

'No. Not just like that. You have to have money. My work deals with money, yes. But if it was only the way you make it sound I don't think I'd be so interested.'

'And you are interested. Sorry.'

'You like to read?'

'Yes.' She turned the book towards him. 'You don't know this man?'

He shook his head. 'I'm just literate. I've never read books.'

He thought of the tall blonde girl he had watched all the evening, and spoken to but briefly, her fair hair short and cut close to her head emphasising her features in a way he had thought attractive, her face in the glimpses he had had of it somehow intimate, yet refusing to offer its secrets indiscriminately, unmoved as if its response must be evoked, and which in the days he had not yet known he was to become too familiar with, seeking always some key to that calm indifference which marriage was not to disturb.

'I suppose I should have read more,' he said.

'Not necessarily. Any more than that I should have

gone into business. I didn't mean to imply that.'

'To return a question,' he said, 'what do you do?'

'I'm not interesting. And for a long time I seem to have been caught with something. I couldn't get away— just getting nowhere. I think now I might break it all. I want to go away, to travel.'

She got up and took the coffee from the stove.

'There's a drop left. Let's share it.'

He thought how still the room was, and he wondered how late they had stayed. He did not want to look at his watch in case she saw him. She asked him if he smoked, but rather as if she realised he did not, and lit herself a cigarette. They talked easily, she drew his words, though she would give, he found, little of herself. She talked freely only of places, or of other people.

He watched her quiet yet strong face, her eyes lifting towards his own or fixed on her hands on the table, the cigarette in her fingers; she had a kind of stillness, not easily disturbed to gesture or movement. Her hands were smooth, the nails cut rather short, he could see the veins soft, not protrusive, but patterned beneath the skin. Occasionally, in a kind of disbelief, he seemed to see himself and the girl sitting there. The room itself might have had no personality impressed upon it, suggesting only transience, and he was reminded of her friend.

He said, 'Your friend—is she coming back?'

'Tomorrow,' she said. She smiled. 'Really tomorrow. Not today.'

He thought of her going away that evening and the other girl not there. But he did not like to comment, he remembered her own words, that she would not intrude.

He said, 'It's late—I've kept you—'

'No,' she said.

They had risen from the table. She came across the room with him.

'It's strange, this,' she said. 'I'm glad you came. It was good of you.'

'It was luck we met,' he said, 'though you're going away and it seems we're very much passing in the night. I've talked more easily to you than to anyone for years.'

'I only went in there tonight,' she said, 'because I—I was afraid to stay here.'

'Afraid?'

'Oh, I've been trying to get away from something. A personal thing. I felt dreadful tonight. And that awful party. You did me good.'

He reached out, touching her arms, and she leant against him suddenly. He looked down on her dark, tightly drawn hair, and he held her gently.

'I don't quite understand—' he said.

'No. Of course not. It isn't interesting. Give me time and I'll tell you. It's very ordinary.'

He said, 'I seem to know you so well. And yet I don't know anything. Perhaps it's crazy.'

'I know. In such a little time. But it's as if that didn't matter.'

'Yes.'

'Oh, I can't let it come back like it was,' she said. 'The way I felt earlier.' She looked up at him. 'I don't want you to go. Is that so wrong?'

peter cowan

'No,' he said. 'Of course not.'

'Perhaps it is. It can only be till tonight—perhaps you should go—'

'That's not very long. I can look after myself till then, perhaps.'

'It isn't long,' she said. 'No.'

In the darkness of the strange room they were themselves strangers, yet knew themselves moved towards something both recognised and accepted, and which they had only to free from irrelevance. As he lay beside her she did not touch him, and he stroked her dark loosened hair, gently, tentatively. Her tenseness did not relax or after a time he might have thought she slept, and then suddenly she held against him, her body soft, heavy, and she said, 'I'm sorry—I—I'm sorry—' and she cried with a harshness she seemed to direct against herself. He was surprised, for he had not thought of her coming easily to tears, and then he knew that of course she did not. In the darkness he could not see her small, strong face, so that in memory it was aloof, as if unmarked by her tears, and he held her quietly, thinking with a mild irony that all this had dissolved into the unexpected, until they drifted to the warmth of sleep.

The light came without clarity into the room, filtered by the latticed verandah and the thin curtains of the window. The objects of the room materialised before him like some fusion of the growing light and his passing from sleep. He looked at the badly lined wall, the dark laths across the plaster squares of the ceiling, the small chest of drawers, the wardrobe, furniture badly made, the clothes upon the chair, the thin strip of frayed carpet. Then he saw that she was watching him, and she said softly, 'Isn't the place dreadful? But it doesn't matter.'

She leant towards him, the covers slipping across her shoulder and her arm, and with a kind of shyness she kissed him. Her hand slid behind his neck, and his mouth found her throat and her shoulder, cooler than the warmth of her body, her small firm breasts. Slowly and without certainty they sought one another, in care and a fear that they might destroy that which was as yet unfound. Yet in a kind of hesitation she gave herself, restraint passing, until she began to whisper to him urgently, pleading, giving endearment, though in something of impersonality which held them both. He knew he did not understand her reaction or her provocation, that it reached out to something in her own private world where he had no foothold. Yet their pleasure and feeling for one another rose and enveloped them and when they lay together, the light now strong in the room, she leant over him, touching his face with her lips, her hands, in feeling that brought him humility and whose cause he knew did not lie only in himself.

After a time she said, 'Hungry, Alan? Should I get tea—or coffee? We could have breakfast—'

He laughed. 'A cup of tea,' he said. 'You have wonderful ideas.'

Before the mirror she drew her hair back to clasp it at her neck. In the thin nightdress her body was full, her thighs unexpectedly heavy, rounded. Her arms lifted to her hair held a beauty that came to him sharply, strongly.

He spoke her name, and she turned her head, laughing. She went in to the kitchen and he heard her movements clearly in the room, setting the cups and saucers upon the table, opening a tin and putting it down. She brought tea and biscuits and they sat on the bed, drinking from the curiously ornamented cups that had been left as good enough for those who might come as tenants.

She said, 'If anyone comes, don't worry. We won't answer.'

'The car is outside, though. They'll see that.'

'It could belong to other people—in the next flat.'

'Are you really going tonight?'

'Yes. I must.'

'I could take you down in the car.'

'To Albany?'

'Yes.'

'You couldn't do that. It's too far.'

'Quicker than the train.'

'But your work, you wouldn't be back—no, Alan, please.'

'That wouldn't matter.' He burst out suddenly, 'What's the good of being my own boss and working all hours of the bloody day and night if I can't get a few of them to myself now and then—'

'No,' she said. 'It's not—not that I don't want you to—it just mustn't happen like that. You can't, Alan.'

'It doesn't make sense.'

'I think it does. Would you take me to the train?'

'Yes. I'll call for you whenever you want.'

'I didn't mean that. Will you stay with me till then?'

He nodded, and she came to him quite simply and implicitly as if she had known him always, and he found her surer, now with nothing of supplication, in demand she had sudden confidence she could fulfil.

Near midday they showered in the small bedroom built off the kitchen against the latticed verandah, the water cold and drumming loudly into the old scarred tin bath. They dressed—he felt incongruous in his suit of the evening before, while she wore shorts and a blouse— and she made lunch. While they were eating they heard a car door slam outside, and she rose quickly, pushing the kitchen door to, locking it. She pulled the blind across the window, darkening the kitchen. He could see through the open connecting door the bedroom window and the end of the verandah. Someone walked onto the boards and knocked at the kitchen door. She sat quite still, looking down at her plate. He felt the faint absurd- ity of one about to be caught in some childish prank, but he saw her face pale and set and he waited whatever she might herself be deciding. A man's voice called her name, self-consciously, as if calling against a conviction of her absence, or his own uncertainty.

The door-handle turned, and then he saw a tall man stoop to peer at the bedroom window. He could see through the faint distortion of the light on the glass a rather sharp face, brown hair receding from the forehead, and the clearly defined line of the parting. He thought they must be seen, and felt a dislike of the person he did not know, whose voice he expected to hear raised in discovery, but they heard the footsteps move uncertainly along the verandah and then go to the single step. For a time in the room neither of them moved as they waited for the car to start. After what seemed a long time, during which the man had deliberately delayed, they heard the car start, and turn, the sound of the motor fading.

'I'm sorry,' she said. She got up and found a cigarette and lit it. 'I knew he would come. I don't know how to explain it—'

'You don't need to,' he said.

She looked down at the table where she traced across the cloth the handle of a small spoon, marking lines and angles that faded from the thin material beneath the metal. She might have seen the small middle-aged man she had not yet met, who was one afternoon in the tidy office in the strange town to come up and speak to her, and with whom, after they had married and the edge of expectancy had been carefully denied between them, she had achieved a comfortable enough understanding in which there was no place for the unexpected or for strangeness, in the years that were untouched before her.

She said, 'I suppose you think I'm—that I've behaved pretty cheaply.'

'No. Perhaps I don't know what I think yet—but that never occurred to me. It isn't like that.'

'I'm glad. Because—well, there was only him.'

He did not make any comment and she said, 'For so long. I've known him so long. And it was getting—I might as well have been married to him, I had no life of my own, and it had all gone wrong, and he made it seem my fault. And he wouldn't go. He kept blaming me. I believed it was my fault. Oh, I can't tell you, but I know now that it wasn't.' She reached out suddenly and touched his hand. 'You've shown me. I've been lucky. And that's why I've got to go away. You can't break something like that in an hour. Later, when I've had time—Alan, could I write to you?'

'You must,' he said. 'I will to you.'

She smiled gently. 'No. Please. You must let me do this myself.'

'I can write to you, surely?'

She shook her head. 'No. I think I hate him. At times so that I didn't know you could feel like that about anyone. About a person. But I don't really. Oh,' she said hopelessly, 'how can you be free after all that time? Perhaps I never will be. I'm going away. I've been trying to plan it for a time now. Just let me write to you when I come back—can I?'

'Of course.'

She smiled suddenly. 'Do you think we'll find we've imagined this?'

'We could. Will we ever know?'

'Yes, one day,' she said.

In the afternoon she packed most of her things, and tidied the place. He helped where he could, and when they had finished she said, 'We could go out for a while if you'd like to.'

'All right,' he said. 'We could walk down to the beach.'

'I've put my things away. Like an idiot. Except the dress I want to wear tonight.'

'That doesn't matter.'

'Do I revolt you like this?' There was a sudden hardness behind the words as if she awaited some criticism, met it in advance. He looked at her in the white shorts and the neat sleeveless blouse.

'I don't follow.'

'I'm sorry. It's just that—he wouldn't have gone out with me like this. I was entirely wrong, it seems. My appearance. I should have been thin and I should have dieted—you can see I'm just not made like that, and I'd got self-conscious and I believed him. He'd have had me think I was repulsive. Perhaps he was right. But I didn't feel like that with you—'

'No,' he said. He held her lightly, his hands on her arms, and she looked up at him, smiling suddenly.

'We mightn't get our walk,' she said, 'if you do that.'

'Would it matter?'

'No. It wouldn't. But—I'd like it to be—as it is between us. If you see—?'

'Yes. We could swim if you like.'

'I haven't for years. And there are no bathers.'

'We'll settle for the walk.' He laughed. 'Come on. Not often you meet a girl who doesn't know how attractive she is.'

'You're a nice person,' she said. 'You don't know perhaps just how badly I needed to meet you.'

They walked down to the promenade, where the cars were parked along the kerbs, and on the beach there were families, the children playing on the loose sand and in the slow wash of the flat sea. At the shops he suggested they buy ice creams and they walked back licking them, in the heat the cream melting over the brown cones.

They washed up and tidied the kitchen, and she wrote a note for her friend who was coming back to the flat in the morning. When they had finished she dressed, and he took the suitcases outside to the car. She came out, locking the door. She put the key in the light-meter box, and came over to the car.

'I didn't know I'd be driving in this again so soon,' she said.

The carriages were drawn up at the platform as they went over the footbridge of the station, the engine backing down to connect with the train. They found her compartment and he arranged her cases. Along the platform people were gathered about the windows and the carriage entrances. She followed him from the compartment out into the corridor, for the moment the only uncrowded space. She held him quickly, as if suddenly she would have kept him, the scent of her dark hair and of the make-up she wore close to him, and she said, 'I will write to you', and he went down the narrow corridor onto the platform. From the window she waved and was lost in the anonymity of other hands, of the white lifting fabric of handkerchiefs, of faces, that drew into noise and distance, and among dispersing people.

The car stood outside the railway station among the lines of parked vehicles. He walked across towards it. To the west there was the glare of the sun, low down, the air hot and still. It was suddenly desolate, empty. There could be no meaning in the asphalted space, the parked cars, the harsh light. From some immense distance he viewed it and it did not contain him. The streets, the way back to the boarding-house, the others he would find there, his daily round, died in the sunlight of the late afternoon.

He would suddenly have driven from the streets and buildings, followed the train to find her when next it stopped, or to have been at its destination waiting when she arrived. But the trees would be drawing about the darkening road, and the paddocks and rises stretched into the distance, it was all as remote as the hot space before the station where he stood.

A car braked sharply beside him, the driver gesticulating at him, moving on past as he walked forward across the street.

Royalton Hotel,
West 44th Street
New York

Thursday night, 2 May 1985

Dear Sal,

It seems foolish to write to you since I've been phoning
you practically every day, but I'm at a loose end. The
Blue Bar across the road is crowded out and I can't fit
into my usual position on a stool in the corner (usual in
the sense that I've sat on it most of the fourteen nights
I've been here so far); and I don't feel like eating at the
Brazilia again which is the restaurant on West 45th Street
which Harry told me about. Well, Harry couldn't
remember its actual address, like all the other good
places and people here he insisted I should visit (sometimes he couldn't even remember their names, including
people), but I happened to walk past the Brazilia the

second day of my arrival and as it's close I eat there frequently. At first the Brazilian owner looked at me suspiciously (despite Harry's assuring me it would be a good place for a woman to eat on her own and drink a couple of bottles of wine without being hassled), but then I told him that an Australian friend of mine who had been in New York recently told me about his restaurant. He at first looked puzzled and then he said, 'Ah yes, you mean Harry with big frizz hair,' and I said yes and from then on he's been very nice to me.

Well, I've been mostly having a good time. Ernest arrived from Europe a few days ago on his way back to Sydney, and it was good to see him, although things didn't quite work out as we'd planned, especially in terms of getting his books published here which is one of the main reasons I came, as you know. I was excited about seeing him because his French publisher has sent me the French reviews of his books which Ernest hasn't seen yet and they say things like 'corrosive humour', 'incisive wit', and they all have very interesting and very French theories about his 'recité' technique. One of the papers devotes half a page to Ernest and half a page to Saul Bellow and Bellow comes off a definite second best! And who but the fucking French could say this: 'We are not the first to discover the Australian novel; even the Australians themselves are beginning to take an interest in it.' Bloody frogs. However, it's all very good for Ernest, and about time he was recognised outside Australia.

Anyway, the first thing that happened was that on

Sunday afternoon he left a message at my hotel asking me to ring him at his, which is new and near Grand Central and looks as if it costs about $500 a night, which I later found out it nearly does. So I phoned and he turned up to meet me at the Royalton and I gave him the reviews which I'd had copied down the road at a photocopying place in West 43rd Street which is run by New York blacks dancing to ghetto blasters which means they don't do a very good job and leave pages out, and I had to go back five times to get it done properly. Well, he was naturally very pleased and excited by the reviews which he read in my room over coffee. Actually it was Ernest who told me to stay at the Royalton when I told him I couldn't afford the Algonquin. Ernest told me it would be all right to stay at the Royalton because according to him Ernest Hemingway once wrote a book there. Our Ernest believes you have to have a literary reason for doing everything in New York. His own hotel is so new no one literary could have yet done anything significant there, but perhaps Ernest believes his stay there will change that. Ernest, mind you, couldn't remember which Hemingway book was written at the Royalton, or when, and no New York literary guide mentions anything about Hemingway ever having stayed there let alone writing a book there, but Ernest swears it's true.

Ernest justifies everything he wants to do in this city by making up something or other about a famous writer having done it, or been there, or drinking there, or living there, or dying there, etc etc etc. He has made up a whole literary geography in his head which contradicts everything written in all the New York literary guides. If you wrote down all of Ernest's made-up literary references you would have a whole alternative literary history of New York. It would confute every PhD thesis ever written on American writers. You would find that all the writers were born in different years to what their biographies say, and you would find them in New York during years in which their biographers claim they were elsewhere, sometimes not even in the United States of America. You would probably find that Henry James was born in England and then went to America later, and vice versa for Wystan Auden. Most likely you would find that Jack London was a teetotaller and that Ralph Waldo Emerson was a drunk. You would probably have Robert Lowell as a small calm man, and Elizabeth Hardwick suffering from uncontrollable mania (though I don't think that Ernest has actually mentioned any women writers). But if he did you would also probably find that Dorothy Parker drank whisky at some oblong table in the White Lion, and that Dylan Thomas died after drinking a martini at the Algonquin. However, Ernest says that a lot of the biographies are wrong, and that it takes a fresh foreign eye to get things right, and that Australians have the best fresh foreign eyes because we have no history or culture ourselves and are therefore not prejudiced by received myth.

I don't suppose it matters, but it's a bit confusing when you're trying to get a literary feel for New York.

Anyway, Ernest suggested we go for a walk and then

back to his hotel where we would pick up Thea who was having a rest and hadn't wanted to come on the walk but would have dinner with us later. (Thea is here with Ernest on a business trip for her company and Ernest said she was tired from all her work and that's why she was resting up.)

So Ernest and I stopped in all these bars which Ernest said so-and-so had written a book in. None of them looked to me as if anyone could write a book in them, they were all grubby little affairs with hardly any room and lots of stools squashed close together at narrow bars with noisy people singing Irish songs and things. He also said as we approached them that he knew the barman in each of them, but no one in them recognised him and then he said that they must have left since he was last in New York. He said that New York is a very mobile city in terms of bar managers. He said it's not like Sydney where staff in restaurants and pubs stay the same for years and years, and you can get free drinks and dinners just by putting their names and their restaurants in your books. In New York they move around a lot, Ernest said, and putting them in your books gets you nowhere anyway because so many American writers put them in their books that the market is over-saturated and they would go broke giving free drinks and meals to hundreds of second-rate writers.

One of the bars Ernest took me to was a very grand bar in a grand hotel attached to Grand Central station by a tunnel which Ernest said all of the writers in the thirties used when they were coming in from out of town to escape their wives. Well, we had a few more drinks there and Ernest told me the reason we were there was because this was the bar where he had picked up a black hooker who had stolen his wallet last time he was in New York. He thought this was something to celebrate. He was drinking toasts to the fact that a black whore had stolen his money. I don't know if he made this up too, but he was very excited about it. It occurred to me that perhaps all the bars we had been to were places where his money had been stolen by prostitutes when he was drunk, and that I was being taken on a guided tour of Ernest-in-the-gutter-in-New-York. The scenes of all his moments of degradation (except he would see them as moments of triumph). You wouldn't exactly think it was something to be proud of, but there you are. You know Ernest, Sal.

Anyway, all this took a few hours and then we arrived at his hotel. Ernest phoned up Thea from the foyer house phone and I heard him say 'What do you mean you don't want to go out?'. Then he said to me that he'd just slip up to the room to freshen up, and he sat me down in the lounge and ordered me a bloody Mary and told me to put it on his account. So I waited and waited and had a few more drinks on his account and then Ernest came down alone. When I asked where Thea was he said she was changing and would be down soon. He muttered about how he always got things wrong with women, he always misread their personalities and moods, and this struck me as probably being true seeing as how it seemed that on his last trip he'd had his money stolen by women in practically every bar we went to.

Anyway, Sal, to cut a long story short, it turned out that he hadn't even told Thea I was in New York or that he was going on a walk with me or that the three of us were meant to be having dinner together. He'd just sprung it on her through the foyer house phone and not surprisingly she was a bit pissed off, not even knowing I was in the country. Not that Ernest and I have been lovers, Sal, well not exactly, but you know, we've known each other for a very long time. Probably he'd taken her on a few walks too, and explained about how many whores had ripped him off. Just the sort of thing to tell your new girlfriend who was seeing the trip as a special occasion between her and you, a shared private journey.

So anyway, Thea made the best of it and was as nice as she could be to me given the fact that Ernest had probably told her they would be having a room-service champagne and oysters and chicken dinner in bed looking out over the New York skyline with a chamber music orchestra playing Gershwin in a corner of their suite.

Ernest said he would take us to the Pen and Pencil. He said this was a famous cartoonists' restaurant where he was well known. He took about an hour to find it, and Thea and I had sore feet in our high heels tramping around while Ernest kept saying 'it's just up this next street' and then pretending he was deliberately taking us the long way to point out more literary famous places, and it turned out to be only five hundred yards from their hotel after all. It was a small classy place but we were the only people in it the whole night, and Ernest said it must have changed from a dinner to a lunch restaurant since the last time he was in New York. And New York's staff mobility must have affected the Pen and Pencil too, because no one knew him. The way things had changed in New York since Ernest had last been there, Sal, you'd think he hadn't been there since 1920.

(... Hang on Sal, I'm just going down to the foyer—forgot to check at the desk to see if Phillip's been trying to phone me ... No, no calls as usual. I ring him about six times a day, Sal, and he's only phoned me four times in two weeks. He says it's not necessary to make all these costly calls. It's not as if I'm going to be away all that long. I get into trouble when I phone him for spending so much money. I think he resents the money because the telephone system here is private enterprise. If it was owned by a left wing government he'd probably encourage me to make lots of calls. Give him a ring for me, please, and tell him to phone me and that I'm worth every penny, though by the time you get this letter I'll probably have phoned him another twenty times. I think he's punishing me for being in New York instead of somewhere like Cuba. Tell him I'm going to Nicaragua to join the Sandanista if that makes him happy ...)

Well, we ate at the Pen and Pencil and when we left Ernest said he'd walk me back to the Royalton, but Thea looked suddenly tired and so he bought me a bunch of tulips instead from Grand Central which I took with me to the Algonquin to have a nightcap. By the way, a funny but awful thing happened on my first night at the Blue

Bar, with a woman called Renata, but I'll tell you about it when I get back.

On Tuesday night I had to meet Ernest and Thea again, this time at the Algonquin, where I'd organised for Ernest to meet this editor called Penny from Simon and Schuster, who had read Ernest's work and was enthusiastic about publishing it, and as Ernest was in town it seemed to me a good idea for her to meet him. So I told her I would be with Ernest and a friend of his and we would see her there in the lounge at six. Well Thea and Ernest turned up and we drank in the lounge for an hour or so with me keeping an eye out for this Penny whom I hadn't yet met myself, only written to and talked on the phone. Ernest was peculiarly nervous, talking very loudly and drinking martinis with twists very fast, which was odd I thought seeing how often he deals with publishers in Australia. Well this woman kept walking around the lounge but I didn't think she looked enough like a New York editor to be Penny and also I thought that she would work out that we would be the people she was looking for, if it was her. Then finally I got up and asked if she was Penny and she said yes, so I introduced her and do you know what she said? She said she hadn't thought we were us, because from reading Ernest's work she had assumed his 'friend' would be a man. So it was a bit embarrassing but she sat down and we all talked for a while. Mostly Ernest and Penny talked about films, and after a while she left telling me to phone her the next morning. I thought it was all very successful, but Ernest was oddly gloomy, and we went into the Blue Bar for more drinks.

You see, on previous nights I'd been talking to the manager in the Blue Bar, a man called Brett, and when he found out I was Australian and in publishing, he told me he'd once met an Australian writer in the bar and had read one of his books and liked it, and it turned out to be Ernest when he was last in New York. This was the one time when Ernest didn't seem to be lying about knowing barmen everywhere.

So in we went, and Thea and I sat down and drank while Brett and Ernest met up again, and they talked for hours and hours because it turned out that Brett had been in the SAS in Vietnam and was writing a novel about it, and also it was the subject of the moment because it's the tenth anniversary of America pulling out of Vietnam and tomorrow there's a big veterans' march in New York. (I suppose there's one in Sydney too.)

I heard Ernest telling Brett that he'd been in the Australian SAS too when as you know he was only in National Service decades ago when there were no wars on, and in any case Ernest used to be in moratorium marches, but you know how he's always reading war books and going to military history seminars and going to Verdun and the Middle East and Lone Pine and hanging around war museums and memorials, so they talked about guns and parachutes and airlifts and 'Charlie' (I think Ernest learnt a lot of this from Pat Burgess when he came back from reporting in Vietnam) and I even heard Ernest say 'the Nam'. At one stage I thought he was going to pull out his Order of

Australia medal and say it was a military hero's medal. And all this time Thea and I had to just talk and drink with each other, and with Thea still quite annoyed that I was in New York.

(Well, I'd better go Sal. How's everything? Have you heard from Tony? Give my love to the girls. Did Sarah pass her exams? If I were you I'd just send Tony a cheery postcard just as if you'd suddenly thought of him, accidentally, and was wondering how he was, just in case he thinks you're pining after him and deliberately not contacting him because you're sad, which I know you are but you shouldn't let him know.)

Oh, and I nearly forgot the point. When we left the bar I told Ernest I'd phone him as soon as I'd phoned Penny the next morning, and he said he wouldn't go out of his hotel room until he'd heard from me about Simon and Schuster. So the next day I rang Penny all ready to go down and pick up a contract for Ernest to sign, and she said she'd changed her mind about wanting to publish him. I was very annoyed and she wouldn't say why, and I am annoyed because they don't know what they're missing out on. I had to ring Ernest and tell him, but I tried to tell him not to worry and that other publishers would be bidding in auctions for him, but it didn't work and he was very depressed. He told me I should never ever again introduce him to publishers because they all cancel contracts when they've met him no matter how much they've said they admire his writing, which isn't true of course. He said he should be kept away from publishers at all costs. He said he should wear a sign saying 'publishers keep away', or swing a bell and call out 'unclean' whenever he was near a publisher. He said he would never go into literary bars again or to writers' festivals or to literary prize-givings or anywhere where he might run into a publisher. He said he must have some smell which repels publishers.

I tried to cheer him up, but it was no good. I said this was a big city and there were hundreds of publishers who would like him as well as his work, but he said it was just as well he was getting out of town tomorrow to leave me clear to sell his books here without him hampering me by his damaging presence. I felt so sorry for him, Sal, I wanted to rush round to his hotel and hug him.

I ended up telling him that if he wrote up his New York literary guide I would take it straight to the office of Michelin in New York and sell it for millions. He said didn't I know the editorial office of Michelin was in Clermont-Ferrand, and if I'd read *Biggles* I'd know where Clermont-Ferrand was, and what kind of an agent was I if I didn't know elementary things like that, and I said I was only joking and he said his literary map of New York was only a joke too.

So, he's left now Sal, and should be back in Sydney within a day or two, unless he stops over at Honolulu to recover from the setback, so give him a ring to cheer him up if you can. And ask him to show you the French reviews.

I'll probably phone you tomorrow anyway to tell you all this.

Lots of love,
Iris.

She cannot close her mind to bacteria climbing cotton threads. She had gone under the knife in the end, and now the thought of any insertion is repellent to her. She explains, her palm beneath her rib cage: 'I feel it start inside me, here, and move down, like I'm closing up to expel you. I'm sorry.'

You tell her don't be. You say it's understandable.

Louise does not offer you time, though. And you are careful not to suggest that time will help. But when one thing is changed, so are all the others. When you wake at seven o'clock you know that she is already awake, wanting to dress, to go home. It had not been the 'companionable night' you'd mentioned; the morning is not companionable. 'This is going to take more than vitamin B6,' she says.

You want to know: If she's able to joke, will everything be all right?

And you watch her gather her things. She won't wait for breakfast, for the balloons.

At half-past eight you move the garden table away from the shedding wattle and set it in the sun. Juice, toast and espresso for one on wrought-iron, once flaring white, now yellow-spotted with blossoms. The reviews, weekend magazine, house auctions circled with a red Bic. Field-glasses. The expectant cat.

You know the balloons by their breathing. They appear above the rooftops. They like to prowl in pairs, always one higher or farther away than the other. On a Saturday morning before all this, Louise had been the first to see them, pointing them out to you, motorless invaders come to hang in your patch of the sky. They had breathed, minutes between breaths. This morning you watch the flames in the field-glasses; a heartbeat later, you hear them. The balloons seem to hang there, palpitating, keeping watch, one red, one blue, both logoed HELM Finance.

They float away towards the Exhibition Building, but that brings you no comfort. As you search in the corners of the *Age* classifieds spread out upon the tabletop, your skin creeps. You turn, look up. Little clouds have drifted in—implanted, you imagine, with monitoring eyes.

You appease them. You sweep the blossoms clotting the yard, water the potted herbs, snip the leaves brown-ing in the windowboxes. You realign the terracotta duck. (Had the cat knocked it? Had a thief?—stand on that bluestone block and one can see into the house.) Then you dump the bagged sweepings upon the mountain of garbage accumulating on the footpath next to Mr Said's unlucky picket fence. Fitzroy Council has been sacked and a scrap of the *Melbourne Times* caught in the garbage is gleeful about that. You look up at the clouds: *My house is in order now.*

You go inside and watch from the bedroom window. Mr Said appears, vigilant, at his picket fence. Perhaps he fears that layers will shift in the garbage mountain, as plates beneath the earth shift. He pokes a broom handle between his palings, and prods and moulds, and gases must be coiling away. There have been spray cans and stones and door-to-door Christians in Mr Said's life. He has repainted the footpath wall, one coat, dimming TOXIC scrawled there with modernist flourish. His windows are screened with rectangles of chicken wire tacked to splintery wooden frames. There are signs on his door warning off anyone promising anything.

Later you lift the Safeway bags from out of the Renault's boot and take them to the front step. There with one hand you attempt to isolate the door key, but it's the neat, decent, elderly man standing in the street who has most of your attention. His glance is moving from you to the house, you to the house, his expression untutored and uncomplicated, like a child who is about to make an ingenuous remark. Do you know him? You don't know him. Does he think he knows you? His hands are on his hips and there is a hat sitting jauntily on the back of his head. He starts towards you.

And there is also a young woman, standing close to but sufficiently apart from him. Her skin is very white, her eyes in dark sockets. She folds her arms, she sighs, all her limbs restless in black, tight, torn, risky tights and layered black petticoats.

You have the front door key now, but then the elderly man reaches you, jerks his head in the manner of a hello, and asks: 'This your place?'

You nod.

'Sam Drewe,' he says, thrusting out his hand. 'This is where I grew up.'

That out-thrust hand: you want to point out that you are trying to juggle keys and shopping bags here. You bite on the RACV tag, the taste of salt-and-iron in your mouth, the keys swinging at your chin, and shake his hand, muffling your name.

He repeats it, as though tracing it in his memory: 'Ross. Ross.' The girl, he explains, is Mary Jane, his granddaughter. She continues to stand apart, suffering, drifting, sharpening only when he mentions her name.

You stand on the front step with your arms burdened but the old man is launched and away. 'I say to Mary Jane, all right, if your professor wants an oral history, come and see where it all happened.' He points at your front door. 'I was born here in 1915, slap bang on the kitchen table. Lived here till the Second War, and haven't been back since.' Then he turns and points to the air above the nearby rooftops. 'See that old chimney? My old man worked there.'

Sam's shoes are dark-tan, gleaming. His shiny-kneed trousers are hooked high at the waist by faded braces. He wears a jacket and a tie; chest hairs and a white vest show where an upper button has popped. Someone has stitched leather patches to his sleeves. You remember the depthless dark pockets of your grandfather's tweed jacket, the tobacco flakes, lint, ha'pennies and pencil stubs caught in the corners of them. 'So, here we are,' Sam says.

'Pop,' the girl says, 'let the man take his shopping in.'

Man? As old as that? A man, thirty-two, was killed today when.

The grandfather steps back. 'Of course. Sorry to bother you. We'll just poke around out here a bit.'

Before you are quite aware of it you are saying, 'Would you like to see inside?'

Need and gratification transform Sam's face and his stumpy teeth worry the offer. He says, 'Wouldn't mind, you know.'

'*Pop*.'

'Just a quick look, love.'

You have the door open, you stand side-on to let them pass. 'Please,' you tell the girl, 'come on in.'

But they fill the hallway and won't budge.

'Go on through,' you tell them.

You see that someone has kissed lips of blood to the surface of Mary Jane's thin neck. She has rings staged down one ear like coils in a spring.

'In here?' Sam says. He pauses under the arch, then crosses the living area to where it opens to the slate tiles of the kitchen.

'Please sit down,' you say.

But the grandfather prowls. The girl sits in the cane rocking chair. Now that she is inside the house she seems to be refreshed, alert for developments. Casting about, she says, 'Do you own it?'

'With the bank.'

'Everything's changed,' Sam says. 'There used to be a wall here.' His hands press flat the air where the carpet meets the slate.

You explain that you needed more space.

'Skylight,' Sam says. 'Those glass door things. Slate floors. You wouldn't credit it.'

The girl is grinning, rocking in the chair. 'They call it gentrification, Pop.'

'Tea?' you ask. 'Coffee?'

'Let's see what tea you've got,' the girl says. She releases the chair to rock behind her and strides into the kitchen alcove. She touches the packets and tins, murmurs the names, and says firmly, 'Peppermint.'

'Sam?'

He is at the French windows, looking out at the jasmine, the wattle, the duck on the bluestone block. 'Whatever's going.'

'He'll have ordinary,' Mary Jane says. She holds the bench lip and scans the open shelves. 'Lavazza. Bertolli. *Totally gorgeous.*'

As she stands on her toes to peer, her shoulder bumps against yours, then sways away. She has chemical-yellow short flat hair, and fluid sinews in her neck. The kitchen space is cramped, so you must edge around her to get at things. It is like the sizing-up steps in a folk dance. You have forgotten Sam. The centre is her willed, ironical, wrinkling nose.

Sam says, 'The toilet was down the back. They used to come around in a horse and cart and collect it, the "night soil".'

Mary Jane shifts her expectations around to make room for this. She says, 'Tell him about Squizzy Taylor, Pop.'

'Next door,' Sam says, 'used to be a sly-grog shop. You'd have someone on watch in the street and you'd go down the laneway there and knock on the gate'—he raps his knuckles on the pine bench—'one, two, three, and they'd open it and you'd give your order. Bloody awful stuff, sort of a whisky. Poison you.'

'Did you buy it?'

'Not me, no, I was just a kid. But we sneaked over the fence and pinched some once. Godawful stuff.'

'Sugar and milk?'

Mary Jane shakes her head. You are standing with her on one side of the bench, facing her grandfather, who is stirring his tea, lost to dreams. You say, 'There's no sugar in it,' and offer him the bowl. He spoons in sugar and stirs again. Mary Jane blows across the surface of her tea. She is holding the cup with both hands, drifting with the wreathing steam. They are both looking down the years.

You ask: 'Did Squizzy Taylor sell the grog?'

Sam gathers himself. 'He was too flash for the dirty work. He was more your spiv, you know, nice suit, big car, the races, them dancing joints and baccarat joints. But he might of, in his younger days.'

Sam's hat is on the bench and his tufted hair is illuminated by the soft sunlight pouring through the perspex dome above him. You are no closer to linking Squizzy Taylor with all this. You say, 'He was a psychopath, wasn't he, Squizzy Taylor?'

You sip your tea, eyeing Sam above the rim.

Sam clatters his cup on to its saucer. Mary Jane swings around.' Killed a few people?' you continue.

Sam measures his words. 'I went to his funeral. 1927. Bloody the whole of Richmond lined the Hill. You can't tell me they'd do that if he was . . . ' His hand rolls, completing the sentence.

Mary Jane has concentrated her attention upon you. You are drawn to face her. You shrug: 'I read it somewhere.'

'So what?'

'Just happened to read it.'

'What Grandpa is talking about,' Mary Jane says, 'is community.'

'Ah.'

Sam says, 'One time he come around our school and give us five bob each to distribute election bills. Another time he gives me a quid, a quid, to keep watch for a two-up game. He'd look after you.'

You nod, drink your tea. 'Did he live near here?'

'Squizzy Taylor? Nah.'

You wait, then say, 'You seemed to imply he was involved with the grog shop next door.'

Sam frowns. 'Not that I know of.'

Mary Jane is watching you, bright, motionless, hard-edged. You can feel the force of it. She murmurs, 'That wasn't necessary.'

You shrug. 'I just thought.'

'Connect,' Mary Jane says. 'That's what a woman would do. Connect and form a wider picture, not pin things down in compartments.' She shivers as she says it, recovers, turns to her grandfather. 'You ready, Pop?'

But Sam has inclined his ear to an approaching clink and clatter in the street outside and his face is expressing delight and can-it-be? 'Well I'll be blowed,' he says.

'What?' says Mary Jane, her face bright, reproducing his. She laughs expectantly. 'What, Pop?'

You say, 'It's the bottle-o. I'll just give him.' You reach down for the cane basket of empties next to the fridge.

'Give us a look,' Mary Jane says. She pulls at the basket's edge, like someone with a practised eye for the half-concealed. This is a moment of risk and reconciliation. Her head is almost touching yours.

'Yellowglen,' she shouts, waving a bottle like a trophy. 'Let's see. Bertolli, we know about that. No-brand mineral water? Bit down-market.'

She releases the basket. You point at her. 'First-year sociology, right?'

'Ha, ha.'

They follow you to the window. You open it and they crowd there with you, watching the advance of the bottle-o and his hard-wheeled wood and iron cart. 'I'll be blowed,' Sam says. The bottle-o halts his cart in the street, shouts, waves an arm, and takes the bottles as Mary Jane passes them through to him.

The bottle-o trundles away with his cart. In Sam's sigh there are elements of grief and love and struggle. 'That took me back,' he says.

Mary Jane closes the window on the garbage and the receding cart. 'God, what a stink.'

'Five weeks now.'

Sam collects his hat. 'Well, Mary Jane?'

You ask them where they're going.

'His place,' Mary Jane says. 'Footscray.'

'Did you drive?'

'Bus,' Sam says.

'Why don't I give you both a lift?'

Mary Jane stands there regarding you as if you have made a confession of passion. She shrugs. 'If you like.'

On the way out she says, 'Don't you use some of these rooms? Do you live here by yourself?'

'Sort of.'

'Sort of,' she says. 'I see.'

She had insisted you take the Westgate Freeway route, for Sam's sake. He had beamed at that. So now you are slowing for the approach ramp, creeping onto the bridge, hugging the centre lane. A wind has come up, pollen-laden and gusty, flinging scratches of dust and grit against the Renault. The windsock points straight out. The car rocks; plastic bags are riding the air, fat between the girders. You are overwhelmed by a fit of sneezing and sniffing and itchy eyes.

'Bless you,' Sam says from the back seat.

'Steady,' Mary Jane says, her hand hovering near the steering wheel. 'Can you see where you're going?'

The Yarra channel is far below. A man, thirty-two, died when.

'Hay fever,' you tell her. 'It's the time of year.'

The car is above a region of docks and oil terminals and streaming smokestacks. Mary Jane smooths the edgings of black lace that pucker about her knees. Her hands bear cuts and scratches and bitten fingernails. 'Out here,' she says, 'it's more complicated than hay fever.'

The down ramp. Growling trucks overtake the Renault. Then the freeway flattens and you are level with noise barriers and banked earth again.

Mary Jane continues: 'You are what you breathe. Ask any doctor around here—cancers, bad lungs, birth defects.'

'Oh, it's not as bad as that,' Sam says.

'It *is*, Pop.'

You can't say to them: *Why do you live here then?* You say: 'How long have you lived here?'

'I don't,' Mary Jane says. She folds her arms.

Sam has his hands on the back of your seat. 'Since the war,' he says, close to your ear.

Mary Jane leans forward. 'Get in the left lane. You want the next exit.'

'Where do you live?' You sneeze again, and sigh.

'Me? A Collingwood squat. Whole group of us.'

Sam releases the seat. He sits back in the corner. You ask, 'Are you all students?'

'What's it to you?'

'Just interested.'

'Think we're dole bludgers or something? Think I wouldn't live in a decent place if I had the money? Turn right at the second set of lights along. You've got all those rooms—I could pay you something.'

Sam apparently has not been listening. All you can see of him in the rear-view mirror is his hat on his bowed head. Born 1915: that would make him over seventy-five.

'When you say you sort of live alone,' Mary Jane says, 'does that mean you've got a girlfriend?'

You shift your shoulders, thinking of a reply.

'All that room going to waste,' Mary Jane says. 'How come you're not living together?' She is facing you, her shoulder against the door. 'Come on, I'm curious.'

The seconds pass. Suddenly Mary Jane shifts in her seat, says thrillingly, '*I know—the New Celibacy*,' and sits back again and stares glumly ahead. 'Next left,' she says. Then, 'Number four, near where that truck is.'

You slow the car, pull into the kerb, stop the engine. A brick fence, shrugged into a comfortable unevenness by time and tree roots; some shrubs and a prickly, unconfined couch-grass lawn; and the house, a neat weatherboard. That texture: it's unnatural. Sam has paid for plastic cladding.

Mary Jane is watching you, but you are not about to be caught out again. You turn, offering Sam your hand between the seats. 'I enjoyed meeting you, Mr Drewe.'

'Mr Drewe,' Mary Jane mutters.

Sam says, 'Ross, was it? Thanks for the ride, Ross.'

'Yeah. Thanks.' Mary Jane hunts for her door-handle. There seem to be several, they confuse her, so you lean across, point, touch, saying, 'Do you need a lift back to Collingwood?'

'Can't. Staying the weekend. Nan's in hospital.'

Sam has left the car and is waiting on the footpath. He appears to be exhausted. You ask Mary Jane, 'Can I do anything? Take you to the shops or something?'

She is suddenly boundless and elusive. She calls, 'No thanks!', grins, and steps lightly out of the car. The door shuts. She clacks her ring on the glass, *goodbye*, and takes her grandfather's arm. By the time you have U-turned she is mounting the front step with him.

On the telephone later that afternoon, Louise says: 'I think I'll just stay in tonight.'

'Fair enough.'

She might be eating something, or sipping a cup of tea. Along the wires you hear a tiny adjustment, a disembodied swallow, then hear her ask: 'What are you going to do?'

'Probably stay in too.'

Later she says, 'Did you see the balloons?'

'Yes.'

'Did you hear about the one that crashed? Not here, in the bush somewhere. It was too windy.' She swallows again. 'Well, I'd better go,' she says, and you echo her goodbye and hang up.

You return to your contemplation of the syringe. When the call came you had been crouched centimetres from its grit-corrupted needle point. You had not noticed it this morning—had discovered it only five minutes ago when you shifted the basil into the last rays of the sun. Better tossed here in your garden than into the gutters where the children idle, but now what? You could put it on the garbage mountain, but like a spined creature stiffening in the darkness it might strike someone.

You crouch near it again. That sharp point, your submissive fingers. This is like being drawn to the desirable rim of a high bridge.

My mother heard it on the radio. They found the boy's body at 4.30 when they were packing up the picnic things, in a metre of water where the bottom of the lagoon shelved suddenly. In the panic it took them twenty minutes to think of counting heads. Then they discovered that another little boy was missing.

The second underwater search in thirty minutes. One child drowned, then another. It's too affecting a beginning, too much to accept. I feel uncomfortable ordering it so definitely. Wise after the event as usual. Full of selective certainties. But I know the second boy was a year younger than the first. Aged six. Lawrence Barker. I forget the first boy's name but obviously I remember Lawrence's. The compounded tragedy, the coincidences of the same name, age and place—Big Heron Lagoon—even their attending the same holiday child-care centre, saw to that. And my mother's reaction when she heard the news.

I'd told her that it was Peter's and Jenna's week with me. I know I'd said they were staying with Lucy and me down at the coast. They were not with Ellen, not spending their holidays at the child-care centre as usual, they were with me. (Somehow my mother's generation has trouble linking the ideas of 'father' and 'children'.) And 'Lawrence' hardly sounds like 'Peter'. But in the drama of a news bulletin enough connections could be made. I could see her making the leaps of imagination and despair. She knew we'd borrowed a friend's cottage at Bundeena, and Bundeena abuts the Royal National Park where the boys had died. So she had plenty to go on. For a long half-hour she was convinced that her grandson had drowned at a badly supervised children's picnic. When she finally reached me on the phone, I had to repeat to her, 'Mother, I can see Peter from here. He's watching "Inspector Gadget". I'll call him to the phone if you like.'

I never called her Mother but I was terse with her. She didn't believe me. She was babbling. Actually, my hand was trembling on the phone. I felt stunned. Peter was sitting crosslegged on the floor in his pyjamas watching television, and yet this evening there was a drowned boy named Barker, aged six.

Another layer of coincidence was making my hands shake. Only the day before, Lucy and I had taken the kids into the park for a picnic by the same lagoon. While my mother sighed and tutted I was replaying the day in my mind like a film, and recalling every frame. I remembered exactly the way the bottom of the shallow lagoon fell away suddenly in the middle. The water was a quieter, creamier green where the fresh creek met the salty white sand of the ocean beach—where, in winter, the higher tides burst through into the lagoon. I could feel the sandy bottom falling away right then, shifting and oozing around my ankles, the cooler currents around my shins, and I kicked away from the water-filled silence. And while my mother gradually calmed down and I turned the conversation around to Christmas plans, it struck me that my supervision of the children had been less than total. Certainly I watched them while they played in the water, but I read a magazine at the same time. I felt warm and lazy. The sun was bright and heavy on my eyelids; I couldn't swear that I didn't close them once or twice. And when I eventually dived in, the water was so bracing after the thick air that I stretched out and swam for several minutes, around a bend and temporarily out of sight.

Frankly, at the time I knew the risk. It occurred to me and I swam on. Worse, I anticipated *something*.

I looked at Peter and Jenna, absorbed by the cartoon, amusement flickering on their cheeks. I stared at them. Peter's hair was wet and spiky from his bath; a trickle ran down his neck behind his ear. Now and then he hummed the 'Inspector Gadget' theme. Despite his dead boy's particulars he moved, he spoke. I went over and stroked his head. To keep things fair, I reached over and patted Jenna's, too. They didn't notice. A little later I began feeling guilty. Waves of guilt swept over me. But I couldn't dwell on the other parents, on what those families were doing right then. I could imagine, but I tried to put them out of my mind. And I succeeded. I was ruthless. I erased their anguish. I burned it out of the air.

Both my children are good swimmers now. That

summer we had them coached, and they still train regularly. Swimming is Peter's only sporting interest. When adults ask his hobbies, he's apt to say, 'My hobby is imagination'. He's one of those sort of ten-year-olds. A sci-fi reader. A dreamy monster-lover. He moons through school classes but knows twenty ancient instruments of torture. He's a 'Dungeons and Dragons' buff. He likes those adventure books where the reader is the hero, and gets to decide which plot strand to follow. Already Peter wants to channel his fate, if only to choose the sword-fight with the skeleton ahead of the possible mauling by the werewolf.

Lucy and I moved to the coast ourselves last year, north rather than south, escaping from city real estate prices as much as other tensions. We bought a cottage at Springstone, a renovated weekender whose high position on Blackwall Hill we believed would compensate for its drawbacks. The views of the bay even made up for the mosquitoes and sandflies which rose from the reeds and mangrove flats at low tide and settled on the house. 'Citronella Heights,' I joked. Lucy is a member of the post-pesticide generation, an advocate of citronella oil as an insect repellent. Last summer we'd spray ourselves before drinks in the garden, before going to the beach, even—especially—before bed. The pungent citronella oil soaked into our clothes, sheets, furnishings, car upholstery. I didn't mind it; the fragrance was nostalgic. It brought back serene times, patchouli oil and incense and women in caftans. But everyone entering our house or car would ask, 'What *is* that smell?'

The children had no faith in citronella. They liked the way pesticides *annihilated* mosquitoes. One Saturday Peter woke with a badly bitten forehead and puffy eyelids. He was struck with awe and admiration for the face in the mirror ('I look like a halfling, a demi-human. I told you that stuff didn't work.'). But his ogre's demeanour had lapsed by bedtime. The first mosquito whine made him frantic. 'They're coming for me!' he yelled. We allowed him dispensation: he was permitted the old poison.

Destruction can be enjoyable, especially with right on your side. It's hard to put more than the broadest Buddhist case for the mosquito. A day I remember from last spring, the Monday of a holiday long-weekend: the arrow on the gauge outside town pointed to Extreme Fire Danger; in the way of city people I was heeding the warning and clearing the bush around the house. What I was doing was really more drastic than clearing. I was hacking into the lantana and scrub with the new Japanese brush-cutter. I was razing things flush to the earth. My blade screamed. Insects flew from the din and lizards scuttled in panic. In the trees above me, lines of kookaburras conspired patiently to swoop on newly exposed centipedes. I was righteous in my destruction: the lantana is an introduced pest, the centipede's bite is painful and poisonous, and so on. I stomped through the scrub wielding the cutter. Rock shards bounced off my heavy-plastic protective glasses, branches snapped underfoot. 'You look like "The Terminator",' Peter said. He approved. He was swinging a scythe. It was too big for him but he swung it anyway. The Grim Reaper, of course, and pleased to be him.

This was the month of unseasonal heat when people in shops and at bus stops first began talking about the Greenhouse Effect. Arsonists were lighting fires in the national parks, and an infestation of Bogong moths, blown by the north-westerlies, descended on the city and coast. The moths had become disoriented on their migration south from Queensland to the alpine country. They turned up in every building. They crawled into cupboards and kettles and shoes, into the luggage lockers in aircraft cabins and the more sinuous wind instruments of orchestras. They flew hundreds of miles out to sea before dropping in the waves. Some made it to New Zealand. Cats and dogs got fat and bored with eating them. (They were big and calorific; on wind-screens they splattered into yellow grease.) Everyone had moths, and those places where bottlebrush trees were flowering for spring—the moths' favorite food was bot-tlebrush nectar—had a hundred times more.

In the hot wind the moths rose in a flurry from our bottlebrushes and showered red pollen on my son's head. Lucy and Jenna had left us to our mayhem. We cut and slashed and raked, but eventually stopped to have a drink. Peter was still charged with an edgy frisk-iness. While I drank a beer he entertained me with his repertoire of murderous noises and death scenes. He mimed axes in skulls and arrows in throats. He did blow-pipes and bazookas. He lurched about with his red-tinged hair, grunting and gurgling. He switched roles from killer to victim. Bullets ricocheted off rocks, scimitars flashed. He could crumple to the ground a dozen ways, holding his entrails in.

The air on our hill was yellow and smoky. Against the blurry horizon he filled me in on monsters. His favorites were the Undead—zombies, ghouls, wights, wraiths, mummies and skeletons. 'They're *chaotic*,' he said. What he liked about them, and gave him the creeps, was their potential for anarchy. Their evil was disorderly. Despite his patient explanations he lost me after that. The bush-fires were on my mind and 'Dungeons and Dragons' is a complex game. But I've flipped through his guide-book, wondering at the attraction. 'A wraith looks like a shadow which flies, and *drains levels* as a wight. A mummy does not drain levels.' I'm none the wiser. I notice they all seem impervious to heroics. 'Ghouls are immune to *sleep and charm spells*. They are hideous beast-like humans who will attack any living thing. Any hit from a ghoul will paralyse any creature of ogre-size or smaller (except elves) . . .'

I knew zombies from those comedy-duo films of the fifties where they chased Abbott and Costello and Martin and Lewis. I knew Malcolm Rydge. This is an easy joke now that I can safely glance out of restaurant windows and not catch him looking in. I can walk the streets and not see him jog past, averting his eyes. I can leave my house suddenly without his car accelerating away. I can return the children to my old house, to Ellen, and not hear his excitable gabble in the kitchen, my name ringing in the air, the abrupt hush, the scramble for the back door.

There was finally a moment, a Friday lunch, when I looked down from the New Hellas, randomly, between mouthfuls of souvlakia, into Elizabeth Street. Malcolm was standing across the road in Hyde Park staring up at my window seat, my regular table. Our eyes met and held this time, in some sort of recognition. There is always someone who thinks you know the secret. Any secret. The secret of knowing Ellen first. The secret of the window table. Ellen had just thrown him out, he told me on my way out. He was waiting for me. It occurred to me later that he could have had a gun, a knife, in that shoulder bag he always wore. He slipped up in his running shoes and shook my hand as if he liked me. His eyes were distracted. His skin was damp and flickery. She had someone else. The voodoo was over, at least for me.

Lucy doesn't scoff at unquiet spirits. Ellen shuts them all out. She drops the portcullis. Her father went for a walk after lunch when she was twelve and never came back. From the verandah she saw him disappear into the treeline, swinging his stick and eating a Granny Smith apple. No one ever found anything. Before it was called Alzheimer's Disease, my mother's mother was always trudging into town to hand in her own belongings to the police. 'I found this handbag in Myer's,' she would say. 'Some lass *will* be in a state.' She basked in her honesty as the cops drove her home again. My mother used to examine her own behaviour for early signs. Now that she doesn't any longer, I do.

Is it a sign that she gets younger every year? That since her sixtieth birthday she's been in reverse gear, hurrying backwards from the end? In the nine years since, she's shed twelve—lopping them off like old branches. Soon she'll pass me coming the other way. And this fifty-seven-year-old Elizabeth (who must have given birth to me at fourteen!) has lately turned into Bettina, having arrived there via Betty and Beth. Doesn't she remember the big party, the guests, the witnesses to her turning sixty? That I gave a speech? That we made a fuss of her? 'What's up with Bet?' her old friends wonder. What can I say? Her old friends look seventy. 'Bettina' looks, well, a cagey fifty-eight. She began getting younger in the 1970s with everyone else. In the 1980s, when everyone else started ageing again, she wilfully stayed behind. Is this a sign? The chin lift? The capped teeth? The bag removals? Lots of purple and gold? Sudden yellow hair? Leopard-skin materials? 'Ocelot,' she says firmly. 'Not leopard, ocelot.' What's the difference? It's not as if it's real skin, animal fur. It's only fabric, cotton blend stretch or something. 'It's what leopard skin *stands* for,' my North Shore sister grumbles. 'She's no chicken.'

Why does Penny always bring our father into it, even into the question of the ocelot-print stretch pants, even nine years later? Because our mother began getting younger as soon as he died? Well, she looked old for a month or two, for appearances' sake, then she started going backwards. 'I just know what Dad would say,'

Penny says. But she never says what he'd say ('I'd prefer not to see those pants on you, Betty.'). 'Maybe he'll let us know,' I could say to Penny. In one of his posthumous letters with the yellow stamps shaped like bananas and a Tonga postmark.

That afternoon the wind carried the sound of fire sirens from the expressway to the coast. They closed the expressway to traffic when the fire jumped the six lanes and surged eastward. From our hill the western sky was a thick bruised cloud fading to yellow. The eucalypts around the house suddenly began to peel. The hot winds had dried and cracked their bark and given the trees a strange mottled look, as if they'd pulled on camouflage uniforms. Now the bloodwoods and peppermints and angophoras were peeling and shedding fast in the wind, dropping sheets of bark all around us, changing their colour and shape before our eyes. Some trees revealed themselves as orange, others were pink, yellow, even purple underneath. All of them seemed moist and vulnerable, membrane instead of wood. They looked as if they'd shiver if you touched them.

All the bushfire-warning literature talks about 'radiant heat'. I'd read that radiant heat was the killer factor in bushfires and I wondered if the trees peeling was some sensitive early-warning system, an early stage of radiant heat. People can't survive more than a few kilowatts of radiant heat touching them. I read that to stand in front of a fire only sixty metres wide was like being exposed to the entire electrical output of the State of Victoria at peak load. Every single metre of this sixty metres beams out the heat of thirty-three thousand household radiators! And now it seemed to be getting hotter even as the sun got lower.

Wary of Peter's vivid imagination, I kept quiet about radiant heat. With the growing clouds of smoke, the trees changing, his eyes were already skittish. 'What holiday is it supposed to be today?' he asked me. Labor Day? I couldn't remember. On rare days things come together: heat, a moth plague, fires, crowds of people. When random factors combine you anticipate more things happening. The drowning tragedy on the news. Maybe the arrival of a letter, mailed from some dozy South Pacific port six months before, from a father five months dead. ('I think the cruise has done me the world of good.') Peter made poison darts fizz through the air, *phht, phht, phht.* 'Let's get out of here,' he said.

In Australia people always run to the coast. Maybe the myth of the bush is a myth. In the car we had less than a kilometre to travel. The heat and the closed windows had activated the citronella oil in the upholstery. It felt like breathing citronella into one lung and smoke into the other.

At the beach we found Lucy and Jenna in the crowd by the rock pool. Everyone seemed to have the same idea. People brushed away moths as they laughed nervously about the smoky wind. Dead moths littered the high-tide line, moths and bluebottles that had been washed ashore. The bluebottles' floats, electric-blue and still full of air, were sharp and erect as puppies' penises. There was a rotting smell from a pile of dead shags. The force of the westerly had flattened the surf; the waves were low and snapping and plumes of spindrift shot away from the beach. People had put up windbreaks, and lounged behind them, facing the sea and drinking beer. One group was drinking champagne and giggling.

'What's that red stuff in Peter's hair?' Jenna said.

'Pollen,' I said. 'From the moths.'

'It'll wash off in the sea,' Lucy said.

At sunset the wind dropped suddenly and by the time we needed to leave for the city the expressway was open again. It was early evening. Jenna and Peter had to return to school the next day, back to Ellen's. I was sorry the expressway had reopened. It would have been an excuse to keep them for a while. Maybe they'd have been stuck with me for days, with the road closed, the lines down. We would have been safe enough. We could always run into the sea.

Lucy kissed us goodbye. The narrow road out of Springstone was clogged with cars, everyone leaving at the same time. On the approach to the expressway the service stations all had fire trucks pulled into the back. Dirty fire-fighters slumped around the trucks, drinking from cans. One man was sitting on the ground trickling water from a hose over his head.

I pulled into the Shell station and filled the tank. I went inside and paid, and bought the kids some drinks.

When I came out I noticed how badly the smoky wind and squashed moths had smeared the windscreen. I began to clean it. Just then a small Nissan truck came in fast and braked hard next to our car. A man in his late twenties jumped out of the driver's seat a few metres from me and headed around to the passenger side where a woman was screaming.

The woman was holding a boy of three or four on her lap. She was screaming in his face, 'You're going to die! Do you hear me? Die! Die!'

For a moment the man stood indecisively at the woman's window. He had wavy blond hair and he ran his hands through it and muttered something to the woman, something mild and self-conscious in tone, but she continued to scream at the child that he was going to die. The child looked stunned, as if he had just woken. I was standing there transfixed, with the squeegee in one hand and a wiper blade in the other. The man saw me looking and gave a wink. He took a couple of steps in my direction. 'Sorry, mate,' he said.

I didn't say anything. Through the windscreen I saw Peter's and Jenna's faces staring at the truck cabin. They both had shocked, embarrassed smiles. The man turned to go into the service station office, but the woman began screaming louder and hurling obscenities and he turned back to the truck.

It was no place to be. I was hurrying to finish the windscreen, but—isn't it always the way?—those splattered moths were stuck fast. I seemed to be working in slow motion. Although I was making brisk, fussy dabs at the glass nothing much was improving. I had a sudden inkling the woman was doing something cruel to the boy that the man and I couldn't see. She was dark-haired, dark-eyed, the man's age or a bit older, and the wide spaces between her front teeth showed when she screamed. The boy had her looks and colouring. It's odd hearing a woman calling a man a cunt, over and over. Peter and Jenna weren't smiling any more. Jenna was pale and cupped her hands over her ears. She was near tears, whereas Peter's expression was confused and distant. He looked straight ahead, blinked, tried a silly scowl. His face was off-centre.

'Die, die die!' the woman screamed again, and began to smack the little boy's face. He started to scream, too. The reaction of the blond man to her onslaught was so mild and understated as he leaned in the cabin window that two thoughts struck me: *that's not his child* and *what did he do or say to her just before this?*

'Please don't do that, you're hurting him,' he said as she continued to hit the boy's face. 'You're making him cry.'

I wanted the man to do something. I wanted him to stop shuffling on the driveway and take over. Do whatever's necessary, I willed him. Get tough with her. By now other motorists were pulling in and staring across at the disruption as they filled their tanks. Two teenagers sauntered past, snickering. I could see the lone service station employee peering out from behind the cash register. There was just enough room in the truck cabin for the woman to swing at the boy while she was holding him on her lap, and she began to punch his head.

'Hey!' I yelled. As if he'd been waiting for a complaint from the general public, the man leaned through the window and tried to grab her arm. She hit him with a flurry of punches, and her screeches and abuse rose in pitch. The boy screamed higher. The man stepped back from the truck and ran his fingers through his hair. 'I'm going for those cigarettes,' he announced, and walked inside the service station.

The woman stopped yelling and began rocking the boy on her lap. She stroked his cheeks, murmuring to him, and pulled his head down on her chest. Gradually, he stopped crying. I put the bucket and squeegee back beside the pumps. As I got back in the car she looked up and shot me a defiant glance. She was still glaring at me, muttering something, as we drove off.

Neither the children nor I said anything. My stomach felt queasy. While I was trying to think of something to say my stomach was turning over. Suddenly I couldn't bear the sickly smell of citronella in the car, the way the air-conditioner re-circulated and revived it. I opened my window to get some air. 'Open your windows,' I said. The smell of fire immediately came into the car. Little specks of ash floated in. Trees were smouldering on both sides of the expressway. Even the grass on the median strip was charred and off to the left flames glowed in a gully.

'Look down there!' I said. I was enthusiastic. I welcomed the diversion of the fire. 'It burned right through here, jumped the highway, and there it is now!'

'Wow,' said Peter, in a low voice. In the heavy traffic we were driving in the inside slow lane, well under the limit, peering out at the fire. The firemen had driven it up against a treeless sandstone ridge. It was fading fast without the wind behind it. But then light burst beside us and there was a roar. For an instant I thought *fire!* but it was the Nissan truck accelerating past us on the inside, on the narrow asphalt shoulder, showering us with loose stones. I saw the three profiles as they passed: the man driving with a cigarette in his mouth, the woman with the boy on her knees. The truck swung back on to the road, swerved around three or four other cars, shot into the outside lane and out of sight.

After I took the children home I drove to my mother's flat. Sometimes I stay overnight with her and head back to the coast first thing in the morning. She has a spare bedroom I've been using for emergencies ever since she moved into the flat after Dad died. I was there for a month when Ellen and I broke up. It was after eleven when I got there this time. I was so drained I could hardly think.

She was in her red tracksuit and gold slippers eating toast. She had face cream on her forehead and cheeks. 'Oh, dear,' she said when she saw me. She extracted a tissue from her tracksuit pocket and wiped her face. 'How are you, dear?'

I quickly said I was fine. Often these days she asks me questions and doesn't listen to the answers. I've just begun to answer and she's on to another question. Sometimes I have to say, 'Do you want to hear this or not? It's all the same to me. I'm just answering you.'

'I'm fine, Mum,' I said. 'I just need a brandy and I'll be fine.' I poured us both a drink and carried them into the living room. It's a small room; I sat next to her on the sofa. 'I was thinking of you watching the news,' I said. 'I hoped you wouldn't worry. The fires didn't get near us. Anyway, Peter and I cleared away all the scrub. No need to worry about fires reaching us.'

'What fires?' she said. 'I've been out. I went to see that Meryl Streep film. I thought she looked a bit horsey.'

'You always say she looks horsey!' I said. 'She's gorgeous. What do you mean, anyway, horsey?'

'You know, angular. Aquiline features or whatever they are. Equine.'

'Meryl Streep's beautiful! Can't you see that? She's the best film actress in the world.'

'Well, she's not my cup of tea,' my mother said. 'She was playing a booze artist, some Skid Row type.' She sipped her drink daintily. She still drinks alcohol in company like a guilty teenager, as if she's new to it, but there are always a couple of empty Remy Martin bottles when I take her garbage out.

'She was *acting*, Mum.'

'What's this about fires?' she said.

'It doesn't matter.' I took a big sip of brandy and swallowed it. 'The whole central coast nearly went up in flames. But it's under control now.'

'Oh, dear,' she said.

'It was weird. All our trees were cracking and peeling. Hot ash was flying everywhere. We escaped to the beach.'

'You must be careful, living up there.' She got up frowning and padded into the kitchen to make me more toast. 'It's the smoke you die from, not the flames,' she said.

'It's the radiant heat,' I said.

I could hear her out in the kitchen muttering something about smoke. 'Don't worry,' I called out. She was making familiar kitchen noises. I listened for her tutting sound, the anxious clicks her tongue made on her teeth when she did things for us. Things would come back to her: events, feelings, memories as organised as snapshots. When she brought me the toast she would lightly touch me on my head or shoulder. A little pat or squeeze. I was a war baby. He was away fighting in the Solomons. For two years it was just me and her. I sank back into the sofa and called out again, 'You really don't need to worry!'

On the last day Bell will remember before the snow, on a blue-grey morning of high cloud, the old woman brings out a *tapsi* rolling with walnuts that she has cracked for the Christmas *baklava*. 'We'll be shut in soon enough,' she sighs, perching on a plaited stool under the grapevine with the *tapsi* on her lap. Bell, her son Grigori's wife, pulls up stools for herself and Chloe, the other daughter-in-law, the Greek one who has come to the village for Christmas; her husband's ship is at sea. The women huddle over the *tapsi* picking out and dropping curled walnuts here, shells there. Chloe's little girl, Sophoula, leans on her mother.

'Me too?' she murmurs.

'Go ahead.'

Sophoula, biting her lips, scowls over her slow fingers. With a trill of laughter Chloe pops a walnut into the child's mouth. 'My darling! Eat,' she says.

'Don't tell me she has nuts at her age?' the old woman says. 'You'll choke the child.'

'Mama, she's three.' Chloe's face and neck turn red.

'Just the same—'

'Oh, I don't like it!' Sophoula spits and dribbles specks of walnut. The shelling goes on; under their bent heads

Chloe and the old woman put on a fierce burst of speed. Suddenly all of them flare bright with sunlight and are printed over with black branches and coils of the grape-vine as a gap opens in the cloud. Bell leaps to her feet and lumbers inside.

'What's wrong with you?' Chloe frowns.

'Nothing. I'm getting my camera.'

'*Aman*. Always photographs,' her mother-in-law sighs.

'It's too cold to sit out here,' Chloe says.

'Oh, please,' Bell wails from the window. 'All stay where you are!'

But the gap in the cloud has closed over by the time she gets back, so that what she will always have is a photograph all cold blues, whites, greys and browns: brittle twigs and branches against walls and clouds, the washing hung along the wire, a white hen pricking holes in mud that mirrors her, and the three heads, black, brown and bone-white, suspended over the *tapsi* of walnuts.

Because she takes all the photographs, she won't find herself in any of them.

Six weeks ago, as soon as she knew for certain, Bell wrote to her parents that they would be grandparents some time in May. 'You're the first to know,' she added, though by the time the letter got to Australia the whole village probably knew. There's no hope now of an answer until after Christmas. But at noon the postman's motorcycle roars past, a fountain of mud in his wake, and stops at the village office, so she wanders down just in case and is handed an Australian aerogram. It has taken a month to get here and is one she will mark with a cross and keep as long as she lives.

Grandma and Grand Pop, eh, scrawls her father. *And about time too. Tell Greg to take that grin off his face.*

'Are they pleased, Bella?' The old woman is kneading the pastry for the *baklava*. Her arms are floured to the shoulders.

'Of course. Dad says, "And about time too."'

'No wonder! Considering that you're thirty-one—'

'Thirty—'

'—or will be when it's born.'

'Hasten slowly.' Bell reads her mother's exclamatory, incoherent half-page, laboriously copied, then goes back to her father's.

It's been three years. You could leave it too late, you know, Bell. With a bub and all that you could find yourselves tied down before you know it. It's hard to think we mightn't live to see our only grandchild. Mum's been having dizzy turns again lately. She's had one stroke, as you know. If money's the problem, I can help you there. Also book you into the Queen Vic or wherever you like.

'What else, Bella?'

'Oh, questions. Money, hospitals. All that.'

'Surely you're booked into the Kliniki?' Chloe stares.

'No, not yet.'

'Well, you'd better do it soon! You don't want to have it in the Public Hospital! *They* have women in labour two to a bed in the corridors, it's so crowded.'

'I think I want to have it at home,' Bell hears herself say.

'At home!' Kyria Sophia is delighted. 'Why not? I had all mine here. Grigori was born in the room you sleep in!'

'It wouldn't be safe.' Chloe raises her eyebrows. 'Not with a first child. Anything can go wrong.'

'Thank you, Chloe.'

'It's the truth. Look what happened to the *papas*'s daughter!'

'The *papas*'s daughter? You know why that happened? She got a craving for fried bananas in the middle of the night and her husband wouldn't go and try to find her any. And sure enough—'

'Mama, the cord got round her baby's neck and strangled it.'

'Mama, not because of the bananas!'

'You're both fools! Of course it was because of the bananas!' The old woman rams a grey branch into the firebox of the *somba*. '*Aman*! How come I'm the only one who ever stokes the fire?' She brushes a wisp of hair out of her eyes and flours her face. White like her hair and arms, it sags into its net of wrinkles.

Lunch, Bell's chore today, isn't ready when the old man comes in from the *kafeneion* and finds her alone in the kitchen. Kyria Sophia has taken Sophoula with her to the bakery to leave the *baklava*, Chloe is at a neighbour's place with the baby. He sits by the *somba*, small and grey and muddy, rolling and smoking one fat cigarette after another. The *makaronia* have to be boiled to a mush, Bell knows, before she can toss them in oil and butter and crumble *feta* cheese over them. Kyria Sophia comes back exhausted hand-in-hand with Sophoula and as if the day's work wasn't enough, now she has her to spoonfeed.

They eat the *makaronia* in silence. At every mouthful a twinge, a jab of pain drills through Bell's jaw. Not a toothache, please, she prays. Not now, not here.

Sophoula pushes the spoon and her grandmother's hand away. 'Yiayia! You have to tell a story!'

'What story?' sighs the old woman.

'A story about princesses.'

'Eat up and then I will.'

'Now!' Sophoula bats the spoon on to the floor. The old woman gets another one and shovels cold lumps into the child's mouth, chanting a story by heart. Whenever she falters, the child clamps her mouth shut. Bell, stacking the dishes, isn't really listening, but when the bowl is almost empty she exclaims aloud in English, 'Snow White! No, Snow White and Rose Red!'

The old woman giggles. 'Zno Quaeet,' she mocks. 'No Zno Quaeet End—'

'Yiayia *pes*!'

'*Aman*, Sophoula!'

'*Pes*.' She spits into the bowl.

After lunch these days Bell sleeps until it's dark. Now that she is into her fifth month she is sleepy most of the time. From under the white *flokati* she can hear Grigori's voice (so he is back from Thessaloniki with the shopping) and then Kyria Sophia's shrill one. When she wakes properly, ready for another long yellow evening by the *somba*, he is still there in the kitchen finishing a coffee. So is Chloe, red from her sleep, with the baby at her breast. 'Hullo,' Bell says, kissing Grigori's woollen crown. She fumbles with the *briki*.

'Coffee again?' Chloe mutters.

'Just one to wake me up.'

'It's so bad for the baby.'

'One won't hurt.'

'Oh well, you'd know.'

Bell turns her back to light the gas. 'Where are the old people?' She touches Grigori's shoulder.

'Milking.' His father's grey head grins in at the window; he leaves the milk saucepans on the sill. 'You got a letter, Mama said. Are Mum and Dad all right?'

'Yes, they send their love and congratulations.' Bell rubs her jaw. There's a hollow ache in her back teeth. She empties the sizzling *briki* into a little cup and takes a furry sip of her hot coffee. The *baklava* is on the table, baked and brought home already, its pastry glossy with the syrup it's soaking in. Grigori's shopping is all around it: oranges in net bags, chestnuts, a blue can of olive oil, lemons and mandarines and—she can hardly believe it— six yellow-green crescent bananas blue-stamped *Chiquita*. 'Oh, bananas! Oh, darling, thank you!' she cries out. 'We were just talking about bananas!'

'I'm so extravagant,' Chloe simpers, 'but Sophoula simply loves them. So I gave Grigori the money to buy her some.' Her eyes dare Bell to ask for one. A pregnant woman can ask even strangers in the street for food. Bell grins at Chloe, remembering her frying mussels one day in Thessaloniki when a pregnant neighbour squealed from a balcony, 'Ach, Kyria Chloe! Mussels! I can smell them!' and Chloe had to let her have a couple. 'She never smells anything cheap,' Chloe grumbled to Bell.

'Is that so, Kyria Chloe?' Bell contents herself with saying. 'Ah, so much lovely food. We'll never eat it.'

'*You* won't.' The old woman comes in and lifts the milk saucepans inside. '*Aman*, the cold!' She slams the window. '*You* won't eat. You're fading, look at you. White as snow.'

'I *will*. That was when I had morning sickness.'

'We don't want a kitten, you know, we want a big strong baby.'

'Believe you me,' Chloe mutters, 'the bigger it is, the harder it comes out.'

'Ah, *bravo*, Chloe, *bravo*!' The old woman clatters the saucepans, straining the warm milk. 'Don't you crave anything, Bella? You must crave something.'

'Why must she?'

'Well, to tell the truth, I'd love a banana,' says Bell. 'It seems like years! Can I buy one from you, Chloe?'

'I'm sorry. There aren't enough.'

'We share in this house, Chloe! If you want a banana, Bella, you have one! Don't even ask!'

'No, no, it's all right.'

Grigori stands up. 'See you later,' he says. He grabs a mandarine and saunters outside.

'Not to the *kafeneion* already?' his mother pleads.

'You just got here.' She stares bleakly after him. 'And what would you expect?' She rounds on her daughters-in-law. 'Doesn't a man have a right to peace and quiet?'

'Auntie?' Chloe has taught Sophoula this English word. 'Auntie Bella? Do they have Christmas where you come from?'

'Yes, of course.'

'Did you go to church?'

'No.'

'You stayed at home at Christmas!'

'We went to the beach,' Bell says.

'At Christmas! You're funny, Auntie!'

'Funny, am I?' Bell crosses her eyes. With a giggle, Sophoula sits in her lap.

'Where's your baby?'

'You're sitting on it. Oh, poor baby.'

'What's its name going to be?'

'I don't know. What's your baby's name going to be?'

'We won't know till he's been christened.'

'Oh, no, I forgot.'

'If it's a girl, they'll call it after Yiayia,' Chloe interposes. 'The same as we did with you.'

'Good idea. I'll call my baby Yiayia.'

'Auntie, you can't!'

'Why can't I? Not if it's a boy, you mean?' Bell winks. 'Then I'll call it Pappou,' and she is rewarded with a peal of laughter so loud that it wakes the old woman.

'Let's eat, Mama,' Chloe says.

'Is it late?' She blinks, squinting in the light. 'The men'll be home any minute.'

'No, they won't.' Bell lifts Sophoula down. 'Can we cut the *baklava* now? I crave *baklava*.'

'Oh. All right.' Smiling in spite of herself, Kyria Sophia cuts her a dripping slice. As Bell bites into it, the ache that has been lying in wait all day drills through her tooth and she shrieks aloud, letting syrup and specks of walnut dribble down her chin. She swills water round her mouth. The women cluck and fluster. Sophoula clings to her mother in tears of fright. The old woman mixes Bell an aspirin and she gulps it. She is helped to bed, where she curls up moaning in the darkness under the *flokati*. The light flashes on once, twice. She lies still until the door quietly closes.

Grigori is undressing with the light on. Bell rubs her watery eyes. The ache is duller now.

'Were you asleep? How's the tooth?'

'Bad.' She probes with her tongue.

He turns off the light and lies on his back with one cold arm against her. 'What's all this about having the baby here at home?'

'No! I'd be terrified.'

'Mama said you said you wanted to.'

'No. She misunderstood. I meant—I just feel—I want to go home and have it.' She holds her breath. 'Home to Australia.'

'How come?'

'Oh. Mum and Dad. You know. Mostly, I suppose. Yes.'

'We can't afford the fares.'

'One way, we can. Dad said they'd help.'

'Ah. One way? I see.'

The moon must have risen. In the hollow glow through the shutters the *flokati* looks like a fall of snow on rough ground. 'I wonder if it'll snow for Christmas?' she says. 'It didn't the other times.'

He snorts. 'You spring a thing like this on me. What I might feel—you couldn't care less, could you! I wanted to stay in Australia three years ago, but no, you uprooted us, you—*felt*—you had to go and live in Greece. And now what? Come along, doggy, I want to go home. To Australia!'

She takes a shaky breath. 'I feel guilty, I suppose. They're old, they're not well. "You could leave it too late," Dad said.'

'You know what a pessimist he is. You used to joke about it.'

'Can we bank on it, though?' She ploughs on. 'It's not as if it would be for ever.'

'It might.'

'We can always come back.'

'Always, can we? Backwards and forwards.' He turns his back to her. 'I'll need to think it over. I'm tired.'

'There's not much time. We've got till the end of February. That's when my smallpox vaccination expires. I can't have another one while I'm pregnant and I can't enter Australia without it.'

Lying along his back, she feels him tightening against her. The nape of his neck is damp and has his hot smell.

Once he pelted past her down a sand dune and was out of sight in the white waves when the hot smell from him buffeted her face. That was at Christmas.

We went to the beach at Christmas when I was little, she remembers. On Phillip Island we had dinner at the guesthouse and then Dad and I followed a track called Lovers' Walk—there was a board nailed up, Lovers' Walk—to look for koalas as they awoke in the trees. First we walked down the wooden pier where men and their sons were fishing. Red water winding and hollowing. Crickets fell silent when I walked in the tea-tree. After sunset the waves were grey and clear rolling and unrolling shadows on the sand. The trees, black now, still had their hot smell.

Some time in the early hours the toothache jerks her out of sleep. Grigori breathes on deeply. Tossing, feverish, close to tears, she stumbles to the kitchen for an aspirin and Chloe, passing through to the lavatory annexe, sees and scolds her. 'You shouldn't take any medicines now,' she says.

'One little aspirin!' Bell's smile is a snarl.

'Any medicine at all.'

'I have toothache!'

'Still, for the baby's sake.'

Bell turns and gulps it down. Back in bed the pain is relentless, it drills into her brain. After an hour, two, of whimpering in her sweat she creeps back to the kitchen and in a flash of bilious light swallows down three more aspirins. No one catches her. In the passage she trips over Sophoula's potty, which they leave outside their door until morning. Splashing away over cold urine, she lets it lie where it fell. Grigori is snoring. 'Turn over,' she hisses in Greek, and he turns.

A rooster calls, the same one as every morning, then hens, then a crow, so loud that it must be in the yard. How long since she last heard a gull? It must be only a couple of weeks. When was the last time she was in Thessaloniki? Gulls are as common as pigeons in the city. It seems like years.

What does tea-tree smell like in summer?

Their bedroom is white and takes up one corner of the house and of the street, 21st of April Street these days, in honour of the Colonels' coup. The two-roomed school that Grigori went to is opposite. They are on one of the busiest crossroads in the village. All through Christmas Day, Boxing Day and the next day Bell sleeps and wakes to the uproar of tractors, donkeys, carol-singers, carts, trucks with loudspeakers bellowing in her windows. Snow falls. She sits sipping milk at the family table in her pyjamas, staggers to the lavatory annexe and back to her cooling hollow under the *flokati*. She coughs. Her head pulsates. She loses count of how many aspirins. The toothache goes through her in waves. Sweat soaks her pyjamas and sheets and Kyria Sophia dries them again by the *somba*. Grigori takes refuge for two nights at his cousin Angelo's place behind the bakery. Children throwing snowballs yell and swear. The baby wails. From time to time Sophoula opens Bell's door, but slams it in panic when Bell stirs to see who it is. Chloe keeps away in case she and the children catch something. Kyria Sophia comes and sits at the end of the bed crocheting with a pan of hot coals at her feet.

Penicillin, somebody suggests, a shot of penicillin, there's a woman down the street who's qualified. Bell says yes, oh yes, please. Chloe is appalled. But no one ever comes to give the injection. Time has broken down. Sand slides shifting under the scorched soles of her feet. The scream of a gull makes her slip and clutch at the stringy trunk of a tea-tree, but it must be the grapevine. No, she is flat on her back, she is clutching the *flokati* when her eyes open. It looks like snow on rough ground. That scream comes again and it's the baby screaming, Chloe's baby though, not her own, that she can hear, then all the sounds of hushing and commotion as he sobs, then whimpering and quiet.

One morning she wakes and is well, clear-headed, free of toothache and of fever. She opens the windows but the shutters won't move. She is weak, look, trembling. But it's not that: snow is heaped on the sill. She patters to the door and stares down the white street. The sun is rising behind white roofs and trees, turning the snow sand-yellow, shading in the printed feet of birds and a stray dog. The stringy grapevine has grown spindles of ice.

Stooped panting over buckets and *tapsia* of water, she spends the day washing her stiff, sour clothes and her hair, stuck in yellow strings to her head by now; and sitting with hair and clothes spread out to dry by the *somba*. She would love a bath, but not in the dank ice-chamber that the lavatory annexe has become. For one thing, other people are always wanting to get in. And in any case, it's not as if they'll notice whether she does or not, not even Grigori: for fear of a miscarriage, now that she has finally conceived they don't make love. She's well again, she won't risk catching cold. She wraps a scarf over her mouth whenever she goes outside. Now and then a twinge through her tooth alarms her, but the riveting ache is gone.

Every day there is washing and cooking of which she does her share. When the sun is out she walks around the village photographing crystals and shadows, tufty snow and smooth. The narrowed river is crinkled, slow, with white domes on its rocks. Ovens in the deserted yards have a cap of snow over two sooty air vents and stare back at the camera like ancient helmets. White hens are invisible except for their jerking legs and combs. The storks' nest is piled high; it could be a linen basket up on top of the church tower. In the schoolyard a snowman has appeared—no, a snow woman two metres tall in a widow's scarf and a cloak of sacking under which her great round breasts and belly glisten naked.

She takes photographs of the snow woman and of children hiding to throw snowballs and of the *papas* as he flaps by, his hair and beard like a stuffing of straw that has burst out of his black robes. The family and the neighbours line up for portraits under the grey grapevine. The old man leads the cows out of the barn and poses for her standing between them on the soiled snow while they shift and blink in the light, mother and daughter.

'You can show them to your parents,' he says. So all the family knows that she is going home. No one talks about it.

She takes time exposures in the blue of evening as the windows in the houses light up and throw their long shapes on the snow outside. As often as not, Kyria Sophia, Chloe, Grigori, even the old man, can be found in one or other of the rooms, the little golden theatres, that Bell used to love being in. Now she knows the sets, the characters, the parts too well. She would rather stay home alone; she is quite happy babysitting. Having read her own few books too often, she reads Sophoula's story books about princesses. If Sophoula wakes, Bell reads aloud with the warm child in her lap. When the old man comes in they roast chestnuts on top of the *somba* until the others come. They listen in to the clandestine broadcasts on Deutsche Welle, which he calls Dolce Vita: these are banned by the Junta and the penalty for listening could be imprisonment, could be torture. He has enemies who would report him if they knew. 'The walls have ears,' he growls, the radio pressed to his grey head; he is hard of hearing himself. His wrinkles are so deep that they pull his hooded eyes into a slant and his lips into a perpetual smile around his cigarette.

On New Year's Eve Kyria Sophia announces that she is

too tired even to dream of making the family *vassilopita*. 'Thank goodness my nephew's the baker,' she says. 'Angelo says he'll bring us one.'

Chloe fluffs up her hair. 'My mother always makes ours.'

'It's a lot of bother for nothing, if you ask me!' snaps the old woman. 'Who appreciates it? Look at all my *baklava* that none of you will eat!'

'Mama, it's a wonderful *baklava*!' Bell hugs her.

'You say that. Eat some then.'

'And what about my tooth?'

'*Aman*, that woman!' Bell hears her whisper to Grigori. 'I could wring her neck,' meaning Chloe, or so Bell hopes.

Then to her further exasperation the old woman looks everywhere and can't find the *flouri*, the lucky coin that she hides in each year's *vassilopita*. Bell gives her the lucky sixpence that she brought from home, the one her mother used to put in the plum pudding.

After dinner, while Grigori and his father are still at the *kafeneion*, Angelo and his mother, Aunt Magdalini, arrive with the *vassilopita*. An elderly doll in long skirts, she falls asleep by the *somba*, steam rising from her woollen socks. Bell wakes her to eat a floury *kourabie*, and again to drink coffee. Angelo has ouzo. It blurs his sharp brown features, so like Grigori's, and makes him jocular.

'What can you see out there, Bella?' She turns from the window. 'Your man coming home?'

'The moon rising.'

'*Fengaraki mou lambro*,' recites Sophoula proudly.

'Good! What comes next?'

'*Fexe mou na perpato!*'

'I'll give you twenty drachmas,' Angelo drawls, 'if you can tell me what the moon's made of.'

'Rock?'

'You lost. It's a snowball, silly. It was thrown so high it can't ever come back to earth.'

Sophoula's jaw drops. 'Who threw it?'

'Guess.' He scratches the black wool on his head.

'A giant?'

'*I* think a bear. There's one up the mountain. There were tracks up there the other day. The hunters are out after her.'

'The poor bear!'

He peers out the window. 'That's not her in the schoolyard, is it? A huge white bear?'

'Silly.' She giggles. 'That's only the snow woman.'

'The snow woman, is it?' hisses Angelo. 'So that's who threw the moon up there!' and Sophoula screams in terror.

Kyria Sophia glares up over her glasses. 'God put the moon there.'

'Supposing she comes alive at night time? Supposing she comes and stares in all the windows while we're asleep?'

'No, no!' Sophoula clamps herself to Bell. 'Auntie, make him stop it!'

'Angelo, please?'

'Of course she doesn't!' cries Kyria Sophia. 'Aren't

you ashamed to put an idea like that in the child's head?'

The door bursts open on Chloe red-faced and tur-
bulent. 'You'll wake the baby! Can't I leave you alone
here for one minute?' She drags the child by the arm
into their room. There they both stay until Angelo and
Aunt Magdalini have gone and Grigori and his father are
home for the midnight ceremony of cutting the *vassilopita*. Then Chloe sidles sullenly in with her black hair
stuck to cheeks still red with sleep or crying. 'Sophoula
will have to miss it. She's asleep,' she mutters.

The old man, as head of the household, carefully
divides the loaf. He sets aside a piece for the church and
then for every member of the family, present and absent.
The lucky sixpence turns up in Chloe's baby's piece, as
it was bound to, and they all pretend surprise. Bell stuffs
the sweet bread into the safe side of her mouth. Next
New Year, she knows, wherever they all are by then, the
flouri or the sixpence will turn up in her child's piece.

The New Year card games at the *kafeneion* will go on
all night. Grigori walking back is a shadow among other
shadows that the moon makes in the snow.

On New Year's Day no bus comes to the village. The
road in has been declared dangerous because the two
narrow wooden bridges that it crosses are thick with
frozen snow. No buses until further notice, bellows the
village loudspeaker. People grumble. This happens every
winter and every winter the government promises a new
road. The mountain villages are worse off, of course;

they'll be snowed in for weeks, not just a few days. Still, since no one has a car, everyone is trapped here while it lasts, except Angelo with his bread van.

Angelo goes on delivering his bread around the villages using chains, risking unmade tracks on hills and across fields to bypass the bridges. Grigori has been joining him lately for the sake of the ride and the company; now he goes on every trip in case Angelo strikes trouble and needs a hand. But Angelo won't take anyone else. 'It's not legal,' he tells everyone, 'and it's not safe.' He broke his rule twice last year, he says, and look what happened. The old man that he took to the district hospital in the back of the van survived; but the woman in labour? She lost her baby when the van hit a buried rock miles from anywhere and broke an axle. 'Never again, not for a million drachmas,' he says. 'Don't ask me.'

So that evening Bell and Chloe, sitting by the small *somba* in Chloe's room with the work done and the children asleep, are thunderstruck when Kyria Sophia—who has made herself scarce all day—puts her head round the door to announce that by the way she and Grigori are off first thing in the morning to Thessaloniki to see her other grandchildren. Angelo is giving them a lift.

'She can't do that!' Chloe cries out, and follows her into the kitchen. 'You can't do that!' Bell hears.

'What? What can't I do?'

'What about *me*?'

'What about you?'

'I brought the children all this way to visit you and it

wasn't easy on the bus and now you take it into your head to go off to Thessaloniki just like that and—'

'Look, when I need you to tell *me* what—'

'—And leave us stranded here!'

'What would you do there, anyway?' Kyria Sophia shouts. 'Your husband's away at sea for two more weeks!'

'I happen to live there. *Your* husband's here, remember? How will he feel if you go? This is your house, it's not mine. I could have gone to my own village for Christmas and New Year when they begged me. *My* mother—'

'You're a married woman. It's your duty to come to us.'

'Duty? Oh, duty? What about your duty, then? Aren't *you* a married woman?'

'You dare to talk to me like—'

'Mama, you have *no right*—'

'Get out of my kitchen, Chloe. You say one more word and I swear I'll hit you. I'll hit you!'

Chloe strides into the room where Bell and now Sophoula too are listening in horror; she slams the door behind her. Thuds and crashes of glass hit the wall between them.

'*Oriste Mas! Oriste mas!*' come her shrieks. 'Now *she'll* tell *me* if I can go or not, will she? Twenty-five years old! *She'll* tell *me* what I can and can't do?'

'Mama, what's Yiayia saying?' Sophoula whimpers.

'Never you mind. She's wicked. She doesn't love you or any of us.' Chloe bites her lips. 'Let the old bitch howl,' she mutters. 'She would have slapped my face in there! She knows she's in the wrong.'

The outside door slams and they jump. Footsteps splash past the shuttered window. The three of them creep to their beds. Bell is still wide awake when at last Grigori comes in and starts undressing in the dark.

'Grigori?'

'You're awake, are you? What happened here? Mama's in a frenzy. She's beside herself.'

'She had a fight with Chloe.'

'And you?'

'Me? No! I stayed out of it.'

'You didn't try to stop her.'

'As soon try stopping a train! If Chloe wants a fight, I suppose that's her business, isn't it?'

'If she fights with her own mother it's her business. If she fights with mine it's my business and yours and all the family's.'

'So I should have stopped her.'

'You were there.' He has slid into bed without touching her. 'And your place in the family gives you the right.'

'Because I'm older than Chloe?'

'No. Because I'm the older brother and you're my wife.'

'Oh. I think Chloe was right to be upset. Is it fair of Mama to go off and leave us like this?'

'One more day of Chloe, she says, and she'll go mad.'

'Chloe's hard to take. It's the children. They tire her out, you see.'

'Mama does everything.'

'No, she doesn't. Chloe pulls her weight. I'm here all day and I know.'

'*You* know! You live in a world of your own! Chloe pulls her weight, does she? And what about you?'

'Tell me, what do the men do here while the women are pulling their weight? Play cards in the *kafeneion*? Stroll around Thessaloniki? If it comes to that, I'm the one who really needs to go. If I don't get to a dentist, I might lose this tooth.'

'Nice timing.'

'For every child a tooth, they say. It's to do with lack of calcium.'

She feels him shrug. 'Drink more milk.'

'I'm awash with milk already. Milk won't fill a rotten tooth, though, will it?'

'Well, bad luck,' he says wearily. 'It's stopped aching, hasn't it? There'll be a bus soon anyway, go on that. The fact is Angelo only has room for two and he needs me.'

'Well, let *me* come, then! Explain to Mama!'

'*You* explain to Mama.' He waits for her to think that over. 'Why all this fuss, I wonder?'

'You're going and leaving me here.'

'It's not as if it's for ever, is it?'

'Oh, that's it. I see. You want revenge.'

'You're happy to go off to Australia and leave me here.'

'Happy? I'm hoping you'll come.'

'It's more than hoping, I think. It's closer to force.'

They are lying rigidly side by side on their backs and

neither moves. 'You'd be taking my child with you.'

She snorts. 'Not much choice at this stage!'

'No. There's not. So I want you to wait.'

'I can't, I told you. My smallpox vaccination.'

'I know that! I mean wait till after it's born.'

She opens her eyes wide in the darkness, so suddenly alarmed that she thinks he will hear the blood thumping through her. 'No. I'd be trapped here then,' she dares to say.

'Trapped!'

'Besides, the whole point is to be home with Mum and Dad before the birth. And then come back. If you want.'

'*Why*? Why does it matter *where* you are for the birth?'

'It just does,' she mutters. 'I'll feel safer there.'

'You're a stubborn, selfish, cold-blooded woman, Bell. You always have been and you always will be.'

'Always?'

'You want your own way in everything. Well, you're not getting it.'

Calming herself, she strokes the long arch of her belly, fingering the navel which has turned inside out and then the new feathery line of dark hair down to her groin. Once or twice a flutter inside her has made her think the baby has quickened, but it might have been only wind. Soon there'll be no mistaking it, her whole belly will hop, quake and ripple. She runs a finger along the lips that the head will burst through. 'What the fuck are you doing?' he mutters.

'Nothing.'

'You're breathing hard.'

'No, I'm not.' She forces herself to count as she breathes slowly in one two three, out one two three.

'I can hear you.'

'No.' She moves to the cold edge and listens motionless, breathing very slowly. He is silent. He has had his say.

She wakes at cockcrow when he gets dressed. She hears the van come, then go. She has stayed in bed through all the flurry of their departure, and so has Chloe. They open the kitchen door to find the *somba* burning with a bright flame, the milk boiled, the baby's napkins dried and folded, the day's eggs brought in from the barn and the table laid with bread and cheese and honey under a cloth.

'Oh, lovely!' cries Bell.

'You see?' Chloe snorts. 'She's sorry.'

'She must have been up all night!' Bell could hug the old woman.

'She was. I heard her.'

'She didn't have to do all this for us!'

Chloe stares and shrugs. 'Why shouldn't she?'

Chloe spends the morning washing and rinsing clothes, Bell taking Sophoula for a walk with the camera. The piles of soft snow were frozen overnight; so were the puddles and the clothes hung out on wires and bare brambles. There are no clouds this morning to block the sun or the faded half-moon, and everywhere they go water trickles and drips and glitters. As they come near the schoolyard Sophoula cringes, pulling at Bell.

'Carry me, Auntie Bella.'

'Why, for heaven's sake?'

'The snow woman's there.'

'It's only snow! It's only a big doll made of snow.'

'It's the wicked witch.' She huddles against Bell. 'She comes alive at night and stares in the window.'

'She does not! Look, she's melted. The poor old thing, she's vanished away.' A heap of pitted snow sits under the pines.

'The moon's melting too, Auntie Bella!'

Sophoula keeps Bell company while she boils the potatoes and fries eggs for the four of them for lunch; Chloe is with the baby in the bedroom. But the child is grizzly and cross now and says she isn't hungry: she doesn't want potato or egg or bread or anything. 'Have a bit of banana?' Bell pleads. One banana is left. Chloe has made them last, feeding them to Sophoula inch by inch and folding the black soft skin over the stump. But no, Sophoula won't. 'I know!' On impulse Bell peels the last banana, flours it and fries it in the pan with the eggs for Sophoula. 'My darling, eat,' she says. The old man trudges in. Lunch is late again. 'Try it? For Auntie? Have some milk with it?'

'Tell a story.'

'Once upon a time,' she slips a spoonful of banana in, 'in a little cottage in the woods—'

Sophoula gags and splutters. The old man stares. 'Eat,' he growls. 'It's good for you.'

'No! Auntie, I don't like it!'

'All right, you don't have to eat it.' Blushing with shame, Bell gobbles the banana herself before Chloe comes.

'There was a banana,' Chloe says when they are peeling fruit into their empty plates later, and Bell tries to explain. Sophoula announces smugly that Auntie ate it all up. So as not to let it go to waste, Bell says, red-faced. 'You know she has them raw,' Chloe accuses. 'No more bananas!' Chloe kisses the child's hair. 'Wicked Auntie! Where will I get my darling some more?'

The old man, groping in his pockets, finds a bag of peanuts in their shells and presses it into Sophoula's hand.

'Is it *safe* to give her nuts?' Bell wonders aloud. 'They'll choke the child.'

In silence she rinses the dishes while Chloe shells peanuts by the *somba*. Abruptly Sophoula hoots and stiffens. Her back arches. Chloe bangs her, shakes her, shoves her head forward, and at last a great gush of sour curds and speckles pours out of her mouth all over her mother.

'Thank God!' Chloe hauls her jumper over her head. '*Aman*, my poor darling!' she moans, dabbing Sophoula's white face. 'They're bad, don't ever eat them! Wicked Pappou!' She pushes the whole bag into the firebox and slams the iron door. The old man plods to his room. 'There,' she says, 'let them burn. He won't tell Her,' she mutters at Bell, who has brought a glass of water. 'Thanks. Don't you tell either, or we'll never hear the end of it.'

It is dark these days before the old man wakes to do the afternoon milking. The torch he takes into the barn lights up the ridge of snow at the door. His approach to the house is a clank and slop of saucepans past the window and a red point and trail of smoke, his cigarette. This time he dumps the saucepans caked with dung and hay inside on the kitchen floor and covers them. 'Who'll strain the milk?' he says loudly to no one. 'Will you boil it or use it for cheese?'

Sullen with sleep in their doorways, the women exchange looks. He is waiting. Chloe tweaks a curl off her baby's damp cheek and kisses it.

'Two daughters-in-law!' barks the old man and they all jump. The baby whines.

'Sssh.' Chloe frowns.

'Two daughters-in-law and I do it, do I? I strain the milk! I make the cheese! It's not enough to look after the cows and milk them. I can do the lot!'

The kitchen door slams. Chloe pulls Bell into her room, where they stand listening behind the door as he unlatches the window and clatters the saucepans. Then the front door clangs shut and his boots crunch away.

'He's thrown it out!' Bell mutters.

'*Two daughters-in-law and I do it, do I?*'

'Sssh. He'll hear!'

'Him, hear?'

'Sssh.'

They creep to the kitchen and turn the light on. In the square of yellow it throws outside, Bell can just make out the saucepans on end against the barn wall. The sun never comes there and the snow is still thick, with a pale puddle in it, a cat crouched at the edge, and all around a wide shawl of creamier snow. 'Oh! What a waste,' Bell sighs.

'Who cares?' Chloe looks in a jug. 'Look, there's all this left from this morning.'

'He's right, though.'

'It's Mama's job!'

'But since she's not here.'

'I have two small children I have to do everything for.'

'Yes, I should have done it.'

'You're pregnant!'

'Only five months.' She sits down. 'I need a coffee.'

'No, come on, let's get out of this place before we go mad! We'll take the children to Aunt Magdalini's. Come on.'

At Aunt Magdalini's, the village secretary's wife tells them that the bridges have been declared safe for the time being and that a bus to Thessaloniki will run in the morning. Rowdy in her elation and relief and scorn of Kyria Sophia, who might just as well have waited, Chloe hauls Bell and Aunt Magdalini's three daughters-in-law along the crusted, muddy street to celebrate her release at the *kafeneion*.

Inside its misted windows men are smoking at small tables, watching the soccer on the grey television screen (the only one in the village) or looking on while Grigori's father plays the champion at *tavli*. The men all sit with their elbows on the chair-back and their hands flat on their chests, glancing sidelong from time to time at the table of women drinking orangeade. When Grigori's father wins the game he sends the *kafedji* over with another round, and the women raise the bottles smiling in a salute to him.

Chloe tells joke after joke uproariously and the other three are soon helpless with laughter. 'What are the men staring at?' she asks, gazing round. 'Oh, Bella, it's you!' She swoops and whispers, 'Bella, look how you're sitting.' Startled, Bell looks. 'Bella, your hands!' She has them open over each breast exactly as the men's are, but women never sit like that. She moves them to the slopes of her belly and Chloe giggles and nudges but Bell is too torpid in the smoky heat to be bothered. When the others are ready to go they wake her. The sky is all white stars, frost crackles as they tread. They link arms with Bell in the middle to keep her from a fall. Scarves of mist trail behind them. They drop her at home on the way to Aunt Magdalini's.

Alone in the cold bed, Bell is awake for the first unmistakable tremor of the quickening.

Before daybreak Bell is up to strain the milk—twice carefully through the gauze—and boil it in time for breakfast. Chloe's noisy desperation surges all around her. At last the kisses crushing or missing cheeks and she is away with the children, the old man carrying their bags to the bus, and Bell has the house to herself.

She scrubs the saucepans and puts clean water on to boil. The table is littered with crusts, plates and cups under the yellow bulb that only now she remembers to switch off; she tidies up. She has packing to do as well, letters and lists to write, but that had better wait until Grigori decides whether or not to go with her.

When her saucepans boil she carries them and another of cold water into the lavatory annexe that the old man spent all autumn building and is proud of. In case he tries to come in and wash, she pushes the heavy can of olive oil against the door. There is no light bulb in here yet, only an air vent and a candle stuck on a plate. She leans over to put a match to it and its flame lights her breasts: they are as she has never seen them, white and full, clasped with dark veins like tree roots. Shuddering in the cold, she stand in the *tapsi*, wets and soaps herself urgently, rinses the soap off. Flames go down her in runnels. She is rough all over with goosepimples except for her belly, domed in her hands, warm and smooth like some great egg.

All the water is swilling round her legs in the *tapsi* before she has got all the soap off but she rubs herself dry anyway, pulls on her clean clothes and with a grunt hoists up the *tapsi* and pours all the water into the lavatory bowl. It brims, then sinks gurgling down in froth and a gust of sweet cold rottenness from the sewer belches up in her face.

Still shuddering, she hugs herself close to the *somba*, propping the iron door open while she crams pine cones in. She sits with her clothes open. Perhaps the baby can see and hear the fire, she thinks: did he see my hands in there, by the light of the candle? They must have made shadows on his red wall.

Here we are in a cold white house with icicles under the eaves and winter has hardly begun, but inside its walls are warm to the touch, full of firelight.

She has a couple of hours before she needs to start cooking lunch, and one full roll of fast film left: she will use them to take her last photographs. Bare interiors of sun and shade and firelight, in which as always she appears absent.

My friends, I'm at a loss for words.

I searched my vocabulary but the only words I could find were FLUMMOX, SCROTUM and PAPOOSE. Words for which I have no possible use.

If only I could find a word like LEPIDOPTERA, which could be useful for all manner of things, especially if I were an order of insect with four wings covered in gossamer scales ... Unfortunately I am not of this species so the word has failed me.

But thankfully I always keep my word. So I have retained the term SYLLOGISM, a form of logical reasoning consisting of two premises and a conclusion, which only brings me to the conclusion that I must choose my words more carefully and thus avoid situations as when I once chose the word PHENOBARBITONE, and fell asleep upon the instant.

In my youth my father gave me his word, which went straight over my head. And when I asked Papa the meaning of the word, he laughed maniacally and sang, 'We'll build a word of our own that no one else can spell ... ' So I am now the proud inheritor of the term XLOXOCLOZIZ-PVERN-PVERN ... Eventually I did discover its meaning, which was on the tip of my tongue, but unfortunately I was mugged by a man who took the words right out of my mouth.

Mind you, I still have the last word ….

ZYGOTE

Kim's father was supposed to come down from Queensland or wherever he lived to straighten her life out for her, give her some good advice, pay her uni fees and so on, or even take her back up there to live with him. He promised he'd be there in June, for her birthday, but for some reason he couldn't make it by the date. Then it was going to be August, then September. She was hanging out for this. She stopped going anywhere, in case he turned up while she was out and the others in the house let him get away without giving him her message, to make himself at home and wait ten minutes. First she used to sew, till the machine broke down, and anyway the whine of the motor was starting to make her nervous. Then she drew, or wrote for hours in her diary. Then she read, lying on her bed in a worn-out old nightie, nibbling at the ends of her hair, but she said the books she was supposed to be studying were so boring that she kept dozing off.

Then things got to the point with her where all she could do was sleep. Awake, whatever she heard threw her into a state of nerves: the wind when it bumped, a bird in a tree outside the window, the water rustling down the gutters when the council workers opened the hydrants. Her fearfulness filled Raymond with impatient scorn, and relief that he was not after all the most hopeless person he knew. The morning a truck poured a ton of blue metal chips down in the lane outside, he came back from the kitchen and found her on her knees in the corner with her head in the dirty clothes bag. He thought of laughing, till he saw that her eyes were bulging. There was a primary school behind where she lived. She couldn't stand the noise the kids made in the yard at playtime, their screaming. It made her grind her teeth and blow her nose till it went red. 'Somebody must be hurting them,' she whispered. 'They're hurting each other.'

'You're stupid,' said Raymond irritably. 'That's a *good* sound. Aren't kids supposed to be a good thing? You shouldn't freak out over something that's *good*. What's the matter with you?'

By October, though she lied about it, she was swallowing day by day in threes and fours the pills she got from her mother and sleeping the time away buried so flat in the quilt and pillows that when he came in he had to feel around to make sure she was still there.

'Get in,' she mumbled, too doped to open her eyes. 'Less go to sleep.'

The nightdress was twisted up round her waist and her skin was loose, like old sacking. She had about as much life in her as a half-deflated dummy, but without complaint she opened her legs, and he kept his face turned away, to avoid her breath. She grunted, that was all, and when he rolled away she made a limp effort to attach herself to his back; but she was a dead weight that could not hang on. Her arms' grip weakened and her torso fell away. The cool air of the room shrank his bare spine. She snuffled, and a light rhythmic click began in the open membranes of her throat. He would have got up straight away except that the tick of her breathing matched itself briefly to his heartbeat, and at the moment of focusing on the leaves outside the glass his mind lost its grip on the edges of the furniture and slithered away into a comforting nest, a sty of warm webs and straw. Then the parrot screeched, in somebody's backyard, and he woke.

He raised himself on one elbow and looked back over his shoulder at her. She was only a small girl, with small bones, and her head too he had always thought of as small. Wandering round the city, the day after she had first dragged him home from a party where he was lurking sourly in a doorway, always too old or too awkward, always wearing the wrong clothes, he had found himself fitting words together in the part of his mind that no one knew about: he practised remarking casually, 'She's buttery,' or 'She's well-toothed'; but he never fell into conversation with anyone who looked interested in that way of talking—Alby certainly wasn't— and now her face, like any drugged sleeper's, was as thick, stupid and meaningless as a hunk of rock. He saw that there was nothing special about her; that he was superior to her after all. She was damaged goods. The pills were not to blame. The pills were doing him a favour by reminding him of something he had always

known was in her, in any girl that age who would do
what she did with him, and you could tell by the moron
face they made when they were doing it, all vague and
grinning. He imagined, propped there in his twisted
pose while his insides congealed again into blankness,
how he would describe her in the café if any of them
stopped talking long enough. 'She was more out of it
than I've ever seen her. Mate, she was'—he would stick
out his flat hands, palms down, and jerk them sharply
apart—'*out* of it. This gig's over. People who can't get
their shit together should just go and *die*.'

It was late in the day. If he got up now he could make
it to the Hare Krishnas for a feed. The girl downstairs
was getting ready for work. As she called to her cat, her
clogs on the cobbles of the lane made a sound like a
tennis ball bouncing. While he pulled on his clothes,
blocking out the irritating click of Kim's open mouth,
he ran his eyes over the floor, checking for dropped
coins, a screwed-up five dollar note, the price of a coffee,
anything he could use.

On the boards between the bed and the door stood a
pair of heavy black rubber-soled shoes. Their laces were
still in bows. She must have yanked them off in her rush
back to the big dipper of sleep, and yet they were placed
tidily side by side, and although they were months old
they still looked new, since the only wear they got was
when she walked over to her mother's every couple of
days for pills and maybe a leftover from the fridge. All
the girls wore these shoes. He felt nothing about the
style. He only noticed the shoes because the neat bows

jigged a memory which was gone before his mind could lumber round to it: something about laces, something about tying a shoe. He hesitated, then he stepped over the shoes and went out of the room. The door clicked shut behind him. The air of the stairs was thick with the smell of cooking broccoli.

Four days passed before he came back.

He too spent them horizontal, in his brother's boarding house room with his pants unzipped, holding across his chest Alby's big acoustic guitar and picking at it tunelessly, or rereading the collection of seventies comics from under the bed: epic acid landscapes, hulking heroes in fur leggings, pinheads, VW buses full of frizzy hair, a stoned cat, girls with huge legs in boots and mini skirts, and a special way of walking called 'truckin''. That world drawn in square boxes and balloons of words, he knew. The real one he was lost in, but so lost that he didn't know he was lost. His father was dead, his mother was stupid, his sister had run away; and as soon as Alby got back he would be on the street again. He lived untouched inside a grey casing through which he watched, dully, how other people behaved, and sometimes tried to mimic them. He saw that they remarked on the weather, and he tried to remember to look at the sky, to see if there were clouds in it. He saw what people ate, and he bought some. He saw that they talked to make each other laugh, and he dropped his mouth open to make the sound 'Ha. Ha.' He saw that when a band played, they heard something; he saw that they danced, and he tried to lift his feet. His whole life was faking. He thought that was what people did.

At six o'clock on Tuesday he cleaned himself up and went out. He passed Kim's mother leaving the Lebanese take-away with a felafel roll in each hand and a heavy-looking bloke coming down the step behind her. 'G'day, Ursula,' he said. She nodded, but the bloke gave him a dirty look and Raymond dropped his eyes. He got himself some chips and ate them as he walked to Kim's, stopping for a look in the window of a secondhand shop that sold things Alby might need: a stringless guitar or a plastic record rack or books with titles like *Chiropody Today* or *Welcome to Bulbland*. The tattoo shop was open. The artist skulked right down at the back, crouching in a burst chair with wooden arms. No thanks. You could get Aids off those needles, though maybe a little anchor, a bluebird . . .

The small concrete yard of Kim's house was scattered with faded junk mail and plastic pots of grey dirt and stalks. He tossed the chip paper against the fence, wiped his hands on his thighs, and pressed the buzzer. She might ask him if it was 'a nice evening'. That kind of talk she picked up from her mother. He directed his eyes upwards and saw grey: a grey sky, grey air. It was not raining. Was that 'nice'? The clog girl opened. Her boyfriend was in a band and once, when he had gone away on tour without taking her and Kim was staying the night at her mother's, the girl, who Raymond believed fancied him, had blundered into Kim's room bawling, wanting an audience for her sob story. She was disgusting. Raymond lay there on Kim's bed, staring up at the girl. He said, 'Oh, go away. Go away or I'll shoot you. To put you out of your misery.' Now, seeing who he was, she turned away without speaking and headed for the back of the house. From the foot of the stairs, before he started to climb, Raymond glanced after her. He saw her shoulder and heel disappear into the kitchen. The bulb hanging there was lit. It swung slightly, and the shadow above it swung too. This he would remember.

Kim's door was closed. There were no voices, and no light showed under it, so he turned the handle and walked straight in. The room was stuffy, and almost dark. He stepped round the low bed, flicked back the curtain and pushed up the window, wedging it open with a hunk of chair leg she kept on the sill. Better air came in under the raised curtain, and at the same instant, in the tree right outside the room, a bird started to sing. He could see it, in against the trunk. It was a small bird but a loud one, and it was shrilling and yelling without any tune, making the kind of racket that sent Kim into fits. He felt a surge of meanness. Holding up the curtain with one hand, he turned his head to watch her wake.

The bed was a turned-over confusion of materials. Only the crests of the folds caught the light. Where was her face? Was she even there? This stupid bird! It was louder than a whole treeful of cicadas and still she didn't hear it. There was a pale bit of her up between the pillows: was it a cheek or a forehead? He stood there with one hand tangled in the curtain, feeling for a nail to hook it back. It caught, but still the light on the bed kept darkening: he was straining to make out her face. Outside, the bird shrilled and thrilled. A bit of her hair had got twisted across her chin. He pulled his hand out of the curtain folds and threw himself to his knees on the very edge of the mattress. It bounced. The smell hit him. Her mouth, half open, was clogged with vomit and alive with a busy-ness of insects. His head and torso jerked back as if on a rein. He made no sound, but across the ridges of his windpipe rushed the shrieking, the squalling of the bird in the tree behind.

He reeled down the stairs and out on to the street. It was almost night. The rooflines of the houses sliced a green and bitter sky. Bells tinkled in showers and some-body was feebly panting, but otherwise the soundtrack had shut down. He kept walking, bumping the shop windows with his shoulder, dragging the soles of his rubber thongs. He blundered past a man sharpening his fingernails on a red brick wall, a bare-faced waitress swabbing terrace tables, a busker unpacking a saxophone in a doorway. He was heading for Alby's, if Alby's still existed; it must, it must, and he travelled slowly, trying to keep himself unfocused, for if he stayed submerged long enough he might surface at last flat on his back under Alby's scratchy grey blanket and open his eyes to see Kim standing crossly beside the bed, trampling Alby's comics with her heavy shoes, scowling at him and biting the split ends off her hair. But the night went on and on, and he ran out of vagueness. It gave out on him. He came to the end of it, and then he knew that nobody on earth, nobody he would ever hear of or meet had the authority to rescue him from the cold fact of what had happened; and yet, as he slunk along the avenue where the mercury vapour lights flushed and whitened, he gazed with stupid longing at the line of spruikers outside the porn clubs, kings of the pavement, big fast-talking dangerous boys in long black overcoats and greasy little ponytails who moved him to awe as angels would, they were so tall, so graceful, so inky with unused power.

He was shoving his spare shirt into a bag when the knock came at Alby's front door. What day was it? Sun was shining. It felt like afternoon. He opened the door and Ursula was standing there. He looked quickly behind her for blokes, but she was on her own. Her face under the sunglasses was fatter, and she was dressed in black.

'Get in the car,' said Ursula.

A taxi was waiting at the kerb, with the door open and the motor running. He hung back.

'Do up your fucking shirt and get in the car,' she said. Her voice was hoarse and she smelt of grog, not beer, something stronger and sweeter. His legs weakened. He had not spoken for two days and he could not speak now. He followed her to the cab. As she climbed in ahead of him, he saw the gold chain round her ankle.

This was one of the few taxi rides of Raymond's life and he was worried that the driver, an Asian in a clean white shirt, would think he was a bludger or up himself for taking a cab at all instead of public transport, and also that he might think he had something to do with this puffy, purple-faced moll who tore in cigarette smoke with all her back teeth showing and kept letting out panting noises and wiping under her sunglasses with the bottom of her dress. She had a flagon of sherry in a plastic bag between her feet and every few minutes she bent over, tipped it sideways and took a swallow. Raymond sat with his hands clasped between his tightly clenched thighs, and kept his eyes on the shiny headrest in front of his face.

The place, when at last the taxi swerved off the freeway and followed the signs to its gates, looked more like a golf course than a cemetery. It was vast, bare and trim. At the end of its curved black road they came to a garden, and in it, a building. Ursula shoved him out, pushing the wrapped flagon into his hands, and he stood there sweating while she paid the driver and the taxi drove away. At the mouth of the chapel some people in a group turned towards them and stared. Raymond thought they were looking at him, but it was Ursula they were watching out for, they were waiting for Ursula to arrive. They must be her friends from before; they were old hippies with grey curls or beards, and the women had hair that was long and stiff, or else cut short like boys', showing their wrinkled eyes and foreheads. One of the men was tall and bony, like a skeleton, with a shaved head and rotten teeth; his hands were tattooed. Ursula kept a tight grip on Raymond's elbow. To the people staring it might have seemed that she was using his arm for support but in fact he was her prisoner, she was yanking him along beside her in a shuffle, in at the chapel door, through a cluster of whispering girls with massed hair and black bodies, and right up the aisle to the empty seats in the front row.

Yellow light fell from long windows at the sides. More people, not many, were waiting in the seats, and someone was playing one of those organs that quiver automatically. Ursula was different now. She was trying to act normal. Raymond heard her put on a voice and say to the woman on her other side, 'What a lot of people have turned up!' The woman tried to put her arm round Ursula's waist, but Ursula went stiff, and the woman, with an offended look, took her arm away and moved across the aisle to a seat further back. Raymond sneaked the flagon under the seat and pushed it out of sight with his foot. As he straightened up someone tapped him sharply on the shoulder. He jerked round. A woman in the seat behind leaned forward and spoke to him in a furtive way.

'What? What?' he said in confusion.

'I said, you were Kimmy's boyfriend, weren't you?' said the woman. She slid her eyes over his face, ears, hair, neck.

'No, no,' he jabbered. 'Not me, no, it wasn't me. Friend of the family, I'm a friend. Of the family.'

His head was shaking itself like a puppet's. He turned his back on her and hunched his shoulders up round his ears. In the front row there was no protection. He could not fold or bend his legs enough; his feet were enlarged, gross, dirty.

The music stopped and a man in a suit stepped uncertainly up to the front and stood against some curtains, facing the people. Raymond did not know whether they were supposed to stand or sit. He glanced behind him for a clue. A couple of the girls were scrambling to their feet, one bloke dropped on to his knees, but most of the people stayed seated with stiff, embarrassed faces. The man out the front said nothing, gave no orders. He did not appear to be in charge: no one was in charge. Raymond realised that nobody here knew how this thing was meant to be done, that nobody here was going to stand up and say the words that would save them.

Then he heard, in the uncomfortable hush, a squeaking and a gliding, the sound of small wheels. Ursula's nails sank into his arm. The curtains at the front were nosed apart and into the empty space where the weak man in the suit was waiting rolled, on a metal trolley, the wooden box with Kim inside it.

Ursula stood up, dragging him with her. Her fingers bit into his inner elbow; and now out of her mouth horrible sounds began, ugly and ridiculous, the noises that bad singers make when they work up to a solo: woh, woh, woh, she went, blank and gaping, gobbling for breath. An old woman darted across and seized her shoulders with both hands but Ursula flung up one arm and knocked her away. In the same movement she struck off her own sunglasses which dangled from one ear and hung half across her mouth, revealing two swollen bruises: her eyes. Out of these sore slits poured a gaze that hit the end of the coffin and bored right in. Ursula at that moment could see through wood.

She turned on Raymond with a crazy mouth. He fought to break away but, like the shrilling of the bird outside the window, Ursula's howling, this horror, exploded and stuffed the universe, paralysed him, swallowed him whole.

Then the bald skeleton with tattooed hands stepped right through the commotion in his heavy boots and put both arms round Ursula from behind.

'Let go,' he said, right in her ear, working at her hands, rubbing at them, getting his thumbs under their grip. 'Urs, it's me, Phil. Come on, Urs. It won't help the little girl now. Lay off the poor bastard, Ursula. Come on, let him go.'

He unhooked her claws and Raymond stumbled back. A rush of murmuring women with handkerchiefs and skirts flowed into the space where he had been, but in the second before they engulfed her he saw her one last time, with her back against the bald man's chest, rearing, her arms pinned up by his grip on her two wrists: her face was a demon's muzzle, sucking in air before its final plunge into the chasm.

Raymond got to his feet in the corner where he had been flung. The air in the ugly chapel settled; the coffin hummed behind him. He could not look at it, but he felt it vibrating in the yellow air, rippling out waves that pressed against his back and propelled him down the aisle towards the door. Ankle-deep in crushed garlands he crossed the porch and stopped on the step of the building, swaying and hanging on to the sides of the archway. He slid his head out into the garden. The last of the cars was pulling away. He heard the sponge and pop of its tyres on the bitumen, saw the blurred hair-masses of the girls packed into the back seat, smelled the exhaust that shot out of its low muffler. It swung round the curve in the road, and was gone.

He let his knees buckle, and sat down hard on the step. He was empty. There was nothing left inside him at all. He crouched there on the chapel's lip, rolling up his shirt sleeve to inspect the site of his bruises. If he could work out where he was, if he could find his way to the gate, he was free to get out of here, to drag himself away.

So when the heavy boots came crunching towards him across the car-park, although the skin of his skull tightened and a thousand hairs grew stiff, he did not raise his head. Maybe it was the gardener. Maybe it was the first person arriving for the next funeral. He kept very still. He made himself narrow. He waited, with shoulders clenched, for the boots to pass.

They halted in front of him. In his stupor and weakness, Raymond fixed his eyes on them. Never in his life had he really examined or considered the meaning of what anyone wore on their feet. The boots were very worn. They were black, and old. They met the ground with leisurely authority, and yet their Cuban heels gave them a lightness, a fanciful quality that was poised, vain, almost feminine. The man whose boots they were, from whose footwear Raymond was trying to read his fate, breathed steadily in and out. He was in no hurry. Still Raymond did not raise his eyes.

At last the grating voice began. 'So you were the one, were you,' it said. 'You were the one who was fucking her.'

Raymond made blinkers round his face with his cupped hands and kept his eyes on the boots. 'No, mate,' he said. 'Not me.' He hardly recognised the sound of himself. 'Oh, I knew her, sure. Sure thing. I knew Kim. Everyone knew Kim. She was a nice girl. But I only came today because Ursula, because her mother wanted me to.'

The boots shifted, emitting a faint leathery squeak. 'Bit old for her, weren't you?'

A whiff of cigarette smoke dropped to Raymond's level and spiked the lining of his nose. 'Listen, mate,' he said, cupping his eyes, keeping his eyes down, 'you've got the wrong bloke. It wasn't me. I don't know who she—'

'Anyway,' said the man, moving his weight on to his left foot. 'She's dead now. No point worrying who was up who. Is there?'

'This is right,' said Raymond. 'Nothing can help her now.'

Over in the garden beyond the car-park a bird uttered three notes of a mounting song, and fell silent.

A butt landed with force on the black ground beside the boots. It lay on its side, saliva-stained, twisted, still burning; Raymond could not resist, at last, the urge to reach out one foot and perform the little circular dance of crushing it. Still he did not look up.

'There is one thing, though,' said the low, harsh voice above him. 'There's one more thing that has to be done. For the girl.'

'I have to go, actually,' said Raymond. He drew in his feet and placed his hands on the step as if to stand. This movement raised his gaze to the knees of the man's black jeans: the cloth was beaten, necessary, seldom washed, carelessly pulled on: as flexible as skin. 'I think I'll get on home,' said Raymond. 'I have to find my brother.'

'Hang on,' said the voice, patiently, firmly. 'You can't leave yet. I want to show you something.'

The boots took two steps back, then another two, then two more. The garden, until now blotted out by the hugeness of the boots, the legs, the voice, spread suddenly into Raymond's frame of vision. This he did not want. He did not want movement, noise, softness; he wanted a permanent berth inside his grey casing.

He raised his chin to argue.

Where one man had been standing, there now were two. Raymond sat in his crouched posture, head back, on the threshold of the chapel. His lips parted to speak, but he could not properly see the two men's faces, for the afternoon sun hung exactly behind their two heads which were leaning together ear to ear, calmly regarding him, calmly waiting for his next burst of excuses; and these died in his mouth at the sight of the corona of light whose centre was their pair of skulls, one furred with yellow hair, one shaven bald as ivory.

The two men stepped apart.

'I know who you are,' said Raymond to the bald man. Again his own voice rang oddly to him, as if his thoughts were forming on his tongue and not in his brain. 'Are you her father?'

'Hardly,' said the bald man, and laughed. 'Don't be a dickhead *all* your life.'

The men looked at each other, swung their heads to take in the moving garden, then fixed their eyes again on Raymond. They're crims, thought Raymond. They've been in the nick. The one with hair was dressed in ironed grey trousers and a maroon blazer with gold on the pocket. He must have a job at a racecourse or out the front of a tourist hotel. He wore boots as well but cheap brown ones, hard-looking, though polished. He glanced at his watch. His hands too were tattooed, with bitten nails.

'Come on, Phil,' he said to the bald man. 'The next mob will be on my back at four.'

The bald man, catching Raymond's eye, clicked his tongue and jerked his head sideways. 'Hop up, pal,' he said. 'We want to show you something.'

Raymond got to his feet warily, brushing the seat of his pants.

'Tsk,' said the man in the blazer, to himself. 'People don't care *what* they wear to a funeral these days.' He took a toothpick out of his blazer pocket, jammed it between his back teeth, and clomped away along a narrow path that skirted the chapel's outer wall. The bald man pushed Raymond lightly between the shoulder blades, and himself trod close behind. A freckled man in a towelling hat passed them and went tramping away across an enormous lawn, wheeling a barrow and whistling with raised eyebrows and cheerful trills. All three men greeted each other in an old-fashioned way, with grimaces and clicks.

Raymond's legs were still hollow and shaky; but as the men marched him Indian-style along the pathway, not speaking, moving forward with apparent purpose, he began to relax. Maybe this wouldn't be too bad. These men, like uncles, had taken him in hand. He turned to glance at the bald one, who winked at him and nodded. It was a public place, after all. What could go wrong? Maybe he could drop his guard and walk like this between them, single file. It was not so dangerous. He could slide from one thing to the next, and the next; nothing much would be expected of him, the rest of the day would roll by as even the longest days do, and by the end of it he would have got a lift somewhere, would have walked somewhere, would find himself somewhere, under somebody's roof, maybe with people, maybe on his own; yes, all this he could handle. The worst was over. He turned again to the bald man, and almost smiled at him.

The man in the blazer veered off the path and plunged into the dense strip of hedge that separated it from the building's side. Between two bouncing bushes of blue flowers he rustled his way, spitting out his toothpick, and with key outstretched unlocked a little wooden door marked *Private*. He held the springy green branches apart for them with turning thrusts of his shoulders; they joined him, pinned against the wall by whippy shrubbery; he went ahead, and one by one they stooped and stepped through the little door, on to a narrow staircase that led them into the underworld.

The shock of it.

Raymond propped on the stair with one leg in mid-air. Above him the door slammed. The bald man coming close on his heels down the ladder would have cannoned into him, but took the strain with his thighs, and Raymond felt, instead of the weight of a heavy body landing against him, merely a dexterous, light brushing. He lurched down the last step.

Here they had not heard of blood or colour. It was a land made of dust, of chalk, of flour. The walls and floor and ceiling were grey, the air was grey, and as his gaze cleared and crept deeper, he saw that the receding alley of huge ovens was grey, that the workers who moved silently away between them were grey. The only sound was a low, steady roaring.

'Like it?' said the man in the blazer. 'This is where we work.'

'He runs the place,' said the bald man. 'He's the one who gives the orders.'

The man in the blazer, flattered, gave a naughty shrug. His hand closed round Raymond's aching upper arm, but gently, and urged him forward step by step until he stood, trembling and dumb, bracketed by the two men, in front of the closed door of the first furnace.

Where is she?' said the bald man. 'He won't want to be kept hanging about.'

'Look up there,' said the man in the blazer, and pointed. 'She's next in line.'

'Ah,' said the bald man in his grating voice, with satisfaction. 'Ah, yes.'

A slot opened high in the grey cement wall, thirty yards away, and out of it, strapped to an elevated conveyor belt, flew the coffin. It dashed down and round the tilted track, skimming fast and cornering suavely on its slender arrangement of rails.

'Yep, here she comes,' said the man in the blazer, giving Raymond's elbow a little squeeze. 'Here comes your girl.'

A single pink posy was still clinging, by an accidental twist of sticky-tape, to the coffin's lid. As the box slid smartly into the last turn of the track and came to a stop beside them at the furnace door, the flowers lost their purchase and sailed in a brief, low arc to the floor. The man in the blazer bobbed down for the bunch. He took a sniff and tossed it over his shoulder into a barrow, while with his other hand, in a smooth movement, he checked a number on the coffin's end and made a mark on a list behind him. He raised his arm in a signal.

The oven door opened.

First, a square of colour: a blossoming, the relief of orange flames. Then a colossal blast of heat which evaporated the moisture off Raymond's eyeballs. He staggered, and the bald man caught him by the arm.

'Steady on,' he said. 'You'll be right.'

Behind them the man in the blazer was deftly unbuckling the straps that had secured the coffin to its sled.

'Here,' he said to Raymond. 'Take an end.'

Raymond's mind had abandoned his body. He obeyed. He turned front-on to the coffin and reached out both arms, but the man in the blazer winked at him and wagged one finger, tick tock, right in his face.

'Uh-uh,' he said. 'Bad posture. Bend those knees, mate, or you'll fuck your back.'

Raymond bent them. His muscles quivered. He slid his fingers under the narrow end of the coffin and got a grip. The bald man played no part in the operation, but stood close by, watching, with his arms folded mildly over his chest. The man in the blazer took hold of the broad end, and nodded to Raymond. They straightened their legs. So light! The box floated up to waist level.

'Little scrap of a thing, was she?' said the man in the blazer. 'Weighs no more than a feather.'

The coffin hovered slant-wise across the open pophole in the furnace door. The heat was tremendous: their eyes squinted, their heads involuntarily turned away, their tongues dried in their mouths.

'Back up,' said the man in the blazer. 'We'll slip her in head-first.'

Raymond shuffled backwards and to one side. The man in the blazer screwed up his face against the blast and flexed his legs just enough to give him leverage. Then, in a series of manoeuvres so rapid, dainty and accurate that in three seconds it was done, he flipped his end of the load on to the lip of the furnace slot, darted back and, nudging Raymond out of the way with his hip, shot the coffin straight through the door and on to the shelf of flame. The door clanged shut. The heat faded. The man took a folded hanky out of his blazer sleeve and mopped his neck.

'A bloke,' he said, 'would be a mug to wear a tie in this line of work.'

Something hard pressed against the backs of Raymond's knees, which gave. It was a chair. The two men stood one on either side of him, each with a hand resting lightly on his shoulder. Like a monarch between courtiers, he sat facing the grey door of the grey oven. When he began to sag, to faint, they held him gently upright, keeping his spine against the chair back. The wrist watch of the man on his right ran madly in his ear.

'Sorry about the delay,' said the man in the blazer. 'We have to squirt a bit of oil on to the head and torso, to get them going. But the feet only take a few minutes.'

'The feet?' whispered Raymond. His teeth, his lips were dry: they rubbed against each other wrongly, snagging and missing.

The bald man, whose shaven skull had flushed a delicate pink, looked down at Raymond with sudden interest.

'You want to see?' he said. 'Open up that door.'

They raised Raymond from the chair and half-pressed, half-carried him forward to the furnace. The other man waved, and the door clanked open. Raymond's cheeks clenched of their own accord, turning his eyes to slits. The heat inside the cavern was so intense, so intent that all he could see was a working and a wavering. The men supported him tenderly, pointing him towards the square of liquid orange.

'I can't—' he said. 'I can't—'

'Yes, you can,' said the bald man urgently. 'Look now.'

Something in there was wrinkling. The small end of the coffin, fragile as an eggshell, was crinkling into a network of tiny cracks. While Raymond stared, greedy in his swoon of shock, the panel collapsed; it gave way to the swarming orange argument, and where it had been he saw a dark-cored nimbus of flame, seething, closer to him than an arm's reach. Its twin centres, their shod soles towards them, were her feet. In the passion of their transfiguration they loosened. They opened. They fell apart.

He could manage only his neck. The rest he let the two men deal with, and their tattooed hands went on holding him together. The long tube of the coffin now lost form. Pouf! It fell softly in upon itself, her last shelter gone. Deep in the fire he made out a humped, curved lump, and beyond that, rising, a denser clod, her head. He opened his mouth to cry out, but the wetness needed for speech was sucked off the surface of him by the oven's impersonal breath.

The furnace door slammed. He tottered like a doll. They lifted him backwards and placed him on the chair. While his seared skin loosened and turned salty, he hung by the shoulders from the men's restraining hands. He drooped there, sightless, beside himself, his own hallucination. Was there music? Someone was whistling,

stacking the notes in jagged steps and executing a long
and detailed flourish: a knot cleverly tied, Kim's shoe,
the brass eyelets in a double row, the impossible twirl of
her fast fingers lacing; a man's voice grew in song, then
the fires roared uninterrupted, while near his ear the
watch chattered, a tiny hysteria headlong, never arriving,
never drawing breath.

'And again,' said the voice.

He half-raised his head, a dog ready for its next
beating, and they bore him forward.

The grey door was open. Raymond looked in. The fire
and the heat were barely a shimmer in the cavernous air.
There was no colour anywhere, except for the maroon
blazer cuff in the outermost corner of Raymond's view.
The furnace floor was covered with ordinary ash, and on
this desert bed lay scattered in a free arrangement three
or four long bones, pale, dry-looking, innocent.

'There,' said the man in the blazer. 'All finished now.
You can go home.'

They turned him and unhanded him and dropped him
on to his own legs, side on to the cooling furnace.

'Go on,' said the bald man. 'Show's over. Buzz off.'
He stuck his hands in the back pockets of his jeans and
jerked his rosy skull in the direction of the ladder.

'I don't know where I am,' said Raymond. He shuffled his feet in the grey dust of the floor. 'Which is the
way?' They would cast him aside: and there was no one
left in the world but these two men.

'Go on—get out,' said the man in the blazer. He bent down and picked up a long piece of wood. Raymond flinched, but without even looking at him the man shoved the head of the rake through the furnace door and began to drag it harshly across the shelf where the bones and ashes lay. The bald man leaned his chin on his companion's shoulder and plunged his eyes deep into the oven where the final disintegration was taking place: the ash tumbled down, as the teeth of the rake ground back and forth. It tumbled down through the grille and crumbled into the under chamber.

'Where do I go?' said Raymond. He felt the words cross his lips, but the voice was a child's. 'How do I get home from here?'

The bald man could not extricate his attention from the graceful behaviour of the ashes. He spoke absently, staring into the furnace where the other man's rake was accomplishing its task. He sighed. Then, with the slow resoluteness of a dreamer waking, he lifted his chin and turned on Raymond eyes as inhuman, blank and depthless as those of a figure carved in granite.

'Home,' he said, 'is the last place you need to go. Don't bother. Don't even go back for your things.' He flexed his arms and shoulders, and let them drop. The ripple of it ran down his torso. His joints were oiled with wakefulness.

Raymond stared. He hung on his own breath. 'Who are you?' he whispered. 'What's your name?'

'None of your business,' said the man. 'But you know where to find me, now. I'm always here. Always on duty.'

Raymond feasted his eyes on the man: his dark limbs, his worn boots, his shining ivory skull. He felt a terrible urge to approach. He longed to offer his forehead to the touch of the bald man's tattooed hand. Appalled, he saw his own grubby foot move out into the narrow space between them; but without taking a step the man was suddenly beyond his reach, balancing easily on the ladder with one arm raised to the latch of the high trapdoor.

'You'll be right,' said the bald man in his low, scraping voice. 'Things'll be different now. Just get out of here and start walking.'

He opened the trapdoor with a quick twist of his up-stretched hand, and leaned back from the ladder to make room, resting on Raymond his calm stone gaze.

Raymond stood in the dust and looked up.

An unbearable diamond of evening sky hovered over his head, scalloped and sprigged at its edges by dark foliage. Air gushed through it, smelling of cut grass; and out of the fresh leaf-masses, there poured down on him a light, nervous, persistent whirring, a multitudinous soft tapping and chewing, a vast and infinitesimal cacophony of insects living, living, living.

Raymond shut his mouth. He reached for the jamb with both hands, planted his feet—one, two—on the steep steps and, helped by a violent shove in the small of his back, hauled himself, flailing, through the shrubbery and out on to the staggering lawn.

(i)

I thought Vince resented me, the kids, the whole mess
I'd got him into. But now I see he cared more than any
of us.

His love was different. He wanted to do something
big. I remember him saying to the doctor: 'If she needs
an operation—I'll work—I'll do overtime—I don't care
how much it costs.' He wanted to spend himself to help
her and when the doctor said there was no operation, it
was as if Vince didn't know what he should be doing. I
can see it now but I couldn't see it then.

I was angry when he wouldn't even pick Sal up,
wouldn't play with her, wouldn't talk to her. And when
Margie was born, he couldn't give himself to her either.
Only to his work and the pub, and he wouldn't speak
to me. He kept the hurt bottled up.

I wanted to understand. I talked to Father O'Halloran
and he tried to talk to Vince, but he wouldn't listen.
And his brother Bluey, who was more of a father to the
kids than Vince was, wouldn't have a word said against
him. 'He's hurting inside, Maise. Give him time.'

But I didn't have the time to give him. Here I was with a new baby and Sal to carry everywhere and Vince with that wounded look in his eyes.

Mum would come every day to give me a hand and I knew she was wanting to say 'I told you so,' but holding back because she could see I had enough to put up with.

And me, really wanting to be a Catholic because I'd come to love the Mass and our Lord, and knowing now I'd have to sin. When I told Father O'Halloran, he said, almost apologising, 'You know what I must say to you, my child.' And I said, 'I know, Father, but I can't have any more. I've got to be free to look after Sally.' I kept going to Mass and he kept giving me the Sacrament, even though I was sinning.

People were saying Sally was born damaged because of VD, and that got to Vince. He'd been wild in the army. He told me he'd been with women in Queensland and New Guinea too. But he was only a boy then and the uniform had gone to his head. I know he wondered if it was his fault because he hadn't kept himself pure but, if anyone was to blame it was me, being so slow in labour. Vince wouldn't take any notice of what the doctor said. He was trying to work it all out for himself inside his head.

I'd just about had enough when Bluey came over to talk to me about the Baths. Margie was walking and getting into all kinds of mischief and little Sally was so helpless. And I knew I should be doing something for her about school because she was over five and bright enough to have some learning. Vince wouldn't even discuss going to Sydney or Brisbane where they have special schools. So when Bluey started talking, I didn't take it seriously. Anyway, I was sure Vince wouldn't let Sally go to a place where other people would see her.

But Vince latched onto Bluey's idea and got angry with me when I couldn't see the point. I wasn't looking for any miracle. I just wanted some help with Sally so I could manage.

I couldn't believe the change. He hadn't touched that child for over four years and here he was waking Sal, taking her to the toilet, dressing her in bathers, wrapping a towel around her and carrying her down to the Baths. And after a week or two, he started with her at night, practising the walking as if he had a mission.

Strange enough, he wouldn't come back to church. He said this was something he had to do by himself. I didn't argue—I didn't want to stop him. And when Bluey started saying that Vince was overdoing it, I had to tell him, 'After all these years, he's come home again, Bluey, and I'm not going to complain.'

Now I can see Vince had made some kind of a bargain. I don't know for sure—I can only guess. It was as if he was saying, 'I've got to do what I'm doing so Sally can walk.'

That's how I want my girls to remember their father. In time they'll come to understand that even miracles have to be paid for.

(ii)

There wasn't any miracle. Oh, I know they went on about Sally's walking as if it was all his doing. And after this disappearing trick, well, he became a saint. My guess was he'd pulled out the throttle for a while and he'd had enough. No staying power, Vince. Couldn't tell Maisie that. She wanted to have him even when it meant breaking her father's heart. But Vince was likeable in those days and handsome. And when he wanted to marry our Maisie, there was no question. It didn't matter that her grandfather had been an Orangeman who hated the Tykes. Vince wouldn't marry her unless she turned and she wanted him so much she would have turned Callithumpian if he'd asked her.

It was sad, not being able to give Maisie a big wedding. We just kept it to the two families—that is, without my Bill. He stayed at home with the sulks. In a way I didn't blame him for that. His father had told him that many stories of what the Catholics had done to the Protestants.

But I didn't hold with Bill when he said the reason little Sal was spastic was the mixed marriage. That's not common sense. Anyway, the doctor explained that it was lack of oxygen during the birth. And the baby was late. If they'd thought of a caesar like they did with Margie . . . But Maisie was in labour for hours and getting nowhere. The doctor was out on one of the farms and was late getting back to the hospital. From the start he suspected there could be something the matter.

Vince kept saying there was nothing wrong with his child. But by the time she was twelve months it was clear to everybody Sally was spastic. That's when he started to drink. Did nothing to help my Maisie, just let her battle on by herself and then later on got her pregnant again.

So there she was, almost ready to drop the new baby and little Sal having to be carried round. It wasn't so much that Sally was heavy; she had skinny arms and legs. But sometimes her body would go rigid—a spasm, they call it—and she could lurch out with an arm or a leg or give you a thump with her head that'd make you see stars. And the poor little kid would get so upset if she thought she'd hurt you. So you'd bite your lip and try not to let on, even if you were starting to feel the black circles under your eyes.

The doctor popped Maisie into hospital a week early for the second baby so they could keep an eye on her. I came over to mind Sally and I couldn't understand how Maisie had managed. You had to do everything for her— lift her to the table, feed her, take her to the toilet, lift her into the bath and out again, carry her to bed. She couldn't even hold a piece of bread by herself.

I knew then who was the saint in that family. He was no help at all. The best that could be said for him was that he did keep his job.

Sally was five and she still couldn't walk. Couldn't even crawl, used to sit or lie all day. She loved to watch little Margie running about. The two girls were good together, seemed to be able to understand one another. Sally would try to talk. Her little face would twist and she'd get something out. Maisie seemed to be able to follow, but it was double-dutch to me. I'd just nod and always try to speak loud and clear for her.

Maisie never complained to me. She just went on looking after her two little girls, and thank goodness he had at least the decency not to get her pregnant again. Then all of a sudden, after having nothing to do with the kids—even little Margie and there was nothing wrong with her—he starts taking Sally to the hot Baths. Gets special permission too because in those days they only had the separate sessions for men and women.

Well, Maisie was like a girl again. Couldn't believe Vince'd come good. He even slowed up on the drinking. Then he started on about getting Sally to walk. He had their lounge room in a terrible mess with bits of rope and railings and chairs back to front. But to give him his due, he'd work with Sal for an hour or so every night.

It was a bit much for the little kid. She was always tired. But when I asked Sal if the Baths and the exercising were worrying her, she gave me a big grin and shook her head. I suppose she liked having something to do instead of sitting about watching other people doing things.

But when Maisie came running round to my place saying there'd been a miracle and Sally was walking, I didn't know what to think. Sal was tottery—her arms waving about as they always did, but she took three steps all by herself and I must admit I joined in too when the priest said a prayer of thanks.

I always knew that little girl had a lot of pluck. Just the way she'd stick at something. One day I saw her sit there half an hour trying to get the pencil onto the paper, holding one hand with the other so she could write an 'S'. And when she went to school and they let her try the painting, she could make pictures an ordinary kid couldn't make. If you could see her with the paper stuck down so she wouldn't move it, and her gripping that brush with both hands, trying to steady herself so she could get the colour onto the paper. Dear God, it'd make you cry with pride to watch that kid. She's got more guts than the lot of us. And now she's at that special school, and they say she'll do her Intermediate Certificate one day. So why they had to cry miracle as soon as Sally took a few steps, I don't know.

I've never discussed this with Maisie. She's doing a great job with her two girls. And if it helps her thinking Vince pulled off a miracle, let her think it. She can do with all the comfort she can get.

(iii)

'There he was, poor bugger, waiting at the edge of the pool—knowing that if he could get there first, he'd be able to walk again, and he had nobody to carry him down. It's a terrible thing, Maisie,' I says to her, 'if the hot Baths could cure our Sal, and nobody's prepared to carry her into the water.'

'But Bluey, the man wasn't cured by the bubbling water,' Maisie says to me. 'He was cured by our Lord.'

'Well, our Lord's not here—but the water is, Maise. Look, you should've seen old Harry—his legs twisted up with arthritis. He walks without a limp now.'

'But that's arthritis. Sally's different,' says Maisie and she slams the screen door on our conversation and goes out to bring in the washing.

I can't explain the special way you love somebody like Sally. It's just different to the way you love ordinary kids. I suppose it's the feeling sorry too—wishing you could make things easier for them. It's hard enough in this world when your body's all right—when you don't have to worry about walking and eating and getting to the lavatory.

Before Maisie had Sally, I used to believe in letting kids die if they were different. But if you knew Sal, you couldn't believe that. She was such a sweetie and I'd joke with her—that was my job each day, to make little Sal laugh. And it wasn't hard because she used to humour her old Uncle Blue.

So when I talked Vince into letting me take Sally to the hot Baths I thought I'd done something pretty clever. And when I'd set it all up, Vince decided he was going to take her himself.

I couldn't believe it. From the time Vince knew Sally had the cerebral palsy, he wouldn't have anything to do with her. And Sal knew—of course she knew. We'd say, 'Dadda's busy. Dadda's gone to work.' But Sal knew all right and that's why I tried to come round every day.

Maise'd given up hope that Vince'd ever change and here he was, getting up at six, taking Sal down to the Baths, bringing her back. He was starting to look like his old self.

And I was feeling pretty proud—believing more than ever that the reading from the Bible was a message.

Then I started to get worried.

Vince got me aside one night. 'Bluey, I've been thinking, if you can do my late shift, I'm going to take Sally to the Baths in the evening session as well.'

'I don't mind doing the shift for you, but it'll be too much. You don't want to overdo it, Vince.'

'If we can have twice as much time in the hot water, it's got to make a difference. Bluey, I can see she's getting stronger and I'm going to get her walking if it's the last thing I do.'

'Listen, Vince, these things are slow. Even with Harry—it was steady. Every day for a month or two before there was any improvement.'

'But if I give it more time. It must make a difference, Bluey. It's got to make a difference.'

Then it got so as he couldn't talk about anything else. He was home every night and he'd get Sally up and start her walking—holding her hands, then letting go. And the kid would fall and you could see the disappointment on his face and on Sally's face too and she looked at her dad and understood what he was thinking.

I couldn't stand it any longer. 'We've got to do something, Maisie. It's too much for Sal—it's not fair to the kid.'

'Come on, Bluey. Sally's never known a father before and now he's giving her all this time.'

'But what if she can't walk? What if he's forcing her and she just can't do it?'

'She's putting on weight and her legs are stronger. Oh Bluey,' she says, her eyes ready to cry, 'you don't know the difference it's made.' And I can see Maisie doesn't have any idea that I've started something I can't stop.

That night—the last night anyone saw Vince—I was at home just finishing my tea and he comes rushing in. He's in a state—I can tell by the way he paces the floor.

'I couldn't stay there and watch them,' he says. 'I just couldn't stay there.'

'Will you calm down, Vince,' and I sit him down and get him a glass of beer and tell him to start from the beginning.

'Bluey, it was terrible. As soon as Sally took the three steps, Maisie runs round and calls her mother and the priest. They all come back and get her to do it again. She takes three more steps before she falls down. And they start calling out "It's a miracle", and the priest says a prayer right there and then, thanking God.'

'But, Vince, you said if she could walk . . . if she could just take some steps by herself.'

'But it wasn't a miracle,' he yells at me. 'She's still the same. I thought she'd be walking like other kids but she's still the same.'

(iv)

Nobody ever asked me if there was a miracle. I could have told them but very few people try to understand zeny giles

what I say. It takes a lot of time and concentration to understand me. The words are clear in my head but they're so hard to get out—like forcing out those steps so many years ago. And when I've made that kind of effort, they won't take the time to listen. Most people— even Nanna—just say Yes dear, No dear, pretending they understand when they don't, as if that's being kind to me.

Margie's the only one who doesn't need to concentrate, but I can't rely on her all the time. Mum tries to listen but she can read my eyes so she takes the shortcut. Lately she's been missing lots of the things I'm saying.

Uncle Bluey used to try harder than anyone else. But after Dadda went away, Uncle Bluey seemed frightened to listen—frightened of what I might ask him.

There was a miracle and it was something I thought could never happen. But it wasn't the walking, as Mum and Father O'Halloran and Nanna thought. I was exhausted after every one of those walking sessions. But I make that kind of effort every day. Every time I walk I have to be careful not to topple. I get there because I'm very determined. I was determined that if Dadda wanted me to walk, I was going to walk. But that wasn't the miracle.

The miracle was that he came close to me and he didn't turn away. He didn't force himself to be kind to me—that would have been even harder to bear. He was so full of the idea of getting me to walk; he dressed me and carried me all the way down to the Baths. In the water he took my arms, telling me to move my legs about. He massaged my legs and my arms and held me tight while the water jets sprayed against me. Day after day he did this. I can still remember the smell of that water and the special smell of his hair and his skin as he carried me close to his body. That was the miracle but he didn't see it. And if I'd tried to tell him, he wouldn't have taken the time to listen.

Mum said he'd made a bargain with God that he would give up his life in exchange for my walking. If that's the kind of bargain Dadda made, it shows how little he understood what I wanted. And if that's the kind of bargain God agreed with, it's no wonder I haven't much time for him either.

October 15th

Dear Scott,

I write to thank you for taking part in our recent weekend conference. Feedback has been very positive on the whole, and we are grateful for your contribution to the success of the weekend. We hope that the very fruitful discussions generated by almost all of the speakers will play some small part in encouraging a more sophisticated and enlightened literary culture in this country.

We enclose your cheque as arranged, and thank you again for your participation.

Yours sincerely,
Christopher Colquhoun
Elizabeth Colquhoun

Convenors

P.S. Scott—sorry about absence of abovementioned cheque but combined bills for damage *et al* add up to rather more than that. You still owe us $679.58—C.C.

October 23rd

Dear Scott,

Re. your letter of October 17th: unfortunately when we offered to cover the costs of your accommodation we didn't really take room service and telephone charges properly into account. We have paid the bill as arranged and we are willing to go as far as the six STD calls and the full breakfast for two, but we're afraid we can't afford the call to Denmark, the towelling bathrobe or the three bottles of Moët et Chandon. As we made a small loss on the conference in any case, we have been obliged to pay for the damage to University property out of the English Department's budget, and the call to Aarhus and the bathrobe and the Moët out of our own pockets. Call it an interest-free loan. It comes to a total of $779.59: minus your withheld cheque, $679.58.

In addition to yours, we have had several other indignant replies to our original thank you note, re. the remark about sophistication and enlightenment. I suppose I can see why you might all have taken it the wrong way, but of course we didn't mean to imply that Australians suffer from arrested cultural development and literary *gaucherie*. We are both finding it very exciting to live and work in such a young, energetic country.

We look forward to hearing from you soon.

Yours sincerely,
Christopher Colquhoun

October 31st

Dear Scott,

Property of the University:

(1) Four chairs: assorted colours (broken) $196.00

(2) One indoor plant (uprooted and unsuccessfully
    repotted) $17.20

(3) One white-board: 200cm. × 150cm. (indelibly
    written on) $129.00

Hotel Extras:

(1) One ISD call to Aarhus, Denmark $142.38

(2) Three bottles of Moët et Chandon (Room Service
    rates) $210.00

(3) One towelling bathrobe (white, size
    Large) $85.00

TOTAL...$779.58

Yours sincerely,
Christopher Colquhoun

November 5th

Dear Scott,

The chairs, or rather the assorted colours thereof, were one lemon, one peacock and two tomatoes. The plant was a maidenhair fern and it did die, yes. Methylated spirits did not work on the white-board; we tried that at the time, as you may remember. The towelling bathrobe is missing from the hotel room and they have therefore charged us for it; I'm afraid they're not very interested in where it could have got to. Have you checked with the person who ate the other full breakfast?

Also, would you enlarge a little on the claim that the call to Denmark was a piece of vital research for your conference paper? We want to be fair about this. As for the champagne, I take your point about entertaining other conference participants, but they'd been quite happy all day with the cask white, I thought. In view of your eloquent remarks at the microphone the next day about French nuclear testing in the Pacific, I should have thought you'd be boycotting their imports in any event.

Yes, I know that $100 isn't very much for (a) two days' attendance and participation, (b) the time, research, expertise and stationery you put into preparing your paper, and (c) the better-paid work you could otherwise have been doing. But it really was all that we could afford to pay, as we explained as clearly as we could when we invited you to give the paper in the first place. Thank you for the information about the Australian Society of Authors rates, and the Australian Journalists' Association rates, and about fees for television appearances. I have put it all on file.

I see from Saturday's paper that you were awarded a writer's grant this year so perhaps that will help to take the financial pressure off a bit.

Regards,
Christopher C.

kerryn goldsworthy

November 23rd

Dear Scott,

Yours of November 10th to hand. Isn't there some law or other in this country about mailing or otherwise transporting fruit and vegetables interstate? A slice of the lemon is floating in my morning tea as I write, but the length of the mail strike took its toll on the two tomatoes, and being bashed about at the bottom of the mail bag has not improved their condition. Couldn't you at least have lined the padded postbag with Happy Wrap or whatever it's called here? (Mind you, what else can one expect from a country in which the generic word for adhesive tape is Durex?) The state of my pigeonhole is beyond description, and the letter accompanying the fruit (tomatoes are fruit, strictly speaking, did you know?) was mostly illegible—though I *did* manage to decipher the bit about colour and metaphor, and with your permission I might work it up into a lecture one day when I'm short of ideas. I do agree that the actual colours of the broken chairs are an affront to human sensibility, and that to describe them as 'lemon', 'peacock' and 'tomato' is to travesty the innate beauty of the objects concerned. You did *ask* what colours they were and I merely transcribed what was on the invoice. It was unnecessary to send me samples of the real thing to prove the point. After all, I, unlike you, have to look at the chairs every day. I have skipped an important staff meeting in order to write immediately and assure you that the point is taken, in the hope that you will spare me the peacock.

Actually, you know, while I've been writing this letter I've been thinking about what you said about colours and the names of colours (with specific reference to house-paint colour cards and 1950's mail-order catalogues for women's fashions) and I think you may have stumbled on something quite exciting. Not just the colour of the thing, but the thing itself. Lemon, tomato. Plum, fawn, duck-egg, lime. Lavender. Charcoal. *Navy*, by God! I could give a sequence of lectures on metaphor, metonymy, synecdoche, synaesthesia, objective correlatives and colour symbolism in poetry. I could even enjoy writing them. In fact, and in gratitude, I am prepared to write off the chairs. Especially since, as you rightly claim, you performed a public service in acting as the agent of their destruction.

Unfortunately that still leaves the plant, the whiteboard, the champagne, the bathrobe and the call to Denmark. You may have touched on some of these things in the letter in which you wrapped the tomatoes and the lemon before you put them in the padded bag. It's hard to tell.

If you have any good ideas about my colour lectures, perhaps you would be good enough to pass them on.

Regards,
Christopher

December 1st

Dear Scott,

'Stumbled on' was an unfortunate choice of words, yes. Of course I didn't mean it like that. I was writing in haste, as you may recall, and no doubt expressed myself carelessly. Of *course* you have given these things some thought. I *know* you're a writer. That's why we asked you to speak at the conference. No, your story 'The Red Wheelbarrow, the Blue Guitar, and the Lilacs in the Dooryard Where the Rainbow Ends' is one I haven't yet read, but I shall make a note of it. (Liz has just come into my office to bring me a cup of tea. She sends her regards. Actually she seems to have brightened up rather a lot lately—must be settling in at last.)

Thanks also for the tip about the accountant. What with British *and* Australian taxes this year and the cost of the move, I do think that professional help is in order and I must say she does sound very good. I certainly had never thought of claiming the cost of dry-cleaning my academic gown as a deduction.

I seem to owe you a few good ideas, so yes, all right; in view of all that we'll forget the champagne and I'll accept your offer of home-stirred martinis the next time I'm in town and we'll call it quid pro Moët.

I honestly don't remember you inviting me back to your hotel room for drinks with the others, that night at the conference dinner, but there was a lot happening at the time and it probably just slipped my mind. The dinner did get rather out of hand, didn't it? I was so exhausted by the end of it that I didn't even go home that night—just crept back to the university and collapsed on the sofa in my office. Liz went off somewhere carousing with some of the other older graduate students—they all *look* fairly quiet, but you'd be surprised. Benedict was away with his aunt for the weekend. That is to say, his auntie. Why are there no fully grown aunts in Australia? Why are they all dwarfed by the diminutive? Do you have any theories about this?

I'm not sure that the Department will accept a lemon tree in a pot as a substitute for the maidenhair fern. It was the only plant we had. Your image of Australian artists in the post-war years as pot-bound, nutrient-starved plants stored on top of each other in a broom cupboard was quite a metaphor, but did you really have to use our maidenhair to illustrate the point? Whence this obsession you seem to have with using physical objects as a means of communication? Don't you realise that humanity invented language in the first place because words are durable and things are not? (Ferns die when grasped, pulled up and waved about; tomatoes rot in the post; chairs collapse when jumped up and down upon by the four heaviest volunteers in the room in order to demonstrate what happens to arts funding bodies when the number of people applying for grants rises in direct inverse proportion to the personnel numbers and budget figures of the bodies concerned.) Don't you know the difference between the signifier and the signified? Aren't the words for the objects good enough for you? And if the words aren't good enough for a *writer*, who *are* they good enough for? Tell me *that*.

The fact that the fern really did turn out to be pot-bound does give some foundation to your claim that it was already moribund before you even touched it. But I'm not at all sure I can grow a tree in a pot from the pips of the lemon that you sent me. Mind you, it's true that I do still have them. I found them in the bottom of a mouldy teacup the day I received your last letter. Three-quarters of the cleaning staff were laid off after the most recent funding cuts and now we're doing all of our own office housework except the hoovering.

I'll try it, though. I rather like the idea of growing something. I don't get the time to do much gardening any more. I must say I was rather taken by your idea of a flourishing young plant as the symbol of a new and fertile alliance between the people who write the books and the people who teach them. As you say, the expressions 'fruitful' and 'sowing the seeds' in this particular case are good examples for my lecture sequence of the way that the metaphorical and the literal can converge. And the fact of its being a *lemon* tree ties the colour thing in very neatly. I could even carry it into the lecture theatre with me to illustrate the point.

What about the white-board, the phone call, and the bathrobe?

Best wishes,
Christopher

December 16th

Dear Scott,

I've had a good look at the white-board as you suggested and I must admit that yes, it *is* a rather effective cartoon on the subject of cultural imperialism, though as an Englishman myself I must say I am rather disturbed by it (is the image of the octopus really *fair*, do you think?)—still, I suppose that's the point, really, isn't it. I don't know that I'd call it a work of art, though.

I agree that we should have provided a supply of the special wipe-off white-board markers, but we couldn't find any; the Department's stationery budget ran out in July. Yes, we should have removed the white-board if we didn't want people to write on it. No, I don't think they do make blackboards any more. Yes, I miss coloured chalk too. And plasticine, yes. I have no doubt that carrying a green texta with you at all times often proves to be a useful habit and yes, it did indeed enable you to draw the cartoon on the spot to illustrate your argument, which incidentally I found very interesting. But carrying it in the pocket of a cream raw silk jacket was an optimistic, not to say reckless, move. No, we are not going to pay for the dry-cleaning. We'll forget about the white-board and call it quits and that's my final offer.

As you also suggested, I did in fact call your friend in Aarhus just out of curiosity and we ended up having quite a chat. A charming woman, I thought. The question of what a Parisienne is doing teaching Australian literature in a Danish university is something I shall no doubt come to understand in the fullness of time. She confirmed your claim that the main subject of her telephone conversation with you was the perception of Australian literature in Europe, with specific reference to your own work, and I must say that I did find that part of your paper particularly illuminating, so I suppose I have to admit that one *would* have to call it legitimate research, yes. However, the phone bill is no longer an issue in any case. Mireille says that regular reverse-charge calls from you, as a noted Australian writer, are built into her Department's telephone budget and she will therefore be happy to reimburse me for the call. Delightful woman.

Now to the subject of the gift-wrapped manilla folder and the assortment of documents therein, which arrived in the mail yesterday morning and thank you very much. (a) The instructions for martini-making: Liz and I spent last evening following these, which may account for the shaky typing in this letter. Don't think I'm not grateful but I couldn't help wondering whether there's a connection bettween your obsession with martinis and your obsession with cultural imperialism, or doesn't America count?

(b) The copy of 'The Red Wheelbarrow, The Blue Guitar, and the Lilacs in the Dooryard Where the Rainbow Ends': I say, Scott, this really is a very good story. Frankly I had no idea that fiction of such subtlety and sophistication was being written in Australia—this story has a truly international feel to it. I'm looking forward to having a proper chat with you about your work the next time we meet.

(c) The dissertation on aunties: if I have understood you correctly, your theory is that it's a question of poetic metre—that the preference for the trochee ('*aun*-ties') over the stressed monosyllable ('*aunts*') is to do with the strain of Irish lyricism in Australian speech, and that since in Australia most women's names get shortened to monosyllables (Di, Pat, Lil, Dot, Peg, Val and Steph), the addition of the word 'aunt' produces an unmusical double clunk, the spondee ('*Aunt—Dot*'), rather than the preferred rhythmic lilt of the catalectic trochaic dimeter ('*Aun—*tie*—Lil*'). Three questions: (1) Have I understood you correctly? (2) Do you have any theories about why, in Australia, most women's names get shortened to monosyllables (Di, Pat, Lil, Dot, Peg, Val and Steph)—i.e. more diminutives, just like the word 'auntie'? (3) *What* strain of Irish lyricism in Australian speech? No, I'm sorry, I take that last one back. I'll try to listen harder for it. Honestly.

(d) The dry-cleaning bill: forget it. No chance. You should be more than able to afford it yourself, now that you no longer have to pay for the chairs, the plant, the white-board, the champagne or the call to Denmark.

As I have just remarked to Liz (who says hello), I am digging my heels in about the bathrobe.

Cheers,
Chris

December 17th

Dear Scott, just a quick PS to yesterday's letter in the form of a departmental memo to let you know two small pieces of good news. First: the bathrobe has turned up! According to Liz, it arrived at the Department in this morning's mail, addressed to the conference convenors. Liz was at the office early and picked it up, and by the time I got to work, she'd already delivered it back to the hotel manager, who refunded quite a lot of the money we'd paid for it. Liz was a wee bit vague about when and where the parcel was posted, and she's thrown away the postbag, so it all remains a bit mysterious. Nice things, those white towelling robes—Liz got herself one a month or two ago. It seems rather too big for her, which means that I can borrow it occasionally. God knows where the hotel one got to, or where it's been all this time. The second piece of good news is that one of your symbolic lemon pips has actually sprouted; we now have a tiny seedling in a terra-cotta pot in the tea-room. I am quite ridiculously pleased. Liz says to give you her love.

1

Years had passed—more years than Alison cared to count—but she recognised him immediately.

Her thoughts were elsewhere, he was the last thing on her mind, but the red flame of his hair singled him out across the crowded airport lobby, raised his face as if in haute-relief from a background frieze of faces.

He hadn't spotted *her*. He was pushing through the crowd, approximately in her direction, glancing back across his shoulder. A woman she had never seen before was at his side.

'Blue!' Alison called across the lobby. 'Blue! Is that you?'

The man turned as she approached, and smiled, and opened his mouth to speak—but the woman at his side spoke first.

'You obviously haven't seen Philip for some years,' she said.

'I'm sorry?' Alison stopped in her tracks.

'No one calls him Blue any more.'

'I don't think you've met my wife,' Blue intervened.

'Suzi—Alison Tully. You must have heard me talk of Alison?'

The wife offered her hand, limply. It was thin: a smooth, fashionable claw, encrusted with various configurations of cold metal and precious stone.

'I don't think so,' she murmured, and smiled, although the smile was also something of a murmur.

Blue was not quite so thin: still red-haired—source of the nickname that had fallen out of favour—and pale-skinned, and with those clear, childlike eyes. But there was a new puffiness to his face and cheeks. Alison recalled a boyish tennis-player, a Finn or a Swede, pale and puffy-faced, she had watched recently on television who, at the time, had reminded her of Blue.

'And this,' Blue turned, 'is little Sebastian.'

For the first time Alison noticed the small child tacking a loaded luggage trolley awkwardly back and forth across the lobby behind his parents. Of course Blue would have children by now, but she was still shocked; and to some extent shocked that she was shocked. Part of her was obviously not yet ready to grant him permission to father children with anyone else.

Even after all these years.

She bent and examined the child: 'And how old are *you*, Sebastian?'

The child's lips remained pressed together, a tight purse.

'Sebastian is five,' Blue answered for him. 'Aren't you, Sebastian?'

Alison forced a smile. She wasn't comfortable with

children; she found the conversations that took place in these circumstances inane. She tried to summon back some other noise from the standard adult-to-child repertoire.

'Have you come to Adelaide to visit your grandma?' she came out with.

'We've come to see both our grandmothers, haven't we?' Suzi informed her.

Alison felt her hackles rise, slightly. She suddenly remembered another Suzi she had known, years before: a school enemy who when she signed her name had always dotted her i's with a cute little circle. It was unfair, of course, but already she had lumped the two Suzis together.

'What are you doing here?' Blue asked.

'Seeing Brian off. To Sydney for a conference.'

'Brian?'

She paused, sensing that he too was a little shocked by the dislocation of an ancient world picture. He also remembered her as he had last seen her: frozen in that time, that place. There were still things in the air between them, she realised; a faint perfume of accusation, and guilt. There had been no clean break, after all; more a slow rending, a long, jagged tear.

'Brian is my hubby,' she said, using the ridiculous word for some reason she couldn't identify.

Blue smiled: 'Of course.'

'How long are you here for?' she asked. 'You must have a meal with us. Brian would love to meet you.'

Aware that she was addressing only Blue, she half turned to include his wife: 'Both of you.'

The woman spoke again: 'We're only staying the long weekend.'

'Then you'll miss Brian,' Alison said. 'But come anyway. You must come. Tomorrow night. Or the next, whichever suits.'

'Give us a call,' Blue said. 'We'd love to come. Wouldn't we, Suzi?'

Suzi was preoccupied with removing the luggage trolley from the tight grasp of little Sebastian.

'Where are you staying?' Alison remembered to ask as they moved away from her into the crowd.

Blue turned: 'At Mum's. Still remember the number?'

If she did, she wasn't prepared to admit it publicly.

'It's in the book,' she said. 'I'll find it.'

2

The table, a big, carved mahogany bench, a family heir-loom, had always been too large for Alison's tiny dining room. The three of them sat clustered at one end, like the last descendants of a once-great family. Suzi had brought flowers: a clutch of daffodils that spilled upwards and outwards from a vase on the far end of the table.

Sebastian was asleep on Alison's bed; the wine and reminiscences were flowing freely. Even Suzi, so remote and suspicious in the airport lobby, had loosened up. Alison had deliberately worn no make-up, and dressed herself in what Brian liked to disparage as 'gardening' clothes: a shapeless jumpsuit. The tactic had worked. Suzi has obviously decided there was no threat from *this* former girlfriend, still childless, but already gone to frump.

'Everyone said that Alison and I were meant for each other,' Blue was telling his disbelieving wife, 'when we first met at university.'

She laughed: 'I couldn't imagine two people more different.'

She was beautiful in a dollyish sort of way, Alison conceded: big eyes, small, upturned nose, hair teased thickly as if to render the head proportionately larger and more childlike.

'No, really,' Blue was telling her. 'It was incredible. We might have been twins.'

'Separated Siamese twins, we liked to tell people,' Alison said, and laughed herself, glowing inside with a warmth that was only partly due to the wine.

She remembered the game they had often played when they first moved in together, guessing how close they must have come to meeting each other in their childhoods, trying to fix actual dates and places when they must have passed within inches of each other, unknowingly.

'I played Joseph in my kindergarten nativity,' Blue, increasingly garrulous, was telling his wife. 'Alison played Mary in hers, same day, same year, a single suburb away. She was head prefect of her girls' school, me of my high . . .'

They had sat in the same audiences for interschool debates, in the same crowds at combined sporting events, and had never met. But fate had no need to resort to accidents, to chance collisions in the street. Their separate paths were always going to cross at university.

'Those were golden times,' he said, and seemed about to add something, but checked himself. *The best times of my life?* The words seemed implicit in his hesitation, or was it just wishful thinking on Alison's part: these were the words she wanted to hear? She poured out another wine, drowning, half tipsy, in nostalgia. She suddenly wished she had dressed up a bit, or performed a more careful cosmetic miracle—tried to remind him of what he had lost.

'So what went wrong?' Suzi said, half tipsy herself, impervious to any undercurrents.

Suddenly Alison had no idea what had gone wrong, or why it had ended. She felt Blue's foot gently pressing against hers beneath the table, and knew he was wondering the same thing.

'What went wrong, Blue?' she held his pale gaze a moment too long.

He increased the pressure of his leg: 'Nothing that I remember. I guess we should still be together.'

Suzi chortled, secure in her girl-charms: 'Don't let me stand in your way.'

'I'll get some coffee,' Alison rose from the table.

'I'll help you,' Blue offered immediately.

He picked up a couple of plates and followed her

through the swing doors into the kitchen, and immediately set down his plates and seized her from behind and pushed himself hard against her back.

'When can I see you?' he whispered, pressing his lips to her ear.

She half turned her head, rubbing her cheek against him: 'I'll be home all day tomorrow.'

Then he released her, and they carried out the coffee things and she was forced to sit with the width of the absurdly big mahogany table between them for the rest of the evening, allowed only the teasing pressure of that leg.

After he had left she groaned aloud with desire and impatience, her threshold of pleasure as low, she felt, as it had ever been: a hair-trigger. It was midnight, and she was drunk, but she rang Brian in his hotel room in Sydney, waking him and inveigling him into a conversation of obscene suggestions and longings: the thrill of long-distance vicarious sex tinged only slightly with guilt that she was using her husband for the first time ever as a surrogate.

3

'I've a bone to pick with you, Blue,' she said.

He watched her with his clear, Finnish eyes, surprised.

'Remember that book I gave you? On your nineteenth birthday?'

They were sitting each side of the big table again, just the two of them. The spontaneity of the night before was gone; he had kept his distance since arriving, having second thoughts perhaps. Had he made love to his doll that morning, she wondered? Worked his lust out of his system? She felt vaguely irritated—and remembered for the first time how irritated he had often made her in the past. His mood swings, his unpredictability.

She offered another clue: 'A book of poetry.'

Still there was no response. The sun poured through a northern window, unobstructed, weightless. Vapour from their two coffees eddied lightly and mingled where it entered the light.

'It had an inscription in it,' she added.

'I *think* I remember,' he answered cautiously, slowing his speech as if sensing some kind of conversational radar trap ahead.

'I found it after you left for Sydney,' she said. 'I was in a second-hand bookshop. And there it was.'

He groped for an excuse: 'They printed more than one.'

'Not with your name in it. In *my* handwriting.'

He screwed his eyes shut, and grimaced: 'Oh, shit.'

'I was *very* hurt, Blue.'

He made an attempt to explain: 'I had to leave town in a hurry. There was no time to pack. The company found me a place in Sydney, but it was too small. And they only paid part-relocation costs. I had to sell everything. Jesus. Ali—I didn't think.'

'I had to order that book from America, specially.'

She decided not to tell him the rest of the story. How she had gone home from the bookshop and angrily dug through her treasure drawer, removing everything of his. His photos and love-letters. The soap she had kept for years since their first love-making: the perfumed soap they had used, together, lovesick teenagers, in the motel bath afterwards.

He tried to regain some sort of initiative: 'I've a bone to pick with *you*,' he said. 'You never wrote to me.'

'*That's* why I never wrote to you,' she told him. 'Because of the book. I couldn't believe you would do such a thing.'

And instantly she felt safe from him—or from herself, from the drunken lust that had overwhelmed her the night before. The fire was dead, and could not be rekindled, not in the sober light of day. Other memories were coming back to her: the real memories, she suspected. A kind of morning-after immunisation was taking place.

She knew he felt the same, but suspected also that he would still go through the motions of desire, halfheartedly, out of habit. Or to save face. Especially now that she seemed reticent. He could never resist a challenge.

'What about last night?' he asked, and pressed her foot again beneath the table.

She removed her foot: 'What about it?'

'You felt something.'

'I felt drunk. It wasn't real.'

He seemed a little stung by this: 'Hubby is real?'

She was stung herself by the way he flung the strange

word back at her, and even more by the fact that he had stored it up all night.

'Just as real as Suzi,' she answered, and then couldn't stop herself. 'Tell me—when she signs her name, does she dot the i with a cute little circle?'

She couldn't believe her luck when he hid his face in his coffee cup, saying nothing.

'She does!'

After some time he looked up to face her, and smiled: 'I'm sure Brian is a wonderful man. You seem very content. I wish I could have met him. And told him how lucky he is.'

He had always had this knack, she remembered, of finding the right thing to say: of spoiling her anger, turning it back on herself, ruined, altered, loaded with guilt.

'I'm sorry,' she apologised. 'I shouldn't have said that. About Suzi.'

'You haven't seen the real Suzi,' he went on. 'I guess she felt a bit threatened. I've talked so much about you since the airport.'

She tried to hide her pleasure in hearing this: 'Another coffee?'

He shook his head and rose from the table: 'I must be off.'

'Before you go,' she said, 'I've something for you.'

She rose herself, and reached behind her and took a slim book from a drawer in the sideboard.

'Here—I'll give it to you a second time.'

He opened the book to the flyleaf and read the inscription.

'I'm sorry I sold it,' he said. 'I can't tell you how much. That was wrong.'

Apologising also had never been a problem for him. If he was wrong, he accepted it easily. She had loved this at first: she had never seen it in other men. But later . . . well, he was so *often* wrong.

'I'll be checking all the second-hand bookshops,' she smiled, trying to make light of her mixed feelings.

They walked to the door arm in arm, and she opened it, and he stepped out and glanced up and down the street.

'How are you travelling?' she asked.

'I borrowed Mum's car.'

'Where is it?'

'Around the corner.'

His eyes slid away from hers, sheepishly, before he added: 'You can't be too careful.'

Hearing this, her heart, still a little wayward from the night before, finally aligned itself with her head: she could almost hear a click. None of his smooth flatteries or apologies could change the fact that it was over. There could be no second innocence, no forgetting, no unlearning.

Or none at least without alcohol.

She suddenly wished she had been more friendly to Suzi, less jealous, more sympathetic. She might even have warned her of the sweet-and-sour road ahead, warned her that life with a man who was well practised in parking his car around corners, out of sight, might not be all it seemed.

But then surely Suzi already knew.

He bent and tried awkwardly to kiss her on the mouth. 'Bye, Ali.'

'Goodbye, Philip,' she said, and offered only her cheek.

In the mottled old bar of a certain peeling old pub, which I fancied for its mottled and peeling qualities, and for the brass rail that just held your foot up nicely—there was talk of it being knocked down to make way for some bit of engineering or other, so I savoured the mottled and peeling qualities and the brass rail all the more for knowing they would soon be gone—in this bar I met a traveller from an antique land.

The traveller was a man with a beer in his hand like the rest of us, and I would not have spoken except that my foot had struck his, and my elbow jogged his, as I had presented myself at the bar, and having apologised it seemed the companionable thing to do to exchange a remark or two: all the more so since I myself was a man in a suit, while the traveller was a man in a jumper with egg down the front, and I did not want to be thought stand-offish. A man in a suit has an obligation to appear egalitarian. It must not be thought that he thinks his suit gives him any rights.

I stood, then, a hand around my beer, a foot nicely held up by the brass rail. On this particular evening I would have chosen to drink something more numbing than beer, something forgetful, something in a small glass, something to stop my heart dead in its tracks. But having jogged the jumper and established my democratic sentiments by apologising, I could not then drink anything but the people's drink. I snatched it up somewhat when it was slopped on the towel, for my hand was shaking, I observed: my pale hand trembled, and I did not wish any beer drinker in a jumper to notice and ask why.

He looked, I could feel him looking, and to throttle his words as they rose into his throat, I offered a remark about the weather. I could not remember the weather, I could not remember anything much: I could only think of a sort of limbo outside, neither day nor night, neither fine nor foul. However, being a person who believed in the social niceties, I knew what sort of remark a blue suit (arranged in its cutting and stitching so as to make little of a paunch) should offer a jumper with a ravelled sleeve and egg down the front: 'Funny old weather,' I said, 'isn't it.'

One thing led to another, and after a small exchange of remarks, his vowels led me to ask where he was from. This is the way these things happen with the foam sliding down the side of the glass. 'And where would you be from, exactly, yourself?' I asked. He put down the beer, wiped his hands on his jumper, took his foot off the brass rail that had been holding it up nicely, and announced: 'I am from nowhere at all, mate. I am a traveller.' Then, shrugging as if bored with his own bombast, he added, 'From an antique land, a land that is out-of-date now.'

'Where, exactly?' I asked, for I was piqued not to be

given a straight answer by this swarthy shifty thick-tongued fellow, making patterns on the floor with his shoe, a worn and soiled tennis shoe that had probably never seen a tennis court. Was he ashamed? or fabricating? 'Oh,' he cried when I insisted, and men near us turned, beers in hand, to stare. 'Oh! There is no use telling you, my friend, you will not have heard its name, and it is on no map now.' He tossed back his beer as if it were some clear fiery liquor, and stared at me for a moment during which I wondered if he might fling the glass to the floor in a flamboyant Slavic gesture. I began to wish I had not spoken to this gent, who, I now observed, was as likely to be simply another reffo ratbag with a chip on his shoulder and garlic on his breath, as someone who might take my mind off things.

I wished now to change the subject and to quell other exclamations that I could see blossoming within the breast of the jumper: I had set him off, asking him where he was from, but I did not wish to hear about his history, or his travels, or his antique land. 'And what is your business, here in Australia?' I asked, not much wanting to hear about that either, but wishing to lead him into quieter waters. He did not hear my question the first time, and I repeated it carefully, making the word Australia sound as un-antique, as prosaic and brick-and-tile as I could, and making my question quite devoid of any symbolic or grandiose possibilities.

The reffo ratbag, or traveller, looked gloomy. He had not smashed the glass at our feet, but now stood with it in his fist in such a grip I expected to see it explode in his hand. 'Oh,' he said with a sniff and a wipe of his nose with the back of his hand. 'I am in the building racket.' He paused and flicked at the egg on his jumper. 'I am a brick-johnny. I hump the bloody bricks.' We were on steadier ground here, I thought, and hoped that after a remark or two about the slump, or the boom, or whatever was going on in the building racket—which might also remind this shabby person that a blue suit might only be making an effort to be polite, and not really wish a long conversation with a brick-johnny—I might be able to turn my back on him and set myself seriously to the business of drowning my sorrows.

But on the subject of bloody bricks this person was prepared to wax eloquent. 'Did you know,' he cried, 'how many bricks it takes to make up a wall? Did you know that bricks can sweat like flesh? Did you know that there is a hollow bubble of nothing in the heart of each and every brick?' He was excited again, and swelling within the green jumper; he came closer so that I could smell garlic and grout. 'I know these things. I know bricks backwards.'

Well, I am not a man to boast, and had no wish to set myself up in competition with this gent, but the fact is that I know a thing or two about bricks myself, and walls are something of an interest with me. If I had thought he knew, I would have asked this expert something that I had heard, and not known whether to believe: I had heard that if a person builds a wall high enough, the bricks at the bottom begin to run like putty under the pressure. I would like to build such a colossal wall, and see bricks turn to water.

However, small walls have been my destiny: I have built many small walls in my time. Walls are something I find soothing, and building another wall is a way of not being in the house. My wife, inside the house, behind her walls, is a good wife, but she does not meet my eye: she does not warm me with looks, nor yet with flesh.

A wall is a good work. I have made walls of bricks, and find it hard to believe that such a substantial item as a brick could be hollow as this man says. I have made walls of stone, flat slabs laid on their end, or chunks fitted in among each other: I have built walls of masonry blocks, I have built walls of rubble and faced them with fragments of marble and coloured stone. Ours is a garden of small walls, of walls within walls. The outer wall is my greatest monument: it is a sort of sampler of the bricklayer's art, with offset corners, edgework coping, and a pair of fine blocks beside the gate on which lions would squat if ours were that sort of street.

'Churchill built walls,' I announced, rather more loudly than I had intended, in order to break into the traveller's flow of speech, for he was still speaking of the bricks and buildings he knew backwards. The traveller was taken by surprise and fell silent: for a moment I felt myself to be a great singer in some opera, and the chorus had fallen silent so that I could sing my aria. But before I could sing—and besides, I had nothing more to say, or sing, on the subject of Winston Churchill and his walls—the man on the other side of me, another man in a suit, turned around and said, 'Yes, and he won the bloody war, mate, beat the bloody Krauts,' and laughed with a look of contempt at the egg stain and the ragged tennis shoes, and turned back to his conversation. He was one of those men who know what is what, about Winston Churchill, or walls, or any other subject you might care to name, a man quite sure of his facts, a man who knew he was going to Heaven, and in the meantime he would put anyone right about any fact they might doubt.

I was not such a man, not a man certain of the world, not a man sure of his facts, not a man sure of Heaven: just a brick in a suit with a hollow bubble at my heart.

I had set this traveller in motion, and it was now beyond my power to stop him: he was determined to tell me all. And I did not mind listening: none of these other beer drinkers, in their suits and certainties, could send the warm shaft of a word into the heart of my fear, but this man, who had seen so much, and whose head was full of some other tongue altogether, might. So I listened, although askance, as befitted a blue suit who had set off the clockwork mystery of a talkative foreign agent.

'I have seen the seven wonderful things,' the traveller said, and the blue suit automatically put him right: 'The seven wonders of the world, you mean.' 'Yes!' he exclaimed, 'yes! You know what I mean. I have seen the pyramids.' He thought, and his eyes narrowed. 'But I would not sit down on them, because the priests mixed smallpox into the mortar, did you know that?' He stared at me, his eyes dark, and I saw the skull beneath the skin:

then he set the skull into motion again with words, which made it once again a face: 'Babylon is in small pieces, in glass boxes, in a museum that is always closed for lunch.' He laughed so I saw his mouthful of gold molars, and he scratched his chest with the pleasure of his wit: 'Babylon is closed for lunch.'

'Pisa, oh,' he waved contemptuously. 'It is short, not tall, and nothing interesting except crooked.' He shrugged. 'Not wonderful, and around the base, you read the signs'—he spread his hand around against the air so the powdered cleavage turned his way, thinking he wanted another beer—'all in a row, Coca-Cola, Pepsi, Marlboro, McDonald's, Esso.' He looked into his beer, dismissing Pisa from him, but I was interested now, and said, 'And the Great Wall? Have you seen the Great Wall?'

He took a while to answer so that when he did I did not believe him, but I listened in any case. A lifetime of truth had been no help to me, so I would listen to a moment of something that was an invention. 'Oh yes,' he said. 'It is in ruins, you know.' He met my eye insistently, filled with a liar's conviction. 'There are two vast'—he gestured vaguely, stuck for words. 'Towers,' he said at last, 'two towers like a pair of pants. And there is a small bit of wall in between. Around is all decay, things half sunk back into the dirt, God knows what!' He was becoming indignant at his picture of the Wall now, but I nodded to egg him on, it was soothing me to hear of these wonderful shattered things. 'All around'—he made a level horizon gesture with his hand—'bare like a table, level like a table, not a soul, not a twig, just the sand, it is all wreck, what they thought would be for ever.'

I was running through the seven wonders trying to remember the others, but he shifted now and called for beer. He was ready for a change of pace and put his hand rather suddenly on the blue arm next to him, my own arm. 'Listen,' he hissed, 'there was a time when I would have been shot for this,' and he began to sing, in a strong voice that wavered with sincerity. It was of course a foreign song, with no words I knew, but with noble sentiments that brought his hand to the green jumper over his heart. It went on for some time, a sad sort of tune sighing up and down, turning over the words of the foreign tongue the way a stream turns over pebbles. The traveller stood at attention as he sang, his large dark eyes glittered with tears, and the muscles of his neck stood out powerfully beneath the skin.

I was mortified, the way everyone was turning to look, and the powdered cleavage looking dubious and hovering near the hatchway, in case Jack the publican would have to be called; I was mortified by so many eyes seeing that it was I who had incited this man to make a spectacle of himself, and bring the sounds of fir forests and wolves into this place of placid gentlemen in hats exchanging a remark or two.

I was mortified, but at last I was drawn down past my mortification; this sighing song drew me along with it so that I could see those dark fir-forests, those wolves snuffing after lambs, those castles of cold stone, those smoking peat fires in humble rooms where soup and rough bread waited in wooden bowls. And although the traveller was still a man whose chest swelled beneath an egg-stained jumper, he was also a man in cossack braid, a man in gypsy tatters, a man in homespun with the mud of his furrows on his boots, a man with waxed moustaches and velvet facings on the top of a prancing horse.

When the singing stopped, we all turned into our glasses to tide us over the moment. The singer took a long swallow, only himself again now. 'I was beaten for that,' he said. 'In the war—you, here, were safe—in the war I was beaten and burned for singing that song, my homeland's song, the song of my people. And I will tell you this, my friend,' he said, and thumped his fist on the bar so an ashtray jumped, 'I would remember his face anywhere, the way he sneered as he beat me, yes, I would know him now.' He glanced around the bar, but there was no sneering here, only lips pursing towards the rims of their glasses.

'And you, mate,' the traveller said, 'what is your past, tell me.' I spoke without care, and found that I had said 'I have no past, I am dying,' when I knew that it is the future that the dying lack, not the past. But it did not matter, this man was not a close listener. 'Oh, mate, we are all dying,' he exclaimed, as if it was easy. 'We are all dying every minute, mate, why, I myself am dying!' He laughed, it was a fine joke, and stood back to make a show of looking me up and down. 'You are a man behind a desk, mate, am I right?' he asked, but did not wait for me to say Yes or No or to tell him what kind of bits of paper were on the desk, he in the blindness of life was rushing on: 'Mate, you have it easy, but I do not complain, I am alive after the beatings, my country is gone but I am not.'

What a smile he gave me then! I saw him in his smile: I saw that he was a man who would never completely die. He was a man who would live to a hundred, a man who had a song, which he would teach to his grandchildren, and make sure they remembered it right. He would make them sing it when he saw them, and then make them laugh with rabbit's ears on the wall, and the way he could make his cheeks go inside out; they would laugh, and not forget, and make sure their own children learned that song, and how to sing it standing at attention, with a hand on the heart.

He was a man who would have plenty of faces at his funeral, and later there would be plenty of fiery liquor in small glasses that would be smashed, and there would be plenty of friends, countrymen, and family to shout his name in heat as the glasses shattered. And those grandchildren, sweet and dark, serious in their funeral best, would be called on to sing the song of his lost country which he had taught them, and all the friends and countrymen and family would grow wistful, tearful, melancholy in a proud glad way, weeping for their vanished nation as well as their freshly buried friend.

Talking to this soiled foreigner, I felt myself no longer part of the world that knew what was what about Winston Churchill and walls. I was joining the world about which those others exchanged glances and winked.

I, who would never have dreamt of allowing an egg-stained foreign ratbag to sing his national anthem to me, much less joined in conversation with him on the subject of the Seven Wonderful Things, had now slid beyond some wall or other. I was outside now, I was joining the greatest ratbaggery of all, the ratbaggery of death.

My mind turned to the things that would remain after me, after my time. When my suit was hung for the last time, what else would there be? I have no songs. I have, in addition to this blue suit, a rectangle of earth, on which there is a lawn and a house and a great many small walls. There are no dandelions in my lawn, no oxalis in my borders, and no aphis on my roses. There are no leaves in my gutters, for in my suburb we do not allow our vegetation to reach higher than a man. I have a wife who will make an appropriate widow, and four pairs of shoes, size ten.

My shoes will be worn by some gent down on his luck in a dosshouse, some other lucky ratbag will make the pockets of this suit bulge with his bottle, oxalis and aphis and dandelions will take root in my lawn, my borders, my roses, and my walls will crumble, slowly, back into the dirt.

A dullness is stealing over me now; I am sick of this histrionic traveller with his tall tales and songs, who will live when I will not. This traveller fills me with longing for how little I have that I could weep over losing. Now a screaming is beginning to swell in my head, and each object in front of me grows a small dark halo. Silence swells around me like a stain and I am afraid. It is dark behind my eyes, my fingers are numb, my body is becoming blind to itself. Somewhere beneath where I stand, I can hear a slow shovel scraping at earth: it is not in any hurry, but it will not stop until it has scraped into the earth, deep enough to make a hole fit for a man.

She can see the bundle reflected in the mirror. It's oblong and lumpy, dirty yellow in colour. The same colour as the shabby gilt frame of the mirror, that large and speckled oval, garlanded with ribbons and roses, cherubs and trumpets. It reflects her own face, too, round and pale like a drowned woman, with crinkled seaweed hair.

The woman in the gilt mirror breaks off a cherub's foot every time she has a birthday. She does it now, pinching the small gilded member between thumb and finger until it snaps off. She has been doing it ever since she began doing it. The *cloisonné* box contains a number of them. It seems likely that she will run out of cherubs' feet before she runs out of birthdays, but the unexpected may happen. It might even be welcome. Birthdays sans cherub's foot will lose their savour. Will she want any longer to pick up the *cloisonné* box and rattle in it all the footloose years? All the footling years, footfallen. Foot-noted. Footsore years and ten.

There is another possibility: that there are left as many cherubs' feet as she will have years. That when they run out so will her birthdays. There's a secret rightness in this that makes her ready to believe it. As though symmetry will be truth. She does not count the number remaining, that would be morbid. Some cherubs have had both fat little feet broken off, disporting completely footless among the roses and ribbons. Some have lost neither, some only one. The fresh white plaster scars age and yellow; with the earlier ones it is necessary to look closely to see whether they are whole or not.

In the mirror her hair has a greenish tint because of the dye in it. She would like somebody to say, what a wonderful colour your hair is, but doubts that she would believe it. She slides a hank of it through her fingers. Maybe, if she tries, she could see it as beautiful. She narrows her eyes, willing beauty to their beholding; a birthday is a day for beauty. Look at this lock, it has a mysterious faint green sheen of the hair of a sea-woman. A woman from Atlantis, Atlantis destroyed by the secrets it knew, look at the narrow-seeing eyes of the woman in the gilt mirror, she knows them too.

But the narrow eyes see the greenish tint of a starling's bosom, portly and worm-hungry, the rusty black of a scarecrow in worn-out mourning clothes. The wise Atlantean woman floats away and drowns in the depths of the guilty mirror. On its surface the yellow bundle quivers and squeaks.

She didn't tell the girl it was her birthday. She wanted to say no, I can't, it's my birthday, but the asking was in such unrefusable terms she'd acquiesced. The girl standing on her doorstep, etiolated as a weed grown under a rock, dressed in fusty black rag-bag garments and metal-studded boots yawning at the sole so you could see her grubby toes like quintupled oysters in a muddy shell. Saying please can I leave him there's no other way. Not in the flat by himself it wouldn't be safe. Please.

The child in the quilted carry-bag, mustard-coloured, shit-coloured in the context, faintly emanant of fashion and coddled trendy middle-class babies a long time ago, among the sprigged flowers worn pale the child has slept till now but now he wakes and squawks.

She takes him out. He's very wet. His yellow jumpsuit is soaked from armpits to toes. She takes it off, and his nappy, leaves him in just a short singlet lying on the bed. There are clean clothes in the carry-bag, and bottles of milk. The child likes the freedom from the nappy, he waves his legs and then is still as though waiting for grace, and pees in a strong arc on the bedcover.

She imagines him gilded, like the cherubs on the mirror, with crisp limbs to break off when the birthdays come, but he's not the right shape. He's limp and thin, sunless like his mother, with none of the juicy baroque flesh that even in plaster the cherubs enjoy. She rubs his legs, holds them for him to kick against, exercising them to make them strong. She had babies once, before they turned into children and then called themselves adults and left home. She knows what to do, provided she doesn't think, provided she disengages her mind and lets her hands do what they know, folding the nappy, pinning it, lifting the small body, supporting the lolling head inside her palm, rocking him against her shoulder when he begins to cry, a thin wailing like the wind in an abandoned house, jiggling on one foot while she sets the bottle in a jug of hot water to warm.

When she's fed him she puts him over her shoulder and rubs his back till he burps. A small runnel of milk slops out, as though he were a vessel overfilled. She's sitting on a chair in the bedroom with her feet on a footstool so she has a deep lap and is tipped back, comfortable, solid, safe. Gradually she recovers the repletions of baby-tending, the slowness, the idleness, the simply being. The communication of love on which a child grows. She doesn't know his name; it doesn't matter. Endearments are the only address he needs.

She wonders what his mother actually said. Of her babbling words all she understood was the urgency: she had to go, she had to have the baby minded. Standing on the step in her safety-pinned clothes and her gaping boots, pushing her carefully clotted hair out of her eyes. It occurs to the woman that the girl may not come back again, that the stammering hurry may carry her far away from the poky next-door flat, that the bottles and the clean clothes are the baby's dowry.

Gently she rocks, calm and solid like a heartbeat. She looks up and sees her face in the mirror, framed in maimed cherubs marking off the years, her face round and pale like a drowned woman, and fitting in to the curve of her neck the baby held close against the greenish-dyed crinkles of her hair. Happy birthday.

Early in the conference there was a party at the Vice-Chancellor's house, a large rambling verandah'd affair where the band, Solomon Islanders, set up their drums on the lawn, spreading their pipes and Spanish guitars beneath the bougainvillaeas. They were playing until midnight and Allen Watts, though he disliked parties, was staying on: it was one of the few occasions when everyone could mix freely—unagendered, though he was blowed if he knew why it had to be at a Vice-Chancellor's when the Peace Conference was sponsored by the unions of the region. Still, the band was good, and he was content to circulate diplomatically, dropping in, so to speak, on the Christians, the ecologists, the clutches of people from community groups, the M.P.s and the various activists. He moved down the garden, away from the band, though the music seemed to follow him—lilting, emphatic, so that he walked with some of the local blokes in mind—those that he had seen that morning strolling the dusty streets of the town; they had flowers in their hair and sang as they went; terrific to see even if it was hard to tell what they were singing, exactly. Here they were in large groups talking, their voices rising above the music, a merry monopoly at the marquee.

Allen sat on a sawn tree stump which faced the card tables that served as a bar.

They were a hotch-potch of fellows really: some in shorts and sandals, or in shoes and socks with white shirts, like public servants; others, the nucleus of the group perhaps, in jeans and T-shirts and dark glasses, looking pretty stiff about it, too, when they stood beside the fellows in lap-laps, whose necks and wrists clicked with beads and teeth. Nearest to Allen, on another log, was a young chap in sports clothes. He turned out to be a local journalist, crackerjack talker too, and very forthcoming about the hypocrisies of his mission education. He went on to describe the life of his parents who were back in the village; they were still hunters and food gatherers. Ten thousand years, Allen thought, ten thousand years you have come in a single lifetime! You know, he almost said, you are the first coloured person I've ever really had a chance to talk with. He was on the verge of saying something when the journalist turned to him and asked, 'Who are you with?'

Allen felt then, quite silly. He was alone: his wife and three children were at home. You didn't bring wife and children to a conference, even if it was the way some union officials would have liked to travel nowadays, to Baghdad, to Moscow, or Tokyo. He had always managed to get to conferences alone and stay on the job: 'Who was he with?' But it was not a personal question at all; the man was asking about the union. So Allen gave him a quick rundown on the union's long-standing involvement in the peace movement, adding modestly—

modestly, because he despised men who made a career out of left wing politics, that he'd been with the union for twenty-seven years and in that time had been to twice as many conferences, of which this was no doubt the most interesting. 'Why?' the man asked.

'Well,' Allen replied, 'it promises to be the most international.' The man seemed unimpressed, or was he distracted by something in the marquee? There had been some shuffling as they spoke. Allen wanted to go on to say that it was imperative that they agree, at this point in the campaign, on a general strategy for the region, and by general, he meant to embrace all the coloured nations, or the blacks, for that was the hard, naked word which people favoured nowadays; but he did not say this as the man was preoccupied. Allen paused. Amelia Rotan came out of the marquee. As she came towards him Allen felt the sweat at the back of his knees.

Had he told the journalist that it was his first real encounter with a black person, he would in fact have been inaccurate, carried away by the promise of the occasion. He probably knew Amelia Rotan better than any other woman, except his wife. Of course this was not saying a great deal, he realised that. He was not a womaniser. Over the years his dealings with women—as secretaries, office girls—had been born of a sexual neutrality, a blandness that he knew was disconcertingly reasonable to some, endearing to others. To Amelia, endearing: when they worked together the previous year—as President of the island's Labor Alliance, she had been posted to Sydney on a work exchange, and Allen had been asked to show her the textile industry—they had warmed to each other remarkably. Allen had promised her any assistance in the future; she assured him of a splendid welcome in her own country if he ever came. Farewelling him at the airport she went so far as to kiss him on both cheeks, in front of the blokes, speaking in the same vibrant key that she was using now, her arm stretched towards him, saying, 'Oh, you white men, you all feel the heat so *badly.*' She slipped the pink tips of her fingers into his hand.

'Terrific to see you Amelia.'

'You mean to say you haven't seen me before tonight?' At the first session the conference had elected her chairman.

'Yes, I reckon I spotted you somewhere.'

'I hope so Allen, I hope so.' Then she was obliged to turn away, address herself to a few compatriots.

The music now was energetic. Up near the band people were dancing, conspicuously lit by the flares which burned in flat bowls on top of tall stakes. In the pool of flickering light, a score of whites were doing their level best to limbo beneath a bamboo pole, successful writhings interspersed with sudden slumps. Allen watched until he was aware of the movement behind him in the marquee. There, amongst his own circle, a solitary black was going through similar motions without a pole. He went a distance slowly parallel with the ground without so much as disturbing his sunglasses. A good deal of laughter when he slipped, contortedly recovered, then in the same movement, and with a yelp, sprang as high as the tent flaps. Applause. Allen decided to top his drink with lemonade.

He went into the house most aware that he was really hoping for a chance to sit and talk with Amelia. He sat in the lounge in the vague—the vain—hope that she might actually follow him. Around the room people were engaged in animated conversation, but he sat on the couch, aloof, withdrawn, and idiotically conscious that he had not behaved as coquettishly as this since he was fifteen. So he took himself in hand and addressed his gaze to the room; inspected the brace of arrows in the amphora beside him, meditated upon the stuffed lizards on the mantelpiece, solemnly observed the wooden masks that hung, gapingly, above the chattering heads of the guests. Then he picked up a magazine that someone had stuffed at the back of the couch.

Flicking through it, he heard the drums step up their beats, the shrieks as the limbo became impossible, even the chattering in the room gathered momentum. It was as hot as billyo, and what the dickens he was doing looking at a magazine like this he did not know: for he had opened at a photograph of a policeman accosting two women. The women, who were bare-breasted and panic stricken, were white. The cop was black. On other pages he sprang into gruesome, obscene action. Allen consulted the cover of the illustrious publication *Deep Cop*, and he was tucking it back into the Vice-Chancellor's couch when she said, 'Doing your homework?'

All the cushions had yielded to take the fall of her body beside him. 'Who do you think reads this stuff?'

He flicked some pages for her amusement.

Amelia placed a hand on his knee. 'Boy,' she said, 'you would be surprised, mighty surprised.'

That rather set him back. Yet 'boy or no boy' she was still smiling, perhaps relieved to have escaped from the others? Allen swallowed irritation and offered her a drink. Yes, she breathed.

He hurried into the hall. Supplies on those tables were low, so he went into the kitchen. He had his hand on the fridge door when a man said, 'What are you looking for, brother?'

It was one of the chaps he'd seen in the marquee. Smiling, with large glistening pores.

'Soda water,' Allen said.

'Soda water?'

'Yes, soda water.' Allen opened the fridge. The man had several companions. One of them was leaning against the fridge, his arm draped across it.

'Soda water. Now, do you hear that, brothers? This cat wants soda water. A quarter to midnight, and this brother cat wants soda water.'

The man against the fridge smiled.

'But, I see there is no soda water,' Allen said.

'Here it is then, man.' One of them kindly passed him a bottle.

'Thanks a lot, mate. I was a dill not to see it.'

'Dill?'

'Yes, a dill. Couldn't see it for looking.'

'A dill. Wow, that's a weird thing to be man, a weird herb.'

Allen guffawed.

The man against the fridge said, 'What you laughin'
at?'

'Where I come from, dill means bit of a dope.'

'You don't belong to one of the big drug companies
do you man. You're not an agent for a multinational
pharmaceutical corporation?' They all laughed: they had
quite a sense of humour.

'No, no, no,' said Allen. He was relieved to be sparkling sober. 'Dill is an Australian expression for someone
who makes a stupid mistake. You call it goofy, I
suppose.'

'That right?' said the fridge man.

'Yes.'

'Crazy,' said the man who had passed the bottle.

'Next time I'll know where to come for soda water.'
Allen moved to go. As he reached the door, someone
said, 'Tell me man, is that all the lady wants, soda water?'

'That's what was asked for as I recall,' said Allen. 'I'd
better go and give it to her, too.' He reached the hall,
soda water in hand.

Then he heard, behind him, 'You give it to her man,
give it to her cool,' followed by hearty laughter—a high
cackle that it was sensible to ignore, and which he very
definitely did, taking the drinks into the lounge and
passing them to Amelia without comment. He sat down
prepared to give her his undivided attention. The conversations nearby went on without a pause. The scent of
Amelia's body was heavy and sweet and it seemed to
occupy most of the couch they were sitting on.

He did not see much of her for the next few days. The conference split into small working parties, each entrusted with the drafting of a model treaty for the nuclear free zone; that in turn to be debated by the full conference later in the week. Allen was happy about this: he preferred the small group to the mass of a conference hall. Though he could, when necessary, marshal demagogic skills, it was with small table discussions he had over the years consolidated his reputation as a skilled and principled negotiator. His only regret was that Amelia was not going to be part of his group; someone needed to check the pussy footing, as it included an Englishman from the Y.M.C.A., another church person, a woman from Canada, a New Zealand member of the Clerks' Union, and two Australians—an Aboriginal girl from Redfern, and a young bloke—bearded, fast-talking, who carried his gear in a string bag, from Friends of The Earth in Melbourne. A very mixed bunch, like the conference itself, Allen thought, though it simplified matters when they acknowledged his age and experience by unanimously electing him Chairman.

He set the discussion going by presenting the union's background paper on the position of the multinationals in the region. Fairly well received, though it was clear that the Church people would have liked to talk about something else. The next session he followed up with a short report on the international ramifications of inflation. When he had finished, the Aboriginal girl said, 'I don't see what this has to do with anything.'

She was a pleasant looking girl, young enough to be his daughter.

'Why's that, Gloria?'

She lit a cigarette. 'Ah, it doesn't matter.'

'No, go on,' he said. In the rowdy days of the student movement he had learnt to bear with the mannerisms of young activists.

'Yeah, go on Glor.,' said Cutter, the bloke from F.O.E.

'Just forget it,' said Gloria.

'Well, we will if you like,' said Allen, 'but . . .'

'Come on Glor.,' said Cutter. He had recovered the matches from Gloria and was lighting his own cigarette. Allen noticed that it was his packet of cigarettes.

'Yes, I think we should explore this,' said the Y.M.C.A. man.

Gloria was looking out the window. One of the working groups had transferred to the shade of a magnolia tree. Stretched on the grass the locals slid away into shadow.

'I was pointing out,' said Allen, 'that unless we come to grips with the basic economic forces of the region, what we decide to do politically is neither here nor there.'

'Yeah,' she said, glancing back into the room.

'Yeah,' said Allen, with a smile.

'What a load of crap,' she said.

The bloke from the Clerks' Union gave Allen a quick look. First time I've had a Grouper on side, Allen thought, waving down the Christian from Canada, who had risen almost from her seat.

'I think we can talk about this calmly,' Allen said.

'Too right we can,' said Cutter, 'providing Gloria has a chance to say her piece.'

Allen looked to Gloria. 'I'm interested in anything Gloria has to say.'

'Because,' continued Cutter, 'if we're going to get into economic affairs the unions have a good bit to answer for.'

'Oh?'

'If we get into inflation and ownership, we get into the energy crisis and Z.P.G.'

'Do you think I could have one of my cigarettes, while you're at it,' Allen said. Gloria was dangling her sandal from the grubby stub of her big toe. To give them a breather Allen lit a cigarette. Then he said, 'Working people . . . '

'Whites,' said Gloria.

'White working people . . . ,' said Allen.

'I notice you don't mention white women.'

'I would if you gave me a chance.'

'Can we get back to this draft resolution do you think,' said the Englishman.

'We certainly can, as soon as we establish a mutual understanding, because I do think that people like Gloria . . . ' He was still very patient.

'People like what?'

'People like you, or Cutter or any of you younger, better educated people with the skills to find out . . . '

'People like what!' she had raised her voice.

'Young activists, young Australians like yourself.' He was still prepared to give a good deal.

'What you mean is blacks like me, black women like me should go under to white men like you.'

'That's not what I said at all.'

'That was the implication, I'm afraid,' said Cutter. 'That was very definitely the implication.'

'That—is—not—what—I—said.'

/ 'Please,' said Christian.

'Please what, you bitch,' said Gloria.

'Gloria,' said Allen firmly, 'Gloria.' But she was already moving. She reached the door before he could speak.

'Fucking union bureaucrat.'

That evening, in the large dining room where everyone ate between sessions, Allen managed to share a table with Amelia and a few of her cronies. Cane cutters, nurses from the local health centre, a union official from the transport workers, all were so spontaneously enamoured of her company that Allen felt himself, his own animation, diminished, as if the sparkle of these local people was bound to set someone like himself back. He was glad when the others drifted off and he had a few minutes alone with her.

She had moved around the table to take the chair beside him. The dining room was almost empty, and from where they sat, beside the windows opening out on to the verandah they could see the others filing across the lawns in the twilight, heading towards the fluorescent bay of the conference hall. She was waiting for him to speak.

He might, then, have proposed a walk about the

grounds, a stroll down to the lily-layered pond, a counting of the toads which had arrived, while he procrasti-
nated, wart-eyed and bloated, on the far edge of the
verandah; he might have said, 'Hey, let's forget about
the shop talk for an hour and walk as far as . . . ' As far
as where? What exactly would he have been proposing?
Instead he said, 'Well, something new happened to me
today.'

'What?' She looked at him directly.

'To my face I was called a so-and-so union
bureaucrat.'

'Who by?'

He hesitated. Telling her made him feel worse.'

'Who?'

'One of our own contingent, as a matter of fact?'

'Who though?'

'The Aboriginal girl.'

'That's understandable,' said Amelia.

Allen looked at her sharply. She was smiling, but she
was not joking.

'Put it this way,' he said, 'it's a new one on me.'

'Oh?'

'To be told that to your face.'

'What was the so and so?'

Allen shrugged. He did not use bad language with
women. 'We'll let that one pass, hey.'

'Come on—tell.' She chuckled. 'It won't offend me,
you know. Or do you think it will?'

'A man can never tell.'

'What a gentleman you are,' she said, still smiling. She

certainly was a handsome woman. In normal circumstances he'd have bitten a person's head off.

The general session: Allen did not like the limelight, and sat well up in the hall, looking down on the platform—on the brilliant foliage of her green sari, the splash of her turban. She seemed to command proceedings with a turn of the wrist, a raised palm. At her signal the most garrulous delegate—for these fellows could really talk, Allen discovered—checked the clock and left the microphone like obedient children, while the next speaker, responding to her call, would be on the platform in a flash, launching himself with an alacrity that made most of the white delegates appear, Allen thought, well—appear insipid. And she was especially effective with the blokes unfamiliar with debating procedure. You could tell their preference for the open-ended village council, where they had all day to reach consensus, all night, if necessary to talk things through until the fences of misunderstanding were removed. But here they were bound by the pseudo trappings of Westminster models where time was cut up and procedures sliced on the assumption that tomorrow the world was going to be different, that things had to be done in a hurry. At times these blokes went off into anecdotes, or oratorically appealed to the gallery (the mob in the dark glasses were together in the top rows—Hawaiians, Allen discovered) and Amelia had to bring them back to the field. She did so with such deftness, such a lack of officiousness, that the discussions moved on with pleasing momentum, a great omen for the future of democracy in the region.

The guest speaker was Portuguese, a little man with a wispy beard and rimless spectacles, like Trotsky's. After the crushing of the guerrilla movements in Brazil he had been exiled to Geneva, and spoke at length about the illiteracy in the third world, the possibilities of combining political education with reading programmes for the peasants. It was good, strong, well thought-out stuff by a man with revolutionary experience, Allen thought.

But it didn't, interestingly, quite gel with the audience. Most speakers condemned the approach as a compromise with the bourgeois, and their vehemence tended to make the Portuguese chap pale into insignificance. From time to time, Amelia would urge local delegates to keep to the main line of argument—for they did go off in a way that suggested that not many had grasped the depth of the man's commitment to action, they seemed to think that he was living in Geneva by choice— but, for a while there the fury of some speakers, especially a few of the Hawaiian blokes, was sufficient to turn the theatre into an arena for tub thumpers. Gloria, he noticed, was up there in the gods, along with the most excited of them.

Amelia was calm. She seemed to have the measure of the Maoists; for that seemed to be the line, Allen thought, as one Hawaiian followed another to the microphone. Maoists or Black Power boys, it didn't matter, and he certainly did not in principle object; at home he was himself solidly to the left of the Labor Party, and while he was not a card carrier with any of the Communists, he was trusted and sought out by them. No, he didn't mind militants, as long as they let others have a go—which they did, responding in the end to Amelia's call, respecting the nobility that she brought to bear upon them, effortlessly presiding over the political realities.

Allen was—it was silly, he knew—rather uplifted by it all. He looked down on her and felt—well, he felt no longer eclipsed by the vitality of the occasion. He regarded her glistening shoulders, the tight green wrap at her breasts, and felt that he had, however recklessly, whatever it takes for a well married man to rise and confront a new woman.

At the end of the session he got up smartly. He caught up with her at the foyer. She was standing with a few Hawaiians. 'Well,' he said with gusto, 'things are really warming up.'

He stood closely beside her. He had, he realised, spoken rather proprietorially, asserting his familiarity as if they were already lovers, or at least as if his resolution, encapsulating the historically inevitable, had made it so. Swiftly she turned to him and said, 'I'm glad you think so Al,' then swung back to the animated, yet strangely expressionless faces of her own circle.

But the snubs, if that's what they were, were almost entirely forgotten the following day. At the end of another lively session the conference passed a resolution which irked Allen, irritated him with its shortsightedness, its negativity, its lack of common sense. He could see the logic of it, but it got under his skin. The conference, having noted the racist roots of the world's nuclear powers, went on to affirm ... 'that we, the Pacific people, are sick and tired of being treated like dogs. You came with guns and fancy words and took our land. You were not satisfied with that, so you took our language and raped our culture and then tell us we should be grateful. We want to tell you we do not like your way of life. It stinks, your brains stink. You worship dead things like your concrete jungles and now you bring your nuclear bomb and want to practise on us.'

Now, no one could deny the historical sense of these feelings. There was no doubt in his mind that racism was tied to colonialism, that colonialism was a product of capitalism, and that whites were, overall, the capitalists. True, but it was all put too forcefully, too crudely, and hardly the sort of thing that would make sense to the blokes back in Sydney. It ought to be raised with the others.

Between sessions he had a short word with Cutter and the chap from the Clerks' Union. They saw Allen's point of view, but Cutter remarked that the opposition to the nuclear industry was bound to become more militant in all parts of the world. The union bloke was more guarded, was obviously unhappy with the resolution, but Allen realised that here he was lobbying with a white collar worker who would sure as anything do him in at home. The Canadian Christian was even more difficult: she cited something from Corinthians and left the conversation for dead.

So much for practicable policies, Allen thought, hoping to get more out of people at the picnic—when they were out of the hot-house of the conference theatre. He would also see if he could get some sense out of Amelia, and having the shape of the conference uppermost in his mind came as a relief. He would be able to approach her on clear ground. Might even get to grips with that Gloria. A day in the bush brings everyone back to the field.

The agreeable picnic plan was to take the coach out of town as far as the base village. From there they would walk up into the hills as far as Tulsa Falls. A pig would be roasted in the ground, and some people from the mountain villages further inland would walk down to the spot to eat and dance with them. The Falls were a mile or so out from the village and the walk was scheduled to take an hour or more—depending on the party: plenty of talking time *en route*.

They were late starting. By the time the drivers had rounded up some carriers, village men and boys who grinned and hopped about as soon as they were nominated, and after some of the party had taken a look at the hills and decided it would be more sensible to have a quiet day at base camp rather than hike into the hot jungle, the dew on the coffee plantations had lifted, and the sun was at their necks. They walked out into a wide-awake morning.

Their path skirted the back of the village, ran past broken, sweet earth of potato patches, between some cane and across a frothy little stream, the village gully trap. They followed the stream on higher ground, then had to cross it again, this time using a footbridge that was a rickety joke amongst the English speakers of the party. Then, very quickly, they were walking into the jungle, where the leaves were sea green and dry, like enamelled kitchen platters. Early jungle: the sun still got to the bottom. Then the path narrowed, became wet, and everyone had to stick to single file, interspersed between the carriers who were setting the pace. As they began to climb Allen lost sight of Amelia who had started slightly ahead of him. Cutter, and perhaps one or two others he knew, were coming up behind. Even if they couldn't talk it was going to be a terrific walk.

The first stage of the track sharply climbed the hill then disappeared at the summit. The way down was a river valley and they picked their way across the high dry rubble of the old river bed, descending in a steady zig zag, the jungle climbing above them on both sides, the white fall of rocks ahead of them, and—a few hundred feet below—the main river, a glinting ribbon. Shouts and groans of self-congratulation from some of the party as they skidded down. Allen wore well, was actually quite fresh when they got to the bottom. Then they crossed the river, re-entered the jungle, climbed again, the sky a series of blue bolts through the canopy.

Climbing the second slope was damper, the track sloshier, as if, in the undergrowth on other parts of the hill, little streams were all the time running down from the top. The trees were green-furred and the vines weak with damp, and the track narrowed again. It was only wide enough for one foot to be very carefully placed before the other. Roots, rocks, clumps often blocked the way, so that you had to get up and over using hands, your tail pointing into the bush. Even before his first fall, Allen was glad to be walking with the carriers who never slipped, who kept going with light, even breaths, their throats barely pulsing. It was a treat to see these blokes in their natural habitat. He hardly minded, really, showing signs of wear.

At the top there was a small clearing, a sudden bald patch on the dank body they had been scaling. Allen sat on a rock in a small patch of sunlight, blowing, shutting his eyes for a few minutes to rest properly. Cutter and the others came up and shared the spot with him. They were chatting about the climb, but Allen was too hot to join the conversation. In ten minutes though—such was the beauty of the mountain air, the nakedness of the morning—he was greatly refreshed. He stood up eagerly when the carriers called. 'Quick. Let's go: the pig will be eaten if we do not keep moving.' Everyone pressed on in high spirits.

Allen let Cutter and the younger push go to the front. No reason why this sort of thing should be a race: dignity in steady progress, steady as she goes, a matter of holding the kneecaps in position while they ran down into even greener, thicker undergrowth. The back firm, hips braced, the green trunks of trees as lamp posts, he walked with a carrier in front and a carrier behind.

When he fell he went down on his backside and slid hard on the heels of the man in front. The complete idiot. He scrambled up, apologising. The carrier smiled,

trotted on, but then at the next scrambling section—
they had come upon a section where the track seemed
to give up, the jungle invaded from all directions—the
man dropped back and lent him a hand. He took the
hand through the most difficult sections. He was determined not to slow the game up.

Climbing, oddly, was easier than going down. The
going down threatened to run you out of control. It was
hard to anticipate the next step whereas going up, the
act of exertion, the will involved, made things safer and
more predictable. So going down, he concentrated on
working into the rhythm of the thing, pressing his feet
evenly, keeping his head erect, as if it was the easiest
thing in the world to know the lie of the land, anticipate
events, keeping his arms high when scaling the knotted
roots that continued to invade the tracks like headless
snakes. And it was a matter of trusting the pace of the
carriers, who continued to go through, down like sleek
canoes, barely slowing for him unless it was obvious that
he needed a hand. He appreciated that, their careful
refusal to coddle him, so that when the going became
especially difficult, he let them take his knapsack without
feeling too guilty at having a personal porter for a
weekday picnic. It was good having his body completely
free. They had been walking for perhaps an hour.

They had now entered dark, face slapping bush, the
real jungle. He had never been into jungle before. The
dampness was stultifying. When they stopped to rest he
spent his time whacking the leeches which had attached
themselves to the legs of his trousers. The carriers came

up and inspected his collar, and once or twice they flicked one out of his hair. Allen had always thought that leeches fixed themselves on to you good and fast. He was once again grateful to the men.

The jungle was silent. Stopping seemed to open up chambers in the hidden undergrowth, and when he heard the crackling, he did not know which way to turn. It was only a few yards away, but quite invisible. It seemed to be moving along slowly at waist height. It moved parallel with the track, crushing its way through the wet. Then broke into view.

Two boys, blackly naked, came out on the track. They carried wooden bowls and spears. A dog scuttled at their heels. The boys waved to the carriers, kept to the track a few more yards, then disappeared into the jungle, taking the short-cut to the picnic. Allen continued to blunder down the highway.

He would have liked to have slowed down a bit. He was at the same time exasperated with himself, making much work of a pleasurable walk, losing all opportunity to talk to people along the way. He would have liked to call to the blokes to slow down just enough for him to go at his own pace. But he did not, so fell once more; face down on a hard, slippery rock, only just breaking his fall with his hands. He lay there until the others helped him up.

'Christ,' he said, 'this pig had better be good.'

'You go, go,' said the first carrier.

'All in good time, mate, all in good time.' The fall had badly winded him.

'Go. Go.'

'Righto, righto,' Allen said. They meant it kindly. He pressed himself forward and up.

The man in front insisted on taking his hand. He clenched tightly: tough skinned, paddy fingers that were surprisingly soft once Allen resigned himself to this degree of assistance.

They went for a while as a pair.

Then, on the next difficult section, when Allen's arm must have been flapping inconsequentially, his other hand was taken by the man behind. Threesome. They walked then, climbing and descending, a small chain, an awkward one at first, then as he relaxed, gearing himself to interdependence, easily. To this extent he gave himself up and felt safer. Yet he had to ask, 'How much further?'

The man in front held up eight fingers.

'Eight minutes?' Optimism.

A repeat gesture. Did he mean eight minutes, miles, or bloody mountains? The man would not, could not, say.

They went on. He considered wrenching loose in order to demand more sense of them. The heat in his chest had knotted. Legs were numb. The uncertainty dragged upon him. It was debilitating. He ought to know, if this was the way they were going, what they were up to. But the men held on to him, pressing and urging him forward, reinforcing progress. If he broke loose he would fall hopelessly. They were champions to be so patient with him. Only a mug would resist. So he yielded once more and they kept, kept going.

He did fall again, but lightly, and it was well broken by the others. Then, without warning, they came out of the jungle into a clearing. They faced a magnificent rock cliff, at the base of which the waterfall pounded into a roaring rock pool. The water drowned anything anybody said as he approached, crossing the clearing towards the party. As he reached the cooking area he managed a wave and an ironic yell of triumph at his belated arrival. He looked around to acknowledge his carriers, but they had left his side, letting him walk the last part alone, as if he were strolling from a cricket field. 'Hi,' he said, sinking to the ground. 'Hi,' someone said, passing him a cold beer.

He forced himself to drink calmly. As he did, the sky darkened; he was not sure whether he sat in the sunlight or shade. After a few mouthfuls, his gaze steadied, the sky reappeared, lucidly blue; yet the very idea of talking sense with anyone that afternoon was preposterous. Amelia appeared. She offered him pig wrapped in the steaming limp rags that once had been leaves. 'Delicacies,' she said. 'Thanks,' he said. He put the food beside him, lay back on the grass with his eyes shut, wondering how the hell he was going to get himself to the bus.

What he most clearly remembered about the return journey were the globules of red that littered the track. They came upon them at regular intervals, and in the dusk of the jungle's afternoon light, they sat on the track like fat insects, big backed and luminously bright. Only when he trod on one did he realise they were not alive. They squelched beneath his foot and edged into the mud. They were walking in the trail of wads of saliva, betel nut dried red and chewed gummy with spit. Most of the party ahead of them must have been chewing it, accepting the offers of the carriers whose pockets bulged with the hardy stimulant. Allen wondered whether it was giving the others hallucinations.

He got to the bus just before dark. As he moved down the aisle to his seat, faces broke into grins, their lips purple and black from the chewing. He sat down. Of course he was slightly feverish by then. Everyone welcomed him, but all he could feel was the paddy fingers of the blacks who had supported him for each step of the return. At one point, it must have been about a third of the way back, he sat down on the track and insisted that they leave him there for the night. 'Come back tomorrow.' He had the interesting notion that a night in the bush would be an excellent preparation for what he had to say the next day. But the carriers giggled, and lifted him up; once on his feet he knew that unless he walked they would lash him to a stretcher and carry him back to the bus. So he pressed on, and arrived; due partly to his final grit, but due mainly to their insistent co-operation, their selfless, unthinking comradeship, their incredible sense of solidarity. At the end he could have kissed them—except that he wasn't French, or Russian! He was helplessly grateful.

He had sat down next to Cutter. Allen could smell the sweet herbs from the pig. Cutter made a confession: out

of sheer curiosity he had broken his golden rule of veg-
etarianism and feasted. 'Won't harm you,' Allen muttered, which inspired Cutter to spend the rest of the
journey discoursing on the universal inevitability of veg-
etarianism. 'Rubbish,' Allen said. 'They'll have you
killing the bloody thing next picnic.' That shut the
fellow up for the rest of the trip.

At the hotel he went to his room immediately; bare
walls, the dumb whir of the air conditioning, the slats of
blinds, broken, dusty—but a haven. He lay on the bed
and tried to sleep. Stilling the aches, taking himself firmly
in hand, he lay expecting to fall into a deep sleep and be
oblivious until the next morning. But he lay awake, still
aching, his mind prickling.

He stood up. He walked about the room, lay down
again. Hopeless. He went to the basin, ran water into
the palm of his hand, bent and sucked. Then he lay prepared to let the sequence run in his mind—the recapit-
ulation and the rehearsal, the succumbing to the
intersecting structure of past and future events. He heard
a cackle in the far corner of his bed: his own laugh! The
act as good as done he sank into sleep. And he slept
profoundly, confident at last that he knew exactly what
to say to everyone.

The next morning he arrived at the conference with
that special clarity which comes after a night fever has
passed. He fancied that the only after-effects of the hike
were his stiff legs and dull backache. The aching abated
when he gained permission to speak. Amelia motioned
to him immediately, and his legs had a new strength

when he took the microphone. The hall was packed. He was soundly prepared.

'DELEGATES.'

'Mr Watts,' said Amelia, 'if you could just stand back a little from the microphone.' She smiled, he smiled in return; she sat with her legs splayed behind the rostrum, cooling herself with a small cane fan, while he stood erectly at the microphone wiping his forehead with a clean cotton handkerchief, a few of the wipes perhaps moving in unison with her fan. He said, 'Certainly, Madame Chair,' then began properly.

He did not often listen to himself in public speaking; he was content usually to know that his voice was going out over a shop floor, or circulating freely in the sheltered squares between factories, coming back at him from time to time if the wind was in the wrong direction and the megaphone weak. Then he was fortified, bolstered, by his own baritone, and sometimes went on longer than he expected, the better to state the full position to the blokes; he did not like holding the floor, but he was prepared to do it when events made it necessary, unavoidable, just as it was now. The microphone was bristlingly clear, and each hole seemed to take his whole voice and throw it skywards towards the uppermost tiers of the theatre where a gallery of black faces bobbed, gleamed, flashed white when someone took it upon themselves to grin. He met a grin with extra warmth, projecting his voice to each tier, to the space between each set of shoulders, as he could hear himself affirming, recapitulating, heartily endorsing all national liberation movements in the region, driving and driving the point as a fundamental expression of his union's support of the conference.

'Hear, hear,' someone called, and not before time, the delay revealing that he really did have to lay out the perspective clearly and that he was monitoring himself with some effectiveness. He placed his statements in steady succession upon one then another tier of the hall, working from the top to the bottom rows then back up again. Then he took the audience in quickly with a side glance.

'Right on man, right on.' And with their support, he was able to elaborate, first of all on the extent to which the struggles of the labour movement are interdependent with those of the region; how, over the years, this had been true, and how, in the future, the prospect of combating militarism, colonialism, the nuclear lobbies, which was to point to nothing less than the power of international capitalism, or to be more precise, the multinationals, rested on evolving a strategy which would unite all oppositional forces in a combined political and economic resistance.

'Yeah.'

And secondly, how in all political struggles it was the easiest thing in the world to adopt the most militant stance, while knowing that it would not only be ineffective, but disruptive of more effective united campaigns, that there was often more to be lost in what Lenin, yes Lenin, delegates, a man who knew a thing or two about strategy—Allen paused, and a few faces did grin appreciatively at the light touch he was able to bring to polemics—what Lenin called left wing infantilism . . .

'Is the speaker about to move a motion?' Amelia, breathing into the microphone, seemed to be consulting the audience. Allen said, 'Yeah,' the smile and mildly American drawl infectiously caught from his supporters at the back of the hall.

A ripple of laughter at his quick reply.

'Then you have three minutes,' said Amelia, which rather put the pressure on him. He had to put the rest very carefully, deftly, with maximum regard for the range of opinion before him, the wealth of cultural back-grounds that the conference had brought to bear upon the issues. So he went on, even before the first call, to say that the draft treaty for a nuclear free zone had to be such that it could be tabled in most councils of the world, acted upon by most progressive forums in all parts of the world, be supported by rank and file members, by workers and peasants, workers and peasants in all parts of the world, the Third and the Fourth World, the Fifth World, if there was one . . . a flippancy which did not work, he had rushed into a gesture rather than a point . . . the point was that we have to endorse a strategy that can be acted upon by all progressive forces in all of all irrespective of nations and races.

He thumped the rostrum. He had said it. He looked about. Silence and smiles. He still had their support. Then she said,

'Tell us another one.'

Gloria. In the high tiers, amongst the grins and gleams of the Hawaiians.

'I will, delegates, I'll tell you another.'

'Come on, then tell us,' she called.

'Yeah, tell us man, tell us.' Some of the men were with her.

Allen looked to Amelia. Amelia was steadfastly regarding the audience, the fan fluttering at her throat.

'I'll tell you,' he heard himself saying, with a bright aplomb, 'that although it is the opinion of some delegates that the labour movement has a poor record on these matters . . .'

'Poor's right.'

'. . . the fact of the matter is that because we have been consistently opposed to all forms of exploitation . . .'

'Poor pig!'

Laughter from men at the back.

'. . . we have been opposed to colonialism in all its forms, to racism in all its forms.'

Until then his voice kept its buoyancy. He spoked cleanly to the wide black faces. He had even nailed Gloria—who could be clearly seen amongst the agitations of the militants she'd fallen in with . . .

'Poor pig!'

So that his mistake was to rise to the bait, to raise his voice and assert, leaning into the microphone,

'Look, there is one thing we should all realise . . .'

'Poor pig, poor pig.' Others had joined in.

'. . . is that racism has nothing to do with the colour of the skin . . .'

'Racist pig.'

'. . . but it has a lot to do with the sort of oppression we find under capitalism, capitalism in all its forms . . . '

'Racist pig, racist pig.'

Some men were standing, chanting and laughing. Gloria stood amongst them, one of them taken up by her support. Allen shouted. He took hold of the rostrum and shouted.

'And if you think that by passing resolutions which say that people's brains stink, that the brains of people like me stink . . . '

'Racist pigs stink. Racist pigs stink . . . '

The chanting rose. Allen stopped, turned to Amelia.

'Do you want me to go on?' He hissed.

The chanting stopped.

Amelia was contemplating her compatriots. She had drawn her skirts further up over her knees, was airing her thighs. The fan went to and fro. In the silence of the hall it quivered in suspension, sucking the air like the wings of a colossal dragonfly.

'Do you want me to go on?'

Had he lost his voice?

Then the chanting started again. It rose and did not stop until he was well back in his seat, until he had moved across the platform, reached the floor, made his way up the steps towards his previous place, mounting tiers that were slippery, especially steep, suddenly smeared with globules of red.

But then, worst of all perhaps, was the dissipation. The

next day, for days and weeks afterwards he was unutterably weary, consumed by an exhaustion that was quite new to him; in and out of chairs his body creaked, and walking from room to room was an expedition. The final session of the conference he was obliged to spend on the hotel settee. He lay almost comatose. The weariness so deep-seated that he was indifferent to the prospect of others thinking he had retired out of cowardice. When the news reached him that the conference had elected Gloria as one of three representatives to the U.N. Committee on De-colonisation he was simply too flat to speak. Then he felt ashamed at whatever had taken the stuffing out of him.

Amelia insisted on driving him out to the airport. As soon as he got back to Sydney, she said he should consult a doctor. Sitting beside her, he wondered how he did not have the strength to challenge her pretext that nothing significant had happened. He grunted. Grunts were about all he could manage; a non-committal glumness possessed him, and in the airport lounge he battled to exchange pleasantries with her. In the plane he sat like a simpleton. He was half conscious of his feeble powers of anticipation and at the same time anxiously confused about the extent to which a man ought to be able to foresee the structure of future events, but he could neither think straight about his recent history, or history in general. Fit only to slump in longing for the plane to take off. Finally it did and he had a rare, lucid thought: as the plane banked over the exquisite atolls and outlying villages of the island's capital, he said to himself, 'What if it bombed the bastards?' Then he lay back, mortified at the thought.

His condition was eventually diagnosed as dengue fever. Symptoms: severe head and backache, bodily exhaustion, fever and tendency towards psychological depression. The knowledge was relief. It helped make sense of a good deal. A clearer pattern emerged, the logic of which he could separate from his health that must have been, when he looked back, skewing perceptions all along; at the party perhaps, at the picnic certainly, the poor job he made of the last session, the agony of those last few steps back to his seat. Not to mention his gormlessness with Amelia! (All for the best though, he realised, in relating incidents to his wife.)

He told her the story in considerable detail. She listened with unfailing sympathy. He went over the events several times, not quite knowing what pattern he was looking for, only dimly aware that he was trying to account for the weird sense of having had, at the time, a telescope, an instrument which brought things clearly forward, if only he'd been well enough to fix them properly into position. But he could see that he was not making much sense to her: he could not bring the experience back. Here, surely, was a measure of the state he must have been in. He would stop talking and walk the house in a low, foul state of mind.

Dragging him further down was the task of preparing the report. A full report was usually tabled to the central committee, and he was usually adept at reports: he wrote them easily and they were often circulated at State and

Federal levels as constructive guides to policy and further action. One Sunday at home was enough for him to turn in an excellent report, but here he was with weeks on his hands at home and he could not sit for more than a few minutes at a time with the conference papers. He would sort through them for the twentieth time and have to lie down. He could not complete an introductory sentence without it buckling under the strain of what was to come. Could he take drugs to speed up his recovery? he asked the doctor. No: only rest would set him straight.

The doctor proved correct. Gradually he began to improve. He was able to get on top of the conference papers.

The difficulty, he then realised, was in shaping the report so that it did not unduly emphasise his own unfortunate, and—the more he had time to think the more clearly he realised it—idiosyncratic experience. The task at hand was to report on the conference objectively. He simply had to convey the range and vigour of the debate. He had to lay out the positions without giving right-wingers a chance to exploit them. He would have, admittedly, to convey some of the sectarianism to be found amongst some delegates, and to some extent comment on the problems of racism in the region. All this could be done straightforwardly. It was a matter of tact. A great deal still rested on maintaining a sense of solidarity.

Once on the mend, his strength came back very quickly.

At twenty-six, Leigh (who is Cass's cousin) is tired of playing the part of bad girl but the habit is difficult to break. She fell into the role quite naturally at puberty—parsons' daughters do—and played it to the hilt, and now it's like a skin she can't shed. The thing is, Cass decides, Leigh knows the ropes of badgirl land, and even though the terrain has become tedious (has in fact become as boring as the Sunday afternoon prayer meetings of their childhoods), Leigh feels comfortable there. And safe.

Safe? In a manner of speaking, safe; because Cass, watching Leigh smooth suntan oil on her bare breasts, knows that Leigh wouldn't even count the Hanlon affair. Leigh wouldn't give it any more significance than Cass would give a crunched fender or a smashed-up headlight. Annoying, yes. Inconvenient. But (shrug) these things happen, and besides, every life needs a little excitement, right?

Nevertheless, it is because of Hanlon that Leigh has called, and because of Hanlon that they are lying towel by towel on Bondi beach, with Deb making sandcastles a few yards off. Not the usual way for Cass to spend a Saturday afternoon these days.

'Come on, Cass,' Leigh had said. 'Live a little.'

'Well . . .' Cass hears herself again, all tiresome caution. She is torn between maternal anxiety and the pleasant pinpricks of risk (*Live* a little? Being target practice for Hanlon?) 'There's this finger-painting thingamy at the public library. I was going to take Deb . . .'

Leigh already has the stroller out. 'Deb needs to be *out*doors, not in. What kind of an Aussie kid are you raising here?'

'But will it be safe?'

'Safe as Sunday School. Hanlon's so dumb, he'll still be watching my flat in Melbourne.'

Leigh and Cass have travelled different roads, but they need each other. We're heads and tails, I suppose you could say, Cass explains to Tom. Though Leigh always counters: *You're* the wolf in sheep's clothing, and I'm the little lost lamb playing wolf to protect myself. (Black and white, Tom hopes; night and day.) At any rate, each plays Best Supporting Actress to the other's role. They grew up in Brisbane, which should explain a lot, and were fed milk and biblical verses in their highchairs.

When Leigh telephoned, the day before yesterday, Cass could feel the rush at the top of her head. 'Leigh!' She was laughing already. 'I don't believe it, I thought you'd vanished from the face of the land! Where are you? Brisbane?'

'God no! Not Brizzy.' Leigh hasn't been heard from for two years, though the family gossip mill has been murmuring Townsville, Cairns, Kuranda, Daintree, Leigh heading further and further north, heading deeper into shady reasons, bad company, offshore boats, *Darwin!* (in a shocked whisper), Cape Trib, Thursday Island (*grant her Thy mercy, Lord*), New Guinea! Then Brisbane again, it was rumoured. Someone had seen her at Expo, her hair un-gelled and unspiked, looking like a normal person, and she'd said *In sales*, giving a phone number. (Selling . . . ? No one dared to ask what.) At the phone number, a male voice went off in a shower of expletives and detonations about that fucking bitch who'd moved on, bloody lucky for her, and if he ever fucking caught up with the slut . . .

Lost traces, lost causes, lost sheep. The family sighed and bowed its head: *Remember, O Lord, thy wayward child and turn not Thy face away from . . .*

'I'm here,' Leigh says. 'In Sydney.' Excitement, sala-mander style, comes slinking in through Cass's eardrum and makes straight for all her nerve centres of tempta-tion. 'Listen,' Leigh says. 'I need a place to crash, it's sort of urgent.'

Cass picks her up at Circular Quay. 'God, you look— ' *terrible*, but what does it matter? Reinstated as bailer-out-in-chief, Cass feels giddy with pleasure.

'Yeah, well. I've been doing a bit of coke. Doesn't go very well with food.' Leigh lights a cigarette. 'How's Deb?'

'Adorable. You'll see in a minute. Tom's home, so I just rushed out.'

'And have you been a good girl while I've been gone?' Leigh asks.

They both laugh.

'What happened?' Cass wants to know.

'What do you mean?'

'You said it was urgent.'

'Oh, that.' Leigh shrugs. 'Nothing much. You remember Hanlon?'

'That bloke you were living with in Brisbane?'

'Him. We hit the road for a while, business you know, but I got tired of doing the dirty work and taking shit, so I—'

'What sort of shit?'

'Oh, you know, the usual. He hit me round a bit.'

'Leigh, why? *Why* do you keep latching on to men like that? You've gotta stop—'

'Yeah, I know. I've tried, I really have. I just can't seem to get turned on unless they're hellraisers. Anyway, in Brizzy, Hanlon set up this little dream of a deal, with me in the hot seat, natch, and it came to me that I could just take the money and run. So I did. Ripped him off for twenty thousand, and headed for Melbourne.'

'God, Leigh! Twenty thousand dollars!' Cass is appalled, her eyes glitter, she is full of plans. 'Well . . . '— she can't stop reeling from the enormity of it—'Well, now you can afford to, you know, quit . . . Quit, uh, selling. You can go straight, get an apartment here, finish your degree . . . '

'Never give up, do you?' Leigh says fondly. In high school, they had been neck and neck. Leigh had won a state medal as well as a Commonwealth Scholarship. A brilliant future, her teachers said, which turned out to be true in a way. 'Still,' Leigh sighs. 'Mackie was worth it for a while.' She winces, then smiles, then winces again, remembering Mackie, the ex-con she'd run off with before the end of her first year at Queensland Uni. 'About going back ... I think about it a lot, but I dunno after all these years.'

'It's never too late.'

'Yeah, yeah.' Leigh is wistful. 'I meant to, actually. Use the money for, you know, uni or something. But I blew it all on coke in Melbourne and last week I saw—'

'You blew *twenty thousand dollars*?'

'Well, not just me. Friends, you know. I threw a few parties. And I guess the word got round because last week—'

'It's all gone?' Cass was awestruck. 'That *entire* amount?'

' 'Fraid so.' Leigh twists sideways in the seat, leaning against the passenger door, to gauge the effect of her words on Cass. 'My coke's at maintenance level, though. It's under control.'

'I get frightened for you,' Cass says. (If Leigh weren't around, what would happen to the world on its axis? What might Cass have to do?)

'Yeah, me too sometimes.' Leigh laughs. 'Anyway, last week I saw Hanlon watching my place. He doesn't take kindly to being gypped, so I thought I'd better bugger of. Hitch-hiked up, left early yesterday and just arrived. God, I'm tired.'

She slept for fifteen hours. She woke, she ate something, she threw up, she slept, she sleeps.

Tom, looking into the guest room before heading for his office (the Saturday catch-up), says: 'God, it's the worst I've ever seen her. She's thin as a whippet.' Except for her tits, he thinks. In spite of himself, he's stirred. The unspiked black hair, longer now, shaggy and glossy, falls across a child's face. He kisses Cass brusquely: 'So how long is she planning to camp here?' Not that he's made uneasy by Leigh's presence in his house, not really. Because this is what Tom has observed: that the children of True Believers go one of two ways, and that there is a delicate ecology within families. To Tom's legal mind (he's a partner in a Regent Street law firm), Leigh is some sort of warranty.

Leigh wakes into high sun. 'Let's go to the beach,' she says.

'Well . . . There's this finger-painting thingamy . . . '

'Live a little,' Leigh laughs, exasperated.

And so they push the stroller along the neat residential streets of Bellevue Hill and down the long asphalt slope to Bondi. Cass is always mildly surprised that no one asks for her passport at that point where the buildings change so sharply.

Cass watches the way the men walk up and down where the sand turns hard, the way their equipment strains against their skimpy briefs, the way their eyes, not even pretending to be covert, scan the rows of oil-slicked breasts: the peacock parade on its mating route between towels and bodies. It still surprises Cass, the lack of self-consciousness on all sides. Bare bosoms are so common that if she rolls sideways on her towel and squints, the beach appears to be strewn with egg cartons, pointy little mounds in all directions. Big ones and small ones, floppy ones and tight little cones. She considers: if I took off my top, would Deb be startled? Would Leigh? (And if *Tom* heard of it?) A man walks within eight inches of her head, flicking sand in her eyes, and manages to spill beer on Leigh's midriff. Leigh sits bolt upright and her splendid bare breasts bounce and quiver.

'Jeez, sorry.' The man squats down, blotting at beer-wet skin with his towel.

'Oh, bugger off,' Leigh says without malice.

'Hey, an accident, swear to God!' The man turns towards Cass and winks. He has very white teeth and a dimple beside his chin. Cass has an urge to stick out her tongue, throw sand at him maybe, and a simultaneous one to run her fingers down through the hair on his chest, across the flat tanned belly, across the blue lycra welt to that bleat of skin on the inside of his squatting thighs. Baby skin, and she can't take her eyes off it. She'd forgotten this: the way sun and salt air and drowsiness and the smell of suntan oil add up to lust. Not lust exactly. More a sort of catholic sensuousness, an erotic languor toward the whole wide world.

'Got some beer in the Esky,' the man says. 'Wanna join me?'

'Sure,' Cass murmurs silkily, eyes meeting his. 'Why not?'

'Be right back.'

Cass stretches like a cat and reaches behind and

unhooks her bikini top. She squirts a glob of sunscreen into one palm and rubs it lovingly on her nipples.

'What the hell are you doing?' Leigh asks. 'Why'd you invite that jerk back here? We'll never get rid of him.'

Cass smiles. This feels good, very good: sun on her white and private breasts, it's like losing your virginity again, a lifesaver watching while she massages in the oil, a slow rhythmic caress, auto-erotic. Watching herself being watched, she can feel what it was that hooked Narcissus.

'A married woman!' Leigh is agitated, Leigh is suddenly and inexplicable angry. 'A *mother*! Put your clothes back on, we're going.'

Cass's eyes go wide. 'You've got to be kidding.'

'You think you're funny or something? You think you're—'

Then chaos comes in a skirl of sand. First, the Esky man is knocked for a sixer, the blue Esky sails in an arc towards the surf trailing cans of Swan Lager like so many bows on a kite tail. After that, it's helter-skelter: screaming, cursing, an assortment of missiles (footballs, cricket bats, a rubber skipping-rope), bodies lunging, bodies falling, blood. There are gouts of blood on the sand. Mothers scream and gather up tots and towels, heading for the concrete steps. Cass scoops up Deb and runs to the water. Children cry and don't know if they're crying from fear or from the sand in their eyes. People wipe their wet faces and find themselves sprinkled with blood. A little further off, a ring of boys gathers to watch and barrack. This is some fight, some thrill.

It's wogs! The wogs started it. They were bothering a white girl, they threw sand in a white lady's face, they kicked a football right into a little kid's head, a little white kid, he's got concussion. Theories fly as fast as punches, as thick as blood. *Go get 'em, send the buggers back where they bloody came from.*

On the concrete embankment that separates beach from shore road, the gasping out-of-condition mothers watch with bemusement, the way one watches a battle scene in a movie. Here and there a ghastly detail catches the eye, but no one can tell who is fighting whom, or who is winning, though it's broken beer bottle time now, it's getting ugly. Time to blow the whistle.

And so the lifesavers come in their tanned and bleach-blond ranks, barefoot, high-cut bikinis exposing their golden buttocks, skullcaps in place, oars from the life-boats flailing at air and insurrection. It's the jousts: there are pennants (the Bondi club pennant, and also—how did they come to be in the mix?—the pennants of the Dee Wy and Curl Curl clubs); there are broken lances, broken oars, there are gasping damsels in a swoon of distress, wearing nothing more than a scrap of fabric between the legs. The venerable order of the Knights Templar of the Bondi Surf Livesaving Club, aided by the Knights Templar of Dee Why, Curl Curl, and Collaroy, runs on the double and tilts at the windmill of Crusade.

Sirens now! It's a full scale rout, it's epic, it's newspaper and television stuff, there are squad cars, an ambulance, an ABC cameraman. (How did the news travel so fast?) And here are the police, truncheons raised, all blue-serge efficiency and ocker sentiment, here are the upholders of the Australian way of decency, *howya goin' mate? it's a free country, we don't mind wogs on the beach if they behave themselves but if they're gonna muck the place up, well they're bloody not gonna know what hit them, are they?* Ah, here are the police running on the double in their shiny black lace-up shoes, here are the police floundering through soft sucking sand, here are the Keystone Cops.

The wogs are fleeing. Born into Palestinian camps, winners of immigration and fitness lotteries, full of street smarts and survival instincts, the wogs are very very fleet of foot. There's a long line haring south toward Cronulla, single file: the wogs (there are only ten of them actually, mostly teenagers, Palestinian kids, a few in their twenties perhaps), then the swift lifesavers (about thirty of these), then the ragtag posse of original combatants (the local Bondi and Darlinghurst boys, beer-bellied, a little flabby, falling back), then the dozen sand-wallowing cops, then the cameraman.

Young boys hop and dance on the sand in a frenzy of excitement, little bookies in the making, calling bets. The line is thinning out now, it's single file with bigger and bigger spaces between the dots. It's going to be a clean getaway, no one's laying odds, the tension's gone. Towels and blankets and buckets and spades and bodies move into the vacuum. Someone turns a radio on. The sand settles quickly.

Where's Leigh? Cass, disconsolate and shaken, spreads her towel and looks about for the stroller and Deb's bucket and spade. Deb, paddling down in the water all this bloody while, is unaffected, and talks confidentially to the shells in her pink hands. Cass sees the stroller, which has travelled thirty feet or so and is almost undamaged.

One by one, the heroes—the local boys—return. *Good on yer, mate!* They swagger a little and flaunt their battle scars: the bloodied mouths, busted teeth, purple welts. It turns out to have been an argument about a frisbee, a Palestinian frisbee which had sailed right across a true blue volleyball game without benefit of visa or *may I please?* Directly in the frisbee's path had been the head of a local boy. *Bloody wogs come out here and think they own the bloody beach.* Little clusters of veterans, hobbling, grumbling, strutting, climb the concrete stairs and cross the street to the Bondi Beach Hotel.

Deb struggles valiantly up from the shallows with a bucket of water and empties it at Cass's feet. Avidly, she watches the sand suck at her offering, watches the wet funnel form. 'Where does it go, Mummy?'

'It goes to China.' A boy says this, a passing teenage boy who, as it turns out, is in urgent need of a listener. He is full of important information which pushes against the aching skin of his body, a body in which he is not at ease. He flops down and arranges all his arms and legs beside the child.

'You got a big bitey,' Deb tells him solemnly, running her small pink and wondering fingers across his cheek. A purple welt, like a brand from a poker, makes a diagonal from mouth to ear.

'Yeah,' he says, speaking to the child but needing her mother's reaction. 'I'm the one that got hit with the frisbee.' He waits. He hasn't quite decided whether to be victim or hero, he needs an audience, a sounding-board. 'I'm the one got the whole thing started.' Cass can see on the surface of his skin—the pulsing tics, the flinches—a *pas de deux* of swagger and self-pity. While his hands offer their services to Deb (packing the wet sand for her, tamping it into her bucket, tapping it neatly out into pristine castle) his toes clasp and unclasp sand. Beneath the backwash of battle, he is locating a surf of emotions. 'And then me mates bugger off to the pub and leave me.' The wound of his under-age status hurts like hell; he feels the purple scar gingerly, and Cass can see him translating, interpreting, deciding: he's victim, definitely victim, abandoned, cruelly neglected. His head is throbbing. 'It's me Saturday off,' he says forlornly. 'Gotta work shift again tomorrow. It's me only day for the beach.'

Cass touches his cheek. 'You should get that cut attended to.'

'Me dad's gonna give me hell, the police and all.' His voice breaks. 'You notice how they only go in gangs?' he asks bitterly, blinking hard, turning away. 'Those bloody cowards, bloody wogs.' He jumps up and runs into the surf.

Cass gathers up towels and Deb, and drags the stroller through sand. No sign of Leigh. The walk home is twice as long as the walk to the beach.

Leigh is in the enclosed back patio, sitting in Tom's favourite deckchair and drinking beer with a guest, a young man in his twenties, olive-skinned, very striking. A clump of the visitor's abundant black hair is matted with blood, and there is a dried crosshatching of blood around his right eye and right cheek. Cass remembers the moment when a cricket bat hit that temple with a sick *thook* of sound.

'Oh Cass!' Leigh calls gaily. 'This is Mahmoud Khan.'

Cass feels shy and ungainly in her own backyard. 'How d'you do?' she says awkwardly, extending her hand.

Courtly, Mahmoud Khan takes it and kisses the backs of her fingers. He smiles with his dazzling white teeth.

'I felt it was the least I could do,' Leigh explains.

Cass, confused, is remembering the single file running toward Cronulla and cannot figure out how Leigh, how this young man . . .

Leigh says: 'I hailed a taxi and followed, and when they ducked up to the road and across and into the alley behind the Khan restaurant . . . ' She shrugs.

'They never catch us,' Mahmoud says, and his accent is broad Australian, more or less, with unpredictable slides and riffs. He smiles his dazzling smile. 'We know Bondi like we know a woman's body, all the ins and outs, we got signals, the buggers can't keep us off the beach. Free bloody country, right?' With the pads of his fingers, he explores the crusted lump on his temple. 'We gotta go in teams, though, for protection.'

Cass fumbled for words: 'I'm awfully sorry . . . I'd, uh, like to apologise . . . '

Mahmoud Khan bows slightly, with only a hint of sarcasm, and Cass feels like a gauche schoolgirl who has just said something particularly banal. She blunders on nevertheless: 'We're not all like that.' Mahmoud Khan bows again and his movement seems to take in the wisteria arbour, the graceful white enamelled chairs, the expensive interlocked paving.

'Well,' Leigh says, jumping up. 'We'll be off.' Moving in front of Mahmoud, so that only Cass can see her, she raises her eyebrows significantly and smiles a little. 'Mahmoud's family runs The Khan's Kitchen. We're going to have dinner there.' She bends over to kiss Deb, gives Cass a hug. 'I'll phone,' she says.

On Sunday morning, Cass wakes at dawn and feels the absence of Leigh in the air. Tom is snoring softly. Is this contentment? Cass wonders dully, studying a long hairline crack in the ceiling. Is this peace? Against the crack, an image interposes itself: Mahmoud Khan is eating Leigh's buttered body. Cass cannot put a name to her feeling. She eases herself out of bed and pads barefoot into Deb's room. In the crib, her daughter's pale ringlets lie damp on the pillow and she bends over to smell the sweet-sour innocent morning breath—which is not entirely regular; which leaves Deb's parted lips in little syncopated riffs. Quick! Cass's hand flies to her own mouth to muffle a sound, an improper noise, some little peep of the body, a lurch of fear or loss, a sob perhaps.

She is almost afraid to brush her lips against her daughter's cheek.

Sunday morning ticks by and she simply stands there, watching, trying to imagine the unimaginable: Deb at ten, fifteen, twenty. Then she tiptoes from the room, pulls on jeans and T-shirt and sandshoes, and lets herself out the front door. Not certain why she feels furtive, *illicit* even, she nevertheless treads softly as a cat past the neat accusing houses, down the long hill, across the desolate patio of the hotel, to the deserted beach. She takes off her sandshoes and ties them together and slings them round her neck. She could be the only person, the loneliest person, in the world. Why? she asks the gregarious gulls. What do I want? She does not know the answer to either question. She walks, giving her heels and toes a little twist at each step for the pleasure of it.

Ouch! Stumbling, clutching at her right foot, she sees the hypodermic she has stepped on. She stares at it in a dazed uncomprehending way, knowing it has a meaning she must grope for. She thinks vaguely of Leigh and Mahmoud Khan and her daughter's cheek damp on its pillow. Then she notices another hypodermic, just ten inches away. Then another. And something else: condoms, she realises. She starts to count them, ten, twenty, thirty, more, just from where she is standing. She shades her eyes and looks about her. There are hundreds of condoms and hypodermics. In a high strange breathy voice, she recites aloud to the gulls: *And she sees the vision splendid / Of the sunlit sands extended* ... Nervous laughter breaks through her lips like bubbles.

This is the spot, she thinks, where Deb was playing with her bucket and spade.

In the distance, she can see the sandsweeper beginning its daily work, the tractor ploughing through sand, the mesh drum gulping in dreck and leaving a plume of pure sifted gold in its wake. She watches it, mesmerised. She knows what she wants now. She wants to go back one half hour in time, to be brushing her lips against Deb's unblemished cheek. She wants to go back two whole days, to the moment when she picked up Leigh at Circular Quay. She wants to go back a decade, a decade and a half, to the day when she and Leigh sat high in the mango tree and showed each other their first underarm hairs. Her foot hurts. She watches the sandsweeper, unable to move.

Over the roar of his engine, the sandsweeper shouts and waves. She cannot catch his words. She is thinking of something she has read about turtles: how thousands of them hatch high up on the beach and begin their mad race for the water; and how the gulls scream and dive; and how only the merest fraction of the baby turtles reaches the waves.

'There's a five acre virgin for sale.' Mother scooped up her avocado pear and drank her cocoa quickly. She pushed the country towns and properties into her shopping bag. 'We'll have a look later,' she said. 'Might be just right for Mr Hodgetts.' She looked at the clock. 'We'll have to hurry if we're going to get all the rooms done today.' Some days I helped Mother like today when I had a half day from the toy shop where she had got me this little job to keep me occupied, as she said, during the long summer holidays. I was screaming mad in that shop, it was so quiet in there. Like yesterday I only had two people in all day, just two little boys who looked at everything, opened all the boxes and took things off the shelves, spilled all the marbles and kept asking me, 'What's this?' and 'how much is this?' And then in the end they just bought themselves a plastic dagger each. I preferred to go with Mother on her cleaning jobs. She had all these luxury apartments in South Heights to do. We got a taste of the pleasures of the rich there and it had the advantage that Mother could let people from down our street in at times to enjoy some of the things which rich people take for granted like rubbish chutes and so much hot water that you could

have showers and do all your washing and wash your
hair every day if you wanted to. Old Mrs Myer was
always first in to Baldpate's penthouse to soak her poor
painful feet.

Just now Mother was terribly concerned over
Mr Hodgetts our lodger. He was a surgeon in the City
and District Hospital; he worked such long and odd
hours Mother felt sure a piece of land was what he
needed to relax him.

'He don't get no pleasure poor man,' Mother said.
'There's nothing like having a piece of land to conquer,'
she said. 'It makes a man feel better to clear the scrub
and have a good burning off.' All doctors had yachts or
horses or farms and it would be quite fitting for
Mr Hodgetts to have some acres of his own.

Mr Hodgetts never stopped working. He used to
come home clomping his boots across the verandah.
Mother said his firm heavy step was Authority walking.
She said it was the measured tread of a clever man pon-
dering over an appendix.

His room opened off the end of the verandah so we
had to pass it going in and out of our own place. He
needed privacy, Mother said, and she put a lace curtain
over the glass part of the door and she got my brother
to fix up a little plate with his name on. The plate had
to be right at the bottom of the door as this was the
only part they could make holes in for the screws.

'Who ever heard of a surgeon being a lodger,' my
brother said.

'Well anyone might be a lodger temporarily,' Mother

said. 'If the Queen came she'd have to stay somewhere till the council got a palace built for her.'

'Not in a crappy place like this.' My brother shoved at the window to open it and the whole thing fell into the yard.

'Well Mr Hodgetts hasn't said he's the Queen, has he.' Mother had to go out to get something for tea then. Thinking what to get Mr Hodgetts and my brother for their tea was a real worry.

'What about lamb's fry and bacon,' I said, but Mother said she thought she had better prepare something elegant like sardines. She was always on about the elegance of sardines and brown bread and butter.

'You'll be giving us celery and yogurt next!' my brother looked disgusted. 'You know I can't stand fish,' he said, 'and tell your surgeon he can take off his cycle clips in the house.' With that he slammed off out. Sometimes he was in a terrible mood, Mother said it was because he couldn't tolerate the false values of society and didn't know how to say so.

'I'll have to hurry,' Mother said. 'It's Mr Hodgetts' ear nose and throat clinic tonight.'

Mother always assisted Mr Hodgetts. He just presumed she would wash and iron his white coat and every night he stood with his arms out waiting for her to help him into it. The first time I saw them dressed in white with bits of cloth tied over their faces I nearly died laughing. I had to lean against the door post it was killing me laughing so much. Mother gave me such a kind look.

'Just you sit down on that chair,' she said to me, 'and

you can be first in, Mr Hodgetts will see you first.'

'But I don't want to see Doctor Hodgetts, there's nothing wrong with me.

'It's *Mr* Hodgetts,' Mother said ever so gently. 'Surgeons is always Mr not Doctor.'

That shut me up I can tell you. So every Friday I had my throat examined and Mr Hodgetts sat there with a little mirror fixed to a band round his head. He peered into my ears too and made notes on a card. Mother fixed up his medical book between the cruet and the tomato sauce on the sideboard. The whole thing was covered with a cloth. Every day we had to bake cloths in the stove to make them sterile for Mr Hodgetts. And Mother made and changed appointments for the people down our street in the back of my old home science note-book.

When Mr Hodgetts went on the night shift Mother took the opportunity to suggest we go to have a look at the five acres.

'We can go on the eight o'clock bus,' she said to him, 'and come back on the one o'clock and you can have time for your sleep after that. We could have a nice outing and take Mrs Myer, it's been a while since she was taken anywhere.'

Mr Hodgetts pondered and then said, 'That's right. The lists don't start till eight pm.'

'The list,' Mother explained to us, was the operations.

'Who ever heard of operations being done all night,' my brother was scornful. 'And they don't wear boiler suits in the operating theatre and who ever heard of a surgeon having his own vacuum polisher and taking it on the bus.'

'Well he can't take it on his bike can he,' Mother said.

It was true the wash line was heavy with grey boiler suits; every day Mother had this big wash, white coat and all.

'Just you hush!' Mother said as I was about to ask her something. 'And you mind what you're saying!' she said to my brother. Mr Hodgetts was clomping through the verandah.

'Oh!' I said very loud. 'I could have sworn I saw a cat hunched on the window.' Of course there was no cat there, I said it so Mr Hodgetts wouldn't think we were discussing him.

'Oh that's nothing,' Mother said, 'your Aunty Shovell once saw a black umbrella walk right round the room of itself.'

Just then there was a knock on the kitchen door and who should come in but our Aunty Shovell.

'Oh!' Mother had to sit down. 'Talk of angels!' she said white as a sheet. 'We just this minute said your name and you walk in through that door!'

'Nothing I wouldn't say about myself I hope.' Aunty Shovell dropped her parcels, lemons rolled from her full shopping bag and she sank, out of breath, on to the kitchen chair. 'Got a kiss for me then?' My brother obediently gave her a little kiss and Aunty Shovell smiled at him lovingly. She had a special place in her heart for my brother, she always said. She even carried a photo of him as a little boy in her handbag. Mother would never look

at it. She said there was too much shy hope and tenderness and expectation in his face.

'Who's our gentleman?' Aunty Shovell indicated the
verandah with a toss of her head. The firm footstep was
on its way back from the wash house.

'Anyways,' she said before Mother could explain, 'a man
who walks like that could never be a thief.' She settled
herself comfortably and didn't make any attempt to leave
till she got Mother to ask her to tea the next day.

In the morning we nearly missed our bus, as my
brother wouldn't get out of bed and Mr Hodgetts took
so long writing up his kidneys and then old Mrs Myer
was late too.

Mother was half under the bus.

'I think there's a big nail drove right into your tyre,'
she called up to the impatient driver. 'You better come
down and have a look.' Mrs Myer was waddling up the
street as fast as she could. Everyone just made it into the
front seats of the bus by the time the driver had climbed
down and been under to check the tyre which seemed
to be all right after all.

We found the piece of land but Mr Hodgetts did not
seem very impressed.

'Look here's a few fencing posts, probably thrown in
with the price,' Mother pointed out the advantages.
'And over there there's a little flat part where you could
put your shed and I'm sure these rocks could be useful
for something.' Her face was all flushed from the fresh
air and her nose had gone red the way it does if she's
excited about things.

'There's no money in wool,' Mr Hodgetts said slowly.

Mother agreed. 'Too right! There's nothing in wool these days and, in any case, if you put sheep here they'd break their necks in no time,' she said. 'And there's nothing for them to eat.'

It was a terrible piece of land, even if it was virgin. There was no shade and it was so steep we had to leave Mrs Myer at the bottom.

'Oh it's so fragrant!' Mother said. 'You know, land isn't just for sheep. It's for people to enjoy themselves.' She waved her arms. 'I'm sure there are masses of flowers here in the spring, you must agree it's a wonderful spot!'

Mr Hodgetts stroked his chin thoughtfully.

'I feel this land is very strong,' Mother urged, 'and what's more it's only two hundred dollars deposit.'

'Why pay two hundred dollars to kill yourself,' my brother said, 'when you could do it for nothing,' and he pretended to slip and fall down the steep rock.

'Halp! I'm falling!' he called and his thin white fingers clutched at the fragments of scrub. 'Halp!' His long thin body struggled on the rock face as he went on falling. He put on his idiot's face with his eyes turned up so only the whites showed. 'Haaalp!'

'Oh Donald be careful!' Mother called. As he fell and rolled we had to see the funny side and we both roared our heads off while Mr Hodgetts stood there in his good clothes and boots.

Suddenly we saw smoke curling up from below.

'Quick!' Mother cried. 'There's a fire down there, Mrs Myer will get burned to death!' She began to scramble down. 'Fire always goes up hill,' she said. 'Hurry! Hurry! We must stop it! Don't be afraid, there's my good girl!' she said to me and we got down that hill much faster than we got up it.

'I am josst boilink my kettle,' Mrs Myer explained from the middle of her fire. 'I sought ve vould all hev tea. I bring everyding in my begs,' she said. 'My leetle cookink is surprise for you!' I don't think I have ever seen Mrs Myer look so happy. My brother was already stamping out the little runs of flame and the rest of us quickly did the same while Mrs Myer busied herself with her teapot.

Mother had a lot on her mind on the way home. It was clear Mr Hodgetts had no feeling for the land.

'And another thing,' she said to me in a low voice. 'There isn't a soul for his outpatients clinic tonight. The street's all been. Wherever am I going to find someone else to come.' She seemed so tired and disappointed. And of course she would have extra to do at South Heights to make up for not being there today.

'What about Aunt Shovell?' I said. 'She's never been examined.' Mother shook her head.

'Shovell's never believed in doctors,' she said. And another burden settled on her. 'Whatever shall I get for *her* tea tonight?'

All through the meal Mr Hodgetts never took his eyes off Aunt Shovell. Mother had asked him into the kitchen as it seemed a shame for him to eat off his tray all alone.

'Mr Hodgetts this is my sister Miss Shovell Hurst, Shovell this is Mr Hodgetts who lodges with us.'

'Pleased to meet you Cheryl.' Mr Hodgetts leaned over the table and shook hands and after that it was all Cheryl. He kept getting up to pass her the plate of brown bread and butter. He kept telling her things too, starting every remark with, 'Cheryl, I must tell you,' and 'Cheryl, have you heard this . . . ?' And then he asked her a riddle. 'Cheryl, what lies at the bottom of the ocean and shivers?'

'Oh,' she said, 'now let me see, what lies at the bottom of the ocean and shivers? I give up!'

'A nervous wreck.' Mr Hodgetts laughed his head off nearly, so did Aunt Shovell. And then she said, 'Pass your cup, I'll read your tea leaves and tell your fortune,' so we all listened while Aunt Shovell predicted a long life of prosperity and happiness for Mr Hodgetts.

'Romance is to be yours,' she said leaning right across the table. 'Miss Right is nearer to you than you think!' Mr Hodgetts sat there amazed.

'Is that so Cheryl,' he said. 'Well I never,' and after tea he asked her if he could take her home before going to his own job.

'We never had the clinic,' I said to Mother when Mr Hodgetts had left for the hospital, walking Aunty Shovell to her bus on the way to his. 'Mr Hodgetts forgot about his clinic.'

'Never mind!' Mother said.

'I never knew Aunty Shovell's name was Cheryl.'

'Yes Shovell, like I said, Shovell,' Mother said.

'Is Aunty Shovell a virgin then?' I asked.

'Nice girls don't ask things like that,' Mother said.

'There's pretty near five acres of her whatever she is,' my brother said.

I thought Mother would go for him for saying that but she only asked him, 'Is my nose red?' as if she cared.

'Just a bit,' he said.

'I expect it's the fresh air,' Mother said and she began to sing,

How do you feel when you marry your ideal . . .
it's a popular song from my youth,' she explained.

How do you feel when you marry your ideal,
ever so goosey goosey goosey goosey,
and she laughed so much we thought she must be really round the bend this time.

Vic and Angela lived right in the town, down by the river. Wes and I lived out a bit, under the hill. As the summer came we spent a lot of evenings sitting out on Vic and Angela's front verandah.

Up at our place, the first that Wes and I had ever shared alone, the darkness seemed to lap around our ankles. The town sprawled out below us, a far-away marquee of lights. But here with Vic and Angela we were deep within a community of sounds. Frogs croaked in the still air by the river. Angela's little sprinkler whip-whipped by the gate. Half a block away Poddy Stratton's T.V. droned under its giant antenna. The girls in the schoolteachers' house behind us sent scraps of laughter echoing across the town.

'I thought they were having a night off,' Angela said. 'The big blonde one told me they all wanted to wash their hair.' A few cars went by. Most were turning up to the schoolteachers' house. The teachers were said to be a 'good crowd' this year. They joined in, they were having a ball.

No doubt we were being observed too, sitting there like a flashback in the light of a kerosene lamp hung by the door. There was a campfire smell from the mosquito coils that Angela had lit for each of us. Vic's was too close, he knocked it over reaching for a can. Angela relit it. While Wes kept playing, discreet runs that went nowhere, as if to himself.

Poddy Stratton liked to surprise us. Prowl up the verge so as not to crunch the gravel. 'Hod enough for you?' He'd pause by the gate as if he'd just seen us. Vic raised a can to him. Wes put down his guitar. They worked in Poddy's garage when it was busy. Angela pulled out a spare chair. She'd been in the town almost a year now and no longer asked 'Where's Maxine?' Everybody knew that by this time of the night Maxine Stratton would be under the weather. Poddy went everywhere alone.

Poddy sat forward, legs apart, and fitted his stubby finger through the ring of a can. His pull was vicious, froth ran onto the floor. 'Cheers,' said Poddy. We all sat forward a little in his honour, our visitor.

'Ye-es,' said Poddy, as if continuing a conversation, which in a way he was. 'It's gunna be a record summer.' His voice was pitched to reach the end of the verandah. He scanned us with his dark, ringed eyes. Poddy after-hours, shaved jowls and sports shirt sleeves ironed out in right-angles above his biceps, had a headmasterly air about him, a self-appointed distance. 'Useta think about putting in air-conditioning.' He wiped his long upper lip. 'That was before your friend Goof took charge of course.' He had assumed from the start where our sympathies would lie. 'I tell you what, everyone's gunna feel the pinch this Christmas. All your university types, your bra-burners, unionists and what have you. They aren't gunna like it any more than we do.'

He waved his hand at us, our bare feet, the ragged deckchairs, the cockeyed flywire door. Which side did he put us on now? We sagged back. Once I had taken him on, look there's a world recession, think what's been done for the etc, but I'd lost energy in the end, retreated—well anyway, it all boils down to, maybe it's just a temperamental, it's not that I'm really into ... (Wes, where are you? ...)

'I hope he doesn't stay long', Angela said in the kitchen. She was trying to light her little camper stove to make a cup of tea. 'He'll wake up Nat the way he carries on.'

'I hate it when we all just sit and take it', I said. 'Pod's pet hippies.' I muttered like this sometimes to Angela, when we were alone. Angela never seemed to hear. She was always doing something, providing something. I hovered behind her with the vague reflex feeling that I ought 'to help'. I tried to wash out some cups in the sink but it was full of drowning nappies.

There was a cough from the bedroom, and a long surprised wail.

'There!' said Angela. She paused on her way out. 'It's all Gough's fault of course.'

I was left, free to prowl. Since Poddy had come, you could disappear behind that beaded curtain in the country, 'women's work'. You only had to turn up with the tea. The flame beneath the kettle flickered near to extinction. Angela must be running out of gas.

Angela's kitchen was a lean-to, tacked onto the back wall of the cottage. The city owners asked no rent on the understanding that Vic would build a proper kitchen. He had laid the concrete slab for the floor. The dark end of the room still held the cement-mixer and a jumble of tools. Into the weatherboard wall, between the louvres, Angela had knocked a dartboard of nails. Here hung her pots, her mugs and nappy-pins, her dusty bunches of drying rosemary and everlastings. Postcards from friends in New Zealand and Bali and Nepal were wedged in between the boards.

From the doorway I could see onto the verandah. Vic now held his son, loosely, high up on his chest, his dark face blank as if to say 'this makes no difference to me'. Poddy was still talking. I thought how people in middle-age seemed to occupy their own features, they seemed overdrawn, stamped with use. Like babies, they were a different species.

I remembered how my own parents used to entertain on summer evenings. They called it 'having a few couples over'. For this my mother would sweep the porch and sponge down the leaves of her pot-plants, wearing a snail curl criss-crossed with bobby pins over each cheek. She would put out guest towels and at the last moment, as the bell rang, shed her shorts and tread into a skirt. Fussed. For a handful of heads on a lit porch—sniper-like my sister and I knelt and picked out favourites—the anecdotal growl of the men's voices, some woman's helpless nervous trill like punctuation, echoing out into the suburb. The vast starry night was undisturbed.

It was in the kitchen, if you padded out in your shortie pajamas, where the women got the supper, heads bent over the hissing kettle, that the evening's true exchange seemed to be taking place.

Were we after all so very different?

And, spying like this, would I have picked out Wes to like, to watch, *mine*, as he yawned, as his bare satiny shoulders curved guard again over his guitar?

The first thing we had done when we came to the farmhouse was to set up the stereo on its packing-case frame in the empty living room. At last, full volume. The wet paddocks, the stolid hill received Zappa, Jeff Beck, the Allman Brothers. This was the environment we were used to.

'10, 9, 8, 7, 6 . . .', shouted Pod on our doorstep one knife-cold night. 'When the hell is blast-off?'

Wes started putting on more and more country blues. Even if we were talking, after a while Wes's eyes slid sideways as his head chased up a beat. Those nostalgic voices were stronger than our own. In the mornings I would know that he had gone by the absence of music. These days he was leaving earlier and earlier for the garage.

I could not train myself to become a morning person. I had counted on this just happening in the country. Change of regime = change of person. Was this part of my work-ethic upbringing or was it really profoundly Zen? Funny how much they all seemed to be linking up; Bad Karma = Reap as Ye Shall Sow etc . . . I lay on the mattress on the floor and tried to think about this. The sun slanted in through the broken venetian blinds.

The Inner Light grows in Silence and Concentration. I had to shut my eyes not to read this on the sun-slashed wall, not to see myself, felt pen in hand, on our first night here. My own uneven letters mocked me like graffiti. Yet still I did not try to remove them, or even cover them up.

In the city, in the big house where I had met Wes, the walls carried signs like a political meeting place. Indian gods behind the kitchen door. Over the stove, a newspaper cutting of Whitlam and Barnard waving after they had announced the conscription amnesty. A big mandala above the fireplace in what had come to be called the meditation room.

I'd thought then it would be easier to meditate in the country, to get up, work in the vegetable garden . . .

The vegetable garden was no more. Such as it was, some lettuce-pale silver beet coiled up like flags and other, unidentified fronds, had disappeared entirely one weekend when we were in Perth. Tours of inspection now included not only the pen where we *could* have chooks, but the vegetable garden's graveyard, its frail wire netting looping among the grass, its scarecrow climbing canes.

Anyway, why were vegetables such an index of virtue? The eating of them, their growing, the disposal of them back to the earth?

. . . *In Silence and Concentration* . . . The 'S' was oversize, it seemed to leer at me . . .

The house was not silent. It was a hollow contained within a sleeve of animal life. In the ceilings and walls, under the floor, rats, cats, possums were they? skittered and thundered on ceaseless missions. The sleeve had holes. At night they gambolled in the passageways with the whispery abandon of out-of-hours children. Now the house itself creaked hospitably as its joints expanded in the heat of the sun. Crows bleated out in the paddocks. The day was cranking open before me.

Some time before we came here, this house had been dispossessed of its land and left to perch as a rental proposition on the crossroads between the town and the hill. A previous owner had tried to turn it into a city house, *à la mode*. You cleaned your teeth over a water-buckled vanity bench. The toilet had just made it inside, wedged in, not quite square, home-tiled next to the shower. (While the old dunny lurked outside among the grasses, its round white pedestal crouching in intimate darkness, its door for ever on the point of being closed.)

A breakfast bar butted across the kitchen on spindly legs where a big wooden table should have been. The fireplace had been boarded up. On the sink a single cup trailed the tail of a tea-bag. The guitar sat in the one comfortable chair.

There was only the country women's programme on the radio. It was like being home, sick, in the suburbs at midday, part of a community of grandmothers and invalids waiting behind lowered blinds. The heat here islanded you to the shelter of your own roof.

Outside the kitchen window the long yellow grasses marched up from the paddocks, consumed the fences, halted at the edge of the firebreak beside the straight gravel road. Although the day was still they shimmered and rocked, an imported pastoral ideal. I grabbed my shoulder bag and shut the front door behind me with a bang that sent Wes's Javanese wind-chimes into brief, oriental applause.

It seemed quieter out on the road. Just the regular swish-swish of my thongs on gravel, throwing up little ankle wings of dust, and a great airy stillness around me. Crows rose and fell in the distance. The sun swamped everything. The drab homespun belly of the hill was exposed, too close behind me. I walked fast towards the haze over the town. I became an engine pumping up heat. I was haloed an inch over with my own heat. I thought about Coca-Cola in thick glass bottles. I thought of shopping centres, as of great humming cathedrals. I thought of pine trees and of wading into the cold oil of the sea on a hot day. Although I had never been to a dinner party, I thought about soft lights and crystal glasses, and the fine picking up of lines of thought. Cheeses and wines, meat in cream, all that refined acid food that made you aggressive and decadent. And interesting. I trod out my own stale band of thoughts, oblivious to the landscape. While my higher mind slumbered, unsummoned for yet another day.

There was always a moment, as Angela and I turned into the main street, that I saw the town as distanced, through a lens, and our approach to it as something slow and heroic, a response to a sudden call for 'Action' . . .

The two women trudge on, faces to the sun, their long skirts blowing against their bodies . . . The pusher rattled a pony-cart accompaniment, a flimsy candy-striped city job that jolted poor Nat sideways, his towelling hat across his eyes, his fat fists clenched on either knee.

'Whòa there boy', sang out Angela, swooping down and straightening him, her long hair still damp from the paddling pool where I had found her, balancing Nat on her naked brown stomach. She and Nat smelled of talcum powder.

The main street narrowed down to vanishing point before us as it sped on into the wheat-belt. The shop-fronts rose into turrets and mouldings, the clock in the Town Hall struck midday against the white-blue sky. But as we entered the town, past the dusty Municipal rose garden, the wide street swallowed us, and the shops broke into their familiar sequence, the Co-op, Mc-Intyre's Newsagency, 'Verna' Hair Salon, the Post Office, Kevin Scragg's, The Bright Spot.

Why was shopping so consoling? A relief from the daily round of giving out, these small smooth purchases bumping against you, a newspaper, stamps, a bucket and spade for Nat, fresh bread, the first watermelon! It was like nourishment . . . especially with Angela who did not worry about confusing wants and needs, who rummaged and fingered passionately while the Co-op girls, school-leavers with engagement rings, clustered around the pusher. 'Isn't he *gor*-geous!' they cried.

The pusher rolled on, Nat unblinking, wedged among the parcels.

'Just a minute', Angela said, when we had nearly passed the butcher's. 'I've got to get a chop for Vic.' Vic was an unrepentant meat-eater. He added a chop or some polony to Angela's wok vegetables and united them with tomato sauce.

'I'll wait outside with Nat', I said. I did not even like to catch Kevin Scragg's eye as we walked past, his knowing salute, chopper in hand. He liked to ask you how you were finding life in the country, and to read your T-shirt, eyes lingering, for the benefit of the other customers. You knew, by the little silence as you made your way to the door, that you were going to be talked about as soon as the bell rang your exit.

I pushed the legitimising pusher back and forward under the window. At the kerb a girl in high-heeled sandals was stowing groceries and a baby into the back of her car. She gave me a quick church-porch smile across the pavement. Loretta Wells—one of the Wells. Did she see me as a sort of poor-white, a younger version of Mrs Boon, who shuffled in to town with a shopping trolley from out near the drive-in?

Through the window I saw Angela's bangles shiver down her arm as she took her tiny white parcel from Kevin Scragg's outstretched hand. The hand held, for a moment the parcel was a tug-of-war with Angela laughing and shaking her head.

'Let's go', she muttered as she joined me, her escape jangling behind her. 'I'm not going in there if he's on his own again.'

Poddy's garage was a block further down the road.

Out in the yard Wes's ute and Vic's Kombi were nosed up next to one another.

'Vic!' called Angela. We stood at the top of the driveway leading down to the black mouth of the workshop. A transistor was playing loudly in its depths. We waited. Vic came out slowly, paused at the door, took out his tobacco.

'Want to come to the Bright Spot with us?'

'Na—got a job on.' He squinted up at us over the paper bandaided across his bottom lip. He clicked his tongue at Nat. I cleared my throat.

'Is Wes about?' I hardly ever spoke to Vic. He wore footy shorts and workman's boots; he propped one shapely leg across the other, leaning on the workshop door. You could glimpse an earring through his tangled hair. 'Wes!' he called out over his shoulder.

Poddy's red beanie shadowed Wes at the entrance. Wes was carrying a coil of rope and the transistor. They were moving towards the yard.

'Any chance of a lift home?' I said.

'No way,' Pod answered for him. 'He's gotta follow me in the truck.' Wes lifted his shoulders above his armful and gave an idiot-grin. He called himself a grease-monkey these days. He marched off, Pod right behind him. With his pony-tail and his big boots he looked like the garage mascot.

'Wait at our place.' Vic gave a nod in the direction of the river. 'Have a sewing circle or something.' He breathed out smoke and smiled broadly at us, conscious that he might have gone too far.

'Do you see yourself living here always?'

'Always?' Angela frowned as if it was a word she didn't know.

I knew it was a low-consciousness sort of question. All because I couldn't bring myself to ask: Are you happy? I drew up hard on my strawberry milkshake. There was a lot of it, it tasted of crushed chewing gum, I felt it flooding through every cell of my body. *Daily renewed sense-yearnings sap your inner peace* . . .

We were sitting at one of the laminex tables in the Bright Spot, the traditional end to our shopping trips. There had been times, when Vic and Wes were with us, playing the pinball machines amongst the town's milling adolescents, that we had recognised the Bright Spot's fly-spotted nostalgic charm. Today we were the only customers. Most of the chairs were stacked on the tables up near the kitchen. A whirring fan bowed to us from the counter.

'Actually', Angela said, 'Vic's talking about moving on. He'd quite like to try opal mining up at Coober Pedy.'

The plastic streamers in the doorway swayed and kicked in a gust of afternoon wind, straight from the desert. A jumpy brightness was suddenly flung across the table.

'Do you want to go?'

'I don't know.' Angela pushed back her fringe and for a moment her small forehead stared out, white, next to her hand. 'I don't mind I guess.' She looked past me towards the door.

We looped our bags over our shoulders and prepared for that moment of darkness through the plastic streamers. There seemed to be a new silence between us as we set off again, into the glare of the long afternoon.

My parents had come to visit Wes and me. This time Evvie, my sister was with them. It seemed crowded in the kitchen round the breakfast bar. Outside the whole country spread, bland in the late afternoon sun. But for all of us the world had shrunk, temporarily, back to this, wary faces across a shadowed table. Between us was the cake-tin with the Highland Tartans border. We ate the cake from it over our crossed knees. Christmas cake, my mother's year-round speciality. Before she left I would give her back the tin, empty. It would come back full again.

Evvie didn't eat the cake. She filled in time examining the kitchen. She was seventeen now; all at once she had very long legs in very tight jeans. Her blouse, satin with little ragged caps of sleeves, was the sort of thing you find by a dedicated haunting of the op-shops. Her blank survey of my kitchen said *Not for me*.

'You've been making jam!', my mother said, smiling.

'Mm. Fig.' She would never know how I had flung the figs, my only crop, into Angela's big pot, bored, martyred, mad with itching ... 'You can take some home with you if you like.' With any luck my mother would forget. Though out of desperation for some proof of this life-style, fruits at last, she would probably persist in pushing the tarry substance across her morning toast . . .

'Still no job turned up for you?' my mother asked me. 'You'll be getting broody if you hang around too much.' Her laugh turned uncertain. She had to go on. 'I'm too young to be a grandmother!'

My father stirred. His big form was hunched up in one of our frail chairs. I hoped she wouldn't go further. I hoped she wouldn't say: 'Mind you, there's a lot less hypocrisy about the young people of today'. But she turned and looked out the window. 'Oh this poor dry countryside', she said. She sighed.

I knew how to look out that window, to see, defined against her, the grasses moving for a moment across that other landscape, *the country*, luminous in fading light, waiting for us.

'How's the guitar going Wes? Do you get enough time to practise?' My mother had turned to Wes.

Wes looked up. 'Oh I get around to it now and . . . haven't had a really good session for a . . . '

'He's been working really hard at the garage', I said.

My mother smiled at him, nodding. 'It's a wonderful chance to learn a trade.'

Then my father did something surprising. He uncoiled his hand from his elbow where it had seemed to be holding him contained. He stretched it across the table, his red, whorl-jointed hand, part of my former life, and picked up Wes's restless fingers.

'These aren't mechanic's hands', he said. He put Wes's hand down gently. He didn't look at anybody. He cleared his throat in a business-like way.

I was sitting, crease-eyed from a heavy siesta, on the front steps of the farmhouse. From time to time I ducked in through the open front door to put the needle back onto my favourite sides of Wes's records. This was something that I was too shy to do when he was home. I felt I probably liked them for the wrong, unmusical reasons, for the feelings they gave me, their melancholy landscapes: I waited for certain songs, to retaste that sensation of the right chord struck, again and again ... Bonnie Raitt singing 'Guilty' and 'I Thought I was a Child', Linda Rondstadt's 'I Never Will Marry', Randy Newman's 'Louisiana' ...

'They're tryin' to wash us away
They're tryin' to wash us away',

I droned, private, flat, stamping empty time on the step below me, calling up something to happen.

The step was still warm from the day, but the glare was gone. Lights began to trace the streets of the town. Dogs barked.

A pair of headlights was advancing up the road with the darkness. I heard the home-coming changing of gears. The ute.

'Did you listen to the news tonight?' Wes called as he came towards me up the path. 'Have you heard?'

'What?'

He stood before me on the steps. 'Gough's been sacked. Kerr's sacked Whitlam.' He wore the half-smile of the news-bringer.

'*When?*' I stood up too.

'This morning. It came through about midday. Fraser's forming a government.' He was edging past me up the steps. 'Pod's been at the pub all afternoon', he called on the way down the hall. 'It's pretty wild down there. You'd think they'd won a war or something.'

He came out again with his guitar.

'Where are you going?'

'They want some live music.'

'You're going back there? Now?'

Wes gave a swift loop of the ute keys over his fingers. His eyes flickered. I felt the wordless authority of his feeling, that chose when he came forward, or kept back.

'I'm going to play', he said.

The fire when it came was swift and stealthy.

On a day when the sun hung venomous, whitening, striking sharp light off leaves, I heard a distant crackling like a friendly winter hearth. I looked out the window and saw a low line of flames snake across the paddock as if it rode along a fuse.

From the verandah, down the hill, a truck was crawling up the road, the fire's keeper. I could just make out the figures of some men by the fence, and then they were lost in billowing smoke.

I thought: Do they know I am here?

The fire took over. The house was darkened. I ran from room to room shutting the windows. A roar

seemed to run under the roof. I heard the windchimes'
futile alarm.

I stood by the kitchen window and watched the flames
pass the house in vast erratic tacks across the grass.

It was heading towards five o'clock and he had missed part of the programme. A bit late, but never mind, there would still be plenty of good racing. He dug in his pocket for the three dollars, handed it to the woman at the entrance, and passed through the turnstile.

Finding a spot was the next question. The place was pretty full; the stand was crowded, and there was a lot of confusion around the gate opening on to the centre of the track where all the riders and their bikes were marshalled. There was no other choice but a position somewhere near the guard rail. From there, he could look down at the riders as they whizzed past.

He walked right round the edge of the track to where he found a gap among the people lining the rail. He spread his hands wide to take hold of the steel tube, and then leaned his weight against it. According to the announcer, there would be a delay before the next race— a junior handicap—was ready to go. The officials were still trying to get a full list of riders together.

He looked up at the sky. Clear now, but with Sydney summer afternoons, you never knew. It could always come down when you least expected it. The track had no roof and, being up here on this hill, was very exposed.

Wasn't there a better place to put it? He could never work out why they put it here where it could only catch all the wind. One good thing about being on a hill though, you could see the thunderstorms coming no trouble at all.

It was getting on for dusk. Twilight. The clouds over Botany Bay were streaked with purple, there was a weird light over the airport in the distance. From here, you could look down on the airport a couple of kilometres away—the planes coming down, going away, the lights, the radar tracking round and round, looking and looking.

A tap on his back, and then someone came up next to him. It was Teddy.

'Ray, old son! How are you?'

'Not bad Ted, not bad, how about you?'

'Actually, I'm a wreck, but I don't like goin' on about it. Know what I mean?'

Ted was always hard to follow, the way he was so quick. He never felt comfortable around blokes like him—they were always sending you up. But when they had both turned away from each other to face the track again, he did think of something to say to him.

'It's like a saucer really, like the radar dish over there.'

'What is?'

'This velodrome. The way it's turned up around the edge. I mean, you can see the likeness, can't you?'

He was conscious then of Ted looking at him sideways for a bit of a while—which made him feel uncomfortable. Then he heard him say—

'Listen Ray, gotta go. Son's racing this afternoon, and I've got to go out in the middle to check his bike. Kid would forget his head if it wasn't screwed on!'

Ted was gone before he could say anything back to him. Not that he felt put out or anything. He was happy to have been saved the trouble.

On the other side of the track, where the grandstand was, people were shifting about, getting themselves ready for the next race. Those who had cushions were moving them around on the concrete seats, trying to prevent the sore arse you got when you sat in the stand. Now the bloke with the hot dogs was starting up, fool that he was. The same bloke every week, yelling 'Doggies! Doggies! Doggies!' while everyone was trying to concentrate on the races. Some kids in the stand were making fun of him; they were calling out 'Doggies!' too.

The kids who were about to race in the handicap had started doing their warm-up laps. With delays like this it was going to be a long night by the time it was all over. He looked at his programme again. Later, the Aces would be riding a One-Hour Madison, and that would be worth watching. The last race he himself had ridden was a Madison, three years ago. Hard to ride, but good to watch. It would be good to be still young enough to start up in something like this, but you couldn't stay a kid for ever.

In the centre of the track, those who weren't doing warm-up laps were sitting around, some on the grass, some on fold-up chairs. The sensible ones had rugs over their legs. With that wind, you had to keep them warm, summer or no summer. It was getting darker, and the northeaster off the bay was starting to get stronger. The only plus was there were no clouds.

He spotted a couple of familiar faces out there in the middle. Chris King and Tony Sutherland. In the programme it said they would be lining up for the Madison too. They were kidding themselves, both of them were around his age, at least forty-five. You can only push yourself so far.

The early races had been boring, the youngsters weren't quick enough to make it interesting. They were nervous at the start and they jumped the gun every time. Restart. Restart again. The problem was with their dads, the way they held them at the line. Hand on the saddle, hand on the bars, all they had to do was let go of them at the gun; but no, they kept giving them these helpful little shoves—and that was cheating. He was glad, in a way, that he never had an old man to give him that sort of trouble.

Now, just before the start of the Madison, he occupied himself looking out over the rooftops, towards the airport and the bay. In his mind's eye, he marked out the expressway, snaking its way towards Kingsford Smith, from that line of orange-coloured lamps. A bright orange, they were; against the ink blue of the sky as it was at the moment, they made a pretty spectacular combination. It occurred to him, also, those colours made a Broadmeadow Club jumper.

The track lights suddenly came on and those colours were lost. The concrete circle turned white. The two straights, the two bends, the whole three hundred metres, all white. A Ribbon of Light—the same sort of thing as they had at the Night Trots, a Ribbon of Light. He was trying to remember the last time he had been to the trots when the bloke in the booth announced that the Madison was about to begin.

'I think we're ready ladies and gentlemen . . . This one is for two-man teams—a series of sprints for points and money. One rider goes for broke in the sprint each five laps, his partner takes it easy, then they swap over.'

He counted the number of teams on the programme. Ten, including Chris and Tony. A hundred and fifty dollars for the team with the most sprint points at the end—ten dollars per sprint along the way.

'There's the gun and, oh mate, is there anything like the Madison for go and excitement?'

Two young Blacktown riders began pouring it on.

'They're hoping to get a break on the field, folks. Pick up the sprint points with no competition. Very cunning . . . But the others are starting to peg them back . . . Never that easy, is it folks?'

He heard a part of the crowd in the grandstand yell 'Nooo!! . . . '

Just after halfway, and old Chris was obviously finding the going hard. He watched as Tony did the next three sprints himself to let his partner get his breath back. It didn't seem to make much difference—they were both starting to drop back . . .

Getting towards the end, they were running fifth on points. Way down compared to the leading team. They still had an outside chance, but they weren't getting anywhere. He focused on the lap board and began to concentrate. There were only three sprints to go, but for the old mates, a win or place was looking to be out of the question. They were still rolling around, almost as if for form's sake, he supposed so they could say they finished.

But then he saw it—a way back up for the two veterans in the field. He added up the numbers again; if they could win the final three sprints, they could still come out on top. And there was a way.

It was a matter of Tony, Tony who looked to be going the better of the two, sticking close to number eight's back wheel. He had been leading a lot of the sprint winners into the home straight, that one; he didn't have a strong enough kick to win them himself, but he was worth following for the slipstream. If Tony could stay behind him and then come around him in the straight, there was every chance of picking up some more points. It wasn't impossible. The hard part, he saw as he looked at the crowd around the gate, was going to be in finding a way to call that idea out to them.

The noise was too loud for him to try and shout across the guard rail. Besides, the speed they were going past, there was no way either of them would be able to hear him. He would have to get down into the inside of the track, where it was quieter, and he could get close enough to them for them to get the message. If he could get inside, he could wave to get their attention.

He pushed his way out through the people massed at his back and walked quickly to the gate further around. A bloke in a dustcoat stood guard; he had a red flag to wave at anyone who tried to get across while the riders were approaching.

'Hey mate,' he called out to him, 'I've gotta get into the middle.'

'Not now you can't. Race is nearly over.'

By the look on this bloke's face, it was obvious he wasn't going to make any exceptions.

'But I've got a message for a couple of the riders.'

'I said you can't get across.'

To make it even harder, this official-type then pushed his fat body against the gate, so that he couldn't slip across while he wasn't looking. That was that. He stood there feeling frustrated, helplessly watching proceedings come to an end. No one gave you a chance; even when you had a few answers, no one ever gave you a chance.

The kid from Blacktown and his little mate went on to win it—all of eighteen years old they were, by the look of them. Sixty-three points to King's and Sutherland's forty-seven.

Soon after, things began to wind up. He didn't want to get caught in the crush of people leaving and so went and sat on an empty seat in the bottom of the stand. From there, he watched them all filing out. At one point, he looked back and up at the rows of seats climbing away behind him. At the top of the stand, in a little booth up there, he saw the announcer switch off the PA and pack up his gear, getting ready to leave.

It was taking a while, but then he was in no hurry to go anywhere. He was happy to sit there and feel the breeze against his skin, so refreshing on a humid night like this. He watched the scraps of paper and empty chip packets blowing down the steps, swirling around on the track itself, like it was time for them to go too.

The last rider carried his machine on his shoulder out of the marshalling area. And following him, the slob with the flag went as well. Just looking at him walking into the tunnel under the stand made him angry; he imagined himself leaning across and putting an axe through his head.

Then, the lights went off. No one seemed to have noticed he was still there.

He would stay a bit longer. On a night like this, the breeze did nothing for the falling-down dump at Erskineville where he lived; it was locked in on all sides, a real oven. He could think of better places to spend a hot night. For instance, what was there to stop him staying right here? He could stay here no trouble at all. He could sleep right here under this grandstand, say, where it was sure to be cool.

The noise of the cars starting up and leaving the parking lot was coming to an end. It was all quiet at last. The only sound came from the rubbish, moved by the wind, scratching along the concrete. He sat there in the stillness for a few more minutes.

He was starting to feel a bit cold, and with that, knew

he really couldn't stay here tonight. When all was said and done, you could never just do whatever you felt like doing. If he stayed here, who was to say he wouldn't be bailed up by a security man, or a cop? All sorts of things probably went on here at night.

He got up to go, and, turning into the aisle, again saw the announcer's booth. It had no door, it was just a plywood box with a sort of canvas awning and open on both sides. He was curious about it, and thought he might have a look inside before he left. He climbed the aisle stairs, the half-dozen rows to the top.

It seemed strange that it was open like this. But then they probably didn't count on anyone being left behind like him; they did lock the outer gates at the end of each carnival.

He sat in the chair. The announcer's microphone was directly in front, screwed down onto a small table. He couldn't see any other gear in the booth itself, no knobs or switches of the sort you might expect. But as he moved his feet around under the table, he felt something there. He looked down and there it was, the amplifier or whatever it was called.

He put his hands around the microphone. It was like being in charge of something up here. The view over everything was perfect, he was beginning to get a good idea of what it would be like to call the races from this spot. It wouldn't be all that hard.

No, not very hard at all. He leaned over again and ran his fingers over the front of the amplifier, trying the various switches. One of them eventually brought on a little red light. He tapped the microphone—there was power all right.

'Ladies and gentlemen,' that's how the other bloke began—'Ladies and gentlemen . . . ' it was funny saying that. He heard his voice carry out and around the velodrome and then return to him. A very strange feeling, it was. It made his fingers tingle. What would happen if he went on? The velodrome *was* out of the way up here; he was pretty sure nobody would hear anything.

And he sure as onions knew what he wanted to say next.

'Yes, looks like King and Sutherland are coming back up through the field. King's got the right idea. He's sticking to that young bloke's back wheel like Tarzan's Grip. Here he comes . . . Yes! A sprint win to King! . . . '

He reran the race for himself in the darkness. Then, a few laps later—

'There's still life in those old-timers folks! King's done it again! Another sprint win . . . They've got it sewn up . . . Yes, there it is, a win to the veterans in the field . . . '

Just as he finished, he had this panicky idea that he should get up and run away. He got out of the chair and went down on his knees to switch the thing off. But in those moments of fumbling around under the table, the silence became obvious again. What was there to be afraid of? There was simply no one around.

He straightened up, and sat back on the chair.

Bugger it, there *was* something else he wanted to do; that is, something else he wanted to say.

He leaned forward and put his mouth close to the microphone. He started softly; with a mike all you had to do was whisper, and it did the rest.

'Ladies and gentlemen ... we've got something special for youse now. An old cyclist from yesteryear—I'm sure you all remember him—Ray Lambert. Yes, that's right, give him a hand. Well Ray is with us here tonight. We thought you'd like to see the old champ do a lap of honour—and he's obliged us ... Go on Ray, off you go ...'

And he saw himself do that three hundred-metre circuit, just like the old days, say after he had won his specialty, the ten-mile scratch race. One hand on the handlebars, the other free and waving to the spectators, or maybe holding a victory bouquet ...

For someone who knew himself to be not much of a talker, he was tickled at the way the words were coming out, the funny sort of confidence that had come over him. He understood he had been waiting a long time for a chance like this. He realised too there were lots more things he felt like saying.

'A couple of other things—before I get off. To the chap at the gate who wouldn't let me through—you're a bloody slug, mate. And a drongo ... And as for that dirty bastard mongrel who took my wallet last week—if I ever get my hands on you, I'll shoot you ... To all the shitheads who've given me a hard time over the years—you can All Go And Get Fucked!!'

A noise. He thought he heard a noise in the parking lot, a door slammed shut or something. Maybe the place wasn't empty at all, and he had been found out. He ducked down quickly to switch off the PA. Just being on made it give off a low hum.

He waited without moving. The minutes passed and he heard nothing more. He was coming round to thinking the noise hadn't been in the car-park, but probably somewhere up the street. Whatever, it was a dangerous game he was playing here, there was no guarantee he hadn't been heard.

And at last there was nothing left but to go—not that he wanted to get going. He had to admit to himself that he was a bit scared of staying here the rest of the night; he was just too much of a coward.

He looked out from the booth for the last time, out over the track, to the airport beyond. Such a terrific view from up here, you felt so on top of things.

There was the radar, still doing its job. He wondered if it was picking him up. Now there was a thought—was it capable of picking him up? He was high enough wasn't he? What do they actually look for, those things? Was it an electrical signal, or something more? If an aeroplane was just a shape in the dark, giving off a signal, what was he?

FOREWORD

The Crowther Galleries are proud to present an event unique in the history of photographic art. Here, in our galleries, we have the work of two great, though very different, photographic artists displayed in a manner that emphasises the aesthetic and historic parallels between them. This is no mere two-man show, but a tandem exhibition in which each photograph can be seen as a comment on another. Indeed, it is more a process than an exhibition—a process which begins essentially as a competition of photographic genius, a show more duel than dual, as if this tandem initially consisted of two bicyclists pedalling the one bike in opposite directions. Yet the process is ultimately one of reconciliation, where each photograph by Edwin Cranberry-Smith is closely complemented with a work by Ralph Lestrange, until the final monumental climax of the exhibition, a piece in which both artists overcome their individual egos in order to create together a work of consummate power. This exhibition must ultimately be seen as a testimony to the spirit of artistic creativity and mutual cooperation. The Crowther Galleries take pride in presenting this remarkable event, including the last work produced by these two great photographers before their tragic, if well-publicised, deaths.

EDWIN CRANBERRY-SMITH (1931–85)

In one of his few revealing moments, Edwin Cranberry-Smith has related the assumptions of his art to his child-hood fascination with collections. He has described his huge, rambling country home, the residence of many generations of children, in which he was the only child. He paints a picture of a labyrinth of a house, a vast emptiness of upper rooms inhabited solely by his col-lections, or, in his own words, 'a kingdom of dust and lightbeams where I was the only king'. He recounts excursions into the overgrown paddocks, his small, del-icate frame draped in billowing shirt and voluminous shorts, trundling through the forests of long grass. It was here, amongst a snowstorm of drifting spoors, that he would attempt to trap, in the gauze of a tall net, the butterflies to add to his collection. Indeed, he was a collector not merely of butterflies, but of collections, since the kingdom of which he was the only king, the maze of upper rooms, was a kingdom of display cases glittering with gelid lepidoptera, with the wings of pre-served hummingbirds, with dragonflies adrift in pools of amber, with beetles' shells pinned to purple velvet like iridescent brooches, with exotic stamps, medallions, stones, and any other thing that either he could find or his father could bring back from one of his long absences.

It is this early mania for the catching, preserving and collecting of living creatures that he particularly relates to his later photographic preoccupation, the collection of moments. For it is undeniable that the underlying motive of his art is the capture of the moment, be it fulgent or furtive, the recognition and the pinning down of timelessness amidst the flux of instants. For Edwin Cranberry-Smith, the only time is the evanescent, yet ever-present moment, and the only universal art is that which can capture the truth and intensity of the infinitely subtle present.

Thus, just as he has presented himself as the child, unspeaking, who listens at the dinner table, who watches silently at doors and windows, as a child's eye bright in a chink of light from another room, so he has said that the collector cannot catch if he is caught, and the artist cannot know if he is known. In following this injunction he has courted privacy and anonymity almost to the point of seeking to become invisible. His elusiveness is not, as some resentful critics have suggested, a contrived programme of self-mystification, but an integral part of his artistic method. In pursuance of this principle, he has cultivated a style of dress, of speech, indeed an overall appearance and manner which have rendered him forgettable, and he suggests that the greatest compliment a stranger can pay him is to ask his name seconds after introduction. If there is one thing that may please Edwin Cranberry-Smith still more than being forgotten, it is not to be seen at all, and he may secrete himself for days on end in some concealed position, in order to capture the magical moments that we can witness through his lens during the course of this exhibition.

RALPH LESTRANGE (1936–85)

Ralph Lestrange, were he alive today, would doubtless appreciate the circumstances of his death. What journalist could fail to do so? And surely Ralph Lestrange is the consummate photographic journalist. Indeed, it might have seemed inconceivable that a populist such as he could possibly be included in an exhibition with an artist of the calibre of Edwin Cranberry-Smith, yet there are many underlying similarities, as this dual project will inevitably reveal to those who approach it with a minimum of preconceptions.

These parallels are perhaps best indicated by Ralph Lestrange's attempts to trace his photographic bias back to the days of his midwestern childhood. Like Edwin Cranberry-Smith's pursuit of insects, his recollections also suggest the hunt as photography's true metaphor, though for him the image is a shade more predatory. Here we have stories of a boy in faded jeans, roaming shadowless at noon across a prairie. It is this barefoot boy, accompanied only by his hound-dog and the rattling music of the prairie snakes, whose hunting of coyotes and wild pigs is seen as the training ground for all that tracking down of royalty, movie stars and millionaires, which was to be the trademark of the man's career.

It is quite probable that his demise will make many a

famous heart now beat a bit more freely, since among those ruthless pursuers of the great he was supreme, with a near supernatural ability to flush out the most reclusive of tycoons, to cast a flashbulb's light upon the shadiest of deals, to catch beauties out in ugly situations, and to expose nobility in moments far from noble. At various times he has been both nemesis and confidant of Princess Caroline and Jacqueline Onassis; he was both perpetrator and recorder of the notorious episode seen through the porthole of Bernard Bauer's yacht, while his photographs of Howard Hughes and Marlene Dietrich are legendary.

For Edwin Cranberry-Smith one might say that photography is art as revelation, while for Ralph Lestrange it might be more accurate to call it 'art as compromise', or perhaps—from the subject's point of view at least—'the art of being compromised'. Yet, for all but those immune to the obvious, his work has increasingly displayed a capacity to capture the life within his portraits of social discomfiture, at times revealing a brooding moral vision. As this exhibition will demonstrate, there is no better argument for the unities that underlie the work of these two artists than the work itself.

Don't fuck up now, keep him tagged, Lestrange, 'cause he's wily as an old fox, and by the look of the hard-hat on that file-clerk's head of his, today's the day all right. There he goes again, one more glance right up the scaffolding he's been staking out the last few days, eyes twinkling away, reading the light, the distance, hidy-holes, those little twin moustaches of his twitching up and down like sparrows in buckshot, walking faster now, Leica cuffed inside his hand,

so move it now, c'mon Lestrange, don't lose the spoor.
This little Pentax sits sweet on the hip, squat as a sidearm,
no telephoto lens today, like a racoon shoot with an elephant gun, no sir, 'cause this one's for the purist, no fancy
lenses from half across the city, no waiting just to snap him
any old how, yes folks, it's one for the aficionados. It's
getting him where he's at, in the act, the legendary
moment, Mr Cranberry-Smith, old chap, the instant of your
shot, whatever the hell your subject is, 'cause there you go,
right into the goddamn cage and up, whatever you're going
to trap inside that timeless bloody moment, a conspiracy of
riggers? dogmen shooting crap a thousand feet up? and up
is where you go, old bean, right up between the girders.

CATALOGUE OF PRINTS

l.a.　*Drunk at The Barley Castle. Sydney, 1984.*
Ilford Galerie paper, 28.0 × 28.6.
Leica camera.

　　This is a scene outside an early-opening
hotel, as is confirmed by the semi-focused
sign 'Breakfast heart-starters' immediately
behind the central figure. This figure appears
to be oblivious to the traffic before him and
the industrial smokestacks at his back. His
pouched and broken face, rising above the
blur of passing cars and caught in a burst of
sunlight, embodies the familiar tensions
implicit in most of the pictures by Edwin
Cranberry-Smith. In this case the desperate,
loose-lipped grimace of the mouth, the eyes'

moist gaze towards the sky, suggest a state somewhere between religious transport and existential nausea, and present us with a paradigm of Cranberrian paradox.

l.b.   *Drunk at The Barley Castle. Sydney, 1984.*
Ilford Galerie paper, 23.7 × 28.0.
Rolleiflex camera.

Here we have an early attempt by Ralph Lestrange to capture the photographer at work. One can see the same figure, the same blur of cars, the same sign, 'Breakfast heart-starters', but the point of view has shifted markedly. The central figure of the original photograph is now almost obscured by a bus-stop at the left-hand edge of this picture, while the focal point is now a shadowy doorway full of refuse. Indeed, attempts to calculate the position of the viewpoint from which the original shot was taken reveal that this doorway would be precisely it. The glint of a lens from within the shadows, and the tip of an Oxford shoe, confirm that Edwin Cranberry-Smith is, in fact, secreted at the centre of this photograph.

Okay, hotshot, just take it easy, like you own the place, company director on an inspection tour or something. No hard-hat here if someone drops a brick on you, like

Cranberry-Smith turns out a little more vindictive than you thought, like I mean not even a bloody pith helmet here, old fellow-me-lad, for a chap on the trail of a sacred cow, 'cause I guess that's what you are, pal, some kind of great white whale. C'mon now, move, be faster climbing up the rivets than in this shuddering gorilla cage, 'cause there he is already, strolling round up there like he's got his umbrella under one arm and *The Times* under the other, hard-hat might almost be a derby, way he saunters with his feet turned out there. So what's he after, love among the foremen? the riveter's epiphany? anything to contradict that critical hint that maybe his drunks and lovers were getting just a touch repetitive?

6.a.   *At The Plaistow. Melbourne, 1984.*
       28.9 × 40.7.
       Mamiyaflex camera.
          Here is a picture illustrating, perhaps more clearly than any other in this exhibition, Edwin Cranberry-Smith's thesis that the most revealing of all relationships is the voyeuristic. The woman, her pale torso exposed amidst the shadows of her room, is a virtual stereotype of exposure, not only in her nakedness, but in her whiteness (exposure's most intimate colour), and in her ignorance that she has been exposed at all. The young man who watches from the shrubbery of the balcony next-door, his face a mask of fear and delight, is yet more intimately exposed, if only for his

conviction that it is he who possesses, at that moment, the power of exposure. Behind such pictures lies the Cranberrian premise that, in being made witness to the voyeuristic act, the viewer himself is compromised, transformed into a voyeur, while the self-consciousness of the aesthetic experience will immediately turn his eyes upon his own guilt, and his voyeurism must ultimately become self-revelation.

6.b.   *At The Plaistow. Melbourne, 1984.*
Cibachrome colour print from 35 mm transparency,
32.6 × 48.0.
Topcon camera.

   This is another quite early attempt to capture Edwin Cranberry-Smith at work. One can clearly see the corner of the hotel featured in the original picture. Here, however, the foreground consists of the upper branches of an abundant maple tree, so abundant indeed, that it makes the picture appear at first to be little more than a mass of maple leaves. However, upon closer inspection of the most densely textured area of green, one can just make out the gleaming of a gold belt buckle, the protruding black cylinder of a telephoto lens and the tip of an Oxford shoe, clear evidence that this is the very spot from which

> Edwin Cranberry-Smith is taking his now
> famous photograph.

Take a step, man, just one little step out on the girder, a tiny step for you, Lestrange, one giant step for photography, pin that old bastard down, yessir, see him sauntering round the catwalks like some tightrope-walker on his Sunday constitutional, while you just hover, whoa there, on the edge. I mean who's the adventurer here Lestrange? Just lookit that journal article, how you run the gauntlet of security guards, dodge bratlets throwing punches, lawsuits, you name it, but then you like to compromise your subjects, serve pap to their slavering fans, what it says, the peeping Tom of the Pentax. Well, Jesus, who's the peeping Tom I wanna know, who does the compromising here? Lestrange, who gives the exhibitionists a bit more to exhibit? or Cranberry-Smith with all that stuff about making the viewer the voyeur? training lenses on old drunks, young lovers, priests, children, dogs, anyone who's never heard of a photo-essay, who can't tell the difference between the eternal moment and an instant replay, talk about aiming a kidney punch at innocence, and there he goes, the old snake in the grass, ducking sharp behind that upright there, near those welders playing cards, too caught up to notice anything, let alone Mr Invisible. C'mon, get out there hotshot, pick up your gold star, your smiley stamp, your tinplate medal, most improved pupil in the acrophobia class.

14.a. *Eugenie. Sydney, 1985.*
28.4 × 34.3.
Mamiyaflex camera.

The story of this picture might be seen either as a parable of artistic dedication, or as an example of the way myths tend to accrete about such talented yet secretive figures as Edwin Cranberry-smith. He is said to have once described his fascination with a singular expression which he had glimpsed upon the face of his wife while they were making love. He described it as a merely fleeting glance, a moment of vulnerability, a privacy laid bare of tenderness and fear as if, for an instant, they were once more their adolescent selves, and sex had become no mere marital habit, but an act of ultimate self-revelation. The story, or myth, suggests that he secretly longed to capture this mysterious, transient glance, and rigged a hidden camera to the ceiling immediately above their bed, its shutter mechanism operated by a remote control device which he would trigger with his foot while they made love. This account has been the subject of some doubt, though it does at least attempt to explain this unique and dazzling portrait of his wife, Eugenie.

14.b. *Eugenie. Sydney, 1985.*
21.3×32.7.
Pentax camera.

Here Ralph Lestrange offers us convincing evidence for the truth of the above account. Though technically flawed by the blurred image of the chicken-wire covering the skylight through which it was taken, this photograph not only shows us the exact original of Eugenie's portrait smiling past the shoulder of Edwin Cranberry-Smith, but reveals the contorted, flailing motion of his foot, and the vague shadow of what appears to be a camera just beyond the skylight's edge. The slight overexposure of the image also hints that this picture might have been taken during the operation of a second flash. However, the technical limitations apart, it seems quite certain that Ralph Lestrange has captured here both the explanation and creation of this remarkable portrait.

What it's like it's like the bridge of sighs, the razor's edge, the strait sharp pathway to some kind of perfect picture, 'cause there he is behind that upright, man, you can just make him out by that little black snub of a lens, that tip of an Oxford shoe, and he's gotta step out further if he wants to get those welders and then, SNAP, gotcha Edwin, gotcha in my Pentax trap, old bean, the ultimate picture, the final definitive portrait of the invisible man, Mr Edwin Cranberry-Smith. So move, Lestrange, tiptoe over easy where you'll get him full frontal, with the snap of a shutter, the quantum leap up the evolutionary ladder from high-paid paparazzo to respected artist, toast of the salon set, Renaissance Man with a Rolleiflex, so creep up close, don't just stand there waiting on the brink of respectability. And here he comes, Lestrange, he's stepping out for the shot, get your Pentax there all set, man, line it up, focal lengths, the light okay, just watch him through the lens then shoot. Yeah, so now he's out, but what the hell? he's turning, what's the fucker turning for? just spinning on his heel, he's shooting, the lens a single eye right in the middle of his face and SNAP, you got him, some strange shot, but Jesus what the fuck, he's coming, hand stretched out and snarling through those little sharp moustaches, 'I'll have that camera, thank you very much!'

23.a. *Untitled. Sydney, 1985.*
Ilford Galerie paper, 20.1 × 23.0.
Leica camera.

Though it contains none of the complex-ities we may usually expect in a Cranberry-Smith image, this is a unique photograph of Ralph Lestrange at work. Half-concealed behind the camera is the broad, seamed face familiar to most of us from a variety of well-publicised damages suits, the hair luxuriant beneath a back-turned baseball cap, teeth worrying the stub of a cigar, while the posi-tion of his feet upon the catwalk suggests that he is taking his shot mid-stride. The composition of this picture is more cluttered than is usual for Edwin Cranberry-Smith, as is exemplified by the manner in which the top of the Centrepoint Tower appears to rise like a bulbous mechanical head from Ralph Lestrange's shoulder.

23.b. *Untitled. Sydney, 1985.*
Ilford Galerie paper, 20.1 × 23.0.
Pentax camera.

Ralph Lestrange has here succeeded at capturing on film an image of Edwin Cranberry-Smith in the act of creating a picture. Here are the business shirt unbuttoned at the neck, the pale slacks worn a little high, the woollen socks, the Oxford shoes. Here is the balance, the perfect centring of a master, though the positioning is perhaps a little more thrust-forward than might have been expected, and the poised detachment of the artist's face is complicated by what one might almost term an aggressive curling of the lip. In the background are some workmen whose expressions, though rather indistinct, appear to betray surprise. The overexposure of the right-hand area of the photograph is due, not to any technical error on Ralph Lestrange's part, but to damage sustained by his camera.

'The camera, thank you!' he's saying in a kind of clipped growl, thrusting out his hand like an imperious beggar, but hell, ol' buddy, you think you're immune to a process that you made your own? You think maybe when you snap a piece right outta the life of some poor slob, when you shut it there inside your camera and dedicate it to eternity in some gallery or bank vault, that just maybe you been stealing a little bit of soul? 'I said I'll have that camera,' and look, he's stepping forward, wants back his soul or maybe just his precious anonymity. 'Why, you—' oh shit, he's lunging, snarling deep down in his throat, grabbing for my Pentax, man. 'Hey, watch it, Edwin,' trying to wrench it from my hand. 'Now watch out, man,' and Jesus, here we, shit no, here we go, both him and me both falling round the Pentax, down a throat of air now falling down into a glistening grey what is it? wet? it's concrete? down . . .

MEMORIAL EXHIBIT

The Crowther Galleries take great pride in this final exhibit, which should be seen not simply as an *objet d'art*, but as a memorial to the art and lives of Edwin Cranberry-Smith and Ralph Lestrange. It is perhaps fitting that these two men, who dedicated their lives to the transmutation of the ephemeral into the permanent, should themselves be remembered by such a unique example of this trans-mutation. It is also fitting, though poignantly so, that two such photographic individualists, initially united by a form of competition, should create their final, greatest work as a mutual self-portrait, hands linked together in a spirit of artistic brotherhood.

richard lunn

Here, at last, the shadows fixed upon the earth of Hiro-
shima, the lampshades made of human skin at Dachau,
those paradigms of a terrifying permanence, have been
transformed into something positive, where terror has
been joined with hope to create a sense of tragedy. Here
we have the beginnings of a uniquely twentieth century
art-form. So it is that we have decided not to allow this
masterpiece to languish as a gallery display, but to place it
at the portal of that most twentieth century of institutions,
the free market. Here is the magnum opus of Edwin Cranberry-Smith and Ralph Lestrange, brought at great
expense by semitrailer from the place of its creation, a monument to artistic harmony and personal reconciliation, the
final imprint of their tragic end, not on photographic
paper, but in stone. With paw-prints and graffiti erased by
the latest of techniques, it is the ultimate in concrete
images, a rock-solid investment and a memorial to two
artistic titans who may be said to have thrown themselves
unflinchingly into their work.

Emery della Carta

Director

Moses stands with his brother Ben in the Hayward
Gallery, London. It is the 150th anniversary of the birth
of Camille Pissarro, a steely-skied Sunday, windy and
wet. Moses is forty-two, grey-bearded, overweight, Ben
a clean-shaven ten years younger. Camille Pissarro, a
founding member of the School of Impressionism, was
born in Charlotte Amalie, the capital of St Thomas in
the Virgin Islands, to Franco-Jewish parents, the third of
four sons. His father, a prosperous trader, sent him to
school in Paris, where Camille early exhibited an artistic
bent, but his father would have none of it, and recalled
him to St Thomas to work in the family business. And
there Camille might well have remained, a humdrum
clerk, but for the fortuitous happenstance of one Fritz
Melbye, an itinerant Danish painter, who whisked the
young man off to Venezuela where they set up a studio
and worked together for two years. Pissarro *père* bowed
to the inevitable. In 1855, at the age of twenty-five,
Camille sailed once again to France, returning to the
Virgin Islands only in the canvases he executed during
his first year as a painter in Europe. Bloody hell, thinks
Moses. What are we doing here?

Moses is plugged into Ben's cassette. 'I don't know

about you, Moses,' Ben had said in the foyer, the second
they'd stepped inside, 'but I always take the tour.' And
before there could be discussion, Ben had plunked down
his eighty p. A blinking Moses had stood and watched
as his brother was instructed in the use of the cassette
equipment, how to wear it, how to fit the earpiece, how
to operate the switches, rewind, pause, on and off,
Moses's mind suddenly zipping back fifteen years, to that
Saturday morning when he had taken Ben into town to
buy him an overcoat. This was that year their parents
had died, when Moses and Ben were living together, the
family house sold, moved into a flat. What Ben had
wanted was a cheap army surplus duffel coat, all his
friends had them, everyone at school, but Moses
wouldn't listen, insisted Ben try on suedes, sheepskins,
things with fur collars, all manner of fancy stuff, overdoing like crazy his new parental role but he couldn't
stop himself, wanting Ben to have the best, and in the
Hayward Gallery, watching his brother being fitted with
the cassette tour, Moses had felt an inexplicable prickle.
Sadness? Nostalgia? That great mad time for ever gone?
Whatever, uncomfortable, uneasy, a stab. And to hide it,
as was his wont, quickly made a joke. 'Wow, you look
gorgeous,' he had said, wiggling his eyebrows Groucho-
fashion, his reward from Ben an exasperated frown.
Whoops, thought Moses, wrong again. Then the attendant had suggested that he, Moses, for an additional
payment of only thirty p., could be plugged into his
friend's cassette. 'Friend?' Moses had said. 'What do you
mean, friend? He's my brother.' 'You want it or not?'

Ben had said. 'Come on, I'll pay.' And slapped down the money—as though that were any consideration—before Moses could speak. Hey, Moses had thought, what's this? What's this aggression? Moses and Ben walked into the gallery side by side, stepping carefully, aswirl with flex. 'Hey, you want to hold hands as well?' Moses had asked. 'Ssh,' Ben had snapped. 'I'm trying to listen.'

Ben has been in England for a year, running the London office of the firm he works for in Sydney, Moses only three days, a lightning business trip. He will be gone in another four. He is staying the week in Ben's Hammersmith flat, hard on the M4, the traffic roaring past in an endless belt, which Moses drowns out with jazz tapes he made up specially and brought for Ben. Cannonball Adderley. Wes Montgomery. Miles and Monk. Ben likes the Beatles and Neil Young and Elton John, but what the hell, Moses thinks, he can listen to that stuff any time, how often does he have me here? Moses stands now, side by side with Ben, regarding a panoramic view of Pontoise, the village where Pissarro first settled, farmhouses, trees, ploughed fields on a rounded hill, a dreary painting, Moses thinks, well, ordinary, what's the fuss? and at once thinks of a marvellous joke, a whole routine, a confusion of Pissarro and Picasso, but when he looks quickly across at Ben, all ready to spring into it, he sees that his brother is serious, intent. Oh-oh, thinks Moses, biting his lip. Better not.

Moses has already disgraced himself once this morning. This was when they were about to get into the car, and Moses had suddenly discovered that he didn't have his wallet. He had run back upstairs. No, it wasn't in the flat. He looked everywhere. Then outside again, maybe he'd dropped it, maybe it was under the car. Moses ran frantically, kicking at leaves, he can't have lost it, it had to be stolen, glaring at Ben as though it were all his fault, finally standing on the stone steps behind the flats that lead down to the Thames, staring at the black waters, money gone, credit cards, hot-eyed and hopeless. And then whoops discovered it in his left trouser pocket, where he always carried it, where it always was. 'Sorry,' he had said to Ben, attempting a smile. And then, as if that hadn't been enough, in the car, sitting beside his brother, his brother the five-miles-a-morning jogger, the health-food fanatic, the vitamin freak, the two nights a week at gym, Moses had taken out and started to light a cigarette.

The cassette informs Moses of Pissarro's attraction to the works of Corot, Courbet and Daubigny, of his meetings with Monet and Guillaumin and Cézanne, of the diagonals, horizontals and verticals he employed in his new compositions, paintings which were praised by the novelist Emile Zola. His use of broad brushstrokes. His interest in tonal nuances. Moses sneaks a look across at Ben, who is completely absorbed, then quickly around the gallery, that is, the small part of it that he can see. God, he thinks, we're going to be here for years.

In 1870 Pissarro fled to London to escape the Franco-Prussian war. He was to remain for a year. 'Monet worked in the parks,' Pissarro later wrote, 'whilst I, living in Lower Norwood, at that time a charming suburb, studied the effects of mist, snow and springtime.' Moses and Ben stand before his famous painting of the Crystal Palace, their attention drawn by the cassette to how all the figures in the painting are walking away, away from the painter, away from the viewer, walking into the heart of the painting, drawing in your eye, and Moses feels suddenly that old stab of guilt, recalling how he sailed away to Europe when he was twenty-six, giving up the flat, leaving Ben with an uncle. Sailed away and was gone for seven years. He's never forgiven me, Moses thinks, looking quickly over at his brother, who just then takes a step forward, eyes narrowed, to examine the detail. Moses, all at once fearful of the flex, hurriedly takes a step forward too. I mean, he thinks, look at the way he snapped at me in the car.

Wait a minute, thinks Moses, it wasn't the cigarette. I mean, not just the cigarette. He was brusque right from the start, right from the minute I arrived. The way he showed me round the flat. This is the way we make coffee. This is how we make toast. Which we don't eat all over the carpet, by the way. That's your plate. When you have a bath, you wipe it out with that rag, O.K.? And I wouldn't mind if you didn't leave the electric towel rail on all night either. Boy, thinks Moses, shaking his head. What a lecture.

Pissarro returns to France. His house has been occupied by soldiers. Only forty paintings are saved of the fifteen hundred he had left behind, twenty years' work. This is in Louveciennes. Pissarro moves back to his beloved Pontoise. The town is changing, becoming rapidly industrial. Pissarro paints the new factories, the markets. He exhibits. He sells nothing. Year after year it is the same. His growing family is often in severe straits. Pissarro's father refuses to help. Well, thinks Moses, sneaking a look over at his brother, don't think I don't know what's going on.

So he's paying me back, Moses thinks. After all these years he's paying me back. Moses ruefully smiles. Well, O.K., he thinks, if it makes him happy. I don't mind. He wants to give me lectures? He wants to be the big boss? Fine. Sure. No skin off my nose. Except, Moses thinks, his smile dropping away, maybe I was a bit of a bully, but was I all that bad? Look, he was just a kid. Practically a baby. Didn't even know how to make a bed, much less how to hang up a pair of pants. So, sure, maybe I lectured him a bit. But who else was going to do it? Who else was there? And listen, Moses continues, we had fun. It was a good time.

During the 1870s and early 80s, the cassette informs Moses, Pissarro worked closely with his friend Cézanne. Inspired by the example of Courbet, they restricted their palettes, brought back their compositions to basic forms, experimented with textures and brushstrokes. Side by side, the two men painted the same views.

'I didn't know Pissarro worked with Cézanne,' Ben says.

'What?' Moses says, caught off balance. But quickly composing himself, nodding, a reassuring smile. 'Oh, sure,' he says. 'Of course.'

Pissarro wrote to his son, Lucien: 'I haven't done

much work outdoors this season, the weather was unfavourable, and I am obsessed with a desire to paint figures which are difficult to compose with. I have made some small sketches; when I have resolved the problem in my mind I shall get to work.'

'Isn't that beautiful?' says Ben. It is a painting of a young peasant girl wearing a hat. 'Look at the sun on the skin, the softness.' Ben moves closer to the painting, his eyes intent. 'You can almost feel it,' he says, and Moses, looking across at his brother, feels again that inexplicable stab. He plummets back ten years. He sees himself standing in the hallway in his old house in England, barefoot, shivering in his pyjamas. It is four o'clock in the morning, winter, dark and cold. Ben is half a world away, a thin, eager voice on the other end of the telephone. He is announcing his marriage. And Moses hears himself too, hears his own voice loud and proprietorial, booming in the dark. What? he shouts. Don't do it! For God's sake, Ben, you're too young!

Has he recovered from that marriage? Moses thinks now. Has he got someone else? We haven't spoken about the divorce, about anything like that. Well, I can't ask him. If he wants to tell me, he'll tell me. I knew he was too young. I told him not to do it. What else could I do?

A woman moves to inspect more closely the canvas before which Ben and Moses stand. 'Excuse me,' cries Moses, warding her off with an upraised arm. 'Can't you see we're *joined*?' And just like that Moses is in tears.

Moses stands in confusion, diving for his handkerchief,

biting his lip. What's happening? Why all this? 'Isn't that superb?' says Ben, of the large *pointilliste* canvas before which they stand, peasants in an orchard gathering apples from a tree, and Moses turns and looks into Ben's face and feels swamped with anger. He is in an instant rage. *What?* he wants to shout. *Don't you know anything? Can't you see? One minute he's painting like Cézanne, the next it's soppy Renoirs, now he's churning out this damn pointilliste stuff. Where's his own personality? Where's his character?* But he doesn't. He smiles. He nods. 'Sure,' he says. 'Very nice.' And then quickly has to turn away, blinded by further tears.

Moses stands with his brother Ben before the exhibition's final canvas, *The Avenue de l'Opéra, sun on a winter morning 1898.* 'It is very beautiful,' wrote Pissarro to a friend, 'to paint these Paris streets that people have come to call ugly, but which are so silvery, so luminous and vital. They are so different from the *boulevards.* This is completely modern. I show in April.'

I didn't want him, Moses says to himself. I was forced. I had to do it. I never wanted him. I hardly even knew he existed until our parents died. Moses stands hot and red, riven with shame. I'm a liar, he says to himself. That flat wasn't fun. It wasn't a good time. It was like prison. It was like being in jail.

Moses stands silent and bowed while the cassette informs him of Pissarro's death, in Paris, at the age of seventy-three, and of the people who honoured his name at his funeral. Renoir was there, intones the cassette, and Monet, and Bernard, and Fénéon, and Lecomte, and

Mirbeau, and Durand-Ruel, and Vollard, and Matisse, Pissarro's fellow painters and friends. Pissarro linked the 19th Century to the 20th, the cassette sums up his life, adding, as coda, how Cézanne, exhibiting in Aix-en-Provence in 1906, signed himself proudly: *Paul Cézanne, pupil of Pissarro.*

'Fantastic,' says Ben. 'That was really fantastic.' He takes a step back, his eyes gleaming. 'Wow,' he says, shaking his head. And now he turns to Moses. He looks at him directly, for the first time this morning, into his eyes. 'Moses, you were terrific,' he says. 'I expected trouble. You know how you are, the jokes, the rubbish. You didn't do any of that. You were terrific. Thank you.'

Moses somehow nods.

Now Ben, smiling, looks around the gallery. 'Oh, there's a bit more upstairs, he says. 'Prints and drawings.' He turns back to Moses. 'But you're tired,' he says, looking at his brother. 'You've had enough.'

'Tired?' says Moses. 'What are you talking about, tired? Come on,' he says, stepping smartly back in. 'Prints and drawings is the best part.'

From the beginning he was a stumbling-block, the Professor. I had always thought of him as an old man, as one thinks of one's parents as old, but he can't in those days have been more than fifty. Squat, powerful, with a good deal of black hair on his wrists, he was what was called a 'ladies man'—though that must have been far in the past and in another country. What he practised now was a formal courtliness, a clicking of heels and kissing of plump fingers that was the extreme form of a set of manners that our parents clung to because it belonged, along with much else, to the Old Country, and which we young people, for the same reason, found it imperative to reject. The Professor had a 'position'—he taught mathematics to apprentices on day-release. He was proof that a breakthrough into the new world was not only possible, it was a fact. Our parents, having come to a place where their qualifications in medicine or law were unacceptable, had been forced to take work as labourers or factory-hands or to keep dingy shops; but we, their clever sons and daughters, would find our way back to the safe professional classes. For our parents there was deep sorrow in all this, and the Professor offered hope. We were invited to see in him both the embodiment of

a noble past and a glimpse of what, with hard work and
a little luck or grace, we might claim from the future.

He was always the special guest.

'Here, pass the Professor this slice of Torte,' my
mother would say, choosing the largest piece and piling
it with cream, or 'Here, take the Professor a nice cold
Pils, and see you hand it to him proper now and don't
spill none on the way': this on one of those community
outings we used to go to in the early years, when half a
dozen families would gather at Suttons Beach with a
crate of beer bottles in straw jackets and a spread of
homemade sausage and cabbage rolls. Aged six or seven,
in my knitted bathing-briefs, and watching out in my
bare feet for bindy-eye, I would set out over the grass
to where the great man and my father, easy now in shir-
tsleeves and braces, would be pursuing one of their inter-
minable arguments. My father had been a lawyer in the
Old Country but worked now at the Vulcan Can
Factory. He was passionately interested in philosophy,
and the Professor was his only companion on those
breathless flights that were, along with the music of Beethoven and Mahler, his sole consolation on the raw and
desolate shore where he was marooned. Seeing me come
wobbling towards them with the Pils—which I had
slopped a little—held breast-high before me, all golden
in the sun, he would look startled, as if I were a spirit of
the place he had failed to allow for. It was the Professor
who recognised the nature of my errand. 'Ah, how kind,'
he would say. 'Thank you, my dear. And thank the good
mama too. Anton, you are a lucky man.' And my father,

reconciled to the earth again, would smile and lay his hand very gently on the nape of my neck while I blushed and squirmed.

The Professor had no family—or not in Australia. He lived alone in a house he had built to his own design. It was of pinewood, as in the Old Country, and in defiance of local custom was surrounded by trees—natives. There was also a swimming pool where he exercised twice a day. I went there occasionally with my father, to collect him for an outing, and had sometimes peered at it through a glass door; but we were never formally invited. The bachelor did not entertain. He was always the guest, and what his visits meant to me, as to the children of a dozen other families, was that I must be especially careful of my manners, see that my shoes were properly polished, my nails clean, my hair combed, my tie straight, my socks pulled up, and that when questioned about school or about the games I played I should give my answers clearly, precisely, and without making faces.

So there he was all through my childhood, an intimidating presence, and a heavy reminder of that previous world; where his family owned a castle, and where he had been, my mother insisted, a real scholar.

Time passed and as the few close-knit families of our community moved to distant suburbs and lost contact with one another, we children were released from restriction. It was easy for our parents to give in to new ways now that others were not watching. Younger brothers failed to inherit our confirmation suits with their stiff white collars and cuffs. We no longer went to examinations weighed down with holy medals, or silently invoked, before putting pen to paper, the good offices of the Infant of Prague—whose influence, I decided, did not extend to Brisbane, Queensland. Only the Professor remained as a last link.

'I wish, when the Professor comes,' my mother would complain, 'that you try to speak better. The vowels! For my sake, darling, but also for your father, because we want to be proud of you,' and she would try to detain me as, barefoot, in khaki shorts and an old T-shirt, already thirteen, I wriggled from her embrace. 'And put shoes on, or sandals at least, and a nice clean shirt. I don't want that the Professor think we got an Arab for a son. And your Scout belt! And comb your hair a little, my darling—please!'

She kissed me before I could pull away. She was shocked, now that she saw me through the Professor's eyes, at how far I had grown from the little gentleman I might have been, all neatly suited and shod and brushed and polished, if they had never left the Old Country, or if she and my father had been stricter with me in this new one.

The fact is, I had succeeded, almost beyond my own expectations, in making myself indistinguishable from the roughest of my mates at school. My mother must have wondered at times if I could ever be smoothed out and civilised again, with my broad accent, my slang, my feet toughened and splayed from going barefoot. I was spoiled and wilful and ashamed of my parents. My mother knew it, and now, in front of the Professor, it was her turn to be ashamed. To assert my independence, or to show them that I did not care, I was never so loutish, I never slouched or mumbled or scowled so darkly as when the Professor appeared. Even my father, who was too dreamily involved with his own thoughts to notice me on most occasions, was aware of it and shocked. He complained to my mother, who shook her head and cried. I felt magnificently justified, and the next time the Professor made his appearance I swaggered even more outrageously and gave every indication of being an incorrigible tough.

The result was not at all what I had had in mind. Far from being repelled by my roughness the Professor seemed charmed. The more I showed off and embarrassed my parents, the more he encouraged me. My excesses delighted him. He was entranced.

He really was, as we younger people had always thought, a caricature of a man. You could barely look at him without laughing, and we had all become expert, even the girls, at imitating his hunched stance, his accent (which was at once terribly foreign and terribly English) and the way he held his stubby fingers when, at the end of a meal, he dipped sweet biscuits into wine and popped them whole into his mouth. My own imitations were designed to torment my mother.

'Oh you shouldn't!' she would whine, suppressing another explosion of giggles. 'You mustn't! Oh stop it now, your father will see—he would be offended. The Professor is a fine man. May you have such a head on your shoulders one day, and such a position.'

'Such a head on my shoulders,' I mimicked, hunching my back like a stork so that I had no neck, and she would try to cuff me, and miss as I ducked away.

I was fifteen and beginning to spring up out of pudgy childhood into clean-limbed, tumultuous adolescence. By staring for long hours into mirrors behind locked doors, by taking stock of myself in shop windows, and from the looks of some of the girls at school, I had discovered that I wasn't at all bad-looking, might even be good-looking, and was already tall and well-made. I had chestnut hair like my mother and my skin didn't freckle in the sun but turned heavy gold. There was a whole year between fifteen and sixteen when I was fascinated by the image of myself I could get back from people simply by playing up to them—it scarcely mattered whom: teachers, girls, visitors to the house like the Professor, passers-by in the street. I was obsessed with myself, and lost no opportunity of putting my powers to the test.

Once or twice in earlier days, when I was playing football on Saturday afternoon, my father and the Professor had appeared on the sidelines, looking in after a walk. Now, as if by accident, the Professor came alone. When I came trotting in to collect my bike, dishevelled, still spattered and streaked from the game, he would be waiting. He just happened, yet again, to be passing, and had a book for me to take home, or a message: he would be calling for my father at eight and could I please remind him, or yes, he would be coming next night to play Solo. He was very formal on these occasions, but I felt his interest; and sometimes, without thinking of anything more than the warm sense of myself it gave me to command his attention, I would walk part of the way home with him, wheeling my bike and chatting about nothing very important: the game, or what I had done with my holiday, or since he was a dedicated star-gazer, the new comet that had appeared. As these meetings increased I got to be more familiar with him. Sometimes, when two or three of the others were there (they had come to recognise him and teased me a little, making faces and jerking their heads as he made his way, hunched and short-sighted, to where we were towelling ourselves at the tap) I would for their benefit show off a little, without at first realising, in my reckless passion to be admired, that I was exceeding all bounds and that they now included me as well as the Professor in their humorous contempt. I was mortified. To ease myself back into their good opinion I passed him off as a family nuisance, whose attentions I knew were comic but whom I was leading on for my own amusement. This was acceptable enough and I was soon restored to popularity, but felt doubly treacherous. He was, after all, my father's closest friend, and there was as well that larger question of the Old Country. I burned with shame, but was too cowardly to do more than brazen things out.

For all my crudeness and arrogance I had a great desire to act nobly, and in this business of the Professor I had miserably failed. I decided to cut my losses. As soon as he appeared now, and had announced his message, I would mount my bike, sling my football boots over my shoulder and pedal away. My one fear was that he might enquire what the trouble was, but of course he did not. Instead he broke off his visits altogether or passed the field without stopping, and I found myself regretting something I had come to depend on—his familiar figure hunched like a bird on the sidelines, our talks, some fuller sense of my own presence to add at the end of the game to the immediacy of my limbs after violent exercise.

Looking back on those days I see myself as a kind of centaur, half-boy, half-bike, for ever wheeling down sub-urban streets under the poincianas, on my way to foot-ball practice or the library or to a meeting of the little group of us, boys and girls, that came together on someone's verandah in the evenings after tea.

I might come across the Professor then on his after-dinner stroll, and as often as not he would be accom-panied by my father, who would stop me and demand (partly, I thought, to impress the Professor) where I was off to or where I had been; insisting, with more than his usual force, that I come home right away, with no argument.

On other occasions, pedalling past his house among the trees, I would catch a glimpse of him with his tele-scope on the roof. He might raise a hand and wave if he recognised me; and sprinting away, crouched low over the handlebars, I would feel, or imagine I felt, that the telescope had been lowered and was following me to the end of the street, losing me for a time, then picking me up again two streets further on as I flashed away under the bunchy leaves.

I spent long hours cycling back and forth between our house and my girlfriend Helen's or to Ross McDowell or Jimmy Larwood's, my friends from school, and the Professor's house was always on the route.

I think of those days now as being all alike, and the nights also: the days warmish, still, endlessly without event, and the nights quivering with expectancy but also uneventful, heavy with the scent of jasmine and honey-suckle and lighted by enormous stars. But what I am describing, of course, is neither a time nor a place but the mood of my own bored, expectant, uneventful ado-lescence. I was always abroad and waiting for something significant to occur, for life somehow to declare itself and catch me up. I rode my bike in slow circles or figures-of-eight, took it for sprints across the gravel of the park, or simply hung motionless in the saddle, balanced and waiting.

Nothing ever happened. In the dark of front veran-dahs we lounged and swapped stories, heard gossip, told jokes, or played show-poker and smoked. One night each week I went to Helen's and we sat a little scared of one another in her garden-swing, touching in the dark. Helen liked me better, I thought, than I liked her—I had that power over her—and it was this more than any-thing else that attracted me, though I found it scary as well. For fear of losing me she might have gone to any one of the numbers that in those days marked the stages of sexual progress and could be boasted about, in a way that seemed shameful afterwards, in locker-rooms or round the edge of the pool. I could have taken us both to 6, 8, 10, but what then? The numbers were not infinite.

I rode around watching my shadow flare off gravel; sprinted, hung motionless, took the rush of warm air into my shirt; afraid that when the declaration came, it too, like the numbers, might be less than infinite. I didn't want to discover the limits of the world. Restlessly impelled towards some future that would at last offer me my real self, I nevertheless drew back, happy for the moment, even in my unhappiness, to be half-boy, half-bike, half aimless energy and half a machine that could hurtle off at a moment's notice in any one of a hundred directions. Away from things—but away, most of all, from my self. My own presence had begun to be a source of deep dissatisfaction to me, my vanity, my charm, my falseness, my preoccupation with sex. I was sick of myself and longed for the world to free me by making its own rigorous demands and declaring at last what I must be.

One night, in our warm late winter, I was riding home past the Professor's house when I saw him hunched as usual beside his telescope, but too absorbed on this occasion to be aware of me.

I paused at the end of the drive, wondering what it was that he saw on clear nights like this, that was invisible to me when I leaned my head back and filled my gaze with the sky.

The stars seemed palpably close. In the high September blueness it was as if the odour of jasmine blossoms had gathered there in a single shower of white. You might have been able to catch the essence of it floating down, as sailors, they say, can smell new land whole days before they first catch sight of it.

What I was catching, in fact, was the first breath of change—a change of season. From the heights I fell suddenly into deep depression, one of those sweet-sad glooms of adolescence that are like a bodiless drifting out of yourself into the immensity of things, when you are aware as never again—or never so poignantly—that time is moving swiftly on, that a school year is very nearly over and childhood finished, that you will have to move up a grade at football into a tougher class—shifts that against the vastness of space are minute, insignificant, but at that age solemnly felt.

I was standing astride the bike, staring upwards, when I became aware that my name was being called, and for the second or third time. I turned my bike into the drive with its border of big-leafed saxifrage and came to where the Professor, his hand on the telescope, was leaning out over the roof.

'I have some books for your father,' he called. 'Just come to the gate and I will get them for you.'

The gate was wooden, and the fence, which made me think of a stockade, was of raw slabs eight feet high, stained reddish-brown. He leaned over the low parapet and dropped a set of keys.

'It's the thin one,' he told me. 'You can leave your

bike in the yard.' He meant the paved courtyard inside, where I rested it easily against the wall. Beyond, and to the left of the pine-framed house, which was stained the same colour as the fence, was a garden taken up almost entirely by the pool. It was overgrown with dark tropical plants, monstera, hibiscus, banana-palms with their big purplish flowers, glossily pendulous on stalks, and fixed to the paling-fence like trophies in wads of bark, elk-horn, tree-orchids, showers of delicate maidenhair. It was too cold for swimming, but the pool was filled and covered with a shifting scum of jacaranda leaves that had blown in from the street, where the big trees were stripping to bloom.

I went round the edge of the pool and a light came on, reddish, in one of the inner rooms. A moment later the Professor himself appeared, tapping for attention at a glass door.

'I have the books right here,' he said briskly; but when I stood hesitating in the dark beyond the threshold, he shifted his feet and added: 'But maybe you would like to come in a moment and have a drink. Coffee. I could make some. Or beer. Or a Coke if you prefer it. I have Coke.'

I had never been here alone, and never, even with my father, to this side of the house. When we came to collect the Professor for an outing we had always waited in the tiled hallway while he rushed about with one arm in the sleeve of his overcoat laying out saucers for cats, and it was to the front door, in later years, that I had delivered bowls of gingerbread fish that my mother had made

specially because she knew he liked it, or cabbage rolls
or herring. I had never been much interested in what lay
beyond the hallway, with its fierce New Guinea masks,
all tufted hair and boar's tusks, and the Old Country
chest that was just like our own. Now, with the books
already in my hands, I hesitated and looked past him into
the room.

'All right. If it's no trouble.'

'No no, no trouble at all!' He grinned, showing his
teeth with their extravagant caps. 'I am delighted. Really!
Just leave the books there. You see they are tied with
string, quite easy for you I'm sure, even on the bike. Sit
where you like. Anywhere. I'll get the drink.'

'Beer then,' I said boldly, and my voice cracked,
destroying what I had hoped might be the setting of our
relationship on a clear, man-to-man basis that would
wipe out the follies of the previous year. I coughed,
cleared my throat, and said again, 'Beer, thanks,' and sat
abruptly on a sofa that was too low and left me prone
and sprawling.

He stopped a moment and considered, as if I had surprised him by crossing a second threshold.

'Well then, if it's to be beer, I shall join you. Maybe
you are also hungry. I could make a sandwich.'

'No, no thank you, they're expecting me. Just the
beer.'

He went out, his slippers shushing over the tiles, and
I shifted immediately to a straight-backed chair opposite
and took the opportunity to look around.

There were rugs on the floor, old threadbare Persians,

and low down, all round the walls, stacks of the heavy seventy-eights I carried home when my father borrowed them: sonatas by Beethoven, symphonies by Sibelius and Mahler. Made easy by the Professor's absence, I got up and wandered round. On every open surface, the glass table-top, the sideboard, the long mantel of the fireplace, were odd bits and pieces that he must have collected in his travels: lumps of coloured quartz, a desert rose, slabs of clay with fern or fish fossils in them, glass paperweights, snuff-boxes, meerschaum pipes of fantastic shape—one a Saracen's head, another the torso of a woman like a ship's figurehead with full breasts and golden nipples—bits of Baltic amber, decorated sherds of pottery, black on terra-cotta, and one unbroken object, a little earthenware lamp that when I examined it more closely turned out to be a phallic grotesque. I had just discovered what it actually was when the Professor stepped into the room. Turning swiftly to a framed photograph on the wall above, I found myself peering into a stretch of the Old Country, a foggy, sepia world that I recognised immediately from similar photographs at home.

'Ah,' he said, setting the tray down on an empty chair, 'you have discovered my weakness.' He switched on another lamp. 'I have tried, but I am too sentimental. I cannot part with them.'

The photograph, I now observed, was one of three. They were all discoloured with foxing on the passe-partout mounts, and the glass of one was shattered, but so neatly that not a single splinter had shifted in the frame.

The one I was staring at was of half a dozen young
men in military uniform. It might have been from the
last century, but there was a date in copperplate: 1921.
Splendidly booted and sashed and frogged, and hierati-
cally stiff, with casque helmets under their arms, swords
tilted at the thigh, white gloves tucked into braided
epaulettes, they were a chorus line from a Ruritanian
operetta. They were also, as I knew, the heroes of a lost
but unforgotten war.

'You recognise me?' the Professor asked.

I looked again. It was difficult. All the young men
strained upright with the same martial hauteur, wore the
same little clipped moustaches, had the same flat hair
parted in the middle and combed in wings over their
ears. Figures from the past can be as foreign, as difficult
to identify individually, as the members of another race.
I took the plunge, set my forefinger against the frame,
and turned to the Professor for confirmation. He came
to my side and peered.

'No,' he said sorrowfully. 'But the mistake is entirely
understandable. He was my great friend, almost a
brother. I am here. This is me. On the left.'

He considered himself, the slim assured figure, chin
slightly tilted, eyes fixed ahead, looking squarely out of
a class whose privileges—inherent in every point of the
stance, the uniform, the polished accoutrements—were
not to be questioned, and from the ranks of an army
that was invincible. The proud caste no longer existed.
Neither did the army nor the country it was meant to
defend, except in the memory of people like the

Professor and my parents and, in a ghostly way, half a century off in another hemisphere, my own.

He shook his head and made a clucking sound. 'Well,' he said firmly, 'it's a long time ago. It is foolish of me to keep such things. We should live for the present. Or like you younger people,' bringing the conversation back to me, 'for the future.'

I found it easier to pass to the other photographs.

In one, the unsmiling officer appeared as an even younger man, caught in an informal, carefully posed moment with a group of ladies. He was clean-shaven and lounging on the grass in a striped blazer; beside him a discarded boater—very English. The ladies, more decorously disposed, wore long dresses with hats and ribbons. Neat little slippers peeped out under their skirts.

'Yes, yes,' he muttered, almost impatient now, 'that too. Summer holidays—who can remember where? And the other a walking trip.'

I looked deep into a high meadow, with broken cloud-drift in the dip below. Three young men in shorts, maybe schoolboys, were climbing on the far side of the wars. There were flowers in the foreground, glowingly out of focus, and it was this picture whose glass was shattered; it was like looking through a brilliant spider's web into a picturebook landscape that was utterly familiar, though I could never have been there. *That is the place*, I thought. *That is the land my parents mean when they say 'the Old Country': the country of childhood and first love that they go back to in their sleep and which I have no memory of, though I was born there. Those flowers are the ones, precisely those, that blossom in the songs they sing.* And immediately I was back in my mood of just a few minutes ago, when I had stood out there gazing up at the stars. *What is it,* I asked myself, *that I will remember and want to preserve, when in years to come I think of the Past? What will be important enough?* For what the photographs had led me back to, once again, was myself. It was always the same. No matter how hard I tried to think my way out into other people's lives, into the world beyond me, the feelings I discovered were my own.

'Come. Sit,' the Professor said, 'and drink your beer. And do eat one of these sandwiches. It's very good rye bread, from the only shop. I go all the way to South Brisbane for it. And Gürken. I seem to remember you like them.'

'What do you do up on the roof?' I asked, my mouth full of bread and beer, feeling uneasy again now that we were sitting with nothing to fix on.

'I make observations, you know. The sky, which looks so still, is always in motion, full of drama if you understand how to read it. Like looking into a pond. Hundreds of events happening right under your eyes, except that most of what we see is already finished by the time we see it—ages ago—but important just the same. Such large events. Huge! Bigger even than we can imagine. And beautiful, since they unfold, you know, to a kind of music, to numbers of infinite dimension like the ones you deal with in equations at school, but more complex, and entirely visible.'

He was moved as he spoke by an emotion that I could

not identify, touched by occasions a million light-years off and still unfolding towards him, in no way personal. The room for a moment lost its tension. I no longer felt myself to be the focus of his interest, or even of my own. I felt liberated, and for the first time the Professor was interesting in his own right, quite apart from the attention he paid me or the importance my parents attached to him.

'Maybe I could come again,' I found myself saying. 'I'd like to see.'

'But of course,' he said, 'any time. Tonight is not good—there is a little haze, but tomorrow if you like. Or any time.'

I nodded. But the moment of easiness had passed. My suggestion, which might have seemed like another move in a game, had brought me back into focus for him and his look was quizzical, defensive. I felt it and was embarrassed, and at the same time saddened. Some truer vision of myself had been in the room for a moment. I had almost grasped it. Now I felt it slipping away as I moved back into my purely physical self.

I put the glass down, not quite empty.

'No thanks, really,' I told him when he indicated the half-finished bottle on the tray. 'I should have been home nearly an hour ago. My mother, you know.'

'Ah yes, of course. Well, just call whenever you wish, no need to be formal. Most nights I am observing. It is a very interesting time. Here—let me open the door for you. The books, I see, are a little awkward, but you are so expert on the bicycle I am sure it will be OK.'

I followed him round the side of the pool into the courtyard and there was my bike at its easy angle to the wall, my other familiar and streamlined self. I wheeled it out while he held the gate.

Among my parents' oldest friends were a couple who had recently moved to a new house on the other side of the park, and at the end of winter, in the year I turned seventeen, I sometimes rode over on Sundays to help John clear the big overgrown garden. All afternoon we grubbed out citrus trees that had gone wild, hacked down morning-glory that had grown all over the lower part of the yard, and cut the knee-high grass with a sickle to prepare it for mowing. I enjoyed the work. Stripped down to shorts in the strong sunlight, I slashed and tore at the weeds till my hands blistered, and in a trancelike preoccupation with tough green things that clung to the earth with a fierce tenacity, forgot for a time my own turmoil and lack of roots. It was something to *do*.

John, who worked up ahead, was a dentist. He paid me ten shillings a day for the work, and this, along with my pocket-money, would take Helen and me to the pictures on Saturday night, or to a flash meal at one of the city hotels. We worked all afternoon, while the children, who were four and seven, watched and got in the way. Then about five-thirty Mary would call us for tea.

Mary had been at school with my mother and was the same age, though I could never quite believe it; she had children a whole ten years younger than I was, and I had always called her Mary. She wore bright bangles on her arm, liked to dance at parties, never gave me presents like handkerchiefs or socks, and had always treated me, I thought, as a grown-up. When she called us for tea I went to the garden tap, washed my feet, splashed water over my back that was streaked with soil and sweat and stuck all over with little grass clippings, and was about to buckle on my loose sandals when she said from the doorway where she had been watching: 'Don't bother to get dressed. John hasn't.' She stood there smiling, and I turned away, aware suddenly of how little I had on; and had to use my V-necked sweater to cover an excitement that might otherwise have been immediately apparent in the khaki shorts I was wearing—without underpants because of the heat.

As I came up the steps towards her she stood back to let me pass, and her hand, very lightly, brushed the skin between my shoulder-blades.

'You're still wet,' she said.

It seemed odd somehow to be sitting at the table in their elegant dining room without a shirt; though John was doing it, and was already engaged like the children in demolishing a pile of neat little sandwiches.

I sat at the head of the table with the children noisily grabbing at my left and John on my right drinking tea and slurping it a little, while Mary plied me with raisin-bread and Old Country cookies. I felt red, swollen, confused every time she turned to me, and for some reason it was the children's presence rather than John's that embarrassed me, especially the boy's.

Almost immediately we were finished John got up.

'I'll just go,' he said, 'and do another twenty minutes before it's dark.' It was dark already, but light enough perhaps to go on raking the grass we had cut and were carting to the incinerator. I made to follow. 'It's all right,' he told me. 'I'll finish off. You've earned your money for today.'

'Come and see our animals!' the children yelled, dragging me down the hall to their bedroom, and for ten minutes or so I sat on the floor with them, setting out farm animals and making fences, till Mary, who had been clearing the table, appeared in the doorway.

'Come on now, that's enough, it's bathtime, you kids. Off you go!'

They ran off, already half-stripped, leaving her to pick up their clothes and fold them while I continued to sit cross-legged among the toys, and her white legs, in their green sandals, moved back and forth at eye-level. When she went out I too got up, and stood watching at the bathroom door.

She was sitting on the edge of the bath, soaping the little boy's back, as I remembered my mother doing, while the children splashed and shouted. Then she dried her hands on a towel, very carefully, and I followed her into the unlighted lounge. Beyond the glass wall, in the depths of the garden, John was stooping to gather armfuls of the grass we had cut, and staggering with it to the incinerator.

She sat and patted the place beside her. I followed as in a dream. The children's voices at the end of the hallway were complaining, quarrelling, shrilling. I was sure John could see us through the glass as he came back for another load.

Nothing was said. Her hand moved over my shoulder, down my spine, brushed very lightly, without lingering, over the place where my shorts tented; then rested easily on my thigh. When John came in he seemed unsurprised to find us sitting close in the dark. He went right past us to the drinks cabinet, which suddenly lighted up. I felt exposed and certain now that he must see where her hand was and say something.

All he said was: 'Something to drink, darling?'

Without hurry she got up to help him and they passed back and forth in front of the blazing cabinet, with its mirrors and its rows of bottles and cut-crystal glasses. I was sweating worse than when I had worked in the garden, and began, self-consciously, to haul on the sweater.

I pedalled furiously away, glad to have the cooling air pour over me and to feel free again.

Back there I had been scared—but of what? Of a game in which I might, for once, be the victim—not passive, but with no power to control the moves. I slowed down and considered that, and was, without realising it, at the edge of something. I rode on in the softening dark. It was good to have the wheels of the bike roll away under me as I rose on the pedals, to feel on my cheeks the warm scent of jasmine that was invisible all round. It was a brilliant night verging on spring. I didn't want it to be over; I wanted to slow things down. I dismounted and walked a little, leading my bike along the grassy edge in the shadow of trees, and without precisely intending it, came on foot to the entrance to the Professor's drive, and paused, looking up beyond the treetops to where he might be installed with his telescope—observing what? What events up there in the infinite sky?

I leaned far back to see. A frozen waterfall it might have been, falling slowly towards me, sending out blown spray that would take centuries, light-years, to break in thunder over my head. Time. What did one moment, one night, a lifespan mean in relation to all that?

'Hullo there!'

It was the Professor. I could see him now, in the moonlight beside the telescope, which he leaned on and which pointed not upward to the heavens but down to where I was standing. It occurred to me, as on previous occasions, that in the few moments of my standing there with my head flung back to the stars, what he might have been observing was *me*. I hesitated, made no decision. Then, out of a state of passive expectancy, willing nothing but waiting poised for my own life to occur; out of a state of being open to the spring night and to the emptiness of the hours between seven and ten when I was expected to be in, or thirteen (was it?) and whatever age I would be when manhood finally came to me; out of my simply being there with my hand on the saddle of the machine, bare-legged, loose-sandalled, going nowhere, I turned into the drive, led my bike up to the stockade gate and waited for him to throw down the keys.

'You know which one it is,' he said, letting them fall. 'Just use the other to come in by the poolside.'

I unlocked the gate, rested my bike against the wall of the courtyard and went round along the edge of the pool. It was clean now but heavy with shadows. I turned the key in the glass door, found my way (though this part of the house was new to me) to the stairs, and climbed to where another door opened straight on to the roof.

'Ah,' he said, smiling. 'So at last! You are here.'

The roof was unwalled but set so deep among trees that it was as if I had stepped out of the city altogether into some earlier, more darkly-wooded era. Only lighted windows, hanging detached in the dark, showed where houses, where neighbours were.

He fixed the telescope for me and I moved into position. 'There,' he said, 'what you can see now is Jupiter with its four moons—you see?—all in line, and with the bands across its face.'

I saw. Later it was Saturn with its rings and the lower of the two pointers to the cross, Alpha Centauri, which was not one star but two. It was miraculous. From that moment below when I had looked up at a cascade of light that was still ages off, I might have been catapulted twenty thousand years into the nearer past, or into my own future. Solid spheres hovered above me, tiny balls of matter moving in concert like the atoms we drew in chemistry, held together by invisible lines of force; and I thought oddly that if I were to lower the telescope now to where I had been standing at the entrance to the drive I would see my own puzzled, upturned face, but as a self I had already outgrown and abandoned, not minutes but aeons back. He shifted the telescope and I caught my breath. One after another, constellations I had known since childhood as points of light to be joined up in the mind (like those picture-puzzles children make, pencilling in the scattered dots till Snow White and the Seven Dwarfs appear, or an old jalopy), came together now, not as an imaginary panhandle or bull's head or belt and sword, but at some depth of vision I hadn't known I possessed, as blossoming abstractions, equations luminously exploding out of their own depths, brilliantly solving themselves and playing the results in my head as a real and visible music. I felt a power in myself that might actually burst out at my ears, and at the same time saw myself, from *out there*, as just a figure with his eye to a lens. I had a clear sense of being one more hard little point in the immensity—but part of it, a source of light like all those others—and was aware for the first time of the grainy reality of my own life, and then, a fact of no large significance, of the certainty of my death; but in some dimension where those terms were too vague to be relevant. It was at the point where my self ended and the rest of it began that Time, or Space, showed its richness to me. I was overwhelmed.

Slowly, from so far out, I drew back, re-entered the

present and was aware again of the close suburban dark—of its moving now in the shape of a hand. I must have known all along that it was there, working from the small of my back to my belly, up the inside of my thigh, but it was of no importance, I was too far off. Too many larger events were unfolding for me to break away and ask, as I might have, 'What are you doing?'

I must have come immediately. But when the stars blurred in my eyes it was with tears, and it was the welling of this deeper salt, filling my eyes and rolling down my cheeks, that was the real overflow of the occasion. I raised my hand to brush them away and it was only then that I was aware, once again, of the Professor. I looked at him as from a distance. He was getting to his feet, and his babble of concern, alarm, self-pity, sentimental recrimination, was incomprehensible to me. I couldn't see what he meant.

'No no, it's nothing,' I assured him, turning aside to button my shorts. 'It was nothing. Honestly.' I was unwilling to say more in case he misunderstood what I did not understand myself.

We stood on opposite sides of the occasion. Nothing of what he had done could make the slightest difference to me, I was untouched: youth is too physical to accord very much to that side of things. But what I had *seen*—what he had led me to see—my bursting into the life of things—I would look back on that as the real beginning of my existence, as the entry into a vocation, and nothing could diminish the gratitude I felt for it. I wanted, in the immense seriousness and humility of this moment, to tell him so, but I lacked the words, and silence was fraught with all the wrong ones.

'I have to go now,' was what I said.

'Very well. Of course.'

He looked hopeless. He might have been waiting for me to strike him a blow—not a physical one. He stood quietly at the gateway while I wheeled out the bike.

I turned then and faced him, and without speaking, offered him, very formally, my hand. He took it and we shook—as if, in the magnanimity of my youth, I had agreed to overlook his misdemeanour or forgive him. That misapprehension too was a weight I would have to bear.

Carrying it with me, a heavy counterpoise to the extraordinary lightness that was my whole life, I bounced unsteadily over the dark tufts of the driveway and out onto the road.

My father sat at the kitchen table much longer than he should have talking about Clarice Carmody coming to Berrigo.

My mother got restless because of the cigarettes my father was rolling and smoking. She worked extra fast glancing several times pointedly through the doorway at the waving corn paddock which my father had come from earlier than he need have for morning tea.

He creaked the kitchen chair as he talked especially when he said her name.

'Clarice Carmody! Sounds like one of them Tivoli dancers!'

My mother put another piece of wood in the stove.

'God help Jack Patterson, that's all I can say,' my father said. My mother's face wore an expression that said she wished it was.

'A mail order marriage!' my father said putting his tobacco tin in his hip pocket. Suddenly he laughed so loud my mother turned around at the dresser.

'That's a good one!' he said, slapping his tongue on his cigarette paper with his brown eyes shining.

My mother strutted to the stove on her short fat legs to put the big kettle over the heat.

'It might be too,' she said.

'Might be what too?' my father said, almost but not quite mocking her.

'A good marriage,' my mother said, emptying the teapot into the scrap bucket which seemed another way of saying morning tea time was over.

'They've never set eyes on each other!' my father said. 'They wouldn't know each other's faults . . .'

'They'll soon learn them,' my mother said dumping the biscuit tin on the dresser top after clamping the lid on.

The next sound was a clamping noise too. My father crossed the floor on the way out almost treading on me sitting on the doorstep.

'Out of the damn way!' he said, quite angry.

My mother sat on a chair for a few moments after he'd gone watching through the doorway with the hint of a smile which vanished when her eyes fell on me.

'You could be out there giving him a hand,' she said.

My toe began to smart a little where his big boots grazed it.

I bit at my kneecaps hoping my mother would say no more on the idea.

She didn't. She began to scrape new potatoes splashing them in a bowl of water.

Perhaps she was thinking about Clarice Carmody. I was. I was seeing her dancing on the stage of the old School of Arts. I thought of thistledown lifted off the ground and bowling along when you don't believe there is a wind. In my excitement I wrapped my arms around my knees and licked them.

'Stop that dirty habit,' my mother said. 'Surely there is something you could be doing.'

'Will we visit Clarice Carmody?' I asked.

'She won't be Clarice Carmody,' my mother said, vigorously rinsing a potato. 'She'll be Clarice Patterson.'

She sounded different already.

She came to Berrigo at the start of the September school holidays.

'The spring and I came together!' she said to me when at last I got to see her at home.

She and Jack Patterson moved into the empty place on the Pattersons' farm where a farm hand and his family lived when the Patterson children were little. When the two boys left school they milked and ploughed and cleared the bush with old Bert Patterson the father. The girl Mary went to the city to work in an office which sounded a wonderful life to me. Cecil Patterson the younger son married Elsie Clark and brought her to the big old Patterson house to live. Young Mrs Patterson had plenty to do as old Mrs Patterson took to her bed when another woman came into the house saying her legs went.

My father was always planning means of tricking old Mrs Patterson into using her legs, like letting a fire get out of control on Berrigo sports day, or raising the alarm on Berrigo picture night.

For old Mrs Patterson's disability didn't prevent her from going to everything that was on in Berrigo carried from the Pattersons' car by Jack and Cecil. Immediately she was set down, to make up for the time spent in isolation on the farm where Elsie took out her resentment with long sulky silences, she turned her fat, creamy face to left and right looking for people to talk to.

Right off she would say 'not a peep out of the silly things' when asked about her legs.

My father who called her a parasite and a sponger would sit in the kitchen after meals and roll and smoke his cigarettes while he worked out plans for making her get up and run.

My mother sweeping his saucer away while his cup was in mid-air said more than once good luck to Gladdie Patterson, she was the smartest woman in Berrigo, and my father silenced would get up after a while and go back to work.

Jack Patterson went to the city and brought Clarice back. My father said how was anyone to know whether they were married or not and my mother said where was the great disadvantage in not being married? My father's glance fell on the old grey shirt of his she was mending and he got up very soon and clumped off to the corn paddock.

I tried to see now by looking at Clarice whether she was married to Jack Patterson. She wore a gold ring which looked a bit loose on her finger. My father having lost no time in getting a look at Clarice when she first arrived said it was one of Mrs Patterson's old rings or perhaps he said one of old Mrs Patterson's rings. He described Clarice as resembling 'one of them long armed golliwog dolls kids play with'. Then he added with one of his short quick laughs that she would be about as much use to Jack Patterson as a doll.

The wedding ring Clarice wore didn't seem to match her narrow hand. I saw it plainly when she dug her finger into the jar of jam I'd brought her.

Her mouth and eyes went round like three O's. She waggled her head and her heavy frizzy hair shook.

'Lovely, darlink,' she said. 'You must have the cleverest, kindest mother in the whole of the world.'

I blushed at this inaccurate description of my mother and hoped the two would not meet up too soon for Clarice to be disappointed.

Sitting there on one of her kitchen chairs, which like all the other furniture were leftovers from the big house, I did not want ever to see Clarice disappointed.

My hopes were short-lived. Jack Patterson came in then and Clarice's face and all her body changed. She did look a little like a golliwog doll although her long arms were mostly gracefully loose. Now she seemed awkward putting her hand on the kettle handle, looking towards Jack as if asking should she be making tea. Both Jack and I looked at the table with several dirty cups and saucers on it. Jack looked over my head out the window. Clarice walked in a stiff-legged way to the table and picked up the jam.

'Look!' she said holding it to the light. 'The lovely colour! Jam red!' Jack Patterson had seen plenty of jam so you couldn't expect him to be impressed. He half hung his head and Clarice tried again.

'This is Ellen from across the creek! Oh, goodness me!

I shouldn't go round introducing people! Everyone knows everyone in the country!'

Jack Patterson took his yard hat and went out.

'Oh, darlink!' Clarice said in a defeated way putting the jam on the shelf above the stove. I wanted to tell her that wasn't where you kept the jam but didn't dare.

She sat on a chair with her feet forward, the skirt of her dress reaching to her calves. She looked straight at me, smiling and crinkling her eyes.

'I think, darlink,' she said, 'you and I are going to be really great friends.'

People said that in books. Here was Clarice saying it to me. She had mentioned introducing me too, which was something happening to me for the first time in my life. I was happy enough for my heart to burst through my skinny ribs.

But I had to get off the chair and go home. My mother said I was to give her the jam and go.

But she asked me about Clarice and Jack Patterson as if she expected me to observe things while I was there. 'What's the place like?' she said.

I remembered the dark little hall and the open bedroom door showing the bed not made and clothes hanging from the brass knobs and the floor mat wrinkled. And Clarice with her halo of frizzy hair and her wide smile drawing me down the hall to her.

'She's got it fixed up pretty good,' I lied.

'The work all done?' my mother asked.

I said yes because I felt Clarice had done all the work she intended to do for that day anyway.

I felt unhappy for Clarice because the Berrigo women most looked up to were those who got their housework done early and kept their homes neat all the time.

I next saw Clarice two months later at Berrigo show.

She wore a dress of soft green material with a band of the same stuff holding her wild hair above her forehead.

'Look!' said Merle Adcock, who was eighteen and dressed from Winn's mail order catalogue. 'She got her belt tied round her head!'

Clarice had her arm through Jack Patterson's, which also drew scornful looks from Berrigo people. When Jack Patterson talked to other men about the prize cows and bulls Clarice stayed there, and watching them I was pretty sure Jack would have liked to have shaken Clarice's arm off.

My mother worked all day in the food tent at the show but managed to get what Berrigo called 'a good gander' at Clarice with Jack.

'A wife hasn't made a difference to Jack Patterson,' she said at home that afternoon. 'He looks as hang dog as ever.'

My father, to my surprise and perhaps to hers too, got up and went off to the yard.

The sports day was the week after the show and that was when my father and Clarice met.

Clarice saw me and said 'Hello, darlink' and laid a finger on my nose to flatten the turned up end. She laughed when she did it so my feelings wouldn't be hurt.

My father suddenly appeared behind us.

I was about to scuffle off thinking that was why he

was there, but he stood in a kind of strutting pose looking at Clarice and putting a hand on the crown of my hat.

'I'm this little one's Dad,' he said. 'She could introduce us.'

I was struck silent by his touch and by his voice with a teasing note in it, so I couldn't have introduced them even if practised at it.

'Everyone is staring at me,' Clarice said. 'So they know who I am.'

'Berrigo always stares,' said my father taking out his tobacco tin and cigarette papers and staring at Clarice too.

She lifted her chin and looked at him with all her face in a way she had. 'Like the cows,' she said and laughed.

Her glance fell on his hands rolling his smoke, so different from my mother's expression. I thought smoking was sinful but started to change my ideas seeing Clarice's lively interested eyes and smiling mouth.

'Your father was talking to Clarice Carmody,' my mother said at home after the sports as if it was my fault.

I noticed she said Clarice Carmody, not Clarice Patterson and perhaps she read my thoughts.

'I doubt very much that she's Clarice Patterson,' my mother said, hanging up the potholder with a jab.

I felt troubled. First it was my father who seemed opposed to Clarice. Now it was my mother. I wondered how I would get to see her.

My chance came when I least expected it. My mother sent me with the slide normally used to take the cans of cream to the roadside to be picked up by the cream lorry, to load with dry sticks to get the stove and copper fire going.

The shivery grass was blowing and I was imagining it was the sea which I had never seen, and the slide was a ship sailing through it.

Clarice was standing there in the bush as if she had dropped from the sky.

'Darlink!' she called stalking towards me holding her dress away from the tussocks and blackberries sprouting up beside the track which led down to the creek separating Pattersons' from our place.

'It's so hot, darlink isn't it?' she said lifting her mop of hair for the air to get through it.

No one else looked at me the way Clarice did with her smiling mouth, wrinkling nose and crinkling eyes. I hoped she didn't find me too awful with straight hair and skin off my sunburned nose and a dress not even fit to wear to school.

She put out a finger and pressed my nose and laughed.

'Why don't we go for a swim, darlink?' she said.

Behind her below the bank of blackberries there was a waterhole. A tree felled years and years ago and bleached white as a bone made a bridge across the creek. The water banked up behind it so it was deep on one side and just a trickle on the other.

I wasn't allowed to swim there. In fact I couldn't swim and neither could any other girls in Berrigo my age. The teacher at school who was a man took the boys swimming in the hole but there was no woman to take the girls so we sat on the school verandah and read what we liked from the school bookshelf supervised by Cissy Adcock the oldest girl in the school.

But how could I tell Clarice I couldn't swim much less take my clothes off? I would certainly be in for what my mother called the father of a belting for such a crime.

'I'll swim and you can cool your tootsies,' Clarice said throwing an arm around me.

We walked down the track crushed together, me thinking already of looking back on this wonderful change of events, but worried about my bony frame not responding to her embrace.

She let go of me near the bank and stepping forward a pace or two began to take off her clothes.

One piece after another.

She lifted her dress and petticoat over her head and cast them onto the branch of a sapling gum. Her hands came around behind her unhooking her brassiere which was something I dreamed of wearing one day and threw it after her other things. When she bent and raised one leg to take off her pants I thought she looked like a young tree. Not a tree anyone would say was beautiful but a tree you would look at more than once.

She jumped into the water ducking down till it covered her to the neck which she swung around to look at me.

'Oh, you should come in, darlink!' she said. She lifted both her arms and the water as if reluctant to let go of her flowed off them.

'Watch, darlink,' she said and swam, flicking her face

from side to side, churning up the water with her white legs. She laughed when she reached the other bank so quickly because the hole was so small.

She sat on a half submerged log and lifting handfuls of mud rubbed it into her thighs.

'Very healthy, darlink,' she said without looking at my shocked face.

She rubbed it on her arms and shoulders and it ran in little grey dollops between her breasts.

Then she plunged in and swam across to me. She came up beside me slipping a bit and laughing.

'That was wonderful, darlink,' she said a little wistfully though, as if she doubted she would ever do it again.

The bush was quiet, so silent you could hear your own breath until a bird called and Clarice jumped a little.

'That's a whip bird,' I said hearing it again a little further away, the sound of a whip lashed in the air.

'Oh darlink, you are so clever,' she said and began to get dressed.

No one at home noticed I'd been away too long. My father was dawdling over afternoon tea just before milking and my mother bustling about made a clicking noise with her tongue every time a cow bellowed.

'It's no life for a girl,' my father said referring to Clarice and making me jump nervously as if there was a way of detecting what we'd been up to.

'She took it on herself,' said my mother, prodding at some corned beef in a saucepan on the stove.

'I'll bet they never let on to her about old lolly legs,' said my father slapping away almost savagely with his tongue on his cigarette paper. 'Landing a young girl into that! They'll expect her to wait on that old sponger before too long.'

He put his tobacco away. 'I'll bet Jack Patterson hardly says a word to her from one week's end to the next.' He stared at his smoke. 'Let alone anything else.'

My mother straightened up from the stove. Her sweaty hair was spiky around her red face which wore a pinched and anxious expression, perhaps because of the late start on the milking. She crushed her old yard hat on.

'I'll go and start,' she said.

My father smoked on for a minute or two then got up and looked around the kitchen as if seeing it for the first time.

He reached for his yard hat and put it on.

'What do you think of Clarice?' he said.

I laid my face on my knees to hide my guilt.

'She's beautiful,' I said.

When he stomped past me sitting on the step he kept quite clear to avoid stepping on me.

I got a chance to go and see Clarice one day in the Christmas holidays when my mother went into Berrigo to buy fruit for the Christmas cake and cordial essence.

Clarice put her arm around me standing at the window watching Elsie Patterson at the clothesline.

Elsie was football shaped under her apron and she carefully unpegged shirts and dresses, turning them around and pegging them again. She took the sides of towels and tea-towels between her hands and stretched them even.

'Why does she do that, darlink?' Clarice asked me.

Berrigo women were proud of their wash, but I found this hard to explain to Clarice.

She laughed merrily when we turned away. 'People are so funny, aren't they darlink?'

She suggested going for a swim because the day was what my mother called a roaster.

This time she took off all her underwear at home leaving her thin dress showing her shape.

'Oh, darlink!' she said when I looked away.

I followed her round bottom with a couple of lovely little dents in it down to the waterhole.

The bush was not as quiet as before. Someone is about, I thought with a bush child's instinct for such things.

'I'll go and watch in case someone comes,' I said, and she threw a handful of water at me for my foolishness.

I ran a little way up the track and when I lifted my head there shielded by some saplings astride his horse was my father.

I stopped so close the flesh of the horse's chest quivered near my eyes.

'Don't go any further,' I said. 'Clarice is swimming.'

My father jumped off the horse and tied the bridle to a tree.

'Go on home,' he said. But I didn't move.

'Go on!' he said and I moved off too slowly. He picked up a piece of chunky wood and threw it.

The horse plunged and the wood glanced off my arm as I ran.

At home I beat at the fire in the stove with the poker and put the kettle over the heat, relieved when it started to sing.

I went to the kitchen door and my mother was coming down the track from the road. I heard Tingle's bus which went in and out of Berrigo every day go whining along the main road after dropping her off.

She had both arms held away from her body with parcels hanging from them.

I went to meet her not looking at her face but seeing it all the same red under the grey coloured straw hat with the bunch of violets on the brim. She had had the hat a long time.

String from the parcels was wound around her fingers and it was hard to free them.

'Be careful!' she said, hot and angry. 'Don't drop that one!'

When she was inside and saw the fire going and the kettle near the boil she spoke more gently.

'It's a shaving mug,' she said, hiding the little parcel in the back of the dresser. 'For your father for Christmas.'

He was hunkered down beside the newly turned earth of the garden bed when the battered old VW swung in through the narrow gate and slid to a skewed stop at the head of the steps. He paused, watching, as the driver's door opened and the girl got out. For a moment she stood, her body hidden from him by the dented red body of the car, an arm laid on the rusty curve of the roof, looking out over the sprawl of the city, the distant windings of the river. The light wind stirred her lank black hair, and she lifted one pale hand to brush a long strand from her eyes.

When she moved he lost sight of her for a moment as she passed behind the car. Then she reappeared at the top of the steps, started down. She stooped a little to avoid the low branches of the apple tree, and he realised that she was nearly as tall as he was. But much thinner.

She stopped beside him on the narrow concrete path, a plastic carry-bag in each hand. The sleeves of her grey cardigan reached almost to her knuckles, and pale-pink apple petals were caught in her hair, hair as black as his own. But she was pale, the skin of her face almost translucent. He felt, in his stocky tanned body, suddenly thick and clumsy. Her eyes were a deep and sleepy blue.

'Hullo,' she said, standing flat-footed in her cheap thongs, the breeze pressing the thin folds of the long green dress against the backs of her thighs. Fine wisps of hair drifted about her face; a face pale, high-cheek-boned, a little too square.

'Hullo,' he said, watching the wide vulnerable mouth.

'I'm looking for number three,' she said, her voice low, as tenuous and insubstantial as the wind.

He stood up, flexed his knees, jerked his head towards the corner. 'Just round there.'

She nodded, moved away, drifted round the edge of the building.

Number three was the lowest, the deepest, of the twelve flats, tucked away at the bottom level of the square three-storey block. It had been empty for nearly a month. No one stayed there long—it was too dark, too airless, too cold; its windows caught little sunlight, even in summer.

He went back to his planting.

Within a few minutes she was back. He heard her foot-steps, heard them pause, sensed her waiting, immobile, behind him. He glanced over his shoulder. The eyes, he saw, were really less sleepy than vacant. No, not that, either; but engaged, their vision turned inward, closed and private.

He raised his eyebrows at her.

'I've got some stuff in the car,' she said. 'Do you think you could give me a hand?'

'Sure.' He got to his feet, followed her up the steps to the car-park, brushing aside the new leaves bursting from the rough knots of the grapevine, dodging under the overhang of the apple tree.

The car was crammed with cardboard cartons, paper parcels, plastic bags. He began to unload, carrying them down to the flat. There was less than he had thought, and it took only a few minutes. Inside the dim flat her few possessions seemed lost, swallowed up in the small cramped emptiness: a stack of records, a player, stained books, unpressed clothes, a few groceries.

He stood for a moment in the dim mustiness of the passage.

'Anything else? Can I help with anything?'

She stood in the doorway of the tiny kitchen. A little bright afternoon sunshine, filtered through the leaves of the peach tree, found its way into the room; against the vibrant green of the light her body, shadowed, took on a two-dimensional aspect, flat, anonymous.

She shook her head. 'No thanks.' Then, 'You're not Australian, are you?'

He smiled a little, almost shyly. 'No, Spanish. My name's Carlo.'

'Mine's Helen.'

'Well . . .'

'Thanks . . .'

He left her, still standing in the doorway, returned stolidly to his flowerbeds.

She came out again a little later, when the sun was edging down towards the distant sawtooth hills, sat on the low concrete wall watching him, smoking a cigarette in sharp quick puffs. He looked at her once, briefly, noting again the paleness, the translucency of her skin, the angular slightness of the body. She wasn't pretty, he decided, wouldn't be even if she were less thin. But there was an openness about her face, an innocent quality that made him think of the faces of young children; an openness denied by the veiled barrier of her eyes.

'You speak good English,' she said. 'Was it hard to learn?'

He laughed. 'No,' he said. 'I've been out here since I was a kid. We speak Spanish at home, but ... ' He shrugged.

'What are those?' She nodded at the plants in the bed, arranged in their neat rows like some small orderly army of grey-green spiders. 'I don't know anything about gardening. What sort are they?'

'Carnations,' he said.

'Oh.'

She seemed almost indifferent, as if her interest was a kind of obligation. She took a quick puff at her cigarette. 'What do you call them in Spanish?'

'*Clavel*,' he said, '*los claveles*.' He grinned at her, white teeth sudden against his dark unhandsome face. '*Clavos de amor, clavos de muerte*.'

With some effort she summoned another question. 'What's that? What's it mean?'

He laughed, turning to face her, squatting on his heels. 'It's a kind of play on words,' he said. '*Clavel* is a carnation, *clavelon* is a marigold. *Clavo* is a nail ... so, "*clavos de amor, clavos de muerte*" . . . nails of love, nails of death . . . carnations, marigolds . . . '

Her eyes seemed to wake a little in genuine puzzlement. 'Why? What does it mean?'

'I don't know,' he said apologetically. 'Just a saying, you know, maybe nothing . . . '

'Oh.'

'Just a saying . . . '

She shivered. 'I'd better go in.'

He looked up at the sun, down at the shadows. 'Yeah,' he said. 'Nearly time to knock off.' He picked up the hose, turned the tap, and began to spray the small plants lightly. 'See you next week, maybe.'

'You come once a week, do you? Every week?'

He nodded. 'That's me, regular rounds. Here Tuesdays, over at Norwood Wednesdays, all over the place the rest of the week.' He smiled. 'If you want a hand any time . . . you know . . . odd jobs . . . just give us a shout. The landlord doesn't mind.'

'Oh . . . thanks.' Then she was gone, and the sun dipped below the top of the big quince tree at the bottom of the garden. Carlo began to gather his tools, load them into his old utility.

He didn't see her when he came to work the next week, although the shabby VW still stood crookedly in the car-park. Through the day he worked methodically, planting, weeding, watering, mowing; passing and repassing her green-painted door. But it remained closed, the opaque glass panel dark and blank.

'She's a quiet one,' said Mrs Sykes from number two, bringing out her garbage in the late afternoon. 'Hardly ever see hide nor hair . . . '

'Doesn't she go to work?' asked Carlo.

Mrs Sykes shrugged, the pale bee-sting of her mouth indifferent in her puffy middle-aged face. Wriggling a finger under the towelling turban she scratched her scalp. 'Never seen her.' She stalked back towards her door. 'I think she's been sick . . . '

Carlo began to trim the edges of the lawn with sharp precise strokes.

On the next Tuesday he had been working for several hours, repairing the grape trellis, training the passionfruit vine along the fence, when he heard her voice calling to him from the doorway.

'Would you like a cup of tea?'

He turned quickly. 'Sure.'

She was standing, hunched a little despite the warmth of the morning, the same shapeless grey cardigan pulled up about her throat, drawn down over her wrists. 'Come on then,' she said, and turned away.

He paused for a moment; he had expected that she would bring the tea out into the garden. There seemed to him a certain impropriety in social visits to the tenants' flats. But, all the same, he followed her into the dimness, along the corridor, and into the kitchen. The sudden coolness of the flat struck at the bare skin of his arms and shoulders, chilled the dampness of his sweaty singlet.

He sat at the tiny hinged table, fiddled with a cigarette, while she lit the gas, filled the kettle, spooned tea into a cheap aluminium pot. He looked idly about the room. It seemed still anonymous, bare. There was little evidence of her occupancy; odd plastic canisters, a few cheap jars, a small transistor radio, a couple of threadbare tea-towels.

She poured the tea, fetched the milk from the tiny refrigerator, opened a screw-capped jar half-filled with lumpy sugar.

He sipped, relaxing a little, aware of some impending break in the wall of her indifference. But he sensed, too, a struggle in her, a hint of that effort he had felt before, the effort she seemed to find necessary to admit outsiders to the private world behind her eyes.

Before he had half-finished his tea, hot and weak, she spoke. She looked, not at him, but down at her own cup, chaliced in her thin hands. Carlo noticed, with a sudden stab of something like tenderness, that the two little fingers were slightly curved, bowed, a curious parenthesis.

'Listen,' she said, 'you told me if there was anything . . . '

The pause lengthened.

'Yes?' he said, at last curious.

'Well,' she said, 'it's not a job or anything . . . ' She raised her eyes suddenly to his, and before she looked down again he caught the quick tremor of some desperate urgency. 'The thing is, I'm a bit light on for the rent. I wondered, could you lend me ten bucks? I'd pay you back next week for certain . . . '

james mcqueen

'Sure.' He was taken aback, embarrassed at her need, and somehow disappointed. He reached quickly into the hip pocket of his shorts, found nothing there. 'My wallet's in the ute . . . I'll get it.' He stood up quickly, and walked out into the warmth and light of the morning. In the parking lot he reached through the window into his coat pocket, opened his wallet, pulled out a note. Turning, he was surprised to find her standing close behind him, and he almost bumped into her. He fumbled the money into her hand.

'Thanks,' she said. 'Next week . . . for sure.'

'No worries. On the dole?'

She nodded quickly and turned to go, hesitated. 'You want some more tea?'

He was sure she expected, hoped for, a refusal. And with some relief he shook his head. 'I better get on with it.'

Her sneakers made no sound as she drifted across the concrete and down the steps, out of sight.

It was three days to rent day, he knew. No mates, he thought, and she must be nervous.

A little later, burning rubbish in the far corner of the garden, he saw her hurry up the steps, climb into the VW; heard the engine grind reluctantly to life. The car reversed into the street, narrowly missing the gatepost, and disappeared. He listened as its uncertain cough slowly faded.

At lunchtime he went to a pub half a mile away for a beer. When he returned he saw that the VW was back in its place. There was no sign of the girl. But towards evening, when the sun was striking deeply into the tiny box of her porch she came out and sat on the concrete floor, back against the wall, legs stretched straight in front of her. As he passed, going towards his utility, sweat cooling and drying, he saw that her eyes were closed. They opened slowly as he passed, and he saw that they were somehow different; less darkness in them, lighter, wider. She smiled at him, said nothing, just smiled, easily, gently. He noticed that, despite the late-afternoon warmth, the grey cardigan was still drawn tightly up to her throat, the ends of the ragged sleeves tucked into her loosely clenched fists. She closed her eyes again, her face open as a flower in the late sun.

Driving away, it occurred to him suddenly that the next Tuesday was a long way off.

The next week the door to number three was closed again, dark and blank as ever. Mrs Sykes, on her way to the supermarket, saw him looking at it.

'Won't see *her* yet a while,' she said, a thin scornful edge to her voice.

'Oh?'

'Resting up, I reckon. Doesn't look too strong, you know, I s'pose all the night work's taking it out of her . . . '

'Got a job, then, has she?'

Mrs Sykes gave him a single pitying glance as she straightened a pink plastic curler and swung away up the steps. 'More like a profession, I'd say . . . '

Carlo watched her go, frowning a little, then began unloading trays of petunias.

An hour later Mrs Sykes was back. 'Come and have a cuppa,' she called to him as she passed. 'No cooking today, that bastard Charlie's taking me out to eat tonight, even if he doesn't know it yet . . . '

He sat on the steps that led to her chrome and laminex kitchen, a kitchen crammed with gadgetry indulgences. Eating sweet bought biscuits and drinking tea, he half-listened to her easy chatter. But all the time he was wondering about the closed door of number three. When he was released by Mrs Sykes he felt relieved, and went quickly back to work, finding a place from which he could observe the door. It's the ten dollars, he thought; I'm not getting done for a tenner just because she lays those big sad eyes on me. But he had a habit of honesty; and knew quite well that there was more to it than that.

He did not see her that day, nor the next week.

On the following Tuesday he considered knocking on her door. But if he did, and she hadn't the money, they would both be embarrassed. And even if she had it, he realised, they would still be embarrassed. So he waited, glancing almost furtively at the door from time to time, aware of growing tension and uneasiness inside himself. It wasn't the money at all; he accepted that now. He had faced the fact, had written it off, discounted it in his mind, weeks ago.

And had almost given up hope of seeing her again. Only the sight of the red VW in the car-park reassured him of her continuing presence in the closed flat.

So he was surprised when, early on a Tuesday morning a month later, she ran, a little breathless, from her door. It was summer, now, and in the full heat and glare she seemed frailer than ever, a wraith floating in her strange long dress and threadbare cardigan. Her paleness was startling beside his deepening tan.

Quickly she pushed a note into his hands.

'I'm sorry,' she said. 'Sorry I was so long about it.'

'That's all right.' He felt awkward, wanting suddenly to touch her, to run a single blunt finger over the fine skin of her cheek. But she had retreated, stood a safe three paces away, watching him with eyes brighter, bluer, livelier, than he remembered.

'Come and have some tea,' she said. 'Later, after I've been shopping.'

'OK.'

She backed away, smiling, then turned and ran lightly towards the dark tunnel of her doorway.

A little later he saw her again, moving quickly up the steps to the car-park. She waved at him, and he raised a hand.

He ate his lunch in the car-park, reluctant to leave in case he missed her return; then went back thirsty to work. The afternoon dragged on interminably as he went about the garden chores, waiting. Finally he took the shears and went to work on the west side of the building, out of sight of the car-park, a conscious rebellion against his new and disturbing dependence. But all the time his ears strained for the sound of the returning VW. It didn't come, and at last he gave up. At five o'clock he packed his tools and left, driving out of the car-park feeling hurt and let-down, and angry at himself because of it.

But he waited for several minutes at the corner in the vain hope of seeing her return.

The weeks passed, the solstice and its celebrations came and went, the heat grew, white dust drifted in from the road and settled on the parching leaves of the peach, the apple trees, the quince. Fruit ripened, the ground grew dry and powdery, and Carlo spent more time watering, weeding, mulching. Sometimes, on very hot days, he came in the evenings, to water the beds. The carnations were in full bloom now, filling the air with their cinnamon scent.

Carlo watched, but saw her only once. She came, late one evening, when the fading day was returning shadow and colour to the garden. He heard the old car lurch through the gate, and saw the familiar battered bonnet quiver to a stop. She was halfway down the steps before she saw him. For a brief moment she paused, then went on, hunching her shoulders a little, looking downward at the hot concrete where her sneakers scattered whispers of dust.

'Hi,' he said.

'Hi . . . ' She raised one hand a little, a half-wave, and

kept going. He watched the door close behind her, and turned away.

She seemed thinner, he thought, as if she were being somehow drained.

The summer crept slowly over the land like a slow bright cloud, leaching the colour from the trees, the sky. Only the fruit, the flowers, grew daily brighter. And as the season faded, so, thought Carlo, did the girl. He caught only brief glimpses of her, now; she seemed intent on avoiding him, and when she could not avoid his presence, avoided the open concern in his eyes. On the few occasions when they met she scurried like some frightened animal to the dark shelter of her flat.

At last, on a day of heat and lowering cloud, a day when sweat started as easily as weeds, he conquered his common sense, his best judgement, and knocked on the glass panel of the door. She was there, he knew; the VW was in the car-park.

But the sound of his knocking echoed emptily, again and again, beyond the door.

He almost turned away, but at the last moment, in a panic of resolution, he twisted the knob ... and the door opened.

Inside, the passage was as dim as ever, as musty, an oppression of thick stale air.

He walked slowly past the kitchen, past the bedroom

with its unmade bed and untidy scattering of clothes; found her in the living room at the end of the corridor. The blinds were drawn, and she lay on the shabby vinyl sofa by the left wall, facing him. He stopped in the doorway, motionless, looking at her.

'Go away,' she said, 'please.'

He walked to the sofa, stood looking down at her. She was shivering a little, her nostrils red and raw, her eyes swimming and dark in bruised valleys. He sat down beside her on the edge of the sofa, feeling the slight weight of her hips against him. Despite the heat she wore the old grey cardigan. Slowly he reached out and picked up her left hand, the one that lay nearest him. She tried to pull away, a movement so weak that it seemed a hardly discernible reflex. Only in her eyes was there a firm strength to her resistance.

'Please,' she said.

With his other hand he slipped the sleeve of her cardigan up her arm until it was above the elbow. For a long moment he looked at the dead-white skin, then gently drew down the sleeve again to cover the needle marks. When he looked back at her eyes again he could see nothing there but pain; and wasn't sure whose pain it was—hers, or his own, reflected in the dark hollows.

'What is it?' he said. 'Smack?'

She lay silent, her eyes fixed blankly beyond him.

'Word games,' he said. 'Funny, we talked about word games once. *El clavo*, remember? It means something else, too . . . a bummer, you know, a bad trip, something that gives you the shits . . . ' Shit, he thought without humour, up to your eyeballs in it . . .

Still she said nothing. He watched the faint veins throbbing gently in her naked throat, starving in the heavy grey light.

'Go away,' she said at last, her voice small and very tired. 'Please.'

He stood up, went out into the bathroom. It wasn't there; nor in the bedroom. He found it, at last, in the kitchen; an old chocolate tin hidden clumsily in the cutlery drawer. Inside it lay the deadliness of the wasp-sharp hypodermic, the tie, the discoloured spoon. There was nothing else—no bag, not even an empty one. He put the tin back in its place, returned to the living room. She hadn't moved.

'Can't you score?' he asked.

She moved her head, a slow side-to-side motion of almost indifferent hopelessness.

He sat down again beside her, lifted her hand, held it clasped between his large calloused palms. She made no move to withdraw it, lay staring tiredly up at the cracked map of the ceiling.

'You haven't got a job,' he said. 'And you're not tough enough to be ripping stuff off. So you're hawking it, right?'

She said nothing, lifted her other hand to wipe her nose.

'Doesn't have to be like this, you know,' he said.

For a moment she dropped her eyes, looked at him,

and he saw in them a curious emptiness that frightened him. But he ploughed on. 'You *can* get off it, you know . . . '

'How would you know?'

He was surprised at the coldness, the immense bitterness, in a voice so faint and distanced.

'Ever tried?' he asked. 'Cold turkey?'

After a long pause she shook her head, faintly, dismissively.

'I'll tell you something,' he said. 'It never killed anyone yet. It's bloody awful, I know . . . But it never killed anyone.'

She sighed then, deeply, tiredly. 'Please,' she said, 'just fuck off, will you? I know you're a nice bloke, but please fuck off . . . '

For what seemed a long time he sat beside her, cupping the thin petal of her palm, gently stroking the soft skin of her wrist with his thumbs, as if trying to massage a little of his rude strength into the ruin of her flesh.

'If you want,' he said, 'we could try.' And realised in a sudden swooping that was close to nausea, the enormity of his commitment. 'I could come every day. In the mornings, at lunchtime, at night. At the weekend.' He paused. 'That's all it would take. A week. I'd bring you some flagons of wine . . . it's a help . . . you could make it . . . I know.'

Slowly she closed her eyes. 'Go away now,' she said. 'Please, I really want you to go now . . . '

For a moment he thought that he felt a slight pressure,

a warmth, in her fingers. He waited, but there was only the faint pulse of her blood.

'All right.' He stood up, releasing her fingers, letting them flow like water from his hands. 'But . . . if you change your mind, just tell me. Any time.'

She nodded faintly.

For one more long and clumsy moment he stood there, his limbs seeming to grow strangely larger, more gross and useless. Then he wheeled quickly away and plunged out through the door, back down the narrow passage towards the heaviness of the hot grey day that lay waiting for him.

Mrs Sykes, pegging out her washing, gave him a thin glance as he clumped past her.

Wordlessly, he began grubbing out fading plants from the dry soil.

The weeks dragged slowly for him. In the evenings, on his way home from work, he often found himself going out of his way to drive past the flats. Sometimes the VW was in the car-park, sometimes not. He never stopped.

And, on Tuesdays, he never went near the closed door again. But it seemed to him that a kind of ache bled through the plain green panels of the door, the dark pebbled glass, stirring a dull answering pain inside him.

He never saw her, and there was no sign, no appeal.

But he waited.

In the coolness of a morning at the beginning of autumn he set out the trays of plants, dug and raked the bed, preparing. The sunlight, even at mid-morning, was cooler now on his naked back. Soon it would be time for a shirt again.

'Did you hear?' asked Mrs Sykes, leaning from her window, nibbling at a Chocolate Royal. 'About her?' She jerked the bright paisley of her rayon turban in the direction of number three.

Carlo stared blankly at her, shook his head.

'Found her on the weekend, they did.' She pursed her lips round crumbs of sticky chocolate; chewed, swallowed. 'On drugs, they said. You know, heroin or something . . .'

'Where is she?'

'Gone,' said Mrs Sykes. 'Dead. You know, an overdose . . .'

Carlo lowered himself slowly to his knees, rested his knuckles gently on the gritty soil, looking downward at the sudden strangeness of his blunt hands so that she would not see his face.

'Why do they do it?' said Mrs Sykes, reaching behind her for another biscuit. 'They must know it'll kill them . . .'

'I don't know,' said Carlo, watching his fingers crumble small clods of soil. A surge of grief and pity swept over him, an almost unbearable weight of darkness that seemed to suffocate him. Yet under the grief, the pity, he felt the beginning of a sickness start in his belly and rise towards his throat, a sickness at the unspeakable guilt of his own relief. For some charge had been taken from him. He felt suddenly light-headed and dizzy at the immensity of his betrayal.

He reached blindly into the tray beside him and dug out a cluster of plants.

'What are you planting?' asked Mrs Sykes.

'French marigolds,' said Carlo, staring down at the tiny plants. 'For the winter.'

'That's nice,' said Mrs Sykes. 'A little bit of colour for the dull days.' She swallowed the last of her biscuit, withdrew her head and closed the window.

Carlo began to scoop small holes for the marigolds, spacing the plants neatly a hand's-breadth apart in the waiting earth.

The family who are buying the house have no respect for its age. Jibby watches them anxiously as they crowd through the old weatherboard rooms, talking in excited voices about renovations, repairs and walls that will have to go. Ada makes a point of not listening. She says her heart would break to hear them talk in such a careless way. Whenever they arrive, she disappears with her walking-stick and it doesn't matter if it's raining.

From the tall kitchen window, Jibby sees her sister hobbling for the river and worries that she'll be chilled all night. It is cold, autumn rain. Arthritis affects them both badly but Ada's is the worst. She jokes to Jibby how her longer bones must be held responsible. The rain is quite grey and heavy. It's only a thin Woolworths rain-coat Ada has put on. Once, Ada would've been the more cautious but since the sale of the old family home and everything in it, she's become stubborn. Ada insists now on these walks across the paddocks and along the river, although Doctor keeps warning about the dangers of a fall.

The home paddock is lumpy, long-grassed and silent

since old Punch died. Jibby feels the loneliness stretching out from his old spot under the camphor laurel. She wishes to hurry after Ada who has moved out of sight but it's quite impossible to leave the house alone with the family. There are four children. They swarm around with sticky, inquisitive fingers, squabbling about who'll have the verandah bedrooms.

'Such a pretty name for such a big river,' says the wife, who occasionally notices Jibby hovering behind.

'There's a story to how it came to be named,' Jibby crooks her finger. 'When the district was first settled by the river, there were no bridges, only fording places. One of the flour wagons tipped over. Wheels caught and over she went. The flour floated past the settlement all day. Covered the water so it looked white as snow.'

'Were you there?'

'No, my dear, we're not that old. That's going way back. Mumma was just a child at the time. The river takes a lot of getting away from,' Jibby murmurs. 'As dear old Mumma used to tell us if it was in flood, the river won't let some people go. It keeps hold . . . '

'Years though, isn't it, since the river flooded?'

'Well, let me see. The last big one came in '64. Ada's the real expert on floods—got all the heights written down somewhere, she has. It was 1964. Almost the biggest flood in living memory, although Ada always says the 1923 flood was much worse in terms of damage. Dear oh dear you can't imagine the rain. Overnight we had 252 points, then 227 the following day and 504 on the third. Almost ten inches in three days. People stood on the hotel verandahs watching the water take things down the main street. I don't know. You forget. What people are like. People became worried about a kangaroo that ended up on the Merewethers' roof! Not that you ever need worry here. Our little hill never looked like going under. Not in any flood. Could be cut off from town but no call ever to worry.' Jibby glances through the windows to the river. Ada would almost be at the big willow by now, her good wool stockings soaked and full of grass seed.

'Did your family run dairy cows?' The wife has a gentle face. Jibby likes her and the way soft, pale hair circles her face.

'Yes, yes but the district is used for grazing now. Once, right up until after the war when the price of butter went down, it was dairying. All gone now. I feel sure we'll never see dairying again. All gone,' Jibby gestures out the window. Fairly recently, a two-storey house went up on the Powers' old farm. Its red bricks and blue roof tiles make the old crooked bails and sheds seem more fragile and unlikely. 'Whoever the silly beggar is who put that new house there will come to regret it. Floodplain that is.' Jibby remembers how it was after all the rain was over: to peer out and see water spreading like a beautiful lake around Mr Power's buildings: people out in rowboats trying to salvage chooks or bits of the favourite farm gate: and odd humps of land like miniature islands. But Ada can't be thinking of the floodplain. She's probably standing by the big willow, watching the river weed swirl past. Her bones will be aching. Jibby thinks she hears her sister's laboured breathing; Ada panting cold air in, looking at the river too wobbly with wave and shadow. Or is it just the hissing rain? Jibby tilts her head.

A child appears suddenly. He hops past, wearing Ada's Sunday hat.

'Darling!' says Sarah—Jibby remembers suddenly the wife's name. 'Darling,' Sarah says, 'that's not very polite wearing Miss Anderson's hat without asking.' The child continues hopping. Round and round the big kitchen he goes until Jibby must close her eyes with the dizziness. A good walloping would fix the naughty little fellow whose grin splits his face. His father Ted tries to reason with his son who thinks he's in the middle of one big game. He is shrieking with laughter until even Jibby has to smile.

'Ooh, you've got a cheeky one there.' Jibby crooks a finger at the small boy. 'What's his name?'

'Jack. I'm terribly sorry,' Ted lunges and grabs for the hat. The dried flowers Ada sewed on so many years ago tear slightly. 'He's just learnt to hop,' apologetically Ted hands the hat to Jibby. 'Oh no, and his nappy needs a change. Sarah, I think the bag's near the front door.'

While Sarah goes to find the nappy bag, Ted plonks Jack on the floor and starts undoing buttons and pulling down a pair of blue corduroy overalls. Ted talks, explaining to Jibby how advanced Jack is for his age in every area except potty training. Without asking, Ted pokes the disposable nappy into the wood oven and shuts the door. 'My old gran had one of these—used to make fantastic pikelets on the top.' He's cheerfully oblivious to the terrible smell of burning plastic. 'Ah, here's the nappy bag.' Sarah reappears with a finely embroidered carpet-bag.

'Beautiful needlework,' says Jibby. 'Did you do it?'

'Me?' Sarah laughs. 'No way. I can hardly manage getting buttons back on. No, you can get them at the Fineflour markets. Let me remember. Umm. Every third Sunday I think. Whatever weekend it was when we were last up. There's an Indian stall there. Really cheap too, some of their stuff.'

'Oh, I see ... Indian? Very pretty anyway.' Jibby remembers her mother's little black boy who used to chop the wood. An Abo, not an Indian. Poddy, everyone called him Poddy because he was as undersized as an early calf that has lost its mother. When the first plane flew over the district, Poddy was so scared he came racing into the house. Jibby remembers it was winter and he had a cold. There were yellow candlesticks dripping from his nose. For ages afterwards, Ada could make Jibby laugh and dear Mumma sigh, by sticking jelly beans up her own nose.

Jibby watches Jack wriggling uselessly under his father's large and capable hands. They look like farmer's fingers but hard though it was to believe at first, Ted is a doctor; a children's specialist and by all accounts a very good one despite his wild curly hair. This time a proper nappy is going on. Ted fastens the pins tightly and re-dresses him, still talking about various aspects of the house, its contents and architecture. There is a damp smudge on the polished floorboards and a strong, salty smell. Jibby feels her back creaking as she bends to mop up.

'Pine, is it?' Ted strokes the soft wood of the dresser.

'Yes, it is some sort of pine, I think. Made in my grandmother's time. The plates were hers too. All fine English china. That big blue and white platter's an Alfred Meakin that came over from England with Grandma. Ah, the roast dinners carved on that were something to see—to feed all the boys on Sundays after the week's work was over.' Jibby stands fingering the ribbon on Ada's hat and feels painfully hungry for a small plate of roast beef with Mumma's thin brown gravy; her five brothers big and friendly along one side of the table. She peers absently into the rain, the smell of baked potatoes a tantalising memory in the wind coming under the window.

'Well, if you'll excuse us, we might just have another look at the bathroom,' Ted says. 'Sarah's found this wonderful tile shop and we wanted to get an idea of sizes. Specialises in all sorts of antique accessories as well. Baths, everything really.'

'Yes, you go. It's always been a lovely big bath.' Jibby drifts in the kitchen, listening. The high ceiling murmurs strangely with the faraway noises of children. Sounds like they're still on the back verandah. Trying not to think of Ada, she decides to make a batch of cookies for the family to eat. Unlike Ada, she can't help enjoying some of the family's visits. She can never remember any of their names but no one seems to mind or notice. Feeling suddenly hopeful, Jibby begins at once, taking the big mixing bowl out in such a hurry she nearly drops it. It is yellow porcelain and full of tiny cracks and the secrets of many a good pudding. Jibby likes to think so anyway, remembering the way her mother used to slap ingredients willy-nilly around and around with a wooden spoon, so the translucent flesh of her arms wobbled and shook. As she'd stir, as she'd dip her hands in to knead and shape, she would talk to Jibby and Ada who'd be sitting up at the table, making fat gingerbread men. Mumma would often say when they were helping her to cook, how lucky it was God had thought to give her two beautiful little girls after years of raising sons.

My little assistants, Mumma said as they stood on tiptoes to watch her poisoning the flour the year the blacks were restless in their camps by the river.

'So help me,' Jibby jumps when one of the children comes creeping round the door. 'You spooked me. What's your name? I'm always forgetting.'

'Emily.'

'That's right. Emily. Such a pretty name.'

'I hate it.' She's been sucking one side of her fringe and it has dried pointy and sharp. She has grey, sad eyes like the river when it's autumn and raining.

'The cat's eating a monster of a grasshopper in your bedroom,' says Emily.

'How do you know it's not my sister's bedroom?'

'Because it's like your bed should be.' She has a shy

girl voice. One bare foot taps against the other and she giggles. 'We reckoned it was your bed because it's the fattest one. Dad says he's never seen such a beautiful quilt as yours, even if the moths are getting it a bit.'

'Ada stitched that,' Jibby says. 'It's Ada's room. Took her from when she was six years old to thirteen, each afternoon before the light went. No electricity then. No way we could do our needlework in the evenings.' Jibby remembers how Poddy the little black boy's eyes would stare through the glass at them as they sewed. And how he'd been sent away the day Mumma found him in Ada's room, fingering the small circles of patchwork.

'I hate sewing,' says Emily. 'I'm always getting in trouble from my sewing teacher. She hates me because I can't do chain stitch for the pincushions we're meant to be making. Do you think we ought to get the cat off Ada's rug?'

'She'll be all right. She won't leave any mess. Not the old grey puss. She's a good girl, getting the grasshoppers. Stops them eating my roses, you know.'

Jack arrives in the kitchen again, hopping. In a small persuasive voice, he asks for a biscuit. 'Pease, pease?' He smiles angelically up, hopping on the spot. He tries again, 'More? More? Biccy?'

'This little fella amuses me,' says Jibby.

'Oh you sooky boy,' Emily tells him. 'She hasn't even made any biscuits yet. Here, you can have one of my fizzers. Just a purple one. Now off you go.' Jack obediently turns round, making energetic hoppy noises as he disappears.

'Going about his business,' says Jibby. 'Look!'

'Well, I'll just go and watch the cat,' says Emily, 'and keep an eye on Jack for a while. It's because of Winnie the Pooh he does all this hopping stuff. Y'know—Christopher Robin goes hoppity, hoppity, hoppity hop.'

Jibby doesn't answer. She looks at the ceiling that is suddenly full of grey mildew and small grey spiders. There's a sadness, a heavy feeling in the air. The kitchen is quiet and waiting now the children are gone. Through the thick glass window comes the spatter of rain getting heavy again. Is it flood rain? Is it an autumn flood on its way? Leaving the butter and treacle to melt together in a pan on the stove, Jibby hurries across to the brown bakelite wireless, wondering if there has been rain in the mountains. Their Dadda always used to say that mountain rain was what really counted in a flood. If the catchment filled up it didn't matter if hardly a drop fell on the town, the shops would be sure to get very wet. Out of the window there are no cows and no Punch in the paddock any more to let Ada know if he felt a flood coming. Ada could always tell if Punch was getting nervous in the skinny paddock by the river. She'd always had a way with horses. Even if Punch was upset, Ada could lead him by his mane through two gates and into the high home run: settle him down with a biscuit of hay. By the big flood of '64 he hardly had enough teeth left for hay and the weight of water in his mane made it drag and catch on the long grass.

Surely Ada must have walked the full length of the river paddock—surely by now? It's a long time since

Jibby was down there but it used to only be a matter of minutes before the boundary fence was reached. She imagines the yellow grass as it swallows Ada's bony ankles and walking-stick; the unsettling decay in every direction. In '64 the flood half-uprooted the border willow so that it has grown sideways through the fence ever since. The fence was built by Jibby's favourite brother Garnett. He said at the time it'd last one hundred years but it hasn't.

Jibby puts a few more chips of wood into the stove, wishing it was spring, not winter, on the way. Woodsmoke hangs more happy and welcoming in spring. She thinks of Ada struggling back to the house and seeing the smoke spiralling away in the wind. It wouldn't be a warming sight. But nothing can warm them up any more, not even a long soak in the tub. Every effort becomes more dangerous. Only the other week, Ada bumped her shin on the edge of the bath. Where the bruise was, an ulcer is forming. Each night Jibby tries to get the healing to begin but the leaking sore is moving all the time down her sister's leg. The problem is Ada's skin is as thin as the fine airmail paper in the writing desk, never used since the old aunt in England died. There's no strength left in Ada's skin to grow over the hurt. The bruise inches around the ulcer in mottled and lavender shadows. All this walking to avoid the family hasn't helped.

There's a dimness in the air and Jibby is frightened, feeling the autumn turning into something worse. The river has been full of change, running with lines of foam

through it in the afternoon southerlies. And now the
rain. Jibby wishes Ada would stop watching it tapping
peculiar patterns in the river. She must be watching the
rain and the river to be taking so long. Seeing the cold
streaming lines instead of their future, 'snug as two little
bugs', says Doctor, in the Henford House retirement
village. It is that name more than anything else which
has made Ada despair—quickly and without hope. She
says they will be like hens in a coop and never be let out,
not ever again.

Ada is meaning to die before the move. Jibby feels the
certainty of her sister's desire as strongly as she smells
the sweet-cooking biscuits. It's a lonely, knowing
feeling, being the sister who'll have to go last. The others
all died years before. Garnett's death, an accident on the
Porridge Creek punt, was the first break. Mumma used
to say Ada and Jibby were God's beautiful afterthoughts
but there's no comfort in that now.

'He's forgotten all about taking us back, Ada ... '
Jibby talks to her baking biscuits. 'We're his afterthoughts at the wrong end of life,' she pokes a knife into
the middle of a hot biscuit and thinks that her cooking
skills aren't what they were. Little bit by little bit, they've
let themselves fall out of all the old routines until they
seem to live mainly on toast and soft-centre chocolates
and endless cups of tea. And the garden keeps reducing
itself round them. There are always the roses by the back
verandah, but further out, asparagus fern is strangling
the tall azaleas and magnolias. The flower beds are
choked with weeds. A young fellow and girl had arrived

at the back door one day offering to fix the beds up a bit. But the pair had looked like they'd crawled out of a drainpipe and she'd sent them off.

The funny thing—funny peculiar, not funny ha-ha—is that Ada can't stop herself returning to her Sunday chore of childhood. Everything else is neglected but not the brass fittings of Mumma's old sewer. Ada polishes and polishes, down on her hands and knees. She won't be stopped by any number of good reasons. She worries that the garden taps are no longer shiny. The other after-noon Jibby heard Ada calling for Poddy. The taps had been Poddy's job. He'd wrap the old red silk scarf Mumma had given him round his head. In summer the sweat would glint on his back, shinier than black metal.

Slowly Jibby becomes aware of an insistent squeak. She wanders from her kitchen, throwing a good-sized handful of tea into the big pot first. It sounds as if a rocking horse is creaking away deep within the house. Their brother John, who left the land to become a carpenter, made Jibby and Ada a rocking horse so big, they were still able to use it when they were eight and nine years old. It was a dappled grey with bright red paint flaring in its nostrils and red leather reins. But the noise turns out to be young Jack getting into mischief again. He's laughing at the rain as he swings the front gate back and forth. White camellia petals fall on the path. Jibby stares at their drift to the ground and at the green-grey bend of river.

'Wain, wain,' Jack is delighted to have captured an audience. 'Wain. It's waining,' he shrieks and swings the gate faster.

'Come inside. Come on inside, Jack, there's a dear little fellow.' Jibby, if she ever knew, has forgotten how to coax a child. She holds her arms out. Jack grins. The camellias shed petals like tears. Jibby would like to suspend her sadness but Ada is such a long time away. By now she must be soaked through, the cheap raincoat clinging and cold. The little boy swings and swings. 'Come along,' calls Jibby.

Jack pokes his tongue out and tips over. He begins to howl, making Jibby run out into the rain. His crying smells medicinal—of Anticols, of cough jubes. Jibby bends over him but he won't stand up. The other three children giggle from the front room. They've been watching through the small squares of rose and blue glass. Jibby hears the strange, snuffling laughter as she hurries down the hallway. It increases her alarm. Only their humped outlines are visible behind the curtains. Ted is in the kitchen, taking the biscuits from the oven.

'Bit black on top. Got them out in the nick of time,' he beams and burns his fingers trying to pick one up.

'Your little boy. He fell off the garden gate.'

'Did he! Well, I wouldn't get too upset. He's always meeting the floor head first. Part of being the youngest y'know. Always the show-off,' says Ted. 'Sarah could tell you all about it. She wrote half her thesis on that subject alone for her PhD. Bit technical but there's probably a lot of truth in it. Sarah's worried that Skye isn't making the adjustment well. For so long she was the youngest, probably the most spoilt . . . '

'I think we'd better make sure your little fella's all

right,' Jibby leads the way back through the hallway.

'Most people don't seem to realise,' Ted grabs a couple of biscuits and follows Jibby, 'that the three eldest are from my first marriage. Jack is Sarah's first. She wants more now, which is why we needed to look for such a big house. And in the country. We both decided it'd be good to make the move from the city. So many advantages. Sarah was the one who spotted your ad in *The Land*.'

Jibby remembers Ada's shock when the real estate man showed them his proposed description:

FAR NORTH COAST BARGAIN: Small, dilapidated dairy on prime river acreage. Lovely, older style home characteristic of its time with high ceilings, entrance hall, stained-glass door surrounds. Three fireplaces, five bedrooms, established gardens. Opportunity to put individual taste into its renovation . . .

The advertisement went on to list household items that would be going at the auction. 'It wasn't much of an advertisement,' says Jibby. 'Ada couldn't get them to change a bit of it.' The word 'dilapidated' had hurt the most. That was the hardest to take, after so many years of love and care.

'The river did make us really interested,' says Ted. 'Well, and the house. But being so close to the river means hours of entertainment for the kids. That's what I immediately thought, having grown up near a river myself. Ahh, there's the monster. Nearly flattened the front gate. Sarah calls his little expeditions search and destroy missions.' Ted runs through the rain to reach Jack who's found two snails to play with. 'You'll have to have a bath now, you scallywag.' Ted hoists Jack onto his hip. 'Poor Miss Anderson. We must seem like the invading army.'

Jibby leans on the verandah railing, staring at the clumps of jonquils. They are Paper Whites—Ada's favourites, Paper Whites. In the rain they look as fragile as their name. Ada should be back. Jibby tries to get the river into focus. It is darker now and glimmers with patterns of rain already past. Ada must be going too slowly through the wild grass that cattle haven't grazed for years and years. The overgrown tracks would be tricky to follow—so easy to slip and fall and to lie still with the river gathering strength.

Ada creeps: the water sounds hiss inside her. She is too full of loneliness to come back to the house. Jibby feels it overtaking her sister—the loneliness coming in every direction. From the river, from the house, from the happy noises of children crowding out of the front room to follow Jack as he hops down the hallway, holding tight to his father's hand. The loneliness has been growing in Jibby and Ada for too long. Sometimes, if it is a really fine day, Jibby lets it fade and falter into the blue loop of river. But loneliness, it always returns. Since meeting the family, Ada has let it fill her up. She walks along the river with it getting tighter and colder inside.

Jibby has tried to make Ada less alone with stories it

takes time to remember or invent. Were swimming car-
nivals really held every summer in a stretch of the river
near their land? The Fineflour floating baths, was that
what they were called? Ada looks so sceptical when she
tries to describe the makeshift palings used to mark
either end of the pool, or the milling group of young
Glover and Donaldson boys who seemed to have a
winner in every race. And she won't remember the trick
they played on Poddy, how they egged him into diving
when he didn't know how. He could not swim a stroke
but they made him leap in with the red scarf in his hair.
He said he thought when he hit the bottom he'd be able
to just walk underwater to the bank that was at least
twenty feet from the springboard. But Ada will not
remember. She bowed her head when Jibby told the
Poddy-tries-to-dive story. Some days she goes silly over
the blacks, what happened to them, and calls dear
Mumma and Dadda killers. Jibby has to sit her in the
Silent Room then. The Silent Room is where Mumma
would wash their mouths out with soap and water if they
were rude. Then she'd make them sit and say prayers for
forgiveness. Ada cries at being locked in the room. Her
weeping is so soft Jibby can sometimes mistake it for
wind on the river.

Luckily, there are a few black and white photographs
in the small grey album. So Ada can't pretend to forget
the day of the reflections. That day they'd taken turns
with the camera. One of Jibby's favourite photographs
is the one of Ada standing by the boundary fence that
runs into the river. Fifty years ago but the day was full

of light and laughter and Jibby won't think of it as past. Ada wears her prettiest striped pinafore and raises her hands over her head as though to dive into the perfect reflection of herself in the water. Singing, she is singing in the year before Poddy disappeared and clear notes seem caught in the dappled grey and white of the photo.

'I must away, Ada,' Jibby mutters. 'Must see what the family's up to.' In the hall mirror she peers at her face. To look makes her feel weepy. The expression she sees reminds her of the warty, squeezed sadness of old caged birds at the show, with no winning tickets on their cages.

In the kitchen the family are eating the batch of biscuits fast. They don't notice Jibby trembling at the door. They chatter away like the early morning myna birds in the ancient old palm outside Ada's bedroom. Jibby turns away from the tumbling, strange words about hobie-cats, rafts and catamarans. She moves back down the hallway where Ada used to get into such trouble for sliding up and down the polished floor. The walls radiate cold but there's no time to go the long way round to the bedrooms for a cardigan. Jibby doesn't bother with an umbrella but pushes her shoes into the gumboots by the back door and struggles into a raincoat. Years, it seems, since she's unlatched the side gate and headed for the river. The rain soon soaks through. The cold settles in her shoulders and moves inwards as she walks. She tries to stride out, to find Ada before the river rises, but her knees totter and cramp. Breathless by the first fence, Jibby looks back at the fine old house, the elegant verandahs, the high pitch of the rusting roof. All, all sold. They don't ever like to admit the final arrangements have been made for the move away. For a moment Jibby mistakes the burst of poinsettias against the western verandah for flames—and cries out before realising. She sighs then, thinking how poor and straggly the flowers are. Far too long since they were pruned back.

A lemon tree looms, yellow with fruit. They are bush lemons, thick-skinned and sweet enough to eat. Mumma used to make pints of sherbet with the milk from Topsy, to drink in the wicker chairs where the winter sun always came. She said no winter cold ever dared come near her lemon sherbet. Jibby latches her fingers around a low hanging lemon but it knots up. The skin across her hand tears as she pulls back through the thorny wood.

'Ada,' she calls and hurries on, slithering. 'Ada,' her voice rises like the wind. 'Little Sis,' as if she calls for a lost puppy. 'Sis Sis Sis.'

The river appears and words babble like water inside her. 'You'll catch your death. No mistake. Ada? We'll run the bath. I've made biscuits and the kettle's on. The family are still there but don't worry. You don't have to worry about them, Ada. They're nice children. Think of the fun they'll have. In the flood, the water up, not having to go to school.'

Ahead, the willows sag for the river. Ada doesn't come forward. Jibby moves closer to the river until she's right at the edge and the slap-slap of the waves couldn't be louder. There is a wild green smell through the rain. There's a rhythm in the sounds of water. Jibby is reminded of a song but its tune is elusive. Ada would know. She always was such a singer.

Something droops against the barbed wire boundary. 'Too wild for reflections today, Ada,' Jibby murmurs as the paddock and fence ripple towards her like a high tide coming in, like the first wash of floodwater over the lumpy banks. There are waves in the grass, as Jibby scrambles to reach the fence. The earth heaves. Jibby feels it moving watery and unsafe beneath her. The dark shape on the fence is moving too, stretching arms out for the sky, stretching up.

'Ada. Ada, the family . . . ' Jibby shuts her eyes against the rain and goes forward. She thinks hard of the children and can picture their colourful, jaunty progress towards their car. It is a big car, red and gleaming. It glides away and inside the mother hands out more food and instructs all the children to wave and wave to the Miss Andersons, who have probably gone for a lie down but to wave just in case they are watching from behind the gauze curtains.

The turning of the screw, stopped by the words, 'The
world is a long journey, Mr McDowell.' Scribner's head.
Scribner bending down to see under the car, 'Taking a
journey, Mr McDowell?'

'The Annual Conference of the New South Wales
Country Cordial Makers Association, Mr Scribner,' he
said from under the car, his voice cramped.

Scribner picked up and held an unnecessary spanner.

Scribner always made himself a part of the situation.

The screw turning completed.

He dragged himself out from under the car. 'The
world *is* a long journey,' he said to Scribner.

Scribner always made himself a part of the situation
and addressed himself to the situation.

He ingratiated himself by slicing, pouring, or serving.

Yet he belonged in no situation.

Slicing, pouring, serving, holding or assisting.

Scribner was also good at quotation, which pleased
him because he liked to hear a good quotation.

Scribner said, 'I myself have been considering a trip to
the city to buy my summer underwear.'

He dusted himself from being under the car and

thought that he did not vary *his* underwear year-long. Why then did Scribner vary his underwear? And why buy it in the city? Was it education or was it because he and his mother considered themselves 'above the town'.

He found himself quite easily saying, yes, that today he would not mind the company of Scribner.

On some days he could not abide the idleness of Scribner or his wandering, picnicking conversation.

He liked Scribner when he felt in a truant mood. He usually fought against this truancy in himself, but yet it did relax him—when he allowed himself to go like a balloon in the breeze. Babbling on with fantasy and speculation.

Being above the town did not save Scribner from being known as a glutton. His mother also, it was said, looked after herself at town functions.

'I was reading only yesterday,' said Scribner, 'talking of cordials—about the brewing of barley beer in Mesopotamia—they kept their brewing recipes secret. O they valued alcohol highly in ancient times.'

'And today also, Mr Scribner.'

'Yes, and today also, Mr McDowell.'

Some in the town had wanted him to go into brewing, but he had decided to go the other way and stay in 'temperance drinks'—aerated waters and maybe egg drinks and milk drinks, which he thought had a future when there was more refrigeration.

'Above the town', but the Scribners, mother and son, never missed a town function invited or not, nor missed a sandwich, a sausage roll, a piece of sponge cake, a pikelet, a cup cake, a scone, a trifle.

Being a Bachelor of Arts was why he supposed that no one minded that Scribner belonged in no situation, did not work at a job. Although he did write letters to Government Departments for those people worried about the right way of doing so.

And Scribner was a speechmaker, invited or not, and always used a Latin line, which he liked, and had enough sense to explain it without implying that you did not know.

Of course, people said, and it was probably so, that the Scribners, mother and son, had little money. That explained, people said, why they ate the way they did at every town function. For a long time it was said that the Scribners had shares, but maybe the Depression had rendered these valueless.

It seemed to answer why they stuffed themselves at every town function.

Scribner made the occasional guinea by writing an advertisement for him, but always took the money offered in payment as some unexpected, though welcome, consideration.

'Isn't there anything you wish to collect from your house before we set off, Mr Scribner? Your valise?'

Scribner said, no, he could go as he was and perhaps buy a toothbrush and toothpowder and stay at the Masonic Club.

He lent Scribner an old dustcoat for the journey up the coast.

'Who told you I was planning a trip to the city, Mr Scribner?'

'O I came across you simply by chance, Mr McDowell. I was taking a stroll.'

That was the whole damn' difference between himself and Scribner. Scribner daily placed himself in the hands of fate. He, on the other hand, worked at making fate do what he wanted. The whole damn' difference.

Yet here they were, in the same car, going to the same destination.

Scribner, he was sure, did not know from day to day his income or even his possible whereabouts. Except that if the town had a banquet, a ball, a garden party, dinner, reception, afternoon tea, Scribners, mother and son, would appear and Scribner would, unsolicited, begin to pour, slice, or serve. They belonged to no local organisation. Or did they consider themselves members of every organisation ex-officio?

The town's social calendar guided Scribner through life. He, on the other hand, organised the social calendar.

Scribner asked about the Cordial Makers Association, saying, 'I always believed that "two of a trade did never agree".'

'Hard times have hurt the Association, but we've agreed on standards. I've opposed Major Adcock's move to put a Jusfrute Factory in every town. Wanted the Association to oppose this. I'm for every town having its distinctive local products.'

He then asked Scribner if he worried for the future, given his style of life.

Scribner replied that he sometimes felt himself to be the embodiment of the Greek god Perseus.

'Which was he, Mr Scribner?'

'Perseus—as though I have the helmet of Pluto which makes me invisible. O everyone expects me to be where I am and no longer notices me. Therefore I am invisible. O and the wings of Hermes because I move where I want and there is always a way—today, thanks to your fine motor-car, Mr McDowell—' Scribner patted the dashboard—'and the Mirror of Athene, which permits me to avoid looking into the dangerous gaze of Mammon or the snakepit called the Opinions of Others, and so I avoid the anxieties of life.'

Scribner, some said, was also close to being mad.

He liked Scribner for talking in an educated fashion and he, himself, found that he talked in a more elevated way when with Scribner.

Both sat over the dusty miles in their dustcoats.

'It has always struck me, Mr Scribner, that as an educated man you could have done more with your talents.'

'What more could I offer life, Mr McDowell? Why I have written a number of immortal labels for your aerated waters!'

It was true that Scribner could always find a new word for 'refreshing' and could tread the difficult line between a 'fancy' invented name and a simple descriptive name and yet still get registration. All Scribner's names for new lines had gained registration. The last had been 'Green River' for the lime.

'One day, Mr McDowell, the label, the advertisement,

will be considered works of art. O yes, demeaned today, but in the future—say in 1950 or 1960 when people fully understand the meaning of Art—I predict that they will be considered the Art of Our Times. The embodiment of our Dreams.'

'You think so, Mr Scribner—that advertising could be, for instance, the poetry of commerce?'

'Indeed, I do. And the machines we use—the sculptures of industry.'

That was a tickling idea.

'Some of the French already do, Mr McDowell. I myself am a French Futurist in Art. Yes, indeed. We wrap our life in words, Mr McDowell. Our poor mundane daily existence would be nothing without the illusions we weave about them. Illusions, Mr McDowell, are the game we play with our selves and life. Words are the "Sparkling Juices from the Fountain of Delight".'

'That was one of your best, Mr Scribner.'

'Thank you, Mr McDowell.'

'Unfortunately, isn't it true that once you recognise these illusions, as you call them, once you see it is a "game", Mr Scribner, don't they disappear? Is that not the case?'

'A painful philosophical truth, painfully true.'

He raised with Scribner his own belief in the 'speech' and the 'business letter' as the practical arts of commerce.

'Noble arts, Mr McDowell, with a long tradition—"When he killed a calf he would do it in high style and make a speech." Why, you're a Futurist yourself, Mr McDowell.'

He told Scribner he did not know about that, but he was against the trend to shorter speeches.

Scribner said with great feeling and some emotion, and not altogether to the point, that the Letter was a failed form. 'We taught the People to write and they never made anything of the Letter. I have read many attempts at the Letter. The greatest condemnation of Mass Literacy has been the failure of the People to produce Great Letters. The Letter to the Editor is also a failed form.'

Scribner was spluttering and salivating with feeling for his words.

'The telephone has harmed the letter, don't you think, Mr Scribner?'

'Ah, but then we must make the telephone the instrument of Art. The Telephonic Essay.'

'I myself plan out each Telephonic Conversation.'

'That is a credit to you, Mr McDowell, but we must not undervalue the spontaneous, the ephemeral, the extemporaneous. Why don't People take delight? Why! the Telephonic Essay is one of the great extemporaneous arts. There is, Mr McDowell . . . '

Scribner was spluttering off again with great gusto for his words. '. . . the art, Mr McDowell, which comes from striving, practice, revision and attachment to the traditions—poetry, painting and so forth—and there is the art which comes from felicitous practice in the daily run of our lives.'

Scribner wiped his mouth with his handkerchief. 'But we don't, but we don't become artists without an act of conscious dedication. No, no, no, there must be dedication to the Muse, dedication of one's Spirit to the idea of doing things superlatively. A dedication to the superlative. And the painstaking accumulation of the supporting skills.'

Scribner fell into exhausted silence, cooling himself by flapping his silk handkerchief, wiping his face, dabbing his neck. He seemed to carry more than one handkerchief.

'I consider yourself to be so dedicated, Mr McDowell,' Scribner managed to get out.

'Thank you, Mr Scribner.'

When he had recovered himself a few miles farther on, Scribner launched off again, saying, 'I consider myself a Dadaist and of the Bohemian Tradition, but I salute you as a Business-man Artist.'

They had passed through the heavy, foreboding bush that closed in on the narrow road between Milton and Nowra, through which they sat silent, inturned, in the cold darkness of the overshadowed road. They grinned and talked a lot when they were out of it and into the open valleys of Berry and Gerringong. It was a relief to see the sea from time to time. Although they could not be lost, there was no way of being lost really, it was good to be sure. They then hugged the embankment around the winding spurs of Kiama, looked and spoke, as everyone did, of the convict fences of the English fields around Kiama.

They were again silent through the tar roads of Wollongong, knowing at that point they had left well and truly behind the outer limits of the district in which they might be known. He did not care for the larger towns where there were more people who did not know you than people who knew you.

'It is a lonely and unrewarding life being the only Dadaist on the coast, Mr McDowell.'

The other side of Wollongong the front tyre was punctured by a piece of broken horseshoe. They lunched at the tearooms at Bulli before trying the Pass and going back into the dark, empty bush before Sydney.

Scribner ordered double servings and blew his nose while the bill was being paid.

As they whined and chugged up Bulli Pass, he joked to Scribner that they were certainly not 'Hope Bartletts' and the Chev was no racing-car. He asked Scribner how one became a Business-man Artist, in his opinion. He did not ask about how one became a Dadaist.

'What is needed, Mr McDowell,' he said, above the motor, 'is to have once *thought the thought*—about striving for the superlative. That's enough, to have *thought the thought*. To have *thought the thought*, understood it, cherished it, as an ideal. Of course, it cannot remain in the forefront of your mind for long, but to have *thought the thought* means that you are then servant of the thought. Some thoughts, you see, contain imperatives and instructions, and once you have had them pass through your head, they affect the spirit. They leave behind instructions to be followed. Some thinking permits of no retreat. One cannot go back, Mr McDowell, to what one was before having come across the thought and allowed it to pass into the mind. Not all thoughts, just some thoughts. We never please an Ideal, Mr McDowell. O no. O no. O Idealism is a taskmaster, Mr McDowell, who makes us permanently dissatisfied with our self.'

He nodded at Scribner's words, trying to keep his own thoughts out of the way so he could fully listen.

'Not a happy state, Mr McDowell.'

'No.'

He had never heard these sorts of thoughts said before. He marvelled that a man like Scribner, who daily placed himself in the hands of fate and did not have goals and plans, should have such ideas. It convinced him that the town was wrong when it thought Scribner a joking matter, which some did, despite his Bachelor's Degree.

He then told Scribner that although the words just spoken were new to him, he had felt similar things. He found that in the town there were too few who could go along with such types of thinking.

'They do not make the conversational possibilities—they keep certain doors closed. Do you know what I mean, Mr Scribner? They do not allow certain thinking to come out because of their tightly closed demeanour. The ideas in one's head become shy and wary. Some people frighten ideas away. And words from your mouth.'

'I am an enemy of those who frighten away my words and ideas, Mr McDowell,' Scribner said with vehemence, hostility.

'I'm afraid there are some in the Science Club even,

who by their general demeanour stop the ideas dead in your head. I must say, Mr Scribner, I find that my ideas are enthusiastic to meet yours.'

'I wish I were more a man of affairs sometimes, like yourself, Mr McDowell.'

'But you are a Bachelor of Arts.'

'All mysteries, Mr McDowell, find their resolution in human practice. A student only lists and classifies the mysteries. Karl Marx, ogre of our Times, said that.'

'Even Mr Marx, then, knows something. They say, I believe, that truth is dispersed among us.'

'But not equally, Mr McDowell. Believe me, in all humility, some of us have more than others. Believe me.'

Although there was little talk over the last miles, Scribner burst out at Sutherland, saying, 'No, damn it, I am not a Dadaist. No, I am not. I am an Everydayist. I believe in the ultimate beauty of everyday things. I'm no Dadaist.'

He did not question Scribner about this or what he meant by it. It was, it seemed, a private tussle. He had feared through the journey the word 'Dadaist'. Not having understood it. He had understood and heard enough for the one day. He did not care to venture further than he had in the conversation. He did not want to ask about the word 'Dadaist', because he did not know what lay behind it. He doubted that Scribner, anyhow, belonged to any of these organisations he mentioned.

His mind, also, was turning to tomorrow, the city, and the Annual Conference.

At Kogarah they stopped and removed their dustcoats and washed their hands in the park, before driving into the city. Scribner went over and stole a flower from a garden in a nearby house, called Denbigh, and put the flower in his buttonhole. This act of theft filled him with apprehension. Annoyed, he refused to accept the buttonhole flower Scribner had stolen for him.

That had been the only irritation of the journey.

Since he was staying at Adams' Tattersalls, he dropped Scribner at the Masonic Club.

'It's good afternoon, or should I say evening, then, Mr Scribner.'

'Yes, and a good evening to you, Mr McDowell. My regards to the cordial-makers of this State. Good conferencing and all that. Conference, they say, maketh a ready man.'

He noticed to his surprise that although Scribner was not a Mason, the doorman at the club knew him and tipped his cap.

Extraordinary.

A few weeks ago, the person writing this story read aloud to a gathering of persons another story that he had written. The chief character of the story that was read aloud was a man who was referred to throughout the story as the chief character of the story. After the person writing this story had read aloud the story mentioned in the previous sentence, the persons listening were invited by the organiser of the gathering to ask questions of the person who had read. The gathering was what some persons might have called a distinguished gathering, and the first person to ask a question was what some persons might have called a most distinguished person, she being the author of a number of books. The first person to ask a question asked the person who had just read whether the chief character of his story might have been a more interesting character if he had been given a name. The person who had just read the story whose chief character was referred to as the chief character of the story had been asked many times previously why the characters in his stories lacked names. The person who wrote stories about characters lacking names understood why his char-acters could have no names and tried always to explain to his questioners why his characters lacked names.

However, the person whose characters lacked names suspected that he had seldom conveyed to any questioner the reason why his characters lacked names, and at the gathering mentioned previously he suspected that his answer to the author who questioned him failed to convey to her the reason for the lack just mentioned. Soon after the gathering just mentioned, the person writing this story decided that he would begin the next story that he wrote by explaining why the characters in that story lacked names. Soon after the person just mentioned had made the decision just mentioned, he began to write this story, 'Boy Blue'.

This is a story about a man and his son and the mother of the man. The man just mentioned will be called in this story *the man* or *the father*; the son just mentioned will be called in this story *the son* or *the son of the man*; the mother just mentioned will be called *the mother* or *the mother of the man*. Other characters will be mentioned in this story, and each of those characters will be distinguished from the other characters, but none of the characters will have what could be considered by any person reading or hearing the story a name. Any person who reads these words or hears these words read aloud and wishes that the characters in the story each had a name is invited to consider the following explanation but to remember at the same time that the words of the explanation are also part of this story.

I am writing these words in the place that is called by many persons the real world. Almost every person who lives or has lived in this place has or has had a name.

Whenever a person tells me that he or she prefers the characters in a story to have names, I suppose that the person likes to pretend, while reading a story, that the characters in the story are living or have lived in the place where the person is reading. Other persons may pretend whatever they choose to pretend, but I cannot pretend that any character in any story written by me or by any other person is a person who lives or has lived in the place where I sit writing these words. I see the characters in stories, including the story of which this sentence is a part, as being in the invisible place that I often call my mind. I would like the reader or the listener to notice that I wrote the word *being* and not the word *living* in the previous sentence.

The man who is the chief character of this story was sitting in the dining area of his and his wife's house at the end of the first hour of a certain morning at the time of the year when the first pink flowers appeared on the branches of the prunus trees in the suburb where he lived with his wife and his son and his daughter in a city in the invisible place mentioned in the previous paragraph.

At the time mentioned in the previous sentence, the son of the man was sitting in the kitchen adjoining the dining area of his parents' house after having eaten a plate of curry and rice that had been put into the oven by his mother during the last hour of the previous evening. At the time mentioned in the previous sentence, the father had in front of him the book *Woodbrook*, by David Thomson, published in 1991 by Vintage, and was pretending to read while he listened for any words that his son might speak. At the time mentioned in the previous sentence, the son had recently returned to his parents' house from the factory where he worked on four days of each week from mid-afternoon until midnight as the operator of a machine. The son worked on only four days of each week because the workers at the factory just mentioned had chosen during the previous week to work for fewer days of each week rather than to have some of themselves dismissed.

Early in the second hour of the morning mentioned in the previous paragraph, the son told his father that the manager of the factory where the son worked had told the workers on the previous evening that one or more of them might have to be dismissed in the near future because fewer orders were being placed at the factory for the parts of the motor car engines and of other machinery that were made there. During the hour just mentioned, the son told his father also that he, the son, believed that the worker in most danger of being dismissed from the factory just mentioned was either himself or a certain man who will be called during the rest of this story the workmate of the son. The son did not have to tell his father why he, the son, was in danger of being dismissed. The father knew that his son had begun to work at the factory more recently than any other worker at the factory. But the son had to explain to the father why the workmate of the son was in danger of being dismissed. Before explaining to his father the matter just mentioned, the son told his father the following details that he, the son, had learned from his workmate or from other workers in the factory.

The workmate of the son was a man a year older than the father of the son. The workmate lived with his wife, his son aged sixteen, and his daughter aged fourteen in a rented house in the suburb where the factory mentioned previously stood, which suburb was often said to be the poorest of all the suburbs in the quarter of the city mentioned previously. The workmate's wife had recently been dismissed from her job in another factory and was looking out for another job of any kind. The workmate and his wife owned only their clothing and the few pieces of furniture in the house that they rented. The workmate owned also a motor car that he had bought during the previous year for seven hundred dollars, but the motor car was in faulty order, and the workmate lacked the money to pay for repairs to the motor car. The television set in the house was also in faulty order, but neither the workmate nor his wife had the money needed to repair the set.

After having told his father the details mentioned in the previous paragraph, the son explained to his father why his, the son's, workmate was in danger of being dismissed from the factory where he worked. His workmate, so the son said, often failed to adjust correctly or to check the settings of his machine, and many of the metal objects that were cut or ground by the machine were found afterwards to be faulty. The workmate wore spectacles with thick lenses, and the son sometimes supposed that the workmate was unable to read the tiny numerals or to see the fine markings on his machine. At other times, the son supposed that his workmate hurried at his work so that he could gain the time for smoking one or more of the many cigarettes that he smoked while he was in the factory.

When the father heard what is reported in the previous paragraph, he wanted to learn more about his son's workmate, but the father did not ask the son to tell him more. The workmate who was in danger of being dismissed was the first person that the son had talked about from among the many persons he had worked with. During the five years before the first morning to have been reported in this story, the only persons that the son and his father had talked about were persons mentioned in the newspapers and magazines that the son read in his room on most evenings. Before he had begun to work at the factory mentioned previously, the son had had no job for more than a year. During the year just mentioned, the son had visited a number of factories as an applicant for one or another job but had not talked to his father afterwards about any of the visits. During the three years before the year when the son had had no job, he had worked at different times in five factories but had not talked to his father about any of the persons he had worked with. During the year before the three years just mentioned, the son had been at first a student in the final year of secondary school but had later stopped going to school and had spent most of each day and evening watching in his room a television set that he had repaired after having found it on a nature strip where it had been left among household rubbish because it was in faulty order. During the year just mentioned, the son had not talked to his father about any matter.

In the first hour of the morning after the first morning to have been mentioned in this story, the man was sitting in the dining area mentioned previously and reading the book mentioned previously when his son arrived home from the factory where he worked. Among the pages that the man had read from the book just mentioned during the hours just mentioned were pages 159 and 160, where the following words are printed inside quotation marks ... *a greater amount of urgent and pressing destitution ... than in any other part of Ireland I have visited, as in addition to want of food which exists to as great an extent as in any other part of Ireland, want of shelter from the inclemency of the seasons exists to a far greater extent ... vast numbers of families have been unhoused and their houses destroyed. You cannot admit them to the workhouse, there is no room; you cannot give them outdoor relief, they have no houses ... their cries may be heard all night in the streets of this town; and since my arrival here I have constantly been obliged to procure shelter in the stables in the neighbourhood for persons I have found perishing in the streets at 12 o'clock at night.* While the son was taking out of the oven mentioned previously the meal that his mother had left for him, which was a plate of chops and rice, he told his father the first of the details in the following paragraph. After the son had eaten the meal just mentioned, he told his father the remainder of the following details just mentioned.

The son had noticed late on the previous afternoon

that the metal objects leaving his workmate's machine had been wrongly finished. The son had then left his own machine and had offered to help his workmate check the settings on his machine and to put again through the machine the objects that had been wrongly finished. The workmate had agreed with the son that the objects leaving his, the workmate's, machine had been wrongly finished, but the workmate had not agreed to let the son check the settings on the machine. The workmate had said that he himself had checked the settings earlier in the afternoon. The workmate had then said that the machine itself was at fault. The workmate had then walked away from his machine and had lit a cigarette and had begun to smoke the cigarette.

After the son had taken out of the oven mentioned previously the plate of chops and rice mentioned previously, he first carried the plate and the chops and the rice to the bench between the kitchen and the dining area, then carried back to the oven door the tea-towel that he had used to protect his hands from the heated plate, then took out a knife and a fork from the drawer of cutlery in the kitchen, then put the knife on one side and the fork on the other side of the plate of chops and rice, then took out from the food cupboard in the kitchen a salt shaker and a pepper mill and a bottle of sauce with the word *Cornwell* and the words *Father's Favourite* on the label, and then shook salt from the cellar and ground out pepper from the mill over the chops on his plate. During some of the time while the son did the things just mentioned, he was facing in a direction such that his father could have seen his face if he, the father, had looked up from where he was sitting with the book named previously open in front of him, but the father did not look up.

During the first hour of each of the three mornings following the morning most recently mentioned, the father was sitting in the position mentioned previously with the book named previously open in front of him when the son returned from the factory where he worked. On the first two of the mornings just mentioned, the father waited for the son to speak while he took his meal from the oven mentioned previously and again after he had eaten his meal, but the son did not speak. On the third of the mornings just mentioned, while the son was taking out of the oven just mentioned the plate of curry and rice that his mother had left for him he told his father that the workmate who had been in danger of being dismissed had not been at his machine when the workers on the evening shift had begun work on the previous afternoon; that he, the son, had asked the foreman of the evening shift where the workmate was; that the foreman had answered that the workmate had been dismissed; that the son had then asked what the workmate had said after he had been told that he had been dismissed; that the foreman had then said that no one had told the workmate that he had been dismissed and that the management of the factory dismissed a person by employing a courier to take to the address of the person a letter telling the person that he or she had been dismissed and a sum of money equal to his or gerald murnane

her pay for two weeks plus any money owing to the person for leave not taken. During some of the time while the son told the father what is reported in the previous sentence, the son was facing in a direction such that the father could have seen the son's face if he, the father, had looked up from where he was sitting with the book named previously in front of him, but the father did not look up.

During the second hour of the morning most recently mentioned, while the man was lying in his and his wife's bed beside his wife, who was asleep, and while the man was waiting to fall asleep, he saw in his mind a scene in a house that was furnished with only a few pieces of furniture. In the scene just mentioned, a man one year older than the man in whose mind the scene appeared was sitting at a table in the kitchen of the house and smoking a cigarette while the wife and the son and the daughter of the man were sitting in the adjoining loungeroom and watching a television set that was in faulty order. The man who saw the scene just mentioned in his mind did not look in the direction of the face of any of the persons in the scene.

During the hour mentioned in the previous paragraph, whenever the man saw in his mind the scene mentioned in that paragraph he told himself that the scene was in his mind and not in the place that was called by many persons the real world. During the hour just mentioned, the man told himself further that the scene in his mind was of the kind of scene that appeared in his mind while he read from a book of fiction or even from the kind of book that reported events believed to have happened or even agreed to have happened in the place that was called by many persons the real world.

During the first hour of the day following the day mentioned in the previous paragraph, the man was sitting in the dining area mentioned previously with the book named previously open in front of him when his son arrived home from the factory where he worked. When the son walked into the kitchen of his parents' house during the hour just mentioned, the father greeted the son but did not look up from the book named previously. After the father had greeted the son as mentioned in the previous sentence, the son greeted the father and then took out of the oven mentioned previously the plate of chicken and rice that had been left for him by his mother and then prepared to eat the meal.

On a certain day in the year when the son was aged five years and had recently begun to go to school and when the father and the son were alone together in the dining area mentioned previously, the father began to tell the son what was likely to happen to him in the future. The son would go to secondary school for six years. Then, so the father said, the son would go to university and would learn there to be a scientist or an engineer. Then, so the father said, the son would work for five days of each week as a scientist or an engineer. The son would be paid much money for his work, so the father then said, and he, the son, would use some of the money to buy a motor car and a house and furniture and books and a television set. At some time in the future, so the father then said, the son would marry, and at some time afterwards he would become the father of a son and a daughter. Late on a certain evening after he, the son, had been living for many years in his house with his wife and his son and his daughter and his furniture and his books and his television set and with his motor car and his wife's motor car in a garage beside the house, so the father said, a visitor would arrive at the son's house. The visitor would knock at the front door of the house, so the father then said, and the son would open the door and would see an old man standing in front of him. The old man would be wearing shabby clothes, so the father then said, and he would say while he stood at the front door that he owned no house or furniture or television set or motor car and that he had no money in his pockets. The old man would then ask, so the father then said, whether he, the old man, might take shelter for the night in his, the son's, house. The son would then look at the face of the old man, so the father then said, and would discover that the old man was his father.

After the father had told his son what is reported in the previous paragraph, the father asked his son what he would say or do after the old man had asked for shelter. The son then said that he would invite his father to come into his, the son's, house and to rest on his, the son's, furniture.

While the son said what is reported in the previous paragraph, the father looked at the son's face. The father then put an arm around the shoulders of his son and said that the scene that he, the father, had been describing was only a scene in a story told by the father.

In the house where the father lived when he was aged from five to seven years, his mother would sometimes ask him whether he would like to hear the poem 'Boy Blue'. The mother would ask the question just mentioned most often in the late afternoon of a cloudy and windy day, when she had not yet turned on the light in the kitchen of the house just mentioned and when the wind was rattling the window-panes and the loose weatherboards of the house. Whenever the mother had asked the question just mentioned, the boy would answer that he wanted to hear the poem. The mother, who had stopped going to school when she was twelve years of age, would first recite the words *Little Boy Blue, by Eugene Field* and would then recite from memory all six stanzas of a poem that she had learned when she was eight years of age from the *Third Book of the Victorian Readers*, published by the Education Department of Victoria.

While the mother recited the poem mentioned in the previous paragraph, her son, the person referred to elsewhere in this story as the man or the father, saw in his mind an image of a room containing a chair on which was a toy dog covered with dust and a toy soldier red with rust, each of which, the toy dog and the toy soldier, was wondering as he waited the long years through what had become of the person known as Little Boy Blue since he had kissed them and put them there and had told them to wait until he came and to make no noise. While the father saw in his mind the image of the room just mentioned, he pretended that the room was not part of an image in the invisible place that he often called his mind but a room in the place that he and others called the real world. The father as a boy pretended that the room in his mind was a room in the place called the real world so that he could further pretend that a person who lived in the place just mentioned would come into the room at some time in the future and would explain to the dog and the soldier mentioned previously why they had to wait and to wonder for so long and so that he could further pretend that he would never again begin to weep while his mother read the poem and would never again pretend to be comforted after his mother had read to the end of the poem and had then looked at his face and had then told him that the dog and the soldier and the room where they were waiting were only details in a story.

The Koreans or the Japanese—*some* animistic nation—
say, 'One's love of a house extends even to the crows
sitting on it.' As of a house surely also so of an era. I
loved the love-on-the-dole decade between 1929 and
1939. Perhaps, because I'd always been poor, I really
didn't notice the crows on the ridges of that decade. If
I did, well, I loved them. It was love 'em or lump 'em
anyway.

I was young; I had no material ambitions, and
wouldn't have minded being as barefooted as a goose
and barebottomed as a Villon cut-throat; I was a liar of
the soaring variety—Perpendicular Gothic; I was naif to
the point of purblindness. Thus endowed, I was safe,
even from myself. Safety encourages happiness. Happy I
was.

The only recollection of a feeling against the era is of
the one that zipped an electric hairline of envy through
the texture of happiness when I had to scurry, running
late on an incandescent day, past a beach strewn with
susso Adonises already grilled walnut. There was I
pounding along on the grass-plots (surely they weren't
nature strips in 1937?) to save my soles, pallid under a
threadbare suit that scarcely performed any function

except keeping me pallid—and respectable; and there were they, straight from Michelangelo, otiose, and not a jerry emptied. And smoking!

Ninety-nine point nine *per cent* of the time I was, however, incontestably happy on almost thirty shillings a week. If I eschewed luxuries such as hats, lottery tickets, cigarettes, singlets, beer, theatre tickets, copies of *Hills Like White Elephants*, and contributions to Spanish Civil War funds, it was only to afford other luxuries such as haircuts, toothbrushes, shoe-polish, soap, sale price underpants and—for I was an artistic as well as a cleanly youth—charcoal and Michelet paper to use at the National Gallery Art Classes.

The almost thirty shillings?

My Uncle Tasker, who had the nature of Genghis Khan embedded in the shape of Alfred Hitchcock, was well-heeled enough to be mean without causing meaning looks, and mean enough to use my delusion that, come 1938, I'd be Honoré Daumier II, to employ me part-time in his business. It was heavily watered-down nepotism. 'I promise you, young fellow-m'-lad, you won't be coddled,' he said, richly, with relish, and exhibiting all his teeth like the Laughing Cavalier. As he was fond of saying, he never broke a promise.

Arcadia Displaye Specialistes was the name of his business. It was in a part of North Melbourne where streets were outnumbered by bluestone-cobbled lanes, more than usually underprivileged-looking lanes through which tomcats with tattered ears, and faces like Mr Hyde's, s-l-a-n-k instead of plumping cosily down to lick their jabots and under their armpits.

The Arcadia products were shop furnishings of elementary and depressing design: plywood display cases
with one corner rounded, display boards with one corner
rounded, nickel-plated *art moderne* display stands.
These, though each looked the same as the other, were
for ever being emotionally designed by the Head
Designer (he was the only one) who was called Rexie to
his pendulous off-white face, and Rosie behind his undu-
lant back. He had melon buttocks, one or other of which
now and then winced—one could almost write winked—
as he stood in front of his little looking-glass combing
his hair into a Cornish Pasty arrangement: up from each
side with a ruffle riding the centre. He wore thick-lensed
spectacles, so that his eyes seemed set in aspic. Rexie's
cubicle (THE STUDIO stated his door) was as neat as a
surgery but had several enlivening touches ... a telephone he had lacquered what he said was 'a soothing
and *subtle* morve', a print of Van Gogh's 'Sunflowers',
and a Beardsleyish drawing of a young man with ama-
ranthine tresses, but otherwise as nude and hairless as a
marrow, peeking into a pond. He was on tiptoe.

I was offsider to the Head Artist, a ferocious man of
fifty who must once have been very good but had drunk
himself down to just good enough. Leo Ryan was his
name. Brandy was his tipple. He smelt like a toadstool,
and couldn't bear a stave of me. His foul-mouthed railings against office slip-ups, which were legion, out-
Leared Lear, and enthralled me. I found it advantageous,
however, to assume deafness or incomprehension when,

in his down-in-the-mouth moods, he fixed me with a red eye, and *whispered* at me, 'You! You haven't suffered! You don't even realise that the privilege of suffering *in the mind* is man's alone! Man's alone!' or 'Look at me! Dead! Trapped! Stale! I used to be young like you! But lock up the wind—it becomes stale air, stale air! You'll find out!'

Most of my chores for this smelly and discouraging man I regarded as crass, and certainly unworthy of the Daumier just under the skin. I arranged branches of crêpe paper almond blossom in front of Leo's painted background at the South Australian Tourist Bureau; finickally dashed in the *minor* stars above his Three Wise Men ... I wasn't up to dashing them in dashingly; daubed large white freckles on three-ply reindeer; and once painted two hundred cardboard butterflies the size of pterodactyls.

In the back regions of Arcadia Displaye Specialistes were three or four men who noisily constructed the display counters with rounded corners, the cut-out chefs that were stood outside cheap restaurants, and so on. They worked under perpetual electric light, and were jockey-sized, quick-tempered, weasel-quick makings-smokers with witty, dirty, whiplash tongues. They had mutton and chow-chow pickle sandwiches for lunch, and nigger-brown cups of tea almost mucilaginous with sugar. They could spit as brilliantly as llamas and, though it cannot have been so, all seemed to be called Arthur.

There were also three females on the staff. Two were, it appeared to me at the age of nineteen, mere children of sixteen or seventeen. One was Brenda, the other was Tootsie, and they were alike enough in a wizened, dank way for me never to know which was which. They shared multiple duties, and were always on the run with their insufficient faces stuck forward like chooks'—making the nigger-brown tea, licking stamps, swaddling display stands in excelsior, cutting silk-screen lettering, spraying stencilled curves parallel to the rounded edges of things. Maybe they were merely girls who'd been dabs at freehand drawing in Grade Six sweating it out until Mr Right fell for them on a cable tram one dazzling Thursday; maybe they were Rosa Bonheurs or Marie Laurencins being nipped in the bud by Uncle Tasker's cupidity, and Miss Guildford-Maggs's languorous nagging. Ah, Miss Guildford-Maggs! Ah, nineteen! Ah, the Nineteen-thirties! Ah, the Depression, where one had to keep down to the Joneses! A-a-ah, Miss Guildford-Maggs!

Right here, I must make it clear that Rexie (peevishly), Leo Ryan (morosely), the Arthurs (busily as leprechauns), Brenda and Tootsie (like put-upon Brontë governesses), and even Uncle Tasker (you may miss the smiling tiger, but he won't miss), everyone of them worked, *worked*—like slaves, like beavers, like gins, like . . . take your pick. Even Uncle Tasker? Even I. Have you ever played ju-jitsu in a narrow shop window with many-elbowed real branches covered with paper blossom, two arc-lights, a nubile dummy in pink organdie, and a placard (with one rounded corner) defiled with words like *picturesque*, *panorama*, *blossom-time*, and *memorable experience*?

hal porter

I found all the workers somehow matily real, and utterly unfascinating. Not so the third female, Miss Guildford-Maggs. She, to me, was unimpeachably fascinating. Work? Hardly a tap, although she was Uncle Tasker's secretary, and oversaw Brenda and Tootsie who were ever to be seen darting rat-like side-glances of venom at her out of their mouse-like fiction of docility.

Miss Guildford-Maggs, cracking thirty, I thought, was tallish, was stately and flexible with it, wandered languidly rather than walked, and had a small flat head set on a long neck that made me think of those herbivorous dinosaurs that munched the uppers of prehistoric trees. A shock-proof vanity sustained her, although her incompetence was notable, and the *non sequitur* antics of her mind gave me the impression that it was based in some organ small as a hazel-nut. God knows why Uncle Tasker kept her ... perhaps her refined telephone talks were suggestive of a superior organisation to the clots who bought Uncle Tasker's products for their suburban emporiums and edge-of-the-city corner shops and country town general stores. Whyever and whatever, her contribution to herself was excessive, I could not see her for the strange offerings she piled on her own altar.

In 1937, women were plucking their eyebrows, *à la* Jean Harlow, vaselining eyelids, wearing fuchsia-coloured materials, snake-skin shoes, and cyclamen lipstick. Albeit in patently cheaper stuffs, Miss Guildford-Maggs went the whole hog, with colours almost passionately wrong and distressingly vibrant. Her eyelids swam with vaseline; her eyebrows were one hair-width only from invisibility.

Externals of any sort I took in my stride. It was the inner mainspring I wanted—in the nicest sticky-nosed way—to understand. I think I thought then that, give or take a little, we all had the same one. The others at Arcadia said and did things I wasn't fazed by. Miss Guildford-Maggs was, however, the very Eiffel of fazers; and given to statements that had the flat sound of cracked truths. It was as though, in seeking her, one came on signposts that bore the correct destination but pointed elsewhere. For example, when one of the Arthurs fell down dead of a heart attack, 'It was,' she pronounced, 'it was reelly the worst attack he ever had.' On the subject of living by oneself: 'If one does prefer to do so, and if one fainds ... and Ai say *if* advaisedly, for it would be quaite unlaikely to occur in any digs of maine ... if one fainds a hair in one's pea soup ...' (Here her protruding eyes delphically protruded a glaze-width more.) '... one could at least be sure that it was one of one's own.'

My first meeting with her was one lunchtime at the Arcadia. She sat in a swivel chair—she *reclined* in *Her* swivel *throne*—in the cubicle she called her sanctum sanctoriarium. It was opposite Rexie's THE STUDIO. With a portentous Borgia nonchalance, she was varnishing her fingernails purple. The interlaced smells of the nail varnish, of some musky scent abundantly applied to her violet dress, and of something simmering in an elderly aluminium saucepan on a gas-ring, repulsed me on the one nostril and, on the other, sent my unsteady imagination skipping in the direction of a kind of Temple of Isis occupied by love-sick priestesses up to no good with potions.

Miss Guildford-Maggs was unable to offer her hand but she offered me a fair section of a parti-coloured monologue. She indicated and named, with ennui if not distaste, Brenda and Tootsie who were playing dumb-struck Charmian and Iras to her genteel-as-buggery Cleopatra.

Brenda was stirring the greyish mess I could see heaving and pouting in the saucepan.

'Ai trust you're being careful not to let it catch, Brenda,' purred the Serpent of old Nile. 'Stir clockwise, and don't let it catch. It is,' she said to me, looking up from under her greasy eyelids, 'a delicate flesh, veal. I rather praide maiself, though Ai do say it maiself, on a rather delicate palate.'

Bred in the country from which I'd just come, veal was abhorrent to me as it is to country people. I con-cealed a gulp of revulsion under a smile of great vivaciousness.

'It's done, I think,' said Brenda through a mouthful of vanilla slice, the flakes from which ringed her feet like larger dandruff.

Miss Guildford-Maggs gave me a minuscule and qual-ified smile as one shrugging, 'A fool, you see!' She next looked at her fingernails, oh, absorbedly . . . she was clearly putting a significant pause in parentheses. She spoke, as a sphinx might, in granite:

'It ... is ... *not* ... done.' She closed her eyes. 'Whatever you maight think you think.' She paused. 'Brenda.' *Brenda* implied by intonation *skivvy*, if not *idiot kitchen drab*. 'Stir clockwise. It will not be done for two and three-quarter minutes.' Her eyes, still closed, she nevertheless turned them elsewhere. 'Ai see, Tootsie, that you've set the tray with a dirty cup. There's a maite of lipstick on the rim. Ai know it's mai cup, and mai lipstick, but Ai've told you ... ' Ghost at cockcrow, Tootsie and the cup disappeared. Miss Guildford-Maggs opened her eyes which seemed luminous and more protuberant. 'Ai'm sure,' she said, 'you'll be very happy in our happy family. Brenda, serve the veal.'

Fascination! 1937! Miss Guildford-Maggs smouldering bitchily in Arcadia!

What slumbrous film star was her model ... Barbara la Marr? ... I'll never know: she was not a good translator. Anyway, I was green. I was emerald green.

From then on, whenever I could, I spent time in research on Miss Guildford-Maggs. Two aspects particularly led me on and on. One was that while all of us in Uncle Tasker's little web bickered *with* each other, and slammed doors behind furious exits, and found it not unpleasant, she bickered with no one. She bickered *at*, from some foxhole on a plateau of her own. It was not pleasant. Why no one told her to shut her dirty big gob, I couldn't understand. I wanted to understand. If this aspect inclined me to earnest, lines-between-the-brow moods (what is Miss G.-M.'s mainspring?), the other aspect outrightly dazzled me. She lied and lied and lied.

She was as far gone a lie-addict as I was. My taste was for the elaborately detailed plot, the train of many carriages all on one branch line, and a cow-catcher ready to scoop away those rash enough to question the train. Her taste, which kept me open-mouthed, was for lies like Dodg'em Cars at Luna Park—no rails, each on its wild own, bump, bump, bump. Swapping lies with her was like swapping a finished jigsaw for the scalenes of many a puzzle.

The time came when I heard her saying, 'Ai do think we've been acquainted long enough for you to call me Maevene?'

I nearly fell off my perch but, in a throbbing voice, said I'd love to; that I was very flattered; that I deemed it ... I shut up. Then, in the unsullied, unthrobbing voice I delivered my fictions in, I said that I was par*tic*-ularly intrigued by her name because one of my grand-mothers had been called Maevene. Maevene Eugénie Charlotte. Paternal grrandmother. The one who died in India. Tragically, but without a whimper. Bitten by a cobra. A white cobra, immeasurably ancient. A *sacred* cobra, I added with some vivacity.

'How in-ter-*est*-ing!' said Miss Guildford-Maggs—er—Maevene. 'It's a very small world. Ai was named after mai grandmother.' We were walking to the tram stop through the cats' maze of lanes. 'She was a raving beauty in har day. The Ruse of London they called har. Ladies and gentlemen stood on the seats of Haide Park to see har sweep bai in har carriage.'

Her eyelids began to droop under her cyclamen tri-corne with its snippet of cyclamen ostrich feather; she was becoming slumbrous and sultry even as she steered her lizard-skin shoes through the sardine tins and dogs' turds.

I tempted myself to outrage.

'She was pregnant,' I said with surprisingly unfaltering clarity for I'd never said this word before.

Maevene stopped being sultry.

'Pardon *me*!' she said sharply as though I'd plunged a hand in her bosom.

'I'm talking, Maevene, of my grandmother Maevene.' I boyishly punted a camp pie tin. 'The one slain by the cobra. In the winter garden of a rajah's palace. She was with child. With children, really. Before she passed away she was delivered of twins. My father was the first.'

'Mai father ...' began Maevene, recovering but still shaken.

'My uncle was the second.'

'Mai father was born in ...'

'So that is why,' I cut relentlessly in, 'my uncle loathes me, hates me, despises me.' He was, as a matter of fact, indifferently jocular to me, and merely thought me whatever he thought a fool was.

'Ah!' said Maevene. 'Ai'm glad you brought that up. Ai would never have mentioned it. But Ai do see, Ai reelly do. Ai sympathise. Ai understand ...'

Fascination! I hadn't the foggiest what she sympathised with, what she understood, where the signpost was pointing. She was a drug I didn't really like, or really dislike.

Maevene and the others at Arcadia were not, of

course, the only city people I was trying to learn about city people from. I didn't, for example, live in Arcadia, but in 28 Collins Street. I had a third-floor back room, from the window of which I could see over the high brick wall of the backyard of the Melbourne Club wherein plane trees, denied municipal surgery, grew like superior weeds. I paid fifteen shillings a week for my aerie, a cell which must once have been a servant's room. This payment included use of a communal kitchen I never used. As well there was a vast bathroom with water so boiling that dangerous steam jetted out when the tap was first turned on; and there was room service. This last was composed of two new experiences for me. One pillow case (the upper), and one sheet (the lower) were changed each week. Lower pillow became the upper, and upper sheet became the lower. It seemed to me dirty, and I thought of it for a long time as a mean city custom like making coffee out of what looked like gunpowder instead of out of a bottle with a turbaned Moor on the outside. The other experience was a breakfast tray which, because I lived on frugal rations, was a bracing as well as a thrilling experience. It was brought in every morning by May, a woman of about forty who could have played football but who was disguised as a sort of blown-up French maid in a bedroom farce—black dress, tiny frilled white apron, tinier frilled cap. Several mornings a week May brought a medicine glass of port wine in with the tea and toast and marmalade. I had my own ideas of what she was up to. 'Now, get that into you,' she would shout. 'You're looking peaky. That'll bring back the

roses. That'll warm the cockles.' I read lustful seductive-
ness into this maternal din. I was terrified, and tossed
the Lorelei's brew out of the window on to the wall of
the Melbourne Club. She intends, I thought, to weaken
my willpower, and sully my virtue. I thought in those
very words. I imagined her dark magnificent eyes,
although embedded in a crumpled rubber face, to be
glimmering with depravity, and when, one morning, I
lied that I had a headache (merely to make polite conversation), and she laid a hot hand on my cool forehead
to find if it were hot, nearly bayed for help. Even had I
merely squeaked, Miss Beveridge, who owned the place,
would have—I was confident of this—appeared in a
Fairy Godmother sunburst, and changed May into something else, a marmoset or an armadillo. Of almost the
same height, weight and shape as May—solid, four-
square, high-bosomed, undumbfoundable, with legs like
jeroboams—Miss Beveridge was as near to being a
Grand Duchess (and a lady) as a lodging-house martinet
with an eye on sheets and her lodgers' morals could be,
even at the posh end of a posh street. Her fingers were
kept almost as apart as frogs' fingers by thick rings, two
or three to a finger, and no finger free ... diamonds,
diamonds, and diamonds. She dressed in beige, wore her
stockings dull side out, and crocodile-skin shoes. Her
hair was steeply terraced, a creamy pompadour ideal for
aigrettes, coronets, or the basket at the base of Sanson's
guillotine.

Although there must have been a dozen others in the
house (we were for ever after-youing each other on the

stair landings) I knew only the one who lived in the ground floor front. Her door, always rosily ajar when I came in late at night, opened off the entrance hall which was crimson-carpeted, darkly panelled, and smelt of burned toast. My knowee was also about forty (looking back it seems I was the only under-forty in the place), and her surname was Kolker, and I called her Kolker because she asked me to. No Maevene nonsense. She was a Jewess, a journalist, smoked black Sobranies so endlessly that her room fumed as if on the point of combustion, and was voluble in an elaborate cultured voice. Since, however, she looked like a gipsy queen, her intense monologues (how people *talked* throughout the Depression!) had the tone of incantations. I'd not have dared to lie to *her*. Perhaps she was lying to me about liars: Hemingway, Lorca, Dos Passos, Sinclair Lewis, Upton Sinclair ... I didn't understand, and didn't deeply listen, and was therefore a seemingly good listener. I kept my eyes intelligently wide open, directing at her the frank gaze that only the unfrank can convincingly direct. Meantime, delicately but nonetheless gluttonously, I kept on eating, for Kolker had a cupboard chock-a-block with food, terribly exotic to me, all bought at Franz the Grocer's at the Eastern Market— rollmops, anchovies, caviar, salami, olives, rye bread, incredible cheeses. I'd have preferred Irish stew, but a tight belt had driven me to caviar, and Kolker's own blend of expensive, freshly ground coffee which tasted to me as I imagine deadly nightshade would. Ah, the Depression, and caviar, and Dorothy Lamour, muted by a room or two, singing on some mysterious lodger's wireless, singing 'Moonlight and Shadows' while Kolker vilified Franco!

I mention May, Miss Beveridge, and Kolker because they resembled Uncle Tasker, Rexie, Leo Ryan, the Arthurs, Brenda and Tootsie in the possession of some quality I couldn't spring in Maevene Guildford-Maggs, and couldn't, anyway, define . . . a saltiness, an awareness of the gravitational pull in others (come down, come down, and be bored with me, my love), a proper organisation of Goods and Bads.

Outside Arcadia and 28 Collins Street, I kept on adding, like a slightly dotty magpie, to my collection of people and places. Places because people wore them as snails their shells.

Kingsley Hall was a place seething with people of kinds I thought fictional because, hitherto, I'd only met them in books given to me by tangible people who, in my youth, were far too fond of this dangerous custom.

Kingsley Hall, a stucco terrace of four two-storeyed houses, was in a one-block-only street behind St Peter's Cathedral and the Eastern Hill Fire Brigade. The street's directory name eludes me. It was generally called the Street of Leaning Trees because its plane tree avenue, aspiring heavenwards, had become so 'picturesquely' skew-whiff that you could bet that, rain or shine, a middle-aged artist and a middle-aged easel would be straddling together at the end of the street.

Kingsley Hall, built *circa* 1870 for the hutching of four ma-and-pa families (children, nursemaid, cook, tweeny), went through this period. Doorways were then cut through the three inner walls to make one establishment which was, first, a private hotel for retired governesses, deaconesses, Anglo-Indian widows, and archbishops' spinster daughters. These menless women were replaced, during the reign of Edward the Seventh, by the women they could have been: Kingsley Hall became a discreetly opulent brothel which left as heritage a number of looking-glasses set high at an angle between wall and ceiling. It was next a boarding house for entertainers of the barn-storming sort: bellringers, contortionists, Shakespearian monologuists looking like Liszt in old age, raddled soubrettes, buck-and-wing dancers, tattooed ladies, itinerants of all sorts whose theatrical baskets could hold anything from a ventriloquist's doll, ageing as its master aged, to a brace of world-weary carpet snakes with *blasé* eyes. By 1937 ... ah, the Depression, the Three Course Meals for Sevenpence, and Ursula Jeans singing 'Twentieth Century Blues' seated on a grand piano (white)! ... it housed those huddling on the fringes of the Arts and the outskirts of spivvery: empty-bellied music students, piece-work commercial artists, door-to-door salesmen from photo-enlarging firms, chorus boys rooming in petulant couples, makers of china masks, amateur confidence men.

I had come to know them fairly well. Indeed, my part-time world much resembled theirs except that my address was less raffish, my desires were less bacchanalian, my country ingenuousness less a hazard than their city guile. I can't recall why my best friends among them were a disappointed writer called Erik who had turned to petty crime, and his voluptuous fast-talking wife . . . or mistress . . . Sybil, an usherette in a cinema.

Sybil was a cut-'em-down gossip. Kingsley Hall was a chest-of-drawers into which a variety of defective, gaudy, shabby, glass-eyed dolls had been shoved out of conventional sight. She dragged them forth, and held them up to me, privately, deriding their excesses and distresses, their tattered nobilities and scruffy *amours* and tinsel exultations. She did this viciously enough, but with a tribal affection. For one only her acridity was undiluted: I had heard her teeth jar often on his name—Max Komesaroff. I'd met many and most of Sybil's subjects but had somehow always missed him. I was befuddled that she ranted most against his openhandedness, and was inclined to agree with Erik whom I'd heard protest in a bai-jove accent straight from a sparkling three-act comedy: 'Reahlly, dahling, Max is a Jew-boy and a Russniak and all that, but he reahlly does scatter the old largesse. He could be J.C., you know, the Second Coming and all that. Lay off, old gel.'

I arrived one twilight to find Sybil alone. The room, in which I'd seen not even a waxed-paper poppy before, reeked of a plethora of jonquils jammed into borrowed vases, a brass jardiniere that usually lived on a pedestal in the hall, a jug, a chamber-pot without a handle, and an enamel milk-billy. Reflected in the canted looking-glasses left over from Kingsley Hall's more lushly improper past this display made a considerable impact.

Sybil made a more considerable one. She held a tumbler of wine. She was flaring.

'That ghetto rat!' she cried. 'That Komesaroff eunuch! Tapping at my door like a charity-worker! Smirking over a great armful of these stinking bloody funeral parlour things!'

I was learning not to flinch when women (that is, pretty women) swore. 'Erik the fool's been picked up for conning some peasant from Woop Woop, and's been popped in the lock-up.' I expressed regret.

'Don't be grotesque,' she said. 'The great oaf's only got himself to blame. He's conned himself in; he'll con himself out. But Big-ears Komesaroff hears the sad tidings, and comes running, pitter-patter, pitter-patter, pitter-patter, laden with a . . . *Look!* A million of these whatever-they-ares! That great fat box of sick-making chockies! Four jars of caviar!' I thought of Kolker pressing midnight snacks of caviar on me. 'And a bottle of muscadine! Muck! As though the wife of the accused should celebrate. As though Komesaroff wanted to pop under the covers with me while Erik's behind the bars. But he doesn't want me to celebrate—he wants me to be wailing and keening. And as for slap-and-tickle—I think he's neuter. How dare he!'

She scolded on, meantime mopping up the muscadine muck. No one knew where Komesaroff worked. Sybil suggested a sewer. By day he was free; between seven and midnight he was invisible, and apparently earning the money with which he lavished impractical gifts—crystallised fruit, sweet wines, boxes of chocolates the

size of the Koran—on penurious donees who, she said
with vehement sincerity, abhorred him. Since I didn't
much mind the unpopular Maevene Guildford-Maggs
who *took*, I thought I mightn't much mind the Komesaroff who *gave*. I said I'd like to meet him.

'Erik doesn't mind him, and look where he is tonight.
You and Erik are dingbats. He's corrupted you. Komesaroff's a creepy-crawly, but if you want to, you can meet
the little runt tomorrow. He'll be at the morning
session—there's a new Loretta Young film showing, and
he lerves those great big tear-filled eyes. You be there,
and I'll *give* him to you.'

I pointed out that I couldn't afford Loretta Young at
the Plaza.

'Don't be grotesque,' said Sybil. 'Your old aunt, Señorita Sybil, will get you in free, gratis, and for nothing.
But wear a fur coat: the caviar king will make your blood
run cold.'

Señorita Sybil! Ah, the cinemas of the Depression! The
Wurlitzers and chandeliers and statues and urns of
authentic flowers, the ankle-deep carpets and marble
staircases! Palaces for the orgies of Tiberius!

The Plaza, where Sybil and her sister usherettes were
dressed like musical comedy señoritas (flounced skirt,
Spanish shawl, lofty comb, black lace mantilla, red velvet
roses), was all Cordoba tiles, iron grilles, seats of embossed
crimson leather, and wall-fountains tinkling from the jaws
of blue ceramic lion-masks. It was in this superbly executed
phoniness that I met Max Komesaroff. In three minutes I
knew what Sybil meant about the fur coat.

I shook his little bony chilled hand, the back of which was decorated by ginger freckles and ginger hairs of the same ginger as those, apparently knitted in moss stitch, on his spherical head. His eyes were of the same tint-lessness as Maevene Guildford-Maggs's, but whereas her glance slid across the air above one's head as if eyes and mind were on a train always pulling out, his drove into one as immediately and as offensively as a harpoon.

He drew a tin of fifty cigarettes from his pocket, and offered me one. I said I didn't smoke.

'Vhy do you not?' His voice had a metallic note. It implied that non-smokers were non-humans.

No one should, suddenly, question liars. I was so star-tled that, instead of fictionising ('My guardian—an eccentric paralytic who infinitely prefers gerberas to people—has forbidden me ever to smoke anything except a narghile'), I told a shameful truth: 'I hate smoking.'

Not for a twink removing the harpoon, he began to smile, slowly to construct a smile in which I was appalled to discern disbelief flowering into utter disbelief. A second or an aeon later I saw compassion break the surface; I spotted *pity*.

'Vhy,' he said, with sorrow, 'do you say this thing? It is not the truth.'

Upon this, my mind instantly ceased to register any-thing more than that he was wearing a suit of pin-striped Vandyke brown material of eye-cutting richness.

'Vhy you do not smoke is the reason you are much too poor. Eh?'

I stood, an ossified gawk, unable to believe the evidence of my senses.

'I speak, you see, alvays the truth. It is because I have this vish to be kind and loving,' continued the monster, the degenerate, the ... the ...

Oh, put down your electric torch, Señorita Sybil, scented and beautiful and all-seeing in your shadow mantilla and roses of red-black velvet, put it down! Leave your caramel-chewers, and glide to my help with your dragon-slaying tongue!

'I have much experience, and see you are not vealthy. I must help you.'

That did it. I took coarse measures—and, lying little gent to the last, delicatised them with High School French, *Je ne suis pas jamais à court d'argent. Jamais! Jamais!* and, that done, 'So sorry I'm leaving you, Mister Markinovich. An important engagement. The Lord Mayor. I'm already late.'

'You are proud; you are vilful.' His eyes filled with liquid. As one slipping a thick love-letter into a letter-box, he slipped the tin of cigarettes into my sportscoat pocket. 'Please, I say, not to be proud because your friend is vealthy.' As though it had heard him say, 'because your friend is suffering,' one large tear departed from his less controlled eye, and plunged dead-straight down his cheek.

'I must run, must run,' I babbled. 'The Lord Mayor. Forgive me. Must run.' Cigarettes and horror and all, I jog-trotted across the foyer floored with imitation Moorish tiles, and out of sight which is something one can very rarely say of oneself.

Sybil told me, later, that he left the Plaza foyer almost immediately after I did. That midnight, as she was going to bed, he came tapping at her door to ask for my address *slyly* tapping, she said.

It was over an hour later when there was a tapping on *my* door. It was not a sly tapping. There, in a kimono of such blinding gaudiness that she looked like Katisha, stood Miss Beveridge with her marchioness's coiffure enclosed and diminished in a net. She spoke, levelly, and with precision.

'Get straight back into bed. We don't want to have you with a chill.' She waited. She slightly moved the bedlamp so the light was not in my eyes. 'Now, listen carefully, young man. You are in my house because I permit you to be. So long as, in my house, you conform to the rules of decent society, I ask no more. I make no enquiries about your comings and goings although you are not yet twenty-one. I am not curious about your friends or your habits, so long as I don't find them affecting the reputation of my house. I do not even mind climbing three flights of stairs at a quarter past one in the morning. I do not mind, you understand, if there's a good reason.'

I couldn't see her face; it was in shadow. I couldn't help but see her score of rings—diamonds, diamonds, and diamonds—blazing whitely in the light. Their mesmeric effect, her beautifully paced and delivered sentences, my own comfortable bed, all soothed me. Although bewildered I was not disturbed, merely felt older, very man-about-town, with a mistress wearing a cascade of silver fox, and a couple of pounds avoirdupois of charm bracelets.

'I *don't* think there's a good reason,' Miss Beveridge was saying, away up there above her exploding diamonds. 'There was someone at the front door for you. He wanted to come up.'

Miss Beveridge stopped dead. Obviously, it was my move. My mind ran empty and, oddly, absolutely silent. What to say? Who wanted to come up?

'My uncle . . . ?' I meant this.

'It was no uncle, young man. It was a foreigner.'

Her voice was so horizontal I still didn't cotton on.

'I will not,' she said, 'not in my house, not at 28 Collins Street, have a young man of your background—or of any background—accepting boxes of chocolates from foreigners. Or from older men—accent or no accent.'

I cottoned on. Max Komesaroff! I steamed with mortification and anger.

'I'm terribly sorry, Miss Beveridge. I'll go down. I'll tell him to go.'

'I have,' she said, 'already sent him about his business.'

My relief at dirty work done for me was so great that my imagination began to frolic.

'Thank you, Miss Beveridge. He's not a friend, merely an acquaintance.' Out came the corny French. *'C'est un original. Mais quel dindon!* He's a Russian aristocrat. White Russian. His parents were hacked to ribbons by the Bolsheviks. He escaped disguised as a vodka-driver.' I think I thought, then, that a vodka was a more elegant sort of droshky, though not *exactly* certain what a droshky was—something with bells on and wolves after. 'He wanders the world distributing largesse. These cigarettes . . . ' They were on my bedside table.

'I see,' said Miss Beveridge. 'Why did he give them to you?' She meant something I didn't understand.

I told her I didn't know. She accepted my artlessness. Her diamonds, diamonds, and diamonds picked up the cigarette tin.

'Have you taken up smoking?'

I was surprised at her. Me, smoking? Mistress-keeping, spying in Lhasa, or jewel-stealing in the Jimmy Valentine manner was possible. Smoking? Not yet, not yet.

'I can't bear them. Would you like them?'

'I shall give them to May. From you. Not, of course, mentioning where they originally came from. I'll say it's in gratitude for the invalid port wine.'

'It's done me a lot of good,' I prattled. 'Fortifying. It warms the . . . '

'Yes,' said Miss Beveridge in such a way that I knew she knew that the stain on the Melbourne Club wall was May's port wine. 'I'll say good morning.' She said it. She switched out the light. She closed the door. I suffered insomnia for about four minutes during which I learned that the direct and dispassionate affection of Miss Beveridge and May was a substantial meal. How right Sybil had been to squall against the jonquils and caviar, the objectification of a creepy-crawly love.

Sybil was, however, only right for Sybil. I? The young are never right.

When one is young one sleeps deep, exhausted from carrying thistledown. One's feelings are of minimal value no matter how theatrically one bangs the cymbals, and agitates the tinpot tambourine. Ah, youth! with its brummy outsize ideals, its outsize ebony heart, its outsize dreams in cheap fancy dress, its crooked gaze, its almost criminal desire to steal only the best from others.

What did I, for instance, having stolen Max Komesaroff's gesture from him, care what happened to him and his chocolates outside the door Miss Beveridge would have just not slammed but might just as well have slammed . . . what did I care?

I cared that I had a Miss Beveridge to not-slam awkward doors for me, that I had Kolker's caviar for a nightcap, and May's maternal wine on my breakfast tray. That morning I drank the port before I set out.

It was a two-miles walk from Collins Street to where Uncle Tasker had staked out his seedy claim amid the lanes of North Melbourne. By the time I'd reached the last lane I had thought myself into feeling years older and sager. I was, nevertheless, singing, although not over-loudly, with aplomb, and a French song at that. Thus engaged, I entered the front door of Arcadia, Rexie's THE STUDIO to the left, Maevene Guildford-Maggs's sanctum sanctoriarium to the right. *Mon Dieu!* My God! The song died and dried in my throat.

Before Maevene Guildford-Maggs trilled out, 'Surpraise! Surpraise! Someone to see you!' I had seen the someone. Max Komesaroff was seated opposite her in the sanctum sanctoriarium. He sat at indubitable ease as if he faced a glowing hearth. Between them, between the refeened bitch and the creepy-crawly, on the top of her typewriter sat the box of chocolates as large as the Shorter Oxford. It was open. Its lid with the bow of royal blue ribbon was as it were off for ever. Max Komesaroff was no longer looking for me. I was the accidental penultimate. With her fingers arranged in a chocolate-choosing gesture ... thumb and middle finger held open-beak-like, the other fingers in fastidious arcs ... Maevene Guildford-Maggs librated hostessishly above what had been turned away from me and the door of 28 Collins Street.

'Would you,' said Maevene Guildford-Maggs, 'care to trai one of mai choc-chocs that your kaind friend has brought?'

One scarcely needs to write another word.

Boy meets girl stuff. Lonely hearts stuff. Dupes of nature, and victims of anatomy stuff. Attraction of opposites stuff. It could even be last-plank-in-a-shipwreck stuff.

Love at first sight?

I wasn't there early enough to see them meet. Earlier, I could have come upon him ... as Maevene Guildford-Maggs had ... lost in the cat-haunted lanes where, just as Miss Beveridge had done, I would have sent him about his business.

His business? A child's business; a tippity-toeing from diminished adult to diminished adult in vain attempts to give away his vanity and himself, his symbolic self, in the form of too many chocolates, and wine too sweet, and flowers too many and too sweet and too scented, and what he called love, a thing too sickly for anyone except Maevene Guildford-Maggs. She had given up expecting, years ago, that a Mr Right would appear with the marsh-mallow truths she could substitute for her terribly untidy lies.

This story, being no more, no more at all than a happy-ever-after one, ends, within two months after their meeting, at the Methodist Church, Footscray, the bride— according to Brenda or Tootsie—looking very nice, for someone as senile as thirty-four, in lilac lace: Rexie's design. This knowledge of her age was a mere fraction of the fund of information the Arcadia people revealed them-selves as possessed of. Max Komesaroff was forty-five, and had owned half a gambling saloon in Exhibition Street which she'd persuaded him to sell for a live-in pawnshop in Russell Street. This was considered by everyone except Leo Ryan to be an exchange both shrewd and prudent, as well as socially advantageous. The last distinction was too subtle for my still rustic perception. I discovered, moreo-ver, why these city people had never told her to shut her big nagging gob. Although maddening them to the point of mayhem, she remained no more than a mean, spoilt child for whom they were sorry. Her real name was, to my amazement, Mavis Maggs.

'You didn't know!' screeched Brenda or Tootsie. 'But everyone knew! How could *she* have a toff's name? Her dad's a plumber at Footscray. A real booze-artist. You must have seen him here when he used to come to borrow from her. He was in and out all the time. You've seen him.'

I hadn't, and said so.

'Anyway, you'll see him at the wedding.'

I wouldn't, and didn't say so. I hadn't been asked, although everyone, including Uncle Tasker, had.

As an accidental and rather tenuous kind of *deus ex machina* I felt I should almost have been best man, and still sometimes wonder if it were the strange behaviour of my paternal grandmother, Maevene Eugénie Charlotte, or the fact that I was vilful and proud at the Plaza, or that I had Katisha in diamonds as a watch-dog at 28 Collins Street, that caused me to be excluded.

Ah, the Depression! Ah, the violinists playing 'Little Grey Home in the West' in the indigo wind at twilight street corners; and the prostitutes in eye-veils and silver fox in the lamplight of Alexandra Avenue; and the El Greco young men with their backs pressed to the woman-warm bricks of bakehouse walls! Ah, the three great spheres of false gold at Komesaroff's, and the people streaming along Russell Street to Komesaroff's with their gospel-true gold-cable bracelets and wedding rings and little hearts with one ruby in.

Ah, Mr and Mrs Komesaroff!

john tranter   Gloria

Gloria handed the doctor a bundle of notes—
typewritten, grubby, scribbled over
and rewritten in different coloured inks.
Masterson adjusted his spectacles
and leafed through the first few pages,
then burrowed further into the mess.
'Yesss, this is interesting, Gloria,
but it looks complicated, full of bother.
Tell me, what does it represent? Hmmm?'
It represented horror, but we didn't
know that then. We dozed, we lazed.
How many of us were there, reclining
peacefully on the grass, sitting in
on the death of the ego. Four? Five? 'Oh,'
Gloria squirmed. 'Oh, it's my . . . well,
memories, where I tell about myself. Talk—
the things . . . you know, where I've been,
what I've done, all that.' Half a dozen of us,
sitting in the pale sunlight in the park
with our sandwiches and bottles of beer: six,
including the troop leader, Doctor Masterson,
who guided the group on its wanderings.
Gloria—twenties, dark hair, freckles

and large round glasses that gave her
the look of a watchful schoolgirl,
wearing a sweet heady perfume that a
teenager might have used—Gloria
frowned and looked down at her hands.
They were twisting slowly in her lap
like dazed, angry creatures. We all
glanced at them, then looked away.
Masterson held a page up to the light
as though something semi-transparent
were hidden underneath the layers of erasures
and white-out, behind the second thoughts
and reconsiderations, a drift, an argument
that might unravel and explain itself
if he stared through it thoughtfully enough.
He puffed on an old pipe, the grey-blue smoke
almost invisible in the hazy light,
though its odour of smouldering heather
drifted over us like a nostalgic memory
and I noticed how the pipe went with his jacket—
dark green tweed, with elbow patches—
to make up a uniform, suited to a character
from an old British movie—a murder mystery
set in some sleepy village before the war—
a doctor, a serious reader, a teacher, perhaps—
and that this message was a kind of pleading:
see me as an uncle, a tutor, a friend,
but not as the fraud I fear I am.

'I think I see what you want.

You'd like one of us to read it out,
is that your plan, Gloria?' He turned
and swung his smile on her like a spotlight.
Was she going to faint? She wavered;
weed under running water. 'Unhhh . . . '
was all Gloria could manage, blushing.
One of the pale animals in her lap
seemed to be on the verge of triumph,
grasping and choking the other, which had
reddened under the sudden attack. A ring—
I hadn't noticed the glittering engagement ring
before—was being twisted violently.

'Well,' she began, 'well, you see . . .
I really can't bring myself to speak . . .
to come out with all that . . . all those . . .
extraordinary . . . events! My goodness!
When I think back over . . . I hoped that
getting it all down in black and white,
turning what happened into a kind of story,
that is, if I could hold back a little way
from all that . . . those terrible memories,
and the good ones, also, because you know
when things are good—so good—they can be
just like a form of torture, too . . . why,
maybe then, with all the blind alleys,
the promises that led to nothing, dreams
that turned into nightmares when you woke—
maybe, crossed out and botched as they are,
it would all fit together, and make sense.'

I noticed her hands were trembling slightly.
She'd been polishing her glasses on the hem
of her print frock, and as she quickly
put them on, she fumbled, and they slipped.
I saw her upper lip was damp with sweat.
She picked the glasses up and pushed them back
on the bridge of her nose with her middle finger.
The gesture was somehow vulnerable, I thought,
or had I read that in a book somewhere—
or seen it in a movie, long ago,
a trick of Bergman's, or Superman's—
she threw a flushed, pleading look quickly
around the group—'And why . . . then you could
perhaps explain it all back to me. Then
I'd know what made it all come out like that,
how—when I was young and full of promise,
so much talent at living—why things all
went so wrong, through no fault of my own,
and everything turned into the most Godawful
mess, and then—' Her voice caught here,
and she struggled to speak—'But I can't—
somehow I couldn't bring myself to spew
forth with all that, in front of everyone,
I just couldn't do that! Do you see?'

She flung a tearful look around the circle
of embarrassed faces like a lasso, but
to no effect. I picked at the grass,
and tried not to look at the others.
I felt sorry for the girl—she seemed

weak, lost, in need of help, and yet
there was something about her voice, her mood—
a clench of hurt, a current of bitterness—
that made me feel anxious and afraid.
I felt sure the story she had to tell—
perhaps not the one she'd given us now,
but some other buried tale too awful
to bring into the light in front of others—
was one that would excite revulsion and fear.
Somewhere in a far recess of summer
monks were playing soccer. The thock
of leather on leather, and their happy cries.

Doctor Masterson's gaze followed her look
at a leisurely pace. He was obviously
searching for someone to saddle with the task
of helping to deliver Gloria's burden
of woe to the world. Looking for a producer,
as it were; a person with tact, someone
who would wade down that black tunnel
that formed Gloria's view of the universe
and bring back treasure, polished, gleaming,
sorted into heaps and counted up;
someone without a stammer or a lisp.
Did we fidget? You bet.

                          'Oh,
for God's sake,' Gloria said quickly,
and took a deep breath. She held it,
turned pink, and let it out explosively.

Then she gave a short mad laugh. The sun
slipped behind a cloud no one had noticed.

'I had a dream,' she began, then paused.
Her voice had taken on a hard edge
and a querulous tone, as though she had to
win some argument against herself.
'What I wrote, and gave you, that was
the track it followed—not my real career,
but an imaginary one. But in that story,
like a pearl within a pearl shell,
lies another dream—perfect, shimmering.
It's the mirror of another life.

'I had a sister. Her name's Karen. She's—
she's not like me, or my twin Marjorie.
We were poor, and grew up in the country,
and our mother always taught us girls
to hold a straight opinion of ourselves,
never to waver, or sell ourselves cheap,
maybe not to win, but to endure.
But Karen, from the start, was hot-blooded,
younger than us, smaller than me or Marjorie—
and when our mother brought Karen home
from the hospital, it was strange, like
she'd found her there—I don't remember
my mother being pregnant, or any talk
of a little sister—that was a joke
we teased her with, that she was picked up
at a bargain sale in town, dirt cheap,

and Marjorie—she started it—we called her
the lost dog, Karen the Mutt, the mongrel.
We were hoping for a pup, to tell the truth—
I'd been promised an Alsatian for my birthday—
and a kid sister was a disappointment.
She was more a foundling than a relative.
Well, maybe the teasing put an anger in her
that she wouldn't have developed otherwise,
then, maybe she was just bad, the blood
tainted, and nothing you could do about it.
Talk about trouble—you wouldn't believe
the things our family came to later on—
divorce, Marjorie dying, Uncle Ben
ruined, all a result of that girl
and the things she caused to happen.
She looked Nordic, like Mum and Dad,
with pale blonde hair and eyebrows,
and bleached white fuzz on her forearms.
We called her 'the Nazi' once—Dad
overheard, and gave us a proper belting.
Grandfather's name had been Larsen,
he changed it to make it more Australian—
the family was Norwegian, or something
Scandinavian, and Mum's mother
came from the Shetlands, a Williams,
like William the Conqueror, a Norman,
descended from the Old Norse raiders.
But Marjorie and I were dark, Celtish,
with black, curly hair and grey eyes—
Dad called us his pair of kelpies.

john tranter

Karen had these bright blue eyes
the colour of cornflowers, that looked at you
and went right through you like a drill
and out the other side.
                                    'Anyhow—
water long gone under the bridge—
in this dream I'm Marjorie, not myself,
I'm standing to the side, somehow,
just accepting everything that happens;
the dream's about Karen, and she's a real
fuckin bitch.' She took a few quick
deep breaths here, and we all did.
She stood up unsteadily, and paced about,
rubbing her temples, concentrating.
The distant traffic was hushed for a moment.
Two magpies quarrelled in a tree.
Gloria seemed a different woman, taller,
with stronger hands and the flexible body
of a dancer, or an athlete. Somehow her
transformation had won her the gift of fluency.

'Just a moment, Gloria—' said the doctor,
watchful as ever, and careful of his charge,
but his moment had come and gone. 'I'm
Marjorie, right?' said the girl angrily,
'and Karen's talking to me, and I'm listening,
so I can remember everything she says.

' "You know Kellyville?" she says. Marjorie
used to live around that neighbourhood.

"I know Kellyville," I say. "Out past
Blackacre way, boy, what a shithole!"
My voice is booming around, a kind of echo—
I can see myself like a reflection.
"Right on," Karen agrees. "I was there—oh,
ten years back, with that animal I married.
Now why would I marry a creep like that? Me,
my father's pet, the original Princess!
Why would I do a fuckin stupid thing
like that? Can you tell me, Marjorie?"

'I didn't know why she married
a turkey like that,' says Gloria, 'but it's
typical of Karen to pick some loser—
most of her boyfriends were junkies. But
it's just a story that blooms within a dream
like a crystal of some mineral salt
growing at the bottom of a forest pool,
and those things don't have a past, that's
the great gift they have for us, their value,
they come unmarked by childhood guilt, they
drag no chain of nightmares in their wake,
they spring from a limbo of innocence.
But people,' she says, and gives that
mad laugh again—'real people
do self-destructive things, don't they,
they bruise and damage those around them
because they've dragged their fears
behind them like a pack of mad dogs,
to the point where they can do fuckall else.

john tranter

Am I right? Yes! They make their own
lack of choice by the choices they make,
and they just have to swallow it,
shit or champagne, like it or not.

'But Karen wouldn't be interested in
that kind of philosophical talk.
She was busy with the story of her life
like it was a movie, or a soap opera.
Marjorie patiently listening, that's me.

' "Poor bloody Blake," Karen says.
"I met him one night—I was dropping pills,
floating and stumbling around in my usual daze
when there he was—a big handsome brute.
He worked hard, drank with his mates,
had a hot car, a Thunderbird
painted red like a fire engine.
And a wonderful place at the Cross,
high up in the heavens, with a rooftop
where we drank whisky and champagne
and looked at the stars in the sky, and the clouds
lit with a pale pink-orange colour
from the lights you could see twinkling
down below. That's what I love
about Sydney—it's never dark, never
like that inky dark you get in the bush
when it's cloudy—here the night sky
is always lit up with a warm glow
from people working, driving about, eating,

making love with the lights on, being alive.
Blake was fun to be with, laughed a lot
when we went out, or when his mates
dropped around with a carton or two of beer;
but then he had another side to him—
Mum would say 'Street angel, home devil'.
When he was at home, he had his moods,
like some captive brooding in a cage.

' "Then that recession came along,
there were a lot of people out of work,
and Blake—he had a fight with his boss,
a big Samoan fellow, and got the sack.
Next thing we're both on the dole,
and then he had to let the car go.
Then we had to get a cheaper flat.
And he starts reading books and magazines.
Going to the library, borrowing books,
reading into the night. I have to
get my sleep, or I get awful . . .
difficult to live with. You know?"
"Oh, I know," I say. "It's like that
with me, with drink. Or it used to be." '

Could it be, I asked myself, our shy
Gloria, the freckles, the cheap frock,
a drunk? No—it's possible, but
hard to believe—but then it's this
Marjorie creature who's speaking, some
alter ego perhaps, the two faces of Eve,

or more . . . under the skirts of rectitude
the nymphomaniac, behind the proper
bank president howls the alcoholic.

'Carry on, sweetheart, get it out,'
says Gloria—Marjorie—' "Well," says Karen,
"Blake's father—he'd been dead for years,
but Blake had been through a bad time
with him, long ago. I knew that Bruce,
the brother, the same age as Blake,
volunteered for service in Vietnam
and never came back, and the father
blamed Blake somehow, for being idle,
for not going too. Bruce was tough,
a heart like an ox, full of courage,
and did things proper, by the book;
Blake was lazy, happy-go-lucky,
good-natured. But the father argued,
picked on Blake a lot, and one day
they had a bad fight—what happened,
the details, he wouldn't say at first.
He didn't want to talk about his past.
Till one night, when it came out—

' "It began with the books. He'd bring them home.
And drink this cheap wine, from a flagon,
and sit up late, reading, mumbling
while he followed the words with his finger,
a chuckle, a murmur, rising and falling.
It got on my nerves. Then late at night,

stinking of that cheap after-shave
he wore, he'd want to read them to me, these
magazines, anthologies. 'C'mon, honey,'
he'd say, 'this is a really great story,
about this elephant hunter, an adventure,
just let me read you some of it.' Jesus!

' "It started out a kind of bed-time game,
like, at first, the stories, they were kind of
sexy—not from cheap tit magazines, no—
books, classy magazines with nice photos,
the models young, with tasteful make-up,
real authors and all that, but kind of . . .
well, you know. Then, later on,
they grew more intellectual—Blake,
he'd done a course, some university degree
by mail, he'd worked on an oil rig
back in the sixties, all that free time,
so he did this diploma and learnt to read
intellectual books. Then, to make it crazier,
soon it was no sex without a story.
That's what he said. Can you believe that?
He wouldn't, or he couldn't do it any other
way, without this stupid fuckin twist.

' "And soon it was just this one story,
time after time, about a blind man,
how his wife's lover—a soldier, captured
in Korea and brainwashed, and turned loose
to assassinate the top men in government—

got his wires crossed and murdered ordinary
men and women—a butterfly collector,
an old rabbi, a man selling toys
on the street—well, this crazy pair
plotted to murder her blind husband,
creeping through the house, playing jokes—
that's sick, isn't it? Don't you think?"

'Karen had this ring on her finger,'
Marjorie—Gloria—said, looking at her own
engagement ring, 'and being Karen it was
some cheap rhinestone article
she'd picked up at the Cross, and she
rubbed it and stared at it, and laughed.

' "Enough is enough," she says, in a flat voice,
"what with the drinking and the crying—
did I tell you that? He'd get upset
when he reached the final episode
where the blind man stabs the soldier—
he'd made a special white cane, sharpened
at the end, and he pokes his eyes out
and blinds him, so they're both stumbling around
covered in blood, stabbing at the air—
and Blake's voice would give out here,
he'd start trembling, staring at the page,
wiping his face. It was like a madhouse,
me in bed in my nightdress—a pretty thing,
a pastel blue silk effect, I bought it
in L.A., on that trip to Disneyland,

remember?—perfume, make-up and all,
Blake drunk and wailing like a loon.
Well, Christ, it had to stop. I said
I was packing up and leaving—then
he told me about his father, how they fought,
and how Blake stabbed him in the face—
Oh God, this is horrible! Horrible!'

'And Karen burst into tears,' says Marjorie—
Gloria—and she starts sobbing too, *her* face
swollen and red. Grief, like a layer-cake!

Doctor Masterson poked at his neglected pipe,
and cleared his throat several times.
He was obviously moved by this complex tale
of wretchedness and desperation. He
grimaced and took some tablets from a pocket—
'Indigestion, please excuse me,' and to Gloria:
'My dear girl—your imagination,
you must use more discipline, more
artistic control—and please sit down,
you make me nervous, stalking around behind me
like that—' he dug some tissues
from his jacket—Gloria's handkerchief
was wet with tears—but in the brief moment
it had taken us all to gather our wits,
she had gathered hers. 'I'm Marjorie, okay?'
she spat out, and plunged onward—
'and Karen's explaining to me about
the fight that mutilated Blake's father:

' "They drank heavily, the whole family—
Blake was an alcoholic," Karen said;
"and the mother was into the cooking sherry.
You remember Auntie Eleanor, Marjorie?
'Just a refresher, for the cook!' she'd say,
folding her apron and picking up
a tray of scones, or whipping up a batter,
but sipping at the sherry in between—
remember? Uncle Ben telling blue jokes
and stuffing cakes into his face—God,
that man could eat like a horse—
and mixing his home brew, everybody
laughing in the kitchen, Old Jack
calling by with a brace of wild ducks—
'Hullo, Missus—I just saw these two
sittin' on the dam, and I reckoned
you could use 'em for dinner, so I
nipped back to the shed and got me gun!'
God, Marjorie, the times that are gone ...
well, like I was saying, Auntie Eleanor,
Blake's mum was like her, but worse.

' "One night—it must have been a Sunday,
and they'd come home early from the Club,
they'd lit the fire in the sitting room,
and turned on a lamp, but the dining room
was dim and shadowy, the mantel clock ticking—
don't they give you the creeps?—the radiogram
playing some dance tune from the thirties
in another room—So there was Jock,

Blake's father, thin as a weasel,
not like the boys; drunk, hacking away
at the roast lamb—he'd wolfed down
his dinner, and he wanted second helpings—
splashing gravy on the good linen tablecloth
they kept for Sunday best, the mother crying,
and Jock going on about the blacks, how they
soak up the government handouts, never work,
drink Blue Ruin, and all that racist shit,
and how Blake's brother was a real man,
never shirked his duty, lion-hearted,
Bruce knew what he wanted, volunteered
for service, killed a few Vietnamese,
and he'd put the Abos in their place.
Blake was keen on a young girl at the time,
part Aborigine, bright, and very pretty.
He swallows as much as he can take, then
he gives a scream like a stuck pig
and a red mist floods over his eyes
and then—it goes blank, no sound,
all dark, he can't remember a thing.

' "Just as well, for what he did then—
the carving knife—Blake had a fetish
about sharpening things, he had
a grindstone, and an Arkansas stone,
and a steel like butchers use, he'd go
whip, *whip*, like that, honing the edge
till it sparkled like a scalpel blade—
in this fit of rage he grabbed the knife

and he cut his father's face about so horribly
that the old man lost both his eyes,
chopped up like soft-boiled eggs. And
the carving fork, with those long prongs,
he drove it right up through his father's nose
with one blow, the thin sinus bones,
right through the floor of the brain cavity,
was how Blake described it. Cut the brain,
a fraction, just a snip, a pointed cut,
right through where your memories are joined,
where you remember things, and store them away.
The ambulance man had to pluck it out,
the long fork, stuck deep in the skull,
and bits of flesh all over the tablecloth.

' "Well, Jock lived—a bit of surgery,
no problem, but his eyes were gone, and worse,
his brain was damaged so that he never
remembered any new thing again.
His early memories lingered on: school,
who he was, old train timetables,
the scent of a pine tree cut down,
a movie he'd seen years ago and could
tell you the plot, telephone numbers,
addresses, bets he'd had on the horses—
but nothing he ever learnt from that day on
stuck. Well, you can imagine Blake, the blame,
the guilt! Whatever he could do to make it up,
he tried, because he really loved his dad.
And then the Aboriginal girl left,

shot through with the father of her baby,
some creep from Tokyo, a priest. The mother
seemed to fade away, Blake said,
hardly eating, pecking like a sparrow,
just a few crumbs here and there,
and in the end she got so thin
she lost her will to live—the bloodshed
had shocked her terribly, and her heart
was weakened by the drink, and diabetes—
so she died, and left them, father and son,
the two of them, together in the house.

' "Like poor Auntie Eleanor, in her last days.
You used to write to me each week—remember?—
when you went to boarding school in the city,
and tell me how you'd go out to visit,
to the old people's home, and read to her
from the family Bible—all that way
alone on the tram, in the evening,
to read the Old Testament, and she'd sob
and hold a dirty hankie to her mouth—
old age, it's a terrible thing. And Gloria,
that bitch, too busy with her books
and her university friends to help out,
too busy drinking gin and having abortions
and being smart and intellectual, and me
stuck on the bloody farm. Oh, I'm sorry,
but those things make me angry. Old Jock.

' "Blake read to him at night—his dad

was blind, and he hated advertisements,
so the TV and the radio were out.
And he refused to listen to the ABC,
full of fuckin communists, he said.
Reading. Every evening. That was fine,"
Karen says, "Blake didn't mind. But you see,

' "every time he'd start to read a story,
poor Jock would forget it by the time
his son had reached the bottom of the page.
'How did that begin again?' he'd say. 'That
sounds like a bloody good yarn. How does it go?'
and Blake would have to start the page again.
There was one story he particularly liked,
from an old *Playboy* magazine, about a guy
who made a living killing elephants.
There was a sex interest in it somewhere,
but Blake never got that far. Over and over,
page thirty-seven, where the story starts
in Nairobi, buying up supplies, then the hero
gets drunk in a bar, and fights a Negro.
Night after night, that page, for seven years.
Then his father had a stroke—he was
getting on, in any case—had a stroke
and sat there in the nursing home, drooling,
eating up money, that's how Blake put it,
and the doctors like a flock of vultures,
till his mind went blank—just nothing—
and he was gone, and Blake was left alone.

' "I picked Blake up," Karen says,
"in a singles bar, soon after that.
I thought: at last, here was a real doll—
he looked stunning in his red convertible—
a big hunk of a guy, built like a house,
a gentle gorilla—someone to sweep me
off my feet and make up for the bad times:
what happened on the farm, Uncle Ben,
working the street, the trouble with the cops.
He wasn't Robert Redford, but he had
a sense of humour, and he took me out a lot.
His eyes were grey, his glossy black hair
fell in thick waves over his collar,
he looked so cute in the clothes he wore,
the roll-neck sweaters, duffel jackets.
He polished up nice, on a lady's arm.
It was fun for a while. He was good in bed,
at first, then he began to get moody, then
the stories started, then the madness.

' "He drank, and in the end he lost his job,
and we were thrown out of our flat, and moved
to that joint way past Kellyville—
we hardly had any money, except for wine—
then to a basement dump in Darlinghurst—
you had to climb down a flight of stairs,
damp sweat on the walls, mould,
dark and freezing in winter, we always
had the light on even in the daytime
and you hardly ever got to see the sky,

and in summer you'd think it would be cool,
but it was suffocating, like a furnace.
And Blake got obsessed about his hair—
he even had nightmares about it—
how it was going grey, and receding,
and then it was falling out, going bald—
I'd catch him with a comb in his hand,
standing in front of the mirror, crying.

' "Then one day, a knock on the door,
and the strangest creature was standing there
weaving from foot to foot in the shadows
like a circus bear—it was Bruce, the brother.
The war was over, and the Vietnamese,
after they'd tortured the poor man
half to death and back, had patched him up
and sent him home again. He looked awful—
big, but bent, hunched over stiffly,
a grey-blond thatch of hair, freckles
that mottled his face like a disfigurement,
and his blue eyes had a crazy glitter.
And there was something wrong with his mouth;
he came up close, and I saw he had a hare-lip
that gave him a strange, sarcastic kind of sneer.
Blake had never told me about that, and then
I realised there were no photos of Bruce—
you'd think when someone close to you
had disappeared off the face of the earth
there'd be a shrine of some sort, but no,
not even a holiday snap, and that was why.

There was a smell about him I didn't like—
beer, tobacco, a kind of animal sweat.
'My brother,' he grunted, 'a souvenir
for my brother.' His big fat paws
held out a parcel wrapped in newspaper—
the back of his hands were matted with red hair—
I felt it, something cold and heavy,
but he wouldn't let me take it, he pushed past
and went through the flat like a robot
calling out 'I want my brother!'
He found Blake half asleep, hungover.
Bruce grabbed him and yelled out loud—
'You fucking mongrel, what did you do?
I want to talk to my dad!'
then he started beating poor Blake
and cracking his head against the wall
for what he'd done on that Sunday
with the knife and the carving fork.
I ran to the kitchen to get something
to hit him with—there was a leg of lamb
I'd just taken from the freezer, I grabbed it
and ran back to the bedroom—he'd taken
a grenade from the parcel, and pulled the pin,
and he was holding Blake against his chest
in a bear-hug, groaning and howling.
I swung the leg of lamb and brought it down
crack on the back of his skull, grabbed Blake—
he'd been beaten nearly unconscious—
and pulled him out of there. We were
halfway down the hall when it went off,

john tranter

a terrible bang!—and I woke up in hospital.

' "Blake said later that he'd crawled back
to try to help Bruce, or to apologise,
but there were just pieces everywhere.
What he saw stuck in his memory
like some horror movie episode
repeating over and over. From then on
he was never quite the same. His skull
had been fractured by the beating, they said,
and his eardrums blown in by the grenade,
so he was half deaf from then on,
though he could hear his 'special voices',
he told me, chiding him for little things
like stealing and dishonesty, and Blake said
'I'm a murderer, but they never mention that.'
Isn't that sad? I cried when he said that.
The doctors patched him up—his eyesight
was never right, and he had to wear glasses,
and they gave him anxiety pills to take
but they made his hands shake, and when he drank
they mixed badly with the alcohol, and then
he'd knock into things and fall over.
And all the time, remembering the grenade,
trying to forget, to blot it out,
then his father, and the meat knife—
he went to group therapy for a while,
but he used to argue, and yell at the doctor.
I was optimistic—he had a medical pension;
there couldn't be any more family trouble—

there wasn't any family, for a start.
I hoped that he could pull himself together.

' "He got his job back with the Samoan,
but then he started stealing—a stuffed bird,
an emu egg, a butterfly display—
and so they had to give him the sack again.
In the end—no medication seemed to work,
and he was drunk or drugged all the time,
with a dull stare like a pole-axed bullock—
he started seeing things, wanting to die—
in the end they put him away, and every night
I think of him locked in there, growing old,
flinching at the voices criticising him,
the endless torrent of memories, the poor man
desperate for things to be like they were,
to turn the clock back, and start again.

' "Oh, Marjorie, I can't bear it!" Karen says,
and a shiver runs through her thin body.
She takes her glasses off and rubs her eyes
and hides her face in her hands.' And Marjorie
was sniffing, holding back a tear, and
Gloria was obviously wrung out, too,
but she had a strange look in her eyes—
they were wet with tears, but they glittered—
she was happy, that was it, her grey eyes
sparkling! She laughed, and hugged herself,
and held her face up to the sky. Then
she sat down at last, with a shudder.

john tranter

The sun drifted out from behind a cloud
and a warm light spilled across the park.
We frowned and blinked in the glare, like
strangers wandering out from a midday movie.

'My notes, please, Doctor Masterson,' she said,
and took back those sheets of type and scribble.
I noticed that her hands were shaking slightly.
Masterson stared at her. No one said a thing.

'Let's start at the beginning, then, shall we,
where I have this extraordinary dream.' Gloria
smiled, adjusted her glasses, and began.

*I follow my course with the precision and the security of a
sleepwalker.*

Adolf Hitler, 1936

Hitler is not just an individual. He is a condition.
Th Th Heine, *Simplicissimus*, 1923

the dark, the sinister . . . ,

   strange man circling through the events of the previous evening, and I lay on a sofa recalling how he declared I was easily the most beautiful woman in the room. Then with a suddenness so complete my eyes shocked open wide, I found myself stepping from a taxi into the cavernous foyer of a hotel. Knowing but passive faces leant from pink and gold reflections and beckoned me to follow through gliding doors over soft carpets to the steel panels closing over the elevator discreetly tucked into a reddened wall. A woman whose brass hair crackled, audibly smacked her purple lips, wreathed perfume around my waist, then hitched her skirt to reveal leather wrinkled thighs. I stood distinct, hat low, distaste concealed. And I paused before stepping through the doorspace, affecting lean elegance, an easy appearance, while glancing into the darkness of the night sprawling from the lobby, yellow lights thin points, traffic lights fullstopping, blue neon hazes penetrating blackness, eerie smudges, untenable. The door slid, imprisoning me in the elevator. I watched the numbers flit upwards, increasing. The door softly opened. I followed a corridor of dim lights and closed embossed doors and oval shaped gilt-edged mirrors. I stopped by one of these mirrors and patted my hair. Elegance transferred to nonchalance and hid indecision. Assured that even a moment's perplexity would appear as a blankness favoured as natural and becoming in a woman, my confidence lifted me into his room and I amazed myself volubly with the view, pan-oramic, a vista of a city beautifully water black and yellow lit, pushing horizons of earth and sky together, guaran-teeing to startle the senses from introspection. Or jet lag. He restrained excitement. Deliberately propelled me to an easy chair. He poured champagne, held the glasses high so the light played through the effervescence and, with a slight bow, he handed one to me. The black mass of night filled the window behind him, silhouetting his red earth colour, the triangular shape of his head sloping away from firm but narrow shoulders. He asked ques-tions about my accent, teasing me of being fraudulent, of disguising my class and origin behind an acquired manner of speaking, therefore belonging to no place, no home, whereas he, even when he was using a language other than his own was readily recognisable as German.

I responded, playing with hands eyes mouth, creating an impression of sheer loveliness and intelligence, vulnerability and kitchen wittedness, a game I had practised so often the art was myself. He rose, stalked around the room, eyes flitting darting behind long lids, smiling, certain I would soon be a pleasant memory of his. Then, spinning on his heels, he cupped my face in his hands, announcing that if I were to stay more than two days in this city, he would get to know me very well. I let my eyes rest on his which, judging by a sudden bright gleam, he misinterpreted in his man's way to accord with his enthusiasm. A quick stride to the window meant to camouflage his apparent glee. But, at that moment, I was deciding behind my eyes if I would agree to be so well known, aware of a fine distinction between the passive action of rejecting and the passive acceptance of life's drift. My husband was elsewhere. His absence need not have placed me in the position of contacting a colleague. Indeed, the wives of colleagues do not, as a general rule, cross the threshold of a hotel foyer in the dead of night to drink champagne for the company. But, whether by adventure or misadventure, my being the wife of a colleague had established the drift. The decision to swim with the mainstream or pick along the rocky edges became a question of fastidiousness. I drank deeply, watching him rove restlessly round the room, his compactness within his clothes reminding me of an equestrian, straight backed and in control. From as many angles as were presented, he surveyed the city's stretch, tossing words and phrases at me over his shoulder. I said,

The disadvantage of a traveller's life is in meeting too briefly people you know you like. He, with a hint of condescension further indicating how surely he believed he had won me, smiled, and corrected my contention to, It is a disadvantage, which is also an advantage. He began to say, When I was in Bolivia ... The unfinished sentence slipped, the drinking soothed, and the lighting in the room softened a slyness lurking round his mouth. His bearing, his presence was evil, the kind of evil I had been taught to recognise as fascist. The doors of the room flew open and a dinner of fine quails under a silver bell and strawberries chilled in silver bowls was wheeled before us. The waiter hovered at our pleasure. Charmed, I enjoyed the dexterous invasion of my senses, curious, watching myself choose whether or not to allow this man to flatter, unfold me into making love with him. We sat close together, eating strawberries by placing them gently between each other's teeth, biting them in half, then slowly pushing the remaining juicy fruit along the inner side of a willing tongue. Our conversation lapsed to gasps and grunts. I leant my head on his shoulder, a sudden aversion for his blue shirt exploding like a sharp rap in my head. The increasingly devilish mouth above my forehead grovelled, bent into my chest, twisting moist and lewd as he fumbled with the clasps of my blouse. When he had undone it, expecting to discover breasts, he shouted instead at the long scar running from my neck disappearing at the top of my trousers before descending into pubic hair. He leapt back, alarmed. A completely cloven woman! He laughed coarse ridicule, and prodded the sensitive skin stretched over the trachea, rubbed his knuckles cruelly over the breastbone, pulled at the top of my trousers to see how the scar finished. Insulted, I tugged my blouse together, adjusted my hat and composed myself as if I had never intended to be anything other than the decorous wife of a colleague. He, slumping in his chair, the back of his head black against the pink upholstery, slipped from my view where walls yawned, corridors narrowed, floors buckled and decay seared my nostrils. I could not find the carpeted corridor I had previously walked along. I fussed at a mirror hanging crooked on a roughened wall. Corrected an eyebrow. The way my blouse tucked in my trousers. But rubble scratched my boots. Dust powdered my jacket. Chips of ceiling plaster fell on my shoulders. Walls dropped away revealing caverns and smaller and smaller rooms. Dejected, I sighed and returned along one corridor when I found him again, surrounded by clowns performing slow tricks on a stage, their faces besmeared white, black around the eyes, devoid of expression. Chalk white suits clad their listless bodies. Suddenly, before I could ask his help, he cracked a whip and the clowns shook and hid their faces in the sleeves of their blouses and cowered at the back of the stage, he herding and shoving them into a huddle. Once assembled, they reached out their arms, fingers flickering the air in front of them, feeling sightlessly as they took small hesitant steps until they were able to paw his clothing, tug at his trousers, unzip his fly. One knelt and began to suck his limp penis. Others fondled, laughing noiselessly, black holes opening wide in white faces, emitting nothing. He stood stiffly at the centre of their attentions, flexed to act. One clown detached from their group, drew him away from the mechanical mouth, and partnered him to dance. Music filled the room, a scratched record of an old fox-trot turning on a gramophone balancing on rubble, and the two danced in habitual timing. The others sat along the wall dutifully, mouths closed to form the shapes of perfectly clean arseholes. I noticed then that he wore well polished black boots over grey jodh-purs. But I could scarcely believe his eyes slid under narrow lids, yellow moon rinds not seeing me alone sig-nalling disappointment mingled with censure. My jacket sat straight. So too did my hat. He danced, controlling his sensations as well as the compliant clown whose face bobbed above his shoulder, blonde hair falling about its cheeks and she may have been his wife. His physical bearing, the tight sadistic lines of his body, attracted my stomach and I lowered my head, slightly jealous of the clown who seemed so joyless in his embrace. I tensed as if to move. Whether forwards or backwards I do not know for the clowns grappled me round my neck, dragged me by the hair and forced me to grovel in the dust at his feet. My tongue and throat choked outrage. They wanted me to lick his boot. When I would not, they tore off my clothes, pulled my breasts, scratched my scar, pinched my buttocks, poked and prodded my vulva and arse. But I shook myself free of them, frowning at the way their clammy fingers sought my flesh. I looked up, one of the creatures still clawing at my neck, another lapping my back with its irksome tongue, and I saw nothing but yellow unseeing slits under his eyelids, a wry smile snarling his lips. Instantly, his face stiffened. He brought down the whip, lashing me fiercely across the back, and my entrails heaved. But I had become so determined to resist and stand alone my skin did not feel the blow nor any humiliation. Without interference, I dressed and left him. As I climbed through a hole in the wall, I realised he stared after me, his mouth agape with wonderment, his whip coiled about his feet. Clowns rolled over, curled into their alcoves, their faces sliding into sleep. Before and behind me, holes continued to open and close, open and close, open and close, clowns lolling stupidly in sleep, and I stepped through and through and through basements of rubble echoing into more, larger and smaller basements as if they were one. But a resilience overcame tears. Repetition did not reduce me, the task in itself becoming a distinctive, thrilling achievement. When I surfaced into the blue evening, he appeared in front of me, militarily elegant in a chauffeur's suit, a riding crop nestling by his calf. With admiration, he clasped my hand and, pressing it, drew me to his chest saying, while staring past the clowns as if they vaulted their spaces, You are the most beautiful presence of the evening. I received the compliment with no surprise, no fascination, expecting it, a few words whose meaning is more oblique than their banality suggests. I looked long at his profile. He looked through his clowns. And around us the city sparked. Car engines fired. Accelerators roared. Brakes squealed. An old car chugged, coughed, fell silent. From the shadows of the foyer, a hotel doorman stretched his arm into the street for a taxi. The uniform broadened his shoulders. He flattened the palm of his hand against the small of my back and guided me to the car door which he opened. I disliked being manipulated from a curiosity in one man to the concern of another to the protection offered by a third. Accepting the doorman's palm as he ushered me forwards, I turned, pointing the toe of my boot into his instep, and kissed him full on the mouth. Satisfied no one could fault my independence, I sat down on the back seat of the taxi. The door slapped shut. The car bulleted through the city's canyons. His chauffeur's face suspended overlapping mine in the rear vision mirror, transparent lids closing over long yellow eyes looking to the back seat, not forwards. The sky catapulted, grey black and forbidding, the car with me as its cargo leaping, never stopping, the bridge rocking buildings giddy overhead, the face in the mirror broadening diminishing distorting, thinning to a hard line resisting boredom. Gloved hands manipulated strongly the vehicle in which I sat, neither acquiescent nor protesting, detached from horror for fear of crumbling, strange, listless on a sofa, its pink upholstery too colourless beneath the black window space, the evening air cool and, if he had been Hitler's driver, did he accept the job as a good one, life's luck to him, motoring blind and in command behind the wheel of a machine through wartorn Europe?, and

be careful on the street close all the doors tight don't
open the window at night i was smuggling arms on my
bicycle german soldiers flirt she said hurry up caught us
going to shoot i get away he hides me in the attic my
hair turned black overnight don't go out by yourself i
hide under the stairs everybody looks a soldier to me
now put away gold take fur i won't need it now who
knocking on the door too loud what is that now who
is it i have to watch out they come boots i climb over
the wall they switch the electricity hid me haystack i
was so hungry never throw out food now i am so
hungry all the time and scared who comes now don't
go out the door there's danger after easter pogroms
don't tell anybody who you are no don't tell them it is
five o'clock now it is too late they'll come again i knew
false passport i change my name to singer the sirens
siren put me up night i leave the next day don't trust
them stole her ring and cut off her finger they inform
me car lights in dark winter he reports me i run through
snow i was in another town i didn't look like it have
to be quiet now don't breathe i get away they come
now up the stairs can't you hear best seats for the
germans stacks of shoes everybody gone now i couldn't

find them if someone leaves the house they might not
come back take your clothes hide the silver it's the same
again now take this it will be useful don't cough don't
make too much noise they hear now walking walking
up knock shadow walls get dusk close curtain don't put
on the light i was on my bicycle don't tell them who
don't trust them don't trust anybody now black cars
maria have sirens they come at night don't tell them
never tell them keep secret don't leave the house they
steal our suitcases hide the whole family till the money
run away now quick mud make soup out of potato
peelings save everything i can't sleep i listen for footsteps and knocking keep awake now look out shut the
door properly test if shut and again close the windows
tight don't trust them the man who worked for my
father gives me away i run i get drunk keep me warm
now don't trust anybody ever the germans come back
thirty years later take jewellery hide it close the doors
all the doors they come now i wait for boots footsteps
on the stairs knock knocking don't let anybody in now
don't go out on the street danger black car night siren
maria don't tell them anything i run through mud in
my dream hide me will you hide me now look look are
they here they can come again don't tell anybody i'm
here i'm on my bicycle smuggling arms i change my
name he hid me in the attic don't tell him who you are
don't tell them anything be careful on the street danger
don't go out the house at easter pogroms stay inside
close doors windows don't put on the light be careful
save all the food come useful i run through snow i was

in another town underground i didn't see the sun don't go out at night stay here i was all alone he hid me attic under the stairs don't tell anybody be careful on the street they steal our suitcases they come now

dad

was in siberia so cold when you blew my nose froze away
drop like stones only grows four months eating garlic
clove whole lot vitamins rats the most intelligent they
don't need it really remember in tasmania there nob dy
to speak didin't needs either only driving coutry drove
into a ditch couldn't see out one eye shoul'dnt go to
any cinema gets nervous what did you eat did you brush
your teeth beer helps acid to my digets digetst digests
only one you said don't want a father drunkard it was
night near a ditch very muddy heavy trucks came and
nearly drove over something saved me threwme away he
said thought you'r a gonner then nearly killed can't see
film gets too much i'm in it look they shot his skull right
off they are chasing running to get my had a russian gun
in the russian army they get st uck german ones always
fired gave me a drink strong young wine in a cy cup they
had to take drink it all down and after on my horse was
rising to the stars like mohammed rising levitate head
hurts where is street what did they say couldn't catch
you tell me now my mother ghost it comes mill owner
of a mill said your mother came to me last night in my
film they chase had officers making sure nobody runs
away had to kill no way out do you think i know i don't

know then forgot polish speaking only russian army
caught shaved my armpits all hair off body every bit
poured disinfectant for lice this man came to a dance
and he said did you hear that they are shooting she said
what comarade to had to get up at four thirty meat
keeping my place safe had lights on left you don't know
who breaks in they're all bandits just tell him know why
your wife left you tell him they were spies read about
that did you must watch the news why didn't you ring
was waiting all the soldiers slept at an orphanage at night
had nowhere else to go they said minus twenty degrees
getting warmer no don't eat much and the tall soldiers
slept there were no beds they slept in baby cots their lrgs
sticking out lots of bugs on the same horse all war long
that was a bay one they don't tell you what hurts can't
i put her there and stayed all year with always fighting
for her was she was like when met wanted to get married
this man very old completely damaged is the beach kind
to strangers went to shop and go to librarry didin't want
to talk to anybody all strangers only read the papers do
you go it's cold don't heat too cold to washing let me
help carry on in siberia taiga such stars very bright stars
they didn't want people to travel so they didin't give
tickets they said all booked out and we waited they
waited on the station sometimes one week and lots of
seats in russia they shot them after the war if they came
very back they were afraid of anybody in leningrad if they
looked healthy because they eat people's meat the like
killed them to keep alive it was a very good horse and
followed me when i fell one night slept in a barn no hat

and the head cold stay was in uniform gave me so i settled there wasn't any way out do you think i'm keeping used the machine cleaned i brought they bring me they had a stretcher out shot off his leg man without a chest though you couldn't see looked normal really and the chest cavity when they took off the blankets there was only bunker in mud that's where sleep i was dozing and as if she still there in did shopping soldiers wer climbing and if they dropped nobody to pick up they were running very brave bog people i've read drag from peat how do you say just dry bread but enough what soldiers eat hard biscuit you soak this well didin't tins survived

I want to go home.
I want to go home.
Oh, Lord, I want to go home.

Charlie Pride moans from a cassette, and his voice slips
out of the crack the window makes. Out into the world
of magpies' soothing carols, and parrots' cheeky whistles,
of descending darkness and spirits.

The man doesn't know that world. His is the world
of the sleek new Kingswood that speeds down the never-
ending highway.

At last he can walk this earth with pride, as his ancestors did many years before him. He had his first exhibition of paintings a month ago. They sold well, and
with the proceeds he bought the car.

The slender black hands swing the shiny black wheel
around a corner. Blackness forms a unison of power.

For five years he has worked hard and saved and sacri-
ficed. Now, on his twenty-first birthday, he is going home.

New car, new clothes, new life.

He plucks a cigarette from the packet beside him, and
lights up.

His movements are elegant and delicate. His hair is well-groomed, and his clothes are clean.

Billy Woodward is coming home in all his might, in his shining armour.

Sixteen years old. Last year at school.

His little brother Carlton and his cousin Rennie Davis, down beside the river, on that last night before he went to the college in Perth, when all three had had a goodbye drink, with their girls beside them.

Frogs croaking into the silent hot air and some animal blundering in the bulrushes on the other side of the gentle river. Moonlight on the ruffled water. Nasal voices whispering and giggling. The clink of beer bottles.

That year at college, with all its schoolwork, and learning, and discipline, and uniformity, he stood out alone in the football carnival.

Black hands grab the ball. Black feet kick the ball. Black hopes go soaring with the ball to the pasty white sky.

No one can stop him now. He forgets about the river of his Dreaming and the people of his blood and the girl in his heart.

The year when he was eighteen, he was picked by a top city team as a rover. This was the year that he played for the state, where he was voted best and fairest on the field.

That was a year to remember.

He never went out to the park at Guildford, so he

never saw his people: his dark, silent staring people, his rowdy, brawling, drunk people.

He was white now.

Once, in the middle of the night, one of his uncles had crept around to the house he rented and fallen asleep on the verandah. A dirty pitiful carcase, encased in a black greatcoat that had smelt of stale drink and lonely, violent places. A withered black hand had clutched an almost-empty metho bottle.

In the morning, Billy had shouted at the old man and pushed him down the steps, where he stumbled and fell without pride. The old man had limped out of the creaking gate, not understanding.

The white neighbours, wakened by the noise, had peered out of their windows at the staggering old man stumbling down the street and the glowering youth muttering on the verandah. They had smirked in self-righteous knowledge.

Billy had moved on the next day.

William Jacob Woodward passed fifth year with flying colours. All the teachers were proud of him. He went to the West Australian Institute of Technology to further improve his painting, to gain fame that way as well.

He bought clean, bright clothes and cut off his long hair that all the camp girls had loved.

Billy Woodward was a handsome youth, with the features of his white grandfather and the quietness of his Aboriginal forebears. He stood tall and proud, with the sensitive lips of a dreamer and a faraway look in his serene amber eyes.

He went to the nightclubs regularly and lost his soul in the throbbing, writhing electrical music as the white tribe danced their corroboree to the good life.

He would sit alone at a darkened corner table, or with a painted-up white girl—but mostly alone. He would drink wine and look around the room at all the happy or desperate people.

He was walking home one night from a nightclub when a middle-aged Aboriginal woman stumbled out of a lane.

She grinned up at him like the Gorgon and her hands clutched at his body, like the lights from the nightclub.

'Billy! Ya Billy Woodward, unna?'

'Yes. What of it?' he snapped.

'Ya dunno me? I'm ya Auntie Rose, from down Koodup.'

She cackled then. Ugly, oh, so ugly. Yellow and red eyes and broken teeth and a long, crooked, white scar across her temple. Dirty grey hair all awry.

His people.

His eyes clouded over in revulsion. He shoved her away and walked off quickly.

He remembered her face for many days afterwards whenever he tried to paint a picture. He felt ashamed to be related to a thing like that. He was bitter that she was of his blood.

That was his life: painting pictures and playing football and pretending. But his people knew. They always knew.

In his latest game of football he had a young part-Aboriginal opponent who stared at him the whole game with large, scornful black eyes seeing right through him.

After the game, the boy's family picked him up in an old battered station wagon.

Billy, surrounded by all his white friends, saw them from afar off. He saw the children kicking an old football about with yells and shouts of laughter and two lanky boys slumping against the door yarning to their hero, and a buxom girl leaning out the window and an old couple in the back. The three boys, glancing up, spotted debonair Billy. Their smiles faded for an instant and they speared him with their proud black eyes.

So Billy was going home, because he had been reminded of home (with all its carefree joys) at that last match.

It is raining now. The shafts slant down from the sky, in the glare of the headlights. Night-time, when woodarchis come out to kill, leaving no tracks: as though they are cloud shadows passing over the sun.

Grotesque trees twist in the half-light. Black tortured figures, with shaggy heads and pleading arms. Ancestors crying for remembrance. Voices shriek or whisper in tired chants: tired from the countless warnings that have not been heeded.

They twirl around the man, like the lights of the city he knows. But he cannot understand these trees. They drag him onwards, even when he thinks of turning back and not going on to where he vowed he would never go again.

A shape, immovable and impassive as the tree it is under, steps into the road on the Koodup turnoff.

An Aboriginal man.

Billy slews to a halt, or he will run the man over.

Door opens.

Wind and rain and coloured man get in.

'Ta, mate. It's bloody cold 'ere,' the coloured man grates, then stares quizically at Billy, with sharp black eyes. 'Nyoongah, are ya, mate?'

'Yes.'

The man sniffs noisily, and rubs a sleeve across his nose.

'Well, I'm Darcy Goodrich, any rate, bud.'

He holds out a calloused hand. Yellow-brown, blunt scarred fingers, dirty nails. A lifetime of sorrow is held between the fingers.

Billy takes it limply.

'I'm William Woodward.'

'Yeah?' Fathomless eyes scrutinise him again from behind the scraggly black hair that falls over his face.

'Ya goin' anywheres near Koodup, William?'

'Yes.'

'Goodoh. This is a nice car ya got 'ere. Ya must 'ave plen'y of boya, unna?'

Silence from Billy.

He would rather not have this cold, wet man beside him, reminding him. He keeps his amber eyes on the lines of the road as they flash under his wheels.

White ... white ... white ...

'Ya got a smoke, William?'

'Certainly. Help yourself.'

Black blunt fingers flick open his expensive cigarette case.

'Ya want one too, koordah?'

'Thanks.'

'Ya wouldn't be Teddy Woodward's boy, would ya, William?'

'Yes, that's right. How are Mum and Dad—and everyone?'

Suddenly he has to know all about his family and become lost in their sea of brownness.

Darcy's craggy face flickers at him in surprise, then turns, impassive again, to the rain-streaked window. He puffs on his cigarette quietly.

'What, ya don't know?' he says softly. 'Ya Dad was drinkin' metho. 'E was blind drunk, an' in the 'orrors, ya know? Well, this truck came out of nowhere when 'e was crossin' the road on a night like this. Never seen 'im. Never stopped or nothin'. Ya brother Carl found 'im next day an' there was nothin' no one could do then. That was a couple of years back now.'

Billy would have been nineteen then, at the peak of his football triumph. On one of those bright white nights, when he had celebrated his victories with wine and white women, Billy's father had been wiped off the face of his country—all alone.

He can remember his father as a small gentle man who was the best card cheat in the camp. He could make boats out of duck feathers and he and Carlton and Billy had had races by the muddy side of the waterhole, from where his people had come long ago, in the time of the beginning.

The lights of Koodup grin at him as he swings around a bend. Pinpricks of eyes, like a pack of foxes waiting for the blundering black rabbit.

'Tell ya what, buddy. Stop off at the hotel an' buy a carton of stubbies.'

'All right, Darcy.' Billy smiles and looks closely at the man for the first time. He desperately feels that he needs a friend as he goes back into the open mouth of his previous life. Darcy gives a gap-toothed grin.

'Bet ya can't wait to see ya people again.'

His people: ugly Auntie Rose, the metho-drinking Uncle, his dead forgotten father, his wild brother and cousin. Even this silent man. They are all his people.

He can never escape.

The car creeps in beside the red brick hotel.

The two Nyoongahs scurry through the rain and shadows and into the glare of the small hotel bar.

The barman is a long time coming, although the bar is almost empty. Just a few old cockies and young larri-kins, right down the other end. Arrogant grey eyes stare at Billy. No feeling there at all.

'A carton of stubbies, please.'

'Only if you bastards drink it down at the camp. Con-stable told me you mob are drinking in town and just causing trouble.'

'We'll drink where we bloody like, thanks, mate.'

'Will you, you cheeky bastard?' The barman looks at Billy, in surprise. 'Well then, you're not gettin' nothin' from me. You can piss off, too, before I call the cops. They'll cool you down, you smart black bastard.'

Something hits Billy deep inside with such force that it makes him want to clutch hold of the bar and spew up all his pride.

He is black and the barman is white, and nothing can ever change that.

All the time he had gulped in the wine and joy of the nightclubs and worn neat fashionable clothes and had white women admiring him, played the white man's game with more skill than most of the wadgulas and painted his country in white man colours to be gabbled over by the wadgulas: all this time he has ignored his mumbling, stumbling tribe and thought he was someone better.

Yet when it comes down to it all, he is just a black man.

Darcy sidles up to the fuming barman.

' 'Scuse me, Mr 'Owett, but William 'ere just come 'ome, see,' he whines like a beaten dog. 'We *will* be drinkin' in the camp, ya know.'

'Just come home, eh? What was he inside for?'

Billy bites his reply back so it stays in his stomach, hard and hurtful as a gallstone.

'Well all right, Darcy. I'll forget about it this time. Just keep your friend out of my hair.'

Good dog, Darcy. Have a bone, Darcy. Or will a carton of stubbies do?

Out into the rain again.

They drive away and turn down a track about a kilometre out of town.

Darcy tears off a bottle top, handing the bottle to Billy. He grins.

'Act stupid, buddy, an' ya go a lo—ong way in this town.'

Billy takes a long draught of the bitter golden liquid. It pours down his throat and into his mind like a shaft of amber sunlight after a gale. He lets his anger subside.

'What ya reckon, Darcy? I'm twenty-one today.'

Darcy thrusts out a hand, beaming.

'Tw'n'y-bloody-one, eh? 'Ow's it feel?'

'No different from yesterday.'

Billy claps the offered hand firmly.

They laugh and clink bottles together in a toast, just as they reach the camp.

Dark and wet, with a howling wind. Rain beating upon the shapeless humpies. Trees thrash around the circle of the clearing in a violent rhythm of sorrow and anger, like great monsters dancing around a carcase.

Darcy indicates a hut clinging to the edge of the clearing.

'That's where ya mum lives.'

A rickety shape of nailed-down tin and sheets of iron. Two oatbags, sewn together, form a door. Floundering in a sea of tins and rags and parts of toys or cars. Mud everywhere.

Billy pulls up as close to the door as he can get. He had forgotten what his house really looked like.

'Come on, koordah. Come an' see ya ole mum. Ya might be lucky, too, an' catch ya brother.'

Billy can't say anything. He gets slowly out of the car

while the dereliction looms up around him.

The rain pricks at him, feeling him over.

He is one of the brotherhood.

A mouth organ's reedy notes slip in and out between the rain. It is at once a profoundly sorrowful yet carefree tune that goes on and on.

Billy's fanfare home.

He follows Darcy, ducking under the bag door. He feels unsure and out of place and terribly alone.

There are six people: two old women, an ancient man, two youths and a young, shy, pregnant woman.

The youth nearest the door glances up with a blank yellowish face, suspicion embedded deep in his black eyes. His long black hair that falls over his shoulders in gentle curls is kept from his face by a red calico head-band. Red for the desert sands whence his ancestors came, red for the blood spilt by his ancestors when the white tribe came. Red, the only bright thing in these drab surroundings.

The youth gives a faint smile at Darcy and the beer.

'G'day, Darcy. Siddown 'ere. 'Oo ya mate is?'

'Oo'd ya think, Carl, ya dopy prick? 'E's ya brother come 'ome.'

Carlton stares at Billy incredulously, then his smile widens a little and he stands up, extending a slim hand.

They shake hands and stare deep into each other's faces, smiling. Brown-black and brown-yellow. They let their happiness soak silently into each other.

Then his cousin Rennie, also tall and slender like a young boomer, with bushy red-tinged hair and eager grey eyes, shakes hands. He introduces Billy to his young woman, Phyllis, and reminds him who old China Groves and Florrie Waters (his mother's parents) are.

His mother sits silently at the scarred kitchen table. Her wrinkled brown face has been battered around, and one of her eyes is sightless. The other stares at her son with a bleak pride of her own.

From that womb I came, Billy thinks, like a flower from the ground or a fledgling from the nest. From out of the reserve I flew.

Where is beauty now?

He remembers his mother as a laughing brown woman, with long black hair in plaits, singing soft songs as she cleaned the house or cooked food. Now she is old and stupid in the mourning of her man.

'So ya come back after all. Ya couldn't come back for ya Dad's funeral, but—unna? Ya too good for us mob, I s'pose,' she whispers in a thin voice like the mouth organ before he even says hello, then turns her eyes back into her pain.

'It's my birthday, Mum. I wanted to see everybody. No one told me Dad was dead.'

Carlton looks up at Billy.

'I make out ya twenty-one, Billy.'

'Yes.'

'Well, shit, we just gotta 'ave a party.' Carlton half-smiles. 'We gotta get more drink, but,' he adds.

Carlton and Rennie drive off to town in Billy's car. When they leave, Billy feels unsure and alone. His mother just stares at him. Phyllis keeps her eyes glued on the mound of her womb and the grandparents crow to Darcy, camp talk he cannot understand.

The cousins burst through the door with a carton that Carlton drops on the table, then he turns to his brother. His smooth face holds the look of a small child who is about to show his father something he has achieved. His dark lips twitch as they try to keep from smiling.

''Appy birthday, Billy, ya ole cunt,' Carlton says, and produces a shining gold watch from the ragged pocket of his black jeans.

'It even works, Billy,' grins Rennie from beside his woman, so Darcy and China laugh.

The laughter swirls around the room like dead leaves from a tree.

They drink. They talk. Darcy goes home and the old people go to bed. His mother has not talked to Billy all night. In the morning he will buy her some pretty curtains for the windows and make a proper door and buy her the best dress in the shop.

They chew on the sweet cud of their past. The memories seep through Billy's skin so he isn't William Woodward the talented football player and artist, but Billy the wild, half-naked boy, with his shock of hair and carefree grin and a covey of girls fluttering around his honey body.

Here they are—all three together again, except now young Rennie is almost a father and Carlton has just come from three months' jail. And Billy? He is nowhere.

At last, Carlton yawns and stretches.

'I reckon I'll 'it that bed.' Punches his strong brother

gently on the shoulder. 'See ya t'morrow, Billy, ole kid.' He smiles.

Billy camps beside the dying fire. He rolls himself into a bundle of ragged blankets on the floor and stares into the fire. In his mind he can hear his father droning away, telling legends that he half-remembered, and his mother softly singing hymns. Voices and memories and woodsmoke drift around him. He sleeps.

He wakes to the sound of magpies carolling in the still trees. Rolls up off the floor and rubs the sleep from his eyes. Gets up and stacks the blankets in a corner, then creeps out to the door.

Carlton's eyes peep out from the blankets on his bed.

'Where ya goin'?' he whispers.

'Just for a walk.'

'Catch ya up, Billy,' he smiles sleepily. With his headband off, his long hair falls every way.

Billy gives a salutation and ducks outside.

A watery sun struggles up over the hills and reflects in the orange puddles that dot the camp. Broken glass winks white, like the bones of dead animals. Several children play with a drum, rolling it at each other and trying to balance on it. Several young men stand around looking at Billy's car. He nods at them and they nod back. Billy stumbles over to the ablution block: three bent and rusty showers and a toilet each for men and women. Names and slogans are scribbled on every available space. After washing away the staleness of the beer he heads for the waterhole, where memories of his father linger. He wants—a lot—to remember his father.

He squats there, watching the ripples the light rain makes on the serene green surface. The bird calls from the jumble of green-brown-black bush are sharp and clear, like the echoes of spirits calling to him.

He gets up and wanders back to the humpy. Smoke from fires wisps up into the grey sky.

Just as he slouches to the edge of the clearing, a police van noses its way through the mud and water and rubbish. A pale, hard, supercilious face peers out at him. The van stops.

'Hey, you! Come here!'

The people at the fires watch, from the corner of their eyes, as he idles over.

'That your car?'

Billy nods, staring at the heavy, blue-clothed sergeant. The driver growls, 'What's your name, and where'd you get the car?'

'I just told you it's my car. My name's William Jacob Woodward, if it's any business of yours,' Billy flares.

The sergeant's door opens with an ominous crack as he slowly gets out. He glances down at black Billy, who suddenly feels small and naked.

'You any relation to Carlton?'

'If you want to know—'

'I want to know, you black prick. I want to know everything about you.'

'Yeah, like where you were last night when the store was broken into, as soon as you come home causing trouble in the pub,' the driver snarls.

'I wasn't causing trouble, and I wasn't in any robbery.

I like the way you come straight down here when there's trouble—'

'If you weren't in the robbery, what's this watch?' the sergeant rumbles triumphantly, and he grabs hold of Billy's hand that has marked so many beautiful marks and painted so many beautiful pictures for the wadgula people. He twists it up behind Billy's back and slams him against the blank blue side of the van. The golden watch dangles between the pink fingers, mocking the stunned man.

'Listen. I was here. You can ask my grandparents or Darcy Goodrich, even,' he moans. But inside he knows it is no good.

'Don't give me that, Woodward. You bastards stick together like flies on a dunny wall,' the driver sneers.

Nothing matters any more. Not the trees, flinging their scraggly arms wide in freedom. Not the people around their warm fires. Not the drizzle that drips down the back of his shirt onto his skin. Just this thickset, glowering man and the sleek oiled machine with POLICE stencilled on the sides neatly and indestructibly.

'You mongrel black bastard, I'm going to make you—and your fucking brother—jump. You could have killed old Peters last night,' the huge man hisses dangerously. Then the driver is beside him, glaring from behind his sunglasses.

'You Woodwards are all the same, thieving boongs. If you think you're such a fighter, beating up old men, you can have a go at the sarge here when we get back to the station.'

'Let's get the other one now, Morgan. Mrs Riley said there were two of them.'

He is shoved into the back, with a few jabs to hurry him on his way. Hunches miserably in the jolting iron belly as the van revs over to the humpy. Catches a glimpse of his new Kingswood standing in the filth. Darcy, a frightened Rennie and several others lean against it, watching with lifeless eyes. Billy returns their gaze with the look of a cornered dingo who does not understand how he was trapped yet who knows he is about to die. Catches a glimpse of his brother being pulled from the humpy, sad yet sullen, eyes downcast staring into the mud of his life—mud that no one can ever escape.

He is thrown into the back of the van.

The van starts up with a satisfied roar.

Carlton gives Billy a tired look as though he isn't even there, then gives his strange, faint smile.

'Welcome 'ome, brother,' he mutters.

I realise now that she must have been in her late twenties when I loved her. I was nine.

('How old *are* you?')

('Old enough to know better.')

('Oh go on, tell me . . .')

(Through the long hot afternoons.)

All I knew then was that she was a grown-up; but I also knew that it wasn't just age that made you one. The girl on the next farm down from ours was twenty-six and had a fiancé but was just a girl. Whereas anyone could see that *she* was grown-up because she was married and had money and her own little house and did whatever she wanted. One summer I stayed in town with her to get away from all the boys at our place. I used to wish that I could be solitary and free like a married woman, like her.

It was lovely, what she used to do.

She would lie in bed dozing and listening to the radio till about ten in the morning, and then get up and eat Saos with sardines or baked beans (or sometimes both) straight out of the tin for breakfast. Then she'd go back

to bed and read women's magazines and smoke cigarettes. If she didn't feel like getting dressed, she
wouldn't. She was extremely fat and always said that
clothes made her hot. They made me hot too, and when
I stayed with her I lived in my swimming costume. At
my house I always had to be fully dressed by the time
Mum served up the porridge, and I had to stay that way
till after tea. *She* used to wear her faded pink nighties
around the house and out in the yard; if she was going
up to the corner shop to buy a loaf of bread, she'd just
slip on a brunch coat.

The bread was another thing: we always had sliced at
home 'because it goes further with all you kids', and
Mum's sandwiches were so thin that the jam crept right
through them and out into your suitcase. But the loaves
that *she* bought had a high crusty top and were divided
into two round humps. When you pulled the halves apart
you had two doughy ends, one rising into a soft mountain, the other making a cavern that just held your
clenched fist. The shop doorway was hung with one of
those curtains made of long coloured plastic streamers
to stop the flies, and she'd already be breaking open the
bread as we fought our way back out like intrepid explor-
ers. Sometimes the hard bright strips would catch around
her neck, or whip across her breasts, around her waist.
More and more would loop in then as she fought, and
she'd laugh like anything while sweat started to trickle
down her face and she'd call back at the shop people as
she cleared the way with her fat little hands.

'Don't nobody help me!'

The black strips were the snakes and all the rest were the creeping jungle. I'd be jumping from bare foot to bare foot on the hot asphalt path, keeping a lookout for enemies. Once she was safe she'd give me the cave half and keep the mountain half herself, and we'd dig tunnels as we traipsed the hundred yards or so home.

Once we got there, we'd eat more bread with jam and butter *and* cream (though my home was a dairy farm, my family only had cream for lunch on Saturdays), or with tomato and onion and sugar and vinegar, or with lashings of golden syrup. And then tinned pears and ice cream. At her place there was dessert for lunch as well as for tea.

We'd be sitting by the fan on the small back verandah, listening to the news and 'Blue Hills'. She'd be drinking Passiona from a Jetty Hotel schooner glass and I'd have Creaming Soda from the bottle.

'Must get the house straight,' she'd sigh next, but we'd stay there watching the dead grass and dust pools in the backyard, the lantana next to the dunny, the paspalum in the empty lot next door. I'd jig around a bit, wishing there wasn't a drought so I could turn on the sprinkler and run under, and she would move slowly around on her chair, rearranging the flesh inside the pink nightie, mopping at the trickle of sweat between her huge breasts, saying occasionally, 'Jeez love, it's hot,' lighting Craven As, stubbing them out in her dessert plate.

After that she'd go back to bed, taking the fan, the radio, the cigarettes, forgetting the ashtray. The house

seemed to abound in ashtrays—including the kind I
liked, with a sort of knob on a spring that you pressed
down to send all the butts into the bowl—but she mostly
used makeshift ones. Apart from plates and cups and
saucers she would use shells and matchboxes and soft
drink bottles of course, but also Nescafe tins, jam lids,
bottle tops, teaspoons, cotton reels (she pushed the butts
down into the hole), vases, lipstick cases, little round
pots that still held lingers of cold cream or rouge.
Though I objected to the smell when my mother had
one of her social-occasional cigarettes, these doodahs of
hers never even made me screw my nose up. Her mess-
iness was simply proof of her freedom.

Yet another sign of her supreme independence was the
bulging red purse which she carried in her fat three-
ringed left hand whenever we went up the street. In her
right she carried the cigarettes in a cracked gold kid case,
and this was deputed to me whenever the right hand was
needed to hold the bread, or a double vanilla cone. (I
don't remember her ever buying anything apart from
bread or cigarettes or ice cream or lollies; nor do I
remember ever wondering where the pears and Spam
and Pecks Paste came from, or the Sweet Mustard Sauce
or Iced Vovos or pineapple rings, or the tins of beetroot
that she would devour, juice and all.) When the girl who
lived on the next farm down from ours took me into
town for shopping, she'd have her mother's red purse,
and she couldn't buy me green frogs and pink-and-white
false teeth because it was 'Mum's money'. Moreover, she
had to go to work every day (she was the secretary at

the Co-op) and never stayed in bed. Even on Saturdays she had to wash her hair and iron her work clothes and didn't have time to talk. And she had to get all dressed up to see her fiancé.

Purse and house, then, were the symbols; but it was clearly marriage that was the source of the freedom. If you were married, even your mother couldn't tell you what to do.

But this wasn't all.

There was yet another version of her that I found as mythic as the one I knew. This was chronicled in a thick flossy-white album that I used to drag out and pore over every afternoon.

While I guess I had the standard small-girl addiction to Brides, my fascination with *her* as a Bride was of a totally different order. I'd stare for hours at that slender, fair, pink-cheeked, curly-haired, excessively pretty girl in the hundred or so manifestations that appeared in the album. Stepping Out The Door From Home. Getting Into The Hire Car. Getting Out Of The Hire Car. Going Into The Church. Signing The Regist-airy. Coming Out Of The Church. Lining Up At The Door Of The Reception. With Mum And Dad And Doug's Mum And Dad. With My Bridesmaids—the pink one ('Janelle, that I went to school with, who's married herself now, with two dear little girls'); the blue one

('Doug's sister Claudie, ditto, but twin boys'); the mauve one ('Glynis, my cousin, same goes for her, except she's got one of each'); and finally, 'Kaylene, my other cousin', the yellow nylon flower girl of whom I was so terribly jealous.

'Why don't you get married again so *I* can be your flower girl?'

'Well . . . Doug mightn't be too happy about *that*!'

And we'd both laugh our heads off!

There was also Cutting The Cake. Throwing The Bouquet. The Bridal Waltz. She wasn't really taller than Doug, but looked it in that one.

'How come?' I always asked her.

'I suppose it was the shoes . . . '

'But then . . . ' (Searching for a comparison. Doug didn't actually feature much in the album, which was only right, for he didn't feature much in my vision of her life.) '. . . Then how come you don't look taller in this other one?'

'I dunno, love. Maybe I'd took my shoes off by that time of the night.'

'Can't you remember?' It seemed to me quite incredible that someone could forget the slightest detail of her own wedding.

'It was a long time ago, love.'

'How long?'

'Long enough.' And she would rearrange herself on the bed, or plump up the pillows. The radio would be playing softly and I'd be up the foot-end, facing her, the album on my crossed knees as I barraged her with questions and comments. The fact that I didn't know any of these people—for not only were we not related, but her family came from fifty miles or so inland—added to the curious interest of the album.

'Who's the skinny man in the suit, next to the lady in the yukky purple?'

And without even checking the illustration, she could tell me.

'Doug's funny-looking, isn't he?' I'd say. 'He's treading on your dress!'

And so we went on, afternoon upon afternoon, through the holidays of a whole summer. We'd also have maybe a little sleep, and she'd smoke and read *True Confessions*, and then Doug would finally slide in and say 'How're my girls?' and she'd get up and put Spam and bread and sauce and stuff on the verandah table and we'd listen to the news and then the repeat of 'Blue Hills'.

When it was dark at last she'd tell him that his girls were very hot and he'd drive us to the beach and we'd dance holding hands in the black night sea, while Doug tactfully went off and had beers with his boring mates at the boring pub. She was too fat for a costume so she tucked her skirt (she wore an old dress for these excursions) into her pants. Her thighs were white and shiny and mine were skinny and brown. Some nights she'd duck right under, clothes and all. Her skirt would fill with air, and balloon right up in front of her.

Then it was the day a letter arrived. Postie delivered it at lunchtime but she just scrutinised the handwriting, and dropped it amongst the litter of out-of-date magazines and half-filled-in crosswords on the table.

'Aren't you going to open it?'

'It's only from Auntie Beryl.'

'Who's she?'

'You know the lady in purple . . . ?'

'Next to the little skinny man in the suit?'

'Yeah, well that's Auntie Beryl.'

I knew now where she fitted in the arcana. 'That's Kaylene's mum,' I volunteered. 'Auntie Beryl's married to Uncle Eric, and they live out of Dorrigo and run pigs. Or try to. And their little girl is called Kaylene.' Of course, Kaylene was the one I was so jealous of.

She laughed. 'Hardly a little girl any more. She was married herself, last Easter.'

'Kaylene! But she's only my age!'

'She *was*, when the photos were taken . . . '

I screwed up my eyes and tried to superimpose the face of Kaylene on to the Bride figure of *her*. But it just looked like a nine year old playing dress-ups. Even more impossible to plant my own skinny mug with its pudding-basin haircut and uneven front teeth on to that symphony of white, that drifting tulle, that sweetheart neckline . . .

So I watched instead as she ate beetroot from the tin with her fingers, slice by slice, and then upended the tin itself into her mouth so that the sweet/sour purple juice poured down her throat. Then she lit a Craven A, and ashed into the beetroot tin.

The letter was still on the verandah table that night as she and Doug and I sat drinking tea and waiting for it to be dark enough to go to the beach.

'Aren't you going to open it?' asked Doug, as I had.

'It's only from Auntie Beryl,' she repeated, but this time lazily picked it up, pried open the envelope, started to read the highlights out loud. 'It's hot as Hades there too, she says . . . if only the drought would break, she reckons . . . The bloke who's got the dairy next door has gone bust and sold up, so Eric's finding it hard to get skim milk for the pigs . . . Even their house cow has gone dry . . . But now for the good news, says Auntie Beryl. Kaylene and new hubby are very happy and guess what? Kaylene is . . . '

A moan seemed to pierce the still night air, and she was off, down the verandah steps and into the backyard, where her nightie flapped like a vast pinky-white moth through the dusk. The letter fluttered to the verandah floor.

Of course at first I thought she'd been caught short, had had to make a sudden dash for the dunny, but she didn't head straight down the path to the outhouse but zotted back and forth across the yard, moaning softly, 'Oh . . . oh . . . oh . . . ' As she passed close to the verandah I saw that her hands were beating at her breasts.

Doug picked up the letter, but didn't bother to read it. He laid it gently on the table and went into the kitchen to get a beer.

'Is Kaylene dead?' I wondered. Though how could that be: Auntie Beryl had said it was good news. I sneaked a peek at the letter, managed to spell out the meaning from Auntie Beryl's irregular handwriting. *Kaylene is already expecting.*

Expecting. I knew that was the polite grown-up way of saying pregnant. That was real bad, to be pregnant if you weren't married. My mother was always warning me. It was called Getting Into Trouble. But now the mystery deepened. Kaylene *was* married. She was married last Easter. So why all the fuss and bother? Especially when Auntie Beryl and Uncle Eric were tickled pink about it (I read on further), and Kaylene's hubby Wayne was over the moon . . .

'Leave her,' Doug said to me, coming back with his beer, 'she'll get over it in a while.' But he'd no sooner had a sip than he got up again and went down the steps to the yard and then her white fluttering eventually stopped as he led her down through the darkness and they disappeared behind the dead passionfruit vine that clung to the old trellis in front of the incinerator. There was murmuring for a long time, then silence, a long sniff, and after more silence he led her back by the hand, and settled her in her chair and made a new pot of tea.

Pouring, he suggested a couple of rounds of euchre to cheer us all up.

She smiled bravely. 'You two go on. I'll just watch tonight.'

As there were only the two of us, I persuaded Doug to play cheat instead. He let me shuffle and be dealer, and I cheated my head off, but somehow game after game he still ended up the winner. Then I caught him cheating in reverse—pretending that he *didn't* have cards, in order to let *me* win. That infuriated me even more. I wasn't a baby!

Looking back, I think I must have forgotten that I wasn't in my own family, wasn't with my brothers, for I reached out and punched him on the shoulder muscle.

Doug laughed. 'Looking for a fight are you?' And he tipped me back on my arm, ever so lightly.

I punched hard.

Doug tipped.

I punched hard. I was out of my chair now, flailing at this man who was not even a relative, just a bloke who used to work for Dad on the farm before my eldest brother got old enough to leave school.

Punch.

Tip.

Punch.

Doug was still sitting but had turned around to face me as I danced like a boxer, beating at his chest with both fists. He was grinning wildly and looking to *her*, as if in the hope (I think now) that this game would distract her from the deep silence she had sunk into.

It seemed however to make no impression on her, and after a while he must have tired of it, for he rose and gently pushed me down onto the old cane lounge that sagged against the verandah wall, and then held my wrists together with one of his huge hands, and held my ankles (for I'd started kicking too) with the other.

'I wish you'd drop dead!' I screamed at him.

Instantly, she broke from her torpor in the way that a

mother animal will turn if you threaten her young one. *'That's a terrible thing to say!'* And moving at a speed that was absolutely uncharacteristic of her she disappeared into the kitchen, letting the screen door slam behind her. It reverberated on its spring hinge.

That she should come to his defence! And against me! This absolutely shattered the sense of female alliance that I had believed to exist between us, and I couldn't feel the same about her any more.

I cried for a long time that night, and the next morning before she got up I snuck down to the post office and rang my mother, and that afternoon I went home.

I only saw her twice after that, and the way I saw her on the first subsequent occasion would have shocked me, if I hadn't already had my myth of her independence ruined.

It would have been a year later. It was summer again, and we sat in the lounge—I'd never sat there before. There was her, my mother, me, and my three younger brothers. She wore a proper dress, and stockings, and bone-coloured shoes with small heels and backstraps. (Her feet were too fat to fit into shoes with sides, and even spilled out over the edges of these ones.) She had powder and lipstick on, and she wasn't smoking. Indeed, there wasn't even an ashtray in sight and my mother had to ask for one, very apologetic. 'Does the smoke bother you, dear? I know how I felt when I was.'

She laughed then in almost her old fashion and her fat heaved in the way I'd loved. 'Go right ahead and I'll sniff in the smell of it. I only don't because Doug thinks I shouldn't now.' She added, 'I'm fine, really I am.'

My mother smiled, but her mouth looked as if she'd stuck sticky-tape across it, and she put her cigarette back in the packet. 'Get off her lap!' she suddenly yelled at my littlest brother. 'Auntie doesn't want a great lump like you all over her.' She wasn't our aunt of course, but Mum made the little kids call her that.

'Oh, he's all right,' she said lazily. 'It's all good practice.' But she pushed him off and smoothed her dress down over her stomach.

So I knew then, and teased the boys with my secret as soon as we got home.

We moved to the city shortly afterwards—perhaps that was a farewell visit—and the next time I heard her name was when a real aunt came down to stay at our place because the uncle's bull was going in the Easter Show. On the first afternoon there was a long mumbled conversation in the kitchen between my mother and my aunt, of the kind that my father called Women's Business. I played patience on the passageway floor and listened, but I couldn't get the full gist.

'The same as the last time?' Mum said, shaking her head.

'The same as the last time,' my aunt gloomily agreed.

I yanked my second-littlest brother in from the yard

and got him to ask: 'When is that fat auntie going to have her baby?'

'Don't be a silly billy!' Mum and my real aunt put on laughs. 'She isn't having a baby. How on earth did you get that idea in your funny old noggin?' And Mum ruffled his crewcut and gave him the middle bit of the chelsea bun.

'Little pitchers,' my aunt said, and stared nastily in my direction. I wasn't offered any bun at all.

By the time of her third failure I was allowed to hang around Women's Business—presumably in the hope that hearing about tubes and ruptions would turn me off Getting Into Trouble. But though I was privileged now with listening status, I was meant to keep my mouth shut. However, Mum and my aunt were so mysterious on this particular occasion that I just had to say, 'What happened to the baby?'

Mum looked solemn. 'I'm afraid she lost it.'

Lost. For a wild moment I felt a giggle start to rise as my mind made pictures of her losing her baby in the way that I lost my hairbrush, my homework diary, my school hat, every morning of the week. Or perhaps as I lost Scrap the cat sometimes, and would call her around the street at night. 'Scrap, here Scrap ... here puss puss puss ... ' At the same time of course I was old enough to know that 'lost' was polite grown-up talk for 'dead', like 'expecting' for 'pregnant'.

But even then I couldn't get a handle on it. 'How come?'

'It was stillborn,' Mum said. 'Just like the last two.'

Still. Born.

Born. Still.

'You mean it came out dead?'

'That's one way of putting it.' Mum pulled a terrible face.

My aunt said, 'Don't they give you homework, in the city?'

I heard nothing about her for a long time after that. Our aunt didn't come down any more because her husband started having trouble with the farm.

('Bloody dairy farmers!' my father would complain. 'When will they learn that it's just not *viable*?' When he'd realised it wasn't viable he'd come to the city to start an equally unviable milk run. 'The money's at the other end,' he used to say when he was struggling with the farm. Now he said, 'There's no money for the small bloke, no matter where he is.')

And so I didn't hear of her, and I almost forgot her, and then we 'dropped in' to the town 'on our way back' from a fortnight's beach holiday when I was fourteen. It wasn't really dropping in, because we stayed three days. And it wasn't really on our way back, because the town was eighty miles north of where we'd holidayed. But that was what they called it, that torture that made me leave the camping ground three days early, when I had just met a boy who had promised to teach me to swim under water. He had a snorkel, and fins, and everything.

It was on the last day that we went to see them, Doug and her. They'd moved too. Doug was now renting a banana plantation up along the coast a bit. He'd had it a couple of years, and it wasn't doing too well. ('Doug's mad,' Dad said. 'He can't beat the bloody combines! There's no hope for the small bloke these days. It's not viable.')

We got there around eleven. 'We'll just drop in for a quick cuppa on our way through,' Mum had said to Doug when she'd rung that morning. The 'quick cuppa' was another of the fictions of that three-day return. I'd sit picking my sunburn through endless hours of talking and tea-drinking, as every single birth, death and marriage that had occurred in the district was annotated. No one of course ever asked if *we* had any news: country people think city slickers don't ever do anything.

'We won't stay for lunch,' Mum had insisted, 'it's too hot for her to fuss. Tell her just a cuppa and a bit of a natter will do us fine.'

We had the cuppa but not the natter, at least not with her, at the two-roomed fibro house at the top of the hill. We sat on the verandah. From there the view swept down through the banana stools that grew in their straight green lines like tropical schoolgirls, their bunches neatly wrapped in bags of blue plastic as if they were breasts or something, something shameful.

'Just can't seem to keep the weeds down,' Doug apologised, seeing Dad eyeing the mess of green that broke through the black-red earth between the rows. 'She should be here soon,' he added, even more apologetically.

The tea was strong even for country tea and my little

brothers starting whingeing for lemonade until Dad yelled at them.

'There's not even cordial, I'm afraid,' Doug said. 'We don't get kids here often.'

'What the children would really like,' Mum gushed, 'is just fresh country rainwater from the tank! That's the thing I miss most, in the city.' But she had tea herself, and when Doug brought the water out in a cracked plastic jug it was lukewarm and had floating specks of algae in it.

'I've changed my mind and I'll have tea,' I said, swishing my water out over the verandah rail and getting a look from Mum.

Doug poured slowly, to make the time last.

'She's usually back by this time,' he said again.

'She goes for walks,' he told us for the third time. 'There's nothing much else for her to do here, I guess.'

In the country when you go for morning tea there are always plates of sandwiches and scones, rock cakes and Anzacs, a boiled fruit cake and a three-layered sponge, and—if you're lucky—lamingtons as well. Here there were plain Saos and stale Arrowroots straight out of the packet, but Mum ate a lot even though at everyone else's place she'd reckoned she was on a diet. The second cup of tea was even stronger than the first, and there was no milk left. It'd been condensed, from a tin.

'That's right, mate,' Dad joked to Doug. 'Don't let the milko fleece the shirt off your back.' And then he stopped laughing quickly when Mum glanced at him, because it certainly looked as if *something* was fleecing the shirt off Doug.

'I told her you were coming,' Doug replied, 'but she doesn't wear a watch of course.'

'Of course not!' Dad agreed, as if wearing a watch was like voting Labor or something.

'She usually just goes for a bit of a stroll ... to get some air ... it gets hot as blazes ... '

'There's a nice breeze up here, anyway,' Mum said, fanning herself with her hand.

'And she just goes down to the south edge of the place,' Doug went on, as if he hadn't heard Mum, 'where it runs into that no-man's-land bit that the Council keeps on reckoning it's going to clear out, and doesn't.'

'Councils!' Dad said.

'Have another biscuit,' Doug said.

'They're lovely and fresh,' Mum said. But she didn't take another.

At last there wasn't any more tea. Doug said he could make up a fresh pot, no sweat, but Mum looked at her watch and said, 'We must really.'

'Must get on the road,' Dad agreed.

'One for the road, then,' Doug joked.

'Twist my arm,' Dad joked back, but we all stood up.

'She'll be real sorry to have missed you,' Doug apologised as we went through the manoeuvre of getting into the car in accordance with our complicated roster of window-sharing. This time it was my turn to squash into the back section of the station wagon, along with the camping gear that didn't fit into the trailer.

'She needs to see people more, that's her trouble,' Doug went on. 'I sometimes think she misses the Bright Lights of town, stuck up here in the sticks.'

(Bright lights of that town! What a joke, I silently mocked.)

'Never mind,' Mum said out the window. 'There's always next time.'

'Sure to be passing through again some time soon,' Dad agreed. He was already starting the engine.

'Bring her down to the Big Smoke for a holiday,' Mum said. We had to call the city that when we talked to country people. It made them think we didn't like it. 'We can always make up the Nite'n'day in the lounge.'

'Or you can have Little Miss Smarty-pants's room, and she can bunk in with the kids.'

'I might just do that,' Doug called after us as we started down the track. 'I might just do that!'

He never did of course, and it was on that day that I saw her for the last time. The others didn't, not even Mum or Dad: it was only because I was sitting where I was, looking out the back of the station wagon . . .

We were nearly down to the road, and the track had veered right over to the south. In that place the banana stools had gone wild, sprouting in great clumps with creepers tangling through and around them. The broad leaves were yellow-brown at the edges and the few bunches that had managed to grow were small, the fruit tiny, wizened, and going black on the stalk. I could hardly make her out at first for she was like a large, translucent, pink jellyfish breaststroking slowly just beneath the surface of a thick green pool of algae. Vines hung around her, great cords with darkened leaves, and as she sank and surfaced back and forth behind this curtain of black-green, her body soft and floating as if it was weightless, I remembered how she'd looked when she had struggled through the bright plastic fly-screen with the loaf of warm bread that she immediately broke in two, and then I thought of Trevor MacKenzie, his arrow-body shooting through the clear waters of the lagoon, and I found myself collapsing into one of those unaccountable fits of the giggles that you get when you're a girl of fourteen.

These were the great days for poets. The heroic days. The days of myth. When the clock was always at quarter to three in the morning. They rolled on the pavements like alchemical twins, breaking each others' heads into the awaiting concrete. They howled their way through plate glass doors and windows. Their blood congealed. Their cars caught fire. When their clothes were taken they wore their neckties. Naked meant honest, as in lunch, dead, cop. For emperor's new clothes they wore sombreros and smoking jackets. They brandished machine guns and straddled mustangs. They shot themselves and others, possessed explosives, attempted assassination, did smash and grabs, died from dirty needles. Waste not, want not, drug poems, prison poems, to say nothing of the madhouse. Nothing will be said of the madhouse.

He was a policeman with the soul of a poet. Or a poet with the soul of a policeman. And who is to say which had priority? A literary agent who could book you. Some people grew moustaches, long hair, shark's tooth medallions, sunglasses, key rings at the hip, the janitorial touch, the payroll guards. 'This is your cover,' they said, giving him a jacket with his picture on the back. 'Start a magazine,' they said, 'get funding from the bored. Make it glossy, sticky, tacky, everyone will want to get into your pages, we'll supply the boys and girls.' They always supplied the boys and girls. 'Then you print the poems and the boys or girls say how they dig the poems and then they get to screw the poets. That's the only way we can be sure to get the poets screwed. Mediated through art.'

He would have preferred it if they'd paid for sex but this was bohemia and he was told that love like verse had to be free. 'But you can deal a little dope,' they said, 'they'll pay for that, get them hooked, that would be a service. Like the massage parlour girls, get them hooked, make them pay back their earnings for dope. You supply the dope so they can write the sort of stoned shit you publish in the magazine,' they said. 'And you get to introduce the chicks,' they said, 'you'll be the M.C. as it were. Macho Chap. You heard of the big banana and the big potato and the big pineapple, well you're the big stud and you don't even have to wear a collar.'

There were poets declaiming Rimbaud in the café noirs, revolution was plotted in their cups and recorded in the potted palms. Coups were conceived over the cheesecake and captured in the kitchen. There were poets' balls, barbecues of skewered kidneys, acid in the punch, sexual harassment institutionalised and licensed. There were anthologies of desire and manifestos of will. Proclamations of ego and performances of id. Speaking in tongues, computerised address lists, minimum fees, cash enslavement, questionnaires on the lone and level sands. State your poetics, state your politics. The poetry of pure sound.

The logic required whole huts of poets writing out material for him. For when he became famous. Success might catch him up. A book. Another book, they demand another book, follow it up. He put his mind to the organisational problems. Translations from the Italian. Get the semioticians to programme the poetry machine. Telepathic theft. All he had to do was get some telepathine and that wasn't difficult.

'Nothing's too difficult for us,' they told him. They had their men out there, combing the hairs of the jungle for telepathine. 'Invite the writers round,' they said, 'feed them chemicals allowing easy transfer of information and plunder their word hoard.' The first experiment made him sick. The psyches.

'So how do I write it?' he said. 'There has to be a better way.'

'We'll send you the lines,' they said, 'install a telex, we've got a line service, we send lines all round the world, we'll fax you.'

'But then they'll know they're not mine.'

'No they won't, they never read, poets never read other people's poetry and the public doesn't read it at all. Anyway, we only send any given set of lines to one person per major language group, more or less.'

'What if they get translated?' he said.

'They'll sound different. That's the point about poetry, it's not what you say but the way you say it, as they say.'

'But what about what you say, though?'

'Well, you don't say very much, it's all a matter of style. The less you say the better, really.'

'Ah,' he said.

'That's right,' they said, 'a sound poem.'

He tried it again, 'ah.'

'Well done,' they said. 'Least said, soonest mended. Never overdo the content, that's how you tell a subversive, by the content.'

'What sort of content?' he said.

'Any sort of content,' they said. 'Just content's subversive in itself.'

'Protection,' he said.

'Protection,' they said.

'So if I deal the dope?'

'Protection,' they said. 'As long as we supply it.'

'Of course,' he said. 'I wouldn't dream of dealing with anyone else.'

'Don't do it either,' they said.

'What about poems?'

'What about poems?'

'Protection for bad poems.'

'That's your lookout,' they said. 'We'll fix the reviews but in the day to day fisticuffs of the poets' café, you're on your own. But if they kill you for your bad verses, we'll revenge you,' they said. 'Never fear, if they get you, we'll get them, don't worry about it.'

'Thanks,' he said.

'You're welcome,' they said. 'Don't mention it. We'd be glad of a chance to off a few poets if you disappear.

Writing about civil rights and human rights and land rights and race riots and wars and rumours of war and conspiracies. Some of them need to be done over every once in a while, hey man, have some of this superdope, what a blast, sprayed with skunk oil, guaranteed to drive everyone away from you for six months; no man, we can't have that old skunk-oil smoker on the programme, he's just too much.'

But this was all low level stuff. His poet's soul wanted more job satisfaction. He studied the aesthetics of it. Get the right recipe and funding will flow. He rebelled against traditional forms. He developed an insignia of the modern. It seemed radical but looked at in the right light it was all right. 'Just challenge the old, the established, the traditional literary order. We've got our chaps there, we need you with the enemy. What the old money won't publish through their traditional firms and established quarterlies is yours.' And when he was on his own, or better still when he had people round, so they could see him actually doing it, he would chisel out a poem or two. Or the odd line thereof. Written on the plaster of a broken arm or a broken wall. Or the frame of a painting, the ripped out title page of a book, a piece of bone or vellum. 'Would you like us to print up some menus?' they said, 'so you can create on them,' these men in button-down shirts, watching their work being done.

So there was always dope around at his place, always chicks, sometimes they'd have a barbecue and roast a dead sheep or a side of an ox. Connections with the meat trade. But the troubadours always embellished the story.

'We drove out to the plains and caught one and hit it over the head till it died and put it in the boot of the car.' Just like getting chicks. Machismo like they promised, poet's licence to kill, rape and shoplift with impunity.

It wasn't too bad being a poet. A different beat but the same old drummer. It didn't take too much time. Not many words. And no one cared anyway. No one needed to understand it. So it wasn't too bad. When you got into it you realised the possibilities of faction. Sexual play. With this poet's lady, and let him know. But a slip of the tongue. The oral tradition. Who's been sleeping in whose bed. 'I thought you guys had a liberated scene.' Get them stoned, get them pissed, bring them home and listen to the bastards. 'Here, smoke some of this supergrass and give us the full story.' A change from watching tv. Here you could write your own plots. Anyway, you could always watch tv at the same time, secure in the knowledge that everything was being taped anyway, he didn't even have to stay awake.

gerard windsor   Botany Cemetery

Incongruities are rife. There is precious little rest for the spirit here.

(i)

Beside the encrusted Italianate wall stands a white Gemini. The front passenger door is open. In the seat reclines a woman in her late thirties. She reads, or at least she has on her lap, a copy of *New Idea*. But she glances up, still with an expression of radical boredom, at any external movement—another vehicle, an adjusted hose, a bird. She sees, she does not register, she is unmoved. Between her open door and an elaborate vault is a man, a little older than herself. He kneels on one knee, and on the other thigh he rests his elbow and leans his forehead into the palm of his hand. In his free right hand he holds a rosary, and with it he makes the sign of the cross, and seems to strap himself. His head slides up and down the slipway of his hand, and he wails at the grim medallion of an old tight-bunned woman on the vault. Inside the car his wife uses *New Idea* as a fan.

(ii)

Only here, in all this city, are there no machines used. The metal bites and slices and opens up the cavity according to the pressure of palm and wrist and shoulder, and heel. The diggers stand in the messy beginnings of the wound, lay down the tough angular clamp, and brace it back against the earth. Then they go on down, in.

The paling ribs are inserted and tapped in, and the exoskeleton takes shape. Its internal organs pulse away rhythmically. They scour and dislodge and remove. They tone up here, strengthen there, they redistribute pressure, they break up the solids, they eject what is extraneous. They murmur as they work. Just once or twice they falter or stutter in their rhythm. The longer they work, the more detritus they accumulate and the more subdued and unreliable becomes the beat of their activity. It is a fast-growing but short life this creature has. It is rare, seldom noticed, perfect in its purpose, and does not draw out its end. Now its organs desist. Just the shell remains. The empty thing is ready.

The blunt-headed, tapering outline is pleasing. Most like a crocodile in its shape, it promises bland unamiability, surprising speed in attack, strong jaws, and the capacity for rapid disposal. Or, like a child's toy, its aperture beckons for the mirror image shape to pass through. The intelligent child works it from both sides. The shape that was made for it rises up and comes out again as easily as it went it.

This is an insertion exercise. The earth is being prepared for the intrusion of a foreign body. It is staked down and forcibly opened. It is not patently diseased, but then it is not yet really anything. It needs the admixture of another, more complex, element. So an injection is prepared. The new unpredictable compound of chemical and memorialised human quirks is implanted. No one can quantify the effects. But the implant represents a gamble: lodged and sewn in there in the hope that there might be produced a new earth. It is a gamble worth running with. That perhaps eventually the ground might quake, the hills might leap like young lambs, the mountains like calves, the cages of the earth burst open, and, of all things, the dead be everywhere and making their appearances to many.

(iii)

He is visited, but he is never allowed complete attention. Sick and dying he was the only figure of interest. But the circumstances of death give a later, and final, twist to the perspective. He is on the western end of his short row. At the eastern end is the daughter of an old friend of his wife's. She has reached here four months before him. She is just thirty-four. She has been murdered. No bond of fellowship between the surgeon and the young woman forces itself on the visitor. This woman is sacred ground. You tread lightly and warily and you do no flippant violence to her. She has earned inviolability. My mother tends the one grave, with its commonplace, almost painless inscription. But her sharing in her own communion of saints takes her every time to say hello, as she calls it, to Carolyn.

My mother does her stations at the graves. It is restrained religion. She is straightforward and severely practical. She snips the grass, she brushes weed and dreck and the build-up of sand. Then she stands back and leaves a decade of the rosary or perhaps three Hail Marys. Never a gratuitous number. Never some unrehearsed aspirations. She has to leave a message that is recognisable. She communicates through the formulas and formalities. Her husband will register that it is her this way. And it is the only approach to a young woman whom she may have met as a child, and to whom no personal words of consolation are possible. So she passes from west to east, from the bent, haggard, consumed shell to the suddenly shattered vessel of energy. Along my mother's beat a thin but sturdy mat of couch grass is growing over the sandy grey soil. It is all her husband wants; any efflorescence would be otiose. There is achievement here already; no one disputes that. These are near enough to old bones, and nothing more is expected of them. They moulder quietly, and the old waves of virtue go out of them. The spirit is stable and satisfied, and no breakouts are looked for or even needed. But to the east, on the grave of the murdered woman, there is the oddest emblem of defiance against arrested life. This grave, this grave alone, is carpeted with horse manure.

gerard windsor

(iv)

The lawn is on a slope of perhaps one in five. Across the
bottom runs a narrow gully. On the other side is a similar
slope, and the two slopes arch around amphitheatrically
to the west, and are hitched together there by the belt
of the vaults of the Italians. On the farther slope are the
white statuary and angular proclamations of the Greeks.
They shimmer towards the north-east. You shade your
eyes against them to the south-east, and the gully runs
away from you towards, of all things, a market garden.
There, along the raised beds edging forward through the
lush greenery of shallots, spring onions, chinese cabbages, leeks, beetroot—all the plenty of the force-fed
bulbs—are the coolie hats. Here, where there should
only be sand and desolation, they move imperceptibly
inland along the lines of their fruitfulness. Then they
turn and ease themselves back again while the smudged
water in the Landing Place at Phillip Bay laps at their
heels and toes. You can see the waves bringing and the
waves taking, in and out along the gully into this place.
This is the Vale of Jehosaphat. Where the nations are
gathered.

The horizon refuses to stabilise. When you lie on the
slope of this shallow bowl, the horizon will not withdraw
its distance. The rim becomes the horizon. The world
loses its infinite seductive possibilities. It is of merely a
child's circumference. All its elements are visible and
operable at once.

The horizon is out of keeping. By the standards of eternal rest. It is jagged metal. The great energy of Bunnerong power station has left this vast one-off fossil. The black, rust-smudged, silver-streaked steel looms over the vaults and the Greeks and the sandy lawn. Chimneys, pipes, conduits, pressure caps, springs, runnels, guylines, stacks—a general exaltation of metal in which all configurations and sizes are rising. But it is silent, it is dead. Besides, the flourishes of cast steel give only a tiny minority their cultural uplift. How many enlightened patrons of a late-twentieth-century aesthetic do you see lazing here? This place is not fashionable. Those that come to lie here have never been enlightened. Those more likely to claim appreciativeness succumb in the end to roses and ash and a plot of earth made sweet by their own romantic dispensation. But this horizon here is striated metal.

I say, it has its appositeness. He is used to the final mercy emerging from the abrupt edges of sharp metal. He is adamant that hope lies only in a detached, cold, steely concentration. He has an ineradicable yearning for the comfort of tears, the rising note, and the velleities and prayers of soft flesh. But it has never been enough, and however fiercely he regrets it, he knows that warm roseate goodwill can never have the effect of the remote gloved hand leaning over the metal.

He sinks back and rests in the carefully disposed suitability of his situation. But between one viewing and the next, the metal is razed. The scrap merchants lumber away with the junk. Now the horizon is flat, bare, utterly without character. He takes it in. So this is not final.

Although he had never been in an aeroplane before, Thomas Awkner was not a complete stranger to flight. His earliest memory was of the day the swing on the back verandah propelled him across the yard and into the fence. The ground rushed beneath him. Borer holes in the wooden paling became mineshafts. Impact was devastating. A loose picket pinched his earlobe and held him captive and screaming until his father could be hounded away from his incinerator behind the shed. Now, as the big jet staggered through the turbulence out over the desert, he twisted that earlobe between his fingers and sweated. He did not like to fly. His own height gave him vertigo.

Flight attendants lurched up the aisles. Drinks spilled. The FASTEN SEATBELTS sign chimed on and off. The thirty seats ahead of him were occupied by what seemed to be a delegation from the Deaf Society. These men and women wore blazers and little berets, and for most of the flight they had been engaged in an informal celebration, creating a disconcertingly visual babble. Words ruffled up by the handful and faces stretched with laughter, impatience, urgency. All Thomas Awkner could hear was the chink of glasses, but for the Deaf Society, he decided, it must have been a rowdy affair. Watching them gave him a thirst. He pushed the button for a flight attendant.

While he waited, he swabbed the sweat from his palms and smiled at the men on either side of him. It was a desperate grin, starched with fear, but it went unnoticed. From up ahead came a sharp, solitary belch. None of the partyers in the aisle seemed embarrassed for a moment.

A flight attendant came, but fear had knotted Awkner's throat so that he found it difficult to speak. The woman raised her sculptured eyebrows at him. Awkner's lips moved, but his voice seemed to be parked somewhere back down in his throat.

'Are you well?' the fat man next to him asked.

'The poor man is deaf, sir,' the flight attendant said. She began to mime eating and drinking. Thomas Awkner flinched.

The fat man scowled. 'I don't think he is. He's not wearing a blazer, or even a beret.'

'For God's sake, man,' the triangular man on Awkner's right protested, 'a man doesn't need a blazer and a beret to be deaf and dumb. He's probably freelance.'

'Rubbish,' the fat man said, 'he's listening to us now.'

'They lip-read, sir,' said the flight atttendant.

'Could I have a beer, please?' Thomas Awkner managed to say at last.

'See? He talks.'

'So what?'

'Sir, honestly, it doesn't mean a thing!'

'Emu Bitter, if I could.'

The flight attendant beamed at him and went to get the drink. Neither man spoke to him. He felt as though he had upset them terribly. He wedged himself between their anger and their outsized bodies, and thought about his two hours in Melbourne. Right across the continent, he mused, long enough to deliver a manila envelope and board another plane home.

Since he was five years old, Thomas Awkner had been running family errands, taking small boxes to strange doors, relaying single words through holes in fibro walls, passing notes to men in grey hats in windy harbourside streets. The Awkners took for granted his apparent idiocy and he did nothing, as he grew older, to unsettle their assumption for fear of losing his only measure of importance in the Awkner web. An idiot, they thought, was the best courier possible. Understanding could be a risk. So the young Thomas Awkner cultivated complete incuriosity; he ignored message or parcel and concentrated on the trip, feasting on the world outside the asbestos house with its smoke and secret talk. But the trip always ended with a return home where nothing more was expected of him. At home, therefore, he did nothing.

He was flying. His father had never flown: that fact made him feel sophisticated. His father was a memory associated with the endlessly smouldering incinerator behind the back shed. Boxes of shredded paper were often brought through the house at every hour of the night. He recalled that long, grey face with its seedy moustache and perennial white stubble. His father died ten years before. An aerosol can had exploded as he peered into the incinerator. Uncle Dubbo appeared out of nowhere to attend the cremation service.

His beer arrived. He drank it quickly and immediately his bladder demanded relief. Lurching down the aisle towards the rear of the plane, he felt as though he was swinging across a ravine on a rope bridge. The turbulence was frightening. He fought against it in the chrome cubicle but he emerged with one hot, wet trouser leg, regardless. Grabbing at coatsleeves and the occasional head of hair for support, he found his way back to his seat and wedged himself between his large fellow-travellers. The two men wrinkled their noses and glanced knowingly at one another, and Thomas Awkner was spared no shame.

All across the continent he sweated. It took time for him to realise that it wasn't only flying that had put fear into him: it was his own curiosity that frightened him. Never before had Thomas Awkner, the courier, experienced the slightest interest in the messages, the mysteries, he bore. What was in the envelope? What did it mean? Why fly across Australia to deliver it in a public place? He longed to take it out of his pocket, hold it to a window, sniff it, rattle it, but these things would draw attention. Whose attention? His newfound curiosity brought fresh fears. Could this mission be *dangerous*? He sweated.

All he had to do was deliver something and come back as always, as though a rubber cord anchored him firmly to that asbestos house in the coastal suburbs. But suddenly it seemed difficult. His filtering process was breaking down. When he went back would he still be able to absent himself from the workings of the family? He had learnt that skill early on, from the year Aunt Dilly and Aunt Celia had dossed in his room with him. Their snoring, their belches and mutterings, their stockings hanging like jungle snakes and their stares across the curtain as he dressed—these things he taught himself to ignore, and fairly soon all the machinations of the Awkner family happened on the grey, outer limits of his awareness. He did not question the prolonged absences of his brothers and his Uncle Dubbo. He never wondered about the huge unmarked containers their milk arrived in, or the boxes of unstamped eggs, the sudden appearance of a television set. Conspiratorial laughter broke through the asbestos walls like cricket balls, and all those years Thomas Awkner studied the discipline of inertia: he watched little, listened little, said little, did little. His schooling was not superb. He had no friends. And when, quite suddenly, the Awkners left town for Melbourne, he found himself alone with his mother.

2

The airport terminal was confusing: so many escalators and shops and purposeful people, and it was difficult to make headway, always casting looks over one's shoulder. He walked into the women's toilets, had to pay for a box of doughnuts he knocked to the floor, and was dragged from a Singapore Airlines queue and interrogated by customs officers. All he wanted was a taxi, and when he did find the taxi rank, the city of Melbourne seemed short of taxis.

After a wait in the sun, a cab eased up to the kerb beside him. He got in.

Pulling away from the rank, the driver asked him where he wanted to go.

'The gallery,' Thomas Awkner said.

'What gallery?'

'The art gallery.'

'Which one?' asked the driver, getting a good look at him in the mirror. Thomas Awkner was not a settling sight. His fine blond hair stood up like wheat to the sun; he had not shaved; the flight had left his clothes rumpled. He stank of urine. 'Which art gallery, mate?'

'The proper one.' He was confused; he hadn't expected this.

The driver shrugged and took a punt and a left turn. 'How long you in town for?'

'Two hours.'

The driver settled lower in his seat. After all, what kind of man stays in a town for two hours? Not the kind of man you told knock-knock jokes to. He drove faster. Thomas Awkner skated about on the seat of his pants, smitten by the strangeness of the place. The buildings were half buried in trees, their lines were soft and their textures aged. It reminded him of Fremantle where he was born: houses standing shoulder to shoulder, old men walking in narrow streets. It charmed him. It flooded him with memories of walking to the wharf with his father. They lived in Fremantle to make it more convenient to visit relatives in prison. The air was full of gulls and the stench of sheep ships and harbour scum. Some days, Thomas walked with his father to the wharf where they would meet strange men and his father would whisper with them in the shadows of hawsers and derricks. The shimmer of the water's surface tantalised him. He always wanted to dive in. He begged his father to let him paddle at the little beach behind the mole, but there was never time and his father mentioned sunburn and rips and sharks.

'You'll sink like a stone,' his father said. They were the only words he remembered from his father.

The taxi stopped with such suddenness that Thomas cracked his chin on the ashtray of the seat in front. It cleared his head for a moment. He paid and got out into the disarming sunshine. He had an hour and a half left. He was to meet Uncle Dubbo here beside the dormant fountain in fifty minutes. It was hot in the sun. The sight of water running down glass attracted him to the building. He went in.

An atmosphere of sanctity was in the place. Tiny lights from heights. A brooding quiet. He decided to wait in there out of the heat until it was time to deliver. He saw his startled face in glass cabinets full of obscure artifacts; he recognised his hooked nose on a Roman bust and his doe-eyes in a Dutch oil painting. He saw pieces of himself everywhere. Normally he could not even bear to see his own reflection in a mirror.

It was thirty minutes before he saw the ceiling and when he did, the oddest sensation touched him. Stained glass—acres of it, it seemed. Fremantle. The old church. He remembered. On the way home from the wharf sometimes, he had followed his father into the old church where the sailors went, and he would be left to stand at the back near the door while his father went down towards the sanctuary to speak to men dressed in grey suits with hats in their hands. Often they would come away with little parcels which his father took out to the incinerator later in the day, but while they were speaking, Thomas was mesmerised by the scenes in stained glass at either side of the church. Every candle seemed to point towards the strange characters and their animals. On the way home, Thomas would dawdle behind his father, heavy with wonder.

In the middle of the gallery, Thomas Awkner took off his coat and lay on the carpet, looking up at the canopy of colours. Time passed beyond him as the panels of coloured light transported him back. He had forgotten wonder long ago and had replaced it with a dejected kind of bewilderment with which he armed himself to fight off the world from the slit-trench of his unmade bed. In those days of wonder, he had not been repulsed by his own image, he had not been afraid of his own height.

A man stooped and touched him on the shoulder.

'Uncle Dubbo?' If it is Uncle Dubbo, he thought, taking in the man's neatly pressed trousers and blazer and the well organised face above them, then the plastic surgeons have done a first class job.

'Sir, you can't lie here all day. There are vagrancy laws in the state of Victoria.'

'Oh.'

When he got up he saw that he'd left a wet patch of sweat on the carpet in the shape of a man, and by the time he had reached the door of the men's toilet people were noticing it. In the glittering hall of the toilet, Thomas Awkner splashed his face with water and looked at himself brazenly in the vast mirror. He was tall. His thin blond hair was matted but not entirely disgraceful. His face was lean and his features thin and (perhaps, he thought, it's the heat) even vaguely elegant. The sight drilled him with that odd sensation again.

He heard a shifting sound in the cubicle behind and was suddenly afraid. He touched the manila envelope inside his shirt. He was a courier. A curious courier. Whatever it was he was carrying, he knew, it was important enough to be wanted by someone else. Perhaps everyone else. Thomas Awkner fled the toilet and walked quickly back to the entrance of the gallery, telling himself with fervour: 'I've got a mission.'

Out under the blinding sun, gelato vans had parked beneath the roadside trees. People sat around the perimeter of the fountain pool. A hot wind stirred deciduous leaves along the pavements and traffic passed, fuming. No sign of Uncle Dubbo. Twenty minutes left, yet. He wondered what he would say to him. A year had passed since he'd seen his Uncle Dubbo, and yet, in all the years through which his uncle had come and gone, in and out of his life, he had never really looked hard at him. Uncle

Dubbo never engaged him in conversation. Maybe he'd put the old man through a few conversational hoops before delivery. How bad did he want this envelope? What would he do to get it? What *was* Uncle Dubbo really like? What did he *do* all these years? What about those grey ghosts, his own brothers? He could barely remember them. Maybe, he thought, a few questions might be the price of delivery, this time. Was it really an aerosol can that blew the old man's head off? What does it all mean? What's my life honestly been about, for God's sake?

Thomas took out his return ticket and turned it over. Stuffing it back in his pocket, he bought an ice cream and sat at the edge of the pool. Two small boys tugged their shirts off and made shallow dives into the water, stirring up a sediment of leaves and potato-chip bags as they skimmed along the bottom and came up gasping beneath the NO WADING sign. People clucked in disapproval. Thomas watched the boys, envious. He had put his jacket on again to cover the bulge of the envelope, and the heat was unpleasant. He watched as the boys duck-dived and came up with coins. A woman next to him, long breasted, long faced, crinkled her shopping bags and rattled her tongue.

'Decent people throw their money in there. To make wishes.'

He looked at her. Reflected light from the water was unkind to her face. He opened his mouth to speak, then closed it again. A moment later he came out with it anyway, grinning like a clergyman.

'Well, so will they when they grow old and stupid.'

She cut him with a stare and turned away. With their hands full of coin, the two boys ran across the pavement to the ice cream vans, footsteps evaporating behind them. When they came back with dripping cones and smeared faces, Thomas Awkner was untying his shoelaces. The woman turned to stare at him. He returned her stare and without taking his eyes from hers slipped sideways into the water. She screamed, brushing drops from her dress, while Thomas Awkner struck out across the mucky pool, ice cream cone in hand, to the cheers of the boys. Cool water rushed through his clothing and he felt like singing. His head cleared and he remembered his father's words. Resting at the end of the pool, he watched the boys finish their ice creams and churn across to where he floated in the shade of the gallery. Behind them he saw the sports jacket and feather-duster moustache of Uncle Dubbo. Thomas lay on his back. He spouted like a whale. He had not been seen. Uncle Dubbo had black eyes. His fists opened and closed as though he might lash out with them at any moment. Thomas recalled suffocating clouds of cigarette smoke, toneless instructions, a plate thrown.

He patted the soggy lump in his shirt. The boys dived around him and he felt the rumour of a laugh in him. The strange city rang in his ears: sound and sight limitless. Uncle Dubbo paced, fists in his pockets. Thomas Awkner floated.

With the clatter of young horses the members of the senior
French class came into the classroom. They were nine large
boys. Their teacher, Jenny Brundall, knew them well. She
never looked at their closed adolescent faces without being
glad she had taught them since childhood, could see in
Colin's dark face the serious intelligent child he would
carry safe into old age, could remember when the king-
fisher glance of Alan Potter's beautiful eyes flashed in a
round baby-face. Alan had changed so much that only the
glance remained in a bony, irregular, secretive face which
would have frightened her if she had been a stranger; after
all, the rosy, solemn countenance of his childhood, disarming as it was, was only another expression of his reserve, for
it had concealed mischief and intelligence. Of the nine,
only Peter Leonard was a stranger, lately arrived from a
boys' school in the city.

She handed out the corrected proses, and discussed
the commonest errors which she had already listed on
the blackboard. The class settled down to work.

In the silence Peter Leonard said, 'What's the matter
with this, miss? I've got *capote* here, and you've crossed
it out. "Without even taking off his overcoat", it says.
What's the matter with *capote*, miss?'

Oh, damn, she thought. It was obscene, that was the matter with it.

'The word for "overcoat" is *pardessus* in this case.'

'What's the matter with *capote*, miss? It says *capote* in the dictionary.'

It gave him some satisfaction to repeat the word. She looked up and saw on his face a slight gleam that told her the obscenity was not accidental, and she felt a sudden intimate shock. When the length of old piping in the grass near one's feet comes to writhing, sliding life it is the lapse of the eye's vigilance that terrifies, more than the presence of the snake. For an instant she stood petrified, her confidence shattered, receiving the impression, from the absolute stillness of the others, that they were forewarned.

'It means military greatcoat, Peter. That isn't what is meant here.' She was tempted to smile, simply because to smile would be disastrous. 'I'm sorry you had to look up such a common word,' she added, speaking smoothly but too quickly, 'and I think you should have been able to find it in your own vocabulary note-book.' To the class she added, 'This is a very good example of the danger of using the dictionary carelessly.' She assumed a bleak, set expression, trying to ward off the idiotic butterfly smile that persisted in trying to alight on her mouth. 'Supposing that one word is as good as another is like supposing that any coat will do, though you know quite well that one doesn't wear a military greatcoat to the office. Words have to be chosen according to circumstances too, so there is a limit to the use of dictionaries. If you use them wrongly you will only confuse your ignorance.' Deplorable, that; she was answering the boy's concealed insolence with concealed spite.

Alan Potter turned on Leonard a bright-eyed, uncommunicative look that indicated secret laughter, and Colin Ellis said easily, 'Would you mind explaining these six lines you've put under this trifling error of mine?' This familiarity was unusual for Colin, and she took it rightly as a gesture of friendship. 'Consider,' his tone said, 'how long we have known you.' This virtue which she had met once or twice before in Colin was the flower of intelligence; stupid people have other virtues, but not that one, thought Jenny. When she had dealt with Colin's mistake, she took up Alan Potter's book. Alan was her best pupil. He was taking Honours French, and she was overjoyed to discover that he was not going to escape enlightenment. As she wrote a correction in his book she said, 'The books have come, Alan. I got a parcels slip from the station this morning.'

All at once she was back with Ivan in the studio on the last day of the vacation. For the first weeks of the term she was haunted by the presence of Ivan and the atmosphere of the studio, but on that last day of the vacation when she was with Ivan her thoughts had been occupied with Potter and the books he needed from the Public Library.

'I absolutely must go and order those books,' she was saying to Ivan, who wanted her to go on posing for the drawing he was finishing.

'A lot of use you are, with that bloody, harried, self-important look on your face,' he grumbled. 'You might as well go.'

Obviously he didn't expect to be taken seriously, for he roared in protest when she got up.

'It won't take an hour, and it's really important. The boy won't be able to follow the course if he doesn't get the books. We don't have Villon and Mallarmé at the School of Arts, you know.'

Ivan probably didn't know what a School of Arts was, but he made no attempt to find out. He had no curiosity at all about the lives of other people.

'Oh, come back and sit down, for God's sake,' he said, with a burst of irritability like tears.

Jenny shook her head. She was painting her face in front of the mirror which reflected Ivan looking at her with a strained, uneasy frown, like an illiterate staring at a newspaper headline that might contain a threat. The claims of a boy in a country town seemed to him completely meaningless.

Jenny was shocked. She had never maintained the importance of anything in comparison with Ivan's work, but that was because it belonged to a whole class of things important enough to devote one's life to, and Potter's reading belonged to it too. She felt strongly that to fail one was to fail all, and was astonished that Ivan didn't think so too. It occurred to her that perhaps Ivan's paintings were important to him simply as things that Ivan did.

It was one of those moments the mind retains for a

long time. Ivan, so deep in the mirror, appeared to have receded into the past, and Jenny thought that this might be the beginning of the end.

Meanwhile, with the detachment of the experienced teacher, she was writing notes in Potter's prose book. After all, she thought, Ivan's work, so austere and so convincing, stated those values she lived by and he seemed not to know. 'The summer's flower,' she said to herself, suddenly interpreting something that had escaped her before. 'The summer's flower is to the summer sweet, though to itself it only live and die.' She was expecting too much of Ivan, who was only called upon to live and die.

'You need the past anterior tense here, Alan, because of the tense in the main clause,' she said, and thought how good it was, after the uncertainties and tyrannies of art, to be back in a world where she knew the rules and applied them.

'If you give me the parcels slip, Miss B., I'll ride over and get the books at lunchtime.'

'I left it in the staff-room.' Just then the recess bell went, and she added, 'Come with me now and I'll get it for you.'

She was careful to conceal her gratification as he was to conceal his eagerness. For years she had practised such tact, had taken care always to be just, to be trustworthy, to be an acceptable authority, and she could not face the thought that one boy like Leonard could frustrate all her efforts, but she knew it was so, and under her discussions of grammar and her thoughts of Ivan she felt the drag of depression and anxiety. In the staff-room she searched her briefcase for the parcels slip with such a look of misery that her friend Margaret said, 'What's the matter, Jen? You look upset.'

She nodded towards the door to indicate the presence of Potter waiting outside as she took the parcels slip out to him, called after him, 'Bring your Honours prose round after school, Alan,' and came back sighing and rubbing her forehead.

'That new boy Leonard wrote some dirt in his French prose. I crossed the word out, thinking it was an accident, you see, and he cross-questioned me about it with a great smirk on his face, so I realised he did it on purpose.'

'The little beast! What did you do?'

'What could I do? I ignored it. If I'd realised when I was marking it I never would have marked the word out, but I've never struck anything like that before. I hope I never do again.'

There was so much anxiety in her voice that Margaret made haste to comfort her.

'The others would never play a trick like that. Imagine Colin Ellis!'

'I'm certain Colin wouldn't, but he's always been a bit of an outsider, and I don't think he has any influence. I don't know what the others would do. I don't really know them. Do you ever really get to know the children in your class?'

'But after years, Jenny?'

'I would have thought so too, but I'm sure they were

all in on it. They were as still as stones while he was talking. Mind you, they wouldn't have the slightest idea that I knew what was going on.' She frowned. 'What's the point of it, then? It's like a story I read about some Oriental aristocrat who was offended by some people so he invited them to dinner and served them food mixed with human excrement.'

Quickly, Margaret put down her half-eaten biscuit.

'Thank you for telling me that.'

'Well, I wondered at the time what satisfaction he got out of it, seeing that they never found out. It's rather the same thing, isn't it?'

'No, it isn't the same thing at all. He isn't trying to insult you particularly, he's just trying to be smart.' She eyed her biscuit and decided to be hardy. 'It will all pass over; the others won't be in it because they like you.'

'Oh, as for liking!' Jenny shrugged her shoulders. She wanted something more dependable than that.

Looking at her severe, handsome face, Margaret thought with dislike of Ivan, as if Jenny's exclamation referred to him too. The two girls were so intimate that Jenny guessed the thought. Once she used to talk a great deal about Ivan to Margaret, but she had stopped because Margaret translated into a limited language of her own the painstakingly accurate information that Jenny gave her, and Jenny in consequence found herself involved in falsehood. Once Margaret, who found the situation exciting and agonising, had said, 'Suppose he met someone else while you were away?' Jenny had considered this as carefully as she considered everything.

'Well, I don't think he'd do any active courting, love. I don't think he'd go to the trouble. If some beautiful passive mermaid came in on the tide, well ... ' She shrugged her shoulders. 'I don't suppose I'd die of it.' I shouldn't like it very much either, she admitted to herself.

Carefully as she had answered the question, Margaret had asked it again, so she realised that it was actually a devious and timid defence of marriage, and ceased to give serious thought to her answers. Time and again she had said, 'I'm not in love with him', but Margaret's ears rejected the words, and at last Jenny realised that this was her moral limit, and she could accept Jenny's affair with Ivan only so long as Jenny was too much in love to help herself. That was a pity, for Jenny very much wanted to talk about her feeling for Ivan and to demonstrate that it wasn't love. Ivan's value for her was that he let her into the world in which she wanted to live; to be near him when he was working was to be near the centre of the world. She admired the work so much that weaknesses in the man shocked her; he was a good artist, but sometimes she thought that given his choice he might have been a bad one. 'I know exactly what it would be like to lose someone you love,' she told herself. 'It would be like a fire's going out for ever. It would be like closing a window, to lose Ivan.'

Jenny knew all about love, for she had invented it. Her parents had been bound together by the real needs of hatred and the false comforts of respectability, and quite early in her childhood she had distinguished the real from the false. As soon as she understood the characters of her parents, she saw that they were bound to make each other suffer. Her mother had no troubles she could display, but was convinced that pity was the only feeling worth inspiring, and her fantasies were so intense that she drew on the air the frail, romantic shape she longed to be. Frantically she tried to make her husband into the villain this situation demanded; if he were five minutes late for dinner there was a clamour, a rehearsal of grievances that rose to a climax of shrieking and sobbing. There was no living in peace with such a woman, for peace was not what she wanted. Jenny often wondered how perfect virtue would have confronted her, but she could not see any answer, and that gave her her first idea of the terrible severity of love, that as soon as one partner failed, both were punished.

To most people her father's behaviour seemed like perfect virtue. It was the cruellest part of her mother's fate, to be told often that she was lucky to have married a good-tempered, easy-going man like Stan. Stan took a quiet pleasure in substituting for the appearance of suffering that would have given his wife a temporary satisfaction, a real suffering she could neither understand nor express. He observed her agitation calmly, prompting occasionally when she omitted an item of her litany, attacking the delicate phantom, his wife's vital part, with no feeling apparent except contempt for such an easy mark. Once or twice a cruelty that seemed innocent but was carefully planned showed the tension of hatred and anger beneath his calm, and compared with this forethought her mother's raging seemed harmless to Jenny.

Love had to exist and to be as strong as hatred, or life would be intolerable. So Jenny set about inventing love, and modelled it on her parents' hatred, an intense demanding passion ruling every moment, requiring her mother's intensity of feeling and her father's diligence. Knowing nothing about social pressure, or the sexual passion and its mysterious connection with one's secret desire to suffer or to inflict suffering, to be extinguished or to live for ever, she supposed love had brought her parents together, which made it seem an unreliable and perilous arrangement. When she grew up she professed the belief that human love was the greatest good, but she thought of it as a beautiful and complicated piece of music, quite beyond her powers of execution; to attempt it and play one wrong note would bring down on one's head an overwhelming curse. So she was always setting tests for love and being relieved when she failed them. If I loved Ivan, she thought, I wouldn't care whether he was a good artist or a bad one. But I do care. It is really the only thing that matters to me.

She was tempted to tell Margaret that Ivan had proposed to her, but she wasn't quite sure that it was true. Certainly, just before she had left to catch her train, he had looked gloomily at the unfinished drawing and had said, 'Can't you get a move to the city? Would they move you if we got married?'

'Not before the end of the year,' she had answered, which meant perhaps that she was engaged. She should, of course, have pounced in a ladylike way, and obliged him to make his meaning plain, but that would have meant making her own meaning plain, which she was, after all, not ready to do. She had never experienced and could not imagine a love that would withstand the rigours of marriage, yet the prompt, whole-hearted refusal hadn't risen to her lips as she had expected.

With the parcels slip in his pocket, Alan Potter went to join the others at the end of the playground. They slouched on the grass, their minds so idle that they stared at him simply because he was moving.

'How's Miss B?' said Leonard, emphasising the initial in a pointed manner.

To show his opinion of this insinuation, Potter allowed his face to sag in a look of idiot amazement while he stared at Leonard.

'She wouldn't change much in two minutes, I suppose.'

'Thought she might have found out what a *capote* was.'

'She was on to you about that,' said Ellis.

'Oh, rot!'

'Yes, she was. She got that gloomy, set look. Always does when she's keeping a straight face.'

'You rave, Ellis, you rave. Where would she find out about a thing like that?'

'There's always the dictionary, son.'

Perceiving the taunt, Leonard muttered in rage, 'Only place she'll ever see one.'

'Shut up,' said Potter sharply, moved not by loyalty to the teacher but by the painful confusion he felt from time to time, when it came over him that a carnival of grotesque behaviour rioted under the sober surface of the world he knew.

'The Honours boy,' said Leonard.

Potter let this pass. It was useless and unnecessary to explain to fools like Leonard the satisfaction that Honours French gave him, the feeling of carrying a gold coin in his pocket and now and then running his thumb over its reassuring milled edge. He needed such a talisman at the moment, since existence was complicated and uneasy; life appeared inviting, yet punished his advances, and he twisted sometimes for slight reasons on the skewers of shame, while every new thing attracted him so strongly that he could never live cautiously. In books he found the passions and the oddities of human behaviour and the words of love and anger safely written down, losing nothing but their power to hurt and to alarm, gaining something that made them more satisfying than they were in life. There was another satisfaction too. The work was hard, and he was pleased to find that he could do it; it made demands, and when he met them he gained not maturity but entry into a world where one did not have to prove maturity or virility, because they were of no account. Voltaire and Verlaine spoke as freely to him as to anyone else; all he needed to bring was the understanding mind.

At the end of the day Jenny was really too tired for the French Honours lesson. During the last lesson of that afternoon she had to concentrate on preserving her self-respect in front of a rowdy Second Year class, in front of which she stood like a desperate matador evading the mortal thrust of ridicule. She came back to the staff-room where the others were getting ready to leave, and the quick succession of small sounds, the whirr of a zip-fastener on a briefcase, the snap of a locker door, the scrape of a chair, which marked the end of every day, convinced her that all days were the same, and she longed to be married, but not to Ivan; she dreamed of a hero of legend intervening between her and 2B.

'Potter left a parcel for you just after lunch, Jenny. I told him to leave it on your table,' said the English master.

Unwrapping the parcel and finding the shabby, sound old volumes with names as familiar as the names of friends, she decided she could give another lesson after all.

'Put your head in as you go past Fifth Year room and tell Potter I'll be five minutes, will you? I must have another cigarette.'

'Don't work yourself into the ground, my girl. How is Potter going?'

'All right, I think. He can when he likes, you know.'

She opened the volume of Madame de Sévigné's letters, reading here and there while she looked for one that would appeal to Potter. All at once she realised that for Potter the barrier of language had disappeared, and she was thinking only of limits in his taste and his experience. I did that, she thought, taking heart, and she stubbed out her cigarette and went to Fifth Year room.

Potter had left his prose book open on the table. She nodded to him, and picked up the prose. He came and stood beside her to watch the correction. It was a difficult piece of translation, an elaborate and formal dialogue between a ladylike but sprightly Victorian miss and a worthy suitor whose proposal of marriage she was determined to parry. As usual, Jenny did not refer to the text-book but read quickly through Potter's version, translating it into English mentally as a test of expression. Suddenly she stopped. ' "Pray rise, sir," said Miss Lydia, no longer able to support so heavy a lover.' '—*Veuillez-vous lever, monsieur, dit mademoiselle Lydia, ne pouvant plus supporter un amant si lourd*.'

Dreamily she turned to the original. ' "Pray rise, sir," said Miss Lydia, no longer able to endure so tedious a suitor', and as she read it she saw again the look of drowned merriment Potter had turned on Leonard that morning. She knew now that it was not ridicule it had conveyed, but complicity, for this was the same thing, though a hundred times as clever. Shock had paralysed her for a moment this morning; now it was the weight of sadness that slowed her thoughts. My life is too narrow, she thought. I invent consolations, I delude myself. She had believed she was communicating something of great value, and now she was crushed by disappointment. That the joke was clever seemed to her the hardest thing to bear; the sentence shed its ludicrous impropriety over the distinguished sentiments the couple were expressing, and made their artificiality ridiculous. It was her kind of joke, aimed at her in hostility or at least with crushing indifference.

Then the boy said, 'What's the matter?' in such a natural voice, so free from guilt, that the world righted itself. After all, it was an innocent mistranslation.

How could she ever have thought he would embarrass himself by embarrassing her? Besides, she thought, it wasn't a boy's joke. Boys weren't much inclined to put themselves in the other person's place. Oh, lord, she thought, I believe I am going to laugh. Miss Lydia and her ponderous suitor appeared more ridiculous every moment, and her sudden intense relief seemed to have weakened her self-control. As she advanced from line to line, underlining and discussing mistakes, aware all the time of the approach of the deadly ambiguous sentence, she set her face in a stern, unresponsive expression. 'Not *lourd*, I think; *ennuyeux* might be better,' she said. There was something in her voice that made the boy look into her face, and though she was certain it was quite expressionless whatever he read there made him look at the sentence, staring until slowly its hidden meaning occurred to him. No matter how slowly, there was no way of stopping it. At last he stood up, snatched his book and said, 'I hate you,' with bitter authority.

What a fuss! Jenny thought angrily, at first, then as slowly as he had deciphered the sentence, she read the meaning of that strange mixture of grief, disgust and indignation in his face. It wasn't a boy's joke; it wasn't the joke of an innocent woman either. It was the coarse, comfortable chuckle of old Margaret in *Much Ado*, when Hero talked of the heaviness of her heart: ' 'Twill be heavier soon, by the weight of a man.' Oh, there was no hiding it; she knew to an ounce what a gentleman weighed.

So there she stood, naked and hideous in the boy's eyes, and likely to remain so for ever, since time had stopped. There was room for everything in that extended moment; she could trace events backwards and lay the blame on Peter Leonard, reflect on the irony of her remark to Margaret, 'Oh, as for liking!' 'Poor kid,' she said to herself now, 'I hope he likes me.' Nothing else could interpret the situation for Potter but a particle of real affection. She even had a vague, surprising idea about love, but it slipped away from her without words. She would have said to the boy, 'Can't you see that it makes no difference what I am?' but she could not say what she was.

As if his own words had just reached his ears, Potter's look of anger changed to a touching look of worry and confusion, and he hurried out of the room.

In ten years' time he'll look back and laugh at himself, she thought. How unfair it was that she should know what it was like to be seventeen and he have no idea what it was like to be thirty-two. Only too well she knew what it was like to be seventeen: was seventeen again herself and tasting disgust, feeling the wretchedness of adolescence giddy in the void of inexperience. Life was dirty, drab and miserable, and she had an anguished feeling of being lost in time, lost in herself. She longed intently for Ivan, and thought her inconsistency comic. Wasn't Ivan the cause of this self-disgust? But the feeling was so extreme that the vision of Ivan rose incongruously innocent, and she thought of everything she liked about him and would like for ever, the simplicity and directness that took the place of humour in his nature, the hardy indifference he felt about making himself ridiculous, and the mildness of temper he tried to disguise with blunder; she thought of the freedom with which they told each other their thoughts and the complete lack of malice in their dealings, and realised that their relationship was thoroughly respectable.

Meanwhile her misery assembled its context from the past, and she recognised herself at seventeen, trying with nausea to reconcile what she knew of her parents with what she had learned about sex.

Love was going to save me, she thought. Love was going to gild the woodwork and repaint the furniture. But I'm like them, though I'm luckier. I never found love, and I did without it.

At least I won't marry. I'll never risk that. She had never liked Ivan better, but she had to be done with confusion and difficult decisions, and, having given her sadness a home in the present, she felt unhappy but secure. It seemed a noble frame of mind, a victory at least over the sordid, and peace of mind seemed to be worth the price she was paying.

The next day in class Potter engaged Jenny's glance, discreetly and deliberately. His look was shy but determined, and there was a gleam in it that indicated his willingness to laugh at himself if she would laugh too. At her faint reassuring grin his face relaxed, invaded by happiness, and Jenny thought with wonder, I could never have done that. She hadn't loved her parents, and this was the first time in her life that she had admitted it. Not because they didn't love each other, but because I didn't love them. What a little prig I was, that I couldn't admit it!

She had a light-hearted feeling that difficulties had disappeared, and the boy had given her something of permanent value, and at last she realised that her old idea of love had vanished. She had discovered something easier, more commonplace, that would do just as well. With amusement she looked at the ponderous old vehicle, high-built and armour-plated, which had carried her across the dangerous desert of childhood, haunted by the sly, deadly serpent and the fierce bird with the poisoned beak. It was time to get down now; the country had changed and the natives were friendly. She was going to marry Ivan, after all.

Glenda ADAMS. (1940–). Born Sydney, studied Indonesian and other languages at University of Sydney. Lived in Indonesia, England, and, for an extended period, in New York, before returning to Australia. Has two short story collections: *Lies and Stories* (1976) and *The Hottest Night of the Century* (1979). Novels include *Dancing on Coral* (1987; winner Miles Franklin Award & NSW Premier's Award) and *Longleg* (1990; winner *Age* Book of the Year Award).

Jessica ANDERSON. (1916–). Born in Brisbane, but lived mostly in Sydney, with a few years in London. Began to write novels at 40, having previously written short stories and radio drama scripts. Her collection *Stories from the Warm Zone* (1987) won the *Age* Book of the Year Award. Novels include *Tirra Lirra by the River* (1978) and *The Impersonators* (1980), both winners of the Miles Franklin Award.

Thea ASTLEY. (1925–). Born in Brisbane, taught in schools in Queensland and NSW until 1967, at Macquarie University, Sydney, 1968–80. Short stories appear in *Hunting the Wild Pineapple* (1979). More than a dozen novels include: *The Well-Dressed Explorer, The Slow Natives*, and *The Acolyte*, all of which won the Miles Franklin Award (1962, '65, '72, respectively). In 1989 she won the Patrick White Award.

Murray BAIL. (1941–   ). Born Adelaide, lived mainly in Australia, though in India (1968–70) and Europe (1970–74) (see *Longhand: a Writer's Notebook*, 1989). Stories included in *Contemporary Portraits* (1975; repub. 1986 as *The Drover's Wife and Other Stories*). *Homesickness* (1980), a novel, won the National Book Council Award and shared the *Age* Book of the Year Award. *Holden's Performance* (1987) won the Victorian Premier's award for fiction. His strong interest in the visual arts is attested to by his study of painter Ian Fairweather (1981) and his serving as a trustee of the Australian National Gallery.

Candida BAKER. (1955–   ). Born London, first visited Australia with the Royal Shakespeare Company in 1975. Now an Australian citizen living in Sydney. Stories are collected in *The Powerful Owl* (1994). A novel, *Women and Horses*, was published in 1990. Has compiled three important collections of her interviews with Australian writers: *Yacker* (1986), and *Yacker* 2 & 3 (1987 and 1989).

Jean BEDFORD. (1946–   ). Born Cambridge, England, brought up in rural Victoria. Won Stanford

Writing Scholarship, 1982. Stories collected in *Country Girl Again* (1979) and, with Rosemary Creswell, *Colouring In* (1986). Novels include: *Sister Kate* (1982), a feminist fictionalising of the life of Ned Kelly's sister, *Love Child* (1986), *A Lease of Summer* (1990).

Carmel BIRD. (1940–   ). Born Launceston, Tasmania. Educated at University of Tasmania, lived in Europe and USA before settling in Melbourne. Her three collections of stories are *Births, Deaths and Marriages* (1983), The *Woodpecker Toy Fact* (1987) and *The Common Rat* (1993). Her three novels are *Cherry Ripe* (1985), *The Bluebird Cafe* (1990) and *The White Garden* (1995). She has written two guides for writers, *Dear Writer* (1988) and *Not Now Jack, I'm Writing a Novel* (1994), and edited two anthologies of Australian writing, *Relations* (ed. 1991) and *Red Hot Notes* (ed. 1991). In addition, she is an experienced teacher of creative writing.

David BROOKS. (1953–   ). Born Canberra, educated Australian National University and the University of Toronto. Has taught in English Departments in several Australian universities. A volume of poems, *The Cold Front* (1983), won the Anne Elder Award. Stories are found in *The Book of Sei and Other Stories* (1985) and *Sheep and the Diva* (1990). Essays are collected in *The Necessary Jungle* (1990). A novel, *The House of Balthus*, appeared in 1995.

Peter CAREY. (1943–   ). Born Bacchus Marsh, Victoria; educated Monash University. Lived in London (1968–70), Sydney, and currently in Manhattan. Two collections of stories: *The Fat Man in History* (1974) and *War Crimes* (1979; winner NSW Premier's Literary Award). *Exotic Pleasures* (1980) contains some stories from both collections. Novels include *Bliss* (1981; winner Miles Franklin Award, NSW Literary Award, and National Book Council "Banjo" Award), *Illywhacker* (1985; *Age* Book of the Year Award, among others), *Oscar and Lucinda* (1988; winner of Booker Prize, among others), *The Tax Inspector* (1991), *The Unusual Life of Tristan Smith* (1994).

Moya COSTELLO. (1952–   ). Grew up in Sydney, lives in Adelaide. Has worked as teacher, editor, and broadcaster, particularly for ABC's 'Science Show'. Stories collected in *The Waters of Vanuatu and Kites in Jakarta* (with Carmel Kelly, 1985) and *Small Ecstasies* (1994).

Anna COUANI. (1948–   ). Born in Sydney of Greek and Polish ancestors. Educated in architecture at the University of Sydney. Has published books of experimental prose and poetry which include *Italy and the Train* (1983), *Were All Women Sex-Mad?* (1982), and *The Harbour Breathes* (1989; a collaboration with photomonteur Peter Lyssiotis). Co-edited *Telling Ways: Australian Women's Experimental Writing* (1988).

Peter COWAN. (1914–   ). Born in Perth, spent most of 1930s as an itinerant labourer in rural areas. Studied at University of Western Australia. Associated with 'Angry Penguins' movement in Melbourne. His seven collections of stories include *Drift* (1944), *The Empty Street* (1965), *Voices* (1988). Has published four novels, including *The Hills of Apollo Bay* (1989). Co-editor of *Westerly*. Author of two biographies, editor of several volumes of fiction and correspondence. AM 1987; Patrick White Award 1992.

Rosemary CRESWELL. (1941–   ). Born Sydney. Has taught at Sydney University, now a literary agent. Stories collected in two volumes: *Colouring In* (1986, with Jean Bedford) and *Lovers and Others* (1989). Edited *Home and Away* (1987), a collection of travel stories by contemporary Australian writers. Under the pseudonym 'Ruth Clarement', she has written collaborative crime fiction with Carol Manners.

Garry DISHER. (1949–   ). Born Burra, South Australia. Lived and worked in England, Europe, & Africa, and has lived in Melbourne since 1974. Awarded Stanford Writing Fellowship (1978–79) and won Angus & Robertson Writers' Fellowship, 1987. Collections of stories include: *The Difference to Me* (1988), *Flamingo Gate* (1991). *The Bamboo Flute* (1992) won the NBC Younger Readers Book of the Year Award in 1993. Thrillers include *Kickback* (1991) and *Deathdeal* (1993). Anthologies: *Personal Best* (1989 & '91), *The Man Who Played the Spoons* (1987).

Robert DREWE. (1943–). Born Melbourne, educated Western Australia. A distinguished career in journalism includes two Walkley Awards. Collections include: *The Bay of Contented Men* (1989) and *The Bodysurfers* (1983), which has been dramatised for television. Novels include *The Savage Crows* (1976) and *Fortune* (1986, winner of NBC Banjo Award), and *Our Sunshine* (1991), a retelling of the Ned Kelly story. His play, *South American Barbecue*, was staged 1990–91. Edited *The Picador Book of the Beach* (1993).

Beverley FARMER. (1941–). Born Melbourne, educated at University of Melbourne. Lived some years in Greece, where she shared village life, taught English, and helped run a restaurant. Stories collected in *Milk* (1983, winner NSW Premier's Award for fiction) and *Home Time* (1985). Novels: *Alone* (1980) and *The Seal Woman* (1992). Her writer's journal *A Body of Water* (1990) challenges generic boundaries.

FLACCO (aka Paul Livingstone). Not so much born as self-created. Stand-up comedian, man of litters, regular contributor to Radio 2JJJ and cultural commentator on David Marr's 'Arts Today' program on ABC Radio National. The Funniest Man on Radio which, considering the competition includes John Laws and Ron Casey, is really saying something.

Helen GARNER. (1942–). Born Geelong, educated at University of Melbourne. Worked as secondary school teacher, journalist, and translator. Her first novel, *Monkey Grip* (1977), won an NBC Award, released as a film 1982. Shorter fiction: *Honour and Other People's Children* (1980), *Postcards from Surfers* (1985, winner NSW Premier's Literary Award). *The Children's Bach* (1984) won South Australian Literary Award. Story included here is taken from *Cosmo Cosmolino* (1992). Has written for film and television, and received a Walkley Award for journalism, 1993. Her non-fiction *The First Stone* (1995) was a national debating point.

Zeny GILES. (1937–   ). Born Sydney, of a Cypriot father and a Kastellorizian mother, educated at universities of Sydney and Newcastle. *Between Two Worlds*, a novel, appeared in 1981 and her collection of stories, *Miracle of the Waters*, in 1989. With Norman Talbot, edited an anthology of stories from the Hunter Valley, *Contrast and Relief* (1981). Has written plays and poetry. Won the *Age* short story competition in 1981.

Kerryn GOLDSWORTHY. (1953–   ). Born South Australia, educated at University of Adelaide, now teaches English at the University of Melbourne. A distinguished editor of *Australian Book Review*, 1986–87. Stories collected in *North of the Moonlight Sonata* (1989). Edited *Australian Short Stories* (1983) and *Coast to Coast* (1986).

Peter GOLDSWORTHY. (1951–). Born South Australia, grew up in country SA towns and Darwin. Graduated in medicine from University of Adelaide, 1974. Books of short fiction include: *Zooing* (1986) and *Little Deaths* (1993). Four volumes of poetry include: *This Goes with That: Selected Poems 1970–1990* (1991). Novels: *Maestro* (1989) and *Honk If You Are Jesus* (1992). With Brian Matthews collaboratively produced *Magpie* (1992). Winner: 1982 Commonwealth Poetry Prize, Anne Elder Poetry Award, SA Biennial Literary Award, Bicentennial Grace Perry Award for Poetry.

Kate GRENVILLE. (1950–). Born Sydney, educated at University of Sydney. From age 26 spent seven years in Europe and USA, completing a master's degree in writing at University of Colorado. Stories collected in *Bearded Ladies* (1984). Novels include *Lilian's Story* (1985; winner *Australian*/Vogel Literary Award; filmed 1995) and *Dark Places* (1994). A practical book for writers, *The Writing Book*, published 1990. With Sue Wolfe, edited *Making Stories: How Ten Australian Novels Were Written* (1993).

Marion HALLIGAN. (1940–). Born Newcastle, worked as teacher and freelance journalist. 1992 appointed chairperson of Literature Board of Australia Council. Collections of stories include: *The Living Hothouse* (1988, winner of Steele Rudd Award) and *The Worry Box* (1993). Novels include *Self-Possession* (1987) and *Lovers' Knots* (1992, winner *Age* Book of Year

Award). *Eat My Words* (1990) is a book about food in its many aspects. Has won many short story awards and in 1990 the Pascall Prize for book-reviewing.

Barry HILL. (1943–). Born Melbourne, educated University of Melbourne. Has worked as teacher, psychologist, and journalist in Victoria and London. Has published collections of short fiction: *A Rim of Blue* (1978), *Headlocks* (1983); a novella, *Near the Refinery* (1980); a novel, *The Best Picture* (1988); poems, *Raft* (1990; winner Anne Elder Award), and *Ghosting William Buckley* (1993). *Sitting In* (1991), an account of an industrial dispute, won a NSW Premier's Award.

Janette Turner HOSPITAL. (1940–). Born Melbourne, moved to Brisbane 1950. Studied at University of Queensland, and in Ontario. Has lived in India, Canada, and USA. Her novel, *The Ivory Swing*, won the prestigious Canadian Seal Award in 1982. Other novels include *Charades* (1988) and *The Last Magician* (1992). Stories collected in *Dislocations* (1987) and *Isobars* (1990). Published crime novel *A Very Proper Death* (1990) as 'Alex Juniper'. Has been writer-in-residence at American and Australian universities.

Elizabeth JOLLEY. (1923–). Born Birmingham, England, of English father and Viennese mother. In 1959 migrated to Western Australia with her husband and three children. Stories collected in *Five Acre Virgin* (1976), *The Travelling Entertainer* (1979), and *Woman* *in a Lampshade* (1983). Novels include *Mr Scobie's Riddle* (1983; winner, *Age* Book of the Year), *Milk and Honey* (1984; winner NSW Premier's Prize for fiction), *The Well* (1986, winner Miles Franklin Award). Autobiographical pieces, speeches, articles, collected in *Central Mischief*, ed. Caroline Lurie (1992). Canada/Australia Literary Award, 1989. Officer of the Order of Australia.

Joan LONDON. (1948–   ). Born Perth, educated University of Western Australia. Lives in Fremantle. Has taught English as a second language, and is a bookseller. *Sister Ships* (1986), her first book of short stories, won the *Age* Book of the Year Award. A second volume, *Letter to Constantine*, was published in 1993.

Angelo LOUKAKIS. (1951–   ). Born Sydney, of Greek parents. Educated at universities of NSW and Sydney. Worked as teacher of English as a second language, multicultural education project officer, and welfare worker. In 1993 appointed literature publisher at Angus & Robertson. Stories collected in *For the Patriarch* (1981, winner of NSW Premier's Literary Award) and *Vernacular Dreams* (1986). A novel, *Messenger*, was published in 1992. His screenplay, *Dancing* (1980), was awarded a prize for production at the Melbourne Film Festival.

Richard LUNN. (1950–   ). Born Sydney, has taught in Australia and England and lectured in creative writing.

Pompeii Deep Fry won the Anne Elder Award for poetry in 1980. Stories collected in *The Divine Right of Dogs* (1982) and *The Taxidermist's Dance* (1990). Winner of *Age* short-story competition in 1987.

Morris LURIE. (1938–   ). Born Melbourne of Polish parents, studied architecture and worked in advertising. Has lived in Europe, Africa, and USA, 1965–73. Stories widely published in UK, USA, and Australia. Collections include: *Inside the Wardrobe* (1975), *The Night We Ate the Sparrow* (1985). Novels include *Flying Home* (1978) and *Madness* (1981). Collections of reportage include: *Hackwork* (1977) and *Snow Jobs* (1985). Has written plays, screenplays, several books for children. An autobiography, *Whole Life*, appeared in 1987.

David MALOUF. (1934–   ). Born in Brisbane of Lebanese and English parents, educated at University of Queensland. Lived in Europe 1959–68. Taught in Sydney University's English Department, 1968–77. Lives in Australia and Tuscany. Poetry collected in *Bicycle* (1970), *Selected Poems* (1991). Novels include *Johnno*, (1975), and *Remembering Babylon* (1993). Stories collected in *Antipodes* (1985). Librettist for Richard Meale's opera, *Voss*. Prizes include: NSW Premier's Literary Award, *Age* Book of the Year, Miles Franklin Award, Commonwealth Prize for fiction, Prix Femina Etranger. AO 1987.

Olga MASTERS. (1919–86). Born Pambula, NSW. From 1940–60 lived in NSW country towns. Mother of seven children, including famous journalists Chris and Roy. In 1955, resumed career as journalist, with *Manly Daily* and *Sydney Morning Herald*. Her first collection of stories, *The Home Girls*, (1982), won a National Book Council Award. Other volumes of stories: *A Long Time Dying* (1985) and *The Rose Fancier* (1988). Two novels: *Loving Daughters* (1984), *Amy's Children* (1987). Journalism collected by Deirdre Coleman: *Reporting Home* (1990).

James McQUEEN. (1934–   ). Born Tasmania. Studied at National Art School, Sydney, completed four-year course in accountancy, at age 40 returned Tasmania to grow orchids. Has won many short story awards. Five novels include: *Hook's Mountain* (1982), *The Floor of Heaven* (1986). Stories collected in: *The Electric Beach* (1978), *Uphill Runner* (1984), et al. *The Franklin—Not Just a River* (1983) deals with a major environmental/political issue.

Gillian MEARS. (1964–   ). Grew up in Grafton, NSW, educated at University of Technology, Sydney. Two collections of short stories, *Ride a Cock Horse* (1988, winner of a Commonwealth Writer's Prize, 1989), and *Fineflour* (1990). Her novel *The Mint Lawn* (1991) won the *Australian*/Vogel Literary Award for 1990. *The Grass Sister*, a novel, was published 1995.

Frank MOORHOUSE. (1938–   ). Born Nowra, NSW. Worked as journalist and as organiser for Workers'

Educational Association. His most recent work of fiction, *Grand Days* (1993), his only novel, is the product of three years' research in Geneva, Paris, and the USA. His many volumes of short fiction include: *The Americans, Baby* (1972), *The Electrical Experience* (1974), *Forty-Seventeen* (1988). Has written for film ("Between Wars") and television ("Time's Raging"). Has held many literary fellowships and received numerous awards, including: NBC Banjo Award, Awgie Award, *Age* Book of the Year, ALS Gold Medal 1989. Made AM in 1985.

Gerald MURNANE. (1939–   ). Born Melbourne, has lived there and in rural Victoria. Worked as school teacher, editor, and university teacher of creative writing. Novels include *Tamarisk Row* (1974), *The Plains* (1982). Stories collected in: *Landscape with Landscape* (1987), *Velvet Waters* (1990, winner of 1991 Barbara Ramsden Award), *Emerald Blue* (1994), though, as in Frank Moorhouse's collections, the collecting offers more than a sum of its individual parts, signified by Moorhouse's term 'discontinuous narrative'.

Hal PORTER. (1911–84). Born Melbourne, educated mainly at Bairnsdale in Gippsland, Vic., worked as schoolteacher and librarian, inter al. Won most Australian literary prizes. AM 1982. His autobiographical work, *The Watcher on the Cast-Iron Balcony* (1963) is justly celebrated. Novelist, playwright, and poet, his seven volumes of stories include: *Short Stories* (1942), *The Cats* *of Venice* (1965), *Selected Stories* (1971). Regarded by many as the doyen of Australian short story writers.

John TRANTER. (1943–   ). Born Cooma, NSW, grew up South Coast NSW. Educated at University of Sydney. Asian editor for Angus & Robertson, 1971–73. Producer for ABC. Publisher, editor, teacher. One of Australia's pre-eminent poets. Collections include: *Red Movie* (1972), *The Floor of Heaven* (1992), *At the Florida* (1993). Edited *The Penguin Book of Modern Australian Poetry* (1991, with Philip Mead) and *Martin Johnston: Selected Poems & Prose* (1993). Won Grace Leven Poetry Prize, 1988, the *Age* Poetry Award, 1993. Awarded a Creative Arts Fellowship, 1990.

Carolyn van LANGENBERG. (1948–). Born Lismore, NSW. Educated at University of Sydney. *Sybil's Stories* was published 1986. In 1995 was awarded a Master's degree in Writing by the University of Western Sydney for *Fish Lips*, a novel.

Ania WALWICZ. (1951–   ). Born Swidnica, Poland, arrived Australia, 1963. Graduate of Victorian College of the Arts, has held several exhibitions. A novel, *Boat* (1989), won the New Writing Prize in the Victorian Premier's Literary Awards. Short fiction collected in: *Writing* (1982), *Travel/Writing* (1989). Performance poet, playwright.

Archie WELLER. (1957–   ). Born Perth, Western Australia. Grew up on isolated farm and spent eight years

in boarding school. Wharf labourer, stablehand, rousea-
bout. Writer-in-residence Australian National University,
1984. Novel, *The Day of the Dog*, (1981), won the WA
Fiction Week Award in 1982. Filmed with James
Ricketson 1991. Won several short story awards. Stories
collected in *Going Home* (1986). Won the Patricia
Weickhardt Award for an Aboriginal writer in 1983.
With Colleen Glass edited *Us Fellas* (1988), an anthology of Aboriginal writing. Playwright, filmaker.

Nadia WHEATLEY. (1949–   ). Born Sydney, edu-
cated Sydney and Macquarie universities. *Five Times
Dizzy* (1982; NSW State Literary Award, 1983), *The
House That Was Eureka* (1984; NSW State Literary
Award 1985), *My Place* (1987, with Donna Rawlins.
CBC Book of the Year for Younger Readers, 1988).
Edited two volumes of writings of Chairman Clift,
Trouble in Lotus Land (1990) and *Being Alone With
Oneself* (1991).

Michael WILDING. (1942–   ). Born Worcester, England,
educated at Oxford University. Holds Personal Chair in
English at University of Sydney. With Frank Moorhouse and
Brian Kiernan, an editor of *Tabloid Story*. Stories collected in:
Aspects of the Dying Process (1972), *Reading the Signs* (1984),
The Man of Slow Feeling (1985). Novels include: *Living
Together* (1974), *The Paraguayan Experiment*
(1985). Edited *The Tabloid Story Pocket Book* (1978), William
Lane's *The Workingman's Paradise* (1980), *Portable Austra-
lian Authors: Marcus Clarke* (1976).

Gerard WINDSOR. (1944–   ). Born Sydney, graduated MA at Australian National University. Worked as editor in Subtitling Unit at SBS television (1982–85). Stories collected in: *The Harlots Enter First* (1982), *Memories of the Assassination Attempt* (1985), and the autobiographical *Family Lore* (1990). A short novel, *That Fierce Virgin* (1988), reflects his Irish Catholic heritage.

Tim WINTON. (1960–   ). Born Scarborough, Western Australia, educated at WA Institute of Technology. Lived in France, Ireland, and Greece. His first novel, *An Open Swimmer* (1982), shared the 1981 *Australian/*Vogel Literary Award. His second, *Shallows* (1984), won the Miles Franklin Award, as did his 1991 novel, *Cloudstreet*. His collection of stories, *Scission* (1985), won the WA Council Week Literary Award. Other collections of stories are: *Minimum of Two* (1987) and *Blood and Water* (1993). He has written for younger readers. *Land's Edge* (1993) is a set of reflections on Winton's relationship with place, particularly the WA littoral.

'Amy WITTING' (Joan Levick). (1918–   ). Born Joan Fraser in Sydney and educated at University of Sydney. Taught French and English in secondary schools. Novels include *I for Isobel* (1989, winner FAW Barbara Ramsden Award), and *A Change in the Lighting* (1994). Stories collected in *Marriages* (1990). Two collections of poetry: *Travel Diary* (1985) and Beauty is the Straw (1991). Received the Patrick White Award, 1993.

I wish to record my indebtedness to The Oxford Companion to Australian Literature, *Second Edition, 1994, ed. Wilde, Hooton & Andrews, in the compilation of these bio-bibliographical notes. Further information about the authors may be sought in the* Encyclopedia of Post-Colonial Literatures in English, *2 vols (1994, Routledge), ed. Benson and Conolly.*

Acknowledgements are due to the following authors, publishers and agents for permission to include the stories which appear in this book.

'Reconstruction of an Event', © Glenda Adams 1979, from *The Hottest Night of the Century*, Angus & Robertson.

'The Milk', © Jessica Anderson 1987, from *Stories From the Warm Zone*, Penguin Books Australia Ltd.

'Hunting the Wild Pineapple', © Thea Astley 1979, from *Hunting the Wild Pineapple and Other Stories*, Penguin Books Australia Ltd.

'A,B,C,D,E,F,G,H,I,J,K,L,M,N,O,P,Q,R,S,T,U,V,W, X,Y,Z', © Murray Bail 1975, from *Contemporary Portraits and Other Stories*, University of Queensland Press, Australia.

'The Powerful Owl', © Candida Baker 1994, from *The Powerful Owl*, Pan Macmillan Australia Pty Limited.

Acknowledgements

'Country Girl Again', © Jean Bedford 1979, from *Country Girl Again*, Penguin Australia Pty Limited.

'The Woodpecker Toy Fact', © Carmel Bird 1987, from *The Woodpecker Toy Fact*, McPhee Gribble, Australia.

'Dr B. and the Students', © David Brooks 1990, from *Sheep and the Diva*, McPhee Gribble Australia.

'American Dreams', © Peter Carey 1994, from *Peter Carey Collected Stories*, University of Queensland Press.

'Frank,' © Moya Costello 1994, from *Small Ecstasies*, University of Queensland Press.

'Xmas in the Bush', © Anna Couani 1983, from *The Train*, Sea Cruise Books, Australia.

'Party', © Peter Cowan 1965, from *The Empty Street*, Angus & Robertson, Australia.

'New York, New York', © Rosemary Creswell 1986, from *Colouring In*, McPhee Gribble Australia.

'Syndrome', © Gary Disher 1991, from *Flamingo Gate*, Harper Collins.

'Radiant Heat', © Robert Drewe 1989, from *The Bay of Contented Men*, Pan Macmillan Australia Pty Limited.

'Place of Birth', © Beverley Farmer 1985, from *Home Time*, McPhee Gribble Australia.

'A Word in the Hand', © Flacco 1995, from *Burnt Offerings*, Penguin Australia.

'A Vigil', © Helen Garner 1992, from *Cosmo Cosmolino*, McPhee Gribble Australia.

'A Miracle of the Waters', © Zeny Giles 1989, from *Miracle of the Water*, Penguin Books Australia Ltd.

'A Patron of the Arts', © Kerryn Goldsworthy 1989, from *North of the Moonlight Sonnata*, McPhee Gribble, Australia.

'The Booster Shot', © Peter Goldsworthy 1993, from *Little Deaths*, Angus & Robertson.

'Look on My Works', © Kate Grenville 1989, from Helen Daniel (Ed.), *Expressway*, Penguin Books Australia Ltd.

'Cherub', © Marion Halligan 1993, from *The Worry Box*, Minerva, Australia.

'Getting to the Pig', © Barry Hill 1978, from *A Rim of Blue*, McPhee Gribble, Australia.

Acknowledgements

'Bondi', © Janette Turner Hospital 1990, from *Isobars*, University of Queensland Press.

'Five Acre Virgin', © Elizabeth Jolley 1976, from *Five Acre Virgin*, Fremantle Arts Centre Press.

'Burning Off', © Joan London 1986, from *Sister Ships*, Fremantle Arts Centre Press.

'Velodrome', © Angelo Loukakis 1986, from *Vernacular Dreams*, University of Queensland Press.

'The Duel Catalogue', © Richard Lunn 1990, from *The Taxidermist's Dance*, HarperCollins.

'Camille Pissaro 1830–1903', © Morris Lurie 1985, from *The Night We Ate the Sparrow*, McPhee Gribble Australia/Penguin Books Australia Ltd.

'Southern Skies', © David Malouf, 1989, from *Antipodes*, Penguin Books Australia Ltd.

'A Good Marriage', © Olga Masters 1982, from *The Home Girls*, University of Queensland Press.

'Nails of Love, Nails of Death', © Olga Masters 1984, from *Uphill Runner*, Penguin Books Australia Ltd.

'Afterthoughts', © Gillian Mears 1990, from *Fineflour*, University of Queensland Press.

'The Annual Conference of 1930 and South Coast Dada', © Frank Moorhouse 1974, from *The Electrical Experience*, Pan Macmillan Australia Pty Limited.

'Boy Blue', © Gerald Murnane 1995, from *Emerald Blue*, McPhee Gribble, Australia.

'Boy Meets Girl', © Hal Porter 1980, from *Hal Porter*, University of Queensland Press.

'Gloria', © John Tranter 1992, from *The Floor of Heaven*, Angus & Robertson.

'Hitler's Driver', © Carolyn Van Langenberg 1995.

'Stories My Mother Told Me' and 'Dad', © Ania Walwicz 1989, from *Boat*, Angus & Robertson.

'Going Home', © Archie Weller 1986, from *Going Home: Stories*, Allen & Unwin Australia.

'Women's Business', © Nadia Wheatley 1984, from *The Night Tolkein Died*, Random House Australia.

'Singing Birds', © Michael Wilding 1994, from *This Is For You*, Angus & Robertson.

'Botany Cemetary', © Gerard Windsor 1990, from *Family Lore*, William Heinemann Australia.

Acknowledgements

'Thomas Awkner Floats', © Tim Winton 1985, from *Scission*, McPhee Gribble Australia, Penguin Books Australia Ltd.

'The Weight of a Man', © Amy Whitting 1961, from Hal Porter (Ed.), *Coast to Coast, 1961–'62*, Angus & Robertson.

Also from Random House Australia

The Grass Sister
Gillian Mears

A haunting novel by the Vogel-winning author of *The Mint Lawn*.

'Only after seven years of not hearing a word have I begun to seek her in every memory, thinking that if the right one will float free, it might yield something important. That like a map or chart, I'll sense her whereabouts by turning the memory around and around in my mind, looking out the window every now and then to compare its details to the landscape.'

A woman sits at a desk in a farmhouse reading old letters. Africa floats in her consciousness like the Australian hills she can see from the window. Seven years ago, her younger sister disappeared near a waterfall on the African mountain range, and now, like a necromancer of memory, the woman begins conjuring up her secretive sister's past so that she can proceed with her own life.

The Grass Sister magically entwines the past and the present as it explores notions of sisterly love and sisterly competitiveness, motherhood, abandonment, and the nature of faded colonials in Africa and Australia turning in on themselves in ways that lead to damage and loss. It is also an affectionate portrait of a father and the kinds of family madness that have shaped him.

The richness and depth of *The Grass Sister* confirm Gillian Mears as one of our finest writers.

Men Love Sex
Edited by Alan Close

Australia's and New Zealand's leading male writers and most exciting new names bare their feelings about love and sex.

Painfully honest, confronting, hilarious and poignant, *Men Love Sex* reveals what men really talk about when they talk about love.

Venero Armanno	Robert Drewe	David Owen
Ian Beck	Jonathan Griffiths	Eric Rolls
John Birmingham	Mike Johnson	John Stapleton
Peter Carey	Stephen Lang	Angus Strachan
Tom Carment	Gerard Lee	Chad Taylor
James Cockington	Damien Lovelock	Clinton Walker
Matthew Condon	Roger McDonald	Archie Weller
Alan Close	Lex Marinos	Peter Wells
Christopher Cyrill	Frank Moorhouse	Tim Winton
John Dale	Mark Mordue	William Yang
Julian Davies		

Blur
Edited by James Bradley

This wide range of talented young voices plots out points on a fictional landscape, resulting in a collection that celebrates difference and multiplicity, and encapsulates what it's like to be young and living in Australia today.

Blake Ayshford	Wendy James	Elliot Perlman
Tegan Bennett	Mireille Juchau	Elizabeth Rogers
James Bradley	Anna Kay	James Roy
Bernard Cohen	Michael Kitson	Mandy Sayer
Matt Condon	Jay Kranz	Jane Sloan
Christopher Cyrill	Angela Malone	David Snell
Luke Davies	Damien Millar	Christos Tsiolkas
Stephen Dunne	Belinda Ogden	Chi Thi-My Vu
Nick Earls	Mark Panozzo	Barbara Wels
Ali Higson	Stephen Pearl	Darren Williams
Chloe Hooper		